continued . . .

"[Quinn] skillfully intertwines the private lives of her characters with huge and shocking events. A deeply passionate love story, tender and touching, in the heat and danger of the brutal arena that was ancient Rome . . . Quinn is a remarkable new talent."

—Kate Furnivall, author of *Shadows on the Nile*

"Equal parts intrigue and drama, action and good old-fashioned storytelling. Featuring a cast of characters as diverse as the champions of the Colosseum, *Mistress of Rome* is destined to please."

—John Shors, bestselling author of *Beneath a Marble Sky*

"Stunning . . . a masterful storyteller . . . It is no mean feat to write a novel that is both literary and a page-turner."

—Margaret George, author of *Elizabeth I: The Novel*

"Full of great characters . . . So gripping, your hands are glued to the book, and so vivid it burns itself into your mind's eye and stays with you long after you turn the final page."

—Diana Gabaldon, #1 *New York Times* bestselling author of the Outlander series

"[A] solid debut . . . Quinn's command of first-century Rome is matched only by her involvement with her characters; all of them, historical and invented, are compelling . . . Should make a splash among devotees of ancient Rome." —*Publishers Weekly*

"For sheer entertainment, drama, and page-turning storytelling, this tumultuous debut novel is well worth reading." —*Library Journal*

BOOKS BY KATE QUINN

The Huntress
The Alice Network

THE BORGIA NOVELS
The Serpent and the Pearl
The Lion and the Rose

THE ROME NOVELS
Mistress of Rome
Daughters of Rome
Empress of the Seven Hills
Lady of the Eternal City

LADY *of the* ETERNAL CITY

KATE QUINN

BERKLEY

NEW YORK

BERKLEY
An imprint of Penguin Random House LLC
penguinrandomhouse.com

Copyright © 2015 by Kate Quinn
Penguin Random House supports copyright. Copyright fuels creativity, encourages diverse voices,
promotes free speech, and creates a vibrant culture. Thank you for buying an authorized
edition of this book and for complying with copyright laws by not reproducing, scanning,
or distributing any part of it in any form without permission. You are supporting writers
and allowing Penguin Random House to continue to publish books for every reader.

BERKLEY and the BERKLEY & B colophon are registered trademarks of
Penguin Random House LLC.

Library of Congress Cataloging-in-Publication Data

Quinn, Kate.
Lady of the eternal city / Kate Quinn. -- Berkley trade paperback edition.
pages ; cm
ISBN 978-0-425-25963-4 (paperback)
1. Hadrian, Emperor of Rome, 76-138--Fiction. 2. Antinoüs,
approximately 110-130--Fiction.
3. Rome--History--Hadrian, 117-138--Fiction.
I. Title.
PS3617.U578L33 2015
813'.6--dc23
2014044118

First Edition: March 2015

Printed in the United States of America

Cover design by Katie Anderson
Cover photographs: woman by Alan Ayers; courtyard by photoshooter2015/Shutterstock;
columns by Tymonko Galyna/Shutterstock

In memory of my first literary agent, Pamela Dean Strickler,
who never lived to read the end of the Empress of Rome saga
but who started it all when she picked Mistress of Rome out of a slush pile.
Pam, I miss you more than I can say. This book is for you.

HADRIAN'S WALL

The best revenge is to be unlike him who performed the injury.

—MARCUS AURELIUS

Chapter I

VIX

Women. Hell's gates, but they ruin everything!

I'm called Vercingetorix the Red, and not for my reddish hair. I've traveled the length and breadth of the Empire, and I've traveled much of it gloved in blood: the men I killed as a desperate boy fighting for his life in the Colosseum, and the men I killed as a steel-clad legionary standing shield-to-shield against the Empire's enemies. My story should be all blood and battle, swords clashing and shields creaking, full of warrior splendor like I'd dreamed as a foolish youth.

So how in the name of all the gods did my gore-and-glory tale get so thoroughly taken over by *women*?

Perhaps all men's stories are overtaken by women. I'm a man of Rome, with all that entails—a citizen, a soldier, a paterfamilias—and all men of Rome think they stride the earth and make it tremble. We make the laws and then punish the lawless; we make the borders and then punish the border-breakers; we record our own glory and then demand our names be remembered—all over the Empire we stride and we bellow, we make and we break. But if men are the makers and breakers of empires, then women are the makers and breakers of men.

This tale of mine isn't the story of Vercingetorix the Red anymore, or even of the Emperor who hated me. That sounds like a good story, I know, but it's not this story. This story belongs to the women—the women in blue, as I like to think of them. So many: the blue-veiled girl who broke my heart and married my enemy, the blue-scarfed girl whose heart I broke and who became *my* enemy, the blue-jeweled girl who married my dearest friend and harbored more than enough reasons to fear me . . .

And the girl who stood before me now in the blue tunic, wide-eyed and bloody-kneed and so young, whom I was sending to her death. Her, most of all.

"*Annia*," I roared, and her eyes flickered over the blood on my hands, the body lying limp at my feet. "*Annia, run!*"

And Annia runs. So fast, just a streak of blue fading away from me, and I wonder, *Can she outrun death?* Because if she can't, an empire falls. You'd think the fate of the Eternal City would depend on someone like me, a warrior with bloody hands and a bloody sword. But it will rise or fall on a woman—and maybe it always does.

But I'm getting ahead of myself. I'm Vercingetorix: "Vix" to my friends, "the Red" to my men, and "that pleb bastard" to my enemies. I've been a slave and a guard, a gladiator and a legionary, a centurion and a legion commander. I've served (in various ways) three emperors, and I've loved (in even more various ways) three blue-eyed women. I'm Vercingetorix the Red, and this is *their* story.

A.D. 118, Summer

As I came striding out of the Imperial palace at dawn, I had three causes to be furious and one to be sick and scared. I hated admitting I was scared, so I focused on the rage instead, and all the reasons for it. For one thing, I was wearing the full, ridiculous parade armor of my rank as tribune in the Praetorian Guard, from the absurd plumed helmet to the ridiculous muscled cuirass, and I hated that armor with every drop of blood in me. Give me a plain legionary breastplate any day. For a second reason, the day was already sweltering hot although the sun had barely risen over the rooftops, and sweat collected where the battered lion skin lapped my neck—the lion skin I'd won when I was promoted for courageous action in Dacia a long time ago, a lion skin I wasn't supposed to wear as a Praetorian, but wore anyway because it meant I was more than a pretty palace guard.

The third reason I was furious? Because on this summer day, I'd have to watch my greatest enemy march through the Eternal City's gates for the first time as Emperor of Rome.

As for why I felt cold and scared, well, I refused to think about that.

I came out into the full glare of sunlight and stopped. My guardsmen were lined up in immaculate red-and-gold rows—Praetorians were good at looking immaculate—and below was the bustle of the Imperial court, chamberlains trying to organize us all for the Emperor's arrival. One of them leeched onto my elbow droning, but I didn't hear a word because I was looking down the marble steps at a woman in Imperial purple who stared past me as though I were not there. I immediately added her to the list of reasons why this was a black, black day. Empress Vibia Sabina had spent the last year ignoring me, and I didn't like being ignored.

"Lady," I greeted her.

"Tribune," she returned coolly.

I felt my jaw jut. People assumed the Empress and I didn't like each other, and that was a reasonable assumption. I didn't get along at all with the old Empress, a rancid Imperial bitch who couldn't lay eyes on me without sniffing like she smelled a drain. But Empress Sabina was a different matter. I'd known her since she was a senator's barefoot daughter and I'd been a lanky young guard in her father's pay. We'd been friends, we'd been enemies, we'd been too many things to count. Now we were an empress and a guard, and if it was my job to keep her alive, I'd be damned if I'd be looked through like I was a window.

Sabina extended a hand to the chamberlain for assistance into her curtained litter. Maybe it was petty, but I brushed the man aside and offered my hand instead, not letting her dismiss me like a slave. Her fingers were narrow and smooth in my big rough paw, and her blue eyes flicked over me once as she settled among the cushions. A supple, sinuous woman maybe a year younger than my thirty-five: a little three-cornered face like a shield, a draped *stola* of Imperial purple, and wide beaten-silver cuffs adorning her wrists and ankles. She looked regal and shackled, and I saw she had her statue face on. When she wore that face you'd never in a thousand years know what she was thinking. Empress Sabina had Imperial purple in her veins as well as on her back:

oceans of patrician-cool self-possession all the way down to the deep and hidden center of her.

But maybe it was a good thing. Of the two of us, Sabina would at least have the self-control to look the Emperor of Rome in the eye and lie like a Greek. I wasn't sure I had the self-control to keep myself from hitting the bastard the moment I saw his smug, bearded face.

We were to greet him at the gates of the city, and the moment was almost here. The air hung like a warm wet cloak as the Imperial procession creaked off into the twisting streets. Rome: that old whore of a city with her overflowing gutters and feral dogs; the plump, brisk housewives with baskets over their arms and vendors crying wares on corners. My city. I hadn't been born here; I hadn't even loved my time here—I'd started out as a slave and a gladiator, and Rome would've been happy to chew me up and spit out my bones on the sand of the arena. But I'd gotten out at the expense of some blood and a few deaths, and then this fickle bitch of a city kissed me instead, sent me vaulting up the ladder in the legions under Emperor Trajan. Trajan came before Hadrian, and Trajan I had loved—but there was no Trajan anymore. Just Rome, and she owned me. Everyone in the city from the idle drunks to the idle rich was pressing along the streets for a look at their new Emperor.

Well, not quite new. Hadrian had put on the purple a full year ago, but he'd learned his lesson from Emperors who celebrated their glory before solidifying it—no one ever said the bastard was stupid. He spent his first year making the rounds of the eastern legions, promising, cajoling, bribing. It wasn't till he was sure of his position that he returned to Rome itself, and he'd sent me instructions for his triumphal entry:

Pomp, Hadrian had written in his terse script. *Sacrifices. Gladiatorial games. Rose petals. Cheering crowds. Oh, and let's take care of the executions on that list I gave you.*

That's why people weren't inclined to cheer. From the back of my ill-tempered gelding I had a fine view over the procession of senators in their snowy rows, and they were a grim, unsmiling lot. A frightened lot, too. They knew the names on that list; Hadrian had had those names rammed down the Senate's collective throat in open session. Men of note; men who should have been safe; senators and former consuls and war heroes who considered themselves untouchable. But no one was safe when Hadrian looked at you—and he made sure we all knew it.

The chamberlains fussed again at the city gates, babbling protocols, but I just swung off my horse and ignored them. So did Empress Sabina; she sat reading a scroll and ignoring the Imperial steward flapping at her. "Lady, the Empress must be first to greet her husband upon his return to hearth and home; if you will array yourself *here*—"

"I will be first," a woman's deep, loud voice intoned. It was that rancid old bitch Plotina, widow to the previous Emperor. "If anyone is to welcome Dear Publius home to the Eternal City, it will be his mother."

Empress Sabina spoke, still reading. "His mother is dead, Plotina."

The old empress in her dark purple silks gave a patronizing smile. "Mother in all but name, Vibia Sabina."

God, but she was insufferable. How a man like the late Emperor Trajan—straightforward, vigorous, with a love of common soldiers and dirty jokes—had ended up with that straitlaced cow of a wife, I had no idea. Politics, I suppose. I was a gutter-born bastard free to marry the girl I loved, and I had, but those of the senatorial class married for power. I'm not sure if any power would've been worth wedding Plotina, with her graying wings of hair and the way she mouthed her words like pronouncements carried down from the gods. She was mouthing more pronouncements at Sabina—the unsatisfactory daughter-in-law who'd taken her place as Empress of Rome.

"You may be Empress, my girl." Plotina lowered her voice, but guards like me always have an excuse to hover. "But only because I made Dear Publius Emperor. Remember that. He certainly will."

"Of course, because we all know he's just aching to see you again." Sabina tossed her scroll aside, swinging out of the curtained litter. "How many letters did my husband write you while he was away, for all those long screeds of advice you sent him every other day?"

A sniff from the old Empress, and then we all took our places. I held my post at Sabina's elbow, watching a drop of sweat ease down the long ribbon of her neck from under her plaited wig. She'd never been a woman to fuss with her hair; she'd shorn it clean off at some point so it covered her head in a silky cap of light brown. But she was Empress now, so someone had jammed a wig over that shocking shorn head. Probably Empress Plotina, who waited with her whole body quivering like a horse at the starting line of the Circus Maximus. Her eyes gleamed fever-bright as she remarked to the air, "Dear Publius keeps us waiting, but that is a god's prerogative. He is a god incarnate, you know."

"Have you been inhaling too much of that Imperial purple dye?" Sabina asked conversationally. "Sometimes I wonder."

I almost laughed, but then the cry went up.

"He comes!"

I looked beyond the gates to see dust, billowing like a storm cloud on the road approaching the city. A great roar went up from the waiting crowd, and Sabina spoke softly. "Are they so eager to see him?"

"They want the largesse they'll get if they cheer, Lady."

"How do you know?"

"Because I made a formal announcement that they'd get largesse if they cheered."

Sabina smiled, her Imperial mask cracking briefly to show the girl who had cantered around the Empire in search of adventure. It was hard not to smile at that girl, even if you sometimes wanted to put a leash on her.

She studied me a moment, and her serious expression returned. "What's wrong, Vix? You're smiling, but you've been coiled tight as a rope all morning. Are you dreading something? Besides *that*," she added with a glance at the approaching storm of dust that was her husband.

I'm dreading a death, I almost said. Five executions were coming, but one would be worse than all the others combined. I'd dreaded it during this whole past year like a leaden weight in my stomach. And it was coming, once this rose-petaled pomp was done. The Emperor had ordered those deaths, and just because he'd changed his mind after the arrests were made—"Leave them alive in their cells till I return," he'd written me, "I will see the executions myself"—didn't mean blood wasn't still going to be spilled.

Empress Sabina knew whose death I dreaded. She dreaded it, too. I saw her hesitate as though hunting for words, but then the trumpets blared, and she remembered to ignore me. I had a moment to resent that, even over the sick swoop in my stomach, but she was right to do it. We were safer that way, both of us. We turned away from each other at the same instant—immaculate Empress, stone-visaged guard; nothing but cool, impersonal space between us—to face the Emperor.

Publius Aelius Hadrian.

He cut a splendid image, I won't deny that. Broad-shouldered, tall, sitting his big stallion like a centaur, red leather reins doubled through his tanned fist. Bearded like a Greek, in disdain for all the long tradition this city had for shorn chins. He'd worn military dress: a cloak of rich purple draped with careless flair across the horse's flanks, a breastplate polished to a meticulous gleam that brought a chuff of approval out of me despite myself. Hadrian's head was bare, the morning breeze stirring his curls, and though that massive handsome head was bowed with a humility designed to please the crowd, I saw the excitement that danced in his deep-set eyes. I felt my pulse give an answering leap of loathing.

It was afternoon before the interminable sacrifices and blessings were complete. My stomach growled and my eyes stung from temple smoke by the time Hadrian swept like a conqueror into the Domus Flavia, sandals slapping against the intricate mosaics. The roaring of the crowds retreated to distant thunder beyond the marble colonnades as Hadrian unfastened his cloak from his breastplate. A slave came forward, but Hadrian looked about him instead and tossed the cloak at me. It fell to the floor at my feet.

Our eyes met for the first time in a year, the first time since Emperor Trajan had died and Hadrian had taken his place. The Emperor and I locked eyes, and I swear I saw a flare of hatred in Hadrian's gaze to match the jump in my heart. I'd felt that same flare the day we first met. Back then I was just a freed slave with a swagger and a chest full of scars; he was a drawling bore with a snow-white toga and a string of senatorial titles. The gulf between two men like that should be wider than the whole Empire, but we put each other's hackles up the moment we met. We'd circled each other, measured each other through narrowed eyes, and I suppose I could be portentous and say that I knew at once how much he would come to blight my life. But I'm about as prescient as a paving stone, and I'd had no idea at the time. I just knew that I hated him on sight, and he felt the same for me. It's just like falling in love, that kind of hatred. It feels the same, that sick swoop in your stomach, but it's all poisoned and upside down.

He pointed to the purple cloak at my feet. "Pick that up."

I didn't move. He'd schemed his way into Imperial purple, and then—for some perverse reason I had yet to understand—he'd made me his watchdog. I'd laughed in his face, but how do you say no to an emperor when he can squash you like a fly? Not just you, but the two daughters you dote on, the adopted son you probably shouldn't admit is your favorite, and the stalwart, beloved wife who raised all three? I had a whole set of hostages for my good behavior, and the Emperor knew it.

"Caesar," I said, and stooped to pick up the damned cloak.

"Excellent," he said pleasantly. "Now, why don't you go fetch our friends? You know the ones I mean. I've a little time to spare before I prepare for the meeting with the Arvals."

The Domus Flavia was a lovely place: marble colonnades catching every breeze, wet green gardens with splashing fountains, cool mosaic tiles set in rippling patterns underfoot. But it was a palace—it had housed great men like Emperor Trajan, but it had housed monsters and madmen too. And monsters and madmen require uglier things in their palaces. Things like dungeon cells.

I let my centurions fetch the other prisoners, but I went for Titus myself—I owed him that, at least. I'd put my old friend in the best cell I could find and softened it up with a yielding bed, good meals, water for washing, even a store of books. But a cell is a cell, and when my friend lifted his head and looked at me, the changes I saw from his months of dwelling in this place shook me. He'd been a lanky, cheerful young patrician with a string of distinguished names and a lineage that went back to Aeneas. Now I saw the shadows under his eyes, the flesh that had fallen away from his body, the gray salting his hair.

How could Titus have gray in his hair already? He was even younger than I.

"Hello, Slight," he said, and I couldn't help wincing at his old name for me. Vercingetorix was too foreign a name for Roman tongues; it had long been shortened to the casual Gallic "Vix"—which just happened to double in Latin as a common adjective, something along the lines of "barely" or "slightly." I'd have belted anyone else who dared call me *slightly* anything, but Titus was allowed. I'd saved his life in Dacia long ago, a brash young legionary rescuing a nervous young tribune, and ever since that day, Titus Aurelius Fulvus Boionius Arrius Antoninus was my friend.

Was. I already had a family hostage to my good behavior—I couldn't afford friends, too. Not anymore.

"Get up," I said curtly. "He wants to see you."

"Your master?"

"Ours."

"Yours, I think." Titus unfolded himself, all long limbs and bony shins. "He made me his prisoner, but you're his dog."

There was cool judgment in his tone, and I bristled. I'd rather have heard hatred. I didn't mind being hated, but I was damned if I'd be judged.

"I'm not his dog," I bit out. "I'm his killer, the one he lets off the leash when he wants blood spilled. Keep it straight."

Titus's words came quietly. "You were never a killer, Vix. A soldier, yes. But not a murderer of innocents."

"Well, that's what I am now." Putting my hand on the hilt of my *gladius*. "So move."

"'A sword is never a killer,'" he quoted. "'It's a tool in the killer's hands.'"

"Juvenal?"

He smiled. "Seneca."

Titus and his damned quotes; he had one for every occasion. "So according to Seneca, am I the killer or the sword?"

My friend met my eyes. The night I'd come to arrest him, he'd been all fury at my betrayal, but now his gaze was sad. "Maybe you're the tool."

That stung. Truth usually does. And it just made me angrier. Truth usually does that, too.

Maybe Titus saw my jaw clench, because he put a hand to my shoulder. "I've been wanting to thank you for something, Slight."

"What?" I gestured. "Putting you in here? You didn't thank me when I arrested you!"

"You've done your best for me since then." A shrug. "No, I meant to thank you for not letting my wife in to see me, after she told me she was expecting a child. I worried she'd miscarry, as much as it upset her to see me here."

"Don't mention it," I said, and gestured him out the door. "I didn't do it for you." I did it for *me*, because every time my friend's wife looked at me, her eyes were stony with condemnation. I couldn't blame her, but I hated facing her. I'd been the one to drag her husband away on what should have been their wedding night, her half-dressed and pleading as I dragged him from their wedding bed, him trying to reassure her even as I marched him across the flower-strewn mosaics. "Hope she doesn't weep all over the atrium today," I said brusquely. "The Emperor hates crying women."

"Faustina doesn't weep." There was pride in Titus's voice. "Too brave! Far braver than me. I'm sure our daughter will take after her—"

I put an arm out and checked him as he passed me. "Stop."

"Stop what?"

"Stop being friendly," I said brutally. "We're not friends. Not now. I'll get the order to kill you in a few moments—"

"And will you carry it out?"

"I'll have to, won't I?" I stepped closer until we stood chest to chest. "I've got a wife too, you know."

"Of course."

I stared into his eyes, seeing fear, but well-mastered fear. He was almost as tall as I was, something few men could say, but I could have snapped his aristocratic bones in half. He'd never been a fighter, Titus.

He was a man of honor, with all it entailed. He wouldn't kill me, if our positions were reversed.

But I wasn't a man of honor. I'd survive, and so would my family—even if I had to kill a friend to do it.

"Come with me," I said, and yanked him away from the cell toward the man who—whether we liked it or not—was master of us all.

SABINA

When Sabina's mother-in-law had become Empress some twenty years ago, she had paused picturesquely in the massive doorway of the Domus Flavia upon entering for the first time and announced, "I hope to leave this palace the same woman as I enter it." Plotina had made sure all Rome knew that story, told with respectful nods for her humility and modesty.

When Sabina entered the Domus Flavia last year as Empress, she hadn't bothered with humility and modesty. Her first words in the Imperial palace had been to the director of the Imperial archives: "Give me everything you have on the previous Empresses of Rome."

He had blinked: a thin, bright-eyed man named Suetonius, ink-stained and irreverent, trailing a forgotten tail of parchment from a scroll thrust through his belt. "Which Empresses, Lady?"

"All of them." Because Rome had had so many Empresses, some of them infamous. Those names were still whispered: the Empresses who had been exiled for adultery or beheaded for plotting. But what about the others? Emperor Domitian's wife with her spotless reputation, except for those faint uneasy rumors of how she'd engineered her husband's assassination . . . Empress Livia, who boasted of weaving Augustus's tunics with her own hands, but was as clever as any man in Rome . . .

The Empresses who *survived.*

How? Sabina had wanted to know, plunging into the scrolls Suetonius brought her. *Teach me quickly, because no one's going to put a sword through my neck if I can help it.*

And Hadrian would certainly put a sword through her neck, if he had even an inkling what she was hiding.

"Vibia Sabina," he had greeted her at the city gates just an hour ago, raising her from her curtsy with a gesture. His eyes moved over her, and Sabina felt a moment of pure, undiluted panic. *He'll see,* she thought. *He'll know.*

No, she thought, and smoothed her face to blandness. *He won't. He'll never know.*

"Caesar," she replied, and saw his eyes flare dark excitement. At hearing the title, not at seeing her—and certainly not in any kind of suspicion. Sabina had breathed easier. One hurdle cleared.

Sabina had not taken her eyes off her husband during the procession through the city. She watched him from her silver litter behind Hadrian's big horse, consuls and lictors pacing along behind. Most men would have been dazzled, and he *was* dazzled; she could see that in the giddiness of the smile every time he raised his hand and got a roar in return. But he was *working* too, Sabina could see that. She could all but hear his thoughts when they paraded past the ruins of the Pantheon, that ancient temple to all the gods of Rome: *Burned down forty years ago. Rebuild? Note: Check funds.* When his eyes fell on the Ara Pacis, the great frieze Emperor Augustus had erected to celebrate the peace and prosperity his family had brought to Rome: *Imperial family as lodestones of divine favor; yes, that always goes over well. Note: Parade family unity.* Working, always working, even in his moment of triumph.

But once the parade was over and they entered the Domus Flavia, Sabina saw him smile. And that made her skin prickle, because her husband always smiled at the prospect of blood.

"Ah," he said idly as a line of shackled men were led in. "The traitors."

A ripple went through the crowd of watchers at the sight of the five men. Two renowned former consuls; a fierce Berber-bred legion commander with the loyalty of thousands; a popular former governor of Dacia whose wife gave a moan from the crowd as he was led in . . . But Sabina's eyes flew past the first four pairs of shoulders, whether shrinking inward or held proudly erect, to the fifth man. *Titus.* Her heart squeezed, and for a moment the secret that weighed so hot and heavy in her breast was forgotten. Poor Titus looked so thin and worn in his shabby tunic, she hardly recognized him—and she'd known him since she was eighteen and he just a year or two younger. He was her brother-in-law and oldest friend; he'd once courted her hand in marriage; he'd stayed a friend when she turned him down. He'd eventually, to her great delight, married her younger half-sister. And now, somehow, he was her husband's enemy.

Sabina found her fingers cutting into the gilded arms of her chair.

Hadrian was lounging back in his own. "Read the charges," he said benignly, and bent to scratch the head of the hunting dog at his feet.

Sabina did not listen to the charges as they were read. They were absurd anyway; trumped-up nonsense about a conspiracy against the Emperor's life. The five men in shackles shared no conspiracy between them. What they shared was the former Emperor's favor; popularity in Rome and among the Senate as her husband had never been popular. Men who could make trouble for a new Caesar. *So perhaps my husband is wise,* Sabina could not help thinking. *Removing all his potential enemies at once, at a single stroke on the beginning of his reign.*

But not Titus. Titus was no one's enemy. Former Emperor Trajan had thought the world of him, had even considered appointing him heir—but Sabina's husband inveigled his way onto the throne instead, and so here was Titus in shackles. *What would this day be like if Titus and not my husband were the one wearing the purple?* Sabina couldn't help but wonder with a pang of thwarted longing. *Certainly my sister would make a far better Empress than me.* Beautiful Faustina, so tall and lovely, clutching her baby in her arms, managing a desperate smile for her husband as he stood there in chains. Titus smiled back at his wife, and Sabina's heart contracted. *Dear gods, he cannot die today. He cannot!*

"Well," Hadrian drawled at last, looking from sweating face to sweating face as the charges were concluded. "I understand the Senate has ratified the arrests. And has recommended execution?"

A general mutter of assent. That decree had been forced through the Senate House, and from the furious glances flying about the room, humiliation still lingered on every senatorial mind. It had been the scandal that rocked all Rome, this whole past month.

"Executions?" Hadrian snapped, voice suddenly icy. "Did I specify to the Senate that I wished these men dead? Where was that written, Senators?"

The new Emperor's deep-set gaze roved the atrium, and everyone froze under it. Pages, senators, slaves, guardsmen—not one person moved.

It wasn't written down because you didn't write it, Sabina thought. Hadrian never committed himself so absolutely to anything—in case he wanted to change his mind later. *But everyone in the Senate House knew what you wanted, and they gave it to you. So, my mercurial husband, what are you doing?*

"Precipitate of you, Senators," Hadrian tutted, "to order executions without my presence."

More silence.

"Or perhaps the blame lies with my Praetorians?" Gaze roving to the Praetorian Prefects, who looked puzzled because they would have had very specific orders indeed about the charges he brought before the Senate. "Praetorians can be . . . overeager."

Sabina's gaze shot to Vix, standing behind the Prefects in that ridiculous overdecorated tribune's armor. His face was impassive as granite, but his eyes burned for one furious white-hot moment. Because Vix had had his orders too, and had been very far from eager to carry them out.

"I'm to stop off on my way back to Rome," Vix had said in bitter horror after Trajan's death in faraway Selinus. "And kill all your husband's enemies for him."

"All his enemies?" Sabina had quipped, just as bitterly. "That's too long a list for one man. Even you."

A thick silence had fallen in the atrium, Sabina realized, and she shook her whirling thoughts of Selinus aside. The Emperor had called for wine; he accepted a goblet from a scuttling page boy and swirled the blood-colored liquid inside with a genial expression. His eyes drifted over his prisoners again. The two former consuls were staring at the Emperor with watering eyes; the provincial governor's mouth opened and closed as though a plea had dried up on his lips; the legionary commander stared back defiantly. Only Titus wasn't looking at Hadrian at all—his gaze had never wavered from Faustina, drinking in the sight of her and their baby daughter, too. The daughter he had never seen, and who might never know him at all.

Hadrian's gaze lingered a moment longer, and the whole room seemed to hold its breath.

"Well, if it is the Senate's decree that these men should die," Hadrian shrugged, "who am I to argue?"

Sabina's breath froze. A shiver went through the whole room. Hadrian's gaze passed over the rows of heads, and she saw a faint smile on his bearded lips.

"Execute them."

Titus bowed his head then, inhaling a deep, slow breath. Vix looked like he had turned to stone. One of the other condemned men let out a cry, and the silence in the atrium broke. Vix's fellow Praetorians shouldered forward to seize shackled wrists; the noise was rising, murmurs and cries mounting from the watching senators. Hadrian looked pleased at the commotion, one hand still toying with his dog's floppy ear. Sabina knew if the prisoners began to scream, it would all slip away from her.

Quickly now, just as you planned.

She threaded away from Hadrian's side, making for her sister. She linked an arm through Faustina's and brought her forward, toward the Emperor's chair. "Look as beseeching as you can," she murmured. "And keep the baby from crying." Faustina was rigid, her eyes screaming horror, but she nodded and tucked the baby's soft head closer against her shoulder.

"Caesar," Sabina said, speaking to pierce the din. "I beg a boon for my brother-in-law, Titus Aurelius. He has never seen his own daughter—surely you would allow him a farewell with your *niece*?" Underlining that last word. "Annia Galeria Faustina the Younger— had she been a boy, my brother-in-law would have named him in your honor."

Hadrian frowned, but Vix's hand snapped out and halted the Praetorians who held Titus by the arms. Sabina gave him a flash of her eyes in thanks as she brought Faustina to Titus's side, turning with a swift gesture so everyone could see the picture they made: the poignant little family with their heads humbly bowed for an emperor's mercy. Sabina could see the court ripple at the sight. Hadrian had insisted on an audience for this show of casual terror; well, she would use it.

"Your brother-in-law"—Sabina emphasized the *your*—"will obey the Emperor's wishes in all things, Caesar. Even to the matter of offering his life. I do hope you will grant this small boon."

Hadrian studied Titus a moment, and then his smile burst out like sunshine. Such a genuine smile, no one in its light could be anything but warmed. "Indeed," he said, and rose to clap Titus upon the shoulder. "Brother-in-law! Congratulations upon your marriage to my wife's sister. I had quite forgotten."

Lie, Sabina thought. Hadrian forgot nothing.

"The Senate has been hasty indeed, in condemning *you*," Hadrian said. "Overhasty. Perhaps I should refuse them their way in this, eh?"

"Family is so important," Sabina murmured, and refused to recoil as Hadrian's gaze snapped to her. *Do not blink*, she thought, staring back at him, and felt sweat begin to roll down her spine. *Do not blink, and show no fear.*

Faustina was quick to sink to her knees, looking graceful even with a squirming baby in arms. Titus followed suit, but he kept his gaze steady on the Emperor.

"You," Hadrian said at last, carelessly, "I will spare. Rise, Titus Aurelius."

Titus bent his head, perhaps to hide the tears Sabina saw spring to his eyes, and kissed the Imperial ring. There was an audible rustle through the atrium. Vix's hand rose again, signaling his Praetorians, and he strode from the atrium with a hard face as the other four men in their shackles were dragged after him. The old general strode out with his head high, but one of the ex-consuls collapsed shaking and babbling and had to be hauled along by the elbows, his fingers twisted from the doorjamb with a snapping sound that echoed in Sabina's ears like cracks of thunder.

But only four men would die today. Not five. And the man who had been spared was one of the wealthiest in Rome, as well as one of the best-liked. "Caesar is merciful," Titus said as he rose, and Sabina heard only the faintest quiver in his voice.

"Caesar is always merciful," the Emperor continued in the same affable tone.

Tell that to the four men you just sent to their deaths, Sabina thought.

"Besides," Hadrian continued to Titus just as affably, dropping his voice so only those nearest could hear, "if you prove inconvenient we can always execute you later. Do feel free to go, and acquaint yourself with my niece elsewhere. The sound of fretting children annoys me."

He turned his back on Faustina's wax-white face and Titus's inaudible swallow, snapping his fingers for his stewards, his secretaries, his freedmen and attendants. "The meeting with the Arvals next? Yes, and the Senate tomorrow. After that . . ." He began flipping between the pile of wax tablets in a secretary's arms; Sabina glanced at her sister and saw them retreat through the atrium without ceremony. "Quite a full calendar for the next month. Gladiatorial games . . . festivals . . . donatives . . . Really, why must an emperor's early years be entirely taken up with public addresses and trivia?"

A few hours back in Rome, Sabina thought, and he was already bored with it. Travel had always been where her husband's heart lay. *Perhaps I should encourage that.* Troublesome husbands were better kept occupied. Surely that went double for troublesome and occasionally murderous husbands. Sabina spared another glance behind her and saw a final flash of Faustina's blue skirts. They were gone, all three of them, baby Annia's angry cries fading to safety, and Sabina's heart contracted violently and then began to beat again. Four men would die this day, and she grieved for them. But not her sister's husband. Not her oldest friend.

I could not save them all.

"Caesar." Vix had returned in his lion skin and his cuirass and his steel-gray gaze. "Are the condemned to be given the opportunity to take their own lives?"

"They are not." The Emperor's eyes lifted from his wax tablets. "Behead them."

Vix did not move.

"Bring me their heads," the Emperor said. "No less than an hour."

"Four's a good many necks, Caesar," Vix said. "Can I have a day?"

Sabina felt a wild urge to laugh. Vix usually had that effect, making her laugh when she should have been weeping or weep when she should have been laughing. Maybe because he didn't seem to know what fear was. Where other men faltered, Vix just went bashing on through, generally with that same contemptuous show of teeth he gave Hadrian now, his russet head thrown back and his scarred arms crossed over his breastplate.

Hadrian looked meditative. "Maybe I require five heads after all, not just four. I could add yours to the pile, Vercingetorix. No one who squawked at the execution of my brother-in-law would quibble at the addition of an ill-tempered, ill-bred guard."

Vix's grin disappeared. "Caesar," he bit out, clipping the honorific off like an insult—and Sabina stepped forward fast, laying a hand on Hadrian's sleeve.

"My dear," she drawled. "Does it suit an emperor's dignity, trading threats with a guard?"

Vix gave her a contemptuous glance. Hadrian considered her for a moment as well, and Sabina felt pinioned between two broad walls: two tall men vibrating with tension as though they might fly clawing at each other and crush her between them.

Hadrian's gaze passed over Sabina's head, meeting Vix's eyes again. "Four heads," he said, and his eyes had a blank, anticipatory shine. "One hour. Vibia Sabina, come with me."

She felt the spike of ice through her throat again, but laid her fingers over his. "Of course." His flesh had a stone coolness, as though the skin were only a thin coating over granite. She had forgotten it, that cold touch of his. He might have been absent from Rome only a year, but they had not touched flesh against flesh in far longer than that.

Hadrian led her a step or two across the atrium, away from Vix, who had gone to his bloody duty, and toward the pool in the center of the room under the open roof. Others still clustered, Praetorians and freedmen, slaves and courtiers, but none within earshot—and the Emperor stopped, bringing her about to face him. "Do not try to maneuver me, Vibia Sabina."

Sabina kept her voice bland. "Is that what I'm doing?"

"Yes. You maneuvered me into pardoning your brother-in-law, and you are now attempting to turn my temper away from Vercingetorix."

"I was thinking of your safety," she managed to say. "And mine. Vix may be a savage, and gods know he's as dense as a brick, but he has a strong sword. I never particularly wanted to be Empress, Hadrian, but I have no intention of being sent off to Hades by some madman with a knife because I don't have a good protector at my back."

Hadrian smiled faintly. "How blunt you are."

"You used to like that about me."

"Did I?"

"You used to like a great many things about me." There had never been love between them, even in the earliest days of cool-headed courtship, but there had once been friendship. Sabina still missed that old camaraderie, when her husband had been an eager world traveler with a thirst to see everything the Empire had to offer.

Hadrian began to walk again, idly circling the pool, his hard hand bringing Sabina with him by the elbow. It seemed an apt moment for a few honeyed words, so Sabina sweetened her voice. "Thank you for sparing my brother-in-law's life. It was kindly done."

"No. It was done for a purpose." Hadrian spoke prosaically. "Execute four men, demonstrate ruthlessness. Spare one, demonstrate mercy."

"You'd already decided to spare Titus?" Maybe her desperate little tableau with Faustina had been entirely unnecessary. She felt a moment's anger at the thought—all the racking of her brain these past months, trying to think of a way to extricate him from his fate.

"I had decided to spare *one* of them," Hadrian corrected. "Your brother-in-law, I thought, might be best. The death of the legionary commander sends a message to any of my other generals who may prove overambitious; the deaths of the consuls gut the Senate and tell them not to cross me. Titus is a dullard of no particular ambition, and he is family. I assumed you would trot out some little plea for his life, and I decided in advance to grant it." Hadrian looked down at her: capricious, amused, merry-eyed, cold. "Had I wanted him dead, his head would be in a basket regardless of your pretty pleading."

"I see."

"I hope you do. Don't attempt to manage me in future."

Sabina laid her challenge down, not flung at his feet like Vix's but gently unsheathed and offered hilt-first. "Then what is it you *do* require of me, husband?"

His eyes went over her, considering. "You look well, you know. Most Imperial." His gaze lingered on the purple draperies, the very proper wig over her shorn head. "You say you have no great wish to be Empress, but now that you are, I suppose we *should* have a chat about that."

"Let's do," Sabina said sweetly. "Difficult to stay within your lines if I don't know where you have drawn them."

Secretaries, chamberlains, senators hovered, impatient for a moment of the Emperor's time, but Hadrian kept them at bay with a glance. "I am told you spent much of this past year sulking in the country."

"Plotina was only too happy to shove me out of the way, so I stayed with my sister and her mother. Faustina had a difficult confinement."

Hadrian brushed that aside. "Your place was at the palace. Not in seclusion." He paused, and Sabina's pulse leaped. *He suspects, dear gods, he knows . . .*

Hadrian spoke. "Were you dallying with a lover?"

Sabina couldn't help it; she burst out laughing. Slightly hysterical laughter, but Hadrian didn't seem to hear that. He just lifted his eyebrows.

"I assure you," Sabina managed to say at last, with utter truthfulness, "I was not dallying with any lover." Very, *very* far from it.

"Then what?"

"I don't like Rome, Hadrian, and I don't like the former Empress either. Why is it such a mystery that I wished to avoid both?"

His lips twitched, and he began to walk again. "That is, perhaps, fair."

Sabina breathed a little easier, moving along at his side. She'd always been an excellent liar, but Hadrian's ear for deceit was honed like a hunting dog's nose for blood. She had absolutely no desire to test his instincts in any lengthy discussion about what she *had* been doing the previous year. "As you wish."

"What I wish, now that I am returned to Rome, is that you confine yourself to your new duties as Empress. Do not seek to advise me, manage me, or embarrass me. In the past you've shown a tendency for all three. I have been indulgent." His voice was calm. "No more."

"I see." She spoke steadily. "Wear purple and be silent, is that it?"

"Be chaste, as well. You may have had a lover or two in the past—"

"Come, Hadrian. I'm no harlot, and I never was." Outrage pricked Sabina's throat as though she'd swallowed a thorn. *A handful of discreet and fully acknowledged dalliances outside a marriage we both knew from the beginning would have no passion in it; just a handful compared to your endless parade of bedmates, and now I am the bed-hopping whore?*

"You have been both discreet and moderate in your bedmates," Hadrian allowed. Generous of him. "But now you are an emperor's wife, and discretion is not enough. You are a symbol of Rome's virtue. I was willing to turn a blind eye in the past, but an emperor cannot be made a fool of. Do I make myself plain?"

No use asking if Hadrian meant to give up his own bedmates: the strapping young slaves and handsome soldiers with whom he stocked his bed. "You make yourself very plain indeed, husband."

He looked annoyed at her coolness. "A touch of gratitude would be appreciated. After all, at least I do not require heirs of you. I know how we would both dislike that prospect."

"Quite." It *was* something to be grateful for. They had not shared a bed in years—Sabina had known from the beginning of their courtship that Hadrian preferred male flesh, and it had not troubled her in the slightest. Hadrian had his men and she had her liberty; it had left them free to be friends instead. But they were no longer friends; she no longer had her liberty—and he still had his men.

The words burned her tongue, but she forced them out. "Thank you, Caesar."

He dropped her hand, summoning his dogs, his aides, and his guards with a snap of his fingers. "Return to your chambers. I meet with the Arvals next, and your presence is not requested."

Old Empress Plotina heard that as she approached, and she looked smug. "Dear Publius," she began, but he strode past her without a glance, calling for his secretaries.

"I don't think it matters anymore who is Empress or former Empress, Plotina," Sabina said. "Dear Publius means to do it all without interference from either of us."

Plotina sniffed as she stalked out after her protégé, but Sabina did not think Hadrian would be hanging on her advice as he had when her patronage had been worth something. The words of a curse rang through Sabina's mind, and she could see the letters stark and black as she carved them: *May the Empress die alone, neglected, bitter, and without power.*

But I am the Empress too, Sabina thought with a wrench of her stomach. *And I am just as alone, just as neglected, just as bitter—and just as powerless.* How many empty echoing years stretched out before her? Sabina had no notion, but the dread of it raked at the back of her eyes like hot claws.

The atrium had emptied, the court trailing off whispering of the men who had died, wondering if more men were to die and what their names would be. Sabina had been left alone with only a few slaves and pages, maintaining their posts at the walls and barely hiding, through lowered lids, their curiosity.

Sabina didn't know how long she stood there, hands folded uselessly over her purple silks, but at last she heard boots on the mosaics behind her. She schooled her face, turning to face Vix because she'd know those footsteps anywhere. He had been almost friendly earlier that morning—his gray eyes had grinned at her in their old way, as he'd used to grin at her when he was a cocky boy. But she turned now and saw him grimmer than he'd ever looked in his life; a scarred soldier with no pity left in him. He had his *gladius* in one hand, unsheathed, and a sack in the other.

Both dripped blood.

Sabina's hand went to her mouth. A ripple went through the watching pages and slaves, and she heard a faint moan. Someone bleating idiotically, "Is that—"

Vix whipped around at the voice. "What do you think it is?"

Sabina swallowed hard on the well of nausea in her throat, unable to take her eyes from the bulging of the sack. "He will be hated for this," she heard herself whisper.

Vix's voice had a harsh grate like iron on stone. "Do you think he cares?"

She gave another hard swallow. A drop of blood collected at the bottom of the sack in Vix's fist, fell with a thick *plop* to the mosaics.

"The two consuls begged," Vix said. "The governor of Dacia knelt for me—tried to be brave. The commander—Hell's gates. I used to *serve* under him in Parthia—"

"Stop." Sabina cut his words off with a sweep of her hand. They were drawing eyes, she saw—the Empress and the Praetorian speaking so vehemently—and she lowered her voice. "They're dead, Vix. Gods know I pity them, but they had no chance for mercy. At least Titus isn't among them."

"I may still have to kill him." Vix's eyes were like pits. "Tomorrow. Next year. Who knows? Your husband made me into his killer, and God knows he loves to kill things. I wonder how long he'll stare into this sack here, when I lay it at his feet."

Sabina met his gaze. "I'm sorry it had to be you."

"I don't want your pity."

"We used to be friends—"

"I can't afford friends. And you spent the last year ignoring me."

A secret could be a heavy thing; Sabina had discovered that during the past year. It could hang in the pit of the stomach like a burning stone. "You have no idea why—"

He pushed past her, his armored shoulder brushing her bare arm.

His footsteps went on without slowing in the direction the Emperor had taken. Sabina closed her eyes a moment, summoning a face like marble. She wanted a basin to vomit into, a pillow to rage into, a shoulder to cry into, and she would have none of those things. Because an Empress was never alone.

All hail the Empress, she thought savagely. *Vibia Sabina, Empress of the seven hills, mistress of Rome, lady of the Eternal City.*

CHAPTER 2

ANNIA

A.D. 122, Spring
Rome

Annia Galeria Faustina never meant to cause trouble. Trouble just happened.

"I won't do it again," she promised every time she did something wrong, and meant it. She tried to follow the rules. It wasn't her fault she kept finding cracks between them.

"Just be gentler," the housekeeper scolded. "Girls should be gentle!"

"Gentle is boring." Annia liked to play hard, and guests took her for a boy sometimes, approving of her scabbed knees and the ferocious scowl she wore when she sent the *trigon* ball flying clear up to the roof of the villa. "That boy will conquer us a new province someday," the guests would chuckle, and then they were embarrassed when Annia's mother said with amusement, "She's a girl." After that, they somehow didn't approve anymore.

"That child should be inside sewing, not climbing on roofs!" Annia had heard two old ladies whisper, appalled because she'd gone climbing after the *trigon* ball and then fallen off the terra-cotta roof. But she didn't cry. Annia never cried. Her father had told her the story of the Spartan boy, the one who let a fox chew his vitals open rather than cry and give his position away to his enemies. Annia tried letting one of the meaner vineyard dogs chew on her foot, biting hard on a stick first so she could match the Spartan boy for stoicism. But the dog wouldn't chew hard enough to get any real blood flowing, and then the nurse-maid came and made all kinds of silly fuss.

"You're going to get in trouble one of these days," Annia's mother sighed.

"I'm always in trouble," Annia complained, because how was she supposed to know she shouldn't let dogs chew her toes off unless some-body *told* her?

"No, real trouble, my love. Because you're not afraid of anything, and that's tempting the Fates."

Annia shrugged. She had long decided, when her father told her the story of the Three Fates, that they had it in for her. And this morn-ing her mother wanted to take her to the Domus Flavia, where every-thing was breakable and the whole world was watching. *That* was tempting the Fates. "Don't make me go!"

"Well, we all leave for Britannia soon. I'll be back soon enough, but this could be your aunt's last chance to see you all year."

"I just saw her at the old Empress's funeral." The woman her mother had always called Old Stoneface Plotina had gone up in smoke on her funeral pyre not two days ago, and that had been quite enough stand-ing still and being good to last Annia all year. "Aunt Sabina doesn't like me, anyway."

"Whatever gave you that idea?" Annia felt her mother's hands tying off the end of her plait. "Of course she likes you."

"No, she doesn't," Annia said with deep conviction. And the shut-tered look on Aunt Sabina's face as Annia trailed into the Imperial gardens in her mother's wake was almost vindicating. *Told you*, Annia thought, meeting those inscrutable eyes.

"You shouldn't have brought her, Faustina. She'll end up packed in a box." The Empress waved a hand toward her quarters, where a stream of slaves bustled. "My maids are trying to pack the entire palace."

"They need me to supervise," Annia's mother decided. "I am packed already."

"I'm sure you are. Are you certain you want to come all the way to Britannia?" The Empress patted the stone bench beside her. "Sea travel, in your condition—"

"Nonsense, I've never felt better." Annia's mother gave her rising stomach a proud thump. "It's good breeding stock I come from! My mother never had a moment's trouble, and neither will I."

The Empress still looked anxious. She was fingering something in her black silk lap; Annia craned her neck to see what. Something dirty-looking. "I am sorry, you know," the Empress went on. "Titus hates travel, and I really have no idea why Hadrian insisted he escort me. I'm perfectly capable of crossing to Britannia myself."

Annia didn't really remember the Emperor—he'd left last year on a grand tour of Germania and Gaul. She knew, however, that the Emperor didn't like her father, which was very strange. Everybody liked her father.

"Can I come to Britannia?" she blurted out.

Her mother laughed. "You'd challenge a Druid to single combat, and then he'd cook you over a fire!"

"I'm not afraid of any old Druid," Annia said scornfully.

"What a fearless girl you are," Empress Sabina commented, which was really just a way of saying, *No, I don't like you and I don't want you coming along to Britannia or anywhere else.*

"Run and play for a moment," her mother said, and Annia went up the garden path around a statue of a satyr. But she doubled back through the myrtle bushes, behind the bench where her mother and her aunt sat. Whenever her mother told her to go play, that meant that interesting things were about to get said.

And sure enough: "All right, Vibia Sabina. What's that dirty thing you're clutching?"

A rustle as Aunt Sabina passed something over—a folded-over tablet made of lead or something else dark and heavy.

Annia's mother took it with a groan. "Sabina, really. You made a *curse tablet?*"

"Five years ago. Feel free to call me foolish."

"Who did you curse? Let me see . . . ah. *'To the goddesses Diana, Hecate, and Proserpina. I invoke you holy ones by your names to punish Empress Pompeia Plotina—'* Well, you couldn't pick a nastier old cow to curse, may the gods keep her rotten soul, but I've never taken you for superstitious!"

"Yes, well, I was in a state. She spent fifteen years calling me a whore—she made Hadrian Emperor—she turned him against Titus and got him stuck in that cell—"

"It was all I could do to keep a suitably sad expression at her funeral pyre," Annia's mother admitted. "I wanted to dance round the flames singing!"

"So did I." Aunt Sabina didn't sound like she wanted to sing and dance, though. She sounded thoughtful. "When I first returned to Rome as Empress, Hadrian was still off in the east—I didn't have anyone to share the palace with but Plotina, smirking and giving me orders. And I remembered a rather nice old witch in Pannonia when I was traveling years before, who told me all about curses and how to make them . . ."

"I'd say your witch knew her work." Annia's mother continued reading off the tablet. "'May the Empress die alone, neglected, bitter, and without power.'"

"Strange, really," Aunt Sabina mused. "She spent her whole life working toward one thing: getting Hadrian made Emperor. And once she achieved it, she was finished. Hadrian tossed her aside like an old shoe. Frustration and bitterness and getting exactly what she wanted— that was what killed her."

"Now you're being fanciful. What killed her was a burst heart!"

"I'm not sorry she's gone." Aunt Sabina's voice hardened. "But it's still strange . . . I spent a good many years wishing her dead. Now that she is, I think it will make very little difference. I'm still Empress, after all. And like her, I'll die alone, neglected, bitter, and powerless."

"You," Annia's mother said briskly, "are not just being fanciful, but morbid."

"I am being realistic. The Emperor only summons me to Britannia because he's discovered there are ceremonial duties I can discharge. The kind of staid public appearances that bore him. And I have to obey." A shake of Aunt Sabina's sleek head. "That's not power of any kind, Faustina."

"Then what is it?"

"Duty. Empresses live by it. I married a madman, and the Fates put him on the throne—that was a terrible thing. Now I'm to go to Britannia and preside over the dedication of temples and the drone of dinner parties, and that's merely dull—but I can't escape either duty."

Annia decided she didn't like duty. When she grew up she just wasn't going to do it.

"Looking the brighter side of things," Annia's mother said at last, "now that the old cow is dead, you won't have anyone calling you a whore across your dinner table."

The Empress laughed, and Annia tried to wriggle closer. All this talk about curses and hearts bursting was fascinating. But she bumped against a stone nymph, and before she could make a grab, over it went and the carved hand broke off.

"Annia Galeria Faustina!" her mother called. "Stop eavesdropping!"

"Sorry." Annia winced, crawling out of the bushes. "I didn't mean to break it—"

"I'm glad you did," the Empress said. "I've always hated that nymph. She has the most sickly expression."

Annia's mother laughed, rising. "You two say your good-byes. I'm going to go take charge of your packing, Sabina. Or we won't be ready to leave until Saturnalia."

Don't leave me, Annia thought, eyes traveling a touch uneasily to the curse tablet still lying on the stone bench, but her mother was already gone. And the Empress of Rome didn't look all that happy about it either, Annia thought.

"Well—" The Empress rose, fluid and swaying in her black *stola* as she dropped her shawl over the curse tablet. She moved like one of her cats, a kind of lithe, connected glide. "What did you hear, little eavesdropper?"

"Nothing," Annia said instantly.

"Really? Because you strike me as quite an observant little thing. Just like your mother."

Annia offered her most wide-eyed expression, the one she adopted whenever anything turned up broken. *You kill people*, she thought. *You write people's names in curses, and their hearts burst.* She didn't know what Aunt Sabina meant about being powerless, because killing people with curse tablets sounded like power to Annia. It was children who were powerless. Children couldn't do *anything*.

The Empress was still surveying Annia top to toe. "What?" Annia asked, edging backward.

"You'll probably be as tall as your father by the time I come back. You already have his hair."

"No, I don't," Annia objected before remembering that empresses weren't supposed to be contradicted, and neither were family, and Aunt Sabina was both. But did that count if they were *wrong?* Because Annia's hair was a soft sandy red, not brown like her father's with his little bits of gray.

"Right here"—Aunt Sabina touched a finger to the crown of her head—"you've got a stray lock that sticks up no matter how hard you smooth it down. Just like your father's."

Annia touched her hair, defensive. "People think I'm a boy," she found herself saying.

"Why do they think that?"

"The way I play."

"And how do you play?"

Annia jutted out her jaw. "To *win*."

Aunt Sabina didn't smile, as most people did. People smiled with indulgence or they smiled with reproof, but they smiled, and Annia hated that. "Win what?" the Empress asked quite seriously.

Annia shrugged. "*Everything*."

"And you shall win." Aunt Sabina knelt down so she was on eye-level. "You shall win everything; I'll make sure of it. Even from Britannia, I'll be watching for you, Annia Galeria Faustina. I'll imagine you starting your lessons, and playing with slave children, and scraping your knees. I'll send you presents—a pot of woad like the old warriors used to wear, because you'd rather have war paint than dolls . . ."

I would, Annia thought, but didn't say so. The Empress already seemed to know her far too well. The silence stretched.

But Aunt Sabina only smiled. "Let's go find your mother."

Annia kept the Empress in front of her the entire walk back through the gardens, warily. "Hug your aunt good-bye," her mother said as they left, but Annia shook her head. "No," she said, even though it made her mother frown and Aunt Sabina veil her watchful eyes with her lashes. Because Annia wasn't afraid of heights or spiders, strangers or blood or the dark—but strange, fascinating, curse-casting Aunt Sabina definitely made her nervous.

VIX

Gesoriacum, a port in Gaul

Any soldier has his good-luck charms; the things that sift out through the rough passage of nomadic campaigns. The things that *matter*, for whatever reason. I had my own collection stowed in my pack. An amulet of Mars, given me by my father to keep me safe in battle. A gold ring with the engraved letters PARTHICUS, given off former Emperor Trajan's own hand when I saved him from a Parthian archer. An earring, silver and glinting with garnets, from a woman I cared for and shouldn't have. A blue scarf from the hair of yet another woman, one I still cared for. Small things, because a soldier never accumulates more than he can carry on a long day's march.

But I'd somehow accumulated more over the years. I'd accumulated people, people I couldn't divest as easily as I'd cut off my friend Titus. I couldn't really afford carrying people about in my heart, not with an emperor's enmity hanging over my head—but I did. And my heart was singing that morning in Gesoriacum as I thought, *She's here!*

I was supposed to be doing any number of things: making preparations for the Emperor's imminent arrival, reading a stack of reports from those officious little supply clerks called the *frumentarii* with their endless tattling of the latest rumors. And I was ignoring it all, rushing down the dock with my heart fluttering in my throat, because my wife had finally disembarked.

She let our daughters tackle me first, both of them pelting across the docks with their dark curls flying. They were getting big, but not too big yet to swoop against my armored chest, one in each arm. I smiled at their mother over their heads, and she smiled back.

"I got *seasick*," Dinah complained, wrinkling her nose. My eldest, a fastidious little thing even at eight. At least, I thought she was eight. Children, even my own, all looked more or less the same age to me: small. "I threw up *everywhere*."

"So did I," Chaya confessed, looking worried. My second daughter always looked worried. She'd been born in the middle of an earthquake in Antioch; the world to Chaya was an uneasy place where even the ground under your feet couldn't be trusted. "Antinous didn't get seasick! It's not fair!"

"Sorry, girls, you both inherited my stomach. Next time I'll send for you by road." Since it was summer and the seas calm, I'd had my family brought to Gaul by boat—even on a calm sea, I'd have been heaving my guts up just as badly as my little ones. I kissed their dark curls, setting them down so I could take my wife in my arms at last, but my tall son came at me next, and I clasped him by the shoulder rather than embracing him because he was sixteen and getting too big to be tousled and hugged. "Hello, Narcissus."

"I hate it when you call me that," he complained, ruffling a hand over his curly hair. Narcissus was the boy in the myth who was so beautiful he'd fallen in love with his own reflection, and my adopted son Antinous put him to shame: straight-nosed, honey-haired, near as tall as me but far more graceful, with a lean-muscled body like a young Apollo and cheekbones that could cut marble. Unlike Narcissus, though, Antinous had not one drop of vanity.

"Antinous got in trouble," Dinah said gleefully from my hip. "On the boat—"

"Tattler," he accused her.

"You got caught kissing a *girl* in the hold!"

I gave him a look. "Was it someone's wife?"

"She kissed me!" He grinned guiltily, and I could see his beautiful Bithynian mother in his smile. She hadn't been a great passion of mine, just a girl who had kept my bed warm, but I felt enough responsibility to take charge of her young son after she died. I knew what happened to pretty children like Antinous when they didn't have anyone to care for them. Even though I hadn't sired him, he'd long since become my son. There's more in life than blood.

"It was a clerk's wife Antinous got caught kissing, and a painted little flirt of a thing she was, too," my wife said tartly, and my heart jumped to hear her voice. I pushed through all my various children and at last, at *last*, scooped their mother up into my arms.

"I see you missed me, Tribune." Mirah wound her arms tight about my neck: my russet-haired wife with her short freckled nose and her eyes a warm blue against the green scarf she'd tied about her hair to keep it from tangling in the wind. My wife, a Jew like my own mother, a Jew with all the fire of her hotheaded cousins who swore that one day they would liberate Judaea from Rome—all their fire, but a good deal more sense. Sense, fire, and sweetness too, and when you put those things together with that snap of laughter in her blue eyes and enough skill in the kitchen to make angels weep, you had a very grateful ex-legionary and current desk mule who counted himself lucky.

My daughters were wrinkling their little noses and complaining about the dockyard stench, and I laughed. "We won't be staying long." Not in obscene and teeming Gesoriacum with its docks swarming with sailors and pickpockets; the air smelling of brine and unwashed bodies; the views over the rooftops all roiling ocean and the sails of triremes and somewhere beyond it, mist-bound Britannia. A fascinating sight any day, but today I just snugged my wife in to one side and led my family to their temporary home.

"I like it," Mirah decided, fists on hips as she looked through the atrium to the tiny wall fountain that managed to fill the little garden with a pleasant plashing sound. Antinous was loping through the atrium like a young colt, and the girls were squealing and squabbling over the little chamber they'd share. "Of course, I'll have to cover that fresco—"

"Later," I said, and tossed her over one shoulder.

"Put me down!" Mirah laughed, squirming against my grip. "*Vix!*"

"Antinous," I said, and pointed at the girls. "Take 'em out and keep 'em out till midafternoon."

"Done." I heard his laughter as he steered the girls through the atrium, and I didn't even wait for the door to thud closed before I was carrying my wife toward the bed.

"Put me down," she was saying, drumming her fist against my back. "This is very undignified!"

"And you're very disobedient. I should beat you." I tipped Mirah into the middle of the wide sleeping couch. "Go on, scold me. You're so pretty when you scold."

She dissolved into laughter and I dissolved into her, my tart and tender wife. My breastplate and greaves clattered down into a pile on the floor, her gown billowed down on top, and her russet hair came loose from its scarf in a warm banner. I kissed her and kissed her, moving over her, moving through her, and then I kissed her again because I had too many unkissed months to make up for. "Missed you," I murmured into her mouth in the quiet that came after, her warm forehead still pressed against mine on the pillow. "Hell's gates, but I missed you."

"Are you still sorry I insisted on coming to Gaul?" The ripple of laughter still came through her words, lazier now.

"No," I admitted. "Though I should be. You should have stayed in Rome, you and the girls."

"What, moldered there another eight months like we did when the Emperor dragged you all over Germania doing Prefect Clarus's job . . ."

"Someone has to." The last Praetorian Prefect had been summarily fired after the four executions at the beginning of Hadrian's reign—the Emperor had managed to dump most of the blame for those executions on him. "Your overhastiness in making the arrests caused great ill will in the Senate," was how he put it, eyes dancing with amusement at the man's astonishment, because after all, he'd done nothing but follow orders. His replacement, Prefect Clarus, was a wine sack, so I did all the work while that bloated prick enjoyed the rank.

Mirah was still arguing. "Maybe the Emperor will station you back in Rome for the next leg of the journey? He could take Prefect Turbo with him instead."

"He trusts Turbo more than he trusts me. When it comes to leaving one of us out of sight for months, anyway." Marcius Turbo was the other Praetorian Prefect—there are always two, largely so you can have one kill the other if someone gets too big for his boots. Turbo was a grizzled, matter-of-fact old soul as rough around the edges as I was; he had a mind for administration and he was practical enough to work directly with me once it was clear that his fellow Prefect was useless. Turbo handled the administrative duties in Rome while I handled the Emperor's security when he traveled. It was a sensible arrangement, but I didn't like it. For one thing, it took me away from Mirah, because I usually refused to take her along. "You should have stayed behind," I grumbled, but couldn't resist tracing a slow circle around the point of her shoulder. "You'd be safer."

"You really think the *Emperor* will concern himself with the likes of us?" She gave me one of those wifely looks, amused at my thickheadedness. "Just to keep you reined in?"

"He likes keeping his thumb on people—even little people. I don't want you anywhere near me if he gets in one of his moods."

"What moods?"

"When he decides he wants to punish someone." My stomach tightened at the thought of Hadrian's idle, shining gaze turning on Mirah.

"What does it matter if we're under his eye or not? If the Emperor of Rome wants to find your family, he can find us!"

"But I want you out of his sight." An old argument, and I attempted to distract her by nuzzling her neck. But she remained undistracted. In fact, her eyes had a mutinous glitter that meant *challenge*.

I lifted my lips from her throat and leveled a hard stare at her instead, the one that shriveled my centurions inside their breastplates. "Glare all you like, Mirah, but you and the children will keep to your own apartments as long as we travel together. You don't visit my quarters in the Praetorian barracks, not ever. You'll stay out of sight, and I'll come to you when I can, just as I do in Rome when I'm not toddling along in the Emperor's shadow."

She gave a scowl to match mine, turning on one side to face me. I ran my palm slowly over the slope of her hip, banded with alternating stripes of shadow from the shutters of the window. "Isn't it good," I persisted, letting my hand slide to her knee, "that I can at least *afford* to keep you separate?" It did pay well, the Praetorian Guard. "And I'll be able to see you more often. Hadrian sent me ahead to make preparations—as soon as he arrives, I'll press to make the crossing to Britannia to prepare again. I'll stay ahead of him, lay preparations for his retinue wherever he goes, and let the centurions tramp around in his shadow for a change. It means I can arrange my own days," I insisted, aware I was losing the argument though she wasn't saying a word. "You know we might be going as far as northern Britannia, after Londinium? My mother and father settled near Vindolanda. Never mind you getting the chance to meet them, I haven't seen them since I was eighteen—"

"There are other places we could go, you know." Mirah's voice was noncommittal. "Besides Britannia."

My hand dropped from her hip.

Her eyes met mine. "If you despise the Emperor so much, we could leave Rome altogether."

I groaned, flopping over on my back. "That again?"

"You agreed you'd think about leaving the Emperor's service," Mirah persisted.

"I have thought on it," I mumbled. "I am thinking on it."

Mirah raised her eyebrows. "And?"

"You think the Emperor will be accommodating if I tell him I feel like quitting my post?"

"You'd find a way, Vix. You *always* find a way when you really want something."

I had no answer for her. My stouthearted wife had been born and raised in Rome, but she'd never uttered a word of complaint coming with me on my legion travels. She'd gone with me all over Parthia; had shared tents and wagons and cramped temporary apartments while I marched on Trajan's eastern campaigns. She'd tipped spiders out of her wine and swept sand out of her sheets; she'd given birth once in a tent and once in the wreckage of an earthquake and raised her babies in the makeshift camps of the east, and now the rented rooms of the west—and I couldn't blame her if she wanted a proper home. Somewhere I could share her bed nightly rather than creeping in every third day like I was visiting a whore; somewhere she could pray to her own God without being spit on by Romans who thought Jews mutilated babies. And when the last rebellion in Judaea had been put down and Mirah's parents had decided to leave Rome for their home province, well, I suppose I couldn't blame her that she'd set her sights on joining them.

"I wouldn't have dreamed of asking you to leave Trajan's service." She snuggled into my shoulder. "I know what he meant to you. But from everything I've heard about Emperor Hadrian, he's a different sort of fish altogether."

I called him something fouler and more anatomically unlikely than a fish. Mirah smacked me whenever I swore where the children might be able to overhear, but not when we were alone. She'd probably store the curses up to use herself when she next broke a plate.

"Don't think you can change the subject by swearing, Vercingetorix. Trajan is *gone*. And we aren't chained down by legionary pay anymore. We could travel in comfort *and* live well when we arrive in Judaea. My parents do, and Uncle Simon—you've read their letters. We don't have to take farmland; I know you're a city dweller down to your bones, but we can take a house like this one in Bethar." Her voice softened. "All my family are there, and they love you like one of their own. Uncle Simon used to fight with you in the Tenth Fidelis; he's told me all the stories how you've saved each other's lives! So why don't you want to join them?"

I knew why, but I couldn't tell her. I'd been a soldier since I was nineteen years old, and now I was past thirty-five, and I didn't know how to do anything else. What would I be in Bethar, sitting about a house all day watching my children grow and my sword rust? A former gladiator, a failed bodyguard, a renegade legionary? A man with no master, no honor, no cause—a man with nothing at all.

I sat up on the bed, ruffling a hand over my hair, and Mirah sat up too, molding her soft form against my back. Her voice was muted against my shoulder. "You despise the Emperor, Vix. So why are you so bent on serving him?"

She wasn't wrong. I'd happily watch Hadrian choke on his own blood.

But Hell's gates, I couldn't let it happen on my watch.

Look. It wasn't much, being a palace guard, but it was what I *had*. Every Praetorian in the Guard braced instinctively when I passed by, because they knew I'd roast them over a slow fire if I caught them slacking. I'd told the whole Guard I'd turn them into men of Rome and not some choir of eunuchs, and I had. They called me a gutter-mouthed flogger who buggered goats, but it wasn't my job to be liked. It was my job to be respected, and I was. Because I did my duty, and I did it well.

"Do you even know how to fail?" I remember a girl teasing me once—the girl whose earring I still carried in my pack alongside Mirah's blue scarf. She was right, that girl. I *didn't* know how to fail. I didn't know how to stop doing what I was so good at: guarding a man I hated, a man who understood me and used me against myself.

But how could I tell Mirah that? How can you tell your wife that you need a master as much as you need her happiness? That she probably shouldn't have married me at all, because she didn't deserve to deal with all the dark worries I carried with me alongside my collection of good-luck tokens?

So I gave her knuckles a kiss where her hands had twined around my shoulders, and rose. "I should be returning to duty."

Mirah let out her breath in a short rush, and I thought I heard her mutter something in Aramaic. "When does the Emperor arrive?"

"God knows." I shrugged into my tunic, slid into the armholes of my breastplate. "He's summoning his bitch of an empress to join him first, so it might be as long as a month. He's still reviewing legions in the south."

Mirah didn't move. I focused on tying my sandals, adjusting my campaign tokens. I flung the battered lion skin across my shoulders, and I couldn't help glancing up. She still sat in the middle of the bed, her russet hair tumbling down her naked back, her small capable hands linked around her drawn-up knees, looking at me. At once I became absorbed in readjusting the *gladius* at my side.

"I don't understand," she said quietly. "I really don't."

I shrugged. She looked at me a moment longer, and then she slid off the sleeping couch and back into her clothes. "I'll be back tonight," I said, feeling helpless and defensive, resentful and aching all at once. "I'm glad you like the rooms."

She gave me her little sideways smile as she tied up her hair. "I do like the rooms."

But she'd like them better if they were in Judaea.

ANTINOUS

"They're staring," Chaya whispered, peeking around Antinous's hip. "Those men!"

"Just ignore them, little monkey." Antinous gave her hand a squeeze, smiling down at his sister. "Drunks at a wine shop will stare at anything."

"They only stare if *you* are along with us," Dinah said, skipping on his other side.

"Don't be silly!" Antinous moved his sisters past the cluster of bleary-eyed drunks. Ex-legionaries by the look of them, with whores straddling their laps. He could hear a mutter as they passed—*Pretty, pretty; I'd ride that boy like a mule*—

Antinous raised his voice, deliberately loud. "Shall we go back, girls? I'll help you unpack!" But he could still hear the mutters behind, and lip-smacking noises. *Pretty, pretty . . .*

Whenever Antinous saw his own face reflected in a bowl of water or his adopted mother's small hand-glass, he stared at it in puzzlement. A face. The same face he'd always had. A straight nose; a chin just starting to prickle with a man's beard; a mop of curly dark-blond hair. Just a face, and yet all his life it had made trouble. Other boys came at him fists raised because of that face, thinking that he was too pretty to know how to throw a punch (as if anyone raised by Vix would grow up not knowing how to fight!). Now that he was older, the other boys glared and accused Antinous of looking at their girls. Either way it meant he had no friends his own age. And strangers were no better. As long as Antinous could remember, he'd heard mutters when he passed by, just like the mutters from the wine shop. His very first clear memory was of a hard-faced woman in Germania, a neighbor who had taken him in when he was orphaned very young: "You're a beauty, aren't you?" Pinching his chin in sharp fingers. "Just like your mother. I can make a few coins off you someday."

Antinous couldn't remember his mother—just a vague impression of honey-colored hair like his own. He wondered if her face had made problems for her, too. If the thing the world called beauty was always more trouble than it was worth.

"Back already, Narcissus?" a voice hailed as Antinous and his sisters came round the corner. "I thought I told you to stay lost for the rest of the afternoon!"

"The girls got bored." Antinous smiled at the tall figure standing with one shoulder jammed against the lintel. His second clear memory from childhood was of that same granite-hard figure in battered armor, looming in the doorway of the woman in Germania. Those shoulders in their lion skin had blocked out the sun, and Antinous had thought he was looking at a god. *Maybe I was.* The only reason that hard-faced woman hadn't made any money off Antinous or his face was that Vercingetorix the Red had tossed him over one shoulder and snarled, "He's coming with me."

Dinah and Chaya released Antinous's hands, flying to their father. Vix dropped a kiss on each dark head. "Inside. Your mother wants you."

"Yes, Father," they chorused, and that made Antinous sigh just a little. They were Vix's daughters, blood of his blood, so of course they called him *Father.* "What do I call you?" Antinous had asked as a boy, paralyzed with shyness, knowing with all his heart what he *wanted* to call this godlike man who had rescued him.

But no. "You had a father, not that you knew him, and it wasn't me," the brisk reply had come. "So *Vix* will do."

Antinous couldn't remember the man who had sired him. All he had in the world was a tall centurion in a lion skin, and he loved that man more than life. *Father.* But he only called Vix that in his mind.

"Walk with me?" Vix asked. "There's a decent bathhouse and gymnasium opposite the barracks, and I could use a sweat."

Antinous hesitated. "Mirah won't mind?"

"Why would she?"

Because she gets jealous, Antinous thought. It was better when Vix wasn't there—then she smiled when Antinous crouched down to play with the girls or helped hoist the laundry basket. "Not many boys know how to braid hair or bleach linen," Mirah would say, as she'd been saying since Antinous was a little boy trying so hard to be the *best* son, the *best* brother. To earn his place. "You're a gem among sons, Antinous!" She said it with such unconscious affection, *son*. But when Vix came home from his travels or his long guard shifts . . .

Well. *Jealous* wasn't the right word. There wasn't an envious bone in Mirah's body; Antinous knew that. But he couldn't help but notice that whenever he came into that laughing, shoulder-thumping embrace with his father, when the two of them teased and joked and got out swords to spar—well, Mirah looked sad. As though wondering why the God she prayed to so fervently hadn't given her a son of her own for Vix to tease and spar with. A son who *could* call Vix "Father."

"Your mother will be another hour at least moving all the furniture," Vix was saying, oblivious to Antinous's musing. "Best thing we can do is get out of her way. Why do women do that, anyway?" he wondered, swinging out of the doorway. "She'll move every couch into a different room, then decide she liked it better the way it was!"

"Let's run while we can," Antinous agreed.

He slouched along easily at his father's side, companionably silent. They were almost of a height, and Antinous almost as broad through the shoulder, but there the similarities stopped. Nobody whispered foul things on the street when he walked with Vix. His father moved with a ferocious swagger like a man who owned the earth. Antinous wondered sometimes if Vix had ever been unsure of anything—if he'd ever been Antinous's age, wondering what the world held in store and what was his place in it.

Mostly Antinous thought the answer to that was *No*.

"Emperor Hadrian," he asked finally. "Arriving soon?"

"Yes." His father never had much to say about the man he served.

"And he's traveling to Britannia afterward?"

A savage chuckle. "If he doesn't drown on the crossing."

Antinous let it drop. He'd never seen the Emperor except as an occasional distant figure on parade in a purple cloak, but he knew his father hated the man. Something to do with Emperor Trajan's death, and his father's transfer from his beloved Tenth Fidelis to the Praetorian Guard. Get Vix going, and he'd convince you Emperor Hadrian was responsible for every evil in the Empire.

"So," Antinous asked. "You aren't going to scold me about kissing the clerk's wife on the boat, are you? Because Mirah already burned my ear off—"

Vix laughed. "Better she saw you kissing the clerk's wife than the clerk."

"Oh, he made a try at me, too." Antinous squatted down on his heels, stretching a hand out to a dog skulking through the gutter. The poor thing looked half-starved. "Mirah just didn't catch that part."

"Good. You know how she'd be about the sin of it."

"And you're not?" Antinous whistled softly at the dog. "Come here, boy—"

"You're sixteen! It's your time to play. Not your fault if all the girls and the boys fall at your feet."

Antinous had to admit there were advantages to having a face like his, even if it caused trouble. Around the age of fifteen, he'd started noticing that it was easy to get women's attention—they sort of fell on him if he smiled. Men, too. The clerk's wife had been soft and buxom in his arms; the clerk had been rough and demanding, and Antinous had enjoyed both. He gave another low whistle and the dog sniffed at his hand. "There," Antinous crooned, feeding him a crust left over from the rolls he'd bought his sisters.

"You should have a dog," his father decided.

"Mirah says she's not running a menagerie so I can't keep bringing home strays to patch up." Wistfully Antinous managed to stroke the stray dog's nose before it went dancing out of reach. "And you know how the girls are about fleas—"

"Bugger that! A boy needs a dog. After we get to Britannia, maybe. Bad enough having two little girls vomiting their way through the crossing without adding a vomiting dog." Vix tousled his hair. "Let's get ourselves to the gymnasium, and we'll spar a few rounds, Narcissus."

"Don't call me that," Antinous groused, but he liked the nickname, and his father knew it. Because Vix, unlike most people, valued what Antinous could *do* rather than what he looked like. He'd insisted from the first that Antinous learn to fight, learn to ride, learn the sword— had stood back, called corrections, picked Antinous up by the scruff of the neck when he fell down, praised him when he succeeded. *Made me useful*, Antinous thought. *Not just pretty.*

Vix could call him Narcissus, but nobody else. Vix—unlike the drunks and their whores, the clerk and his wife—saw past his face.

"I want the spear this time," Antinous said. "The spear has longer reach."

"And a *gladius* has edge *and* point to kill your enemy. Practice with that."

"Race you for it?" Antinous said, seeing the bathhouse with its attached gymnasium loom up ahead. "First to the door wins!" And he took off, feinting through the crowd like a shadow, knowing his father in all his armor and fur would never catch up.

"Bloody *cheat!*" he heard Vix howl behind him, laughing.

I love you, Father, Antinous thought. But didn't say it.

CHAPTER 3

SABINA

Londinium

Sabina made huge sad eyes. "Please, Titus?"

"No," her brother-in-law said. "You are my friend and my Empress, but this is too much to ask. Sit beside Servianus at dinner?"

At Titus's side, Faustina shuddered.

"Surely you can't object to our Emperor's illustrious brother-in-law as a dinner companion," Sabina said, straight-faced. "He's the most virtuous man in Rome, after all."

"He's a crashing bore," said Faustina. "He spent the last dinner party telling me about the declining standard of virtue among Roman wives."

"While looking down your *stola?*" Sabina asked.

"No. He really is the most virtuous man in Rome."

"And a man of no taste," Titus decreed. "Virtue or not, no man of true discernment would fail to look down my wife's *stola.*"

"If I put him beside Hadrian," Sabina persisted, "he'll drone all evening about Hadrian's need to appoint an heir, and that puts Hadrian in a black humor for days. And since the Emperor and I will be taking the road for Vindolanda soon, and you two will be going back to Rome, I'll have to bear all that black humor myself. So indulge me?"

Titus sighed. "Very well, I shall fall on the sword. Show me to Servianus's couch."

"And I'll tackle the Emperor," Faustina conceded. "Let's see if I can't coax him into a better mood, shall I?"

Sabina watched her sister's smile turn from something steel-edged to something brilliant as she sallied into the triclinium: a column of sunshine-yellow silk with fine gold chains webbing her blond hair, and a swan-feather fan setting up a gentle flutter just like her lashes. *No one can dissemble like my little sister,* Sabina admired. You'd never guess that Faustina had once stared at Hadrian in utter terror that he would take her husband's life. She was hanging on his every word as though they were the best of friends, and soon Hadrian was preening under her admiration and promising her a lavish gift as soon as her child was born.

Let it come easily, Sabina thought, making a little prayer to the goddess of childbirth. Everything *seemed* to be going well so far—the voyage from Rome to Londinium hadn't bothered Faustina or her swelling belly a jot. It was Titus who groaned and heaved over the trireme's railing when they made the crossing, while Sabina stood at the prow with her sister, the wind blowing their cloaks flat over her own narrow form and Faustina's rounding one, as they squinted over the banks of oars to see who would catch first sight of mysterious, mist-wrapped Britannia.

To be traveling again—Sabina's whole mood felt lighter, the moment she stepped down from the trireme and smelled cool, mossy air that decidedly wasn't Rome. Even traveling in the enormous entourage of slaves and chamberlains and courtiers that Hadrian felt appropriate to an empress's station, she felt light enough to fly. Even in her husband's company.

"Caesar," Faustina was saying, beaming admiration like a lighthouse. "I do hope you have devoted some time in all this traveling to your poetry? I much admired the mourning hymns you wrote for Empress Plotina—"

"Perhaps I should write some verses for you," Hadrian said, tucking Faustina's hand into his arm. "Surely eyes as lovely as yours have inspired rhymes by the dozen. Tell me . . ."

"I believe," Titus murmured, watching Hadrian escort Faustina to her dining couch, "that your husband is flirting with my wife."

"He may not care for women in his bed, but he does like their flattery." Sabina watched her sister flutter and coo. "And he always thought

Faustina would make a better empress than me. In which he's quite correct—any time I have to think 'How would an empress behave?' I just think, 'How would my little sister do it?' Gods know what I shall do when she's not close enough to *ask*. Couldn't you both just stay here in Britannia with me?"

"In all this mud?" Titus shuddered. "Give me a marble rostra and a brick forum over a glorious vista of forest, any day." He led Sabina after Hadrian and Faustina. "Surely you'll be back in Rome soon?"

"Who knows where Hadrian will want to go after Britannia? Though of course, he may not take me with him." Sabina couldn't help a slight frown. An empress's entourage complicated her husband's journeying considerably—Hadrian had already had to send Vix and a party of stewards and guards north, just to prepare for their arrival in Vindolanda in ten days' time. If Hadrian decided to send her back to Rome when he continued on . . .

Well, at least she had this time in Britannia. The provincial governor had lent his large and gracious *domus* for the Emperor's personal use, clearly anxious to prove that civilization thrived even on the edge of the Empire—the couches were draped in silver wolf pelts; a platter of sumptuous local oysters was being ushered out; the slaves were all matched redheads in embroidered linen. One, a handsome page boy with a silver wine decanter, stood in the far corner tittering softly with the lute player, and to Sabina's amusement, he had to be nudged to fill the wine cups as the guests settled themselves. Hadrian gave the boy a glance, just to show that he had noticed. He noticed everything.

"Massilia!" Faustina was exclaiming. "Goodness, I cannot imagine. In Rome we all heard of your generosity in passing out donatives. And there was something about a wall, wasn't there, when Caesar toured the northern border in Germania?"

"Yes." Hadrian smiled, tossing an oyster shell to the mosaics. "You will see more walls soon enough—one of my many plans, for both Germania and Britannia."

Titus smiled from his couch, and Hadrian's eyes fixed on him with a sudden sharpening of attention.

"Do you laugh, Titus Aurelius?"

Sabina saw a sudden flash of worry cross her sister's face. But Titus was entirely placid, returning the Emperor's heavy-lidded gaze with a cheerful smile, as though he had never spent months in one of Hadrian's cells under threat of death. "Why, yes, Caesar. I laugh at myself— if I were ever so unfortunate as to find myself at the northern edge of Germania, I would never stay long enough to build a wall. But I'm a dull, plodding sort of fellow with no imagination or ambition."

"Are you." Hadrian's voice did not make it a question. "Sometimes I wonder."

"Oh, look," Sabina said brightly. "More oysters. And that dish with sow's udders that you're so fond of, Caesar. I ordered it especially to please you."

Hadrian's thoughtful gaze rested a moment longer on Titus, but at last his eyes shifted. "Thank you, Vibia Sabina. Most thoughtful."

"In my day," a deep voice rumbled from Titus's far side, and Sabina knew without looking that it was Lucius Julius Ursus Servianus because Servianus prefaced most of his statements with *In my day*. "In my day, one did not eat so richly, even at an Imperial table." Servianus shook his head: reputedly the most virtuous man in Rome, Imperial brother-in-law thanks to a long marriage with Hadrian's colorless and little-liked elder sister, and such a vision of silvered wisdom in his old-fashioned synthesis that Sabina could not imagine he had ever been young. "It is such indulgence that ruins our Empire," Servianus concluded, and gave a sniff at the dish of pheasant, sow's udders, and ham in a pastry crust that had just been laid before the Emperor.

"Ham in a pastry crust is ruining the Empire?" Sabina couldn't help saying. "Goodness."

"No, it is indulgence that will be our ruin! Bread and vinegar, that would do us better. And serious discussion, not gossip and poetry." Servianus cast a disapproving glance at Faustina, who was feeding tidbits to Hadrian's hounds and listening admiringly to the verses the Emperor had composed when his favorite horse died. Better mourning verses, Sabina thought, than the ones he'd composed for the old Empress's funeral. "The succession has not yet been settled; is that not more important than building walls? I have spoken with the Emperor

many times about young Pedanius Fuscus, such a promising boy, yet
the Emperor has not yet confirmed him as heir—"

"And why should I do so?" Hadrian interrupted, sounding much
cooler than when he had addressed Faustina. "Because he is your
grandson?"

"Because he is your great-nephew, Caesar." Servianus sounded
reproachful. "He carries the blood imperial!"

Hadrian snorted. "The blood imperial is no guarantor of genius."
The red-haired page boy whispering behind them with the lute player
had let out a sudden titter at some murmured joke, and Hadrian sent
a sharp glance. "Cease that, boy!" The page subsided.

Servianus gave a great *harrumph*. Everyone in Rome knew that he
prided himself on speaking his mind, even to their feared and mercurial emperor. Many admired him for that, even if they found him tiresome. Sabina just found him a fool. *You don't speak your mind to the
Emperor because you lack fear*, she thought, looking on as her white-
bearded guest prepared to pontificate. *You speak your mind because you
think being the Imperial brother-in-law is all the shield you need. And
someday, Hadrian will teach you differently.*

"Emperor Augustus," Servianus said ponderously, "adopted the
young men of his own family as sons as well as heirs, training them in
his image—"

"Yes," Faustina murmured. "And didn't *that* work out well."

"Nevertheless—"

Hadrian was looking irked, Sabina saw. Everyone else kept silent,
but Servianus went blathering on. *Shut up, you old idiot.*

"If you would adopt young Pedanius Fuscus, Caesar, you would
discover for yourself his worth. High spirited, healthy—"

"I will give the matter of an heir my attention," Hadrian snapped.
"In due course."

The pretty page boy in the corner whistled softly. Not at them,
Sabina noted—at a slave girl who had silently entered to refill the water
jug. *To a slave boy, all this Imperial drama is nothing more than background noise.* But Hadrian heard the whistle and gave the boy another

glance as Imperial secretary Suetonius came to the couch with a murmur. "Forgive me, Caesar, a dispatch from Rome . . ."

Hadrian broke the seal in a sharp movement, his bad mood expanding like a storm cloud, billowing almost visibly through the triclinium. Servianus wagged his head sadly. "In my day—"

"Even in your day," Sabina said, "surely it was no courteous thing to pester one's Emperor with trivia."

"The matter of an Imperial heir is not *trivia*, Lady. A woman's understanding—"

"I said the matter would be settled when I wish it settled." Hadrian held out his cup to one side. "Wine."

The red-haired page was still ogling the slave girl with her water jug.

"*Wine!*" the Emperor barked, and the boy looked startled. He scurried to the couch with another nervous titter. *Don't laugh*, Sabina had time to think. *No one laughs in Hadrian's presence unless he's telling the joke*— But the thought was a mere flash, as Hadrian turned in a sudden motion and struck the boy. Not with a closed fist, but with the sharp stylus he had used to break the seal on Suetonius's dispatch.

The slave screamed. The sound tore through the triclinium, cutting off Servianus's droning and the soft rustle of the fans. Sabina saw blood splash, bright and shocking against the tiles. The boy doubled over, his scream dying off into a whimper. Sabina's mind was still frozen on the sight of the red droplets falling so vividly on the mosaic tiles, but she found herself moving, off her couch and past Suetonius, who clutched his scrolls gray-faced. Sabina reached the slave boy, crouched beside him. "Let me see—" And she wished she could unsee, because his eye was ruined and blind, oozing onto his cheek. The other eye fixed with dulled horror on the Emperor, and Sabina felt the same horror on her own face when she looked at her husband.

Hadrian stared down at the moaning slave boy, and Sabina saw none of his usual masks. Just a strange blank excitement, and something in the bright gaze that heaved and shuddered like a subterranean creature trying to be born. She had seen the same look on his face four years ago, when he ordered Vix to bring him four heads—and on a few other occasions since then, which she mostly preferred not to think about.

The Emperor gave a small shiver and then he blinked, and as quickly as that, it was gone. He stretched out a hand in a curiously precise movement and dropped the bloodied stylus. Everyone watched it fall, and then Faustina's hands flew to her mouth with a small sound of nausea and the thickened silence broke.

"You have an irritating laugh, young man," Hadrian told the slave in an absent voice, "but I suppose it didn't warrant blinding. What may I give you in compensation?"

"My eye," the boy whimpered behind the wad of cloth Sabina was holding to his bleeding socket. "My eye—"

"You want your eye back? That, I'm afraid, is beyond even an emperor's powers." Hadrian snapped his fingers for Suetonius; he had to snap twice before the stunned secretary looked up. "Take him away."

Sabina spoke without thinking. "Is that all?"

"Should there be more?" Hadrian looked puzzled. "I suppose his value has been decreased. I shall see that the governor is compensated for the damage of his property."

The slave was led away, still hunched over and whimpering. He was perhaps sixteen, Sabina thought, and anger roiled low in her stomach. A rise of outrage that utterly swamped caution.

"Titus," Sabina said, rising. "My sister appears to be feeling ill. Why don't you escort her out? Servianus, perhaps you will accompany them."

Servianus, too white-faced and appalled to say anything about how in *his* day no one blinded their slaves at dinner, went shuffling toward the doors. Titus needed no urging to put his arm around Faustina, who looked as though she were about to vomit. He sent a look of dire warning over her bowed head to Sabina, but she ignored it. "Leave us," she said crisply to the rest of the petrified slaves.

Sabina waited until the Praetorians closed the doors, and then she turned to her husband, folding her arms across her breasts and surveying him. He was chewing on a handful of grapes, tossing every other one to the dog at his feet. "Do you intend to scold me, Vibia Sabina?" he said in the mild tone that usually meant trouble.

Only she didn't care, just now, if it meant trouble or not. Four years dancing about his moods, wearing purple and being silent—enough.

"You idiot," she said.

Hadrian's head snapped up like a darting snake, the remaining grapes spilling from his hand to the floor. "Pardon me?"

"Yes, yes, you're very frightening," she said. "What are you going to do, put out my eye, too? I don't think you want a Cyclops for an Empress."

"I could take your tongue." Hadrian snapped his fingers at the dog at his feet; she rose with tail wagging, and he caressed the graying ears. "A silent Empress would be most desirable."

Sabina wanted to swallow, but her husband would certainly notice if her throat moved. "Let me offer you some advice, Hadrian, before you render me mute. You are going to die if you continue your reign as you have begun it."

Hadrian's eyes crinkled in a sudden grin of genuine amusement. "How dramatic."

"There you go again." Sabina flung up her hands. "Slinging threats one moment and laughing the next, like the flip of a coin. That's the kind of thing that makes people nervous. Emperor Caligula and Emperor Domitian made people nervous too, the way their moods shifted. Look what happened to them!"

A multitude of expressions chased over the Emperor's face, as though he were trying to choose a reaction. *Just let yourself be puzzled like a normal human being*, Sabina thought in exasperation. But if Hadrian was undecided, well, at least it gave her time to keep talking.

So Sabina kept talking, and fast. "Tell me something. What Emperors of the past do you admire?"

"Augustus," Hadrian replied automatically. "His administration, particularly. And Trajan, too, though those Parthian wars of his were foolishly unnecessary."

"Trajan and Augustus." Sabina nodded. "Fine Emperors both. They did great things—"

"Are you saying I have not?"

"Of course you have." Swiftly. "You've ordered temples repaired and more temples built; you've hosted games and given largesse; you've forgiven public debt. But what else do you plan to do in your reign? What will be your legacy?"

Hadrian hesitated, still looking affronted at her bluntness. *But no man can resist a chance to boast of his legacy,* Sabina thought, *even if only to a woman.* "I mean to remake this Empire," he said at last. "All of it."

Of course Hadrian would be grandiose—no small ambitions here. Sabina gave an encouraging tilt of her head, all eager willingness to be impressed.

"Rome has become insular," her husband said, and his words began to tumble as though he had been holding them inside for years. "A gaggle of bored senators who have never traveled farther than their summer villas, and they think themselves fit to pass judgment on matters in Gaul and Syria? No. Traveling is key. Augustus understood that; he traveled whenever health and time allowed, and so will I. I will see with my own eyes what needs to be done. I will *understand* my Empire before I attempt to govern it."

"And once you understand it?"

"There are things I already understand." Hadrian was off his couch, striding and gesturing. "First and foremost is that the Empire is big enough. We cannot forever be conquering, or this Empire will be nothing but a collection of sullen subjugated provinces around a marble hub. It is time to unite what we have. Roman law will be the whip, and Greek culture the light, unifying us within borders that I will mark so that no emperor who comes after me is tempted to expand beyond them."

He turned to stride back the other way, beginning to wave his arms in enthusiasm. An old habit, Sabina remembered—it had been so long since Hadrian allowed himself spontaneous enthusiasm about anything. "What else?" she prompted.

"Our legions must be consolidated as well. I mean to fight no wars, but war always comes when an Emperor least expects it, and the legions must be ready. Kept fierce and fit—but not so much that they become restless and begin to make trouble. That is a knife's edge to find and balance upon, but I mean to find it." Striding faster. "I mean to raise temples and bridges and aqueducts throughout the provinces—I will have my whole Empire made beautiful, not just the Eternal City. And our laws, dear gods, but they need organization! We need to systematize the judgments and rulings that have been made over the years, and resolve the resulting inconsistencies—"

Sabina felt a thrum of excitement run through her veins. *This man,* she thought, looking at Hadrian's sparkling eyes and swift excitement, his enthusiasm and his energy and his waving hands, *this man is an emperor worth having.*

A pity he could not be this man more often. Well, perhaps she could make him see that. If he didn't take *her* eye out, or her tongue, for saying so.

"Worthy plans," she said, interrupting him full-flow. "Marvelous plans. And you will accomplish none of them, Hadrian, if you do not curb your dark side."

He stopped, startled. Startled was good. Startled kept him from reacting.

"You wish to emulate Trajan and Augustus?" Sabina went on. "They were loved. They were good men—"

"And I am not?"

"Of course you are." Sabina wasn't mad enough to counsel the Emperor on what was goodness and what was evil; Hadrian frankly didn't seem to understand the difference. But on the *appearance* of goodness . . . Well, if there was anything Hadrian understood, it was appearances. "You are a good man, but you cannot deny you have a temper—and that it gets the better of you sometimes. You have shown you can hand out executions without blinking, and you take a harmless boy's eye out of sheer irritation. You strike fear into your subjects from the Senate on down."

"They should fear me," Hadrian said, and his face was cold again. "So should you, Vibia Sabina."

Oh, I do. But she kept talking anyway, forcing her hands to lie quiet in her lap rather than fisting her gown into sweaty handfuls of silk. "I know what little regard you have for a woman's opinion, Hadrian. My purpose as Empress is to look impeccable and wave at crowds. But I have the blood of Caesars in my veins: My great-uncle was an Emperor you admired, and my father could have been an Emperor too had history fallen out a little differently. I've observed the doings of Caesars all my life. And I can tell you that unless you control your temper—unless you put a better face on for your people—you will never accomplish any of the great things you plan. You will be dead on the floor with a blade in your back, because that is what happens when emperors make their people nervous."

"And what would calm their simple little minds?" Hadrian's eyes lay on her like a pair of blades. "A pretense of placid temper? A few jokes and smiles? The mask of a good man?"

"It would be a start," Sabina said quietly.

Hadrian regarded her, unblinking. She stared straight back, allowing the silence to fall. *Let me not be dead for this*, she thought, and felt her palms sweating.

"You have been very presumptuous with me this evening, Vibia Sabina," her husband said at last. "And I am done listening to a woman's prattle. Leave me."

Gladly, she wanted to scream, even as she slid off the couch and made for the doors. *But did you hear me? Did you hear anything?*

She had no idea. But she had to try one more time. Because she heard her sister's voice on the other side of the doors, and Faustina's words were indistinct but they had the high edge of fear.

"Pretend mercy," Sabina said, looking over her shoulder at her husband. "Pretend it, even if you cannot feel it—and start with my sister's husband. Trajan might have thought about appointing him heir, but it didn't happen, so stop eyeing him suspiciously. You got the purple, not Titus, and you have it in you to be a great Emperor. I want to see you put these grand plans of yours in place, Hadrian. I want to see that very much."

"You want to see me pretend?" Hadrian asked benignly. "I am pretending I am not angry with you. Leave before I change my mind."

VIX

Vindolanda, Northern Britannia

I suppose there isn't a man in the Empire who doesn't put on a mask from time to time—to fool his fellows, to shield his thoughts, to hide his anger or his heart. We all hide ourselves from time to time. Emperor Hadrian was the only man I knew who was *always* hiding—who had a series of masks so myriad you could go mad trying to figure if any of them was real.

There was Scholarly Emperor. Hadrian put that one on most often over dinner, reclining on one elbow and gesturing with the cup of wine in his hand as he expounded on some point of Stoic philosophy or defended the artistic merits of Terence over Plautus. Scholarly Emperor liked to appear a modest man; he always demurred (initially) whenever the guests begged for his opinions or his poetry—but Scholarly Emperor got irate very quickly if the dinner guests weren't won over instantly by his brilliant arguments. I got used to directing a pointed stare over the Emperor's shoulder, from my post at the wall, to any guest who argued with him too long. "The man with forty legions to command is always right," I told one guest bluntly, and the arse not only took my advice but stole that line for himself.

Scholarly Emperor wasn't far removed from Judicial Emperor. Judicial Emperor was a trifle more remote, the gestures restrained from eager intellectual enthusiasm to formal, marble calm. Hadrian became Judicial Emperor during his public audiences, or when he raised a hand for the cheering crowds. Judicial Emperor was godlike, remote; but I trusted him more than the others—at least he was always fair.

Judicial Emperor relaxed to Sporting Emperor on hunts or rides. The long words contracted to casual slang, and the hand that waved a lecturing finger in support of some philosophical point converted into a fist gripped around the shaft of a hunting spear. Sporting Hadrian was a good deal less formal, but he had a vicious streak—he'd crack you across the head with that spear shaft if you got between him and his prey on a hunt.

There were other masks Hadrian used from time to time. Mercurial

Emperor, with a lightning-quick line of jabs that could turn cruel or funny or both depending on his target . . . He had made old Servianus go scarlet with humiliation recently, lashing him with a jeering epigram that mocked his last speech in the Senate. And there was Autocratic Emperor, who scowled and stamped and clearly thought his footsteps shook the heavens.

But what in the name of all the gods was this new mask he had worn ever since coming from Londinium to Vindolanda? Who was this even-tempered man who dealt patiently with his petitioners, who teased me about my poor horsemanship, who graciously offered to read Suetonius's latest treatise once it was finished?

I had no idea, but I never trusted the bastard when he was this good-humored.

"A wall," he was saying now—standing a little ahead of me on the makeshift bridge over the river, looking very much the soldier today in a breastplate and a common legionary's cloak. He had the usual brace of hounds at his heels, a bare minimum of guards, and a handful of pebbles he was slinging one by one into the rushing water. "A new bridge here, six or seven piers at least. It can provide the foundation for the wall. Stretching west"—and one pebble plopped into the fast-flowing river, disappearing west.

"West," I echoed. "How far, Caesar?"

"Until it meets the sea."

I blinked, trading glances with my second-in-command, who looked as startled as I. "That's eighty miles, Caesar!"

Hadrian grinned, and it surprised me. Since when did he waste his smiles and his charm on someone like me? In his eyes I was for killing people, not idle conversation about building plans. "I can already see that wall," he continued. "Quarried stone, with a clay and rubble core. At least twenty feet broad—maybe thirty. Fifteen high; that should be enough if I couple it with a ditch to the northern side." Swift gestures. "Signaling turrets, guard posts with barracks for legionaries . . ."

"How much will that cost?" I tried to calculate the sheer value of stone, of laborers, of cattle and wagons. I didn't know if I could count that high. "And how long will it all take?"

"Years," he said, and tossed another stone in the water. "What of it?"

"But why?" I couldn't help asking, since he seemed in a mood to answer questions. "Who needs a wall here?"

"Because this is Rome." Stabbing a finger at the squelchy patch of ground on which we both stood. "*That* is not." Stabbing a finger at the squelchy patch of ground just thirty feet—the width of a massive wall—away.

I looked to the south: windswept moors, craggy hills, dappling clouds. I looked to the north: windswept moors, craggy hills, dappling clouds. "It all looks the same to me, Caesar."

"Ah, but it isn't." Hadrian glanced over his shoulder at me, and his eyes sparkled. Damn it, why *was* he so good-tempered lately?

He turned, gesturing me to follow. "I ordered another wall built along the northern border when we were in Germania," he said as I fell in beside him. "You remember?"

"A timber wall, Caesar. Not a stone monstrosity like you're planning here. You'll need the whole Britannic fleet for hauling building materials. Probably all the garrison legions, too."

"Exactly. I want them busy. The legions here have been troublesome in the past. I'll pour all their discontent into an eighty-mile wall."

"Have them conquer the north." I jerked my chin toward the distant purple hills across the river. "That'll soak up their discontent better than a wall. And you won't need any boundary to tell you what's Rome and what's not, because it will all be Rome. The whole island."

"I don't *want* the other half of the island, Tribune. Scrubby hills too steep to plow, even scrubbier cattle, and if we're lucky, a few paltry silver mines. And a bloodbath to get it—if these miserable little tribesmen in southern Britannia are bad, the northerners are even worse. Fighting them on their own land, struggling for every square foot of bramble and thorns?"

I traded another glance with my second. His name was Boil, a fair-skinned Gaul built like a siege tower who was the last of my old tent-brothers from the Tenth Fidelis, and we'd been brothers-in-arms long enough that I knew he was thinking the same thing I was. "A bloodbath for the other half of this island?" I said. "Sounds like our kind of fight, Caesar."

"Oh, I don't doubt you could do it, Tribune. *If* I gave you at least three legions. But at the end, we'd still have nothing but scrubby cattle, sullen slaves, and a few paltry silver mines."

I shrugged, surprised at the twinge of hope I'd felt when he said "three legions." *Stupid barbarian, he will never give you legions.* "You'd still own the whole island, though. Not just the bottom part of it."

Hadrian laughed. "You don't like half measures, do you?"

"No, Caesar."

"Then put your Praetorians to aiding in the wall's construction, and satisfy yourself by making it the most splendid wall anyone has ever seen. I'll have a good segment built as a sample before I leave Britannia, as an example to spur them when we leave."

"At fifteen feet high and thirty feet across, even a short segment of wall will take months, Caesar."

But he wasn't listening; he was striding ahead making plans with waves of both hands. It was my old friend Boil who said softly, "Looks like we'd better get used to this rain?"

"Looks like."

It wasn't just the prospect of the great wall that galvanized the Emperor's energy in Vindolanda. He tore through the region like a fire, evaluating, gesticulating, ordering. I tramped along behind him, and his odd cheer didn't break once.

And that just made me and everyone else more nervous. Because consistency was never Hadrian's strength, was it? We were far too used to the parade of masks.

"I tell you this, Senators," I heard that old windbag Servianus say to a cluster of the Emperor's advisers, just before he decided he'd had enough of Britannia and went back to Rome. "In our Eternal City, the Emperor was much absorbed in small things. Now he strides upon a wider stage. If no one can know his mind, can anyone guess what he may do next, upon such a stage?"

Nobody knew, but they all worried. They whispered of a slave boy in Londinium whose eye he had put out in a fit of temper. They whispered of a certain chamber he was rumored to keep in his ever-expanding villa springing up just outside Rome, a chamber he called his Hades, and into which no one but the Emperor had ever been allowed to go. They whispered of what he might keep there, because sometimes laughter was heard and sometimes sobs. I didn't know if I believed that rumor—I'd certainly never been inside.

But . . .

We were a full month in Vindolanda before I was able to make the day journey I'd wanted to make since the moment we'd arrived. The journey back up the road I'd last seen at age eighteen, when I first left my home for the Eternal City. It was a gray, blustery morning the day I finally turned off that muddy road and slid down from my horse.

Mirah gave me one of those looks of wifely amusement, bright-eyed in the red cloak that brought out the color in her cheeks. "You're nervous, Vercingetorix!"

A little. My parents would find me so changed—what if they didn't like what they saw? I didn't altogether like what I saw in the mirror anymore, after all.

My daughters squealed at the mud on the hillside, refusing to get down from their mule. "That's girls for you," Antinous groaned, but he led the mule along behind me. I slid my hand into Mirah's as I climbed, and she gave my fingers a squeeze.

I saw the crowning roof of a snug little villa. Cow byres behind; those were new. Things were prosperous, then. I swallowed and felt the quick pressure of Mirah's fingers. Rich grass ran up the slope toward the house, and hedges flowered against the villa's walls. My feet took me unthinkingly around the east wall, where I remembered there had been a meager excuse for a garden.

There still was. Someone had put in a fruit tree, but it looked pinched and leafless, and the herbs in their pots weren't much more than twigs. I smiled. He still wasn't any good at gardening, then, the broad-shouldered man in a blue tunic who squatted among the herbs with a trowel.

My feet were soundless on the grass, but the man whipped about before I got a step farther, dropping his trowel and drawing the dagger at his waist instead. He was up in a crouch and ready to face me in an eyeblink. And though his shoulders were bent and his hair entirely gray, his crisp *secutor* stance could have graced any arena in Rome. And had.

"You haven't gotten slow with age," I told my father. "But you still can't garden worth a tribune's arse."

He dropped his dagger and I dropped Mirah's hand to go to him. We'd neither of us admit it, my father and me, but when we came together in a thunderclap of an embrace, we were both crying.

It was downright frightening the way my mother and Mirah took to each other. It didn't start quite smoothly—Mirah was unaccustomedly shy (anyone who knew my mother's history would be), and there was a certain awkwardness when the children came forward. My mother took one look at my son as I introduced him and smiled warmly. "Antinous! Vix wrote that he called you Narcissus; you certainly deserve the name—"

Mirah looked just a little stiff, then. She stood between Dinah and Chaya, one arm about each, and I could see her arms tighten protectively. Our girls were pretty pink-cheeked little things, but it was Antinous everyone noticed first: his carved Bithynian face that broke into such a radiant smile, his lean-muscled height, his curling hair the color of dark honey . . . And my wife gave a sigh and a few pent-up tears, month after month, when she saw the evidence that her own belly hadn't decided yet to produce a boy just as beautiful. She'd conceived our two girls easily, but Chaya's birth had come very hard indeed, and my wife hadn't quickened since.

My mother must have seen the little shadow of disappointment on Mirah's face, because she turned with all her quiet warmth to the girls and clasped them against her. They were shy with strangers, but she addressed them fluidly in the language of the Jews, and Mirah smiled and replied in the same tongue. My mother had a low, melodious voice that could charm shy children and savage emperors in any language, and soon my daughters forgot their fear and my wife her diffidence, and all four of them were chattering away. "Vix!" Mirah exclaimed, switching out of Aramaic. "No wonder our girls are so dark-haired. They look like their grandmother!"

"I am officially old, if my firstborn has given me grandchildren," my mother announced with a smile. "But do call me Thea, so I don't feel quite so ancient!" She was only in her fifties, and barely looked it: a tall woman with threads of silver through dark hair, and in her red linen gown and tooled sandals she had the same serene elegance I remembered from the days she'd worn silks and pearls. My mother had been an emperor's unwilling mistress, and the Fates had brought her here to this cozy villa on a hilltop in Britannia. Never mind how.

The conversation had changed to Aramaic again, and Antinous was warming cups of wine for Mirah and my mother so they wouldn't have to get up. "I see you've raised this boy well," my mother approved. "Do tell me . . ."

"Our women want to chatter," my father announced. "Let them."

We went wandering, my father and I. Past the garden and up the slope, to another wooded hill thick with flowers. "Apple trees," he said, ducking under a branch. "Blooming very late, this year. I walk here every morning with the dogs."

"When did you finally lose that old three-legged bitch of yours?"

"God love her, she lasted a long time. These are all her descendants." Three puppies frisked at his heels: two curly-haired, one sleek and black. "Maybe your girls would like a pup?"

"Dinah hates fleas and Chaya's afraid of getting bitten. But I promised Antinous a dog."

We walked in silence a little ways, both grinning when we noticed I was walking just like him: hands clasped behind me at the small of my back. Antinous often walked that way, too, copying me since he was a boy, though his Bithynian blood gave him a liquid grace neither my father nor I could match. I had too much barbarian in me for grace, and so did my father, who stumped along as gnarled as a badger, his shoulders bent but still burly. He'd never been sure of his age, but he had to be past sixty, and unlike my mother, he looked older than his years. Well, he'd lived hard. The last few decades might have been easy, but the ones before had been all arena fights and blood and chains.

I showed him my campaign tokens; told a few stories of my campaigns. He told me of my younger brother and my three sisters; all grown. "Your brother's a stonemason—he'll be working on this wall of the Emperor's, and right pleased about it. He never wanted the sword, not the way you did." A quirk of his mouth. "They none of them gave me trouble the way you did."

"I turned out all right, didn't I?"

He turned and walked backward, appraising me. "Praetorian Prefect, eh?"

"Tribune. I do the Prefect's job, because he's an idiot, but he gets the title." I shrugged. "It's a pisser of a job."

There was a certain wry sharpness in his voice. "I killed Romans, and you serve them."

"I order them around! In fact, I'd have had a legion of my own to command if not for the Emperor."

"And that's an improvement? Romans made me fight, and now you're fighting for them?" But the quirk of his mouth had more pride in it this time. "A legion of your own, how did you manage that?"

"The Tenth Fidelis was supposed to be mine." My old legion. Emperor Trajan promised it to me at the end of the Parthian wars. Then Hadrian became Emperor, and you know the whole blasted rest of *that*. I told my father, briefly. "Hadrian's a bastard," I concluded.

"Most emperors are." My father ducked around a sapling without looking.

"You'd have liked Trajan." I'd wept like a baby at his death, and not because I was losing my legion. Trajan was the best man I'd ever known outside my father and maybe Titus Aurelius. "Emperor Hadrian, though . . ." I hesitated. "He's my enemy."

We'd reached the top of the hill, coming out from the flowering trees. There was a crumbling stone wall at the top, and my father leaned against it, folding his broad arms across his chest. "Tell me."

I told him, all of it. The many masks, and the man behind them.

My father sounded noncommittal. "Anything good to be said for him?"

I thought of Hadrian's rampant enthusiasm as he told me all about his wall. "He's got vision, I won't deny it. But what does that matter? He once threatened to have Mirah and the children killed if I didn't do his bidding."

A wordless rumble in my father's chest, like a lion's growl. I stared out over the hill.

"He threatened them," I said. "And I let him. I still *serve* him."

My father waited, scarred as an old oak, but not as yielding.

"Did he *break* me," I managed to say, "or did Rome?"

"No one could break my son." His reply came calmly. "Not the Young Barbarian."

My old gladiator name. How foolish it sounded; so foolish I almost laughed. "Not so young anymore."

"And grown more stubborn, not less." My father looked at me. "Nobody's broken you, boy. Not the Emperor, not anyone. You're just biding your time, like I taught you to do in a fight."

I felt my eyes sting. "If I'm just biding my time, why did I let him make me his tame dog?"

My father shrugged. "Why did I make so many kills in the arena?"

"You were a slave." I rested my fists on the crumbling wall. "You had no choice."

"Still felt like a black-souled bastard for doing it. You know how many I've killed? Men, unarmed prisoners, boys young enough to count as children. Women—there was one dressed like an Amazon. I still think about her. I've taken more lives than you, I'll wager. They called me the Barbarian, and I earned it. But I didn't *stay* the Barbarian, and you won't stay anybody's dog."

I looked down at the wooded hills, seeing Hadrian's bearded face. "Sometimes I think about killing him."

"I don't recommend it," my father said, reflective. "It's a lot of trouble, killing emperors." He should know.

"Mirah wants us to leave Rome. I reckon I could, get far enough away from Hadrian to make it not worth the chase, but . . ."

"But you've never liked running."

"No."

"So what's your plan? Keep taking everything he dishes out; smile and say 'Thank you, Caesar'? I know you, boy. You'll slip your leash someday, and then you'll crack him open like an egg, and that'll be the end of you."

"I have ways of keeping my temper." I smiled a little. "You see, I slept with his wife—"

My father nearly fell off the hilltop. *"What?"*

"Empress Sabina. Five years ago, in Selinus after Emperor Trajan died. I had her right under Hadrian's nose, and he never knew." That's what I thought of, every time he maddened me with his pompous jests or his whispered threats. It should have been the noble thought of Mirah and the children that held my temper in check, but I wasn't so noble as all that. It was the thought of the Emperor's supple wife lying under me that kept my jaw locked, no matter what the Emperor himself might be saying. *Your wife laced her arms around my neck and said, "Shut up and take me,"* I'd thought silently to Hadrian, so many times. *How does that feel, you bloodless bastard?*

I'd never say it—it would be death to say it. But I *could* say it if I wanted to. And that helped.

"You always had more balls than brains, boy," my father observed. "The Empress of *Rome?*"

"At least it helps me keep my temper, that memory." Which was something, because otherwise I wasn't proud of it: the one time I'd betrayed my wife. It had been from grief, not any great passion—Sabina and I had both been so ravaged by Trajan's death, we hardly knew what we were doing—but I'd still done it. With a woman who had ignored me ever since.

"My foolish Roman son," my father said, shaking his head, and we trailed down the flowered hill with the dogs loping between our feet.

ANNIA

Rome

Of all Annia's cousins, Marcus Catilius Severus had to be the worst. He was about her age, maybe younger; he had curly dark hair; and he was more boring than a white-washed wall.

"What's it made of?" he was asking, shading his eyes with his hand as he looked up at the huge dome of the half-completed Pantheon.

"Poured concrete," said Annia's father, looking down at them both. "Coffered inside, with a central oculus. Do you know what an oculus is?"

Marcus nodded. "I study famous buildings," he said, and sounded so pompous, Annia wanted to smack him. *Show-off.*

The building site for the great temple was deserted: all scaffolding and marble dust, littered stone-cutting tools and stray boards, drapes flapping in a wind that had gone cool now that summer was done. "I saw to it the workmen had a day's rest, as hard as they worked to finish the dome's exterior," Annia's father said as they approached the scaffolded portico—which took quite a long time, because everyone in Rome seemed to have a respectful greeting for her father as he passed by. "See the roof? If it were a bright day, you'd see the gilding flash. I told the Emperor I would finance all that gilding, Annia, so I reckoned you should see it. If just so you know why I can no longer afford to dower you." A fond tweak to her ear.

"Thank you for inviting me along, sir." Marcus marched as stiff as a little old man as they made their way inside, and Annia glowered at him. She adored these afternoons with her father, especially now that he had finally come back from Britannia. A good many fathers would have had only a curt nod for a daughter, but Annia's father was always willing to snatch an hour or so from his endless petitioners and Senate gatherings just to take her to the theatre for a pantomime or the Campus Martius to watch the chariots dash. She didn't want to share this precious time with boring Marcus, who had been shoved off on them because his mother had another headache. As if he were so smart, knowing what an oculus was. Annia knew what an oculus was too; it was a hole in the roof!

"Titus Aurelius," a sonorous voice hailed from behind, and Annia groaned inside. *Oh, Hades, not him!* The only person in the world more boring than her cousin.

Old Servianus came ducking through the scaffolding, raising a gnarled hand. He'd come back from Britannia recently, declaring his bones too old for the northern climes. "What he really means is that the Emperor doesn't take his advice on anything," Annia's mother had hooted, "so why bother freezing in Vindolanda just to be ignored!"

"I came to inspect the temple," Servianus went on, and heaved a sigh. "Corinthian columns! The Emperor insisted. In my day a plain Doric column . . ." As he droned on, Annia looked at the boy on whom Servianus was leaning like a staff. He wore a plain tunic like Marcus's, and the same *bulla* amulet about his neck all boys wore, but there wasn't anything else the same. This boy was taller, fair haired and stocky, at least nine—he laughed when Marcus offered him a little bow.

"Fortuna smiles upon me," Servianus concluded at last. "I wished to call upon you, Titus Aurelius, to discuss the uniting of our families— and here we stand united under the roof of all the gods! A good omen."

Annia's father sounded amused. "Our families uniting?"

"A marriage. My grandson, Gnaeus Pedanius Fuscus Salinator"—a thump to the shoulder of the stocky fair-haired boy—"and your daughter."

Annia's eyes, which had begun to wander around the temple, snapped back to the stocky boy.

"My daughter is very young," her father said mildly. "I hadn't planned on marrying her off until she was, oh, at least eight years old. By ten she'd be too long in the tooth, of course. But eight seems a reasonable age."

Servianus looked at him closely, but her father appeared perfectly serious. Only his eyes danced, the way they did when he laughed inside.

"A betrothal will suffice until they come of age." Servianus waved a hand. "Settled now while the children are young and obedient—"

"Some more obedient than others," her father murmured.

"In my day—"

"When *was* your day?" Annia piped up, even though she knew it was rude. Servianus reared back, and Annia's father gave her that glance of quiet authority that could stop anyone dead in their tracks.

"Marcus," he said, "why don't you escort your cousins to see the portico?"

"Yes, sir." Marcus rotated in place like a little legionary, and Annia found herself marched off on one side while Pedanius Fuscus slouched along on the other. They turned to face each other the moment they were outside among the scaffolding.

"Gnaeus Pedanius Fuscus," she said, folding her arms across her chest.

"Salinator," he corrected. "That goes on the end of my name."

"Doesn't *Salinator* mean brine?" she asked. "Why are you Gnaeus Pedanius Fuscus Brine-Face?"

He looked irritated. "It means salt. One of my ancestors instituted the tax upon salt."

Annia thought there were more impressive things to be remembered for. *Brine-Face.* "Married," she said instead, dubious. "Us?"

He gave a shrug. "Your father's the richest man in Rome. Or one of them. And my grandfather says I'll need a rich wife."

"Why?"

"I'm going to be Emperor." Pedanius said it as a fact. "My grandmother was Emperor Hadrian's sister, so I'm his great-nephew." He gave her a long superior blink. "You should be honored. Ugly girl like you—"

Annia just stuck her tongue out, but Marcus burst into speech. "Don't say that." He'd been standing there framed between two scaffolded columns, his gaze turning back and forth between them, and his face was flushed with indignation. "She's not ugly!"

Pedanius Fuscus laughed, and he swung himself up to sit on the lowest level of scaffolding. "I can say whatever I want. I'm the next Emperor. My grandfather tells me that every day."

"'A mouse does not rely on just one hole,'" Marcus said, looking triumphant.

Annia and Pedanius both stared at him. "What's that mean?" Pedanius asked, suspicious.

"It means, have another *plan.*"

Pedanius looked at him, feet swinging, eyes narrowed, already looking big and broad in his boy's tunic. His sandaled foot lashed out and caught Marcus square in the chest, sending him stumbling.

"Apologize," Pedanius said. "Or I'll have you exiled someday."

Marcus straightened. He looked down at his tunic and brushed at the muddy sandal print. He said nothing.

"Go on." Pedanius grinned. "Apologize. Or maybe I'll *execute* you once I'm Emperor."

Marcus's flush deepened. Annia started looking around. Her father and old Servianus were still inside the temple. All she could hear was the flap of drop cloths in the cold wind.

Pedanius hopped down from the scaffold and rested both hands on the column behind Marcus's head, trapping him. "It's treason to disobey the Emperor."

Annia glanced down at the scattering of workman's tools that had been left behind by some careless builder, and her eyes found a small wooden mallet. *"It's astounding what a good craftsman can accomplish with just a mallet,"* her father had said once. She picked it up, hefted it, then brought it down in a sharp clip on Pedanius Fuscus's hand where it rested on the column.

He yowled, snatching his hand back. Marcus let out a yelp too, probably from the yell right next to his ear. A few red drops landed bright in the pale stone dust under their feet as Pedanius danced up and down clutching his hand, and Annia saw that she'd broken his thumbnail in half.

Father had been right. It really *was* astounding, what you could accomplish with just a mallet. She tossed it to the floor at Pedanius's feet. Marcus stared at her, wide-eyed, and so did her prospective husband. He was trying to stare daggers at her, but his eyes were too bright and wet to glare. He looked like he was about to start blubbering.

Annia reached out and grabbed Marcus's hand. "You're not Emperor yet," she told the Emperor's great-nephew. "And Marcus is my cousin, not yours. So you can't tease him."

She turned and towed Marcus back toward the temple's entrance, but she heard Pedanius's voice rise behind her. "I'm telling my grandfather."

"Tell him a girl made you cry," she said, turning back to see the tears of rage spill over his lashes. Probably no one had ever hit him before, just stood around telling him he'd one day be master of Rome. "Now you really are a Brine-Face," she added for good measure, looking at the salty tracks on his cheeks, and dragged Marcus back into the temple.

Old Servianus was looking peevish. "—most definitely a matter to be considered in the future," her father was saying graciously. "Your grandson is a fine boy, most worthy of consideration. Ah, Annia, did you forget to bring young Pedanius Fuscus with you?"

"He's coming," she said. "He hit his hand with a mallet."

"That's a lie," Marcus whispered under his breath.

"Is not," Annia whispered back. Brine-Face *did* hit his hand with a mallet. She just hadn't mentioned that she'd been the one swinging it.

Pedanius came foot-dragging into the temple, glaring at Annia and Marcus. Annia gave the glare back as good as she got, but Marcus just returned it with a proud look. Annia couldn't say which Brine-Face seemed to resent more.

Years later, she would still remember that meeting with such clarity—the half-built temple, the flapping drop cloths, the droning overhead—and wonder how the adults could have been so oblivious to the fact that their children had just become mortal enemies. "Mortal enemies," Marcus scoffed when Annia said as much later. "Don't be dramatic!"

"Am I wrong?" Because Marcus remembered that day with the same steel-edged clarity, and she knew Pedanius Fuscus did, too. Like it was important, more important than just a broken thumbnail and a few childish insults. And later when they were all grown, Marcus didn't seem to find Annia's idea quite so silly.

"I think the Fates were watching," he confessed. "I think they tied a knot that day. His thread, yours, and mine."

"Now who's being dramatic?"

But at the time, of course, they were all too young and ignorant to do anything but glare at each other. And Annia ended up glaring at Marcus too, because when Servianus finally dragged his sullen nephew away, Marcus gave Annia's hand a squeeze and she realized they were still standing with fingers interlocked warm and damp.

"Don't marry Pedanius Fuscus," he said suddenly. "Marry me."

"Oh, *Hades*," she said in disgust, and wouldn't talk to him all the way home.

CHAPTER 4

VIX

Vindolanda, Northern Britannia

"Nothing like a good kill to clear the head," the Emperor said happily, wiping his long knife across one sleeve. A doe lay at his feet, an arrow broken off in her haunch. Hadrian's dogs had brought her down after a long chase across the rain-spotted hills, but they didn't finish her off. They knew to down the prey, then pull back in a ring to let their master finish the job. I'd watched the doe look up at Hadrian with huge liquid eyes as he drew the knife across her throat. "You look grim, Tribune," the Emperor observed, gesturing for the huntsmen to bind up the doe's carcass. "You aren't fond of these hunts of mine?"

"No, Caesar." I didn't much like killing animals. Not for sport, anyway.

"Is it in the killing of men, then, that you find your release?"

I eyed him. "Depends, Caesar."

He laughed, still full of even-tempered good cheer in that way that made me uneasy. "We travel south soon, and then make the crossing to Hispania—as soon as the first segment of wall is done. Perhaps Fortuna will favor you there with your preferred choice of game, Tribune."

I felt a pang of wistfulness, because I'd enjoyed these months in Britannia. Watching the wall rise was a daily fascination; the steep hills gave me the chance to condition my Praetorians on ruthless marches; and my family was close again. Mirah had spent the summer helping my mother with the supervision of the hillside villa, both of them chattering in Aramaic while Dinah and Chaya played inside with the end-less red-haired babies my sisters had produced while I was gone.

I still slept away from Mirah, of course. Spent most of my nights at the fort working late on endless rosters and supply lists and *frumenta-rii* reports; rising early because Hadrian apparently never slept and was always off either hunting or interviewing petitioners by first light. But as often as I could, I returned to the house I'd left at eighteen and fought practice bouts with my father or shared a mug of mead with my stonemason younger brother, who spoke eagerly of the wall that he was helping to raise. It was making his fortune for him, that wall.

No, I wasn't really in any hurry to move on. Not from my mother, who couldn't quite stop reaching out to touch my cheek whenever she saw me, as though memorizing my face in case I was gone another fifteen years. Not from my father's rock-silent, rock-steady presence. And I didn't think Mirah would be so happy to journey on to Hispania, either. She'd turned to me in bed the last time I'd been able to stay, her voice diffident in the dark. "You know I've always been in favor of Judaea, Vix." Her fingers found mine on the pillow and twined through them. "My family being there, and our people. But if Judaea sounds too strange to you . . . We could settle here. After all, *your* family is here. We could be happy."

"Not our girls," I said, trying to joke. "Did you hear Dinah com-plaining about the mud, and Chaya crying about hearing wolves? Proper little prigs, our daughters are turning into."

"Because they're *Roman* girls, and do we want them to keep growing up that way? They'd get used to the mud and the wolves." Mirah's fingers tightened. "They love your family—all right, your father terri-fies them, but Antinous really shouldn't have told them all those glad-iator stories." Voice softening, then. "It doesn't have to be Judaea, Vix. If we could stay here—"

"I'll think on it."

"You're always thinking," she sighed, and I kissed her then to quiet her. But kisses never distracted my wife for long, and I could see the question in her eyes.

We could be happy here, Vix. So how—

"Tribune?" Hadrian asked, and I looked at his bearded face.

"Hispania next, Caesar," I said woodenly. "I'll begin laying preparations."

"I know, I know." His eyes sparkled, and he swung up into his saddle in one easy flowing motion. "You'd rather conquer the rest of this wet little island. My bloodthirsty dog of war!" He shook his head at me and set off at a thundering pace for Vindolanda.

It was my fault, what happened when we got back. A guard must be alert, and I was too absorbed in my own thoughts. Hadrian had swung off his horse in the courtyard before the *praetorium*, dealing with the rush of secretaries and scribes thronging to meet him, and I was ordering the horses away when I heard a voice calling.

"Vix!"

I looked up with an absent frown. A familiar honey-colored head was fighting its way toward me through the crush of the courtyard. "Antinous, what are you doing here?"

"I know you don't like me visiting you at the fort, but I had to show you." Proudly Antinous presented me with a bright-eyed, big-eared ball of squirming black fur. "Your father gave him to me, said I could have my pick of the pups if Mirah didn't mind! Isn't he beautiful?"

I should have sent Antinous away. I'd been so firm on my rule that my family did not mix with the people I met as Praetorian. I should have sent Antinous home, and I was forming the suitable stern words even as I gave his new puppy's ear a tweak, when Hadrian's sudden laugh caught me off guard.

"Tribune, what a surprise." The Emperor sounded knowing, and I turned, my arm still slung absently over Antinous's lean young shoulder. "And here I thought you always turned up your nose at bum-boys. I don't blame you for changing your mind; he's a pretty one."

I'd shrugged off far worse bits of spite than that during my years at Hadrian's side. I doubt he even meant insult; the Emperor merely looked amused. But Antinous flushed a slow dark red, and my arm tightened too late around his shoulder as I saw the danger. Because my son had never seen the Emperor up close, and in the common breastplate and mud-splashed cloak he'd donned for the hunt, Hadrian was just another bearded huntsman. And my adopted son shoved his new puppy at me, took two furious strides forward before I could yank him back, and drove his fist into the Emperor's nose.

I saw droplets of blood fly as Hadrian toppled astonished into the mud.

"He's my *father*, you foul-mouthed bastard," Antinous shouted, coming for him again. "And I'm no one's bum-boy!"

Miraculously, I got him before the Praetorians descended, dropping the puppy and doubling an arm about his shoulder. "Antinous, no—" I yanked him back so hard he almost fell to the mud, thrusting him behind me as the guards closed in a sudden ring. "Stay back, it's nothing to draw blades for!" But my hand fell instinctively to the hilt of my own *gladius* as I saw Hadrian uncoil from the ground.

"Caesar, are you hurt?" I heard Antinous give a sudden convulsive gulp behind me as he heard the title, as one of the Praetorians approached Hadrian to blot his nose with some hastily torn strip of cloth. The Emperor waved him aside. He touched his swelling nose delicately, and I saw his tongue dart out to taste blood. He looked up then, his eyes blasting me from notice and fastening on my son, and my surge of terror nearly welded my hand to the *gladius* hilt.

Because all that affable, inexplicable good temper of the past few months had dropped away like a pantomime mask.

Hadrian spoke softly, eyes never leaving Antinous. "I didn't know you had a son."

"Adopted," I managed to say. Hoping he would be more merciful if he thought Antinous didn't share my bad barbarian blood.

"He requires instruction," the Emperor stated even more softly, "in polite behavior."

"He does," I choked out. "I will punish him—"

"No."

The guards edged closer, swords unsheathed.

"Stand down," I growled, "stand down!"

They inched back, eyes never wavering from Antinous. My son stood still as a statue behind me, the puppy whining nervously between his feet, and I felt a quiver of fear go through him. A quiver of a different kind seemed to go through Hadrian; he squeezed his eyes shut and brought a hand to his own face, giving his bleeding nose a vicious pinch. I saw more blood trickle down to his lips, and he said something strange. "Merciful," he murmured, and his tongue lapped to taste blood again. "Merciful."

When he lowered his hand he was smiling. It would have chilled my blood, if I hadn't been so desperate for any sign my son would get out of this alive.

"In Londinium, I blinded a slave who annoyed me," Hadrian told Antinous in a pleasant voice. "For striking me, boy, I could take your hand. So get out of my sight, before I give in to temptation."

"I'm—" Antinous quavered, and his voice had broken three years ago to a light tenor, but it cracked now like a child's. He looked like a child suddenly, my tall and handsome son. "I apologize, Caesar, most humbly. I did not recognize you—I wouldn't—"

"No." Hadrian was still smiling, but I didn't believe this smile. This wasn't the carefree grin he wore as he watched the progress of the wall, striding up and down outlining his giddy plans for a full eighty miles of stonework. This smile was just a poorly constructed copy. "You did not recognize me. For that, boy, I will allow you to take your leave."

Antinous stood frozen, pinned by the twin points of Hadrian's eyes, but I wasn't. I pushed the puppy into my son's arms and sent him toward the gates with a massive shove. "Go home," I whispered, "and stay there."

He gave me one wide-eyed look and fled.

"Keep him out of my sight," Hadrian said, and the cordiality dropped from his voice. He was allowing a pair of slaves to fuss over the nose, bringing a basin of water. "You have no idea how hard I find it, Vercingetorix, to extend mercy to those who hurt me."

I felt a tiny hot thread of anger weaving through my fright, now that Antinous was safely gone. "He didn't recognize you, Caesar!"

"Then you've raised a son as ignorant and barbaric as yourself, Vercingetorix." Hadrian laughed, glancing in the direction Antinous had gone. "But he's pretty, I'll say that. Pretty as an old man's dream."

The fear left me then, and I inhaled pure red rage. It filled me, swamped me, and I took two fast steps forward until I stood nose to nose with the Emperor of Rome.

Lay a finger on my son, and I'll kill you. I didn't say it because it would get me killed, but I shoved it out my eyes, all my pent-up threats. Then I turned and began to stalk away, shaking with the effort to keep my hands off that Imperial throat.

But Hadrian must have made some gesture, because two of my own Praetorians caught me by the arms. "Let go of me," I said contemptuously, batting a hand off my shoulder, but they seized me again. If I'd had Boil with me they wouldn't have dared; my second would have my back over any Emperor—but these were boot-licking Praetorians, and they wrenched me around to face the Emperor.

"Release him," Hadrian said, and the hands holding my arms disappeared. "Remove yourselves." The guards and the secretaries and the rest of the entourage retreated out of earshot, although they were all gaping. Hadrian stepped closer, his face quite serene.

"I exhibit mercy," he said, "and you glare threats at me?"

"You threatened my son," I snarled. "My *son*—"

The dagger flashed in the Emperor's hand before I could react, sharp point coming to lodge just under my chin. My muscles bunched, but I willed myself stone-still. Hadrian was no career soldier; I could have beaten him with shield and *gladius*—but he was the finest hunter I'd ever seen. I knew how efficiently he could cut a throat.

"Vercingetorix," Hadrian said calmly, and the knife's point traced a small circle just under my chin. "You are useful to me, and so I allow you a certain latitude. But my tolerance is not infinite."

"Yes, yes, now you threaten me," I snarled, still not moving. "We both know how this dance plays out, Caesar. You tell me to curb my tongue and do what I'm told, or you'll cut *my* hand off."

He regarded me, pitying. "Oh, Vercingetorix. If I truly wanted to punish you, I wouldn't mutilate you. I'd just bugger you instead."

His knife tip sank a fraction deeper, and I felt a drop of blood slide down my neck. I looked past his unblinking gaze, saw the Imperial entourage whispering among themselves and straining to hear what their Emperor was saying. But no one was close enough, and for an instant I wondered if I'd heard wrong. I looked back to Hadrian, saw his placid, peaceful smile, and I knew I hadn't heard wrong.

And I was suddenly terrified.

"You see, I know what would happen if I threatened to take your hand off, as I threatened to take your son's. You'd just bundle up the bleeding stump and hit me with it." His knife traced slowly from my chin along the line of my jaw, toward the corner of my eye. That eye began to water, but I didn't dare blink with the point pricking my lid. "But you're proud. All warriors are." The knife traced back down my neck. "I could crack that pride in half, and do you know how I'd do it? I'd have you stripped and spread-eagled, and maybe it would take six Praetorians to keep you still, and maybe it would take a dozen, but they'd hold you down for me. I don't like my bedmates scarred and crude, and I don't like them unwilling, either. I prefer them handsome and eager, and for an emperor, there are plenty like that. But I'd use you till you bled, Vercingetorix. I'd make you my whore while everyone watched."

My mind flashed utterly white, like the moment when a savage streak of lightning dazzles the eyes. The lightning passes but you're left on the ground, screaming in terror. And my mind was screaming, clutching the blank whiteness, trying not to fit images to his unspeakable words.

"I'd make you take up your duties afterward," Hadrian went on placidly. "Make you stand watch in that lion skin you won for bravery in Dacia, while every soldier in Rome snickers because I used Vercingetorix the Red like a dog uses a bitch. And I'd smile every time I looked you in the eye, and I don't think you'd be holding my gaze with your head thrown back, not like you are now. You'd look away. And I'd like to see that, Vercingetorix. I'd like to see that very much. But it would break you, or at least, it would if I did it properly. And you're useful to me whole."

The knife disappeared from my neck, but my raw skin quivered where the point had lingered. I felt sick and cold and violated. There were no words. None at all.

"So keep on being useful to me, won't you?" He reached out and patted my head, like he'd pat a dog. Or a bitch. "Because if I can't use you, I might as well break you."

I turned my back on him then. A Praetorian never turns his back on his Emperor and a man never turns his back on his enemy, but I could not look at him anymore. I could *not*. I closed my eyes and clenched my teeth, but it was no use. I vomited, bending double to void my shame onto the stones. Over the roar in my ears I could hear the guards murmur blankly, wondering what was wrong with their iron-hard tribune. And I could hear Hadrian's voice, crooning low as if to a lover.

"Good dog."

ANTINOUS

"You look like you could use a drink," said Arius the Barbarian, and poured Antinous a cup of wine directly from the amphora, no water. Mirah looked up, brows creased, as Antinous took the cup and collapsed onto a stool.

"I struck the Emperor." Antinous downed the wine at a single swallow, not feeling the burn. He was still shaking, seeing the Emperor's eyes bore into his. Emperor Hadrian, the dark creature of his father's bitter stories. "Sweet gods, I struck the *Emperor!*"

"Not wise," Arius said mildly, and that was when Vix kicked the door in.

"Father," Antinous began, but Vix crossed the room in three long strides, and Antinous felt himself hauled up by the throat. His cup fell to the floor, and Mirah gave a sharp gasp.

I shouldn't have called him Father, Antinous thought disjointedly.

"Mirah," Vix said, his voice low as a whisper and barely recognizable. "Pack Antinous's things. He is leaving."

Antinous's heart lurched. "I am?"

"The Emperor wants you out of his sight," Vix said, "and I don't even want you on the same damned *island.* I'm sending you back to Rome."

No, Antinous thought, *but it was fair. Of course it was fair. You struck the Emperor, you stupid boy. So many years being the perfect son, and now you ruined it. Of course you're being sent away.*

Dimly he heard Mirah retreating, heard his grandfather shepherding the girls back from where they peeked around the door—"Go bake bread with your grandmother, now." Heard the door shutting, leaving Antinous alone with his father, who still held him by the throat and had eyes like black pits.

"Vix—" Antinous rasped, but Vix shook him like a rat.

"You idiot boy."

"I didn't know! How could I know it was the Emperor? Just a bearded man—" Even now, Antinous didn't have a very clear vision of Hadrian's face, just his eyes. He'd been too frightened to see more.

Vix's hand dropped. Antinous slid down, misery welling in him like a new spring. His new black puppy nosed at his elbow, whining. If he hadn't been so eager to show Vix the puppy—

"You're right," Vix was saying. He sounded tired. "You didn't know him for who he was. That's my fault. I should have shown you at some point . . ."

He seemed to lose the thought, sinking down on a stool and locking his fists together. He was shaking, Antinous saw in shock—his invincible, godlike father, shaking as though he'd been terrified out of his wits.

"Would he truly have taken my hand off?" Antinous ventured.

Vix let out a harsh little laugh. "Hell's gates, don't you remember any of the things I've told you over the years? What he's capable of? I nearly *lost* you today. I nearly lost my—"

He bit that off, staring down at the floor.

Antinous felt a lump rise in his throat. "I'm sorry."

No answer.

The lump turned into a stone. "Where are you sending me?" A void opened in front of him, the one he'd felt when Vix first took him in; the fear that if he wasn't good enough, wasn't clever enough, wasn't obedient enough . . .

"I'd send you to the Tenth Fidelis if I could." Vix sounded listless.

"A stint in the legions—that would knock the urge out of you to go round hitting strangers. But you're too young."

Relief stabbed through Antinous like a spear. *I don't want to be a legionary*, he thought—had been thinking in the back of his mind for a long time. But how did you say that to the consummate legion man?

"The Tenth Fidelis can wait till you're older," Vix went on, and Antinous's stomach clenched again. "For now it'll have to be the *paedogogium* back in Rome. You can board at the school with the other boys your age; get some proper training; learn some manners. Keep your dog with you . . ."

School. Antinous supposed it could be worse. "For how long?"

"A year? Two? Who bloody knows?" Vix rose in a violent movement, reaching for the amphora. He poured wine out in a splash, hands still shaking, and downed it all at once.

Antinous rose too, feeling the black puppy wind anxiously about his ankles. "I'm sorry," he repeated, his voice still hoarse from the force of Vix's grip. Vix had never lifted a hand to him in all his life. Had never needed to. And now . . . Antinous bent and picked up the puppy, hiding the tears that sprang to his eyes.

"In a way I'm proud of you." Vix still stood half turned away, staring into his cup. "You didn't let even the Emperor of Rome call you a bum-boy."

"I—"

"That's good." His father spoke tightly, still not turning. "It's good to know you'll draw that line where it needs to be drawn, when you'll be on your own in the *paedogogium*. There are plenty of opportunists in Rome who will take advantage of a good-looking boy like you, if you let them."

Antinous cleared his throat. "I'll help Mirah pack."

But his father swung around, shoving another stool across the floor with one foot. Antinous sank down as if struck, and so did Vix. For a moment Vix just rubbed his callused hand across the base of the wine cup in a slow, aimless motion. "There have been women, I know. Men, too," he said finally. "You had the women, and the men had you."

Antinous felt a crimson flush mounting his cheeks. "Everyone does it—"

"Boys, maybe. But you're almost a man. And you're going out of my reach, where I can't protect you as you turn into one." Vix's hands gripped the wine cup so tight it nearly shattered. "Don't let anyone *use* you, once you're out there on your own in the Eternal City. You're young and you're handsome, and they'll try. There are men in Rome who like nothing better than a handsome boy too innocent to guard his own arsehole. And once you're a man grown, if you're letting men spread your cheeks—well, you'll be laughed at for a useless bum-boy and a whore. You'll be shamed." A short laugh. "Listen to me ramble. I don't need to tell *you* this; you're the one who defended your own honor today."

"Nobody calls the legionaries bum-boys," Antinous managed to say. "And you've told me plenty of them like to . . ."

His father waved that aside. "If you're in the legions, it's different."

"Mirah wouldn't say so. She says it's all sin."

"That's what her god says, not—"

"Isn't he your god too?" Antinous knew the answer; he was just being evasive. His father might murmur the prayers along with Mirah because it made her happy, but Vix believed in luck, in fortune, in Rome, and in himself. Not in any particular God, Mirah's or any other.

Vix shrugged. "Mirah's god might be mine by birth and blood, but it's Rome we live in." Confirming every one of Antinous's thoughts. "As long as we're in Rome and not Judaea, Rome's rules govern us. Not Mirah's god. And a man's honor and what he does to keep it or lose it—that's something Rome's rules govern, too."

But why? Antinous clamped his lips, feeling stubborn. *Why does Rome say some things you want are allowed, and some are not? Who made the rules?* That was what he really wanted to know. *Why?*

"You're right when you say the legions are different," his father continued. A man who rarely wondered *why.* "Plenty of times there aren't enough women to go round, so no one cares if you'd rather bugger your *contubernium* mate than go without altogether. But when you've got wider options, people aren't so forgiving. You can't be anybody's *mount,* or the world will despise you—that's just the way it is." He looked at

Antinous. "I'm glad you wouldn't let the Emperor shame you today. I don't ever want to see you used and belittled. Not you."

It was his father who looked shamed, Antinous thought. Shamed and shaken and gazing at him with anxious eyes, begging Antinous to understand.

"I understand," he mumbled at last, and averted his gaze.

"Good," Vix said. "End of lecture." He poured more wine for them both. Antinous gripped his cup, still feeling his cheeks glow hot.

"I'm sorry," Vix said gruffly, noting his blushes. "I—it's the sort of thing you have to say, when your boy strikes out on his own. Especially when he strikes out a year or two earlier than you ever thought he'd have to go . . ."

Antinous's throat filled. "You'll miss me?" he managed to ask. Because he didn't think Mirah would, not really. Much as she loved him, he didn't share her blood or her faith: He had too much dilution through his life from the Roman gods worshipped everywhere else. He couldn't do as his father did and just murmur the prayers to make Mirah happy; Vix didn't mind doing it, but Antinous did, and he knew it made Mirah feel as though she'd failed in raising him. *No, she won't miss me much.* And he didn't really think his sisters would, either. They loved him, but they had their mother, their mother's prayers, their own secretive girlish games just for two. They had no need of Antinous.

No one did.

"Of course I'll miss you!" Vix sounded baffled. "What kind of question is that? I'll be counting the days till you rejoin the family."

Antinous smiled then. Something he couldn't have imagined doing, this wretched afternoon.

"You know, I'm almost jealous?" Vix reached out, covering Antinous's hand with his rough one. "I've never hit that bastard Hadrian, no matter how many insults he's heaped on my head. But he calls you a bum-boy, and you damn near break his nose." Squeezing Antinous's fingers, so hard they hurt. "A fist like that, you won't need me guarding your back in Rome."

"Still wish I had you," Antinous said. The puppy yelped and spilled to the ground as Vix rose, yanking Antinous up into a crushing embrace.

"Hell's gates, boy. You don't take care of yourself, I will storm into the next world just to beat your shade black and blue—"

Antinous scrubbed at his stinging eyes. "I promise I won't fail you. I won't *disappoint* you—"

"You won't. You couldn't." Vix pulled back, gripping him by the shoulders and giving him one of those fierce looks. The kind that made Antinous feel tall as a mountain. "Just keep out of trouble, don't hit any more emperors, kill anyone who calls you a bum-boy or hurts your dog"—looking down at the puppy gazing up huge-eared and anxious—"and stick to bedding girls because you can do whatever you want between the sheets with a girl, and it's all a deal simpler. That's my last bit of fatherly advice."

More than enough, Antinous thought with a twist of shame in his stomach. Because he could think of having a girl soft and sweet-smelling in his arms, and enjoy the thought—but there were other times too, like the clerk on the ship to Gesoriacum who had turned him with rough passion against a wall, and that had been something else entirely.

You want to know why I really hit the Emperor, Father? Because it's what you'd do if someone called you a bum-boy. Not what I'd do. I did it because you'd expect me to be insulted.

And he'd never in all the world be able to say so.

ANNIA

Rome

It was a very big party: women in jewels and bright silks pretending they liked each other; senators in wreaths pretending they were listening to each other; slaves with silver decanters and golden platters pretending they weren't eavesdropping on everyone. Annia could see her mother, all emeralds and turquoise silks and a belly round as a melon, happy and laughing and not pretending anything at all, and there was her father ignoring a pair of hovering senators so he could talk with cousin Marcus, who hung on his every word. Good thing Marcus was occupied; he'd be sure to tattle if he saw Annia now. She'd broken something again, and she had absolutely no intention of getting caught.

Annia scouted the room. Everyone seemed to be watching the choir of boys hired from the *paedogogium* to sing Greek songs, the group of them arrayed like young gods in their silk tunics and oiled limbs. The boys were all tall and well-built, but one was more beautiful than a god—he had hair the color of honey and a sweet tenor voice. The women, Annia saw with a giggle, looked like they wanted to eat him. So did a lot of the men. Either way, nobody was looking at her.

Perfect.

Applause burst out, and Annia swept the pieces of the glass dish into her skirt hem and trotted out into the gardens. Live peacocks wandered arrogantly through the hedges, and she kept her distance because she'd already tried to ride a peacock once and the results had not been good. She skirted the couples kissing in dark alcoves, finally finding a laurel bush under which she began to sweep the broken bits of glass.

"What are you doing, little monkey?"

Annia whirled. "Nothing." It was the boy from the *paedogogium*, the beautiful one with the fair hair. "Why aren't you singing?"

"That was the last song." He looked amused. "You're hiding something."

"Am not." Annia shoved the last bit of glass under the bush with her foot. It clinked.

"Don't worry, I won't tell." He smiled. He had a beautiful smile, the kind that crinkled his eyes and put deep dimples in his cheeks. But there was something false about it.

"Why are you sad?" Annia asked suddenly.

"Why should I be sad?" He squatted down so he was level with her height. "I'm at a beautiful party in the most illustrious city in the world, talking to the most beautiful girl in the house. I have no reason to be sad."

"You're sad," Annia stated. It was in his eyes, brown eyes that looked just a little wistful even over that dimpled smile. "Why?"

"Perhaps I'm lonely." He sounded thoughtful. "In a way, I think I've always been a little lonely."

"Why?" she asked, genuinely curious. Because Annia couldn't remember ever being lonely. She had her father telling her what an Ionian column was; her mother telling her what a good sister she was going to be when the baby arrived; the housekeeper telling her to stop climbing trees before she broke her neck; Marcus droning the latest verse from his tutor. There were too many people in Annia's life ever to get lonely. "Why?" she asked again.

"I'm new to the *paedogogium*, only here a month, and everyone but me seems to know the career they hope to take. I don't believe in my mother's god or want my father's career, and I can't say that to either of them. I have more would-be lovers than I ever have friends. And I have no one to tell any of this to but"—touching the tip of Annia's nose gently—"you. So I think I should know your name, little monkey."

"Annia Galeria Faustina."

"Antinous," he said, and rose to give her a graceful bow, his fair hair shining in the lamplight.

"Don't be lonely," Annia instructed him. "Be my friend." And she seized him by the hand and dragged him, laughing, to meet her father.

SABINA

Hadrian's Wall

"What are you doing here, Vibia Sabina?" the Emperor asked.

"I wanted to see it by moonlight." *Half the truth.*

"It is quite a sight, isn't it?" The Emperor came to stand beside Sabina, arms folded across his chest. He wore the legionary dress he affected when staying at any fort—Sabina had steered him gently, there, pointing out how the legions liked it, and she couldn't deny it suited him, tall and imposing as he was. Sabina had a cloak of wolf pelts, soft gray fur pinned at the shoulder with a silver circle brooch, and she'd taken off her horrid braided wig. The muffled clank of their

Praetorians came from behind as the guards shifted their feet, but in the soft blackness of the night it might have been just the Emperor and the Empress, looking at the white ribbon of the wall.

"Did it come out as you'd hoped?" There had been a lengthy ceremony this afternoon where the engineers had formally presented the short finished segment. Hadrian had clambered over everything, asked questions about everything, and finally pronounced himself pleased. But now he was frowning.

"I wish they could have built more."

"You only gave them three months! Even just a mile or two of finished wall is impressive on that schedule." A waxing moon swelled in the scatter of stars overhead, turning the grassy hills as dark as pitch— but flung across the stretch of black, a broad band of white stone gleamed. "That was a good idea to have it plastered and whitewashed. It looks twice as impressive."

"Thank you, my dear."

Sabina looked at him in surprise. She could not remember the last time he had called her "my dear." Since the night in Londinium where she had advised him to wear the mask of a good man even if he could not be one, he seemed to have been regarding her rather closely, as though watching for signs of meddling. *Advice is one thing*, Sabina thought, *but given sparingly*. So she had stepped back and kept to her duties: attending the dedication of an altar to Neptune and another to Oceanus; presiding over the discharge ceremonies of old legionaries; keeping up her correspondence with Rome. Doing her duty, and doing it faultlessly. Hadrian gave no praise, but . . .

My dear.

"So—" Her husband rocked back on his heels, staring at the moon-drenched stretch of stone. "Do you think my wall is just a foolish expense, as so many others do?"

"On the contrary. You didn't just build it to control trade across the border, or to give the legions something to do."

"Didn't I?"

"Publius Aelius Hadrian always has multiple motivations," she teased, but very lightly. He used to like her teasing, but his skin was thinner as Emperor. "You want to be sure that later Emperors don't undo this policy of yours."

"And which policy would that be?"

"Your belief that the Empire is big enough as it stands." She nodded out at the wall. "You said you wished to enclose our territories in borders, so future emperors will hesitate to go beyond. With something as permanent as this wall marking the boundary, they will not."

"Most people consider it a fault, that I have no wish to go beyond."

"Most people are fools. It was a bitter thing to force down everyone's throat, giving up Syria and Parthia and the other territories Trajan conquered . . . but that didn't mean it was wrong. We could never have held those territories. Even Trajan knew that, at the end." She had loved her great-uncle, but his blind love of victory had to be counted a fault, at least when it led him to overreach. "Nobody wanted to hear you say the Empire was getting too big, but it was."

Hadrian quirked a brow. "Are you flattering me, Vibia Sabina?"

"Is it flattery if it's truth?" Perhaps it was both. Sabina rubbed a thumb along the band of the gold-and-iron ring Hadrian had put on her finger at their wedding: gold for flattery, soft but pretty; iron for truth, hard but strong—both were layered together in her ring and in her marriage, quite easily. "I didn't like hearing you say you were undoing Trajan's victories, either," she found herself saying. "But now I'm proud of you."

Hadrian preened just a little, and Sabina smiled, surprised to find how sincerely she meant it. She might not *like* her husband very much, but there were things she had always admired about him. "So, is it a journey to Hispania next?"

"Gaul first. I will build Empress Plotina a fitting temple at the city of her birthplace. After Gaul, Hispania. It is time I made an appearance in the province that reared me, and Hispania will prove a fitting launch to visit Africa and Mauretania."

Africa. Sabina caught her breath, envisioning huge dappled cats and tawny skies and the great Iseum that Cleopatra's daughter had built in mourning for her lost Egypt . . .

Wait, she told herself. *Wait.*

"You are silent, Vibia Sabina." Hadrian slanted a brow at her. "I'd expected to hear you pleading to come along."

"Oh, I long to see Africa and Mauretania and all the rest," Sabina said frankly. "But an empress cannot always have what she wants. I believe I could be of use to you in Africa; the system of grain dispersal there is something I've been looking into—but if you feel I would be more useful in Rome, then back to Rome I will go." Sabina looked at him, matching his look of regal calm. "I go where you need me, Caesar."

"That was not always your way."

"It is, now."

Hadrian regarded her, eyes glittering in the moonlight. "I meet tomorrow with my secretaries and my legates," he said at last. "To discuss the next leg of our tour, and what matters must be seen to in each province. Attend, if you please. I would hear your opinions. And now, I will bid you good night."

"Good night, my dear."

He gave her a smile, a friendly smile, and she inclined her head in turn. He tramped off toward his quarters, his Praetorians clinking behind, and it wasn't till he was gone and Sabina was left with her own guards that she allowed herself a small, soundless laugh.

"Lady?" one of her guards ventured. "Do you wish to return to your quarters?"

"Not one bit," Sabina said. "Wait here."

"Lady, a Praetorian's duty—"

"Is to wait when his Empress tells him." Sabina tossed the hem of her furred cloak over one arm. "Your Empress wants a closer look at the wall."

Her footsteps quickened until she was skimming the frosty grass— how long had it been since she had the freedom to *run* anywhere? She reached the outer staircase that led to the top of the wall and took the steps two at a time, reaching the top in a final burst of breath. Skidding to a halt, she laughed up at the star-wheeling sky. "Gods," she heard herself exclaiming aloud in wonder, "it's glorious!"

The whitewashed stones drank the moonlight, bouncing it back so the wall was lit as bright as day. The fort on one side was just a collection

of guttering lights, torches that glowed a sickly orange in comparison
to the stark light of the stars, and to the north there was nothing but a
sea of black and the whistling of trees. Someday, perhaps in five years
or so, the wall would stretch out in both directions, an infinite gleaming line from horizon to horizon, but for now it was just an oasis in the
night, the whiteness disappearing abruptly a mile in either direction.
When Sabina looked down at her own hands, they looked like they'd
turned to ice-white marble, and her wolf-skin cloak to pure gleaming
silver. "Glorious," she said again softly, and felt the beauty stab in her
throat like pain.

There was another reason she'd wanted to be alone here, alone
under the moon, and she slowly drew it out from under her cloak. A
letter from her sister, along with a small package; both arrived this
afternoon. Sabina opened the package first, and something small fell
into her hand: a cameo of carved glass, showing an exquisitely etched
profile white against blue. At the sight of that profile—a child's short
nose and stubborn chin, her unruly hair and the eyes that had been
carved almost to glare . . . "Oh," Sabina said softly, and her throat
seized with pain of an altogether different kind. "Oh," she said again,
and her hands shook as she broke the seal on the letter.

Annia as she looks now, her sister had written. *I shall have her carved
again next year, if you are still away from Rome. This way you'll always
know what your niece looks like, no matter how long you're gone on your
travels!*

Clever Faustina, always assuming letters might be read by outside
eyes. *Niece.* Sabina had trained herself to use that word from the
first day.

"You should hold her," Faustina had said after the birth, coming to
Sabina's bedside with an armload of blankets. The villa was deep in the
hills of Toscana, a quiet estate where Faustina's mother had retired
after widowhood—she'd welcomed them with open arms and a house
emptied of slaves, acting as midwife herself so there would be no witness who could say the Empress of Rome had given birth. Faustina and
her mother looked after everything, and afterward stood like two
blond sentinels with a wailing bundle held between them.

"Even only once," Sabina heard her stepmother say, "hold your daughter!"

Over the mass of blankets, Sabina had seen a dome of forehead like a rosy peach and a pair of furious waving fists, and she shut her eyes before she could see more. "My niece," she said firmly, or as firmly as she could after being racked by two unending days of labor. "I have to think of her that way. Always, not one slip. Not if she's to be safe. So take her away. Please."

Niece.

Never daughter.

Think it, Sabina thought, staring at Annia's stubborn carved profile. *Let yourself think it, just once. There's no one here on the wall but you.*

Daughter. My daughter. Mine.

She found herself on her knees on the stones, head bowed, gulping for breath and gripping the tiny cameo so hard it hurt.

Astounding how easy it had been to fool everyone. Hadrian as the new Emperor had still been traveling in the east all year; in his absence, the court in Rome had not demanded Sabina's attendance. Faustina had retired to her mother's villa in the country for the final six months of her official confinement; Sabina had let it be known she would accompany her sister—and Faustina had returned to Rome a proud young mother, presenting her firstborn in the arms of its wet nurse to all her friends. "No one suspects?" Sabina had pressed, returning to Rome sometime after Faustina. Returning once she was sure her milk had dried up and her body returned to its narrow shape. "You're certain no one suspects?"

"Not a one. I've been playing proud mother all over Rome."

"Do people snicker?" Sabina had asked with a stab of shame so deep it was almost self-loathing. "Only seven months since you and Titus married—"

A graceful shrug that stirred Faustina's ripples of blond hair. "If they snicker, they do it behind my back. And they aren't precisely wrong, you know, if they think I have no morals. I don't. I *would* have seduced Titus before the wedding, if I could have. I tried. He was too principled!"

Principled or not, people had snickered at Titus, too. Titus, who had extended his blessing on the plan from the cell where he'd been immured, and who had proceeded to claim Annia for his own once he came out of it. Dear gods, how much Sabina owed her best friend and her sister!

Sabina blinked her stinging eyes. She read the page of news Faustina had written her—Annia's latest scrapes, breakages, adventures—and then she touched the cameo with one fingertip. "I miss you, little one," she said softly. "I know you don't miss me." Annia had looked so wary, that afternoon she'd been brought to say good-bye. *The way I was staring, she probably thought I wanted to eat her.* Sabina hadn't been able to *stop* staring. At those freckles, at those blue-gray eyes (*my eyes, you got my eyes*), at that unruly reddish hair (*your father's hair, definitely*). Wondering what else Annia had inherited.

"You had grass stains on your knees," she told the cameo, remembering so clearly. "Of course you did. My love for adventure and your father's love for trouble? Of course you're a girl with scabbed elbows and grass stains rather than a lapful of embroidery. You'd like it out here on the wall—I'd wrap you in this wolf-skin cloak and point up at the stars and tell you all the stories behind them . . ."

It was a good thing she'd been whispering to herself, because an annoyed male voice came through the dark then and interrupted her. "You aren't supposed to be out here alone, Lady."

"Vix." Sabina looked over her shoulder, palming the cameo and letter back inside her cloak. "How does anyone as large as you manage to sneak up so silently?" she managed to say. Her heart was beating hard, as though she'd been caught doing something illicit. *Weren't you?* the thought whispered.

I haven't been caught yet, the Empress thought grimly. *And for Annia's sake, and my sister's, and her husband's, I never will be.*

Vix was coming up the stone steps, helmet tucked under his arm. He threw an inky shadow across the wall, tall as a colossus. "What are you doing up here?"

"Seeing the wall." She drew up her knees beneath her wolf skins, propping her folded arms on top. "I had to sit like a statue this afternoon during the formal presentation, while the Emperor got to clamber all over it. He can be adventurous"—Sabina pillowed her cheek on her folded arms—"but I have to look docile."

"I haven't met an empress yet who was docile." Vix came to stand over her, looking out over the darkness north of the wall.

"Well, we need to give the appearance of docility, anyway."

"You can't even manage that, Lady."

His voice coming down through the dark was dourly amused. Sabina tilted her head up at his craggy shape looming over her. "Why did you come tramping up after me?" she asked. "I've hardly seen hide or hair of you through all these months in Britannia." And long before that, truth be told—he was forever busy with his guards, his slates and dispatches, his endless rides off to the various garrisons. And he never, ever stood guard at her back if he could help it.

"I'm avoiding you." He spoke bluntly. "But I'm also avoiding the Emperor tonight, not to mention my wife. So if it's a choice between rounding you up, going home to her, or guarding him, I'll take you."

"Why are you avoiding your wife?" Sabina had met Vix's wife once or twice, in Antioch back at the informal court Emperor Trajan kept in the east between campaigns. A fiery creature, taller than Sabina, with a glint of amusement in her eye.

Vix grunted.

"Well," Sabina said softly. "I am glad to have you here."

She could feel the cameo in her hand, the carved edges etching into her palm. Annia's small, carved profile. Hard to tell yet in a child's unformed face—but Sabina thought she might grow up with Vix's nose.

The Empress patted the stones beside her. "Sit."

Annia's father hesitated a moment, standing there in the battered lion skin across his armored shoulders, which the moon had bleached to the color of bone, and the lock of his hair that like his daughter's never lay flat. Sabina remembered moving her hand over that lock of hair when they helped each other dress, that afternoon nearly five years ago on the barren hilltop in Selinus.

The day they had made Annia. Not that Vix knew that.

"So you've decided you want my company?" He sat down beside her on the stones, resting his elbows on his knees. "You've done a good job yourself of avoiding *me*, these past few years. Since you became Empress of Rome, anyway."

"I didn't avoid you because I got grand, Vix." In fact she'd missed their old easy camaraderie desperately. They'd been lovers on and off since they'd both been eighteen, but even more than lovers they had been friends. "I thought it would be safer, keeping my distance. After . . ."

"Selinus?" he finished.

Sabina jumping up into Vix's arms, mouths clashing and tasting salt tears, both of them bitter and sick with grief for the Emperor they had both loved. Vix's mouth at her breast, consuming her, marking her as she breathed in his ear, *"Shut up and take me."* "Yes," Sabina admitted, pulling her furs closer. "Not the wisest thing we've ever done."

It hadn't been love, that savage coupling in the wild grass. Trajan had just died, and they had mourned him together, united in their dread that Hadrian would follow on the throne. Making something in that moment for which Hadrian would have destroyed them both; oh, how the gods must have been laughing!

"No harm came from it, at least." Vix shrugged, and Sabina bit her own tongue, feeling the cameo's edges again.

"No. No harm." Her throat was getting thick, and she cast about for something else to say—something that didn't catch her throat as though she were swallowing thorns. "Did you know, Hadrian's spoken of making further reforms to the legion regulations? I told him he should consult with you."

"I don't want him to consult me. If he never says a word to me again, I'll die happy."

The sharpness in Vix's voice made Sabina blink.

"I serve him," Vix went on. "He's got me there. That's what happens when you've got a family—they're the sword for someone like Hadrian to hold over you—"

They are, Sabina thought. *Oh, they are!*

"—but I'll be damned if I help him. Not ever."

"Isn't it easier than fighting him?"

"Is that why you're playing docile Empress all of a sudden?"

Sabina lifted her cheek off her furred knees, raising her head to catch his eyes directly. "Back on Selinus, we'd have done anything to keep Hadrian from taking the purple. But it happened. Like it or not, he *is* our Emperor. So shouldn't we help him? Help him to do great things? I will, if I can."

It was part of the promise she'd sworn to herself, telling Annia goodbye. "I'll send you presents," she had chattered inanely, just to say something that might get through Annia's wary stare. All the while thinking, *I will give you more than presents, Annia Galeria Faustina. I will make this world over for you. I will make it safe, I will make it beautiful. I will make this Empire your haven. I am Empress of Rome, and I swear it.*

"You want Hadrian to change?" Vix flung the words at her like stones. "He's an evil, heartless bastard. He'll never change."

"Probably not." He might never *be* a good man, but if he could just listen to her about the necessity of *acting* like one . . . "Even if it proves impossible, Vix, I think we shall have to try. Because we've seen mad emperors, you and I, mad ones and wicked ones, and I won't let my husband go down that road."

"He's already down that road!" Vix snarled. "He paved that bloody road, and you want me to *help?*"

"What choice do we have?"

Vix let out a bitter bark of laughter, fingering the little medallion at his throat. A medallion of Mars, Sabina knew. It had always brought him luck. She wondered if he still had the silver earring she'd once given him as a lover's token. That had brought him luck, too.

"So what do you mean to do, Vix? Leave Imperial service?" Sabina drew a finger down a fold of wolf fur over her knee, feeling a stab at the thought of losing Vix for good. Of course, he'd been lost to her a long time, long before he ever married his gingery wife. For all the heat that flared whenever he and Sabina drew close, they always ended up pricking each other in the end. Pricking till they both bled. They'd always had different stars to follow, and the draw of the stars had always been stronger than the draw of the flesh.

But Vix gone for good, not even seen in passing anymore with his lion skin and his infectious grin?

We have a daughter, Sabina almost said. *I bore you a daughter, and she's being raised by my sister and your oldest friend.* But it was no way to hold him.

"Will you leave?" she asked instead.

"No." A harsh bark of a laugh. "I haven't got the nerve to flee. Your husband saw to that."

"Why?"

"He threatened me." Even in the dark, she saw his throat move. "And he threatened my son."

"What did he threaten?"

In anger Vix was always a storm of motion: pacing, striding, shouting. But now he was still as a boulder. "None of your business."

Quietly Sabina asked, "Did he carry out any of those threats? Against you, or your son?"

"No."

"You see? He *is* changing, at least in his actions if not his soul. Otherwise—"

Vix rose in a clatter of mail. He dropped his big hand across the back of her neck and raised her effortlessly, pulling her up against him, his fingers sliding around to circle her throat. His hand on her naked skin was as warm as though he'd been sitting by a roaring fire. Even in this cold northern place under the icy stars, Vix could never be cold. His blood ran hotter and faster than ordinary. But then, he'd never been ordinary, had he?

"Sabina." He whispered her name. "Do not talk to me of how much *good* he can do."

He released her, so abruptly she staggered. When she regained her balance, she saw her bodyguard—her perfect Imperial guard, her lifelong friend and sometime lover, the father of the child the world had no idea she'd ever borne—descending the steps toward the ground, almost running. Leaving her alone in the moonlight, on Hadrian's wall.

HADRIAN'S LOVE

It is not death that a man should fear,
but he should fear never beginning to live.

—MARCUS AURELIUS

CHAPTER 5

VIX

A.D. 124, Winter
Hispania

The worst fight Mirah and I had in years, and it started over such a small thing. A letter!

I'd been reading the latest missive from my wife's family out loud, Mirah hanging over my shoulder to look at the words she couldn't read, and I broke off in the middle with a snort. "Sounds like Simon's getting a rebellious streak."

"Why shouldn't he?" We were in Hispania by that time; the girls were asleep, and Mirah had let her hair down for the night so it gleamed in the firelight. "Uncle Simon always agreed with my cousins whenever they talked of liberating Judaea. He just doesn't thump the table and bellow." A smile. "They can be tiresome, I know."

"Still—" I reread the bit about Simon, with whom I'd once shared a tent in the Tenth Fidelis as legionaries. "Simon, turning rebellious? He spent years *serving* Rome!"

"He regrets those years. He was a foolish boy craving adventure, and he paid for that with decades of his life. He's lucky his family took him back, as long as he'd drifted away from the faith. He was a different man the moment he returned."

"I'd rather have the man from my *contubernium* back than some fire-eyed spouter of liberty." The dark-bearded man who'd welcomed me into the tent as a raw green recruit—there's no friend like a friend from the days of war. "Fire-eyed spouters of liberty are all such bloody bores. Not to mention that they tend to die bloodily."

"Maybe it won't have to be bloody this time," my wife said as I put down the letter to build up the fire. The winter nights in Hispania could be cold—I'd be glad when Hadrian's entourage made the crossing to Africa in the spring. "Uncle Simon has high hopes of Emperor Hadrian," Mirah went on. "He let Parthia and Armenia go when he saw it wasn't practical keeping them. Maybe he'd let Judaea go, too."

I laughed. "No."

"Why?" Mirah challenged.

That was where Antinous would have jumped in: made some witty pun, gotten us smiling, then offered to fetch hot spiced wine. But he wasn't here, so Mirah and I kept digging ourselves into the hole.

"Judaea's been part of Rome a good deal longer than Parthia, Mirah. We had nothing invested in Parthia but dead legionaries." I'd railed about the waste of those lives when Hadrian withdrew from our hard-won territories . . . But I'd been battle-sick and heart-sore, not in any mind to listen to the cool wisdom of knowing what was worth defending, and what would be a sinkhole for yet more dead friends.

Cool wisdom. Was I defending Hadrian's decisions now—a man who had threatened to mutilate my son and bugger me in front of my men?

Didn't mean he wasn't right about Parthia. I hated the man, but that didn't make him stupid. "Judaea isn't Parthia," I said again. "Hadrian won't give it up."

"He will if there's enough trouble in the region. He's a coward." She sounded derisive, and why shouldn't she? I'd said far worse than that about the Emperor. "If we make Judaea not worth fighting for—"

" 'We'?" I raised my eyebrows.

"My entire family is in Bethar, Vix. My parents, my sisters, Uncle Simon—"

"And if they make trouble, who do you think will get sent to quash it?"

"Not you," Mirah reassured. "Praetorians don't dirty themselves in provincial struggles."

She didn't say it to sting. I knew she didn't. I let some air out. "Boys I trained will be sent. Men I know."

Her voice rose. "Then that's the price."

"It's a fine thing to talk about price when you're not the one paying it," I shot back. "Rome's given us a fine life—"

"But we aren't *Roman*. Even you. The things you endured as a child—"

"I survived. And I don't whine about it."

"But you don't try to *change* it either. If you could only—"

I heard a sniffle from the doorway. I looked over and saw two huge pairs of dark eyes—Dinah and Chaya, roused from their beds. We'd been louder than I thought.

"I'll tuck them back in." Mirah rose, pushing her loose hair back. "We shouldn't be quarreling over this anyway."

"Why?" I said. "Because we'll wake the children, or because you're right and I'm wrong and that's an end to it?"

Either she didn't hear me or she pretended she didn't hear me, whisking away to put the girls back to bed. I looked down at the letter that had caused all the fuss, and I tossed it in the fire.

We slid between the bedcovers that night without saying a word. Mirah's voice didn't come until long after the lamp had been extinguished. "Is there something *wrong*, Vix? Ever since sending Antinous away . . ."

"There's nothing," I said, and rolled away from her.

But there's no fooling a wife. Not a wife like mine, anyway. She curled against me, rubbing her hand across my chest. "Are you sure?"

I kissed her to silence her, pulling her over me, but I couldn't make love to her that night, much as I ached for her. Because I was *lying* to her—because I'd never told her what Hadrian said to me in Britannia. If I had, she'd explode into rage on my behalf. And she'd ask one very simple question.

"How can you serve him?"

And the answer was, *Because he broke me.* And I'd die before I'd say it, so I turned away from her again on the pillow and gazed long and silent into the dark.

SABINA

Rome

"I made her laugh twice," Sabina reported as she slipped from Faustina's chamber to the atrium, and Titus's worn face relaxed into one of the first smiles she'd seen since her visit began.

"I knew it would do her good to see you." He took Sabina's hand, squeezing it. "You're very good to come all the way from Thrace."

I'm not good at all, Sabina thought. *Good* was to take a child with parentage that could never be revealed and raise it as your own knowing you might be executed if the truth were uncovered. That was *good*; that was a depth of good that could never be matched or repaid. Sabina did not count herself as *good*, not compared to her sister and her dearest friend. It was no more than common decency, surely, to rush to your little sister's side upon learning she had lost her baby son to a fever. Sabina had dropped the letter half-read and ordered a trireme to carry her from warm spice-scented Thrace to cool marble Rome.

Little Marcus Galerius Aurelius Antoninus. Her nephew, whom she had never had the chance to meet. Lived no more than a year and a half, but he had put lines of grief around the eyes of Sabina's little sister, and fresh gray in Titus's hair. Sabina could see that very clearly, standing in the sunny light of the atrium as Titus talked of his son. "He looked like your father. That's why we named him Marcus. Terribly wise eyes, for a baby! Annia claimed he understood every word we said . . ."

Sabina felt a pang of a different kind, hearing Annia's name. The fever that took little Marcus hadn't touched Annia, and Sabina felt a warped, shamed pang of relief that if a child had had to be taken to the doors of the underworld, it hadn't been *her* child.

No, she thought. *I may have sailed from Thrace to comfort my sister, but that doesn't make me good. Not at all.*

"Annia was a surprisingly good big sister," Titus was saying, passing a hand over his hair. It was a gesture that belonged to a much older man, Sabina thought. Someone Servianus's age. "She can't cross a room without knocking something over, but she'd rock the baby so gently—"

"Titus." Sabina cupped her brother-in-law's worn cheek. "My dear, dear Titus, who's looking after you while you're looking after Annia and Faustina? How are *you* faring?"

"'The life of the dead is retained in the memory of the living,'" he quoted. "According to Cicero, anyway. So my son will never die."

"Cicero is generally a comfort in bad times," Sabina agreed. Titus's face twisted, and she reached up and drew his head down against her shoulder. They stood in the atrium for a moment, Sabina on tiptoe as Titus breathed unevenly against the stiff folds of her *stola*. When he straightened, his face was calm again.

"Will you be rejoining the Emperor in—where is he, Athens?"

A year and a half of traveling had covered many provinces. Dry Hispania, restless Parthia, beautiful Mauretania where Sabina had walked the crocodile pools of the great Iseum. "Hadrian's hashed things out among the Parthians, thrown up a great many temples, inspected the legions, so it's on to see the ruins of Troy next." Sabina drew Titus's hand through her arm, and they drifted out of the atrium down toward the gardens. Titus's villa sat on the northeast edge of the city, almost in the country—beyond the garden walls rolled vineyards and lush summer hills. "I'll try to catch the Imperial party before they sail back to Athens."

Hadrian and Sabina had spent one of the early years of their marriage in Athens—it was a place her husband adored, arguing happily with bearded scholars while Sabina wandered sunburned and happy through the temples of Delphi. They'd meet each night tired and happy and spilling over with things to say to each other, Hadrian so excited he waved his arms to illustrate his points. That had been long ago, but in Hadrian's ravenous delight to be back in the land he admired so much more than Rome, Sabina thought she could see traces of that bright-eyed young philosopher again. Just traces, but still . . .

Titus was looking sad. "I suppose you'll be making sail soon."

"I'm afraid so. Hadrian wasn't pleased when I left him."

"He likes having you at his side, then."

"So it seems." Hadrian didn't always take her advice, but he was at least willing to hear it—and he had not had any more of those murderous lapses in temper in many months. A half-mad slave had set on him with a knife in Hispania, and rather than having the fellow tossed to the lions, Hadrian merely had him disarmed and taken away. "The fellow was clearly mad," the Emperor mused. "I suppose a flogging will do for punishment, instead of execution."

"Why not pardon him?" Sabina had dared to counter. "Send him to your physicians to be treated, and let word of your compassion spread."

Hadrian had given a noncommittal *hmph*, but he had taken the suggestion. Progress indeed.

"The Emperor continues to ignore me." Titus rippled a hand over the rosemary hedge. "Perhaps he will be content to let me live quietly and out of sight."

"You are far too capable to live as quietly as you wish, Titus."

"Capable? At the moment I do nothing but wrangle Servianus in the Senate. He has been good enough to call me 'decently respectful for a mere boy.' You know he wants to marry Annia to his grandson?"

"We're not worrying about Annia's future husband already, are we?" Sabina blinked. "Little Pedanius can't be above eleven. I'm to bring him back to Mysia with me—Servianus battened down on me as soon as I arrived in Rome, droning on about how it's time the Emperor's greatnephew took his place at Hadrian's side."

Titus actually had a smile for her mimicry. "Well, Faustina doesn't favor any talk of betrothal at such an age either. Servianus didn't like that. 'For a woman so light-minded and full of levity to impose her whims on the future of the Emperor's heir—'"

Sabina thought of her sister, folding and refolding one of her son's small blankets and trying valiantly to stop crying. "Let's hope she's full of levity again, and very soon."

A child's shriek interrupted them, and a pair of figures careened around the hedge. A tall boy, laughing and sun-bronzed, calling over his shoulder, "Come on, you can run faster than that!" Behind him came Annia, deadly serious as she pelted at his heels, and at the rear ran a black dog bouncing and barking. All three skidded to a halt, the boy running a hand over his tumbled hair, Annia scrubbing her hands down her dusty tunic and giving her father a sparkling grin.

"Lady." The boy gave a graceful bow. More a young man than a boy, and a very handsome one: a young Adonis wearing a linen tunic and an infectious smile. "I apologize," he said, nudging the dog back from Sabina's skirts. "My tutors at the *paedogogium* would surely wash their hands of me if I bowled over the Empress of Rome. Or let my dog shed all over her hem—" He glared at the creature, which lolled its tongue and laughed up at him.

"This is Antinous." Titus gave a cordial nod to the young Adonis. "Did you know our old friend Vercingetorix had a son?"

"No, I didn't." The things one learned about old lovers. Ever since that night on the wall in Britannia, Vix turned into a pillar whenever he entered Sabina's presence: tall, granite, utterly mute.

"Titus Aurelius helped my father find a foster family for me, after my mother died," Antinous explained. "Before my father had a home of his own into which he could take me—"

"Your mother was a lovely girl." Titus smiled. "As often as I sat eating her lamb stew in those cold German nights when I was a tribune, I owed her son consideration once I learned he'd come to Rome. Annia brought him up to me at a party . . ."

"The first friend I made in the Eternal City!" Antinous tousled Annia's hair in affection before giving a graceful bow to her father. "Thank you for your many kindnesses, *patronus*." Sabina heard real warmth behind the formal words. "I've never known much about my mother. My father, well, he's everything brave and kind, but he's no wordsmith. All he could ever tell me was that my mother was Bithynian and beautiful, and he doesn't even like saying that because then his wife scowls and asks *how* beautiful."

"Most wives would," Titus agreed as Sabina laughed. "That fiery wife of Vix's—did he haul her with him to Thrace?"

"No," Antinous said. "He wanted to, but after Hispania she decided she'd bring the girls back to Rome. Tired of going back and forth across the Empire like a message case, I suspect. But now my schooling's done, she's agreed I'll go join my father wherever he's accompanied the Emperor to next." Antinous's carved and handsome face glowed at the prospect of adventure, and Sabina gave a small internal sigh. When she'd been Antinous's age, all she'd wanted to do was see the world. Now she'd seen most of it, from the wild places of the west to the hot places of the east—but the price for seeing all those horizons had been so much higher than she'd ever imagined.

Be careful what you wish for, Antinous, she thought with a sudden tang in her mouth like a bite of iron. *What if you don't get it? Or even worse, what if you do?* He looked eager and happy, bouncing on his feet to charge the future, and the Fates ate such youths and their dreams alive.

Listen to me, she mocked. *Saying "at your age" as though I were an old woman.*

But wasn't she an old woman? You were old when your life was finished, surely, and at forty years old her life *was* finished. A child she could not acknowledge, a lover who would not acknowledge her, and nothing ahead but empty years in an empty bed, and endless empty smiles beside a man she had to keep from becoming a monster.

Well, there was a reason they called it duty instead of pleasure.

Handsome Antinous was talking on, looking down at Annia. "I'll miss you especially, little monkey," he said, and laughed as she tackled him in a massive hug.

Sabina smiled at the sight. "Join my entourage, Antinous," she said on impulse. "I travel to rejoin the Emperor soon, and I always have room for one more page."

Antinous hesitated. "My father thought I should avoid the Emperor. I, well, I didn't make a very good impression when I first laid eyes on him."

Sabina laughed. "You don't think I see much of the Emperor myself, do you? Except for public functions, and I can certainly excuse you from those. And you'll reach Greece quite a bit faster traveling on *my* trireme."

Antinous's face lit up. "Then thank you, Lady. I would be honored."

"If I have to take little Pedanius Fuscus, I certainly don't mind taking you." Sabina stole one last glance to memorize the pattern of Annia's latest freckles—*I must have another cameo made to take with me, she is growing so fast*—and turned away, Antinous falling in at her side. "What kind of impression *did* you make on the Emperor, there must be a story there ..."

ANNIA

Rome

Marcus's voice drifted up toward Annia. "What did you do *this* time?"

She poked her head out the window of her chamber, looking down on the garden path below where he stood with his armload of scrolls. "Nothing."

"You don't get locked into your room all day for nothing." Marcus was a regular visitor to Annia's house—every time his dreary mother had a headache (and she had more headaches than a hundred-headed hydra), he got dumped here and Annia had to entertain him. And that was impossible. He wouldn't play *trigon* with the slave children ("My mother says they'd give me fleas"), he wouldn't let Annia teach him to tumble or stand on his head ("My grandfather says I'd break my neck"), and he wouldn't sneak rides on the chariot horses ("I don't sneak"). What was Annia supposed to do with a visitor like that?

"I'm hungry," she said instead, before Marcus could keep asking questions about why she was in trouble. "Can't you steal me a honey cake?" Annia wasn't to be allowed a single sweet until her punishment was done, and the smell of cakes was wafting clear from the *culina*.

"You're not supposed to—"

"Just go steal me a cake! Antinous would." Antinous wouldn't even have to steal; the cooks would be blushing and pouring them into his hands.

But Marcus just looked up at her through curly dark lashes, disapproving. "What *did* you do this time?"

Annia blew out a rebellious breath, running her finger along the stone window ledge. "It was just Brine-Face again."

Pedanius Fuscus, whom she saw almost as often as Marcus, and who at a brutish eleven was turning into the bane of life. A year ago he'd nearly drowned her in the atrium, holding her down in the central pool to make her stop calling him Brine-Face, and every time he hauled her up she'd spit it out through her teeth while coughing up water. He hadn't gotten in trouble, of course. When his grandfather came along, Pedanius made it look like he was pulling her out of the pool and not pushing her in. Old Servianus had reprovingly told Annia (still coughing up water, as Pedanius gazed on virtuously) that she was behaving like a barbarian.

And two days ago had been something even worse.

"He said something awful," Annia told Marcus briefly. "And I hit him. Brine-Face is off to Greece now, but I'm still supposed to stay in my room until I apologize to his grandfather, and I *won't*."

Her father had been angry with her, and that hurt. "Your mother is feeling quite fragile enough without your misbehavior," he said shortly, and took Annia's mother off to Baiae. "Just the two of us, Faustina," Annia had heard him murmur into her beautiful hair. "We'll look out at the sea and read poetry by the brazier—and perhaps make another son."

And Annia's eyes pricked because even if she had another brother someday, she wouldn't stop hurting for the one who was gone. The brother she'd walked all over the house with his fat feet balanced on top of hers and his tiny fingers clinging to her thumbs.

The brother who was dead—and who Brine-Face had laughed at.

"What did he say?" Marcus asked as though he'd read her mind. He did that sometimes.

"He said the gods killed my brother because of me. Because I was already such a boy, there wasn't room in the house for two." A slow breath full of rage. "And then he *laughed*. That's when I hit him."

She hadn't told anyone what Pedanius had said, even when her father demanded to know why she'd behaved so badly. She hadn't wanted to see her mother cry again. So she was stuck in her chamber, in disgrace and craving honey cakes she couldn't eat.

Marcus looked up at her, thoughtful. "Wait there."

"Where are you going?" Annia called. He didn't answer, just flapped a hand. He was back in a few moments, looking vaguely guilty. To Annia's surprise, he reached for the vines along the wall under her window, and began to climb.

"You'll fall," Annia warned, but he kept coming. He was skinny but strong. Annia leaned down and extended a hand to pull him up onto the ledge, where he sat with feet dangling.

"Here." He produced a handful of honey cakes from his tunic, only slightly squashed. "You're right—you don't deserve to be punished this time. Pedanius gets other people punished for what *he* does. He does the same thing to me, and everyone believes him."

Annia grinned, dividing the cakes and handing Marcus half. "Can you be my brother?"

He smiled. He had thin cheeks, but his smile was nice. "Why?"

"I still want a brother," Annia confessed around a mouthful of cake. "Very much."

He considered that, nibbling much more politely. "I'd like being your father's son. But I can't."

"Why not?"

"If I were your brother I couldn't marry you."

Annia stared at him. He'd said that before, but it had been a long time ago, and it sounded just as stupid now as it had then. "What?"

"I'm going to marry you," he said as if it were self-explanatory, still nibbling. "Once we're old. Twelve or—wait!"

Annia got up from the window ledge.

"Wait, I'm coming in—"

Annia slammed the inside shutters with a howl of outrage, leaving him sitting on the ledge outside.

Marcus's voice floated through the shutters, plaintive. "What did I *say*?"

VIX

I didn't bother with Roman stoicism when Antinous arrived in Mysia. I grabbed my boy in a vast hug, crushing him against my breastplate. "Hell's gates, did you fly all the way from Rome?" I'd hesitated about having Antinous join the Imperial entourage, considering why he'd left it in the first place—but it was so long since I'd seen him! I hadn't admitted to anyone just how much I missed my son.

"I came by Imperial trireme." Antinous pushed down the sleek black dog who bounced about our feet barking. "If Empress Sabina's on board—down, boy!—the gods send nothing but fast winds."

I pulled back enough to look him over. Nearly two years since I'd sent him packing to the *paedogogium*. He'd grown taller, but it was more than that. The last awkward lankiness of boyhood had given way to broad-shouldered, slim-hipped leanness; his childish freckles had been replaced by sun-bronzed silk-smooth skin; the uncertain fits and starts of motion had become lithe, well-trained grace. "Look at you," I said. "I send a boy away to Rome, and you come back a man."

He flushed. "You think so?"

"I know so." We hadn't marked Antinous's manhood by any of the usual ceremonies, largely because Mirah and I couldn't decide which to employ: the *toga virilis* where Roman youths marked the end of childhood by donning a toga for the first time, or the blessing by which Jewish boys announced their status as men. I'd argued for the *toga virilis*, and Mirah argued for the blessing, and neither had seemed quite right for our mismatched household where a Greek boy had been raised by a Jew and a barbarian.

Besides, I didn't reckon manhood came from any ceremony. I'd marked myself a man when I made my first kill. At least my son had reached his manhood more gently than that. "You make many friends at the *paedogogium*?" I asked. "You weren't one for details in your letters—"

Antinous ruffled a hand over his dark-honey curls. "I don't have your knack for making friends. I hang back, and people think I'm haughty. Or I smile, and they think I'm fawning or flirting."

I guessed it was that face of his that made it hard for him. When Antinous stood unsmiling he looked so marble-carved that people just gaped like he was a statue on a plinth. When he smiled, the marble statue came to such radiant life that people began stuttering. He wasn't haughty and he wasn't ingratiating, he was just *shy* sometimes; but a face like that didn't allow him to be shy because it made men jealous and women ignite. I guessed it hadn't been an easy two years for him in the ranks of all those spotty ambitious boys.

Antinous was prowling through my quarters with his dog at his heels, giving a hoot at the piles of slates on my desk and the dirty tunics I'd left on the floor. "You live worse than a beggar when you haven't got a wife around to keep you tidy!"

I smiled. "How is Mirah?"

"Full of fire. Goes to the scribes every other day to dictate letters, for her mother and Uncle Simon and the rest of them in Judaea."

"A great believer in letters, your mother." Even out here on the edge of the Empire, Imperial messengers brought me a stack of missives every day: reports from my informers, updates from Prefect Turbo in Rome . . . and scrolls with Mirah's words in a scribe's neat script. She couldn't write, but that didn't stop her sending me letters.

"I thought she'd come with me," Antinous was saying as he emptied his pack. "She made me read every letter you sent out loud, till it fell to bits. She misses you."

"And I miss her," I said briefly. "But she's tired of traveling. The girls need a home to settle in."

That was only part of it. It wasn't even our prickly discussions about going to Judaea or freeing Judaea or whatever came in her uncle's latest rants. A year ago when we were about to depart Hispania, I'd woken one cold morning to find Mirah weeping over her monthly blood—heavier than usual, and she insisted it must have been the beginnings of a child.

"Maybe," I'd said, putting my arms around her. "We don't know, do we? Far too early to be sure." I'd been trying to comfort her, but she'd flared up at me.

"It *was* a child. It was, and it would have been a boy. One of our own—"

"Not that again—"

"—and for once someone would have looked at *my* son instead of Antinous!"

"Well, I'm not one of those arses who tosses a woman out if she can't push out sons," I'd said irritably. "So stop fretting. And quit bringing Antinous into it, because it's not his fault we don't have a boy of our own blood!"

Her blue eyes were bitter. "You love him more than your own blood."

I'd picked up my helmet and greaves and slammed out. Gone through my day with a black scowl, and when I came back Mirah wound her arms around my waist and I murmured into her hair with the taste of guilt thick and sour on my tongue. Because I tried to hide it; I tried to keep it from her that Antinous was the one I loved most. Mirah thought it was because he was a boy, but it wasn't that. I didn't know what it was. I just knew that I loved him best—and Mirah knew it, too.

We hadn't spoken another word about it, just fallen into each other's arms with fierce kisses and patched things up that way, the best way. But when Hadrian's entourage moved on from Hispania, that was when Mirah said quietly that she'd take the girls to Rome rather than accompany us east. And I hadn't tried to stop her.

Antinous was looking at me quizzically. I forced a smile. I wasn't about to tell him any of it—he loved Mirah like the mother he'd never known. "What's wrong?" he asked.

"Nothing. Just—wondering when you grew out your hair, boy," I improvised, and tousled his honey-colored curls. "You've got more hair than Empress Sabina. And how in God's name did you end up in the middle of her entourage, anyway?"

"I met her at the household of Titus Aurelius, and she was kind enough to invite me. Took quite a liking to me, actually. Her chamberlain and her maids were seasick all through the crossing, so she taught me to play *latrunculi*. She beat me flat most of the time." He gave a little whistle. "A mind like a general, Empress Sabina's got."

"A mind like a snake, more like."

"Do you trust *anyone*?" he objected.

"No, and it's kept me alive long enough to see gray in my hair." Something that still surprised me, whenever I saw the wavering reflection in my shaving water. I was past forty: I had a son grown to manhood, and gray was beginning to salt my russet hair, and weatherbeaten lines had carved themselves about my eyes. Yet I felt no older than the boy standing before me with his sunny smile and his overflowing energy.

"Empress Sabina likes me," Antinous was saying as he settled away the last of his belongings. "She says she'll help me find a position at court, if I want one. Perhaps with the archivists—"

I tilted my head, surprised. "Is that what you want? A court career?"

"It's what they train you for, in the *paedogogium*." It wasn't exactly an answer, and as Antinous leaned down to ruffle his dog's ears, I wondered if he was avoiding my gaze. "I . . . don't really see myself in the legions."

"Why not?" Antinous sat a horse better than I ever would, wielded sword and spear with a grace that was beyond me, and had won his share of fistfights among the other boys as he grew. "You'd be an asset to any legion. You wouldn't have to start as a legionary the way I did— I could contact my old friends in the Tenth Fidelis; get you made a tribune."

He shrugged, definitely avoiding my gaze. "I don't really like killing things."

"You like hunting," I pointed out.

"Hunting's different. You hunt to stock your table, or to kill something that preys on men, like bears or mountain cats. I can do that, but—" He hesitated. "I think about shoving a sword through a man's chest, and it sickens me."

"It should," I said seriously. "No one enjoys that part, Antinous."

"You do." He winced as soon as the words were out, seeing the way my jaw dropped.

"I do *not*—"

"I didn't mean that, I meant—sweet gods, I'm making a fumble of this." Antinous ran a hand through his hair again. "You might not enjoy killing, but you can get past it. You make it mean something. I wouldn't. I've no wish to be a killer." He took a breath, meeting my eyes square. "*Or a legion man.*"

I don't know what look he saw on my face, but he stood with his shoulders braced as if for a blow. "Well," I began, but couldn't think what else to say. *Are you going to tell him it's such a shining path, being a hired killer?* I thought of the Dacian king I'd watched die on a solar disk—the Parthian rebels I'd killed in Trajan's wars—the four men I'd had hauled from their cells and butchered at the beginning of Hadrian's reign. Did I want such memories for Antinous?

"Well," I said again, forcing a little cheer into my voice. "It's a good thing you're not my son by blood, then, or you'd—"

His amber-brown eyes flew to mine, and they looked stricken.

"I didn't mean it like that, let me finish—" I nearly groaned at myself. Now *I* was the one making a fumble of things. "I only meant it's good you didn't have to inherit my brains. Because I don't have the wit to be a chamberlain or an archivist or a translator, and God knows you do."

His shoulders relaxed then, relief flowering visibly through his whole body, and the sight made me blink. Had he been dreading this moment, screwing up the courage to tell me he didn't want to follow my path? It had never occurred to me. All I'd wanted when I was young was my father's path; he'd practically had to beat me off it with a stick. I'd assumed Antinous would be the same. I won't say I hadn't looked forward to seeing him in a tribune's armor, my son and I both the same rank, but . . .

I pulled Antinous into another rough embrace, feeling him stiffen in surprise. "You're no killer," I said. "You won't have the nightmares and the scars that I do, and that makes me glad, because you're made for better things. You're fine and clever and brave, and you speak more languages than I've even heard of—we'll get you the best post in Rome, whatever you want. And you'll make me proud."

I gave his shoulder a thump and he thumped mine in return. When we pulled apart, I felt a trifle thick in the throat and he had a grin wide enough to light a legion camp.

"Mind you," I couldn't help adding, "I'd rather you found a post for yourself back in Rome! Not here under the Emperor's nose."

"I promise I won't try to break it again." Antinous's smile was quick and relieved. "I doubt he'll remember me."

"How many people do you think hit him in the face? He'll remember you."

"Then I'll stay out of sight."

"Start tomorrow. There's a hunt in the morning—the Emperor's determined to bag a she-bear he's been tracking in the mountains. He takes an army on his hunts; you could blend in among the retainers easily enough."

His eyes lit. "Can I?"

God help me, I didn't have a single premonition. Not one.

ANTINOUS

"Where'd you get *that?*" Vix asked.

Antinous hefted the long hunting spear. "Stole it right off some perfumed courtier's saddle! It clearly wasn't going to get used even if the bear fell right in the man's lap."

"And you're not using it either." Vix offered a stern look from under his Praetorian's helmet, leading two horses through the press of the hunting party. "You're staying well back of the chase, remember?"

"But my father told me never to go unarmed," Antinous said, innocent. "And I always obey my father!"

"Don't get wide-eyed with me, boy. And are you starting a *beard?*"

"Everyone here has a beard." Antinous rubbed a hand over his night's worth of gold stubble, looking around at the thronging hunting party that had turned out on the wooded slopes of Mysia. Near a hundred men from Praetorians to courtiers, and every one had a beard in imitation of the Emperor.

"Not me." Vix tossed him a set of reins.

"Of course *you* don't!" His father wouldn't follow the Emperor's example in anything—if it got about that Emperor Hadrian had taken a great liking for *air*, Vix would probably try to stop breathing. "But I'm going to be a creature of the court, remember? So I must follow the fashions."

His father groaned, hauling himself up into the saddle with his usual lack of grace. "I should have forced you into legion life."

But you didn't, Antinous thought, rubbing his borrowed horse's nose, and the relief was dizzying. How long had he had that little dread in the back of his mind, wondering if his father would be disappointed in him once he realized Antinous had no desire to follow in his footsteps? A father had a right to dictate his son's path in life, after all, and expect obedience. What would he have done, if his father had put that massive booted foot down and stated that he was going to the Tenth Fidelis?

Tried to do it, I expect. Tried to please him.

But after all Antinous's agonizing, Vix had barely blinked an eye. They'd stayed up half the night pouring wine and making plans instead, debating whether the archivists or the huntsmen or the translators might make a better fit, Vix striding up and down getting excited— "You should consider the law; with that honey tongue of yours, you could wind any judge round your hand like a wet woman!" Antinous had gone to bed with a buzzing head and a smile on his face.

His father's voice broke his thoughts. "Coming?"

Antinous vaulted up onto his borrowed horse. "Wouldn't miss it."

The Emperor came trotting out on his big bay stallion, and Antinous craned for a look. He hadn't laid eyes on the man since he'd nearly broken the Imperial nose, after all, and that hadn't been much of a look. Just a terror-filled impression of muddy height and ice-cold eyes. "Doesn't seem quite so fearsome as I remember."

"He'd still cut your hand off if he felt like it," Vix said. "Don't you forget that."

The Emperor halted his horse, lifting his face to the sky. He sat easy and erect in his saddle, reins looped through his brown fingers, massive spear with its glittering point behind his shoulder. His bare dark head rode taller than any of the guards at his side, his curly hair and purple cloak stirred in the warm air, and his broad chest expanded contentedly as he sniffed the morning breeze. "Hah," Antinous heard him say to no one in particular. "Good hunting weather!"

The thought of losing a hand made Antinous flex his fingers rather gratefully, but he couldn't help saying, "I don't really blame him, you know. He had a perfect right to punish me if he wanted."

Vix lifted a reddish brow. "You have no gift for grudges."

"You have enough for the both of us," Antinous teased.

The Emperor kicked his horse ahead, and his entourage fell in behind: guards, huntsmen, grooms, courtiers trying desperately to look as though they enjoyed all this muddy exertion. Antinous followed his father as he gave the nod to the other Praetorians enveloping the Emperor in a phalanx of spear points. The path climbed, tracking into the wooded hills, and when the Emperor kicked into a gallop, Antinous was only too glad to give his horse its head. To be outside again after droning tutors and stuffy rooms—Antinous inhaled it all, the smells of pines and animal musk, rocks and leaf mold and moss, overlaid by the sweat of the horses, the yammering of the dogs, the creak of leather and chinking sound of armor as the hounds began to cast for a scent.

"See that man over there?" Antinous gave a nod to where the Emperor had pulled up his stallion and leaned back in the saddle to address someone beside him. "The one next to the Emperor, patting his own hair back into place? He's the one I stole the spear from."

"Lucius Ceionius." Vix snorted. "He's a fool. Always playing a part. He told me he's Actaeon the Hunter today—a stag-skin cloak for him, just like the myth, and those two slave girls he never goes anywhere without are supposed to be Huntresses of Artemis."

"Just the thing to bring along on a bear hunt," Antinous agreed. "Matched blondes in green silk and crescent moon embroidery."

"Don't know why, but the women adore him." Vix looked grimly amused. "The man's charmed his way through half the beds in Rome."

"Including the Imperial couch?" Antinous laughed. "I can see him flirting with the Emperor all the way from here!"

"No. Even Lucius Ceionius wouldn't go so far as the Emperor's bed."

"Why not?"

He felt his father looking at him. "He might parade his pretty profile if it gets him Hadrian's favor, but he wants to be consul someday. Maybe even Imperial heir. He'll never get that if he's the Imperial bum-boy."

"Of course not." Antinous fiddled with his horse's mane. In the *paedogogium*, of course, things had been different—you still counted as a *boy* there, free to go look for girls at the local whorehouses, or have a sweaty post-gymnasium fumble with one of your fellow students. Antinous had done both, but it all just made him more lonely. The brothel girls were hard-eyed, and the boys desperate to prove something.

Maybe I'm still a boy, then, Antinous thought. *Because I am desperate to prove something*. Prove he had Vix's confidence, maybe—he looked at his father, so graceless on his horse but not caring a whit that he looked like a sack of millet in a saddle. Vix was so *certain*, sure of everything in his world. He could hold a sword and he could not ride a horse; he was a man of Rome and he had a master he hated and a wife he loved, and that was that. He didn't care for the opinions of others, because certainty came so easy to him: in his loves, his hates, his place in the great scheme of things.

Not so much for me, Antinous thought.

One of the hounds gave voice, and the whole pack bolted off into the thicket. The Emperor raised his spear and gave a shout, cloak billowing as he kicked his stallion in pursuit, and the whole hunting party streamed after him. Antinous was grateful to kick his horse into the thick of things, shedding his momentary gloom. Over the cracking of branches and the thunder of hooves, he heard the roar of a bear and his blood began to pound.

The beast was already surrounded by a ring of spear points by the time Antinous's horse came skidding into the wooded clearing. The she-bear was a storm of teeth and claws and rage, dark fur gleaming in the dappled light from the trees. The dogs seethed and snapped around her, snarling as they dodged the clawed swipes of those enormous paws. A cluster of huntsmen circled with spears and nets, eyes alert. The rest of the entourage circled and milled and laughed.

Poor bear, Antinous thought, and then his eyes went to the Emperor. His bearded face had a look of perfect, taut focus as he yanked his stallion to a halt and came vaulting to the mossy ground all in a single fluid motion. One powerful sling of his arm and his spear flew, true as a god's arrow. Antinous's breath caught as droplets of blood rained like rubies from the dark flank to the moss.

"Sweet gods," Antinous breathed. "He's good!"

His father sounded sour. "Just ask him."

The beast roared, whirling on the Emperor. Two of the huntsmen shouted and jabbed with their own spears, goading her haunches, but Hadrian motioned them away. His eyes never left the bear; he put out his hand and it was filled by a new spear haft even as Antinous reached instinctively for his own. Hadrian went into a crouch, circling the beast as his hunting hounds snarled at his heels.

The bear came for the Emperor in a lumbering rush. He slid out of reach, lithe as a shadow, his spear point raking her muzzle. More blood, and the bear rose to her full height, roaring fury. Antinous saw the muscles in the Emperor's arm bunch clear up to his shoulder as he flung his second spear, dead into the massive chest. The bear screamed at a higher pitch, and the spear haft splintered away as she came down in another rush. Hadrian had another spear and was circling again.

"He'll get mauled!" Antinous felt his own heart hammering in his chest. "Aren't you going to—"

"Jump in and spoil his kill? He'd have me flogged."

A howl raked Antinous's ears. One of the bitch hounds had danced too close; the bear caught her with a tremendous clawed swipe and sent her tumbling end over end. The bitch screamed piteously, blood flying bright, and Antinous saw the Emperor's taut focus change to utter fury. Hadrian winged his spear straight into the bear's ribs, then waded in with the sword at his waist as Antinous came flying out of his saddle and flung himself into the chaos, aiming for the wounded hound. "You she-demon," he heard the Emperor snarl at the bear, "if you killed my dog—"

Antinous was already darting low for the screaming hound, as somewhere in the background Vix bellowed for the guards. Scooping up the bleeding bundle of fur, Antinous caught the rank breath of the bear, the rancid stench of matted pelt and old blood, and flung himself desperately out of the way, turning in time to see the Emperor bring his sword down like a wood ax. The bear's great clawed paw sheared away. Hadrian's sword punched forward again in a brutal lunge, and he buried the blade to the hilt in the great furred breast, giving a savage twist as his teeth bared in a feral hiss.

Antinous tried to still the bitch-hound's thrashing as he darted back out of range. "Easy, girl—" A spot to lay her down, he just needed a space in the throng. She was whimpering and struggling in his arms. "Ssshh—"

The bear gave one last ear-shattering roar as Antinous laid the dog down on soft moss. He looked up to see the bear's blood arc in a hot spray across the Emperor's furious face, and then the beast fell. She made one final lash of her remaining paw and caught Hadrian square across the thigh. Antinous saw the Emperor's leg slew to the wrong side and he yelled his agony through clenched teeth, but the dog was crying out too, and Antinous felt at her torn side through the mass of bloodied fur. Dimly he heard his father shouting, rushing to finish off the bear—someone else saying, "Caesar, your leg—"

The dog's lips peeled back from her teeth in pain but she never tried to bite Antinous even as he pinched the lips of her wounds together. "You're a sweet thing, aren't you? Don't worry, we'll get you patched up." The bear hadn't opened her belly down to the entrails, not quite. "Don't struggle, sweet girl, don't tear it open any worse—"

"A physician!" Vix shouted somewhere behind him. "A physician for the Emperor!"

"Hang the physician," came a deep snarl. "My *dog*—"

"Lean on me, Caesar." Lucius Ceionius, unctuous voice pushing against the edge of Antinous's attention as he probed the dog's side with tender fingers. If he could stop the bleeding—

"He should lean on me!" Young Pedanius Fuscus sounded indignant. "I'm Caesar's great-nephew, he should lean on *me*—"

Antinous barely glanced up as the Emperor limped up beside him: tall, bearded, white-faced, bloody. He was upright, leaning hard on a spear haft, one leg bleeding and bent at a strange angle. "My dog," he said hoarsely. "Is she—"

"I need a bandage." Antinous's fingers were slippery with blood. "Rest easy, sweet girl—"

Huntsmen milled and fussed, but the Emperor just yanked the Imperial purple cloak off his own shoulders. Antinous wadded up the priceless dyed wool and wrapped it tight around the dog. She whimpered, trembling under his hands, and Hadrian gave a tremulous breath. "Easy, easy," the Emperor crooned, sinking down on his uninjured knee to stroke her blood-flecked muzzle. She whined and tried to wash his hand. Antinous looked full into the Emperor's face for the first time, and was astounded to see tears in those deep-set eyes. Hadrian looked back at him, not trying to hide them. "What can I do?" he said simply.

"See if you can calm her, Caesar," Antinous said. "I've got to tie this off."

"How bad is it?" Hadrian's big hands cradled the dog's head, holding her still.

"The claws didn't open her belly. If she doesn't bleed too much—"

"Make it tighter, then!"

Antinous swaddled the dog in more Imperial purple, then mopped the lesser scrapes. Finally he sat back on his heels, brushing his hair out of his eyes. "If she can be stitched up, I believe she'll live."

"You believe?" The Emperor of Rome sounded anxious as a mother.

"My dog got mauled much the same way as a pup—a pack of street curs rather than a bear. He was trotting about in no time after I had him stitched." The Emperor looked so agonized, Antinous almost touched his arm to reassure him. He barely stopped himself—this was the same man who'd once threatened to cut his *hand* off, after all. He gave a smile instead, as comforting as he knew how. "With a little care and luck she should live, Caesar."

Hadrian dashed at his eyes. He'd been all icy calm facing the bear, Antinous thought, but now he looked as though he were about to collapse. "She's my favorite," the Emperor confessed, stroking the bitchhound's ear.

"A brave girl," Antinous said softly. The Emperor's eyes softened in return, and then the rest of the hunting party began to descend.

"Caesar, your leg!" But the Emperor waved them all away, and the improvised litter too as the huntsmen brought it forward.

"I can ride. The litter is hers." The Emperor turned toward Antinous, but he was already lifting the whimpering hound and settling her into the cushions. He straightened to see those Imperial eyes studying him. "Do I know you, young man?"

Antinous felt his heart thud.

"Caesar!" His father called hastily from the other side of the litter. "If that leg isn't set soon, this is the last hunting you'll ever do."

But the Emperor ignored Vix. "I do know you." The Emperor swept Antinous with eyes no longer teary. "Our tribune's son with the quick fist."

Antinous gave the most graceful bow he could manage while covered in dog blood and mud. "I had hoped that would be forgotten, Caesar," he managed to say. "Allow me to offer my sincere apologies for being such an overhasty youth."

"And I offer you thanks for tending my dog." The Emperor gave a nod that turned into a hiss of pain. "Vercingetorix, if your son would like a post, he may have it. Perhaps among the huntsmen. And I think I may have overstated when I said I could ride . . ."

A great rise of noise and chaos then. The dog in her Imperial bandaging was carried ahead at double speed, Antinous was glad to see. He'd sneak down to the kennels later to check on her. The Imperial entourage trailed behind more slowly, the bear's carcass dragged along on a sledge. Young Pedanius Fuscus was bouncing along beside the Emperor's makeshift litter like a puppy: "You should have let me put a spear into it, Caesar, I'd have killed it before it struck you!" The Emperor paid him no heed, lying back on his elbows with lips clamped tight in pain and his broken leg stripped and purpling before him. Antinous hoped it would heal straight. It would be a great crime for as magnificent a hunter as the Emperor of Rome never to ride again— never to fling a spear again with that splendid strength.

His father's growl sounded in his ear. "That's what you call keeping out of sight?"

"I wasn't about to stand there and watch a dog die." Antinous scrubbed his blood-dried hands up and down his tunic. "He cried."

"Who?"

"The Emperor," Antinous repeated softly, and couldn't help smiling. He would never in his wildest dreams have thought to see Emperor Hadrian, his father's dark-souled rival, in tears over the fate of a dog.

"He might tear up over his hounds and horses, but he can see men die without batting an eye." Vix's sourness jarred Antinous instead of amusing him as it usually did. "Be glad he didn't decide to take offense at the sight of you."

"Yes, sir," Antinous said, and found himself thinking that his father's long-despised master might be a cold and frightening man . . . But not a monster through and through. Not if he could shed tears for a dog.

CHAPTER 6

SABINA

A.D. 124, Autumn
Athens

"The Mysteries of Eleusis?" Sabina blinked. She'd been expecting to hear that they were returning to Rome. Hadrian had been gone from the Eternal City a full four years, after all, and with his recent hunting injury—

"We will make time to attend the Eleusinian rites before returning home." Hadrian was writing three things at once, as he so often did, wax tablets piled about his desk in stacks. "I will not miss this chance for enlightenment."

Sabina looked down at her lap to hide a smile. How like Hadrian to just add enlightenment to his list of things to do. *Build wall, redesign legionary training, open soul to mysteries of world.* "An acolyte's role is arduous," she pointed out instead, looking at the crutch he still needed to walk.

"I will take an attendant to lean on. You may take one as well."

"You're allowing me along?" That *was* a surprise.

"Don't be too happy," he warned dryly. "Julia Balbilla will be accompanying you."

"Gods, no!" Julia Balbilla was the newest member of Sabina's entourage, a carefully preserved society matron who was possibly the most tiresome woman in the Empire. "Why her?"

"Because she's one of the richest women in Athens, and her insufferable family is funding half the temples and bridges I've been trying to get built, that's why."

"All very well and good, but you didn't have to stay and listen to her read her own poetry at the last dinner party!"

"Of course I didn't. There are *some* advantages to being Emperor." Hadrian leaned back in his chair with a smile, looking so very human for once that Sabina beamed at him.

"Thank you," she said. "For taking me to Eleusis. Even if I must spend it listening to Balbilla recite insipid little verses about starlight."

"I remembered how much you enjoyed the rites at Delphi." Hadrian sounded reminiscent for once. "You chewed on laurel leaves with the Pythia and said some extremely silly things."

"It was that foul drink the priests gave me. It made my head ache horribly, and had me examining the backs of my hands for hours. Hopefully Eleusis will be more exciting."

"Is that why you wish to go?" he said with a faint cock of his head. "Not for enlightenment, but for mere excitement?"

"An empress's life is a smooth and public thing," she said, careful not to sound petulant. "Rather short on excitement."

"May you find it, then."

And here she was, in Athens where the rites traditionally began. Standing under a full autumn moon surrounded by eager fellow acolytes who did not see her purple *stola* or care what it meant—and Sabina felt more sheer anticipation than she'd felt in a good many long and predictable years.

"What's that old gander going on about?" Vix hissed at her shoulder.

"The hierophant is exhorting the people of Athens. Calling upon those eligible to follow him in the Mysteries of Eleusis." As the old priest raised his white-robed arms to the night sky, Sabina translated his formal words. "'Whoever hath clean hands, a pure soul, and an intelligible tongue—' That means you have to speak Greek."

"So why am I here?" Vix must be too baffled to remember he wasn't talking to her anymore. "I can't speak Greek, I've got more blood on my hands than in my veins, and God knows I'm not pure of soul or heart or anything else. Neither or you. For that matter, neither is the Emperor—"

Next time, Sabina decided, she would ask Hadrian to pick his companions for a religious ecstasy more carefully. People of sensitivity, or at least curiosity. Not large annoyed people vibrating with irritation. "Ssshhh!"

The crowd thronging the great *stoa* of Athens rippled and shivered. Lowly slaves and nobly born citizens, packed shoulder to shoulder with merchants and prostitutes and the Emperor of Rome himself—all reduced under the night's darkness to mere shadows. Hadrian, standing before Sabina with his gaze fixed eagerly on the hierophant, was just another man in a tunic that didn't show in the darkness as Imperial purple.

The moon rose beyond the double vault of columns, full and white, and the hierophant let out a cry. "To Eleusis!"

The cry redoubled from the mass of acolytes, and feet rushed to be first to leave, first to set foot on the white ribbon of road called the Sacred Way. "To Eleusis," Sabina echoed softly.

"We'll be all night walking," Vix grumped, shifting to put his own armored body between Sabina and the buffeting crowd streaming past. "It's a full night's march to Eleusis, and with the Emperor on a crutch—"

"Enlightenment cannot be had without pain, Tribune!" Hadrian sounded almost merry, his eyes glinting under the moon. "We walk to experience hardship; to echo the footsteps of Demeter as she searched the earth in her despair—and to weed out the faint of heart! Do I want our fellow acolytes to say their Emperor was faint of heart? No." He lifted an arm. "If young Pedanius Fuscus will be kind enough to lend me his shoulder—"

Hadrian's entourage could have doubled the year's acolytes, but he'd flatly limited his party to ten. Vix and three hand-selected Praetorians, picked first to provide protection—"What better place to launch an attack than a mob of god-crazed acolytes?" Vix had argued. Hadrian himself walked first inside that ring of guards, flanked by Suetonius with his slate and stocky Pedanius, who Sabina suspected had been chosen for his sturdy young shoulder as much as for family feeling. Sabina brought up the rear with Balbilla, ignoring the other woman's chatter and giving a little skip despite her Imperial dignity.

"Careful, Lady." A hand steadied her arm. "The footing's still uneven."

"So serious, Antinous." She smiled at the handsome boy with his moon-bleached curls, striding along on her other side and earning Balbilla's appreciative glances. Sabina's maids were frightened of the dark or the ritual or both, but Antinous's eyes had lit up when she asked if he'd act as her attendant. "I know you aren't an acolyte," she said now, "but are you hoping to find something in Eleusis anyway? Adventure? The gods? Or just a good drunken celebration?"

He smiled, but his eyes were serious as he turned the question over. "I don't know, Lady. I wouldn't mind partaking as an acolyte, really. My father says it's all foolishness, but . . ." He struggled for the words. "I wouldn't mind seeing something—*more*. The *paedogogium* fills you up with facts: sums to learn, dates to remember, how to pour wine and write a good hand and speak gracefully. But there are things that can't be taught—and from what I've heard of the Mysteries, well, people say you come away with a glimpse."

"A glimpse of what?"

"The ultimate mystery. Death, life, the future." Antinous rubbed the back of his neck, self-conscious. "A peek at the future, anyway."

"Antinous." Vix's voice was sharp. "Go walk with Boil. He could use your eyes."

"Yes, sir." A quick bow, and Antinous jogged ahead to the front of the little Imperial party.

"My dear," Balbilla murmured, squeezing Sabina's arm. "Where did you find that beautiful boy? He's positively mouthwatering!"

The whole procession was passing out of the city. With the torches and lamps of Athens behind, Sabina could see the prick of the stars overhead even more clearly, a scatter of glass chips around the great shining pearl of the moon. Vix was just a dark looming shape, coming up on Sabina's other side.

"See here," he growled, too low for inquisitive ears. "I don't like you dragging Antinous along tonight under the Emperor's nose—"

"You've made that clear, yes."

"—but that's nothing compared to how angry I'll be if I think you have your eye on my son."

"Dear gods, Vix. I'm fond of him, that's all. He made very good company on the voyage from Rome." An eager conversationalist who also knew when to be silent; a boy who could serve at table, make her laugh, or play a good game of *latrunculi*, all with equal grace and enthusiasm.

Vix gave her a look.

Sabina gave it right back to him. "Do you truly see me lusting after a boy young enough to be my son?"

"I've seen fine ladies old enough to be his *grandmother* giving him the eye."

Sabina gave a sidelong glance at Balbilla, her eyes painted to hide the lines and piled curls tinted to hide the gray. "I don't think I'm quite so shameless as that."

Vix eyed her slowly, up and down—her, not Balbilla. "I seem to remember you have no shame at all."

"Flatterer!" Sabina mocked. "Antinous is perfectly well able to shield himself from avid matrons, Vix. What irritates you is the thought that I'd admire your son instead of you!"

He gave another withering glare and turned away. Sabina felt a prick of warmth in her stomach. *He's jealous*, she thought, and grinned. *Imagine that!*

They soon passed over the Kephisos, a flow of moon-glossed water beneath the arches of a new bridge. "I commissioned this bridge, you know," Sabina heard Hadrian expounding up ahead, as young Pedanius made admiring noises. "Quarried limestone, fully one hundred sixty-five feet long—"

"Hadrian," Sabina called merrily, "don't be boring. We're on a mystical procession under a full moon; do you think we care how long the bridge is?"

A brief, sticky silence, and Sabina wondered if she'd been too careless in her night-found happiness. But then at length she heard a chuckle from Hadrian, just slightly forced. "You may," he said, "have a point."

More dark miles as the moon rose. The winding countryside around them, black and mysterious; the pressing crowds of acolytes. "Though the acolytes of Eleusis are called the *mystai*," Sabina explained to Antinous, who was curious. She paused to strip off her sandals, feeling blisters rise on her feet. *Demeter's feet bled.* The rites at Eleusis followed the legend of Demeter, walking the earth to find her daughter, to bring her reborn from death. Pain, death, rebirth; the oldest of cycles. *If my feet bleed, will I find my daughter?* Sabina walked until her blisters burst, then walked on blood-shod. Antinous tread behind her, singing softly in Greek. He had a pure young tenor, heartbreakingly tender.

Balbilla again: "The mystery and wonder of it all, I can already sense it filling me! The pain of the Goddess, the eternal pain, though of course she didn't get blisters, did she? If you're not going to wear your shoes, Vibia Sabina, may I? I didn't anticipate so many *pebbles . . .*"

Hadrian ahead, talking cheerfully, though his bound and broken leg must have sent a ripple of pain through his body at every uneven advance of the crutch. Talking of his forthcoming tour to the Peloponnese, the peacock he would sacrifice to Juno in the ruins of Mycenae. "And then to Sparta; do you know they still hold demonstrations where the boys subject themselves to bloody whippings to prove their bravery?" Pedanius Fuscus trying to pipe in. "I could whip myself to prove bravery, Great-Uncle. I don't fear anything!" Hadrian, sounding indulgent: "I'm sure you don't."

The moon rising, full and soft. At some point, Hadrian called Vix forward. "Vercingetorix, join me . . ." Vix tramping ahead, armor jingling in the dark. Their voices drifting back to Sabina.

"—inspection of the eastern legions, Tribune. What do you make of the men? I would welcome your opinion—"

Sabina smiled to herself, remembering Britannia, where she'd first suggested Hadrian cull opinions from Vix about the legions. *A man may be an enemy and still be useful*, she'd said, and he had ignored her. Or so she thought.

"—getting the legionaries back on regular route marches, keeping them fit during peacetime," Vix was replying, sounding guarded. "The officers, too. You know I saw a tribune of the Sixth Victrix who padded his saddle with *feather cushions?*"

"Really. What on earth is the Empire coming to? Go on—"

Vix went on, and he went on at length. *If I do not leave the Mysteries enlightened by the gods,* Sabina reflected, *I will at least be enlightened about the finer points of legionary training.* "—Men are always transferring between legions; there should be a manual of standard regulations—"

"Yes, they should know the rules are the same regardless of the standard under which they march." Hadrian's shadowy head was nodding. "A manual. Would you like to write it?"

"Me?" Vix's voice scaled up.

"Quit squawking like a startled owl. You may irk me to the point of violence, but that doesn't mean you don't have some sensible ideas. Suetonius, a note if you please . . ."

"Men," said Balbilla. "So insensitive to life's great mysteries. The cosmos opens around them, and they can talk of nothing but legions! I must write a poem about that, the female mythos—"

I am happy, Sabina thought. *Why am I so happy?*

Dawn, showing itself first in the slow retreat of the stars as they curtsied and took their leave of night. The moon fading, the gray line of horizon blushing with pink. And a great hoarse shout rising up from the first of the acolytes, shoving and pushing for their first look at white-walled, many-stepped Eleusis, framed by the endless rush of the sea.

Sabina found herself running to join the flood of *mystai,* but checked herself. Hadrian was stumping forward eagerly on his crutch, Vix's hand under his elbow—Sabina came up under Hadrian's other arm. "Hurry up, husband," she scolded. "Will you keep the gods waiting?"

Hadrian reared back for a moment at her chiding, but she laughed and pulled him along, feeling the happiness rising giddy in her chest like warmed wine. Sand underfoot at last, first dry and slipping, then damp and soft, and Sabina released Hadrian's arm at the same time as Vix, and the three of them plunged into the sea.

A shock of cold as the autumn-chilled wave broke over her head. Sabina laughed, choked, laughed again, then sank under the water and held her breath until she could hold it no more. She surfaced at last, letting the water lift her, and saw that the ocean was full to the brim: everywhere around her the *mystai* were bathing, washing the impurities of the world away. Antinous watched wistfully from the water's edge, and a buxom Greek girl took the advantage of the tumbling waves to fall into his arms. He set her on her feet with a laugh, stealing a kiss. Hadrian was washing himself in ritual motions, his beard sending rivulets of water down his strong throat, his face absorbed and solemn. Balbilla waded arms outspread into the water and promptly fell under a wave.

Vix had already splashed out, water shedding off his broad shoulders, one hand on his *gladius*. *No assassins here*, Sabina wanted to tell him, but you might as well tell Vix to cease breathing as cease preparing for danger. Her heart squeezed, half in pain, half in exquisite pleasure.

"Empress Sabina!" Antinous called. He had her new acolyte's robe ready, conscientious of his duties. "If you wish to change—"

"I do," she called back, "I do." The sodden curls of her wig felt twice as heavy as usual, and suddenly she wanted it all gone. She swept the wig off into the water, laughing as a wave carried it away like a mass of lumpy seaweed, then yanked out the brooches at her shoulders, gave them to the sea as an offering, and let the waves sweep her purple silks away. She floated in the water a moment, naked and weightless. *Free*, she thought. *How long has it been since I felt that?*

An illusion, of course, even if a sweet one. The Empress of Rome was not free to walk naked out of the sea before the eyes of plebs, even for the Mysteries of Eleusis. Hadrian was already glaring, conscious of their Imperial dignity, so Sabina crossed one arm over her breasts as she rose from the water. Antinous tossed her new robe out, the wool unfurling on the snap of the sea breeze, and she managed to catch the bundle one-handed. She tugged it over her head, the plain undyed linen that marked her not an empress but just another worshipper, and lowered the hem modestly as she came out of the ocean. Her blistered feet stung, but it was a clean pain, and she curled her toes into the damp sand. The robe was shapeless, too big; the neck hole slid down one shoulder and she could feel the skirts flapping about her wet legs. Antinous held out a cloak to cover her goose-prickled arms, but she just stood a moment, ruffling a hand across the damp silk of her short hair and gazing at the sea. Empress Vibia Sabina: soaking wet, freezing cold, falsely but gloriously free.

"Lady?" Vix sounded impatient. Sabina tilted her chin over her naked shoulder and grinned at him. A wicked, carefree grin like the girl she'd once been, the girl she felt like instead of the somber marble-carved Empress.

"Yes, Tribune?"

He looked back at her a moment, the stone soldier as she'd become the marble Empress, and then he smiled as though he couldn't resist any longer. A reluctant, invisible smile, more a movement of his eyes than his mouth. His gray gaze went over her, and the Empress of Rome knew why she was so happy.

"Put a cloak on," Vix said finally. "You'll die of cold."

VIX

I'm under pain of death never to reveal what I saw at the Mysteries of Eleusis. There was an ear of wheat; I'll leave it at that. But I didn't even *hear* half their sacred words. I was too busy dreaming dreams.

"What do you know about how to improve our legions?" Hadrian had asked me on that long march along the Sacred Way.

Plenty, I had thought. *Oh, plenty.* I'd hesitated, hating to give him anything, but the problem had been toying too long on the fringes of my own bored mind. I'd chattered to him under the moon, and he'd listened. The bastard had *listened*.

"A manual of standardized legionary regulations . . . Would you like to write it?"

It takes a great deal to startle me. I have fought in battles shield against shield; I have led night raids through country as dark and strange as Hades itself; I killed a Dacian king who had the strength of ten men. I had *never* been quite so startled as I was now.

Hell's gates, yes, I wanted to write it!

The Mysteries of Eleusis take a full nine nights to complete, nine long nights under the waning of the full moon, and I went through those nights in a white-hot haze of inspiration. *A practical manual for the common legionary*, I mused as Hadrian went blindfolded to the priests who approached with torches and fans. Something to do with being purified by wind and fire—he twitched as the torch approached, but Sabina leaned forward and kissed the flames when it was her turn, moving too quickly to be burned.

No, I thought, following behind Emperor and Empress alike as they presented a pair of piglets for sacrifice. *A practical manual for all soldiers of Rome. Why limit it just to legionaries?*

"I want to be initiated," Antinous told me on the dusty toil back to Athens. All through the Mysteries, we'd be trudging back and forth along the Sacred Way. "I know you think it's foolishness, and I know I'm only here to attend the Empress, but she'd let me take the rites if you will. I qualify under the rules—"

"As you please." *A multiorganized system of training, not just the same formations and shield drills. Those fighters in Parthia were lethal—Parthian drill instructors . . . ?*

Days of fasting and rest, allowing the tardy candidates to present themselves. Antinous taking his place among them, glowing under the blindfold. Sabina sleeping the sleep of the dead on the end of that second endless walk back to Athens; me tugging the wolf-skin cloak up over her shoulders against the cold. *Cold*, I thought. *Should be different slants for the eastern and the western legions; training in the cold versus training in the heat . . .*

The fifth day. Sabina and Hadrian and the rest tying saffron ribbons about left leg and right hand as the mark of the newly purified. Sabina in her too-big robe, sliding the shapeless folds up so she could loop the ribbon around one narrow brown thigh . . . Another trudge to Eleusis, but I didn't mind it somehow. It reminded me of the long marches under Trajan in Dacia, when Sabina had been a brown girl stealing away from her illustrious quarters to march beside me. We'd come full circle; here she was marching beside me again, and she was turning just as brown, freckles sprinkling her nose like flakes of gold. We crossed a narrow bridge on our march where old women waited to offer the ritual ribald jeers, mimicking the mortal women who had mocked Demeter in her journey. Sabina gave as good as she got, hauling out all the old legionary obscenities I'd ever taught her, and I even saw Hadrian's mouth twitch when he heard his Empress tell a wizened old crone to go fuck a horse.

Entering the temple grounds at Eleusis, cups were passed filled with something dark and bitter called *kykeon*, but I was thinking of how I could improve the drill exercises for javelin throwing . . . Around me rose shrieks and cries as whatever was in the *kykeon* took hold, but I sat dreaming and the Mysteries of Eleusis passed me by untouched.

Or did they? Because by the sixth night, the Night of Torches, the serenity of the *mystai* was infecting even me. Maybe my thoughts were all of military matters rather than godly ones, but my voice had fallen just as silent, my eyes turned just as reverently to the sky and the waning moon. I found myself laughing like a child, and so did the others: Hadrian's crutch slipped on a stone and tipped him splat into a puddle, and instead of looking vengeful and outraged, he looked at the mud down the front of his tunic and just said, "I look a sight, don't I?" We all dared to laugh then, and when Hadrian called for my arm to support his lamed side, I didn't quite recoil at his touch as I had ever since Britannia. My stomach growled at some point, and I realized I had not eaten in God knew how long. Food had not seemed important.

I'm happy, I thought. *How long has it been since I've been happy?* Happy beyond some momentary flash of comfort when I held Mirah in my arms, or some thrum of physical satisfaction as I finished my sword drills or a good meal? Happy like this; a bone-deep and mindless contentment?

I couldn't remember.

When twilight fell on the Night of Torches, Antinous put a hand on my arm as I picked up my breastplate. "Don't," he said. "It would offend the gods." I padded out barefoot in a plain tunic, just like the rest of them. (Though I did toss my lion skin over one shoulder to hide my *gladius*. I wasn't so far gone in happiness that I was about to go *completely* unarmed.)

Sabina had been trying to retie the acolyte's ribbon about her wrist, but she looked up and gave me the same sparkling glance she'd given me on the edge of the sea with the water sliding down her naked shoulder. "Tie this for me?" Holding up her wrist with the ribbon coming loose, she glanced at my lion skin. "You look like Hercules."

"You look about twenty," I said, truthfully, because she could have been the girl in Dacia all over again. She was still trim as a spear, thanks to her lifelong habit of marching with legions and scrambling after adventure instead of staying at home breeding children and eating sweetmeats. And the shorn hair had an oddly boyish effect on her pointed little face. I suppose she had a few lines around the eyes, but at least she didn't cake on powder trying to cover them up, like Balbilla.

"I feel old sometimes," my Empress confessed, arching her back in a long stretch like a cat. "Old and used up."

"Don't look it to me," I said. And then I glared at Antinous because he too was looking at her admiringly as she stretched.

The Night of Torches is the center of the Mysteries, which is probably why I didn't understand a thing. I'm not sure anyone understood it, but maybe you weren't supposed to—the priests were passing around a lot of that *kykeon* drink. Sabina said it was made of barley and pennyroyal, but I guessed there was more, some draught to confuse the senses, because as the stars came out and the rites began inside the temple, I heard cries of grief and terror among the *mystai*, and the rites weren't at all terrifying. More like absurd. (A stalk of wheat? Really, that was supposed to be a mystery?) I didn't drink any of the *kykeon*, but Hadrian shivered under its effects and I saw the black in Sabina's eyes expanding to swallow the blue as the Mysteries advanced. Everyone stared and moaned, watching the priests, while I just sat with my mind wandering peacefully through shield drills.

There was some sort of play going on among the priestesses, and I don't have to hide the details because I don't remember them. But I glanced to one side and saw Sabina sitting with her narrow fingers linked about her knees; tears were sliding down her cheeks. "What is it?" I asked. On her other side Hadrian gave a great shudder, staring blind into the dark, and then he stumbled to his feet, chest heaving. "Caesar—"

"He is seeing the void," Suetonius whispered. Suetonius, like me, had not imbibed. "Whatever it holds for him!"

"So beautiful," Antinous murmured. He looked awed, as though gazing on something of unimaginable loveliness, but Hadrian wasn't seeing anything so peaceable. He stared around wildly, every muscle quivering. The hierophant struck a great gong, and the whole crowd surged to its feet with a great cry.

Hadrian's cry came loudest of all. His head jerked wildly from whatever dark visions danced before his eyes—and before I could rise, he was gone into the madness.

ANTINOUS

Later, Antinous thought that the *kykeon* must have given wings to his feet as well as his soul. Half a dozen men chased after the Emperor when he gave his great shout and fled the temple, but they soon fell behind and lost themselves in the shadows of the trees. Antinous skimmed behind as the Emperor panted and stumbled, never losing him for a moment. "Caesar," Antinous called softly.

Hadrian jerked to a violent stop, staring about with glassy eyes, and then he gave a hoarse scream. *Why do you scream when the world is so beautiful?* Antinous wondered, his thoughts gliding as dreamy as silver fish through deep water. The world was stars overhead like a carpet of pearls; shadows all around like the warmest of cloaks; moss underfoot as plush-soft as a comforting bed. A place of wonders, and Antinous wanted to weep from the joy of it. He smiled instead, reaching out to touch the Emperor's heaving shoulder, thinking as he did so that his own flesh seemed to sparkle in the moonlight. "There is nothing to fear here," he said in the same soothing tone he had once used on the Emperor's wounded dog. "Nothing at all."

Hadrian's fist lashed out, catching Antinous square on the chin and snapping his head back. He felt the blow as if from a distance; it did not hurt at all. "Well," he conceded. "I did hit you once, Caesar, so I suppose we are now even."

Hadrian gave another cry and fell to his knees, swatting at the air around him. "Back—all of you, back—" Publius Aelius Hadrian: ruler of the world, marble face of countless statues, crawling on hands and knees quaking in terror of a beautiful world. He looked like a cringing dog about to be beaten, and the sight stabbed Antinous to the heart. He squatted down beside the Emperor, stroking one burly shoulder just as he might have stroked a whimpering dog. Hadrian was ice-cold, drenched in sweat, and at Antinous's touch he flinched violently. "Ssshh," Antinous said. "Don't be afraid."

"Get away—" That deep voice that had called the bear hunt with such splendid authority was hoarse from sobbing. "Faces, faces in the mirror—"

"Ssshh," Antinous crooned again, smoothing his hand back and forth across that trembling back. They were quite alone beneath a great overarching oak that seemed to have tangled the moon in its branches. Other *mystai* flitted through the woods around them—he could see the flash of their torches. More than that, he could *feel* them; they were all part of the same moon-drenched dream. The Empress was lost in it too, crying just like her husband, but for something else. *Who knows what?* She would be safe; his father was with her. But the Emperor had no one here but Antinous. "Take my hand," he told the Emperor.

Hadrian lashed out at him again, fists doubled. Antinous ducked this time. Even if the blow to his jaw hadn't hurt, he knew it would in the morning—Emperor Hadrian had fists as hard as Mars; Antinous had seen that on the bear hunt when his hands had clenched and unclenched so helplessly, watching his dog bleed. He ducked those fists as they swung at him, came under the Emperor's arm as Hadrian blundered at him snarling, and then Antinous laughed softly as he doubled the Emperor up from behind in a wrestler's hold.

"Faces," the Emperor was babbling, "in the mirror, dear gods, the *mirror*—"

"My grandfather taught me this hold," Antinous told Hadrian, locking those sweat-drenched arms behind him. "When we were in Britannia. He used to be a gladiator, and he said you could follow this up with a nasty gouge and take a man's eye out. I think I'll just sit you down instead . . ."

Antinous kept talking, low and lulling, as he put his back to the great oak and slid down to the moss, taking Hadrian with him fighting all the way. "Don't struggle, not much use fighting a hold taught by Arius the Barbarian himself . . . Calm yourself, Caesar. Calm. There are no faces. There are no faces, and you are safe."

The Emperor went still all of a sudden inside Antinous's locked arms. The muscles of his broad back were drawn stone-hard against Antinous's chest. "Mirror," he said hoarsely, still staring at nothing, and Antinous felt a great leap of pity. This man he had feared for so long in the abstract, a shadowy demon capable of anything—and then the bear hunt had come, and he had turned from a demon into a man, a man who could fling a spear better than anyone Antinous had ever seen, and then reduce himself to tears over a dog . . .

And now he wasn't a demon or a god or even the Emperor of Rome anymore. Just a man in terror.

"Mirror," Hadrian whispered again, and he trembled inside Antinous's arm-lock and began to weep.

"Mirrors reflect good things too, you know." Antinous risked letting go of the Emperor's wrist, pausing to make sure he wouldn't lash out again, then put a hand to the Emperor's ice-sweated forehead and pulled it gently back, directing that glassy tear-dimmed gaze up at the sky. "Stars, see? The mirror is full of stars."

"Stars," the Emperor whispered in a cracked voice. Then his head fell against Antinous's shoulder, and he wept like a child. His face was contorted in agony, utterly naked in its grief, and it gutted Antinous. He pressed his lips to the curly hair, feeling tears in his own eyes.

"You poor broken soul, how long has it been since you've wept?" His arms tightened around the Emperor, and he felt Hadrian's tears slide warm and damp down his shoulder. He pressed another kiss to the Emperor's forehead, as the stars wheeled and the world turned and his fellow *mystai* reveled. "Weep your eyes dry and be at peace, Caesar. You are safe with me."

VIX

It was all chaos. Some of the acolytes cried out in terror like Hadrian; some were transfixed by rapture like Antinous. There was dancing and singing, wandering and fighting, and any of the revelers might have trampled Sabina to her death. Because as Hadrian bolted from the temple with Boil and Antinous and the rest of the Praetorians in pursuit, the Empress of Rome lay boneless and weeping on the temple floor. "Empress," I snapped, shaking her by the shoulder.

"The world is so large," Sabina wept. "So large and dark, and she is gone."

"Oh, Hell's gates." I picked her up and threw her over one shoulder.

The *mystai* were fleeing in all directions, seizing torches, buffeting me as they spilled from the temple and ran for the trees. I carried Sabina out of harm's way, deep into a dense little woods that I judged the *kykeon*-mad crowd would probably assume was full of demons. There I slung her down with her back against a tree, and squatted before her. "Sabina?"

"Tree," she observed. "So much *tree*."

"You're flying higher than an arrow, aren't you?" I looked around me for Suetonius or little Pedanius Fuscus or any of the others. They'd disappeared into the crowd, but they weren't a Praetorian's responsibility. Hadrian was, but Boil had called the other guards after him. I reckoned my old friend could keep the Emperor from trying to stab himself or take a flying leap off a cliff.

I sat down beside Sabina, my back against the same tree, the lion skin over my shoulder brushing her arm. At first I saw flashes of white as acolytes darted past, but eventually the sounds of revelry faded away. Maybe they'd charged back into the temple to moan and pray. I don't know how long we sat there, but my mind was cool and empty again.

Sabina sat as I'd first placed her, hands limp in her lap, small head tilted back, looking up at the black waving branches overhead. "Dark," she mused. "So much *dark*."

"At least you're not crying anymore." I'd only seen her cry once, after Trajan died, weeping for our lost emperor and her lost freedom both. It had broken my heart. "What made you cry tonight?"

"The play." Her voice was quiet, surprisingly lucid. "Didn't you see it? Demeter searching for her lost daughter Persephone . . . I saw her, wandering in the dark, and whenever I tried to reach toward that beautiful red hair, she was gone."

"Who? Persephone?"

"Persephone, Proserpina, Kore, Annia. She has so many names."

"And that made you weep like your heart was breaking?"

"Yes." She gave a single bitter laugh. "We're all supposed to be searching for her—that's why the priests gave out torches. We're to search all night; and by morning they'll ring another gong as a symbol of when she was found and returned to her mother." A sigh. "The hierophant didn't say what we're supposed to do if we already know where Persephone is. Or if we know she'll never be returned to her mother."

"You're still drunk," I decided.

Her head turned, and her eyes caught mine. "Oh, Vix," she mocked, but her tone was gentler. "So much *Vix*."

"I'm not going to get any sense out of you tonight, am I?"

"Mmm." She closed her eyes. "It feels a bit like when I was a child and I had fits of epilepsia. I feel my head contracting in about itself, and then the world goes flying away in shards. Only I'm still awake—if this were epilepsia, everything would go dark until I wake with a splitting headache."

"Do you still have those fits?"

"Not since I was twelve." She smiled. "You might have had something to do with that."

So I had.

"Here comes the headache." Sabina massaged her temples, watching the sky for a while, and then suddenly she rose and went to throw up into a distant bush. "That's better," she said, wiping her mouth as she came back. "I caught a glimpse of Balbilla—she's torn her robe off to bare her breasts and is dancing in a Dionysian frenzy."

I thought of my duty as a guard. "I suppose we should make sure she doesn't dance off a ridgetop."

"Why bother? She's perfectly lucid."

"How can you tell?"

"Because no woman lost in actual Dionysian revelry holds her stomach in quite that carefully as she revels."

I laughed and offered Sabina my flask of barley water. She rinsed her mouth and then went prowling a little unsteadily among the bushes in the other direction and came back with a fistful of sprigs. "Wild mint," she said, and began chewing on a handful of leaves. "So my breath doesn't stupefy an ox."

Some of the *kykeon* must have still lingered, because her legs gave out all at once and she flopped on her back on the moss. "What are you thinking about, Vercingetorix?"

"*Pila* drills," I said honestly.

"Ah." She smiled through the dark; I could hear it in her voice. "That manual Hadrian asked you to prepare with Suetonius."

We hadn't spoken so cordially to each other in a long time. I'd hardly spoken more than two sentences to her in years—since the wall in Britannia, where we'd stood under another moon like this one. A moon not quite round, but full of promise.

"You're taking notes for your manual already, aren't you?" she asked me. "Really, Vix. Millions have waxed lyrical about the Mysteries of Eleusis, and all you can do is scribble *pila* drills!"

"Suetonius said the same thing," I admitted. "But he's cross at me. This manual of mine will take him away from his latest treatise."

"He's writing a treatise? I shall make sure I sponsor it, so it does well." Sabina linked her pale arms behind her head in the grass. "Is it like the treatises my father used to write?"

"Nothing like. Those were serious works. Suetonius, well, he's got a mind like a gossip trap. The most rubbishy collection of rumors, omens, portents, and stories you've ever heard." I grinned. "He's very cross with me, thinking he'll have to put his next book aside to take my notes on improved training regimens."

"He'll live."

"Sabina . . ." I hesitated, winding my fingers around each other. "Why did Hadrian ask a common legionary to assist with legion reform? The Senate won't like it."

"He doesn't care. Don't you know him by now?"

"Nobody knows him." I still felt that, very strongly. "And I still don't know why he picked *me*."

She turned on one side in the dark, propping her cheek on one hand. "Because he thinks you're the best man to do it."

"But he hates me."

"You're still useful. He never lets a little thing like hatred get in the way."

"He threatened my children," I said. "And he threatened to have me held down and then fuck me till I bled."

A small breath in the dark. "Ah," Sabina said quietly. "It sounds like him."

I didn't know why I'd told her—I hadn't told *anyone*. It just came out of me like poison from a lanced wound. "He made it clear I was dirt," I said. "That he could turn me into one of his bum-spreading whores if he wanted to. And now he hands me power."

"And you're flattered." Sabina's eyes were just a gleam in the inky shadows. "Aren't you?"

I ruffled a hand across my hair. "Look, I don't hate the bugger any less than I ever did. But these changes he wants to make?" I wrestled with my own words. "If I'd gotten the Tenth Fidelis, I'd have shaken everything up, trained the men my way. And I don't have the Tenth Fidelis. But if the Emperor likes my notions of legion reform, every soldier in *Rome* will be trained my way. Do you know what that means?"

"It means you'll do it," Sabina said.

"God help me, yes." I flopped on my own back beside her. "On the wall in Britannia, you told me he could be a great man. I didn't believe you. And I'll still say it—he's not a *good* man, not by any means. Not like Trajan. But when he's on a tear like this and out to change the world . . ."

"You can't look away," Sabina finished. "Because, as bad as he can be, you want to stick around and watch, just see what he'll do next. Don't you?"

No. I dropped an arm across my own eyes. *Yes?*

"So . . ." Sabina's cool fingers touched my shoulder, slid down to my hand, and she tugged my arm away. "You'll help him in this? Help him be the Emperor he can be?" Her fingertips glided like butterflies over my palm. "The way I asked you on the wall in Britannia?"

"Quit trying to seduce me into it." I raised myself on one elbow opposite her, aiming a glare through the shadows. "I'll help. All right? So don't lie there looking so damned pleased with yourself."

"How do you know how I look? It's pitch dark."

I always know how you look, I almost said. *Always have. Always will.*

I had a past that came before Mirah, and Sabina ran through that past like a blue ribbon, sinuous and maddening. Of any woman in my life who wasn't my mother, I'd known Sabina the longest. We'd met as children inside the marble reaches of the Colosseum, a slave brat and a pearled doll, awkward and already fascinated with each other, and here we were more than thirty years later in a dark grove, a sleek empress and a battered guard. No longer awkward, maybe, but still fascinated with each other. I couldn't deny that, not in this sacred place where the absurd but gripping truth of the Mysteries still held me fast. I knew Sabina better than any woman alive. I didn't need to see her face, so close to mine in the dark, to know that her mouth was curved in a faint half smile, that her elegant shorn head was cocked toward me, and that her narrow fingers lay on the moss between us waiting to be touched.

I didn't touch her. I'd betrayed Mirah once before in the arms of the Empress of Rome. Once was enough.

Sabina's hand rose through the dark, and I felt her featherlight touch on the one piece of my hair that seemed to stick up no matter how short I razored it off. "Vix," she said quietly. "How often do you think of Selinus?"

That barren isle where I'd lost Trajan, where Sabina and I had lain together for the last time, her mouth opening under mine like a budding flower. "Every day," I whispered. Every day I thought of it, because that was how I stopped myself from lashing out at her husband when he needled me. *I had your wife, you bastard. How would that hurt your precious pride?* I didn't say it but I thought it, every time he mocked me—only now he'd left off mocking me. Instead he asked my advice and valued what I said and gave me power, and I had to take pride in that.

But I'd still gotten into the habit of remembering how Sabina felt under me, the scent and the taste of her, and that was a bad habit to have. Because I knew exactly how she'd taste if I reached out through the dark and speared her mouth on mine as I'd done on Selinus.

"I think of it." Her breath touched me, smelling of mint. "Every time I lay eyes on you, Vix."

"Hell's gates," I whispered back. "What did we do on that hillside? What witchcraft did we *make?*" It was only grief that had pulled us together, so why had that one final time left her lingering in my blood like a poison?

"We did make something on that hillside, but it wasn't witchcraft." She took a breath. "Vix—"

ANTINOUS

Antinous could feel the *kykeon* seeping away. His mind stopped its dreamlike whirl up among the treetops, and his jaw began to hurt from where the Emperor had struck him, yet he felt no urge to move. He sat with his back to the tree and the Emperor of Rome inside the circle of his arms, and he gazed up at the sky. The world was still a place of miraculous beauty. He did not think he would ever see it any other way, ever again.

The Emperor had long ceased weeping, Antinous saw with a huge swell of tenderness. He had thought Hadrian would pull away, but the curly head still lay against his shoulder, and he had not pushed free of

Antinous's encircling arms. Hadrian's whole terror-tautened body had relaxed to limpness, and he was silent as a tomb. Antinous did not mind. He spoke for the both of them, whatever the mood took him to say.

"My mother talks of her god's infinite wonders. I wonder what she would say about all this . . . but she'd never come. Her god is too jealous. I think that's why I can't believe in him."

And "Don't worry for your Empress. My father is with her. He'd protect her against the hordes at Thermopylae if he had to."

And "I know what I believe in now. This—peace and beauty and stars . . ."

The Emperor sighed, so Antinous knew he was awake. A question had been forming in him. It was time to speak it aloud. "What faces do you see, Caesar?" he asked quietly. "What faces make you so afraid?"

A long silence. Finally the Emperor spoke, his voice husky and cracked. "The faces in my Hades."

"What is your Hades?"

"Pray you never know."

Antinous turned his head a little so his cheek rested against the Emperor's hair, and realized he wanted to press another kiss there. *I am happy*, Antinous thought wonderingly. *I am so happy.*

The Emperor's head turned too, tilting toward him. Antinous saw dark eyes gleaming like pieces of jet. Weary eyes, and lonely. So lonely his soul hurt. *Surrounded by crowds, and still so lonely*, Antinous thought. He understood that, even though his own loneliness was so different: the child waiting alone for a god in a lion skin to claim him; the boy playing alone among stray dogs because his sisters had their own games and their bond of blood; the student at the *paedogogium* who sat alone because he had no friends; the lone son who could not speak to his father about so many of the things that troubled him. Antinous was so often alone, in one way or another. Little Annia had seen that when she first laid eyes on him, observant young thing that she was.

You are never alone, he thought, looking at the Emperor of Rome. *But you are still as lonely as I am.*

Hadrian's bearded lips brushed his, as tentatively as though he had never offered a kiss in his life. Antinous's breath caught in his throat, the blood tingling in his veins. He threaded his hands through Hadrian's curly hair, and he felt the Emperor's wide strong hand cradling his cheek. Hadrian turned in Antinous's arms, his hard chest against Antinous's, and he could feel the thump of the Emperor's heart. That hunter's heart, which had probably beat calmly while facing down a maddened she-bear, was thrumming fast as a bird's wings. Hadrian's mouth was fierce against his, and Antinous fell into the kiss like he'd fallen into the whirl of *kykeon*. They sank down into the moss, twined together like vines, and Antinous set his lips at the hollow of Hadrian's collarbone, kissing him with a tenderness that rose fierce and protective in his own throat. Who felt protective of an emperor, the lord of the world ringed by spears and safe from all danger? But Antinous felt it anyway, and he wrapped Hadrian in his arms and held him, murmured to him, opened to him under the welcoming moon.

VIX

Sabina was about to tell me something, but I laid my hand on her bare ankle and she went silent. Slowly I slid my hand along the curve of her leg, the rough hem of her robe pooling over my wrist as it pushed up. "What were you about to say?" I asked, and my voice was hoarse in my own ears.

She was silent. Her flesh was warm and smooth, and I could feel her breath coming uneven. My fingers found the saffron ribbon she'd tied about her leg above the knee, the mark of an acolyte like the matching ribbon at her wrist. I ran my fingertips along the taut band for a moment, and then I slid one finger beneath and slowly tugged it loose. I twined the bit of silk between my fingers, and it was still warm from her skin. "Hell's gates," I whispered. "Don't tell me this isn't witchcraft you're working on me."

She said nothing. I saw her biting her lip in the dark, and I remembered how cool and fresh those lips tasted, like water from the world's purest spring. I gripped the loops of the ribbon in my fist, so hard they bit into my fingers.

Sabina lifted her hand, plucking the other saffron ribbon away from her wrist. She slid it about my neck, her fingers whispering over my skin, holding each end in a small hand as she tugged me down toward her on the moss. Tugged me toward her with nothing more than a frail strip of silk, and the whole slim coil of her body arched up toward me and her lips were just a hair's distance from mine when I moved over her. I loosed my fist from the other ribbon's loops and laid the band of silk across her throat, stretching it between my fists and pressing her back into the ground. Then I eased up until she was at arm's length again, my fists sunk into the moss on either side of her head, the ribbon stretching taut between them across her supple throat.

"No," I said thickly. "No."

She still had me around the neck with her own length of silk. She could have tugged the ends again, brought me down full length against her, and she had to feel how hard I wanted it. All she had to do was tug, and I was trying to summon Mirah's face to mind, keep myself from following that tug like a dog. They called me the Emperor's dog, but really I was his wife's. God help me.

Sabina let the ribbon slide away down my neck. "No," she said, and I didn't need to see her face to know she wore one of her wry smiles. "So much *no*."

I released her. Stood up. She rose too, her bare arms gleaming like silver in the faint starlight. "You'll be cold," I said, and slid the lion skin from my shoulders so I could drape it about hers. Her small shoulders were wrapped for a moment inside the circle of my arms, and I lowered my head so I could press my lips briefly against the crown of her shorn head. "I've always loved that short hair."

"Why do you think I keep it this way?"

It was nearly dawn as we made our silent way back to the temple. We had almost cleared the trees when I saw the honey-colored head of my son. He was sitting against a tree of his own, eyes closed either in sleep or in reverie, and I saw a darker head resting in his lap like a child's.

Antinous opened his eyes and saw me, just as I saw that it was Hadrian who slept with his head in my son's lap. The Emperor looked white and worn and innocent somehow, like a terrified child at last relaxed into slumber. "He was frightened," Antinous said simply. "Something he saw under the *kykeon*."

"Did it affect you as badly as it did him?" I asked, because it had been a night for dreams but also for nightmares—and I loved my son so much, I'd have slain every night terror in all the cups of *kykeon* in the world, just to keep his sleep serene.

Antinous smiled at me, and his smile was a dazzling thing, sweet and dazed and utterly beautiful. "I have dreamed and danced and marveled. And now I have wakened, and found the world is still a wondrous place."

He's still drunk, I decided.

"Thank you for looking after the Emperor," said Sabina, and the three of us raised the Emperor of Rome in his slumber. The hierophant was ringing his gong, and all around people stumbled to answer the call, wild-eyed and dazed. Persephone had been found; death defeated once again. There were only minor rites left over the next few days, and then the final trudge back to Athens.

The Mysteries of Eleusis were over.

CHAPTER 7

ANTINOUS
Athens

Two days after the Mysteries ended, the Emperor summoned him.

Antinous had always found waiting an agony—waiting for his father to return from his latest war; waiting for Mirah to conceive that son who would have healed the little wound in her heart. Waiting usually meant time for doubt to grow, time for Antinous to convince himself that this was the war his father would never return from; that Mirah never would birth that son and would be giving Antinous that mournful, half-resentful smile for the rest of his life. But there were no doubts this time. Antinous knew the Emperor would summon him, and he waited those two days serene as a lotus floating on a pool.

It wasn't lotuses he smelled now, but lemons—the delicate waft of lemon trees all around, as Antinous made his way through the grove where he had been told Hadrian waited. "I could delay a bit," the Praetorian who had summoned him ventured. It was massive, square-built, red-faced Boil, who had been like an uncle to Antinous as long as he could remember. "I don't like it, Caesar summoning you without Vix. I could say I couldn't find you, wait till your father gets back from inspecting that cohort outside Athens—"

"That's all right."

"But—"

"Please?" Antinous said simply.

Boil sighed and let him go ahead into the lemon trees.

The Emperor sat on a marble bench reading from a wax tablet, staff propped beside him and three dogs panting happily about his feet. He did not look up as Antinous came to stand before him.

Boil's footsteps retreated from the edge of the trees, leaving them entirely alone, and still Hadrian continued to read. Antinous's black dog had put his hackles up at the Emperor's hounds; Antinous bent and ran a hand over the pricked ears. "Hush, Caesar."

Hadrian's head jerked up, startled out of his deliberate silence. "I beg your pardon?"

"The dog," Antinous explained. "His name is Caesar."

"That is very nearly blasphemous."

"My father named him. He said he'd like to be giving a Caesar the orders for once."

A sharp glance. "Your father is rude."

"He is," Antinous agreed. Hadrian's eyes were cold. The same eyes Antinous had seen when he first struck the Emperor. Cold enough to pierce Antinous's serenity, but not shatter it. *I do fear you*, he thought. *I'm not stupid, after all.* No matter what had happened between them during the Mysteries, this man was dangerous. How could the Emperor of Rome not be? But he was also the man who had pressed a tender kiss between Antinous's shoulder blades and murmured sweet, broken words in the dark.

From that moment, Antinous knew the Emperor would call for him again. *Because there is more to you than this cold and frightening face and you let me see it.*

He returned that intimidating stare with a smile, and Hadrian's eyes slid away. He tapped his stylus, and Antinous continued to look at him steadily, still smiling.

"Your name," Hadrian said at last, brusque. "I have forgotten it."

No, you haven't. This Emperor was famous for remembering the names of everyone he ever met, lowborn or high. "Antinous," he replied gently.

"That's right." Hadrian made a mark on the wax tablet. Very much the master of the world today in his purple cloak, eyes hooded and aloof, hair gleaming in the dappled sunlight, his broad arms decked with gold bracelets. Confident and haughty; a man who looked like his own statues; not the same man who had ever wept in terror under a night sky. And yet he was. Antinous thought he could still feel the vibration of the Emperor's heart against his own, as though they lay chest to chest instead of separated by a few feet of lemon-scented breeze.

"You made pleasant company in Eleusis." The deep voice was careless. "You shall be appropriately rewarded."

He tossed a purse at Antinous. A good few sesterces, Antinous judged from the weight. He let the purse fall through his fingers to the grass.

Hadrian glanced up from his tablet again. "You wish for more, boy? I do not overpay my whores."

He said the word *whores* so sharply. It should have cut like a knife, but it did not. *Because you don't mean it*, Antinous thought, *I know you don't*. He wished he could stretch out a hand to the master of the world, but he knew he'd be rebuffed. "I want nothing from you, Caesar," Antinous said, and reached out to the hunting dogs instead. "Nothing except your company."

"I prefer variety in my bedmates." Another mark on the wax tablet. "I already had you once. That was enough."

Antinous almost laughed. Since the day he first started lengthening from a boy to a man—and even before that, truth be told—he'd seen his own face reflected in the gaze of men and women alike and recognized the answering flare for what it was. If there was anything Antinous had learned growing up, it was when he was desired. No one had *ever* wanted him just once. "Forgive me for contradicting you, Caesar, but you do want me again."

The Emperor's eyes narrowed. "You think that pretty face gives you leave to say whatever you please to your Emperor? Or that I cannot find another dozen boys just as handsome as you?"

"It wasn't my face that drew you in Eleusis, Caesar," Antinous said. "And it wasn't your purple cloak that drew me." What a rare thing that was, for either of them—because if there was anything Hadrian knew, surely it was the flare *he* saw in the faces of those who looked at him. For Antinous that flare was lust and for the Emperor it was ambition, but it was still the same kind of greed. Something they had in common, Antinous and the Emperor.

"What an innocent you are." Hadrian did not make it sound like a compliment. "I knew exactly who you were in Eleusis, boy. I knew you were your father's son Why do you think I bedded you? To insult him."

"Ouch," Antinous said, reflective. "That would hurt, Caesar. Except . . ."

"Except for *what*?"

"You said you didn't remember my name."

Silence stretched. Hadrian's three dogs were pushing for Antinous's pats, wagging their tails. His own small Caesar growled, and Antinous hushed him. The Caesar on the marble bench sat still as stone.

"Take your gold or not," he said at last. "You are dismissed."

Antinous straightened. "You know where to find me, when you are lonely again."

"I am never lonely," Hadrian snapped.

"Forgive me, but you are." Antinous wanted to curve his hand around that bearded cheek, but the Emperor would probably strike him if he tried. Poor chained dog of a man, snapping at any hand outstretched in comfort. "You are so lonely you could die, Caesar. So am I, sometimes. But not at Eleusis, and not here. Not with you."

Such a strange mix of feelings surged through him in place of that bleak loneliness. Tenderness: the urge to press a kiss between those scowling eyes. Protectiveness: the desire to massage the tension from those knotted shoulders. A dash of fear, looking at those iron-hammer fists and knowing how much they wanted to lash out.

And passion—sweet gods, passion to buckle the knees. Nothing Antinous had ever felt before: not with the giggling buxom girls of Rome, not with the lean boys of the *paedogogium*. Antinous looked at the Emperor through the dappled light of the lemon trees, and all he wanted was for those great fists to uncurl and tangle through his hair again—for that bearded mouth to claim his own.

"You are dismissed," the Emperor said again, at last. "Take your gold and go."

"I'm no whore," Antinous said softly. "And you want me to stay."
He had never been so certain of anything in his life.

"Don't be ridiculous." The Emperor rose, wincing as he put his
weight to his half-healed leg.

Antinous put a hand out to steady him. "You're hurting," he said.
"Lean on me."

"I will not lean on you! If I wish for a companion, I will find someone more suitable. You're nearly a grown man, too old to be whoring
like a bum-boy." Hadrian's face had flushed with high color; he spat the
words out like icicles. "Your father should have taught you better. I will
point that out, when I tell him what his son has become."

A frightened animal will hurt you. Antinous had learned that long
ago, playing with strays in the street. The Emperor might look angry,
but it was fear behind the anger—and his words hurt, but not for the
reason Hadrian thought. They hurt because Antinous could see his
father's face, full of disbelief and rage, if he found out his son had fallen
into the arms of an enemy.

Your enemy, Antinous thought defiantly. Not mine. Not that his
father had lied to him, telling all those dark tales of the Emperor—Vix
seemed to believe every one. But Antinous looked at Hadrian, who
hadn't taken a step but somehow seemed to be standing closer, his chest
heaving like a bellows and his eyes like desperate pits, and found he
could not believe the stories. He did not want to believe them. This
could not be a man who had blinded a slave or ordered executions for
sport. This man couldn't even look Antinous in the face, he seemed so
afraid of what he might find there.

"Go," the Emperor said for the third time, his voice hoarse.
"Leave me."

"No," Antinous whispered, and reached for the Emperor's hand.
He felt it jerk under his touch: the hand of a hunter, callused from
spears and reins rather than perfumed and soft as one would imagine
an emperor's hand. Those rough fingers were still balled into a fist as
Antinous bent his head and kissed the Imperial ring.

The fist unclenched beneath his lips. The Emperor's hand curved
around Antinous's cheek. An inarticulate sound came from Hadrian,

a sigh and a stifled oath all at once. Antinous was the one to step closer, until they stood chest against chest just as they had in Eleusis. He fit his lips with infinite care to that clamped, trembling mouth. Hadrian's lips opened under his with a groan, and then Antinous pulled the Emperor's head against his shoulder as those hunter's arms came hard about his waist.

"You are not a whore," Hadrian said into Antinous's tunic, the words blurred.

Antinous laughed.

"What?" At once the voice was angry. "Why do you laugh at me?"

"You do not apologize very often, do you?" Stroking the dark curls. "More contrition is called for, Caesar, when one slings such words as *whore* and *bum-boy*," he said gently.

The Emperor's jaw clenched, and Antinous saw the anger in his eyes. His grip about Antinous's waist tightened, brutally hard as his kisses had been under the Greek moon. Antinous felt no fear at all, only an edge of excitement. He wanted to be held in those arms forever.

Then the anger was gone as though the Emperor had pulled a curtain over it. "I am sorry, Antinous." His voice was stiff, but he had still said it. *Said my name*, Antinous thought, dizzy as though he had drunk a bucket of *kykeon*. He took the Emperor's arm and drew it over his shoulder to support his injured side, and they wandered deeper into the grove of lemon trees. They left the dogs behind to frisk, and where the branches overhead laced the thickest, they stopped and spread out the Imperial purple cloak. Under the starlit oak it had been fast and rough and desperate, terror seeking safe harbor in comforting flesh. This was different. Hadrian lay almost helpless thanks to his half-healed leg, his mouth clamped so tight from fierce emotion that he could hardly speak, only look up at Antinous as though he had no idea what he wanted or how to ask for it. He looked terrified. So Antinous stretched over him and made love to his Emperor, slow and sunlit and tender, and through it all, Hadrian's eyes watched him dazed and wondering.

"Caesar," Antinous said afterward, just to say it. Because his heart was vibrating in his chest, and because the Emperor's callused fingers were still linked tight through his own.

"I return to the Eternal City soon," the Emperor said, staring up at the interlaced branches. "In the spring, once my travels in Greece are completed."

"Do you?" Antinous caressed the rough knuckles with his thumb.

"You will accompany me back to Rome." It was an order, not an invitation.

"Of course." Antinous laughed. It had not occurred to him to doubt it.

"You will be assigned to my trireme, your father to the Empress's."

"Yes, Caesar."

And for the whole long voyage back to Rome, once the sea lanes were open, it was blue sky and blue sea and a bed rocked by Neptune's long swells and the rhythmic movement of the oars, and Antinous had never in all his life been so happy.

SABINA

A.D. 125, Spring
Rome

"What does he want?" Faustina's voice was pitched low under the commotion of the Imperial box. "Why did he invite us?"

"He invited a great many people to watch the races, Faustina. It may mean nothing." Sabina linked fingers with her sister behind cover of their fans.

Faustina's eyes were pools of worry as she watched the newly returned Emperor in his throng of courtiers. "I thought he might have forgotten us, as long as he's been away from Rome. But the way he *looked* at Titus, when the senators first presented themselves. Like he was thinking which piece went on which spear . . ."

"No spears," Sabina said sternly before the panic in her sister's voice could rise. "Don't even think it. Hadrian has been *much* more good-natured ever since Eleusis." She hadn't traveled with her husband on the voyage back to Rome, but Sabina had reports from the Emperor's trireme saying that he had never seemed so good-humored—and what was more, his cheer had *held*, even though he was back in the Eternal City, which he so disliked. "Perhaps he just wants to thank Titus for gilding the roof of the Pantheon."

"Perhaps . . ."

Sabina followed her sister's gaze. Titus had retreated to a quiet corner of the Imperial box, flanked by little Annia and her cousin Marcus. The children stared raptly at the sea of color and humanity in the Circus Maximus below: the raked sands, the flower petals raining down, as Titus pointed. "The largest arena for sport in the Empire—two hundred fifty thousand Romans! See the gold dolphins at the starting line? They tip their noses down, one to mark each lap . . ." Everyone else in the Imperial box was angling for the seat closest to the Emperor, but Titus's attention was all for the children.

Wise, Sabina thought. She saw the way Hadrian's eyes flicked to her brother-in-law over the rim of his wine cup—what could be more thoroughly harmless to a suspicious emperor's eyes than a man surrounded by children?

Or perhaps Titus is merely the kindest father in Rome. Annia and her cousin were both gazing up at him like he drove the sun. It made Sabina's heart squeeze beneath her Imperial purple *stola*, not in envy, but in love. She might not have chosen well when it came to the father who had sired Annia—there were those who might call a bloody-handed ex-legionary a decidedly questionable choice—but she had at least chosen well in the father she *gave* her daughter afterward.

"Mother!" Annia came whirling up, dragging her cousin. "Marcus is a *traitor*. He won't cheer for the Reds!"

"Rank treachery!" Faustina forced a little lightness into her tone, smoothing Annia's flyaway hair. Annia looked puzzled, as if she felt the anxiety in her mother's touch. *My observant girl*, Sabina thought. *Nothing gets past you, does it?*

Trumpets sounded. Sabina took a last look to measure just how much Annia had grown—seven years old, and so tall!—and took her place at Hadrian's side as he raised his arm to begin the festivities. Cheering rose below in a dutiful swell, redoubling as the slow parade of chariots began with their prancing horses and preening charioteers. A star charioteer would always get a bigger ovation than an emperor in the Eternal City, Sabina thought with some amusement.

"Does Caesar wish to dispense the prizes?" Titus approached the Emperor with a bow and the customary basket of painted wooden balls, every one of which would be lobbed into the crowd and redeemed by some lucky pleb for a prize: a slave, a bullock, a side of ham. "Young Pedanius Fuscus has volunteered to throw them—"

Whatever Hadrian said was lost then, because Titus got the greatest roar of all from the crowd below. The plebs of Rome had put their hands together for their Emperor; they had surged to their feet for their charioteers—but when Sabina's brother-in-law came to the fore, they stamped and clapped and shrieked.

"*Titus Antoninus Pius!*" someone shouted, and other voices took up the shout. "*Pi-us! Pi-us! Pi-us!*"

"'Pius'?" Sabina whispered to Faustina. "When did that nickname start?"

"For his piety in helping restore the Pantheon?" Faustina shrugged. "For those massive consignments of oil and grain he gave from our personal stores after the winter shortages? Or maybe for the way he used to offer our father his arm whenever they walked out—you know how people love a show of filial piety."

"But it isn't a *show*. Titus does everything so quietly; he doesn't court approval."

"Which is why they give it to him." Fierce pride flashed like a vein of gold through Faustina's voice. "Servianus might call himself the most virtuous man in Rome, but *Rome* knows that title truly belongs to my husband."

Sabina looked at her oldest friend, standing at the rail of the Imperial box, pristine toga fluttering, head gleaming, hand half-raised to quiet the crowd. But they wouldn't quiet, not until he had lifted an arm in salute, and smiled at the answering roar.

That was when Hadrian's gaze turned to ice. And so did Sabina's heart.

"Look how they cheer for the prizes," she said brightly, whisking the basket from Titus. "How the plebs do love getting something without cost! Let Pedanius throw the balls out, Caesar, it will be the only thing to quiet them—"

Young Pedanius strutted up, flexing his arm for the first throw, and Sabina managed to flatter everyone back to their seats, Titus sliding at once to the rear of the box. But Hadrian did not smile once, even when the first race finally began in a storm of hooves and sand. Everyone else was leaning forward, calling encouragement to their favorite teams, but the Emperor sat back in his wrought-silver chair, one foot rubbing along the back of the dog at his feet . . . and when he crooked a finger at Titus to approach, the Imperial eyes were full of blank, cold speculation.

Like he was thinking which piece went on which spear, Faustina's words whispered, and Sabina repressed a shudder.

Annia saw that look, too, and her small hand shot into her father's as he rose. "Let go, little monkey"—but Annia just gripped tighter. Titus at last gave a chuckle and let her follow as he took the chair beside Sabina, and Annia scrambled up to perch on his knee. Hadrian looked irked, and Annia gave him an expression of doe-eyed innocence that would have made Sabina laugh had she not been so vibrantly afraid.

"Tell me, *Pius.*" Hadrian's eyes looked like lamps gleaming from a hidden niche. "Why are you alive?"

Sabina's fingers clenched about her wine cup, and she saw Annia's eyes narrow. But Titus looked calm as ever.

"I could speak theologically, Caesar, and say that I am alive because the Fates spun a thread with all six of my names on it, and thus I came squalling into the world. Or I could speak for my wife, who says that I was born for the purpose of making her happy, which I seem to do even though I drive her mad by leaving my togas unwound all over the *tablinum.* Or I could speak with strict truth"—a half bow from his seat—"and say that I am alive by Caesar's gracious mercy."

"Are you being flippant with me?" Hadrian asked.

"Not at all," Titus said sincerely. "I'm being pedantic. I always get pedantic when I'm nervous."

Sabina wanted to jump in again, anything to divert this conversation, but part of Hadrian's keen attention was focused on her, and so she continued to sit like his vision of a perfect Empress: serene and silent, her gaze fixed on the race below, never interfering. Her husband had at last begun including her again in his travels, in his decisions—but he'd banish her back to the palace to rot if she interfered at the wrong moment. *Wait.*

Hadrian took a bunch of grapes from the silver bowl at his side, tossing one to the dog panting happily at his feet. "You're sweating, Titus Aurelius."

Annia sat stiff as a doll on her father's knee, not fidgeting or bouncing as she normally did, but she must have made some movement because Titus looped an arm about her and gave a squeeze. "Naturally I'm sweating," he said. "I'm terrified."

"Seven years ago"—the Emperor popped a grape into his mouth—"I decided a demonstration of mercy was called for, and spared your life. But I may decide to change my mind. Do not think some small degree of popularity among the plebs renders you immune from my displeasure. Crowds are fickle."

"They are, Caesar. I am only cheered because I am known to loan money at four percent interest instead of twelve."

"Twelve percent at market rate? That seems high. The reports I see indicate six percent. Do make a note, Suetonius." Hadrian lifted a finger at his secretary, but his eyes never shifted from Titus, and Sabina's pulse continued to pound. Everyone else in the box was oblivious to the small drama unfolding between their three chairs; only Faustina had strained eyes, watching the conversation she could not hear. Annia's blue-gray eyes were fixed on the Emperor in cool distrust, and Sabina had time for a small, absurd prick of pride. Her daughter might be just a child, but she knew perfectly well that behind all these bland phrases, her father was being threatened.

"If I may ask what I have done to draw Caesar's ire?" Titus still sounded equable, as though he were talking about chalk for his togas or slates for his *tablinum*. "I am a thoroughly undistinguished sort of fellow, after all. I was born to an old name, and my family has been rather fortunate in its investments, but in myself I am nothing. Low-interest loans and a few famine-relief consignments to the city are hardly original acts; a dozen other men in the Senate House do the same."

"Agreed," the Emperor said, spitting out another pip. "But they are not cheered as you just were. It makes me wonder if the crowd looks at you and remembers that Trajan had some notion of appointing you heir."

"I doubt anyone outside this box knows that. And would it be any use telling you I don't want the purple?"

Hadrian's idle tone dropped at once. "Spare me the obligatory protestations."

"You think I have any desire to be where you are, Caesar?" Sabina heard her brother-in-law's voice resound, that clarion ring of authority that came so unexpectedly from a man otherwise so mild. "To be Emperor of Rome is to be worked to death in this mausoleum of a palace, or forever moving between provincial wastelands. Never alone and forever worrying—that is not a life I wish."

"The next race is being called, Caesar," Sabina murmured. But Hadrian's gaze remained locked on Titus, and Titus never broke the stare.

"Believe me, Caesar," Sabina's brother-in-law went on. "I have no wish to change the life I have. I consider myself a lucky man. I have funds enough to invest in Caesar's building programs, I have the most beautiful wife in Rome—begging the Empress's pardon"—a nod to Sabina—"and I have a daughter whom I hold so dear that I'm happy to keep her in expensive playthings as fast as she can break them."

Sabina saw Annia's fingers curl tight through a fold of Titus's toga. The small knuckles were white, and she was glaring at the Emperor like a little Medusa.

"I have friends," Titus went on, "I have health, and nobody has any interest in assassinating me. The most taxing decision I made all year was whether to buy my wife emeralds or sapphires for Lupercalia. So no," he finished. "I don't want to trade places with you, Caesar. Not ever."

"Are you quite finished?" the Emperor asked Titus, and spit out another pip.

"Yes," Titus sighed.

Trumpets blared again, but Sabina wouldn't have been able to say if it was because the race was begun, won, lost, or because the arena had caught fire. She wished the arena *would* catch fire. *Distraction*, she thought frantically, *distraction* . . .

And the Fates provided it—with a little help from Sabina's daughter. At the same time as a man's voice murmured from behind Sabina's chair, "Forgive me for intruding, Lady—" Annia's eyes widened and she flung herself off her father's lap, upsetting the bowl of grapes and a frail glass goblet that went *smash* all over the tiles.

"*Antinous!*"

Sabina turned to see her favorite page in his flawless white tunic, just stepping into the Imperial box from the passage behind. "A message, Lady," Antinous said, handing Sabina a scroll. His bow was impeccable even when he had a little girl clinging to his hip. "You asked to see the new list of candidates for your *alimenta* program, the girls petitioning for state dowries"—looking down at Annia with a smile. "You certainly don't need a dowry, Annia Galeria Faustina!"

"Control your daughter, Titus Aurelius," the Emperor snapped, frowning, and Titus beckoned Annia, and Antinous murmured, "Please forgive my interruption—"

But Annia clung like a limpet. "Where is Caesar, where is your *dog?*" she demanded as though determined to keep that thick threatening silence from falling again around her father, and Sabina jumped right in beside her.

"Titus, I know you were a patron of Antinous's; you will be delighted to see he is with my household . . ." Social niceties, she kept them flowing and ignored Hadrian's frown because hadn't he made it clear that social niceties were an empress's business?

"*Patronus*," Antinous was saying with another bow for Titus, and an utterly infectious grin. "How very pleasant to see you again. I will never forget your kindness to me while I was in the *paedogogium*."

"Nonsense, Antinous." Titus offered his own smile, despite the strain still visible about his eyes. "I am glad to see travel agreed with you."

"Very much, *patronus*."

That was all. Antinous would never put himself forward; he was already backing away with a parting ruffle for Annia's hair. But Hadrian was looking on with a frown—a thoughtful frown, not that icy glare that could freeze men in their tracks.

"You act as patron for my pages, Titus Aurelius?"

Titus looked puzzled. "I knew Antinous as a child, Caesar."

"Then perhaps your young protégé will be the first to congratulate you." Hadrian tossed the rest of his grapes to the dog, his frown turning into a smile of such benign approval that Titus's brows shot up. "Since I have decided to appoint you as one of next year's consuls. Judging from the crowd's reaction to the mere sight of you, it will be a popular choice."

And after keeping his composure through so many veiled threats, *that* was when Titus looked flummoxed.

There was bowing and thanking and all kinds of politeness—Hadrian looking gracious; Antinous beaming from his place against the wall; Annia looking at the Emperor as though she didn't trust his smiles *or* his gifts. *I do not blame you, little one,* Sabina thought, because behind her flurry of congratulations she was as puzzled as Titus.

What had this all been, this Imperial flexing of claws? Another of Hadrian's elaborate games, threats presented and then replaced on a whim with rewards? Or had he simply decided Titus's popularity would be better harnessed than squashed?

Faustina was claiming Titus's arm with relief all over her beautiful face, curtsying her own thanks, and the rest of the box was beginning to notice the fuss. Sabina stepped away, allowing Servianus to stump in and demand the news, and went to join the tight knot of children at the corner of the Imperial box. Young Pedanius Fuscus was whooping over the rail—the Whites charioteer had crashed spectacularly on the turn below, Sabina saw vaguely, and was being dragged behind his runaway horses. Pedanius might be cheering, but Annia was ignoring the arena, her small body as tense as Sabina's as she stood beside her serious-looking cousin Marcus.

"Tell me something, Annia." Sabina looked down at her daughter's face. "You ran over to Antinous just to distract the Emperor, didn't you?"

"Did not," Annia said.

"Did too." Sabina smiled. "You were still as a mouse till you saw a way to make a fuss. And you never sit still for anything."

Annia's scowl was pure Vix.

"Don't worry," Sabina reassured her. "I won't tell. You were very helpful."

"Antinous helped too," Annia said, and Sabina looked for her favorite page. She'd invited him to take a post in her household, at Hadrian's irritated request—Antinous had somehow ended up on Hadrian's trireme rather than Sabina's, on the voyage back from Athens. "I don't care to have the boy underfoot when he once tried to break my nose, Vibia Sabina. Take him into *your* service if you insist on sponsoring him!"

She had—and she made a point of never taking him with her if she was accompanying the Emperor on any function. That was for Vix, who didn't favor his son's new post. "I offer to send him to the Tenth Fidelis as a tribune, and he'd rather pour your wine?" Vix had complained.

"You had better not still be thinking I have a lustful eye for him," Sabina said tartly.

"Maybe he has an eye for you." Vix's eyes had crinkled the way they did ever since Eleusis. That way that could still turn her stomach over and over as though she were a girl. "At least my son has good taste."

Annia was still looking worried, chewing on her lip as she looked across the box at her father, and her cousin Marcus followed her eyes. "Why was the Emperor talking to your father for so long?" little Marcus whispered. "What happened?"

"He made him consul," Annia replied. "What's a consul?"

"A consulate"—Sabina supplied the answer—"is the highest rank to which a man of Rome may aspire."

"If he is not emperor," Marcus corrected, and began droning something about the required terms of service.

Annia just looked up at Sabina. "Why?" A whole host of questions hovering behind that one wide-eyed word. *Why is my father in danger? Why is he now consul? Why did the Emperor do it?*

And the Empress had to wonder as well. Because she would have laid any odds in the Empire that mercy had not been on Hadrian's mind when he first crooked his finger at Titus across the Imperial box.

ANTINOUS

Hadrian's Villa

"This isn't a villa. It's a small city!" Empress Sabina looked out over the nest of marbled buildings stretching out around them. The Imperial party had arrived for the first glimpse of the Emperor's fabled new domicile, his resting place outside Rome from which he could rule an empire in peace, and Antinous had to school his face into utter innocence.

"Very beautiful," he said, handing the Empress out of her litter, and hoped his surprise wasn't too obviously feigned. He'd never been much of an actor.

"Let us hope Hadrian thinks so." She tilted her head at her husband, swinging off his horse and making for the architects. "He's complaining already."

"—first set of porticoes, not right at all." Hadrian's critical voice drifted clearly back to Antinous's ears. "Far too sprawling compared to the plans I drew—"

Don't overdo it, my love, Antinous thought with a ripple of inward laughter. All those frowns and tutted sighs as the Emperor strode up the marble steps, and Antinous knew it was all to make him laugh, because Hadrian had seen everything already and loved it, and so had Antinous. Two nights ago they had been lying in bed, Antinous listening to the Emperor's heartbeat as Hadrian expounded on his much-awaited villa. "Four years leaving the architects to their own devices;

doubtless they mucked everything up! I should have stayed in Rome if I wished to see it all done as I wished—"

"And died of boredom," Antinous had laughed.

"But I've dreamed of building this villa all my life." How he could worry, this ruler of the world! "What if it falls short?"

"Then let's go tonight." Antinous sat up, tossing the covers back. The Emperor blinked. "What?"

"Let's set that restless mind at ease." And they had taken two guards and two horses and sneaked out of the Eternal City like a pair of errant schoolboys escaping the *paedogogium* in search of whores and wine. A long midnight gallop under the moon, helpless with laughter, racing their horses till they lathered white. "Gods," Hadrian gasped when they pulled up. "Antinous, the things I do for you!"

"Quick, Caesar!" Hurling himself off his horse, he tossed the reins to the guard who stood as stolidly as though deaf and blind. "We'll have to move fast if we want to be back unseen!"

"And why should the world not know that I decided to view everything a few nights early?"

"Because it's more fun this way!" Antinous shouted over his shoulder, taking the steps three at a time. Hadrian had sprinted after him, broken leg now healed to full strength, and he tackled Antinous at the top and got him in the same arm-lock Antinous had put him in Eleusis. He had held Antinous there till he begged mercy, still laughing, then kissed him till he begged mercy again.

And now Hadrian was striding about as though he had never seen it before.

"Those poor architects," Empress Sabina said. "Look at them sweating. I do hope he doesn't throw them to the lions."

He'd never toss anybody to the lions, Antinous thought. Though his Imperial lover wasn't above *pretending* he might. "I encourage dark rumors," Hadrian had laughed, some months ago when Antinous asked rather tentatively about some of the more sinister tales that swirled about his lover's name. "People work harder not to annoy me when they think I'm a touch ruthless!"

Antinous wondered what his father would have thought of that. *Likely refused to believe it.*

"If you will note the presence chamber, Caesar—" The chief architect groveled into an airy vaulted chamber as the Imperial party flocked after. "Built as you specified—"

Hadrian frowned. "*Blue* mosaics?" And Antinous had to bite his lip to keep from laughing, because two nights ago the Emperor had dragged Antinous into this chamber and stood behind him using his hand to point, alight with excitement. "I wanted the colors to echo the provinces I've seen! The south wall, you can't see in the dark, but that should have a mosaic in shades of green, like the forests in Gaul. Gold on every statue, like the golden plains in Mauretania. And finally . . ." Pointing Antinous's finger to the tiles beneath their foot, as his lips moved over Antinous's ear in that lazy pattern that made him tremble. "Sapphire-blue floors, like the seas we sailed over from Athens. Remember?"

"I remember," Antinous had whispered.

"All very Greek," Servianus was saying now, peevishly. He was in an ill humor because of course he'd wanted to bring the boy he'd been pestering Hadrian to adopt as heir—"My grandson should be present to see the legacy you have built, Caesar"—and Hadrian had snapped, "I didn't build it for him, I built it for me."

Antinous could have told Servianus that the worst way to get Hadrian to do anything was to nag. He'd been the Emperor's companion for six months, but he'd known that at six *hours.*

Six months. *Can he still make me so dizzy after six months?* Just watching Hadrian go striding through this vast villa was enough to melt Antinous's knees. Hadrian was so much the Emperor today, toga falling about him in crisp folds as he surveyed a banqueting suite equipped with wrought-silver couches and declared "Fit for the Empire's finest guests!" in such round tones that Antinous had to cough to hide his splutter of laughter. Two nights ago, Hadrian had wandered through those couches in a mussed tunic and muttered, "Fit for the Empire's greatest bores."

And both men were his, somehow: the grand Emperor in Imperial purple, and the laughing man with his trail of dogs. Both treasured *him*, Antinous, Bithynian boy from nowhere.

"And the smaller triclinium, here, for when Caesar wishes to dine alone. The pool will reflect the sunset . . ."

"I want a line of lemon trees," Hadrian decided, "so the fragrance blows on the evening breezes." And the architect took notes, and Antinous swallowed a lump in his throat because that was for him, too: lemon trees, for the grove outside Athens.

"Antinous?" Empress Sabina was looking at him. They had fallen behind, Antinous idling in reverie as Hadrian and the rest of the party made their processional way to a set of blue-tiled baths. "What are you daydreaming about?"

"Nothing, Lady." Antinous banished his smile as he caught up with her sunshade, feeling the usual vague pang of guilt as he looked at his lover's wife. Because it was an odd thing to be bedding an empress's husband, even if he knew there had never been any particular passion between them. Perhaps he felt the guilt because he *liked* Empress Sabina—had liked her ever since their sea crossing from Rome to Mysia, when she had taught him to play *latrunculi*. He liked the way she played with ruthless relish, annihilating his pieces one by one, and then swearing as filthily as any legionary when he ambushed her from behind. He liked the fact that she could be all candor one moment and all mysterious silences the next; could be a barefoot urchin strolling a deck and also mistress of Rome in elegant olive-green silks and bands of jade as she was today. A dual woman as Hadrian was a dual man, and maybe all emperors and empresses had to be that way. Maybe he liked Empress Sabina so much because she was like Hadrian.

"Don't be absurd!" Hadrian had snapped the one time Antinous had ever made the comparison. "My wife is as irksome as any woman ever born, and I cannot think why I did not divorce her years ago!"

"Because she understands you?" Antinous suggested.

"Of course she doesn't!"

"What do you think of it all, Lady?" Antinous ventured as they strolled into yet another audience chamber. "What do you think of the villa?"

"I think it's like him." The Empress tilted her head at her husband, who strode on into the gardens. "It's all curves, just like his mind. Color and charm and nothing straightforward."

You do understand him, Lady. And Antinous had a sudden mad urge to confess everything, to look into those thoughtful eyes lined with crushed malachite and say, "I love your husband more than breath." Because he could talk of Hadrian to no one, he held his whole over-flowing heart in silence—and that was as it had to be, as he'd asked it to be from the start. Only a few Praetorians knew, the ones Hadrian had threatened into silence with words so soft and deadly that even Antinous's blood ran cold. "You are a dangerous man," he'd said, trying to laugh off the moment as the men tramped out white-faced, and Hadrian had looked at him with that cold gaze he showed even Antinous sometimes and said, "You wish for secrecy. I give it to you. Do not complain about my methods."

I do wish secrecy, Antinous thought, and felt a bleak twist in his gut because he wished for it still. Because of his father—and he knew that it angered Hadrian. "I do not like to sneak, boy. Not on the account of a thug like your father."

He is not a thug, Antinous wanted to cry out, but there wasn't any use trying to make peace between those two. Too much hatred there for that, and sometimes Antinous wondered if Empress Sabina didn't lie at the root. Because he'd seen her walk out of the trees in Eleusis at his father's side, wearing his father's lion skin about her small shoulders, their hands almost brushing, and there was something there in his father's closed face whenever Antinous spoke the Empress's name after that. *Is that why you believe the worst of him, Vix? Because you desire his wife?*

But that was not something to be spoken of either. Just a small unhappiness, really—a little dark sliver in the joy of these past months. No mortal had uninterrupted happiness; only gods had that, and he was no god. Mortals paid for bliss with grief.

Make it only a little grief, Antinous prayed nightly. *Let my father not find out.* For another day, for another year, for forever—Antinous lived hour to hour, not letting himself think of the future, of how long Vix could be kept in ignorance. *Let him not find out now, that is all I ask.*

They'd passed through more gardens, a vast green space with pools and fountains and overgrown statues of Pan and Silenus. Handsome Lucius Ceionius with his silly dressed-up slave girls was declaring they must host a party of maenads with everyone in vine leaves, but Hadrian strode on to the heart of the villa.

"This is for us," he'd told Antinous when they visited alone. A circular colonnade enclosing a silent pool, and floating on the pool, a tiny marble island of a domicile. "A villa within the villa. A room to work and read, a private bathhouse, a sleeping chamber. Big enough only for two." And he turned and took Antinous's face in his hands. "No one to enter unless by *my* invitation. The bridge to be drawn up, so no one may disturb us. You understand?"

"I understand that I love you," Antinous had replied, and Hadrian's face had filled with bewilderment.

"Why?"

Antinous laughed. "Is there a *why* with love?" The Emperor shook his head and held him even tighter, rendered speechless for once. Antinous did not really know if Hadrian returned his love in the same measure—there were so many claims on an emperor's heart and mind and time; could one person ever truly hold full sway? Sometimes the Emperor looked at him, and Antinous had no idea what was passing through that complicated mind, only that it was dark and paralyzing and sometimes filled Hadrian's nights with torment. Nights when his Imperial lover disappeared without comment and came back after hours, spent and exhausted, and people whispered of some imaginary Hades and the things that happened there. Antinous learned not to speak on those nights, just draw Hadrian's head into his lap and hum quietly until the taut muscles gave way to sleep.

And the Emperor had created a place in this villa just for them— for the two of them alone. "I need you," he had said fiercely in the dark as Antinous first gazed on it. "Gods, but I need you!"

I know, my love. I know.

"I will dine here this evening." Hadrian gazed at the little *domus* now in full sunlight, not looking at Antinous by so much as an eyelash. *He has better control than I.* Antinous knew his own gaze followed the

Emperor sometimes like a flower followed the sun. "Alone," the Emperor continued. "If I might arrange for a list of books to be brought—"

He scribbled a brief list and passed it to the side without looking. Antinous stepped forward and took it silently. "Vibia Sabina, you may wish to see your quarters. I remember your liking for dawn views . . ."

Antinous unfolded the note.

> *Oh sweet boy like a girl,*
> *I watch you though you will not glance my way.*
> *You are unaware that you hold the reins of my soul.*

Anakreon—Antinous had studied the poet at the *paedogogium*. Hadrian did that so often: slipped him notes right under the nose of the entire court. Scraps of poetry, sometimes from his favorite Greek poets and sometimes verses of his own. *You hold the reins of my soul.*

Antinous had no gift for verse, not like Hadrian or Anakreon. *I love you*, he thought simply, *I love you*. And his heart was full.

SABINA

"Tribune Vercingetorix is here to see you, Lady. To discuss your guard arrangements now that you will be residing in the villa—"

"Send him away."

"He won't be pleased," one of Sabina's favorite maids laughed, hefting a basket of Sabina's tunics for unpacking. "He has an eye for you, Lady. Stands *far* more watches on you than he has to!"

I noticed, Sabina thought. She'd noticed other things too, ever since Eleusis. Wondered if Vix's eyes rested on her more often, lingered more warmly than they used to. Found herself taking his hand to alight a flight of stairs, when she'd never needed help in her life to get up and down a step. Realized that even in these brand-new quarters in the Emperor's villa—quarters she had seen for the first time this afternoon during Hadrian's official inspection—she had somehow already calculated in the back of her mind just how these chambers might be emptied at night. Emptied innocuously so that no one, from chattering Balbilla to her sharp-eyed maids, would notice the way had been cleared for a single man.

That is how foolish empresses get their heads struck from their shoulders, Sabina told herself. *Especially empresses whose husbands have told them quite explicitly to remain chaste.*

The new litter of kittens gave a *mrow* from their basket beside Sabina's sleeping couch. Antinous was on his knees beside them, tickling the tiny paws. "They've settled well, Lady," he said. "Since the Emperor is to dine privately tonight, would you like me to send a message inviting Titus Aurelius and his family to dine with you?"

"No, Titus is still quite busy enough getting used to the idea that he's to be consul." Four days since that afternoon at the races that brought Titus's sudden promotion to Imperial favor.

Antinous's face glowed. "Very astute of the Emperor, Lady. There could be no better choice."

"No." Sabina pointed at the page in Antinous's hand. "Is that the list of books the Emperor wanted?"

"Yes, Lady."

Sabina crossed the chamber and took the note.

It was Antinous's involuntary snatch that told her she was right. His hand fell back to his side, and he flushed scarlet. Sabina looked down and in one glance read the verse scribbled in Hadrian's terse scrawl.

Oh, dear gods. How much she would have given to be wrong.

"Anakreon," the Empress managed to say, hardly hearing her own voice over the thudding of her heart. "Hadrian always did like his verses."

Antinous went even more crimson, twisting his hands before him. "Lady . . ." he whispered, but his voice trailed away.

Sabina read on. There was only one word after the poem.

Tonight.

She didn't know how long she looked at the sheet. When she lifted her eyes, Antinous went crashing to his knees.

"If you're wondering how I knew"—Sabina crossed to close the door of her chamber on the chattering maids in the next room—"it was the way you blushed this afternoon when you read it."

There had been other signs over the past months: glances, gestures so small they meant nothing unless one added them together. And then there was the matter of Hadrian showing Titus favor, his mood changing from hostility to benevolence as soon as Antinous entered and made it so innocently clear how he revered Titus.

That was the reason Sabina's brother-in-law had been made consul. To please Antinous.

"Lady—" Antinous's amber-brown eyes were anguished, staring up at her. "I never meant to cause you humiliation—"

"Oh, get up, Antinous." She raised him with a crook of one finger. "You think it's a surprise to me that my husband beds handsome young men?"

"No, Lady." Antinous rose, looking as though he were about to be crucified. "But one doesn't speak of such things . . ."

Sabina turned away, giving him a chance to compose himself as she ran her fingers along the inlaid frame of her sleeping couch.

"'Tonight,'" she said at last, still not looking at him. "Is this the first time Hadrian has—requested you?"

"No, Lady."

"I see." Sabina wished she could ask for how long, but Antinous was right: One did not speak of these things. An empress was serenely blind to her husband's lovers, be they girls or boys. Empress Plotina had set the standard for that, her nose riding the air too high to ever see the common soldiers who traipsed in and out of Trajan's bed.

But those soldiers were willing, Sabina thought. *Not helpless youths.*

She turned, folding her hands at her waist and choosing her words carefully. "You are a citizen of Rome, Antinous," she said. "Not a slave to be forced, even by an emperor."

Antinous was silent. Sabina tried again. "The Emperor may lust for you. I am sure many do. But you may refuse him without fear. He might be displeased, but he would not punish you—for all his faults, he does not relish unwilling bedfellows. And a free man of Rome may not be forced into any man's bed like a slave on an auction block."

Antinous's face had begun to clear, but now it flooded with color again. "I—" he began, and cleared his throat. He looked at her, and his eyes burned like brands. "Lady—I'm not unwilling."

Oh, Sabina thought. *Oh.*

"It started at Eleusis," Antinous said in a rush.

Eleusis. Six months this had been going on? Sabina's heart plummeted to the pit of her stomach.

"I found him in the trees after the Night of Torches. The *kykeon* madness; I soothed him. He wasn't *Emperor* then, he was a man as frightened of the void as any of us." Antinous trailed off, lashes veiling his eyes, but not before Sabina saw the light in his gaze. *Oh, sweet boy*, she thought, looking back at the rolled note in her hand. How clever Hadrian was in his wooing, irresistible as he had the power to be when throwing all his passion into one single aim. Stealing a moment before his entire court to write his beloved a love note, just like a god coming down from on high to beg a mortal girl's love. Antinous looked as starry-eyed as though he wore the favor of Jupiter himself about his arm.

"He has had other handsome lovers besides you," Sabina said finally. What to say that might penetrate Antinous's radiant happiness? "You hear the jokes people make, about the line of pretty pages outside the Imperial chamber? You think you are something unique to him?"

"I am," Antinous said simply.

Sabina had to turn away, bending to pick up one of the kittens. The little ball of fluff purred and flexed its tiny claws in the silk of her *stola.* "You do not know him as well as you think, Antinous. Do you know where he is now?"

Antinous's answer was prompt. "With the architects."

"Wrong. He is in his Hades." Antinous and the rest of the party had been dismissed by then; Sabina had been the only one close enough to hear as the architect pressed into the Emperor's hand a key of black iron. "Your Hades, Caesar. Built exactly as specified."

"Excellent," Hadrian had said, and looked at Sabina. "Make my excuses, Vibia Sabina. I require a long stint."

"Do you know what he does in his Hades?" Sabina looked up into Antinous's beautiful, puzzled eyes. "Do you have any idea?"

"Do you, Lady?"

"No. And I have known him far, far longer than you."

Stubbornness was falling over Antinous's face like a curtain. "There is no Hades, Lady, not the way the rumors paint it. He goes off alone sometimes to brood, that is all. He always comes back the better for it. He told me so."

I'm sure he did, Sabina thought. *Clever, clever, clever.* "Break it off," she said. "For your own good, Antinous, break it off."

But he was already shaking his head, his eyes clear and guileless. "I will leave your service, Lady. I will leave court if you wish it—I would not cause you humiliation for all the world, as kind as you've been to me. But I cannot leave him. He needs me."

Sabina wanted to slap him back and forth until his head rattled. Was there no one more stupid, more blind, more fanatically stubborn than a boy in love? *You young fool*, she wanted to rage, but she didn't rage at him and she didn't strike him either. Antinous had stars in his eyes and a heart full of poetry, and all the blows and curses in the world wouldn't make a dent in either.

Instead, she gave back the note with Hadrian's verse. Antinous took it, his fingers tender on the parchment in a way that tore at her breast. He hesitated a moment, and then his gaze under those long honey-colored lashes rose.

"Lady," he said, and now there was anguish in those eyes instead of stars. "My father—I know you and he are friendly. Will you feel it your duty to tell him . . . ?"

Vix, she thought, and the pulse that stabbed through her was pure, leaden dread.

"No," she managed to say. "No, I will say nothing." Vix's curses wouldn't do any good, either. All she could hope for was that this passion burned out before Vix knew a thing about it.

But it has burned already for six months, she thought. Much longer than any of Hadrian's other affairs had lasted, to be sure.

"Thank you, Lady." Antinous fell to his knees before her again. "For not telling my father."

"You should be the one to tell him."

He flinched. "I will, Lady. I will, but . . ."

She allowed the silence to stretch. "Tell him," she said, and turned and swept from the room, almost running. Wishing she could run all the way back to Britannia, reach Hadrian's wall, and keep running into the wilds north of it, before Vix ever found out her husband had seduced his son.

CHAPTER 8

VIX

A.D. 125, Autumn
Rome

"Give us a kiss!" I greeted the girls as I came through the door. Chaya stood on tiptoe to peck my cheek, but Dinah squealed.

"You're all sweaty and dusty!"

"So I am, but your mother doesn't mind." I grabbed Mirah in a bear hug, squeezing till she laughed. I didn't see her as often as I liked, even if I wasn't traveling the provinces anymore—I berthed most nights at the Emperor's villa outside the city.

"Where's Antinous?" Mirah asked as I set her back on her feet. "I made his favorite beef stew."

"Well, he *told* me that he'll be sitting up with a sick dog all night. But I think he's got a woman." I discarded my cloak. "The other Imperial pages tell me he ducks out most nights from their quarters, and he had a nice gold chain about his neck yesterday that he couldn't explain without blushing."

"Hmm. And you think that means some woman's keeping him?"

"Julia Balbilla, I'd wager." I unbuckled my sword belt, tossing it over the back of my chair. "She's handsome enough—one of those painted, well-preserved types who manages to look forty when she's fifty. Yesterday I saw her pinch his bum when he poured her wine."

"A court lady keeping your son like a pet, and you're not outraged?"

I shrugged. "He's a man grown, Mirah. He can do as he likes. Let's have that beef stew—"

She dished up, and then because it was Shabbat she bowed her head after we'd all assembled at table, and murmured the ancient prayers. I usually murmured the prayers with her because she liked it, but tonight I just looked at her through the soft lamplight. My lovely Mirah, with the freckles across her nose like a sprinkle of ginger, her hair falling loose the way I loved to see it, her voice low and serene. Our girls flanked her like twin acolytes, ten and eleven now, alike as two rose-buds in their smocks of matching pink wool. My girls were good as gold, and my wife could have married a wine merchant with a villa in Rome and land in Judaea but she'd chosen a hot-tempered legion man instead. It was more than I deserved, and I was a bloody fool to have ached for any woman but Mirah. In the dark groves of Eleusis or any-where else.

And to my shame, I couldn't deny that I ached. Things had been different since Greece. My eye stayed on Sabina longer than it should have, noticing her swift swaying grace as she moved ahead of me while I escorted her, and why was I escorting her so much lately, anyway? Why did my hand keep writing my own name in beside hers on the roster, and not giving that spot to Boil instead? I'd torn up a whole month's worth of rosters this afternoon and given him every single slot at her side, cursing myself for a fool.

Women. Didn't I say they ruined everything?

"Uncle Simon writes from Bethar," Mirah said as we finished our prayers. "He's befriended a rabbi in Jaffa, Aqiba ben Joseph—they've been studying the prophecies of Balaam."

"Who's that?" My stew was rapidly disappearing. I'd worked through midday with Suetonius on the legionary manual, composing a new system of ration distribution. "Balaam?"

"One of our prophets, surely I've told you before!" Mirah chattered on as I got myself another bowl of stew. I got more for the girls as well, grinning because Mirah was too busy waving her spoon and quoting holy verse to notice that her daughters were nearing the bottom of their bowls. "*I look into the future and I see the nation of Israel. A king like a bright star will arise in that nation.*' Think of it, Vix!"

What I thought of it was that Judaea didn't stand a chance of breaking away from Hadrian's grip to make a free nation of anything, but I didn't say so. It was Mirah's dream, and for her happiness and for her family who all lived there, I hoped it would come true. I had my own dreams, too.

"My manual," I said when Mirah ran out of prophecies to quote and dived into her own cooling stew. "You should see how it's coming along. Boil and I talked through two shifts about training the legionaries in the fighting styles of past *and* potential enemies, learning to use their own tricks against them—"

I would have babbled on as she had, but I stopped because I could see the little smile on her face. The kind of smile wives get when they're being tolerant and just a little disapproving. "What?"

Mirah shook her head. "I wish you hadn't taken this manual on. Isn't it something of a betrayal?" She nipped up another bite of stew, decisive. "Rome stamped on you as a boy, and you want to make her armies even stronger so she can stamp on even more boys?"

"It's not just that." I thought of the painstaking work of the past months, stealing my sleep, stealing my time—and yet the visceral white-hot excitement I felt underneath of knowing how it would all unspool. Boys not yet born, growing up someday to fight and defend in the way that *I* was setting down on my midnight-scribbled notes. Boys living longer, perhaps, because of the rules of battle *I* laid out. Hadrian's white wall hemming the north of Britannia, manned by Roman soldiers a thousand years hence, every one of them trained to my standards and vigilant as eagles. I could feel the eagle tattooed on my arm pulse at the very thought. "It's important," I said. "It's important to *me*." Just like Balaam and his prophecies were important to her.

That faint smile again. "Well, tell me about it, then."

Suddenly I didn't want to. I went back to my stew, and Mirah looked quizzical but applied herself to the girls, who were soon chattering away, and as soon as dinner was done I pushed back from the table. "I should ride back to the villa tonight."

Mirah's arm snaked about my waist as I reached for my sword belt. "I was hoping you'd stay."

I kissed the top of her head. "Tomorrow." When I could bring Antinous with me, because dinners were always easier when my son was present. His jokes, his bright cheer, his deft way of easing the conversation whenever Mirah and I prickled at each other . . .

It was full dark by the time I reached Hadrian's villa. I found my Praetorians on night duty, standing rigid at the moat around the Emperor's tiny central villa. I could see the faint glow of a lamp inside the shuttered windows, but the wooden footbridge that spanned the little moat had been taken up—a sign Hadrian was not to be disturbed. By anything. "What if I get word a mob is marching on us?" I hadn't been able to resist asking, the first time he immured himself.

"I trust you to hold the bridge like Horatius and let me sleep."

It had made me smile. Since when did Hadrian learn to joke? Since when did he trust me? And who was Horatius, anyway?

My Praetorians reported quietly. "Caesar has *company* tonight," one said, and the other shot him a quelling glance. I was about to retire back to the barracks, when I caught sight of a shadow on the little islanded villa's doorstep.

A pair of dogs. The bitch-hound who had been swiped by the bear in Mysia, long recovered and lying placidly on the doorstep by the water . . . and a smaller dog, black as a moonless night, with a red leather collar.

I had made that collar.

I saw my own hand reach out, saw myself point toward the dim lamplight from the Emperor's chamber. "Who is with him?"

My Praetorians looked at me, and they both blanched. My stomach rolled sickly.

"Who?" I whispered.

One of them shuffled. "Tribune—"

"Put the bridge back."

"Tribune, we were ordered—"

I jumped down into the water surrounding the little villa. It wasn't deep despite its grand title of moat. I waded across, grabbed the marble lip of the far side, levered myself up dripping and shaking. "Tribune," one of my Praetorians called, and I could hear them scrabbling to put the bridge down, but I ignored them. I thrust the dogs out of the way, I drew my sword, and with one blow of the hilt I shattered the bolt that had been drawn from the inside and kicked the door in.

What do you see, when you cannot bear to see?

The details come slowly, a series of fractured images, as though your mind hopes you will take it better if you see only a little at a time. A warm pool of yellow lamplight falling over rumpled blankets. A pair of cups. A tray with the remains of a meal. A spider, descending from the ceiling on a frail thread of silk. I focused on the spider, because I didn't want to see the rest.

A young man, curly-haired, bare-armed, sitting cross-legged on the bed's rumpled blankets, fingering the strings of a lyre. Surely the most beautiful young man in the world, his skin gilded in the light, his long fingers sensitive on the lyre's strings, his wide mouth half-smiling. His eyes heavy-lidded as he turned his head, as a muscled arm slid about him from behind, and an emperor's lips whispered something in his ear.

My Emperor.

My son.

Surely I didn't have time to see all that. Surely it could have been no more than a split second, the instant I kicked down the door and the instant their eyes flew to me. But I swear I had time to see Hadrian's lips trace my son's ear and see Antinous's mouth turn and hunt for his, before Antinous's head jerked up and he let out a cry at the sight of me. The cry went through me like a knife, and I lunged at the Emperor.

Praetorians were the only men in Rome allowed to keep their swords in the Emperor's presence, and I had mine now, the hilt of my *gladius* gripped in both hands. I was ripping across the room, roaring as I came, and Hadrian's head snapped up, but he was empty-handed and would never be able to stop me. It was Antinous who stopped me, lunging from the bed with liquid speed. "*Stop!*" he shouted, and his shout broke into a sob as we collided and went down with a great crash.

He struggled with me, wrestling for the *gladius*, and somewhere distant I heard the clatter of the wooden bridge across the little moat, the thudding footsteps as the other Praetorians came running. Antinous scrabbled for my sword and I struck him away, rolling to my feet. I stood at the foot of the bed with sword still tight-clenched in my fist and my chest heaving as Antinous drew himself up naked and vulnerable beside the sleeping couch. My eyes blurred, skittering past him to where Hadrian still lay.

He leaned back deliberately against the cushions, folding his arms across his chest with slow precision. He must have called off the other Praetorians while Antinous and I were struggling, because I could hear them tramping back over that damned footbridge. My ears roared like waterfalls.

"Well," the Emperor said at last. "Apparently your son was mistaken, that you would be staying in the city tonight."

My eyes flew to Antinous. He flushed scarlet all over his naked skin: a young and defiled Apollo with the lyre lying broken at his feet. "How long?" I whispered.

"I—"

"*How long?*"

His eyes filled with tears then. "Since Eleusis."

The better part of a year, and I'd never known. I'd never even suspected. "You hid this?" I asked, and my whisper cracked.

Antinous's voice was as broken as mine. "I already knew what you'd say."

"Not you. Him." I pointed at Hadrian. "*You* hid this?" Why hadn't Hadrian rubbed it in my face at once: the debauchery of my son?

"Your son wished secrecy," the Emperor said, still quite at ease.

And I'd thought it was foolish overpainted Julia Balbilla buying Antinous gold chains. He had the chain about his neck, and another about his wrist. Chained like a bitch-hound, and used like one. As the Emperor had once threatened to chain and use me.

My eyes went back to Hadrian. "Oh, you bastard," I breathed, the words leaving my throat like a mouthful of glass shards. "You bloody-handed stone-hearted sick-minded bastard."

"Don't," Antinous whispered. "He didn't—"

My roar could have shattered stone. *"HE MADE YOU HIS WHORE!"*

I came at the Emperor again, and this time I think I would have run him through. I would have opened him throat to groin, gelded him and made him eat his own cock, and then the Praetorians outside could have struck the head off my shoulders and mounted it on a spike. But Antinous flung himself between us again. "He didn't force me, I came to him of my own—"

"You stupid boy," I snarled. Antinous still wrestled for the sword; I released my grip on it so he staggered back, and then I lashed him across the face and sent him stumbling. *"Stupid* boy," I said as the *gladius* fell from his hand, and realized I was near weeping.

A heavy hand spun me, and now it was me stumbling as Hadrian slammed me against the wall. I hadn't even seen him leap up from the sleeping couch. "I will spill your guts across the floor with your own blade," the Emperor said calmly, one arm braced across my throat and one foot braced on my sword hilt, "if you lay hand on Antinous again."

"Do not say his name!"

"I'll say it whenever I like." He kicked my *gladius* across the room in a clatter of steel against marble. "Do not think you have the right to give orders here."

"I have every right!" I tried to swing at him but he swatted my fist away, his arm still sinking like an iron bar into my throat. "He's my son," I rasped, swinging again. "You think I'll allow him to be turned into your toy?"

"Sweet gods, Vix—" Antinous's voice rose. "That's not what I am!"

"It's all you'll ever be in the eyes of the world. A boy who spreads his cheeks. And I'm not allowing it, not for one moment." I looked at Antinous over the Emperor's shoulder. "You're my son, and I'm taking you from this murdering stink-pit whore-master if I have to drag you in chains."

"Did you adopt him?" Hadrian asked conversationally.

It stopped me, and it stopped Antinous, who had begun half-hysterically to shout over me. "What?" I said, and my balled fist dropped.

"It's a legal matter." The Emperor dropped his arm from my throat, stepping back to stand quite naked and at his ease. His eyes glittered. "Antinous is not your son by blood. So, did you adopt him formally?"

"I—" Law? Who talked of such formalities? He'd been an orphan who needed shielding, so I'd taken him in. It had been as easy as that. "Your buggardly law doesn't—"

"No." Antinous's voice was hoarse, but he spoke clear. "No, he never adopted me formally."

"Then he is not entitled to the obedience a son owes a paterfamilias." Hadrian spoke with cool logic, as if he were droning some point of legislation in the Senate. "Antinous is a grown man of legal age, without guardian, without father; a citizen of Rome. You may not drag him anywhere, Vercingetorix, in chains or otherwise."

"Spout law all you want," I spat. "He's my *son*."

"I'm not!" Antinous shouted, and he might as well have pinned me to the wall with a spear. "I'm not your *son*, Vix! You made that clear from the first day. I'd have called you Father, damn it. I *worshipped* you. But you weren't having it. You wouldn't let me call you by anything but your name. You never did. So why bother claiming me now? The only reason you care is because you fear what the world will think of you for raising a bum-boy."

"No—" My voice cracked. "Hell's gates, no, I didn't *mean* that—"

"I'm not your son." Antinous's voice sank to a whisper, and that whisper sank hilt-deep into my heart. "I never was."

I stared at him. I stared and stared, looking at my boy. *My boy.* "Antinous—"

"I stay here." Antinous raised his chin; he came to stand at the Emperor's shoulder. "I'll stay with the one who needs me."

"Needs you?" I pushed away from the wall. I was shaking everywhere, and dear God—dear God, what had happened to my son? What poison had Hadrian whispered to him? "Is that how he got you into his bed, by playing your sympathy? He threatened once to fuck me, Antinous; spread-eagle me and use me like a bitch-hound if I didn't bend to his will, and that's who you want in your bed?"

"I don't believe you," Antinous flung at me. "You'd say anything, you—"

"*I'm not lying!*"

Hadrian never blinked. "Don't listen, Antinous. He'd say anything to turn you against me."

"You bastard," I snarled. "You filthy—"

"Get out," said Antinous. Tears pooled in his eyes, but his voice was steely as a spear. "Get out, Vix, just—get out."

Children. Why does any man want them, whether they come to him by blood or by love? Either way, they cut your throat in the end. You're a father with a defiled son, you have a father's right to rescue him from a madman who will ruin him or kill him or both. It was the truest thing in the world. But he looked at me with amber-brown eyes— the boy who wasn't my son any longer—and he turned away from me. Walked to the side of a power-mad whoremongering liar. I looked at him, and I wanted to shake him, scream at him, beat him to a pulp. Call him fool, child, *son*. But the sight of him was killing me where I stood, ripping my chest further open with every breath.

Burying my friends in Parthia, nearly losing Mirah in the great earthquake of Antioch, even losing Trajan—none of it had hurt like this.

"Lie in his bed then." My voice scraped. "You won't stay there long. He'll discard you like an old tunic once he's bored with your arsehole, and find himself a new one just as tight."

Antinous flinched, but I dragged my eyes away from him to Hadrian. The Emperor, who had already dismissed me from attention and was shrugging into his tunic. "You will die screaming," I said. "And that is a promise."

"You raised a hand against me," Hadrian said pleasantly. "And you insulted Antinous. I'd nail you to a cross for that, but I will leave your fate to the son you just spat on." He looked at my son. "Antinous?"

My son turned his back on me. "Let him go," he whispered. "Just— let him go."

I felt every word like another blade through my chest. "How much of this was about getting at me?" I asked the Emperor.

Hadrian looked at Antinous, and he curved a hand around my son's pure young face. "Nothing was about you," he said, and kissed Antinous between the eyes. "You're nothing."

I actually laughed. There's a point, in rage or pain or both, when there's nothing left but laughter. "You're good," I said. "Hell's gates, but you're good. You nearly had *me* convinced these past years, the way you play-acted the good man. I really thought you might be capable of change after all. Capable of . . . more. What a fool I was. Almost as much a fool as you're making of my son."

Maybe I'd have stalked out then, exited this grotesque little tragedy like the bit player I was. Maybe I'd have grabbed for my sword and tried one last time to carve Hadrian's heart out. But there was the incongruous sound of laughter outside, a woman's laughter and a man's too. "It can wait until tomorrow, Lady," a voice was protesting. "The Emperor does not wish to be disturbed—"

"Nonsense, the bridge is down, that means he's free to be seen. This is too good to wait!"

My Praetorians spoke in an uneasy unison mumble. "I wouldn't go in, Lady—" But when did Sabina ever listen to anyone? Her light footsteps crossed the bridge, I heard her cooing briefly at the dogs, and then she came tripping into the chamber. She'd attended a funeral today; some ancient former consul whose death had merited fanfare and speeches— she still wore the same slim black gown she'd worn to the solemn procession; the same ebony circlet around her sleek shorn head. She was reading from a scroll in one hand and turning half over her shoulder to speak to Suetonius, who had followed her in, smiling.

"Caesar," she said with another laugh, still half-turned, "I've finally had a chance to read Suetonius's treatise, *The Twelve Caesars*! It's—"

Sabina looked up from her scroll then at the scene frozen before her. Antinous still naked and gilded in the lamplight; the Emperor beside him with his rumpled hair and beard; me disarmed and broken with my sword across the room and my cloak half torn away. Sabina's blue eyes swept over everything, and that was when the rage swamped me. Pure fire-red rage, drowning even the broken stabbing pieces of love and guilt, because I knew her face so well, better than any woman's alive—hadn't I told her that at Eleusis?—and there was no surprise on her face. Not one drop.

You knew, I thought. *Oh, you bitch. You knew.*

"Your husband is bedding my son," I said, and was pleased at how level and conversational my voice came out. "But you knew that."

The ebony circlet about her hair glittered as she lowered her head a moment. "Vix," she began softly.

From the whirl of molten rage in my heart came perhaps the stupidest thing I have ever done. But I was so far past sense, so far gone into wretchedness—all I wanted was to share this agony, dish back some of what that bastard of an emperor and his bitch of an empress had leveled on me. So, I didn't think twice; didn't think of Mirah, or the girls, or my own life. Just stretched my mouth into a taut, vicious grin and lashed out with the only weapon I had.

"Don't worry, Sabina. I'll take an apology from you, as long as you get on your knees to make it." My hand shot out; I gripped her arm and I yanked her up against me. "Of course, you're used to going on your knees for me."

Sabina went stiff against me, as though she'd turned to stone. I looked over her head to Hadrian, and I ran a deliberate hand down his Empress's hip. "Maybe you made my son your whore," I said. "But your wife's been my whore for years. How do you like that, Caesar?"

Hadrian's face didn't move. But it hardened slowly, till he looked like one of the marble statues of himself that dotted this whole blasted villa.

"I broke her in, as a matter of fact," I taunted. "Long before you married her. Made her bleed, but she didn't bleed long. She took to it like a duck to water. She was moaning under me three times a night in her father's house. In Dacia too, after you were stupid enough to marry the bitch and think you were getting a virgin bride. You were my commander, the fine legate on his grand horse, and I was the common legionary fucking your wife half the night and spending the other half laughing at you. And the entire legion was laughing with me."

"*Vix!*" Sabina's voice snapped like a whip as she wrenched herself away from me, but I was too far gone to stop.

"You can tell him about Selinus, if you like." I looked back at her. "You had a black dress that day too, in mourning for Trajan, and I had it up around your hips in no time. And Eleusis, let's not forget Eleusis, he was off seducing my son while I was riding you among the trees—"

"You *lie!*" she cried out. "Nothing happened in Eleusis, nothing—"

I smiled. If Hadrian could lie, so could I. "What about the rest of it, Lady? Deny that, you deceitful bitch."

She was silent. Her gaze went to Hadrian, standing marble-faced with beasts raging in his deep-set eyes. To Antinous, white and shocked. Even to Suetonius, turned to a pillar at the doorway, still clutching his precious manuscript. Our gruesome tableau of fury and shame and pain.

Hadrian's foot was still resting on my *gladius*. Slowly he leaned down and took it up, and I just hoped he would run Sabina through first so I could see her bleed. His face quivered, the affable mask I'd seen him wear for so long utterly shattered, and I didn't care. Let him kill me. I should have died with *my* emperor, Emperor Trajan—should have put a sword through my own breast and thrown myself on his funeral pyre rather than serve his monstrous successor.

Antinous moved. Very slowly, he put two fingers on Hadrian's fist, white-clenched about my *gladius*. Just two fingers, resting gently on the Emperor's rage-heated skin.

Hadrian shook his touch away. He raised the *gladius*, leveling the tip at my teeth. He'd ram it through my mouth, and I'd have time to feel my teeth splinter before the blade tore through the back of my skull.

"Go ahead." I spread my arms. "Kill me." But Antinous sank to his knees. My son, on his knees before that man. My heart snapped then like an old twig.

"Caesar," he whispered, leaning his head against the Emperor's knee. "Spare them. Please."

ANTINOUS

It was done.

It was done, and as soon as they were alone, Antinous crumpled to the floor. He folded his shaking arms about his head, shutting out the world and all its cruelty, and felt the sobs come. He sobbed like a child, rocking back and forth, naked and cold in a room that smelled of agony and shame.

Father, he thought, *oh, my father!*

But Vix was gone. And Vix had never been his father.

Antinous had been the one to hold the Emperor when he sobbed at Eleusis. Now it was Hadrian's strong arms that slid around him. "Oh, my star," he said quietly. "Don't waste your tears."

"I want my father," Antinous wept. *"I want my father."*

"He does not want you." The Emperor's wide hand smoothed his hair. "But I do. Is that not enough?"

Antinous felt the Emperor pulling him from his huddle against the floor, pulling him against a broad chest that smelled of Imperial purple dye and hunting dogs. Antinous sobbed his agony into that chest, Hadrian's cheek against his hair, the Emperor apparently content to sit in the wreckage of his ruined bedchamber as long as Antinous had tears to shed.

And he had many—for Vix, for Mirah, for his sisters. All lost to him.

Everyone lost but Hadrian.

"Oh, my star," Hadrian said again, and kissed his swollen eyelids.

"'My star,'" Antinous echoed. His voice was hoarse with misery, but he had no more tears left to fall. "Why do you call me that, Hadrian?"

The first time he had ever dared call the Emperor by name, much as he had always longed to. It had not seemed right, somehow—but from the kiss Hadrian pressed into his hair, perhaps the Emperor had been longing to hear it as much as Antinous had longed to say it. As much as he had longed to call Vix *Father.*

"You talked of the stars, that night on Eleusis," Hadrian said. "The stars in the sky, in all their beauty. But I saw only one star." Another brush of the lips then, kissing away Antinous's last tears, so tenderly. Hadrian was rarely tender; his passions were more likely to bruise and inflame than soothe or comfort. "I saw my star, and it was your face."

ANNIA

Rome

"Good aim."

Annia leaped to catch the *trigon* ball as it bounced off the garden wall, spinning to see who had spoken. A legionary, she thought, standing at the top of the garden steps—tall and weathered-looking in a well-worn breastplate, and he had a lion skin tossed about his shoulders. Russet hair, a shade or two darker than Annia's, and gray eyes that looked at her curiously.

He nodded at the figure she'd chalked on the wall as a target. "Who's that?"

"Nobody," she said shortly. "Are you waiting to see my father?" He wasn't the usual sort of client who came to their house. Mostly they were old and had spotless togas and hissed at Annia like ganders if she made so much as a peep.

This man didn't hiss at her. "Your father's occupied, your housekeeper tells me. So I'm waiting on him. Who are you smacking with that ball?"

Adults always had to know *why*, and then they were never satisfied with the answer. "My cousin Marcus," Annia said, and she knew it was rude but she turned her back on the visitor.

"What did your cousin Marcus do?"

She hurled the ball again, right at the chalked circle she'd decided was Marcus's head. "We were playing *trigon*, and I smacked him in the face with the ball and bloodied his lip. And he was *noble* about it and he said it was an accident and went off to get mopped up. But it wasn't an accident; I hit him on purpose because he was lecturing me about how I should talk softer and walk slower and practice my weaving, and I wanted him to shut up."

Annia stopped. She scuffed a toe through the grass, waiting for the man to look disapproving. But he just tilted an eyebrow.

"I shouldn't have hit him," she heard herself saying. "He's annoying, but I still shouldn't have. I'm always hitting people, even when I don't mean to. I play too hard. I do everything too hard, and I get in trouble."

"What's your name then, little trouble?"

"Annia Galeria Faustina."

The visitor smiled. "Titus's girl."

Annia bounced the ball savagely against the wall again. She wanted to hit, when she got in moods like this. Hit or *be* hit, it didn't matter. Marcus should have hit her back, when she'd smacked him in the mouth with the ball. He just stood there with a look of surprise on his face, and then told her girls shouldn't hit boys, and that had made her angrier than ever.

The visitor, whoever he was, had descended into the garden holding out a big rough hand. "Throw to me," he said, and nodded at the ball in her clenched fist.

"Why?" She knew he wasn't here to play *trigon*.

"I'm bored and I hate waiting. Let's play." He shrugged off the lion skin. "Try to knock *me* off my feet, little girl."

Annia felt her eyes narrow. "Don't call me little girl."

"What, you aren't little? You aren't a girl?"

Annia whipped the ball at him. The visitor snagged it easily out of the air.

"Soft," he said, and tossed it back. "I thought you could throw hard."

"I can!" Slinging the ball at him again.

"You throw underhanded," he said. "Try side-arming it like this—"

The ball crashed into her stomach. Annia *huffed* in surprise.

"Too slow," he mocked, but not meanly somehow. Annia could tell.

"Throw as hard as you can," she challenged, bouncing on her toes.

"I'd knock you down."

She narrowed her eyes again. "Will not."

His arm looped. Annia's hands whipped up, but the ball streaked between them, catching her square in the mouth. Her head snapped back, but she lunged in the same motion and caught the ball before it could rebound into the grass.

"Still caught it," she said, and cuffed at her stinging lip. She saw a smear of blood on her hand, tasted the metal tang of it. Smiled.

"Catching it with your teeth doesn't count," he said, and came toward her. "I split your lip."

Annia spat blood into the grass. "So?"

His rough hand tilted her chin up. He really was tall. Her father was too, but he had a way of bending toward you so you felt welcomed rather than intimidated. This soldier stood with his shoulders thrown back, like he didn't care if he scared you into feeling small.

Well, *she* didn't feel small. She squared her shoulders right back at him.

"You're not crying," he observed.

"I never cry."

"My girls would be crying."

"Babies." Annia spat blood again. "Throw the ball again. *Hard!*"

He threw it for her, snapping it like a whip, and she caught that one even though it stung her hands. She threw it back with a whoop, and he gave a bellow of *"Release pila!"* and heaved it back. He ran Annia all over the garden, had her skidding into walls, diving behind bushes, falling into hedges. She scraped both her knees; she opened both her elbows, her lip puffed up twice its size, and she felt herself grinning ear to ear.

"If you get any more flesh wounds I'll have to carry you to the medicus." One final toss. "Let's call a victor."

Annia saw blood drying on her scraped knuckles and gave them a swipe across her skirt. "Do I still throw like a little girl?"

"You've got promise," he conceded. "Do you always play this hard?"

"Yes." She scowled. "I shouldn't. I can't. I *tell* myself I'm going to behave, be proper like Ceionia Fabia. A girl who does her weaving and knows how to curtsy—"

"Ceionia Fabia sounds like a bloody bore."

"She's what girls are supposed to be. Not me." Annia peered at him through her fringe of sweaty hair. "I get all full of bad temper. And when I do, I usually hit something or break something. I have to hit, or I hurt."

"I get moods like that," the soldier said matter-of-factly. "*Gladius* drill gets it out of me. Don't suppose you can train with a *gladius?*"

Annia shook her head.

"Have you tried running it out?"

"Running what out?"

"The bad. Have you got a good stretch here where you can run?"

Annia pointed to the gate at the end of the garden, the long stretch past the place where her father's horses were stabled to the more distant stretch of orderly vines that bordered their villa. "It's half a mile down to the vineyard and back."

He waited. Annia cuffed at her lip again. She hitched up her skirt a bit and went into a jog.

"*Faster, legionary!*" came a bellow behind her. "*You lazy clay-brained lackwit!*"

She turned, running backward, and yelled back at him. "I am not lazy!"

"Then run faster!" Cupping his hands around his mouth. "Run till you throw up! And if you still feel like hitting somebody then, it's because they deserve it, and not because your temper's biting you!"

She whipped back round and put her head down, feet flashing from the grass of the garden to the white dust of the track where the horses were sometimes exercised.

One full lap. Down through the hedges out of sight of the legionary; the full half mile to the wall that bordered the vineyard; giving it a slap; turning about and sprinting back. Sweat trickled down her neck inside her tunic, and her feet burned. The legionary probably didn't think she'd do it—run till she threw up.

She'd show him.

VIX

"What have you done to my daughter, Slight?"

I heard Titus's voice behind me. I knew that voice so well, though I hadn't held a conversation with him in so long.

His daughter's flying red mane was disappearing toward the vineyard. I braced myself before I turned to face him, dreading the moment I'd have to meet his eyes. Maybe that was why I'd been so willing to dawdle in the garden, throwing a ball to a little girl . . . Titus stood in his snowy toga with his armload of scrolls, consul of Rome with all it entailed, and as I met his gaze I saw that his thin, gentle face had a wry expression. "What *have* you done to my daughter?" he repeated.

"She's running off a fit of temper," I said. "Fierce little thing you sired there."

"Gets it from her mother." Titus smiled strangely, studying me a moment. "Is that why you came, to get a look at my daughter?"

"No, why would I? I was waiting for you." But I thought of little Annia's steely glare, the fierce smile she'd given me as she cuffed blood off her lip, and a little pang of guilt stabbed me. Because I loved my girls, I'd have died for them in a heartbeat . . . But in all stark honesty, they *bored* me. So pretty, so good, keeping their dresses clean and sewing their straight seams and never misbehaving; crying at a skinned knee or a barking dog or a glimpse of a spider. I'd never once played *trigon* with either of my girls. Dinah would squeal in disgust at the thought of getting her hem dirty, and Chaya would be too mortally afraid of scraping her knees.

"So—" Titus looked at me, and I looked back. "Why *have* you come to see me, Slight? Seven years, and you turn up without a word of warning. Seven *years*."

There was muted anger in his voice, and I bowed my head under the sting because I deserved it. "I've come to say good-bye," I said, and the words felt strange in my mouth. "Maybe it's been seven years, but—but you're the only damned person in Rome I wanted to bid farewell."

"Ah . . ." Titus let out a long sigh. "Well, come in."

I felt every bit the hulking savage in that beautiful airy villa on the edge of the city. Every graceful line of carved couch or still pool of water spoke of wealth, of peace, of happiness. I saw Titus's beautiful fair-haired wife across the atrium, a column of smoke-blue silk sharing a laugh with the housekeeper—I saw the enormous crowd of petitioners outside his *tablinum* eager for their consul's advice, his authority, his calm certainty. I'd cut myself off from my friend in part to protect him, but why had I bothered? Titus was loved by Fortuna, he always would be: Titus Aurelius Antoninus Pius, as they were starting to call him. I was the one cursed.

His petitioners stared at me as I passed, and I saw one or two whisper behind their hands. One of the Praetorians who had seduced the Empress, or tried to rape her, or perhaps shared her bed, along with Prefect Clarus and Imperial secretary Suetonius, who had also been dismissed. No one could be sure what the real reason for our dismissal was, behind the bland and formal words, but everyone whispered. It must have been something very untoward indeed, though, to merit losing my place at the Emperor's side.

"Don't pretend you haven't heard," I began, as Titus closed the door of his *tablinum* behind us.

"I'd have to be deaf and dumb not to have heard." Titus sat back, looking at me across his heaped desk. "The whole city's buzzing."

"About which part?" I said it brutally. "That I fucked the Empress, or that the Emperor fucked my son?"

"Actually, the part that has people buzzing is just how little anyone seems to really know." Titus quoted the official announcement that had come from Hadrian's pen. "'Tribune Vercingetorix and Prefect Clarus of the Praetorian Guard, and Imperial Secretary Suetonius are to be dismissed because they behaved toward Empress Vibia Sabina in a more informal manner than respect for the Imperial family requires.' No one quite knows what to make of that, 'more informal manner.'"

"That's the point." Less humiliating for the Imperium altogether, even if everyone had salacious suspicions. Hadrian merely dismissed us, and let the world speculate why. People would suspect adultery, but no one would know for certain. His humiliation would remain private.

"Why Suetonius and Prefect Clarus as well as you?" Titus asked.

"My guess?" I shrugged. "Suetonius because he heard me tell about Sabina, and my Prefect because he was my direct superior and if he didn't know I'd bedded her, he should have. Or maybe just because dismissing three of us distracts from the fact that the only guilty one is me."

Titus indicated an inlaid chair, and I sank down into it. Now the questions were mine to ask.

"Did you know?" I looked at him. "About Antinous and the Emperor?"

"No." The answer came without hesitation. "I don't concern myself with gossip about the Emperor's lovers. Had I known, I would have told you."

"Everyone else knew," I said. "No one told me."

Titus's voice was quiet. "Antinous's position isn't the scandal you seem to think. If the Emperor takes a handsome young man to his bed, it's hardly worth noting. Very few people even realize he is your son."

"He's not my son." I looked away. "He made that very clear."

"Don't cast a son away like trash." Titus's voice went suddenly cool. "I lost my boy to the shadows of death. You think I wouldn't trade places with you?"

"You'd wish your son alive again so he'd someday be despised and used by a madman?" I flared. "No, I don't think you want to trade places with me."

My old friend was silent, but his cold gaze never wavered. I remembered the nervous young tribune I'd rescued in Dacia, and I couldn't see him anywhere.

"I'm sorry, Titus." His eyes hooked it out of me. "I'm so sorry about your son."

A long moment, and then Titus finally sat forward and filled two cups with a golden wine the color of Antinous's glinting hair. "And I'm sorry about yours, too."

We drank. Probably an ancient vintage that cost as much per amphora as a year of my old tribune's pay. It might as well have been a dram of vinegar in my mouth.

"Sabina is here, you know," Titus said at last. "Faustina and I invited her, when the news of your dismissal became public. We thought it might help alleviate the talk."

"Don't tell me where she is in this big house of yours. I might still be tempted to wrap my hands about her throat and squeeze till her face turns black."

"She's hurting every bit as much as you, Vix. You realize the Emperor could divorce her? Exile her? *Behead* her?"

"Yes." And I felt a certain thrum of guilt for that, but the rage was still sharper. "She knows better than anyone what her husband is, and she still let Antinous go to his bed without a word of warning. Because for Sabina, whatever Hadrian wants he gets. Even my son."

For that, I refused to regret what I had done.

Titus went on. "The Emperor could have killed you *both*, you know!"

Hadrian would have killed me, right there in the bedchamber with my own *gladius*, but Antinous had gotten down on his knees. Begged for my life, begged for Sabina's, and the Emperor had listened.

I have to hit, little Annia had said, *or I hurt*. How well I understood that. I'd seen my son go down on his knees before Hadrian, and now I hurt all the time and I wanted to hit everyone. Everyone in Rome but the man opposite who looked at me with such quiet eyes.

"So you are leaving," Titus said at last. "Where will you go?"

"Bethar. In Judaea."

"Why Judaea?"

"Because I don't care where I go, and Mirah wants to rejoin her own people, so I might as well make her happy."

God, but my wife was happy! I'd seen the incredulous flash of joy cross her face when I walked through the door stripped of my Praetorian armor and said without preamble, "We go to Bethar as soon as we can make the arrangements." Joy; she couldn't suppress it even when I explained the reason. Even as shock rippled through her eyes when I told her what had happened to our son, even as I stood there fighting off sobs, I saw the happiness overtaking her sorrow for Antinous. And I had the urge to hate her. Because how could she be happy when we'd lost our son?

She must have seen the look on my face, because she came to me and drew my head to her breast. "We won't speak of Antinous," she said. "Not until you are ready. Not ever, if that is what you wish."

Not ever? I'd thought, and wanted to howl. *I don't want to write him off as lost! I want him* back! But the tears came then, and I let it all go and sobbed in her arms.

Titus's voice broke my bitter thoughts. "How will you live in Judaea? I can't imagine you outside a soldier's life."

I shrugged. I'd made myself serve Hadrian for seven long years, too afraid to step outside a soldier's career and all its certainties. Now I felt remarkably little curiosity about the future and whatever it might hold. "I'll get by."

"If you need—"

"Don't you dare offer me money, you sod. I've got coin saved."

"What can I offer you, then?"

I hesitated. "Nothing."

"I'll keep an eye on your son," Titus said quietly. "When the Emperor discards him, he'll find a friend in me. Always."

The words burned my mouth. "Thank you."

We wandered back to the gardens, silent, shoulder to shoulder. I remembered pulling him out of a mud puddle in Dacia, hearing his incongruously polite voice coming out of the barbarian dark. Drinking sour *posca*, me laughing when he poured his out in horror at the taste. Eating lamb stew together in a rented room where a young Antinous crawled over the floor . . . I felt the urge to cry again. I'd been weeping these days like a woman.

But I didn't cry. I smiled instead, because I saw a dusty little red-head standing in the garden, hands on knees, panting like a dying dog.

Another figure stood beside her, a little boy waving a cup of water under her nose, but she pushed him aside as she saw me.

"I ran," Annia gasped, "till I threw up."

I raised my eyebrows, impressed despite myself. "How many laps to the vineyard and back?" I inquired in my sternest centurion's voice. Might be the last occasion I ever had to use it.

She held up three fingers, too winded to talk.

"She threw up *everywhere*," the boy at her side protested. "She's *insane*."

He had a puffy nose to match Annia's split lip. I pointed. "This is the one you hit with a ball?"

She nodded, tiny chest still heaving.

"Still want to hit him?"

She shook her head.

"Worked then, didn't it? The running."

Nod.

"What are you teaching my daughter?" Titus murmured.

"Lessons to live by," I murmured back.

"You shouldn't let her run like that, sir." The little boy bowed for Titus. "It's not proper. Girls aren't supposed to run—"

"Oh, *Hades*," Annia gasped. "Now I want to hit you again."

She veered off wearily toward the garden gate once more, and before I realized it, I laughed. Not much of a laugh. But it was there, as I watched that red-haired imp lurch into a grim jog, the skinny boy running after her. "See? See? She's *insane*—"

Titus laughed too, and we looked at each other and the laughter faded into smiles. We stared at each other, and then I yanked him close and gave him a thump on the shoulder that nearly put him on the ground. "Good-bye."

"Good-bye, Slight."

I took my last walk alone through the high-arched anteroom, over those brilliant mosaics that were too good for my boots to walk on. Just before I left my best friend's house for good, I passed by two silent silk-clad women. One was Titus's wife, Faustina, and the other had close-cropped hair and red, swollen eyes like she'd been crying. At the sight of her, I felt a swell of fury like none I'd ever felt in my fury-filled life.

I spat between Sabina's sandaled feet and moved past her without stopping. I was done with her. I was done with Hadrian. I was done with Rome.

And I would never, ever be back.

HADRIAN'S GOD

Nothing happens to any man that he is not
formed by nature to bear.

—MARCUS AURELIUS

CHAPTER 9

SABINA

A.D. 127, Summer
Rome

"It's *very* improper," Faustina sighed.

"Very," Sabina agreed.

"Borderline scandalous."

"Undoubtedly."

"I'm a bad mother for allowing it."

"Terrible."

From the terrace of Sabina's villa they watched the small figure emerge from the dawn mist: a blue tunic with feet blurring below and red hair flying above. Annia Galeria Faustina the Younger, out for her morning sprint.

"At least she's not naked," Sabina consoled, holding her silver cup between two hands as they peered over the long stretch of gardens. "Didn't the Spartan girls run naked for the glory of their city? I'm surprised Hadrian hasn't brought back *that* tradition along with everything else Greek. Of course, he'd probably be more interested in naked boys . . ."

Faustina groaned, thumping her forehead on her older sister's shoulder. "Did the Spartan girls run four miles at a stretch? That's how long it is, when Annia takes the far loop round all the grounds!" Sabina's villa lay adjoining her sister's, their vineyards almost overlapping; they could walk to each other's atrium without calling a litter. But Annia always took the long way. "Her feet are as hard as a legionary's, and she's as freckled as a slave girl—"

"It suits her." Sabina feasted her eyes on her daughter: tall and tousled, her long legs pumping lean and strong under the hem of her blue tunic. Annia moved with easy speed toward the line of the vineyard wall, bare feet hitting the soft earth and springing free again, her braid of red hair thumping against her back. She looked as though she might take flight at any moment. "Watching her go by is the best part of my day."

"She does find it easier to sit still after she's had a good run," Faustina conceded. "I don't have the heart to forbid her, improper or not."

Annia came to the low boundary wall, cleared it in an easy leap, and sped toward Sabina's adjoining stretch of vines. Her face as she ran was clear and serene, not the resigned boredom she so often wore when she was stuffed into some embroidered dress and standing on display. If there was anything Sabina could conclude after watching her daughter every morning, it was that Annia was happy as long as she was in motion.

"I don't know how she gets up so early." Faustina stifled a yawn: a vision of ripe blond beauty even at dawn. "Who gets up at this hour if they don't have to? I'm only up myself to help *you*, considering the occasion. You should be in your bath by now."

"Not till she's out of sight."

Annia crossed the grass, diving between the vines. A quick flash of wind made flesh, and then she was gone.

Run forever, Sabina thought, and raised her cup in silent toast. *Run forever, my love. I wish I could run with you.*

But the Empress of Rome could not run anywhere. The Empress of Rome was in semi-exile.

Why didn't Hadrian divorce me? The question still whispered to Sabina, every day she rose from her solitary couch. Why hadn't her husband sent Praetorians to her terrace, demanding her head? Disgraced Empresses had died such deaths before, like Claudius's Messalina; or else they were exiled to lonely islands to rot, like Tiberius's loose-moraled Julia.

But no Praetorians with knives ever came, nor did any banishment to barren islands. Sabina's seclusion in this small private villa at the edge of the Eternal City was pleasant, if dull: She could rise every dawn, take her cold mint tisane and drink it on the quiet terrace, spend the days as she pleased. Her mornings were no longer taken up by petitioners and courtiers; few came to call on an empress whose title was all but empty.

So why leave me the title at all? Sabina thought. Because she had barely laid eyes on Hadrian in the past two years, and yet she was still his wife. It was *puzzling.*

"Enough musing, Sabina." The sun was rising, the summer heat sifting down to banish the morning mist, and Faustina was plucking the cup from her hand. "Into the bathhouse with you. If you're to be at Hadrian's side today, you are going to look *magnificent.*"

"I doubt that will change his mind about reinstating me, if that's what you hope for."

"He has to take you back at some point, doesn't he? And this is the tenth anniversary of his reign; the entire city will be watching. If he understands he has to have you on his arm today—"

"Why?" Sabina felt the old frustration rise in her chest as they entered the bathhouse steam. "Why now? He needs me for nothing. Why trot me out today?"

Faustina eyed her shrewdly as the bath slaves fluttered with towels and strigils. "Do you wish he would divorce you?"

Sabina considered that. "Mostly I wish he would make up his mind one way or the other." Slipping out of her robe. "This in-between state is very wearing."

"Would you marry again?" Faustina sounded genuinely curious.

"I doubt it. I'll not be having children, after all—you must have them for me, so I can spoil them." Sabina gave her sister's rising belly a pat before she stepped down into the blue-marbled pool. Four years since Faustina's son had died, four years of prayers to Juno and Diana and Isis—and at last Faustina's stomach was swelling again. Sabina sent silent thanks to whichever of those benevolent goddesses had worked her magic. She had so hated to see the sadness in her sister's eyes. She was meant for laughter, not tears.

"You will behave yourself when you see Hadrian, won't you?" Faustina pressed as soon as Sabina resurfaced, slicking back her short hair. "No matter how much he provokes you!"

"I have no idea how he'll greet me. Whether he'll snub me, laugh at me, or ignore me altogether." She couldn't help but be curious—curious, and more than a little nervous. If that didn't sum up her entire life with Publius Aelius Hadrian . . .

"It doesn't matter what he does," Faustina instructed. "Make him see the advantages of having you at his side again."

Sabina laughed. "I can't *make* him see anything."

"Then behave yourself for noble reasons." Faustina folded Sabina's fallen robe. "Until the Emperor divorces you, you are still Empress of Rome. And an empress has duties."

"Oh, she does," Sabina sighed as a slave began to scrape down her wet shoulders. "Very well, I shall be impeccable. You know exactly how to hit me in my weak point, don't you?"

A sparkling smile as Faustina fanned herself in the steam. "What are sisters for?"

Hadrian's tenth anniversary. It was an occasion worth celebrating; Sabina couldn't deny that. At the bloody beginning of his reign, no one would have guessed Hadrian would cling to his throne for a full decade. *And I had my part in that,* Sabina thought with a small flash of pride. However difficult Hadrian found his mask to wear, it seemed firmly fixed in place. He was a good emperor. A just one. A hardworking one. Even (mostly) a merciful one—he'd spared Sabina and Vix both, hadn't he, when he could have had their heads on spears?

So perhaps my life's work is done, Sabina thought as she came from the bathhouse swathed in towels. Her maids were laying out her elaborate silks, the curled wig she never bothered to wear when alone, the shackles of bracelets and necklaces and rings. *I shall put it all on like a cart horse shrugging into its harness, and go do my duty.*

And perhaps the Emperor would finally set her free.

ANTINOUS

Hadrian was reading one petition, signing another, and dictating to a secretary as Antinous brought the dogs into his study. "Caesar," Antinous murmured into the general commotion, and Hadrian raised a hand. The throng of pages and secretaries and guards filed out, and he called for the dogs.

"Come here, my girls!"

Antinous released the gilt leather leashes so the hounds could lope across the mosaics, tails wagging. Hadrian dropped caresses among those sleek heads until the doors closed behind the last Praetorian. Then the Emperor rose to take Antinous in his arms for a long kiss. Antinous had the same sensation of floating that he'd first felt in a lemon grove in Greece. He raised a hand to the Emperor's face as they kissed, touching the furrow traced almost permanently between those heavy brows, and Hadrian dissolved into laughter against his mouth because it was a joke between them by now—Antinous's way of telling him to cease working and for the love of all the gods don't think so hard. "That's better," Antinous murmured against Hadrian's lips, feeling the furrow disappear under his fingers.

"Blue," Hadrian said, once he'd pulled away far enough to look Antinous over in his blue tunic. "I like you in blue. I'd hang sapphires around your neck, but you'd refuse to wear them."

"I'm afraid so." Of all the ornaments his lover tried to give him, the only one he kept was a gold ring set with a modest topaz. *The color of your eyes*, Hadrian had said, kissing Antinous on the throat as he slipped it over the fourth finger on the left hand, where a vein was supposed to run to the heart. Antinous never took that ring off, but he turned down the pearled fillets and the emerald cloak pins as tactfully as he knew how. He still remembered Vix's eyes sliding over him, that night when he'd been surprised wearing nothing but the gold chains about his neck and wrists that had been Hadrian's first gift. *Tarted up like a whore.*

The usual shaft of sheer agony pierced him at the thought of his father, but there was nothing to do but shove it away. As he had been doing for two long years. "The Empress has arrived," he said instead, briskly to hide the momentary pain thickening his throat. "She's waiting in the atrium."

"I don't know how I let you persuade me," Hadrian complained, his arms still resting easy about Antinous's waist. "I don't *want* the Empress present for the festivities!"

"You can hardly exclude her on such an important occasion," Antinous pointed out patiently, as he had been pointing out ever since the celebrations were first being planned. For a tenth anniversary nothing would be overlooked; everything had to go well. Antinous felt a twinge of anxiety, knowing exactly how people would be looking for omens today. "It would cause talk if you exclude her. Do you wish that to overshadow a day of such triumph?"

"It will cause far more talk if she is seen at my side as if all is forgiven. All is not forgiven. She humiliated me."

"Rome does not know that." The vagueness of Sabina's offenses kept gossip roiling, but no one was certain precisely why she was out of favor—only that she was. "Besides, who could humiliate you? The god of Rome!" Antinous kept his tone gentle. He had learned that a light touch was needed on prickly matters. And there were few matters that prickled Hadrian more than his Empress.

"I still don't see why you are such an advocate of Sabina's." Hadrian held up a hand, matching his fingers with Antinous's.

"Because she was always kind to me." But it was more than just kindness. *I cost you your husband* and *your lover*, Antinous thought every time he contemplated the Empress of Rome. That guilt bore at his stomach like a wire. To see her restored from solitude and shame to the place she deserved seemed the least he could do. "She is still your wife," he said mildly. "The women of Rome look to her, and they can't do that if she's nowhere to be seen. You need her on your arm."

"I'd rather have you on my arm," Hadrian said, and pulled him close for another long kiss. "Where everyone could admire you."

"Better if they don't." He'd *prefer* if they didn't. Antinous held his post only as the Emperor's page, handler of his dogs and pourer of his wine. A bedmate, certainly, but no one important. Hadrian saved his gestures of love for private moments, thank the gods. It made Antinous anonymous and comfortable, hardly to be noticed. Safe in the shadows.

"You will be late," Antinous said after another kiss, bumping his nose softly against Hadrian's. "Go make the Empress welcome!"

Hadrian slanted a brow at him in warning. He would listen to gentle argument, but never nagging. Antinous made a face of wide-eyed apology, and Hadrian laughed. "Oh, my star. Let's get this rose-petal pomp over with, and then I'm taking you on a tour of the east. Egypt, Parthia, Syria . . ."

"If your health allows." Antinous looked at the Emperor's fingers, still linked with his. Hadrian's knuckles were swelling again, and looking painful. Just the summer heat, he insisted, but Antinous worried. *He pushes himself so hard.* His ever-busy, ever-working lover who would not admit he was unwell even when he was weaving from fever—sometimes Antinous wanted to throttle him, and all from love. "Does the physician say it's a summer malady or—"

"Bother the physician," Hadrian said, as Antinous had known he would, and swept out to the atrium.

A crowd had gathered to wait, pressing at once around their Emperor. Antinous took the dogs and melted discreetly back, but Empress Sabina noticed him at once. She noticed everything.

"Antinous."

"Lady." Antinous approached her where she stood beside her sister. How different the two of them were for sisters: Faustina tall and ripe and merry-eyed as a fertility goddess; Sabina small and cool and elegant with her face like an oblique shield. *The deepest rivers flow with the least sound,* Antinous thought of the old quote by Quintus Curtius Rufus. If Titus Aurelius's wife was a laughing stream, Hadrian's was very dark still water indeed.

Do you resent me? Do you hate me? Are you happy to be out of the public eye, or are you slowly dying of loneliness in your exile? Antinous had no idea. The Empress's opaque blue eyes gave away nothing.

He still wanted to help her. "You look very fine, Lady." She wore the same shade of sea-blue as he did: a chiton with a pattern of Greek keys stamped in gold about its rippling hem, and a gold diadem with long filigreed strands hanging to her shoulders like the one Helen of Troy was said to have worn. She had made herself a Greek queen, and Antinous knew Hadrian would approve despite himself—because she never put a foot wrong. *Except, perhaps, in loving my father.*

The Emperor came to claim his Empress, and eyes turned everywhere as Hadrian's gaze traveled over his mysteriously disgraced wife. Antinous wished he could have seen acceptance there, however grudging, but his lover's eyes were cold. The Empress returned that stare calmly, and a wave of unabashed admiration rose in Antinous. Gods only knew, Hadrian's anger turned him into jelly (little as he ever saw it), but Empress Sabina wasn't giving away so much as a flicker of nervousness.

"Argive Helen," the Emperor said at last, giving a nod to her Greek diadem.

"Jupiter Optimus Maximus," she returned, surveying his crisp toga and wreath. "All you're missing is a lightning bolt in one hand. Don't we make a handsome statement? How did you put it, 'The best that is Greece and the best that is Rome, brought together in harmony'?"

Hadrian's eyes did not thaw. "Not such great harmony as that, Vibia Sabina."

Sweet gods, but Hadrian could hold a grudge every bit as ferociously as Vix! It made Antinous wonder sometimes just what Empress Sabina had ever been thinking, to try to balance between two men with such ever-lasting tempers.

Well, I tried that, too. In a different way. But such a balance would always fail, sooner or later: in the end, the scales crashed and the choice had to be made. *I chose Hadrian.*

He would make that choice again a thousand times over, and never hesitate. If only the pain of making it didn't still linger like an unknitted wound.

"Shall we settle for the appearance of harmony, Caesar?" Empress Sabina tucked a hand through Hadrian's arm, and the Emperor's tenth-anniversary celebration began.

"For such a momentous occasion, it's a damned dull one!" Antinous heard Lucius Ceionius drawl, yawning behind a pair of slave girls dressed in nothing but peacock feathers. "Even the crowds look bored!"

But isn't that extraordinary? Antinous wanted to say as the procession descended through the streets of Rome. At the *paedogogium* he had studied the Year of Four Emperors—back then, Rome would have been agog to celebrate any emperor who made it a full ten years on the throne. But titans like Vespasian and Trajan had ruled since then, and here was Hadrian following in those giant footsteps, giving out peace and prosperity with such ease that his people were not even excited by it anymore. The parade with falling rose petals, the gladiatorial displays, the coins and prizes flung into the crowd—Rome took it all as her due.

It was not until the sacrifice at the Temple of Jupiter Optimus Maximus that the city's boredom evaporated.

The sun had just appeared from behind a cloud, striking the gilt-bronze roof to brilliance as the priests led out a white ox bathed and bleached to the color of snow. The beast stared impassively at the sacrificial knife, as though quite willing to die for the glory of the emperor who stood bearded and grave in his toga—the Emperor who turned his head to find Antinous in the throng and gave him a tiny circumspect smile. Antinous felt that upwell of tenderness, seeing not only Hadrian where he stood now, but Hadrian bare-shouldered in bed scribbling poetry, and Hadrian laughing till his eyes overflowed. Hadrian shouting in irritation; Hadrian remote on his throne; Hadrian in rippling motion on his horse. The many faces of Publius Aelius Hadrian, and Antinous loved them all.

I'd die for you too, he thought. *Just like that bull.*

Maybe his eyes said it too clearly, because Hadrian didn't look away. Just stood staring with that expression he sometimes had when he looked at Antinous. An expression of bewilderment, as though he did not understand what he was looking at. "I don't," he had muttered, the one time Antinous laughingly said as much. "I don't understand why the gods gave you to me. I will never understand it."

Understand that I love you, Antinous thought, sending a kiss with his eyes. *Nothing on this earth can be simpler than that.*

Hadrian was still staring. The priest waited, holding his sacrificial knife with a puzzled expression, and Antinous quickly dropped his gaze.

That was when the rustle of the crowd became a flurry of whispers. Antinous glanced up and saw that the Emperor had turned away from the priest and was holding out his hand.

To Antinous.

Heads craned. Shock pierced Antinous like an arrow. He took an automatic step forward, pulled by those fierce eyes, but he stopped again, giving his head a minute shake. *Hadrian*, he thought, stunned. *No!* He already had his Empress at his side where she belonged; his Greek queen, his match in the eyes of the world.

But Hadrian was stepping away from her, making his way toward Antinous with jaw clenched in defiance of the whispers, eyes wide with that strange bewilderment as if he did not know why he was moving. He halted, still staring, and Antinous felt a wash of crimson flood to his cheeks as all faces turned toward him. He cast his gaze down, rooted to the spot under so many eyes. Hadrian still hesitated. *Go back to your Empress*, Antinous begged him silently. *This is not fitting!* Not fitting in so very many ways: not here, not today, not before the temple gods, not before all the people of Rome. *And not me. I am not fitting!*

But Hadrian came to his side. The Emperor of Rome came to a page, brushing people out of the way if they did not move fast enough. Antinous jerked out a bow as he always did when there were people to observe them, but Hadrian put a hand to his cheek and raised him.

"Caesar," Antinous whispered. "What are you—"

"Take your place," Hadrian said, not lowering his voice, and drew Antinous's hand through his arm. "Take your place where you belong." A breath, and he spoke even more loudly. "Dearest and most beautiful of stars."

He led Antinous to the front, gripping his hand tight. Standing at his side, as close as Empress Sabina stood on the other. Antinous did not dare look at her—that carved profile under the diadem was just a blur on Hadrian's other side. He stared straight ahead, feeling a roar in his ears. Whispers rose all around him like a sea of snakes.

From the corner of his eye, he saw Hadrian look fiercely around, glaring at the whispering entourage, the hissing senators, the shocked priest. "Continue."

They did. But no one had eyes for the sacrifice—only for Antinous.

"Caesar," he whispered as the priest's prayers stuttered out. "*What are you doing?*"

"Bringing you out of the shadows." Hadrian gazed straight ahead, his lips clamped tight, the picture of cool arrogance. "I will not hide you any longer."

"I like the shadows—"

"But you belong at my side. You. No one else."

The way they stare, Antinous thought, feeling his heart rise into his throat. Sweet gods, he might as well have been utterly naked. He had been stared at all his life, but not like this. "They look at me as if I crawled from a gutter," he whispered. He saw it in their eyes, the disgust Vix had warned of: a bum-boy standing before all Rome, before the temple that *was* Rome, on the Emperor of Rome's arm.

"Let me step back," he begged in another whisper as the knife descended and the bull went to its knees in a pool of blood.

"I need you."

Not for this, Antinous wanted to cry out. To discreetly share an emperor's bed; that was his place. To stand at the Emperor's side on the most momentous public day in recent memory; that was Empress Sabina's.

She will hate me for this, he thought in black, barren certainty. *They will all hate me.*

Hadrian's hand raised his chin, another gesture to send hisses fluttering through the crowd. He ignored them, staring into Antinous's swimming eyes. "No one will scorn you," he said, and he no longer looked fierce. He looked tender, as tender as he ever looked when they were alone and he could let the mask of a great man drop. "You have my word."

Oh, my love, Antinous thought sadly, *what a dreamer you are. There are some things even an emperor cannot command.*

SABINA

"He did it to slight you!" Faustina huffed loyally. A feast at Hadrian's great villa was to mark the end of the anniversary festivities. "All the world knows about his lovers, but to show one off at his side like an empress—"

"Not just any lover, Faustina." Sabina looked over the lily-decked atrium: buzzing, roiling with gossip only barely contained to a whisper. The slightly bored pleasure that had previously marked the festivities was gone; everyone in the room craned their eyes for the Emperor. "Antinous is different."

"And he's a sweet boy, but he's not an *empress*, and he can't be treated like one! Everyone knows that. Remember the stories about Emperor Domitian and that Jewish slave girl he was obsessed with? Even *he* never brought a concubine out on his arm standing in for his wife." Faustina shook her head, blond curls dancing. "The Emperor can divorce you or he can reinstate you, but he has no right to shame you."

"I don't think he meant to," Sabina said. "I don't believe he was thinking of me at all."

Conversation suddenly stilled. Sabina looked up. The Emperor had arrived, toga changed for a Greek robe and a wreath, his eyes gleaming and his arm openly about Antinous. Old Servianus hissed audibly at the sight, and he was not the only one. Sabina heard muffled gasps, stifled titters—and at the sound, Antinous faltered in the doorway.

But Hadrian pulled him closer and pressed his lips deliberately against the honey-colored hair. The Imperial eyes looked at the throng, cold and challenging. Across the atrium, senators and generals and their wives all bowed before the Emperor and his lover.

"I think," Sabina said slowly, "that my husband is in love."

I should have seen it, she thought, stunned. But the thought followed itself with *Why? Publius Aelius Hadrian has never been in love in his life.*

The Emperor was calling for wine, calling for dice, declaring he felt lucky. A page brought him a cup, but Hadrian waved him to serve Antinous first. Antinous sipped shyly, handsomer than ever with his fair curls bound back under a Greek fillet, his limbs tanned and oiled and glowing against a snow-white synthesis. He was just beginning to smile when Servianus stumped up with his mouth pinched tight.

"Caesar," he said. "I fear you must excuse me this evening. I am an old man, and I have had"—his eyes slid over Antinous as though he were covered in sewer slime—"quite enough."

Hadrian's eyes went from happy to vicious in an instant.

Oh, gods, Sabina thought. This was going to end very badly if that old idiot did not shut up.

"You will stay, Servianus," the Emperor stated. "At least long enough to throw a turn of dice with Antinous."

"Please, Caesar—" The Emperor's lover tried to smile, giving Servianus a respectful bow. "Do not keep anyone from their beds on my account."

Hadrian's eyes drilled into the old man's. "He will stay to play a round with you."

Servianus's nose quivered as though he smelled something foul. "Caesar," he hissed. "As your brother-in-law I have the right to speak—this is *disgrace*, this is—"

Someone safely out of sight at the back of the crowd laughed. There were little ripples of agreement, almost too small to be heard but they were there, and Antinous turned as red as an open wound. "Caesar," the young man whispered, and then lost his voice and slid away from the Emperor's arm.

Sabina saw murder in her husband's eyes and found herself moving before it could blossom like a poisoned rose. Someone had to stop this before there was blood on the tiles, and it might as well be the Empress of Rome. She brushed past Servianus, so quickly that her sea-blue hem frothed at her feet like a wave as she came up beside Antinous and slid an arm through his.

"Goodness, Servianus," she said, and gave a titter of amused mockery. "Such fussing over a game of dice! If you are so determined to retire, I will take your turn." She felt Antinous's pulse beating fast inside his arm and gave his elbow a squeeze. "Antinous, do throw the dice for me, I have had abominable luck—"

"I will join you," a quiet voice said at Sabina's other side. Titus was there, giving Antinous a cordial nod. He had a set of dice in hand, though Sabina did not think Titus had ever played dice in his life. "If you would give me the pleasure, Antinous? And perhaps you might tell me more about the *paedogogium*; my wife is to bear what she assures me is a son, and I am already pondering whether I should send him to school or hire tutors at home—"

"Of course, *patronus*," Antinous said with a sudden smile of utter relief, and the chattering broke loud and nervous over the room. Old Servianus looked dour, shaking his white head. "A shame," he whispered venomously to his nearest crony. "In my day no man of this Empire would pay honor to a—"

But Sabina lifted her voice loudly before he could name just what he thought Antinous was. "Faustina, join us!" and even if Faustina had earlier thought Antinous's presence a slight to her sister she still came forward, loyal as a rock. Soon there was a riotous game in progress with Antinous at its center like a young sun.

"Thank you, Lady," he whispered when Sabina bent her head to blow on the dice cupped in his palm. "I thought—I thought you might hate me."

She looked up into those amber-brown eyes, startled. "Dear gods, Antinous, who could hate you?"

"Most of this room, I imagine." He tried to smile as though that were nothing, but Sabina saw the rigid set of his shoulders.

"They may think what they like of you," Sabina said. "But they will not dare say it, that I promise. Chamberlain!" she called. "Seat Antinous beside me at dinner. The brightest young man in Rome, and certainly the most charming!"

"Antinous is to sit at the Emperor's side, Lady," the chamberlain said nervously, and everyone looked to see how she would take that, but Sabina only shrugged.

"Sit him between us then, what of it?" She kept up the laughter through the many courses of dinner, hanging on Antinous's shy words, offering him the choice bits of each dish, pulling every guest into the conversation until every person on every couch had been forced to acknowledge the Emperor's lover with at least a few civil words. She kept the tension at bay with silver-bright chatter, seeing the gratitude in Antinous's eyes, and seeing nothing at all in Hadrian's.

She was not surprised to feel her husband's hand on her elbow the moment the guests rose and dispersed into chatter. "Walk with me." His grip brooked no disagreement.

"Are you angry?" Sabina kept her voice low as they drifted to where the atrium lay open to the vast moonlit gardens. "I'm sorry to interfere, but I saw how you looked at Servianus."

"I would not have harmed that old fool."

"No?" They stood looking out over the shadowed trees, the noise and laughter of the party dimmed. "You wanted him dead on the tiles."

"Yes. But it would have displeased Antinous—a death on his behalf."

"You would not displease him?"

"Not for the Empire or anything in it." Hadrian's bearded face was immobile, but he looked over his shoulder, and Sabina saw the way his eyes followed Antinous's graceful figure. *So much for my hope it would all burn itself out,* Sabina thought. She had thought it all just lust, at least on Hadrian's side, but this was far more dangerous.

Publius Aelius Hadrian was indeed in love.

"If you feel so tenderly toward him," she said, "then why did you expose him to public scorn?"

Her husband's chin jerked. "No one will dare say—"

"Servianus dared. He is only the first."

"Antinous said they would. He said . . ." Hadrian trailed off. "You were the one to put Servianus in his place. Not me."

She could feel the rage biting him. Rage at himself, she thought, and spoke gently. "To silence mockery is a woman's gift. Men may own the world, but they can do little against scorn. Even an emperor."

"You came to Antinous's rescue." Hadrian said it stiffly. "They could have laughed, and he would have been shamed, and I could have killed them all but that would not have healed his shame. You stopped that. It was kindly done."

"I don't like to see anyone shamed."

"Even your husband's bedmate?"

"I like Antinous, Hadrian. I have always liked him. But he's shy, for all his beauty—he doesn't want notoriety, no matter what those like Servianus might think." Tilting her head. "So why *did* you bring him forward like that, on the steps of the temple?"

Hadrian looked down at her. "I was not trying to slight you, if that is what you imply."

"Not at all." Sabina felt the night breeze blowing sharp and fragrant, stirring the gold strands of her diadem. "You do nothing without calculation of how it will *look*, Hadrian. You know how this will look. Why did you do it?"

He ran a hand along the carved marble of the nearest pillar. "I can't—hide it any longer. I should. But I cannot."

"Why?"

He was silent for a moment, fingering his beard. "'Passionate love,'" he quoted at last, slowly. "'Relentless, twists a cord under my heart, and spreads deep clouds on my eyes . . .'"

"That's not one of your verses," Sabina said. "Anakreon?"

"No, Archilochus." Hadrian's head bowed. "I should hide Antinous. I should dismiss him altogether. It is not fitting, for one of my station to feel what I do. But I looked at him on the steps of the temple today and I could—not—" A long breath. "He steals all my good sense away."

Sabina remembered Vix's smile, that invisible one that started and finished all in his gray eyes when he looked her over. "Maybe I felt the same once."

Hadrian glanced at her sharply. "That crude, bloodthirsty legionary?"

She shrugged. "Can we choose, Hadrian—even those of us with Imperial blood? Cupid strikes where he will."

"I expected more restraint from you. Better sense."

"Because I am Empress?"

"Because you were *born* with the control for which I struggle. Do you need a Hades to keep yourself in check? No." He sounded exasperated. "If I am to be made a fool by love, Vibia Sabina, surely one of us must maintain decorum!"

The unfairness of that stung. *He is allowed to be in love, but not me.*

Never me. "So you will have your scandal, and I will be respectable for the both of us?"

"Yes."

"Hardly just, is it?"

"I do not care," said Hadrian coolly. "I will not give him up, and I am done hiding him. He is the star of my life. The Empire will accept him, or I will cram their scorn down their throats."

"He will still be made to feel shame."

"And in return I will give him the world." Hadrian's brown hand curled into a slow fist against the marble column. "It will be enough. It will *have* to be enough."

Sabina heard the thickness in his voice. She glanced back inside the atrium and saw Antinous standing at Faustina's side. Faustina had called a dozen women over and they were all cooing and laughing. "If you wish to make the court accept him, start with the women," Sabina advised. "The senators are swayed more by their wives than they think. Faustina looks to have things in hand—if she takes Antinous under her wing, the others will do the same."

"Surely your sister sees his presence as an insult to you."

"She is generous of heart. She likes Antinous—and even if she did not, she'd befriend his cause if I asked."

"And you'd ask? Even if I sent you back to that villa at the edge of Rome tomorrow in disgrace again?"

"Yes."

"Why?"

Sabina looked her husband up and down. "Love is good for you," she said. "Frankly, I hadn't thought you capable of it. You have no idea how happy I am to be wrong."

She said it to be flippant, but realized she *was* happy. It surprised her, because she was still angry too. She wished she could haul off and give Hadrian a good slap for his hypocrisy, letting himself gorge on the thing she wasn't allowed to taste. But—

But she was still happy for him.

A flare of temper went through Hadrian's eyes at her frankness, but she held his gaze and slowly it banked. He reached out, tilting her chin up with his hand. "It was Antinous," he said slowly, "who advised me not to divorce you two years ago. When I dismissed Vercingetorix."

"Antinous?" That she had not anticipated, not at all.

"He said you had always been kind to him. And," Hadrian conceded, "he pointed out that I would just need another empress, to take on those formal duties you handle for me, and if I divorced you half the women of Rome would be jockeying. I would probably end up with some pseudo-poetic harpy like Julia Balbilla."

"Gods forbid!" Sabina mocked.

"So, I did not divorce you. As angry as I was."

"Was?"

"Still am," he said evenly, and she could see it in the set of his teeth. "But even if Antinous had not advised against it . . . Well. You anger me sometimes to the point of loathing, but I find it difficult to be rid of you."

"Why is that?"

"You know me better than anyone in this world, Vibia Sabina."

"Even Antinous?"

"He does not know me at all, thank the gods. And I intend to keep it that way." Hadrian released her chin. "I am planning another grand tour, you know. The east—Judaea, Parthia, Egypt. I take Antinous with me."

"He will enjoy that. He always wanted to see the world."

"Come with us."

The breath left Sabina in a rush. "*What?*"

"Antinous told me I needed you, but what I really need is him. *He* is the one who needs you, as a shield against the world's scorn. Given that, you may come with us."

So I am not to be divorced and freed, Sabina thought with a twinge of disappointment. Perhaps if she had left Antinous to twist under the scorn of ancient spluttering Servianus . . .

But I could never have done that. And so I am to be Empress again.

And an empress had duties.

At least along with duty there would be Judaea, Parthia, Egypt. The world. Not a busy palace stagnant with sycophants. Not a lonely villa where her one joy was a daily glimpse of her speeding daughter.

It is enough, Sabina thought. *It will have to be enough.* And lowered her eyes for Hadrian, choking down her last pangs of regret, and said, "Thank you, Caesar."

Hadrian tilted her chin up again. "Do not make me regret it."

ANNIA

A.D. 127, Winter
Hadrian's Villa

It was just a flight of shallow stone steps beside the Greek theatre, leading down to a set of black doors. Annia had seen the theatre before—a few months ago, right after the Emperor's tenth anniversary and before he'd broken his collarbone on a boar hunt, her father had taken her to a pantomime here. No one had paid any attention to the actors because they were too busy watching the Emperor sit with his arm about Antinous. Annia remembered the theatre, but she hadn't seen these black iron doors set below the earth.

"That's the Emperor's Hades." Pedanius Fuscus sounded nervous. "He buggers little slave boys in there and dismembers them—"

"Does not," Annia scoffed. The Emperor didn't like children—it was why she and Marcus and Brine-Face got tossed together out in the Imperial gardens whenever her father and their grandfathers went to attend Hadrian at his villa. But she knew perfectly well that even if he didn't like children, he didn't dismember them *or* bugger them.

Annia took a step down toward the Emperor's Hades. Her breath frosted in the air; it was the cold time just before the year's turn. "Don't go down there," Marcus said, eyeing the black doors. "It's evil."

Another step. "I want to see."

"You can't," Brine-Face said. "*I'm* allowed because the Emperor favors me, but—"

"No, he doesn't!" Pedanius was always bragging about his great-uncle's favor, but if he was such a favorite, why was he out here with the children?

Pedanius bristled. "My grandfather says the Emperor is going to make me a member of the Salian priesthood soon, to show the world I'll succeed him—"

Annia snorted, bounding down the rest of the steps. The door handles were black iron, fashioned in the shape of screech owls, the bird sacred to Hades. She pushed back her warm red cloak, crouching down to look through the keyhole. "It's just a passage."

"You shouldn't be looking," Marcus said, and then, "What else?"

"A lamp . . ." A wall bracket shaped like another screech owl, and a guttering lamp lighting a dark stone passage. Annia's pulse jumped in an uneasy little thrill. "I can almost see a—"

A roar like Jupiter in the heavens shattered their solitude. *"What is the meaning of this?"*

Annia's hand leaped off the iron screech owl. Marcus let out a croak and Pedanius squealed like a piglet. A tall and furious Emperor stood gazing down at them with eyes like black thunder.

Maybe he does dismember children.

When he spoke again it was in a deadly whisper, and after the sky-breaking roar Annia found that more terrifying than anything. "Come. Here."

Annia bolted up the steps to Marcus's side. His fingers slipped instantly through hers, and Annia was glad. Her mouth went dry as parchment as the Emperor looked down at them. He wore a long tunic as dark as the iron doors, his beard was wild, and one arm was bound in a white sling. His face was flushed, his eyes glittered, and he didn't seem to feel the cold at all. *He's sick*, Annia found herself thinking inconsequentially, in the midst of her fear. The Emperor hadn't just postponed his travels east because of a broken collarbone; he was also *sick*.

His eyes devoured them as he said in that near-whisper, "What do you brats think you are doing?"

"I told them not to trespass," Pedanius babbled. He was fourteen, big across the shoulders, and his voice had long since deepened to a man's, but now it scaled back up in a child's squeak. "I warned them, Great-Uncle—"

"Silence."

Brine-Face went red. The Emperor's eyes moved from Pedanius to

Marcus and Annia, and she flinched inside. He was going to beat them to bloody ribbons.

"Strike us if you like, Caesar," Marcus blurted out suddenly. "But not in anger."

The Emperor blinked. "What?"

"Strike us because we trespassed," Marcus explained, "not because you are angry. An angry man is one who has lost control of himself, and the loss of control is contrary to all Stoic principles. If I may paraphrase Epictetus—"

"Shut up!" Annia hissed, seeing the Emperor's eyes narrow.

"—'If any be angry, let him remember that he is unhappy by reason of himself alone,'" Marcus babbled. "Not to mention the precepts of Seneca—"

There was no stopping Marcus on one of his nervous rants. He was spilling Zeno and Seneca and Epictetus at the speed of a chariot on the last lap, and the Emperor glowered like a thundercloud, which just made Marcus quote even faster.

"Boy," the Emperor said at last, "shut up."

Amazingly, Marcus gulped and fell silent.

"You with the quotations. Whose brat are you?"

"Marcus Annius Verus, son of Marcus Annius Verus, grandson of Marcus Annius Verus. Though I am frequently addressed as Marcus Catilius Severus in honor of my great-grandfather upon my mother's—"

"There is another famous quote," the Emperor said. "'Be succinct in your answers.'"

"Yes, Caesar. Who said that, Caesar?"

"I did. You are a student of Stoicism?"

"My tutor is a Stoic, Caesar, and I look to follow his precepts."

"By boring us all to death with your chatter?"

"By making no excuses and by always speaking truth," Marcus whispered.

The Emperor smiled in wintry amusement. "You won't live long if you speak nothing but truth, boy."

Annia could *see* Marcus trying not to quote, but he lost the battle with temptation. "'The point is not how long you live, but how nobly you live.'"

Emperor Hadrian laughed sourly. "Outquoted by a brat," he said. "I think I will spare you punishment, little Verissimus."

Truthful one.

"It's a better nickname than Brine-Face," Annia couldn't help whispering, and Pedanius looked like he wanted to kill her.

"You remind me," the Emperor said, still looking at Marcus, "of myself at your age."

"Th-thank you, Caesar."

"It was not a compliment. I was a dreadful little pedant." The Emperor brushed past them, down to the black iron doors. "Shoo."

"Yes, Caesar. Thank you, Caesar." Marcus bowed.

"And tell your grandfather I'm appointing you to the Salian priests," the Emperor tossed over one shoulder. "It is quite an honor for a child of your age, but you've bored me enough this afternoon, so please don't compose some elaborate speech of thanks."

Marcus stared openmouthed. The Emperor disappeared inside his Hades, and Annia craned her neck. She got a bare glimpse of a rough passage of undressed stone, of more screech owl lamps, a flash of something that might have been silver . . .

"The Salii?" Marcus whispered.

Annia grinned. "You're going to look silly. The Salii do all that dancing around in costume on festival days—"

Pedanius stared slit-eyed at Marcus. "The Salii?" he said at last. "My grandfather said *I* would be get that post. *Me.*"

"Maybe you would have," Annia told Brine-Face. "But *you* just babbled like a coward in front of the Emperor. Marcus faced him down."

VIX

Judaea

My mother had told me something back in Britannia that was beginning to haunt me. She'd been fingering her lyre as we watched Mirah plait flower chains for the girls, and my mother said, "I do hope you realized you married a Jew."

"Why should that matter?" I blinked. "I'm a Jew, too. So are you."

"Not really." My mother gave a graceful shrug. "We were slaves, and slaves have neither God nor nation. We have nothing at all, and it gives us the power to choose where our home lies. And you may have been born to the chosen people, Vix, but that doesn't mean you were ever *of* them. Your wife is."

"She was born and raised in Rome, just the same as—"

"It doesn't matter. Her heart lies in Judaea."

"Is that your way of saying you don't like her?" I asked wryly.

"Oh, I like her very much. She's good for you. But she is of God and you are of Rome."

"God and Rome get along well in enough in our house."

My mother's dark eyes studied me. "Good."

"What did you choose?" I couldn't help asking. "If you're not much of a Jew, you're certainly not a Roman either. Where's your home?"

"It lies in your father." The melody under her fingers stilled as her gaze rested on the burly figure spading earth in the garden—the figure who lifted his head to smile at her, as though he'd felt her eyes on him like a caress. "My home, my country, and my god together. As I am his."

I'd been settled in Judaea for two years now . . . And those words were still echoing through my head.

Mirah had wept when we finally stepped off the ship onto Judaean soil: dropped the bundle she had been carrying and fell to her knees. "Thank you," I heard her whisper, and she pulled the girls close to her sides and kissed their dark heads over and over until they began crying, too. As I stood there with my *gladius* and dagger in a bundle, feeling so very strange.

We settled in Bethar: a fortified farming town, terraced and prosperous, rising from the high country southwest of ruined Jerusalem. Mirah wept again as we came through the gates. "Home," she said, pressing my hand, but I felt only strangeness. In Bethar's pressing crowds, I had the only breastplate, the only shaven chin. I'd spent most of my life as one of many, a legionary among other legionaries, a guard among other guards—and now I was the one who stood out.

Mirah's family held a great celebration to welcome us. Her mother roasted an entire calf, my wife was swallowed up in the eager arms of her aunts, and our girls were soon running through the garden with enough cousins to field a cohort. I leaned against the wall watching, and when Simon found me there, he switched from Aramaic to Latin.

"It passes." He smiled when I looked at him in surprise. "The strangeness you're feeling. It goes away."

I swirled the wine in my cup. "How long did it take you?"

"A year to stop thinking in Latin. Two years to stop dreaming about the legions. Five before I stopped bristling whenever my cousins cursed the Emperor's name."

"Feel free to curse Hadrian," I said. "But if you curse Trajan's name, I'll beat you to a paste."

"Trajan, Hadrian." Simon shrugged. "It's all the same to me."

"And you call yourself a legion man?" I said, outraged.

"Not anymore. All those years in the ranks?" He shrugged. "Wasted youth."

I looked at him. A big man, first in my *contubernium* when I arrived fresh from my training; tough-grained and solid as the earth in his polished breastplate; his curls cropped close and his chin stubbled. He'd looked humorous, weathered, and competent, and I'd yearned to be just like him. He had the same expression now, hard and amused, but he wore a striped robe and a full beard and looked nothing like Simon the legion man. He was Simon ben Cosiba of Bethar, and I wondered if I knew him at all.

"Don't worry," he urged, seeing my expression. "It passes!"

"Maybe I don't want it to," I said. "Maybe I don't want to stop thinking in Latin and dreaming about the legions."

"That's Rome talking," he dismissed. "It's like a poison dream, Vix. You stop taking the poison, and at first you crave it, but then you see it was making you weak all along. You'll see."

"Will I?"

"Rome made your son a whore," he said, face darkening. "Think of that, when you start doubting. If it were my son, I'd have—"

I dropped my wine cup and grabbed Simon by the front of his striped robe. "Friend or not, I will tear your throat out if you use that word about him again."

"Mirah said—"

"Mirah shouldn't have gone telling you about my son's shame, even if you are her favorite uncle. It's not your business, Simon, so don't you *ever* call him a whore."

"Vix!" Mirah called across the little garden, her face glowing. "My mother says we can take a house nearby! There's—" She stopped as she saw my spilled wine, my fist at Simon's chest. "Vix, what are you—"

"It's nothing," Simon said, not taking his eyes from mine. "I spilled his wine, and now he's threatening to dump mine over my head."

I exhaled the rage, uncurling my fist from his robe. "That's right."

Mirah looked doubtful, but she took my arm and steered me away. Toward safer things.

We soon had a house with a walled garden and a small courtyard forever overflowing with laughter and chatter and cousins. "You're a lucky man," they told me, and yes, I was. I had a beautiful wife; I had two daughters who were starting to flower into young women; I had coin enough to support them in comfort and take my ease in my sunny courtyard. I knew men who did just that, men like Mirah's father, who basked in grandchildren and books. "You could grow a beard," Mirah teased me, "become a venerable patriarch!"

"What does a patriarch do?"

"Well, I don't see you studying the sacred scrolls like my father." She kissed me soundly. "There's any number of trades you could take to fill your time. Perhaps buy a wine shop? There are other retired soldiers in Judaea—you could make a way station for them."

"You've been thinking about this, haven't you?" I couldn't help asking.

"I know my husband isn't the sort to lie idle." A laugh. "But at least you could run a place where the war stories can be told in comfort!"

I did buy a wine shop, though I wasn't much good at running it. What did I know about how to store wine and keep mice out of storerooms? The part I did best was toss out the rowdy drunks; everything else I left to a capable widow who could have run a naval fleet, never mind a wine shop, so I left her to it and soon the days were empty again. I made a stab at working leather, then—made my girls a pair of slippers apiece that fell apart on their first wearing. Wasn't any good at working leather, or smithing, or any of the other pastimes Mirah suggested. I wasn't any good at *peace*. And before I knew it, two years had passed and I was still dreaming of the legions. The legions and my mother's noncommittal words.

I had letters from Titus, who gave me news of his own family—and of Antinous. Antinous, still the Emperor's perfumed boy, and that stabbed like a fresh wound. I'd had some vague but vibrant hope that one day I'd turn around and see Antinous on my doorstep; free of Hadrian, free of everything. I'd have flung my arms about him with all the joy in the world . . . but I didn't see him. I didn't see my son, and maybe I never would. Why should he come back to me? I was a bitter, aging legionary with bloody hands and a cruel tongue; I'd failed at running a wine shop or even making a pair of shoes, and I'd failed my son. Why should Antinous give me any thought at all?

Two years, then approaching three. Dinah turned thirteen, fourteen, flowering into her monthly blood with Chaya starting right behind her as though she were too afraid to be left in childhood while her sister advanced ahead. "You're women now," Mirah told them, though the only difference their new status made was that Mirah stopped wearing her hair loose in the evenings the way I'd always liked it. "It's not fitting in a mother of grown girls," she said briskly, and she bustled about in dark gowns that hid her lithe slenderness and made her look like a dowager. She smiled at me tolerantly when I said that I missed seeing the fall of her russet hair at night, and I started going to my wine shop in the evenings. Simon met me there sometimes and I would see his eyes on me, shrewd and thoughtful. "Do you still dream of the legions?" he asked once.

"No."

Simon held me in his gaze. He had eyes like Hadrian's, bottomless and deep-socketed, and the beard was like Hadrian's too, and his restless way of moving. Simon could intimidate people with that burning energy and those deep-set eyes, but I'd learned to lie under Hadrian's gaze, and I stared back until my old friend shrugged.

"I told you it would pass."

"You did," I said. "Join me at the bathhouse tomorrow to spar?"

"No, I've my own affairs to handle." I didn't know what those affairs were. Simon was no patriarch to laze in the courtyard with scrolls and grandchildren.

I didn't ask. I should have.

It was after he'd departed that I heard that the Emperor was to visit Judaea. Perhaps next year, maybe the one after that. "After he travels through Parthia."

"Corrupt boy-fucker," someone snickered from behind me, and I stood up and swung. God knows I'd called Hadrian worse, and to his face—but I swung my fists in his defense anyway, or maybe Antinous's defense, and I broke a man's jaw and his hand before the widow I employed managed to get her hissing imprecations through my rage. "It's your shop," she said, eyeing me with what I realized was dislike. "But you'll never turn a profit if you beat the customers!"

I looked at the drinkers sitting at my tables. Two or three retired legionaries dicing in a corner, but the rest were men of Judaea, hard-eyed and hostile as they looked at me. I turned and slouched out, and behind I heard a soft, contemptuous mutter. "Romans and their fists!" I could have turned and started swinging again, but if I came home with skinned knuckles one more time, Mirah would just look at me in disappointment—or worse yet, indulgence. Or she wouldn't notice at all, because she was wrapped in her prayers. So I sat down in the street outside with my back to a wall, stinging hands dangling useless between my knees. I couldn't go home because my wife would be singing softly throughout the house, and the girls would be chattering in the Aramaic they spoke more than they spoke Latin. All three of them so happy, all of them *home*.

And I was so wretchedly lonely I sometimes thought it would kill me.

CHAPTER 10

ANNIA

A.D. 128, Spring
Rome

"I look ridiculous," Marcus said.

Annia propelled him along the passage. "Yes."

"That's all I am to you. A joke in a silly costume!"

"Just make my mother laugh, Marcus? She's hardly so much as smiled yet. I thought maybe . . ." A gesture at Marcus's ceremonial garb, which he'd donned for his first performance as one of the Salii. The leaping priests of Mars were supposed to be warriors of old, and the antique breastplate and the red cloak weren't so bad, but the spiked helmet looked like a phallus, and the tunic was bloused and flounced and embroidered within an inch of its life. "Just make my mother laugh, and I'll owe you a boon." Any boon would be worth a smile from her mother, who was still recovering from childbed. The twins had come so hard, and the fever afterward had hit so swiftly.

She's well now, Annia thought, towing Marcus along again. *I just have to make her happy.*

Annia's mother *did* smile just a little as they came into her chamber and Marcus doffed his spiked headdress. "What have we here?" she exclaimed. "A leaping priest on the verge of his debut?"

"It's a very great honor, my grandfather tells me," Marcus sighed. "But nobody *understands* the ritual. Ovid wrote about it, and even he didn't understand it."

Annia rejoiced then, because her mother laughed outright. "Will you practice it for us, nevertheless? If I'm not to be at the festival—"

Marcus seized a tasseled cushion and struck a pose. "Imagine this is a shield fallen from the heavens during the reign of Numa Pompilius—"

"I'll take the baby so you can clap," Annia volunteered to her mother, settling the softly gurgling bundle against one arm the way the wet nurse had shown her. Marcus went through his ritual jigging with absolute gravitas, and by the end, Annia's mother was helpless with laughter. "What does all that gibberish in the song even mean?"

"I'm not sure," Marcus confessed, straightening. "Cicero attempted a translation and didn't make much headway. There's a line—a corrupted line, I think—that might mean 'I shall be as a kiss to grief.'"

Annia's mother looked at him a moment, and then suddenly pulled him into a hug. "And so you are," she said softly. "So you are."

Annia smiled down into the baby's blankets. "Can I take Fadilla to the festival? I won't drop her, I promise!"

"I'm sure you won't, because you're an excellent older sister. But Fadilla stays here." Faustina took the little bundle back into her arms, another smile lighting her face. Aurelia Fadilla, Annia's new baby sister, and thank the *gods* she was thriving. She'd been born first of twins, and the boy who followed lived only an hour.

That was why Annia's mother had lain so quiet in her bed this past month.

"You really should be my brother, you know," Annia told Marcus later. "My parents adore you."

He looked exasperated. "I am not going to be your brother, and that is final!"

To Annia's surprise, the rites of the Salii weren't as ridiculous as she thought. She could pick out Marcus at once among the twelve identically garbed boys. The others were about as nimble as cows, but Marcus went at it with steady grace and a serious expression. He did everything like that, Annia thought, whether it was his lessons, a game of *trigon*, or an absurd religious ritual. "I want to do things well," he'd explained to her. "Even if I don't win." Annia hadn't seen the point of doing something well if you weren't going to win, but maybe Marcus was right after all.

"Well done, young Verissimus!" the Emperor shouted down, able to applaud now that his arm was well out of its sling, and turned to Marcus's beaming grandfather. "When I leave on my travels, send me word on how his studies progress. He shows promise."

The Salii performed their leaping dances on each successive day, but it was the enormous final banquet at the Temple of Mars that everyone looked forward to. Marcus made a brief appearance, when the boy priests cast their wreaths to the banqueting couch that was supposed to belong to Mars himself (as if a god were going to just drop in for some wine and some roast parrot!), and Marcus's wreath landed right around the brow of the god's statue.

"You did that on purpose," Annia said when he came sliding out into the garden.

"I didn't, I swear!" Marcus took off the silly helmet, now that they were out of sight of all the feasting adults inside. "I hate being the center of attention. I felt silly."

"You didn't look it." Annia made a jump at an overhanging tree branch, swinging from her hands.

He tilted his head at her. "Will you let go of that?"

"Why?" She grinned down at him. "I like being taller than you." When she turned nine, Marcus had shot up in height suddenly, so his eyes were level with her own.

Marcus cleared his throat. "Annia, about that boon you owe me—"

"Watch out," she groaned, seeing a familiar stocky figure come storming along the twilit path. "It's Brine-Face." She dropped down from the branch, but before she could even call out a good insult, Pedanius flattened Marcus with one punch.

"Get up!" he shouted, and his face was scarlet. "Get up, you prancing ass, you looked like a fool out there. You in your penis helmet—"

Oh, Hades. Annia went for him, letting out a yell, but Brine-Face turned and shoved her so hard she tumbled off her feet. "Get up!" Pedanius tried to kick Marcus, but Marcus managed to roll out of the way, grabbing Pedanius's foot. Brine-Face dropped a knee on Marcus's chest and sent his fist smashing into Marcus's face again, and Annia saw blood. "You took *my* place in the Salii, my grandfather said I'd have that place, and the Emperor gave it to *you*—"

Marcus's fist shot upward, and he caught Brine-Face a good clip on the jaw. Annia cheered, scrambling up, but Pedanius just doubled up his own fist and swung again. "What'd you promise the Emperor, Bum-Boy? What's he giving you next—"

Annia flung herself on her enemy's back, locking her arms about his neck, and Marcus took the opportunity to plug a fist into Pedanius's ribs. Pedanius yelled, and then he yelled again on a higher note when Annia sank her teeth into his ear. That was when she felt a strong hand at her neck.

"I don't know who I should I be rescuing here," an amused voice said. Annia looked up at Antinous, who was trying to look stern and failing as he hauled Annia off Brine-Face and then Brine-Face off Marcus. "Young Pedanius, you seem to be getting the worst of things."

"I was not!"

"Were too," Marcus mumbled around his bloody lip.

"I was beating you to a pulp, you sniveling—"

Annia lunged at Pedanius again. "You're the one sniveling," she yelled, as Antinous held her back. "Don't you *dare* say we began it this time, you hit my cousin *first*—"

"He took my place," Pedanius snarled, for once too incensed to try to shift the blame. "He took my place with the Emperor!"

"Easy—" Antinous had Annia by the neck of her dress, but she lashed out with a foot and got Brine-Face square in the knee.

"See?" Pedanius howled. "She's a barbarian, she started it—"

"I did *not* start it!" Annia shrieked. "You're always coming at Marcus and me, and someday I am going to make you *sorry*—"

"Calm down, Annia." Antinous ignored the shouting, giving Pedanius a little shake. "I saw you go for them first, you little bully. It's not how a man of Rome behaves, and you might not have your toga yet but you're old enough to behave like a man."

Annia exhaled furious vindication, but Pedanius just sneered. "*You're* not a man at all, just the Emperor's catamite. Filthy little Greek he likes to fuck—"

"Don't you call him that!" Marcus shouted, and Annia pulled her foot back for another kick, but Antinous overrode them. His face was still and hard as a statue, and just as lovely.

"Call me what you like, boy," he said quietly. "But do not insult the Emperor."

"You don't dare speak to me that way," Pedanius bristled. "You're a whore. And everybody knows he'll throw you in the gutter with the other whores when you're too much older, because he only wants young ones sucking his—"

"Go whine to your grandfather." Antinous gave him a clip on the ear like swatting a dog, and Brine-Face stumbled back with a yelp. "Don't insult the Emperor again, and leave off bullying children. Hear me, boy?"

Pedanius tried to draw himself up proudly as he scurried up the path, but Annia let out a derisive hoot. Antinous gave her a clip on the ear, too. "That's enough out of you. Taunt a bully, and he'll just come back for revenge."

"Brine-Face always comes back anyway," Annia stated.

Antinous looked rather amused at her grim tone. "Why is that?"

"Gods know," Marcus said wearily. "I think it's fated. Pedanius Fuscus against Annia and me—the Greeks against the Trojans—"

"Don't be silly," Annia snorted. "He hates us because *you* got to join the Salii, and I whacked his hand with a mallet. And because he's a bullying coward."

"I won't argue about the bullying part," Antinous agreed. "And I thought he always seemed a nice lad . . ."

"Everyone thinks that. He puts on a good show." Annia turned to Marcus. "And if it's Trojans against Greeks, at least make us the Greeks! The Greeks *win*!"

Marcus scowled, and Antinous laughed outright. "Hell's gates," he said, and shook his head. "I wouldn't take on you two brawlers for all the gold in Egypt."

"You're going to Egypt with the Emperor, aren't you?" Annia felt a wistful pang in her chest.

"Well, Numidia first. And Parthia, and Judaea. Then Egypt."

Antinous tucked a lock of her hair back behind her ear. "Shall I bring you back an obelisk?"

"You'd have to bring it in pieces," Marcus said, ready to start dissecting the technical difficulties of transporting an obelisk. Annia just looked up at Antinous, standing there like a young god, his rich hair catching the lamplight.

"I'll miss you," she blurted out. Antinous coming to pay respects to her father and always taking time to toss a ball with Annia or teach her *latrunculi* . . . Antinous helping her clean up the latest bowl she'd broken so no one would find the pieces . . . Antinous giving her a wink across the room at boring parties . . .

"You won't miss me," Antinous said lightly. "You'll be too busy getting tall and beautiful, and when I come back you won't even remember who I am."

If I get tall and beautiful enough, can I marry you? Annia thought. Not that Antinous would ever love anybody but the Emperor. Anybody could see that—it shone out of his face like sunlight.

"I won't forget you," she said instead. "No matter how long you're gone."

"And I'll think of you every day, little brawler." Antinous opened his arms to give her a hug. "The very first friend I ever made in Rome. I won't forget that."

Annia hugged him back fiercely. "Promise?"

"On the River Styx." He bent down to kiss her cheek. Annia turned her head at the very last moment, so his lips brushed hers.

"Ha!" she crowed. "So you *do* kiss girls!"

"Only the most beautiful ones." Antinous laughed again, a sound like a ripple of gold coins.

Marcus looked at Antinous, outraged. "You got my boon!"

Antinous gave Marcus a man-to-man nod. "She'll get round to you," he whispered. "Trust me—just wait a few years." Annia poked her tongue out at them both, and Antinous grinned. "Come inside, you little gladiators, before you get in any more trouble."

"*We undertake to be burned by fire, to be bound in chains, to be beaten by rods"*—Annia chanted the gladiator oath, slinging one arm around Marcus and the other around Antinous—*"and to die by the sword!"*

"I have no intention of being burned by fire or bound in chains," Marcus objected. "It sounds *most* uncomfortable . . ."

ANTINOUS

"Not that one doesn't appreciate an ecstatic welcome"—Empress Sabina looked out at the men and women of Carthage, cheering in the deluge of rain—"but what have we done to merit it?"

"There has been no rain to speak of in Carthage for nearly five years," said Hadrian, and began to reel off the drought's effect on various varieties of local crops. Of course he had all the facts at his fingertips, Antinous thought with a smile. There seemed to be nothing on earth the Emperor did not know, and yet he was always questing for more. More knowledge, more understanding, more insight—it enchanted Antinous. His own brain was uncomplicated as a cup of water by comparison, and yet it was to him that this restless, complex, insatiable mind kept returning. *You have earned the love of a man like this,* he reminded himself. *That is cause for pride—no matter what rude little boys like Pedanius Fuscus or condescending old men like his grandfather think.*

The Imperial party had only just disembarked in Carthage when the sky opened. Crowds in Rome would have called it a bad omen, but the men and women of Carthage danced and called out Hadrian's name.

Antinous couldn't help it. He took off into the crowd with a whoop, seizing an aged matron by the hands and whirling her in a circle. She beamed and hung a garland about his neck; Antinous kissed her on both cheeks and then found his hands grabbed by a pair of little boys who stood with their mouths open under the rain like a pair of baby birds. He opened his mouth too, and the drops tasted like sweet, cool freedom. Freedom from Rome; from avid eyes; from disapproving stares and quivering nostrils and sneering voices calling him the Emperor's he-bitch.

"Antinous!" Hadrian was shouldering through the crowd after him, half-alarmed and half-laughing as the Carthaginians started to hang garlands on him too. "Bringer of rain!" the call went up. "Hadrian Caesar, bringer of rain!"

"They think I control the rain?" Hadrian asked later, half-amused and half-outraged. "Really. I design walls to contain the Empire; I entirely revitalize the legions; I erect so many new roads and temples that my footsteps might as well spring up marble columns the way Persephone's were said to spring up flowers. And after all that, I am hailed for a cloudburst?"

"Acclaim is acclaim," Empress Sabina pointed out as Antinous brought a towel to drape about the Emperor's wet curls. She had danced in the rain too, wiggling her toes in the mud—not the Empress of Rome, not the Greek queen in her diadem, but simply a woman enjoying herself, whirling through the raindrops with such glee that she looked no older to Antinous than little Annia.

"I'd rather be acclaimed for something I actually *did*," Hadrian grumbled. "After Carthage we'll travel to Numidia—I'll review the legions. Then back across the sea before the autumn storms, to winter in Greece." Hadrian captured Antinous's hand in his own. "We can take part in the Mysteries again!"

"Are you sure?" A thread of anxiety disrupted Antinous's contentment. He brushed Hadrian's hair back to feel his forehead—warm, even after the cool drench of the rain outside. Ever since that long stint of bed rest recovering from the broken collarbone, these bouts of sickness seemed to come and go, bringing fevers and spells of nausea . . . And there had been that troubling redness that patched and hardened the skin of his arms so painfully. "There is so much walking at the Mysteries. If you were to have a relapse of fever on the road—"

"Bother my health." Hadrian gave him a slanted look, warning him not to speak of it further before others. He had always projected such endless energy; he hadn't wanted anyone but his physicians to know when his health troubled him. "You worry like a mother!"

"You never listened to your mother," Empress Sabina interjected. "You just might listen to Antinous."

"Promise me," Antinous persisted, despite the unspoken warning. "Promise me you will not overstretch yourself?"

"A small promise." Hadrian twined his brown hand about Antinous's neck and kissed him, though the chamber was full of guards and courtiers. Antinous heard the Praetorians stir uncomfortably, but he made himself ignore it. *You do not need the world or its approval, not as long as you have him.*

Away from the Eternal City, at least they had a smaller and less openly disapproving audience. The Emperor had a skeleton entourage on this round of traveling. The young and adventurous of the court still scrambled to stay at his side—Antinous was amused to see flamboyant Lucius Ceionius declaring himself much taken with the glories of Carthage, acquiring triplet Nubian slave girls who followed him about dressed in nothing but gold anklets. But old Servianus and any number of worthies who usually fought to travel at the Emperor's side had stayed in Rome.

Because of the Emperor's whore, thought Antinous. No matter how often he told himself the insults didn't matter, they still made him go rigid on the inside. Not just from pain, but from the effort it took not to flinch.

At least here the contempt was quieter. And whenever the eyebrows *did* rise—when Hadrian captured Antinous's hand as they rode side by side, or received a deputation while lying with his head in Antinous's lap—Empress Sabina fixed the starers with a cool gaze until the grimaces disappeared. *May all the gods love her*, Antinous thought, *because I certainly do.*

Carthage, and the lands around it. Long loops on horseback through that sparkling, never-ending rain. "A cut in taxation for those who would utilize all this outlying land," Hadrian decided. "For those who cannot be urged to farm the outlands, there will work on the walls."

"More walls?" Antinous asked. "You're mad for walls, Caesar!"

"I intend to mark the borders of Numidia and Africa, just as I marked the border of Britannia and Germania. I'm reviewing the stone quarries; there should be abundant granite—"

"Have you considered using mud-bricks?" Empress Sabina perched on the edge of the table to peer at the plans. "Might fare better under this heat."

"She's right, Caesar," Antinous was quick to chime in. Hadrian gave a blink, and Antinous held his gaze. How many times had he said it to his royal lover? *Married to one of the most intelligent women I've yet to meet, and you've limited her to waving at crowds and sitting alone in a villa?*

Not anymore. Antinous didn't know what had made Hadrian decide to bring the Empress, but he was glad of it. *I owe you so much, Lady,* he thought, watching her slim fingers trace the map where Hadrian planned his wall. *I will do what I can to pay it back.*

"You may have a point, Vibia Sabina." Hadrian said grudgingly, and tapped the map where she had traced a line. "Mud-bricks. I shall investigate."

Sabina smiled her thanks behind Hadrian's head, and Antinous dropped her a wink.

A sunny, rain-scented spring saw them through Carthage, and then the Imperial party moved on. The winds of Numidia smelled of sand and cinnamon, ruffling the hair and sparking the blood, taking breath from the lungs and firing the soul . . . It was on a sweltering day late in the month of Juno that Antinous and the Empress watched Hadrian make inspection of the legions.

"He's something rather special to see, isn't he?" Empress Sabina said. "I haven't watched him address the legions before."

"He's a wonder," Antinous said softly.

They both fell silent, watching: the Empress from her Imperial carriage, Antinous astride his bay colt at her window. For days they had watched the Third Augusta go through its paces, and the men stood in serried rows waiting their emperor's verdict. And striding up and down before the men, Hadrian: huge and powerful in a spit-polished breastplate and greaves like any soldier in the field, his hands as callused as any that gripped a sword in the crowd below. And he was bellowing at them, not in rage but in fierce approval.

"Military exercises," he shouted, "have their own rules, and if anything is added or subtracted from them, the exercise becomes too insignificant or too difficult—"

"I've heard that before," Sabina said. "From who?"

Antinous's stomach twisted. "Guess."

"—and of all the difficult exercises," Hadrian bellowed on, "the most difficult was the one *you* performed! Throwing the javelin in full battle dress." He paused, eyes raking the crowd, and he gave a slow salute of his clenched fist. "I approve of your eagerness!"

The men were too well disciplined to cheer, but Antinous saw a fierce ripple go through them. Hadrian grinned, raking a hand back through his hair, and the resemblance tore Antinous's heart in its similarity.

"Vix," the Empress said slowly. "*Vix* said that, about the javelin exercises. At Eleusis . . ."

"Yes."

Hadrian had moved on to single out a Spanish cohort, something to do with a wall reinforcing a new fortress. "A wall requiring much work, and you constructed it in not much longer a time than it takes to build a wall of turf!" Hadrian clapped their centurion on the shoulder, nearly flattening the man. Another of Vix's gestures, Antinous thought, stomach still twisting knots in itself.

"I commend Catullinus, my legate! Because he directed you to this exercise, which took on the appearance of a real battle . . ." Hadrian went on striding up and down, overflowing restless energy, leaving men shuffling and beaming in his wake, and Antinous's heart stabbed because it was his father all over. The blunt soldierly phrases instead of the scholarly metaphors; the striding and the bellowing and that stabbing gesture of the outstretched fist—

Vix to the life, Antinous thought, and his eyes stung.

"It must be a trifle odd," the Empress mused, "seeing your lover turn into your father."

Antinous gave a shaky little laugh. "I should be used to it, Lady. He does this whenever he addresses the legions."

"Does he, now?"

"Yes. They eat it up." The men weren't quite cheering, but they were banging their spears softly against their shields to the rough cadence of Hadrian's voice.

"However." Hadrian stopped with a ferocious scowl, and the beating of spears stopped. "The cavalry skirmish did *not* please me. A cavalryman should ride across from cover and pursue with caution—"

The cavalrymen in question looked red-faced and determined, clearly ready to charge off and try again on the spot. Antinous had seen that expression too, in the Praetorians that his father had dressed down with that same benign ferocity. He had to look down at his horse's mane again, biting fiercely on the inside of his cheek because he was not used to it, no matter how many times he watched Hadrian address the legions. *I want my father,* he thought, and the sight of his horse's mane under his fingers went blurry.

"Hadrian must not realize he's doing it," Sabina said.

Antinous blinked his welling eyes. "Oh, he does." How many times had Hadrian said it? *I have no love for that crude lout who once dared call you a son, but he is the ideal Roman legionary made flesh.* So when Hadrian addressed the legions, he looked to the legions' best example of how to appear. All very logical, really. Except that it was like a spike through Antinous's eyes, seeing his father appear like a mirage from nowhere.

Oh, Vix, Antinous thought with the familiar anguish sharp on his tongue. *Do you think of me at all? Or did you finally get a son of your own blood from Mirah—a son to make you proud instead of shamed?*

"Tell me . . ." The Empress interrupted Antinous's bitter thoughts. He looked at her, running a finger along the ivory handle of her fan, and her face was somber. "Does Hadrian still hate your father?"

Do you find his name as painful to say as I do, Lady? Antinous thought. *I think you do.*

"The Emperor has learned from his example," Antinous temporized. "His ideas—not just about how to present himself to the legions, but how to train them in peacetime, keep them occupied and fit." The notes for the legionary manual that Vix had left behind: Hadrian had gone through them page by page in the days just after Vix stormed out, mocking every line—"The spelling, dear gods, was that barbarian utterly illiterate?" But he had had those notes compiled, documented, polished into the manual now distributed to legions across the Empire.

A painful pride had risen in Antinous when he looked at that manual, wondering if Vix would ever know his enemy had made his dream real. "But yes, Lady—despite all that, Hadrian still hates him."

"I suppose he would." Empress Sabina was still staring down at her fan. "Hadrian doesn't forget an insult."

"I think he would forgive the insult to himself. But he will never forgive my father for insulting *me*."

Sabina's eyes lifted toward Antinous then. Her attention was like a weight. "Have you forgiven him?"

"Oh, yes." Antinous felt another twist of pain go through him like a spear. If Vix were somehow transported here before him, he'd drop to his knees weeping and beg for his love. *I would do anything to feel him thump my shoulder and call me "Narcissus" again.* "But the Emperor doesn't forgive those who offend me as easily as I do."

"Is that why you don't tell him half the insults you hear?" the Empress asked. "Don't look startled, Antinous. I have ears—back in the Eternal City, Servianus never stopped going on about filthy cata-mites, and you never once mentioned it to Hadrian. Or those courtiers sniggering that you should join Lucius Ceionius when he dressed up as Jupiter, be his Ganymede with a gold cup—"

"I don't tell him, because Hadrian would kill them," Antinous said simply.

Sabina looked amused despite herself. "And here I thought you were utterly blind to his faults."

"I know that he is a dangerous man." Wasn't that part of the appeal? The way Hadrian's eyes glittered when he was angry, the way his fist curled slowly on the arm of his chair—it could send Antinous's pulse racing as much as his smiles. The edge behind the charm, the power in those arms that held him so gently. "He'd kill on my behalf; I know that. And I love him, so it's my duty to see he never does. Save others from him; save him from himself. That night with my father, he was a breath away from murder." Sweet gods, but Antinous still had night-mares about that moment! He woke with a scream choked off in his throat, just at the moment when Hadrian *swung* that *gladius* and sent Vix's head spinning to the tiles.

"But you were able to stop him," Sabina said softly. "Whenever I dream of it, I wake up thanking the gods that you were there."

Antinous was surprised. "You dream of that night too?"

"Oh, yes."

He looked at her: as tanned as Hadrian from the Numidian sun, a dusting of freckles across her small nose, henna tattoos on her hands, and a patterned veil thrown over that elegant shorn head. "Tell me something, Lady," he said, diffident. "Are we friends?"

"How can anyone resist being your friend?" The Empress smiled, which was not quite an answer. In her way she was as oblique as Hadrian. Another restless questing mind; definitely not the clear cup of water Antinous knew himself to be. *Had you been born a man, would he have loved you instead of me?* Antinous wondered.

Maybe. Maybe not. Perhaps complicated questing minds needed cups of cool water in which to calm themselves. Needed uncomplicated sorts like Antinous. *And my father.*

Antinous was still glad Sabina had not been born a man.

"Forgive me for being presumptuous, Lady," he dared to say, his voice gentle. "But you are lonely. I see it every day."

She blinked, surprised. Perhaps because he had never said anything so intimate before. Antinous wondered how he dared now. Perhaps because the wear of traveling had ground away the stifling formality of Rome. Perhaps because she had become his ally, his lover's wife so unexpectedly deciding to befriend him when she might easily have made his life miserable.

Or perhaps because they had danced in the rain at Carthage, and he had seen exactly what his father saw in her.

"You think me lonely?" Her eyebrows arched, very imperious, but Antinous was not intimidated anymore by *imperious.*

"I was lonely myself for so long," he said. "I know the signs. And if you will forgive me for saying it," he added, looking down at his horse's mane, "you look even lonelier when anyone mentions Vix."

"Do I?"

"Yes." A breath. "You love him, Lady."

The Empress of Rome gave a slow blink of her lashes, confirming nothing and denying nothing, but Antinous was used to seeing past these Imperial faces with their expressions like shields.

"I knew it even before he said those things about you, the night he discovered me with the Emperor." Antinous shifted a little in his saddle. "You hide it well, Lady, but he was never one for concealing anything. His eyes used to follow you like a lion's."

She was silent a moment, looking away over the ranked legionaries, but Antinous saw the moment when she gave in to curiosity. ". . . Like a lion follows its prey?"

"No, that's how he'd look at his wife. Hungry, a little wistful sometimes, like she was out of reach." Poor Mirah, not even aware of her competition. "Vix watched you like a lion watches a lioness."

"And how does a lion watch a lioness?" Sabina didn't even try to pretend nonchalance this time.

"He doesn't need to tend her, because she hunts her own prey. He doesn't need to shield her, because she kills her own enemies. He doesn't need to look for her, because she's always at his side." Antinous couldn't help grinning. "And the mating is fierce."

That earned him a cool glance that could have come straight from Hadrian. "You are impudent."

"Apologies, Lady. I do not mean to be. I only see it because it is what I feel every day—but for Caesar." Antinous picked up her small hand and kissed it, making enormous soulful eyes. "Forgive me?"

She laughed, rapping him over the head with her fan, and he found himself laughing too. He had never made friends easily—before Hadrian he mostly had lovers or would-be lovers, and after Hadrian he had those who despised him and those who sought to use him.

But I have a friend now, he thought, looking at the Empress of Rome. *A true friend.* It warmed him as much as one of Hadrian's kisses.

An enormous roar went up from the men of the Third Augusta: Hadrian had finished his speech. He stood fist raised, sunlight blazing off his breastplate, and then he bounded down among the men. They drew back a little, awed and still cheering, but he moved among them like a colossus. *Teasing and joking and generally being irresistible,* Antinous thought.

"Tell me—" Sabina began to descend from her carriage, and Antinous swung off his horse to hand her down. "Would Hadrian ever take Vix back, if you asked him?"

"He would do almost anything that I asked him." Which was why he tried so hard to ask for nothing. "But even if I asked for my father to be allowed back, and the Emperor agreed, Vix wouldn't come."

"Still—why not ask? We're to travel to Judaea at some point."

"Oh . . ." Antinous ruffled a hand through his hair. "If we travel to Judaea, I think I will be far too terrified to see him."

"Why?"

"Because what if he kicks me away?" Looking down at her, standing at his side and barely coming to his shoulder. "I'll likely never travel to Judaea again, after all, and he'll likely never leave it. If he spat on me there, it would be the end of all things."

Empress Sabina said nothing. But she slipped her hand into his arm, and his sore heart eased. She was one of those rare people who was not afraid to let a silence fall, he thought, and he relaxed in the quiet comfort of her presence. By the time Hadrian bounded up, Antinous was able to offer a wholly sunny smile.

"Ha, I like a good speech!" Hadrian seized Antinous around the neck, kissing him heartily. "Shall I tell you something else, my star? I've just had word the Senate voted to give me the title of Pater Patriae."

"What, again?" Antinous knew they'd voted to give him that all-illustrious title before. Very insincerely. "Do you mean to accept this time, Caesar?" It gave him a slightly wistful pang. *I miss my father so much, and my lover becomes father of all the world.* A sign from the gods, perhaps?

"You know, I think I shall." Hadrian sounded delighted. "I don't like titles I haven't earned—Emperor Augustus turned down the title too, until he felt he merited the honor. But by now, I think I *have* earned it."

Empress Sabina studied him, smiling. "I think you are right."

Antinous looked at his ally, his friend, his lover's wife, and wished he could give her—what? *Happiness? Freedom? My father's love?* He tugged Hadrian's head down instead, whispering in his ear.

The Emperor looked surprised. Antinous nodded. "That's what I want," he said firmly. Not something for himself. Something for Sabina.

Hadrian shrugged, turning back to his wife. "What if I made you Augusta at the same time as I become Pater Patriae, Vibia Sabina?"

She looked startled again—twice in one conversation, Antinous thought with glee. That had to be a record for the enigmatic Empress of Rome. "Me, Augusta? Have *I* earned it?" she asked, sounding wry.

Hadrian looked meditative, and Antinous didn't nudge him this time. "I think you have," he said. "Your work with the share farmers in Africa, bringing their complaints to my attention, and your advice on the border walls . . . My Augusta," Hadrian repeated, sounding it out, then looked at Antinous. "My Augusta and my star. What else does a father of his people need?" He began moving toward his quarters, one arm about Antinous, Sabina gliding in their wake. "Where shall we go after Numidia, eh? Greece first, I think, but after that? I think Judaea . . ."

Not yet, Antinous thought with a quick catch in his chest. *Let's follow the winds first, the winds that smell like sand and cinnamon. Follow them anywhere, just not Judaea!*

"Judaea," Hadrian decided. "After Greece."

Then let Greece last forever, Antinous thought as his heart kicked. Because he was not ready to face his father. Not now.

Maybe not ever.

VIX

Bethar

There's nothing worse than a girl who thinks she's in love. Dinah was fourteen now, dreamy and dewy and mooning over the blacksmith's boy from the south quarter of Bethar, and Chaya was sullen because she didn't have a boy to moon over yet. I finally warned that if they didn't stop their sighing and squabbling I'd strap them both. That sent them sniffling off to their chamber, making me think of a little red-haired girl boasting that she never cried, not ever, and Mirah went on calmly eating.

"They're young and filled with storms," she said. "It means they'll be ready to marry soon." I could see my wife settling back in her chair, ready to discuss every eligible son-in-law in Bethar, and I pushed back from the table.

"I'll be gone a day or two."

Mirah brightened. "Are you going with Uncle Simon? He so wants to speak with you . . ."

"No." I paused. "I thought I'd go to Lydda. Thereabouts."

Her face fell. She knew what I wanted to see there. "It will only make you unhappy, Vix."

I cut her off. "What does Simon want to talk with me about?" My friend had been traveling lately, speaking vaguely of unnamed friends. I'd offered to come with him, but Simon looked at me a moment and then gave a noncommittal refusal. "Where's he going this time?"

Mirah gave me the same blank look her uncle had. "I don't know."

I grunted, reaching for my *gladius*, and then I hesitated for a moment before I reached for my lion skin. I'd given off wearing it in Judaea—"You look like some pagan demigod," Mirah scolded me—and besides, the pelt was old and patchy. Pathetic. But I set my jaw and flung it over one shoulder, and Mirah looked at it and set her cup down with a rattle.

"*Why* are you going?" she said, low-voiced. "Why can't you stay and talk about who the girls should marry, and if we should hire a new doorman for our gate with the streets getting so restless? Why won't you stop pacing and scowling and wanting to revisit your legion days?" She spoke Aramaic, because she spoke it everywhere and that included speaking to me, even though I still thought and spoke and dreamed in Latin. And right now, it angered me. "Stay, Vix."

"I won't be more than a night." I heard Dinah and Chaya squabbling in the next room, and I raised my voice. "*Hell's gates, will you two stop mewling!*" And I banged out of the house before either of them could start to weep in earnest.

Girls in love. Is it any wonder I fled to visit my old legion, now that the Tenth Fidelis was stationed in Judaea?

I kept my hand to the hilt of my *gladius* as I walked. I didn't know what had changed in the last few years, but the heat seemed to linger in the streets, and it made throats scratchy and tempers sore. I saw more fights break out in my wine shop; I saw men clustering on street corners stabbing fingers at the air as they argued some point that I never heard because such conversations fell silent whenever I passed. Years ago when rebellion had roiled across Cyrene and Cyprus, Mirah had said that Romans looked at her with distrustful eyes and flung mud at her in the market. These days the Jews flung mud at me when my back was turned, at the man who still looked like a Roman with his shaved chin and his *gladius*, and I didn't like to think what it meant.

I didn't know how to present myself at the legion's winter quarters, so I gave some muttered story about an old veteran's petition and plunged between the orderly rows of barracks, breathing in the familiar smell of a legion: leather and metal, sweat and horse dung. I pressed through, looking for the *principia* that sat at the core of any legion's camp, and then I threaded the lines of petitioners to the shrine at the far end. I stepped behind the screen and I stopped because she was waiting for me.

"Hello," I said softly, and my hand rose of its own accord to caress her. The legion's eagle, the most precious of her standards, a proud winged bird staring at me with fierce pride from her perch on the standard pole. "I carried you," I told her, stroking the cool wings. "Do you remember your old aquilifer?"

Of course she didn't. I'd carried this same eagle in my hands, and I still carried her in my heart, but she stared out proud and uncaring. I was infinitely replaceable, just one of many beneath the wings she spread across the Empire. She didn't serve me; I served her—and the moment I'd heard the Tenth Fidelis was coming from the Parthian border to be stationed in Judaea, I'd yearned to see her again. Maybe I'd thought it would cure me. But she just gave me her arrogant stare, lovely and unforgiving, and my hand fell away from her proud head. I pushed out of the shrine with my eyes blurred, and that was when an unbelieving voice called my name.

"Vercingetorix?" Quick footsteps behind me, and I swiped a hasty hand across my eyes. "Vercingetorix the Red?"

"What?" I said, turning, and it came out in a growl.

"It *is* you, sir!" A centurion was coming toward me, a man with a broad dark face and an even broader grin. I fumbled for the name.

"Africanus?"

"That's right." To my surprise, he saluted. "You traded nearly a month's pay to my centurion to get me into your century when you first made rank. The first thing you said to me was that I had a damned unoriginal name."

"I did say that." He'd been a muscled youth then; now he had to be a man of forty with gray in his hair. When had we all started going gray?

"I'm up for Primus Pilus soon," he was saying proudly. "Like you, sir."

"No need to call me *sir*. I'm no legion man anymore. No Praetorian, either."

"We heard." He gave a cheerful leer. "You couldn't keep your hand out from under the Empress's skirts, was that it?"

I gave my best centurion's glower and was pleased to see him brace just a bit. "I'm just here to see the eagle, since she was near."

"Then you're still a legion man, sir. You should come to the barracks with me—there's plenty who remember you!"

"I haven't set foot on Tenth territory in more than fifteen years."

He looked at me quizzically. "You made the jump from legionary to aquilifer," he said as if explaining to an idiot. "Then centurion, then Primus Pilus, and then you'd have commanded the legion. Every boy who joins the Tenth Fidelis knows your name. 'Vercingetorix the Red, the man who made it all the way from the ranks to the commander's tent.' They invoke you in their prayers, hoping for your luck."

"Tell them they don't want my luck," I managed to say through my astonishment. "I never got the legion, did I?"

"You'd have had it if Trajan lived, bless his name." Africanus shrugged. "You know we still train with gladiator drills, not just your old century but all of them? And the Emperor approved the use of Parthian drill instructors the way you were always pestering about, and there's a regulation manual—"

My lips were stiff. "There is?"

He dragged me off with him, and there were men here who remembered my name, and boys who hadn't been born when I left the Tenth but still looked at me as though they'd expected me to be eight feet tall. They begged for stories of my old fights, and asked about Judaea: "Is it true they cut the cocks off their baby boys? The Emperor says he'll put a stop to that—"

"Good luck." I thought of Mirah's firebrand cousins. "And they don't cut the cocks off, they just take a slash at the skin—"

"I've heard things are tense here," Africanus said more seriously. "I've got a cousin somewhere in the Tenth Fratensis, and he says things are getting hot around Jerusalem's ruins."

"When is Jerusalem anything but hot?" I thought of the men who quarreled on the street corners in Bethar, and shivered.

I was borne off to the bathhouse where the steam and the sweat loosened tongues and the men asked what Empress Sabina was like under her skirts. "We've got a statue of her with the Emperor's in the *principia*, and if she's that stiff and stony in a bedroll—"

"She's not."

"Then what's she like?"

"Limber," I said, and there was lewd jeering. None for Hadrian, though. "The Emperor will review us when he comes back from Greece," Africanus said. "And he'll not find us lacking. You should hear what the Third Augusta said of him; everything investigated down to the last tent. He wasn't too proud to sleep and eat the way the legionaries did, either—"

No condemnation in their voices; no contempt for the man who had followed Trajan. They were a fit and sun-bronzed lot, clearly busy and content, and my heart ached. "Hadrian's a bastard," I said harshly, but they just shrugged.

"You screwed his wife. Sure, he's got a pretty boy he's buggering, but you can't expect an emperor to look the other way when you shaft his wife, can you?"

I stiffened, but if anyone remembered the little boy who had trotted after me on the Parthian campaigns, they didn't connect him with the Emperor's favorite.

I rode back to Bethar on a tide of rude jokes and good wishes.

When I approached with my wine-heavy head and my eagle-heavy heart, I saw Simon in the doorway, and I glowered.

"So Mirah told you I went to see the Tenth? You should have come with me. I *asked* you to when they first arrived, and you spat on the ground!"

"My niece," he said, "didn't tell me anything. But she's been crying, and normally that means you've been an ass."

I was sore, snappish, and snarling, in no mood to be scolded. "I know you never wanted me to marry Mirah," I snarled. "Hard to watch your favorite niece marry a man you used to whore with in your legion days; I understand that. But you don't care to remember your legion days, Simon ben Cosiba, so I'll be damned if I'll have them held against *me*. Because I love your niece. I came here for her, and I've *stayed* here for her, and bugger you to Hades and gone if you spit at me. Because if it weren't for Mirah, I'd take my swords and go back to the Tenth Fidelis in a heartbeat."

His voice was quiet. "Would you?"

"I'm not like you, Simon. I'm not anything but a soldier. I never was." My eyes stung, remembering the gleam of the eagle, the smell of the legion, the rough laughter and the familiar cameraderie. "Hell's gates, but I miss it."

He turned to go. "Maybe you don't have to miss it."

"The legion?"

"No. Being a soldier."

I barked out a bitter laugh. "What exactly do you propose I do?"

"You could still fight, Vix." Simon glanced over his shoulder, eyes gleaming dark in his bearded face, and once again he reminded me oddly of Hadrian. "Just not for Rome."

CHAPTER II

ANTINOUS

A.D. 128, Autumn
Eleusis

"Well, my star?" The smile in Hadrian's voice came clearly through the blackness of Antinous's closed eyes. "What did the *kykeon* show you this time?"

Antinous opened his eyes to the light of dawn. His head rested in the Emperor's lap, his lashes were tear-wet, and his mouth held a foul taste. He saw the massive tangling branches overhead of the oak tree—the same oak where he and Hadrian had lain together that first time at Eleusis. "Nothing," he said slowly. "I saw . . . nothing."

"No starry visions?" Hadrian stroked a hand through Antinous's hair.

"No." Antinous tried to swallow the sour taste on his tongue. Every muscle in his body hurt. "What did you see?"

"No terrors," the Emperor said softly. "Just your face."

I was the one to see terrors, Antinous thought, and his stomach roiled. How could that be? As soon as they had come to Athens for the winter, he had been every bit as eager as the Emperor to take the rites at Eleusis again. They had linked hands through the long night walks, washed each other's hair in the sea, and Antinous had exploded in laughter watching the Emperor try to hold his sacrificial piglet still. They had found the oak that was their tree, drunk the *kykeon* out of a single cup, and Antinous had swallowed eagerly, ready for that soul-widening bliss he remembered so well.

But this time there had been no starry void. There had been nothing but—blankness.

"Well, we can't catch the mind of the gods every time." Hadrian shifted Antinous's head off his lap with a kiss, already rising to return to the temple. "Better to dream of nothing than to dream of monstrous faces!"

No. *Nothing was not* nothing. The nothing had been darkness; lonely, swirling, lightless emptiness. Far more terrifying than any loom of monstrous faces. Antinous sat up, squeezing his eyes shut, and it was there again, black and implacable, pressing in from all sides—

Panic roared inside him, fast as a flame. He gagged, vomiting on hands and knees into the dry grass. *Get out of me*, he thought, his stomach jerking and heaving, and he did not know if he meant the darkness or the *kykeon* that had caused it. *Sweet gods, get out of me!*

"Easy." Hadrian steadied him, an arm about his shoulders. "You're shaking," he exclaimed, and pressed a hand to Antinous's cheek. "And you're ice-cold—"

"I fear I have seen the future." Antinous sat back on his heels, gasping as though he had sprinted a mile. His stomach still roiled, nauseated and voided, and his eyes burned. He didn't want to blink. If his eyes closed even for a flash, the black could rush back in. "I have seen the future, and it is a dark one."

He feared the Emperor would blanch—gods knew, Hadrian was superstitious; he'd study star charts and seek out strange rituals and buy magic charms from the east to test if they worked. But he tended to choose the omens he wanted to believe and those he did not, and this morning he was evidently in too good a humor to want it spoiled by darkness of any kind. "My moody star, don't borrow trouble!" Hadrian pulled Antinous's head against his chest, sounding fond. "It was just a dream."

Antinous burrowed into the Emperor's shoulder, trying to slow his racing heart. "You're right," he managed to say. "Just a dream." A dream brought on by a cup of pennyroyal and barley and strange herbs.

But he could not shake his foreboding, not for the rest of the rites at Eleusis, not for the serene winter they spent in Greece, not in the spring when they moved on to Ephesus. He would wake in the night under the comforting weight of Hadrian's arm and see swirling black. *The future*, he would think. *The future is empty.*

And then he would think, with increasing dread, *Whose future?*

He did not get his answer until summer, when Hadrian took them all to Antioch and set his sights at once on the great flat peak rearing up to the southern horizon. "I always meant to climb Mount Casius. To make sacrifice to Jupiter at the temple, during the sunrise hour when the sun shows itself only to the mountain's peak . . ."

"Oh, gods," Sabina had whispered to Antinous. "We're going up the mountain at dawn, aren't we?"

"We are," Antinous sighed. A dawn hike up a steep mountain—just the thing for a man with a tendency to fevers and joints that swelled!

But Hadrian was breathing easily enough at the summit, gazing out over the mountain's peak into the rolling gray mass of cloud. "One could see Jupiter himself from these heights!"

Antinous looked at the Imperial entourage panting and staggering up the mountain track behind them in the cool predawn darkness. "I think you killed your court."

"That is merely a bonus," Hadrian said, and they both laughed.

All across the barren stone outcroppings of the summit, Hadrian's courtiers were flinging themselves down. Empress Sabina was still on her feet, however, and Antinous came to offer her a water skin. She tipped it gratefully over the back of her neck, flushed rosy as a girl. "I used to be able to march at legion pace and never fall behind," she complained. "I've grown soft and useless!"

"Not useless, Lady." He smiled. "Beautiful."

"Flatterer." She put her hands to her back and stretched, lithe as a cat. "Good to see you smile, Antinous. You've been too solemn since the Mysteries."

His smile vanished, and he looked out at the swirling mass of clouds wrapping the peak. *Gray*, he told himself. *Not black.* It was no premonition; it was just cloud.

"Caesar!" A white-robed priest descended from the peak-roofed temple crowning the mountain's flat summit, and a flower-crowned bull had already been prepared, pawing at the stone. The rest of the Imperial entourage hastened into place as Hadrian strode forward, and Antinous heard a distant rumble of thunder as the priest effused. "—surely Caesar will strike a coin to commemorate his visit to our temple? Naturally we will erect a statue—"

"And another to our divine Empress," Antinous heard Lucius Ceionius proclaim. "Artemis, lady of the wild, as you were proclaimed in Aigeae! Carved as you stand here, I think."

"What, sweating and rumpled?" Sabina gave a low-voiced laugh, as Hadrian waved a hand in acceptance of the priest's flattery.

"Dewy and glorious," Lucius corrected. "Far above petty mortal women who would fuss over such things as dust and blood. I can see you, ice-white Phrygian marble with a moonstone diadem upon your brow. I would dress myself as Apollo to match you, gold glory to your silver allure . . ."

Amusement pierced Antinous's formless foreboding for a moment, and he leaned down to murmur in the Empress's ear. "Lucius is trying to seduce you."

"Since Eleusis," she agreed. "Very flattering at my age. Though one has to wonder if he has gone mad. Does he forget what happened to the last men accused of being too *informal* with me?"

"Perhaps the Emperor might be persuaded to look the other way?" Antinous said lightly, though he knew it unlikely. *I'm not sure he would allow that even if I were the one to ask it. Which is a pity, because I think you need a lover, Lady.*

The Empress looked at him as though she knew what he was thinking. "Do you see me filling my bed with a man who theme-costumes his slaves and thinks the two finest things in life are beautiful clothes and other men's wives?"

"He might make you laugh." Antinous rather liked Lucius, for all his vanities. *He'll actually* speak *with me, without looking down his nose or sneering.* "And he's right about one thing, Lady—you would make a very fine Artemis. Wild and laughing and always out of men's reach."

Hadrian's voice interrupted the priest, who was droning over the bull with its wreath of blossoms. "Shouldn't we wait?" he demanded, eyes scanning the heaped dark clouds that still wrapped the mountain in near-night. "Surely the sacrifice must take place at the moment of dawn, when the temple is touched with the first rays of the sun—"

"I assure Caesar that it *is* dawn." The priest sounded nervous that he could not sweep the thunderheads away at the Emperor's command. "The clouds but hide the light of the sun."

He began his chanting again, raising the sacrificial knife, and it all happened so quickly. A final peal of thunder, shockingly loud overhead—Sabina flung her hands over her head, crying out, but her cry was drowned in the great spine-ripping *crack* from the heavens, as a jagged shaft of blue-white light lanced from the clouds and struck.

Antinous opened his eyes to a vista of swirling black cloud overhead, his ears ringing like anvils. *This*, he thought in a moment's disjointed panic, and tasted *kykeon* sour and seductive on his tongue. *This is what I saw. Swirling dark and swirling fear—*

The Empress's voice broke through the ringing of his ears, then. Her voice, raised in fear as he had never heard it in his life. "Hadrian! Caesar!"

Terror swept Antinous. *Hadrian*, he thought, *sweet gods, no, no—* and then the words were gone and there was nothing in his skull but a huge reverberating scream. He stumbled to his feet, everything in his vision lined by a nimbus of jerky light as though still limned in the moment when he'd seen the lightning strike—but even that strange jerkiness could not hide the horror of what he saw: the sacrificial bull lying stone dead upon the sacred rock, its garland of flowers gone stiff as its legs.

And Hadrian flat on his back beside it, staring eyes gazing at the churning sky.

No. No, it could not be this—it could not be death at dawn, darkness claiming his light. That could not be what the vision at Eleusis meant. *My future*, he had thought. *It was* my *future, not Hadrian's!*

Antinous realized he was shouting the Emperor's name as he crashed to his knees beside the limp form. Sabina was already there, shaking Hadrian's big shoulder—she looked up, trying to raise her voice, but he could hear nothing, feel nothing but his own terror. *No, no, not him*—still howling Hadrian's name, as thunder rolled through the heavens and the lightning played and flashed like a mad god's smiles.

"*Antinous!*" Sabina's hand cracked across his cheek, cutting him off mid-shout. He stared at her, chest heaving, still tasting the deadly promise of the *kykeon.*

"Antinous, stop." The Empress's voice came quiet. "Don't you see? He lives."

Antinous heard his own voice come in a cracked whisper. "He lives?" Hope burst in his chest as violent as a sun being born, and he looked from Sabina's face to Hadrian's.

Take my life, Antinous offered the uncaring gods, looking at that beloved, bearded face. *Take my life if you require a sacrifice—but spare his.*

Hadrian's chest rose—fell—rose again. Antinous's own chest hitched violently. Hadrian's eyes fluttered in a slow blink, coming into focus. His lips moved, and Antinous knew the words. *My star.*

He let his head drop against the Emperor's chest in a silent gasp, as Hadrian began to laugh. He clasped the back of Antinous's neck, sitting up, and Antinous felt the press of lips against his hair. He stayed where he was, on his knees on the bare rock, as Hadrian bounded to his feet still laughing. *You live,* he thought numbly. *You live.* He felt as though the heart had been torn from his chest and then stuffed roughly back in.

The priest and the rest of the court began to fuss then, but Hadrian brushed them all away. His eyes sparkled, and he spread his arms to the heavens.

"Hadrian Caesar salutes you!" he called to the gods, "Hadrian Caesar, bringer of rain—" and as though in answer, thunder rolled again and the rain began to fall in sheets.

SABINA

The ringing in Sabina's ears had more or less faded away by the time she came from her private baths at the palace in Antioch. Her maid was waiting with a clean bath drape, looking worried. "Don't worry, the lightning didn't strike *me*." The girl smiled back; a little African no more than eleven whom Sabina had spotted when she came to watch the mud-brick walls rise. The girl had been trailing an engineer, half-starved and beaten and wearing the saffron robe of a whore, but she had something of Annia's defiance in her chin. Sabina claimed the girl and, when the engineer protested, gave the order that he be flogged for so misusing his property. Hadrian had looked exasperated, but with a glance at Antinous's watching face he said, "The Empress may please herself. The women of Rome are hers to govern, as the men are mine."

He has *changed*, she thought. And gave a prayer of thanks to the listening gods that he was not dead—not killed in the shaft of lightning like the bull. What would Rome be without Publius Aelius Hadrian?

That thought chilled her bones. He had no named heir. If that lightning had taken his life, the throne would be empty, Sabina widowed and irrelevant, Antinous's heart shattered in pieces . . . And very likely, the Empire in chaos. *Hadrian Caesar, bringer of rain*, she thought. *More like the bringer of peace.*

Long may he live to keep bringing it.

"Antinous," she said as she came into the atrium outside. "I thought you would be with the Emperor."

"He's bathing." Antinous sat at a marble bench, hands hanging between his knees. "In great high spirits."

"Well," Sabina acknowledged, still toweling off her damp hair. "It was a rather dramatic morning. You will not be surprised to hear that Lucius Ceionius plans a costume of storm gray with his slave girls dressed to match as rain clouds."

She expected Antinous to laugh, perhaps tease again about Lucius trying to seduce her, but he didn't even look up. "Do you count it as a good omen, Lady? The lightning striking so close to our Emperor as he makes sacrifice to the thunder god?"

Sabina piled the towel into the arms of her little maid and went to sit beside Antinous. "The Emperor seems convinced it is a good omen. Why should we argue with him?"

"Because he won't *see*." Antinous's head jerked up, and to her astonishment she saw that his eyes were red-rimmed. "It means ill for him, Lady. I'm sure of it."

"But the Emperor wasn't harmed." She touched Antinous's shoulder. "Not a scratch. What kind of ill omen is that?"

Antinous hesitated. "Perhaps it foretells his death."

"The only times he's ever been kept to his bed were when he broke his leg on a bear hunt—the hunt where he met *you*—and the hunt before this tour east where he broke his collarbone."

"It wasn't just his collarbone that summer, Lady—the reason he delayed this journey east. He had fevers all summer, and his joints pained him—"

Sabina felt her bath drape start to slide down her arm, and pushed it back up.

"He kept it quiet because he didn't want anyone thinking he was growing weak." Antinous's voice rose. "He pushes himself too hard! This sprint up the mountain for a look off the top of the world, and those days marching with the legionaries just to prove he can keep up with the youngest of them—he won't take care. Now it's Jupiter himself sending omens, and he still won't listen." A ragged sigh. "The lightning didn't kill him, but what if his own habits do?"

"Antinous." She cupped his carved cheek in her hand. "He would not want you to worry so."

"But I do." His eyes were pools of anguish. *Hadrian does not deserve such love,* she couldn't help thinking. *What has he done to earn such a treasure?*

But Antinous had earned it—he had a soul made of love if Sabina had ever seen one. If he wanted peace of mind about his beloved, she would see he got it. "Take me to Hadrian. Now."

Her husband was soaking in his private baths, muscled arms spread along the hot pool's marble lip as the water lapped nearly to his shoulders, head tilted back and eyes closed against the wreathing steam. "Antinous," he said without looking up. "The steam has me dizzy; I think I may need your arm to rise—"

"It's not the heat making you dizzy," Antinous said. "I've told the Empress."

Hadrian's eyes snapped open. He looked at Sabina, and she didn't think it was bathhouse heat that put the slow flush into his cheeks.

Sabina folded her still-damp arms across her breasts. "Antinous is worried."

"I'm a trifle singed by the lightning, but—"

"Please, Caesar?" Antinous pleaded. "Show her."

Hadrian stared another moment, and then he rose slowly until the water lapped his hips. Trickles sluiced off his shoulders over the springy hair at his chest, along the muscled arms that could still down a boar with one strike—but he swayed as he rose; Sabina could see that. "See?" he said, defensive. "Perfectly well."

"He has fevers." Antinous sounded miserable. "He has one now, I'd say. Headaches come too, and aches in the joints. And his skin hardens in patches, and at its worst it's so painful he can't bear to feel cloth on it."

"That was two years ago. The summer before we left Rome."

"—and you were so dizzy you couldn't sit a horse, which is why you postponed the journey east," Antinous plowed onward—Antinous of the exquisite manners, overriding the Emperor. "You're dizzy now, aren't you? I can see you swaying—"

"No," Hadrian snapped, even as Sabina saw he *was* unsteady in the water. "You are mistaken."

"Perhaps I overstep," Antinous said. "But I do it for your own good."

Hadrian's head jerked up, and Sabina saw the flash of anger in his eyes. She expected him to lash out, give Antinous a cut with that whip-sharp tongue, but he controlled himself. "Don't fuss at me, my star," he said gruffly, and reached for the strigil.

Antinous stepped down into the pool beside him, water floating his tunic around him. He touched the frown lines between Hadrian's eyes, a gesture Sabina had seen before—usually it made Hadrian laugh, but now he just jerked away, still frowning. Antinous withdrew his hand, taking the strigil from the Emperor instead, and motioning him to hold out his arms. "I do worry," he said, very quiet, and scraped down one muscled shoulder. "Perhaps too much."

Hadrian melted at once, looking placating—*Hadrian*, placating. Sabina would never had believed it if she hadn't seen it with her own eyes. "The fever is nothing, Antinous, you can see for yourself! And my skin troubles me sometimes, but it's just irritation from this eastern heat—"

"And if it gets worse? Hardened and rashed, as it did that summer in Rome?" Antinous drew the strigil down the Emperor's muscled back, sounding mild but still very firm. "It got very bad then—don't be defensive, Caesar; I know how much it troubled you!"

"Well, it's not troubling me now." Hadrian looked over his shoulder, cajoling for one of Antinous's smiles, but the young man just gave him a steady look.

Sabina stepped forward then. "Antinous is right," she said coolly. "You do push yourself too hard, Hadrian. If you wish to avoid fevers and vomiting and dizziness—in the desert heat, in the *summertime*, which is quite enough to make anyone ill—then you will take greater care of yourself."

"I do not need minding!"

"You do, because when you are ill, you are short-tempered and you lash out at everything." Sabina raised her eyebrows. "That incident in Parthia?"

Hadrian scowled. Settling disputes among the ever-quarreling easterners recently, he'd lost his temper when Parthia's king mocked Rome's lavish gifts by sending a few threadbare gold-embroidered cloaks. Hadrian had put the cloaks on three hundred condemned Parthian prisoners, and had them all sent to the arena and slaughtered. Sabina had been surprised; he'd all but given up the habit of petty vengeful gestures like that. If he had been in the grip of a fever and a headache at the time . . .

"Ill health is not good for your temper *or* your reputation for mercy," Sabina continued, unfolding her arms. "So allow me to be firm with you, husband. Take greater care of yourself, or I will begin fussing over your health before the rest of the court until the rumors of your imminent demise spread back to Rome, and you are deluged with senators all panting to establish themselves your heir before you finally totter off to the underworld."

Hadrian's eyes narrowed. "You wouldn't dare."

"She would." Antinous gave Sabina a tiny smile over Hadrian's shoulder. "And I'd aid her."

Hadrian looked from Sabina to Antinous and back again, and let out a bark of angry laugher. "Hadrian Caesar," he said, "ruler of the known world, marked by Jupiter himself with the gift of lightning, and yet I cannot rule over a wife and a lover?"

Sabina and Antinous looked at each other, and then back. "No," they said in unison.

The Emperor had a glint in his eye that Sabina remembered from the days when his mask had been less firmly in place—days when the habits of bad temper and petty vengeful gestures had been common. But Antinous touched the frown lines between his eyes again, and this time when Hadrian laughed there was no angry edge. He captured Antinous's hand and kissed it. "I yield, my star—I yield. Now for the love of all the gods, dry me off!"

He came splashing up the steps to stand on the mosaics, and Antinous splashed out too, relief all over his face as Sabina fetched a stack of towels. Hadrian spread his arms as Antinous dried him, and Sabina took a towel herself and stood on tiptoe to tousle Hadrian's wet curls. "You go to Parthia next," she asked, "to deal with all those administrators you've been ranting about, the ones you think are skimming profits?"

"They *are* skimming profits, and I'll see them hanged for it."

"Perhaps take a month to rest here first," Sabina suggested, sliding the towel away from his hair.

"A few months," Antinous said firmly, standing back with his own damp towel.

"I haven't got the time—"

"Then stop being Emperor!"

Hadrian laughed again. "We'll see," he said, sliding an arm about Antinous and kissing him heartily. "We'll see," he said again at Sabina's glare, and then astonishment wiped her mind clean as Hadrian bent his head and kissed her, too. His beard was scratchy against her face, and his lips warm. *The first kiss I've had in years*, she thought inconsequentially even as she clung to him. And it had been longer than years since a kiss had come from her husband. *Surely more than a decade*. Hadrian drew back, his lips leaving hers with a faint smile for her surprise, and Sabina turned her head to see Antinous smiling too, in that quiet way of his.

"I should go back to my desk," Hadrian began, and both Sabina and Antinous exclaimed "*No!*" in the same breath, and suddenly they were all laughing, even Hadrian, as his empress took him by one wrist and his lover by the other, and they bore him across the bathhouse to the couch that lay behind air-thin curtains. "Pin him," Sabina laughed, "you have to *force* him to rest!" And Antinous got the Emperor of Rome in an arm-hold and wrestled him efficiently to the wide white-draped couch.

"I surrender," Hadrian groaned, more helpless with laughter than Sabina had ever seen him. He spread his arms wide, grinning, and Antinous burrowed into his chest on one side and Sabina on the other. "I should be working," Hadrian complained. "I intend to make a good many reforms on the treatment of slaves in Rome, did you know that?"

"I did not know that, Caesar," Sabina said.

"Antinous said it would please him." A long kiss for Antinous, leading to another and then a third, but Hadrian left his arm about Sabina's shoulders, and she curled against his heavy chest, warm and tingling from the heat of the bath, feeling the Emperor's heartbeat under her cheek. She closed her eyes a moment, wondering when she had last felt so content, and when her lashes rose again she saw Antinous smiling at her across Hadrian's chest, head tucked in the curve of Hadrian's other shoulder. She lifted her hand and he matched his own to it, the long fingers overtopping hers. *Understand the Emperor or not*, Sabina thought, *we will keep him alive*. And she could swear the thought passed from her mind to Antinous through their fingers, because they squeezed at the same time.

Hadrian kissed Antinous again, with more heat this time, and Sabina laughed a little and sat up. "I think I shall leave you." She bent and brushed her mouth across Hadrian's in farewell, feeling the silent amusement curve his bearded lips against hers, and then she rose and drifted smiling through the curtains toward the bathhouse doors.

"Wait—" A quick footstep behind her, and she saw that Antinous had risen from the couch to follow, pulling the curtain momentarily between them and the Emperor. He gave one of his heart-catching smiles, and then he bent his head and kissed her once on each of her naked shoulders above the bath drape.

Sabina drew back with a startled smile. "What—"

"Don't think that was pity," Antinous said. "That was for me. Because I can see why my father cannot forget you, Lady—I see it very well."

Sabina felt bemused and rueful, warm and astonished, and she could not stop a soft laugh. *The handsomest young man ever born finds me beautiful*, she thought, and gave a little push at his chest. "Go back to the Emperor, Antinous!"

A salute like a legionary. "Yes, Lady. And thank you—for everything."

She watched them a moment through the thin curtains, shadowed by the dim lamplight. Antinous slipping down over Hadrian with tender haste, Hadrian's strong hand pulling him close as their lips met again. Hadrian's muscled arm curving about Antinous's lean shoulder, Antinous dropping kisses one by one like pearls on a string along Hadrian's throat. The murmured caresses, the soft laughter. Sabina felt a stab of wistful envy for their happiness. *They could travel the world alone and be happy*, she thought. Antinous with his black dog at his heels and Hadrian in his Imperial purple, a solitary pair dazed by their own bliss.

Hadrian does not deserve such love, she had thought just a little while ago. Perhaps he did not. But it was still something her soul warmed to see. She smiled again and stole away.

The following morning, Hadrian bid her join them for fruit and bread and iced infusions of mulberry and honey, and he announced that he meant to make a desert caravan to Palmyra. "A journey in easy stages," he said, answering Sabina's stern look. "I had thought only to take the men of my court, but I believe I will take you, Vibia Sabina. To take charge of me, since I am inclined to run rough-shod over my star here." A squeeze of Antinous's fingers lying content in his own.

Sabina raised her cup. "To Palmyra," she said. "Bride of the desert."

"To Palmyra," Hadrian agreed, raising his own cup, and Antinous did the same. "And then Judaea, eh?"

Her husband ruled long years, Sabina reflected later. But that year that followed their triple toast—that was the best one.

Before it all fell to ruin.

ANNIA

A.D. 130, Summer
Rome

"You aren't wearing *that*, are you?" Ceionia Fabia wrinkled her perfect little nose. "It's so short it's improper. Everyone will see your ankles!"

Annia shrugged, looking down at her filmy blue hem. "I'm growing." She was nearly as tall at twelve as Pedanius Fuscus was at seventeen. "And so what if people see my ankles? You're always flashing *yours* for the boys!"

Ceionia was far too demure to bristle, but Annia could tell she wanted to. She was Annia's age, smooth-haired and smooth-faced and unspeakably proper, and their respective mothers were always pushing them to be friends. Either girl could have said *that* was never going to happen, but since when did mothers listen to anything?

Ceionia turned away from Annia with a sniff. Her father, Lucius Ceionius, had gone east to dance attendance on the Emperor, so Ceionia had been corralled into Annia's household for today's festivities. Which Annia didn't find festive at all: Brine-Face's first walk to the Forum as a man of Rome.

The waiting crowd rippled, and Ceionia's eyes flashed under her downcast lids. "Do you see Pedanius Fuscus yet?"

"Get your ankles ready."

It was always an occasion when a boy donned the *toga virilis* for the first time. Everybody knew Servianus had pinned his hopes on the Emperor returning from the east to see Brine-Face become a man—"otherwise he'd have surely put on his toga at fourteen," Ceionia whispered. But the Emperor had taken his entourage to Judaea rather than return to Rome, and so Brine-Face had his toga.

Annia could just make him out across the heads of the crowd, his hair gleaming barley-brown in the morning sun. This morning he'd have put aside his childhood tunic, taken the *bulla* amulet from his neck, and hung it up for the household gods, and according to law, that made him a man. Annia didn't understand why. Girls didn't get a ceremony when they became women. All she'd gotten when she started her monthly bleeding was a demonstration with cloth pads and a warm hug from her mother, and a lecture from the housekeeper about not running around flashing her ankles for Marcus anymore. What *was* this obsession with ankles, anyway? She wished she could ask Marcus that—he was standing behind her now, not hearing Ceionia's little kitten-claw digs—but Annia poked his elbow and instead asked, "Why aren't *you* getting your *toga virilis* yet? You're more a man than Brine-Face."

Marcus fingered the *bulla* about his neck, watching Pedanius strut past alongside his grandfather. "I don't think I'm ready. I'd still rather stay up late reading than start my obligations as a man. I should be more resigned to my duty before I put the toga on, or I won't do it the honor it deserves."

"Prig," Annia teased, but thought Marcus could have done justice to a toga. Even in his boy's tunic he was slender and strong, his face high-cheekboned and serious, like he could mount the Rostra at any moment and give a speech. But it was Brine-Face at the Rostra today, new toga gleaming in the sun, accepting his formal congratulations with an easy white grin, and getting a roar from the crowd.

"He'll be needing a wife soon," Ceionia speculated. "Since he'll be emperor someday . . ."

"Says who?" Annia snorted.

"Who else can the Emperor choose but his great-nephew?" Ceionia patted at her smooth hair, wound crownlike around her head. "Peda-nius will need an empress."

"Not you. Empresses kill people"—remembering Aunt Sabina and her curse tablets—"and you can't even kill a flea without squealing."

After Brine-Face's ceremony, Servianus hosted a great feast and invited half of Rome. "Where are you going?" Marcus whispered as Annia slid behind her parents and began sidling toward the gardens.

"No one will notice if I'm gone," she whispered back. "My father only said I had to *come*, not that I had to *stay*."

"You should train for a lawyer," Marcus disapproved.

She thumped him on the arm. "Go sit with Ceionia. She's angling to marry Brine-Face, but she'll cast her lashes at you, too."

"I wouldn't mind that. She's pretty."

"Just like a boy," Annia said, nettled, "getting his head turned by *pretty*."

"Not just pretty, properly behaved. A man likes that once in a while."

"You're not a man yet!" Annia made a face as he disappeared into the triclinium. Now she *really* needed a run.

Servianus was always extolling austerity, so of course his villa and gardens were some of the most sumptuous on the Palatine Hill. Annia reckoned there was a good half mile down the length of the sculpted terraces and back, and she took off at an easy speed, relishing the rich summer grass under her bare, flashing feet. Down to the gate, turn and back, and she let her strides lengthen. The trees flashed past and the wind tore at her hair; the soles of her feet stung and her blood pounded in her ears. She finished her third circuit at a flat sprint, skidding to a halt by her discarded sandals and sticking her head under the foun-tain's spray. Raking a hand through her wet hair, she laughed aloud even though she was still gasping for breath.

She remembered that soldier, the russet-haired one who had taught her how to run. *Run till you throw up*, he'd said. *And if you still feel like hitting somebody after that, then it's because they deserve to be hit.* Annia hadn't seen that soldier again—he'd left Rome, and there had been some sort of scandal her father refused to talk about. She wished he would come back, so she could thank him. Because the running helped. It helped *everything*.

She could feel her heartbeat slowing, the contented tiredness leaking into her muscles. She looked down at herself, and saw happily that the blue dress was a sweaty wreck. She could go back in and her mother would make a great fuss—"Goodness, child, I must take you home!" She said it scoldingly, but Annia never got punished. Not when it was a really boring party they were fleeing. She prepared her penitent face, scooping up her sandals.

"What are you doing?"

Annia looked up to see Pedanius Fuscus standing there, muscled arms folded across his chest. "Nothing." She started to move past him, then hesitated. She knew what her father would want her to say, and if he were here he'd give her one of his quietly formidable gazes.

"Congratulations," she added with a bump of a curtsy. "Upon reaching your manhood, Pedanius Fuscus."

His hand caught her arm as she began to brush past. "Let me show you something."

"What?"

"Over here." He had a gleam of sweat on his upper lip, and she was close enough to see that his jaw was rough even if he was only seventeen. "Come on."

"No." That was how silly princesses and nymphs got themselves abducted in the myths her nurse told her. Persephone, wandering off all by herself like an idiot, easy prey for Hades to snatch. "I don't want to go anywhere with you," Annia said, and yanked her arm free.

But he grabbed again, and he shoved her back into the garden with both hands this time. "I'm a man now," he said as she stumbled back against the fountain. "So you do what I say."

"Boy or man, you're still just Brine-Face," she retorted. "I'm going inside."

"No," he said. And took a step toward her.

Annia gave an insolent shrug, and then she whirled and bolted. "Catch me if you want me," she mocked over one shoulder. Pedanius could *never* catch her. He was big and slow, weighed down in heavy folds of toga. She'd cruise ahead of him just long enough to hear him curse, and then she'd sprint off with a laugh.

But Annia veered away from the terraced gardens, because that way was just one long open stretch and she'd never lose Brine-Face there. She didn't know the gardens here as she did her own; she bolted laughing through a stone archway, leaped a small lily pond in one long vault, and then her laughter ended. Because she'd come into the stone enclosure of the *nymphaeum* with its quietly plashing water, and the *nymphaeum* was enclosed on three sides. She was already turning and gathering herself for another sprint, but Pedanius was in the entranceway, breathing hard, blocking her way entirely with his wide chest and planted feet. They were a long way from the noisy triclinium where her father laughed with his grandfather.

Annia wasn't afraid. It was just Brine-Face, after all. "Out of my way," she said.

He grinned. "No."

She feinted at one side, but he just batted a big arm, and all that training he boasted of with his sword instructors had done its work, because Annia went down with a crash, the whole side of her head ringing. The breath left her in a whoosh, and she felt Brine-Face's big hand in her hair, yanking her up to her knees. Her whole body vibrated with shock as she looked up at him.

"My grandfather says I can have a slave tonight," Pedanius said. "Any one I want. He says it's the other part of being a man, and that's a joke, because I've been having slave girls for years. They aren't any sport; they just lie there."

That was when Annia felt fear curling through her stomach in cold tendrils. She tried to jerk away, but Pedanius gave her hair a yank that sent sparkles of pain all over her scalp. "I wanted a proper whore," he went on. "A courtesan with long legs who knows how to please a man, but my grandfather's too cheap."

Annia clawed at the big hand in her hair, but her nails were too short and bitten to draw blood. *Why didn't I ever grow my nails out long like Ceionia?* she thought wildly. *I could rake his arm open to the bone!*

"Maybe it's better this way." Pedanius gave her head another hard shake. "I'd have to pay a whore, and I don't have to pay you. I'm going to be Emperor, and you're going to get on your knees and tell me so."

"I won't," she managed to say. But she was already on her knees, and she could see a bulge under his toga. *Oh, Hades*, she thought, and the word kept going around her head in circles. *Hades, Hades, Hades*—"I won't!"

"Yes, you will." Pedanius grinned again. "Because I'm going to fuck you."

"I'll kill you." She hated how high and unsteady her voice came out. "My *father* will kill you!"

Pedanius laughed. "You won't dare tell him."

"I tell my father everything." Yanking against his fist. "I'll tell him you ruined me!"

"I said I was going to fuck you, not ruin you."

"What—what do you mean?"

"You don't know anything, do you?" Pedanius looked nervous, but he looked giddy too, flushed and eager. He gave his hips a jerk. "I'd make you open your mouth and suck on it, but you'd just bite me like the little snake you are. And I can't fuck you up the front without ruining you. So I'll go up the back, like the Emperor takes that Bithynian he-bitch who dared call me a bully. And if you try to tell anyone, they'll examine you and you'll still be a virgin, and they'll call you a liar."

You're an idiot, she wanted to shriek. Like her father wouldn't believe her if she came to him bleeding from *anywhere*. But she didn't have any scorn to pour into her voice, just fear, and all she could manage was a whisper. "He'll still believe me."

"But my grandfather won't. He already thinks you're a whore, the way you run around flashing your legs. If your father comes to him, he'll just say you tempted me and then you'll be ruined anyway without me fucking you at all. Not even stupid Marcus will marry you then."

Marcus. What she wouldn't have given to see Marcus wander up to the *nymphaeum*—but he was inside, talking Stoicism with her father or flirting with Ceionia.

"Say it." Pedanius wagged her head side to side with his fisted hand in her hair. "Call me Caesar. Do that, and I won't make it hurt too much."

Oh, Annia thought inanely, *I think it's going to hurt a lot.* She hardly understood the things he was saying he'd do to her but she was certain they would be painful. She lashed out at the bulge under his toga, but he gave her a casual slap that rang Annia's ears. Somehow that shocked her more than anything. *Brine-Face*, she kept thinking, *this is Brine-Face.* The boy who hit only when nobody was looking, who tattled to his grandfather whenever anyone hit back. Brine-Face, who she'd always found about as frightening as an oyster. Brine-Face, who was releasing her hair and stepping back out of reach.

Annia tensed, still on her knees but gathering her toes under her so she could run. But there was nowhere to run.

"Say it." He pointed at her. "'Caesar.'"

She swallowed, still eyeing the bulge.

"Say it!"

She tasted bile. "Caesar." The word was treason, and it tasted like ash.

"Emperor Gnaeus Pedanius Fuscus Salinator."

"Emperor Gnaeus Pedanius Fuscus Salinator."

"That's a start," he crowed, still sounding like that strutting little boy she'd whacked with a mallet when she was four years old. What she would have given for a mallet, because he was hauling up the folds of his toga.

"I'm not taking this off," he informed her. As if she cared. "It should happen in the toga, because only men get to take virgins. Down on your hands and knees."

No. She was full of terror, but she pushed the word out. "No."

He grabbed her by the hair again, shoving her down on her hands and knees. She heard him behind her, hauling at his toga. Felt her own pounding blood, tasted rancid fear. She was trembling like it was the last lap of a sprint, one of her bad sprints where she was running out a red haze of temper. Only now there was nowhere to run.

Annia felt his hand hauling up her skirts. Felt air on her naked thighs, and such a rush of shame she almost vomited. Felt him come closer, the brush of his toga against her spread legs. "You're ugly, but I like your legs," he said, still sounding nervous but also excited. "Maybe I'll take you in the front after all, if you promise to wrap those legs around me."

Annia squeezed her eyes tight shut, her heart hammering in her throat, and kicked behind her with one foot. A stiff kick like a donkey, the knee bent and the foot flexed hard. *The angle*, she thought desperately. It had to be just right—she'd been sizing it up as he forced her down. If she caught him wrong, he'd just swear and get on with it.

She missed the groin. But Pedanius let out a yelp as Annia's heel slammed into his ankle. He staggered, and Annia lunged out of reach, scrambling to her feet. She could hardly see through her flying hair, but Pedanius was on the ground clutching his ankle. He was still blocking the entrance of the *nymphaeum*, and she backed up to leap across him like she'd vaulted the little lily pond.

But she couldn't run away like that. She couldn't.

"Coward," she hissed, and rage billowed up in her like a red monster. "You couldn't *fuck* me if I was the last girl in the Empire!" The first time she'd ever used such a foul word, and it fed the rage like kindling to a fire. Maybe this was the ceremony that turned girls into women, rather than some idiotic ritual of putting on a bundle of chalked cloth. You became a woman the first day a man attacked your virtue. "You won't ever be Emperor," she said, "*never*." And she cocked her head back and spat on him. Right on the folds of his new toga.

He howled, swinging for her. As soon as his fists lashed out she stepped forward and stomped—stomped with her horn-hard foot, with all the strength of those long legs he'd admired, and which had run so many hard miles. Stomped right where the housekeeper had told her to stomp. "Right in the balls, little mistress. Kick a man there, and you can walk away at your leisure."

And she did. Walked calmly away from the *nymphaeum*, hair hanging lank and sweaty in her face, her vision still sheeted red and her blood roaring. Behind her Pedanius retched up a bellyful of wine between shrieks of agony, his new toga already stained where he had pissed himself. Annia felt queer and cold, triumphant and sick, and her face was blank as stone.

"You look like the sack of Troy," her father said mildly as she came to his dining couch in the triclinium. Old Servianus clucked disapproval. *Don't say it,* Annia thought, staring him down. *Don't you dare say, "In my day girls lay there obediently when boys fucked them up the back." Or I'll kick you in the balls, too.*

Her father was looking at her quizzically, and so was Marcus from his stool. "Are you all right? What happened?"

Annia let out the last of the red rage in a long breath, and all she felt now was sick. "Nothing I couldn't handle."

CHAPTER 12

VIX

Bethar

The message was so brief. Just a few words in a graceful hand, but they set my heart to pounding.

Titus Aurelius was good enough to tell me you live in Bethar, Antinous had written. *Would you welcome a visit?*

I looked up at the supercilious Imperial freedman who had delivered the scroll. I couldn't speak, just nodded and carried the letter inside. Mirah was chopping turnips, and one glance at the way I stood tracing the signature with my thumb must have told her everything. Maybe she had prepared for this moment, since Hadrian and his entourage arrived in Judaea a few days ago. Because she took a deep breath and laid down her knife.

"I know you love him. But if he is asking to visit us here, he cannot come. I cannot have him under this roof."

Anger flared in me. Mirah met it in my eyes, and her own were full of sorrow.

"I'm sorry, Vix. But we cannot welcome him here."

She spoke in Aramaic. I replied in Latin. "He has a name, Mirah."

"I know." She switched languages, placating me. "And I love Antinous. That has nothing to do with this, so don't let us quarrel."

We *had* been quarreling lately, but so was the whole region. Bethar was a kettle on high boil, a pile of tinder so dry a single spark would have set it ablaze—but at the moment, I didn't care. "If you love him, why won't you see him?"

"It's our girls. Don't you see? The Emperor's catamite under the same roof as our daughters, just as they're coming to marriageable age? What will that do for their reputations?"

My voice rose. "Do *not* use that word." I wouldn't hear it from Simon and I was damned well not going to hear it from Mirah.

"I don't like that word either," she sighed. "But the whole *Empire* knows what Antinous is. He rode on the Emperor's right hand when Hadrian entered Judaea, didn't he? Uncle Simon said he wore a purple cloak like a prince, with his hair curled like a woman!"

"I don't want to hear you call him a *woman* either, Mirah." I hadn't gone with the rest of the crowds to Jerusalem when Hadrian first came to make his inspection, but I'd heard plenty from those who had been there. Those few who knew about my son and pitied me silently. Nobody dared pity me openly.

"I grieve for the boy he was." Mirah reached for an onion. "But I can never approve of the man he's become."

"He *wrote* to me. To us." I pulled his words back toward me, pain spiking my throat. For the last year I'd been able to think of little but Antinous—ever since I heard Hadrian was at last coming to Judaea. Over and over again, I'd sat down with parchment and tried to write him, wondering if he could bear to see me after the words that had passed between us. Longing to see him, no matter what words he had said to me.

And he'd written. Not four days after arriving in Judaea. My golden boy, reaching out for—what? My love? My forgiveness? My help? How would I ever know if I turned him away?

"He wants to see me," I heard myself saying. "And he's my son."

Mirah went on chopping. "Once, maybe."

I felt that flash of hard anger again. "He's still my son." He would *always* be my son. His falling into Hadrian's net didn't change that. His falling into Hadrian's net didn't change that. His repudiating me as a father didn't change that. The world's opinion of him didn't change that.

Nothing would.

"He's not your son by blood, and thank God for it." Mirah slid chopped turnips and onions alike into the stew pot, moving with her usual quick grace. "It would do our girls' prospects no good at all to have a catamite for a blood brother—"

"*Do not call him that!*" All in an instant, anger was boiling over into rage. "You *raised* him, Mirah! You raised him, and he loved you like a mother. And if I receive him here, you'll smile when you see him."

"I can't smile." Her chin trembled. "Not at what he's become. It breaks my heart, Vix."

And you are breaking mine. I wanted to cry and I wanted to hit her. Antinous was my son, but apparently he was no longer hers—and she didn't seem to see why I was angry. She just looked at me with tender pity, as though I were a child failing to understand a hard truth.

"It just condones what he's done, if I smile and pretend nothing is wrong as he walks into my house—"

I actually felt my hand lift at that. I brought it down in a hard slap against the wood of the table, and Mirah fell back from the look on my face.

"This is *my* house," I said in a hard voice. "And when my son comes through that door, you will smile for him. I don't care if you have to fake it, but you will smile."

There were more bitter words said after that, but in the end I gave the Imperial freedman his reply, just one word long. *Tomorrow.*

Five years. Five years since I'd last seen him. He'd be twenty-four, but I kept seeing the boy I'd first taken in. The little boy who had pointed at my lion skin and crowed "*Yion!*"

I don't know what I expected when I opened my door to him. An oiled and painted bed-toy like the mocking rumors painted him? An embittered young man made old before his time? The child I remembered so well?

Instead I saw a young god standing lightly at my gate in his plain white tunic and blue cloak, poised as though he had just alighted from a winged chariot. A man grown, lean-muscled and hard of jaw, his curls tied carelessly at the back of his neck and his brown eyes somber.

I wanted to fall on him with open arms. But I couldn't bear it if he recoiled, so I just gave a nod. "Welcome."

He nodded back. "Thank you."

Mirah and I had reached a ferociously fought-out compromise. She and the girls stood in the courtyard, a pretty trinity in an array of blue gowns, and Antinous smiled for the first time as he came to stand before them. "You look well," he said to Mirah.

Don't be hard, I begged her silently. And her mouth curved as though she hadn't meant it to, curved with a love that couldn't possibly be false. But she didn't move toward him.

Antinous didn't seem to expect it, because he turned to the girls, standing round-eyed and stiff as spears. "Dinah—sweet gods, you're a vision. I always knew you'd be beautiful. And Chaya, I hope you're not letting your sister have all the suitors!"

My daughters just stood there, looking at each other nervously. They didn't fully understand why their adopted brother was such a heated subject in our house—Mirah shielded them from salacious gossip—but they could sense their mother's tension, and they pulled back like skittish kittens as Antinous moved to embrace them.

"Girls," I barked, but Antinous's arms dropped before I could tell Dinah and Chaya to embrace their brother. His face was sad, and a little silence fell.

"Come," I said at last. "We'll walk."

"All right."

"Wait," said Mirah. Stepping forward, she touched Antinous's cheek just once. She murmured something in formal Hebrew, a tongue I'd never mastered, but Antinous answered her in the same accents and a smile touched his lips.

"What was that?" I asked as he followed me out of the gate into the busy street.

"A blessing," he said. "She blessed me."

A blessing. It was more than I had hoped for, but I still didn't know if I could forgive her for wanting to bar her door against him in the first place. Mirah and I had slept last night with our backs to each other.

"She'll bless me," he said, "but she won't have me in her house, will she?"

I tried to find an excuse for his mother that was an honest one, but all I could say was, "Her God won't allow it."

He shrugged, his face cool and hard. "I'm done apologizing."

We walked down the dusty street, skirting an ox cart. Antinous's dog trotted at our heels, a lithe black shadow. He pricked his ears as a stray cat hissed at him, but Antinous snapped his fingers, and the dog bounded back between us. "The girls are beautiful," Antinous said. "So tall. I somehow thought they'd still be four years old and begging for rides on my shoulders."

"They cry a lot." I kicked a pebble out of my way. "Mirah says it means they're becoming women."

"She never did have a son, then? I knew she always hoped."

"I think she believed coming to Bethar would be a blessing on her womb, but"—a shrug. "At least we're *in* Judaea, now. She counts that blessing enough."

"And I'm sure she feels less a failure," Antinous said, that edge in his voice again, "if she doesn't have to look at me."

That stung me like a clip on the chin. I'd always hoped I'd kept it from him, Mirah's tiny resentment. Apparently not.

A cluster of bearded boys no older than Antinous broke off their fierce arguing to watch us go by with hostile eyes, and one of them made the sign against evil. "Don't mind them," I said. Ever since Hadrian's arrival, you could hardly turn around in Bethar without seeing fists being shaken and voices raised in outrage. "They despise all Romans these days."

"I'm used to being despised," he said lightly. "But why the glares for all Romans?"

"Your master isn't very popular in Judaea." I refused to use his name. "We get word he's planning to make circumcision punishable by death and rebuild Jerusalem as a Roman city with temples to Jupiter—he's got Greek notions and Roman laws, and the people here don't like either. If he goes through with all his plans, they'll be burning his temples and shattering his statues."

"That won't bother him." Antinous clasped his hands at the small of his back, and it stabbed me. That old habit he still had, of walking like me. "He's to rename Jerusalem as Aelia Capitolina, did you hear?"

I thought of Mirah's hothead cousins and their curses against Rome. Thought of the older men, the men like Simon who didn't thunder and curse, but simmered and brooded. "Taking their city's ancient name away and christening it after himself," I said. "Does he think that's going to go over well?"

"He wants to see Rome united, all the provinces. Not by force of legions, but by light of common culture. Is it so wrong?"

"Greek culture." A culture of soft women and womanish men, as far as I was concerned, and Antinous's current status didn't exactly contradict me. "The Jews have their own way of doing things, you know that."

"So I've told him, but he's got his own ideas." He imitated Hadrian's deep voice. "'They can keep their own god and their own prayers, but when they're mutilating their baby boys who are growing up to be *my* citizens, that's where an emperor gets involved.'"

His mimicry of Hadrian's irritable cadences was perfect. I felt the urge to spit. "Don't talk of him," I said brusquely. "Not unless it's to tell me you've come to your senses and crawled out of his bed."

"Then we won't have much to talk about." Antinous's voice was mild, but I heard iron under it. "He's my world."

I swung around on my son. "And what does he give you in return? The world holds you in contempt. A man of twenty-four still acting the woman for—"

"Stop," my son said quietly, and his tone brooked no argument. "Just—stop."

We both stopped, standing in the middle of Bethar's dusty road. Antinous looked me in the eye, so handsome in his jewel-blue cloak that it speared me. Beauty like his wasn't a blessing; it was a curse. "This was a mistake," I said hoarsely, and turned to go back to my home.

He caught my arm. "Do you still hate me?" he asked, and I heard the catch in his voice.

"I hate *him*." My voice scraped my throat like a blade. "Never you."

He sighed, relief pooling in his eyes. And as that question had tormented him, the question that tormented me came ripping out of *my* throat.

"Did you mean what you said at his villa?" I couldn't meet his eyes. "That you weren't my son—all because I wouldn't let you call me—"

"No," he said. "No. I didn't mean that."

"Because you *are* my son." I had known that almost all his life, felt it thrumming true in my bones—how had he not realized? "And you can always call me Father."

"Can I?" His voice was muted. "Or can I only call you Father if I leave him?"

"Why can't you leave him?" I heard myself imploring. "Leave that vicious madman and come *home*."

"This isn't my home." Antinous gestured around the streets of Bethar, the terraces rising upward in their walled ranks, the bustle of trade, the foreign chatter of Aramaic so different from Latin's terse clip. "It will never be my home."

"It could be." I would have gotten down on my knees in the street to beg him, but he looked so hard. So young, and so hard. "This could be your home. You could run the wine shop with me—"

He gave a bitter laugh. "You tell me you're happy here, running a wine shop and stagnating? Neither of us belongs here."

That stung me. My eyes slid away.

"I have another idea," Antinous said. "Come with me."

"What?"

"We're to leave Judaea soon for Egypt. Empress Sabina's been there, but not Hadrian—"

I felt a stab at how casually he used the Emperor's name.

"—we're to go to Alexandria first, then take a barge up the Nile. Come with us!" Antinous was the one pleading now. "You belong with *Romans*. Not here among people who curse at the sight of you—"

"The Emperor would have my head on a spike!"

"No. He's changed, I tell you—"

"Snakes shed their skins, but it's still the same snake underneath."

"—he wouldn't acknowledge your presence, maybe, but he'd turn a blind eye. Let you travel with the Imperial party; it's like a small city on the move. Join us." He hesitated. "At least—for a time? Just a little while!"

"Join that parasite court?" I said. "Hadrian thinks he can march into Judaea, spin a few edicts and laws that will have the people here rioting—"

"Hadrian does nothing without consideration, nothing. You know how hard he works? The toll it takes on his health—"

"He'll leave everything here in turmoil, stir up the muck for people like me to wade in, and take you off for a jaunt up the Nile without a backward glance." I felt the hatred boiling in me again. "And you tell me that maybe, just maybe, he'll indulge his boy's whim and let me come along for the ride? That's supposed to make me give up my family and forgive everything?"

"I just want to talk with you again." Quietly. "Hadrian may never travel back to Judaea."

"Then we don't have anything to talk about." I drank him in, whole and healthy and stubborn, and I lingered on every detail because I'd probably never see him again. "Not as long as you're the Emperor's plaything."

"Sweet gods, but you can be a bastard," Antinous said.

We stared at each other. I could have left it there, but I reached out and I wrapped him in my arms. So strong, so tall, and yet all I could feel was the light weight of the little boy on my back, crowing, "*Yion!*"

"Stay," I said thickly. The black dog whined at our feet.

"Come," he said.

And there really wasn't much more to say than that.

The bathhouse in Bethar was sparsely attended. The people here didn't approve of the Roman habit of social bathing, so there was no one to watch as Simon and I took over the empty gymnasium and squared up behind our wooden shields. A brief salute, and we went at each other in short stabbing thrusts: the legion drills we'd practiced for years. Simon didn't ask what had happened with Antinous. He already knew, and not just because Mirah told her uncle everything. Simon seemed to know everything that happened in Bethar; in all of Judaea and the provinces around her, for that matter. "The Twelfth Deiotariana is poised to come from Egypt," he'd say. "If there's trouble, that is, when the Emperor departs." And if you asked him how he knew what was happening in bloody *Egypt*, he'd just smile.

"Another bout," I said shortly after winning the first. Sparring was a physical release when I felt so emotion-roiled inside. Simon nodded, deep-set eyes glittering at me across the weed-threaded sand, and waded in. He might be well into his fifties, but he was still hard-bodied and fit, his drills as crisp as though he'd just come from the legion yesterday. I sometimes wondered why he kept himself fighting trim when he was so eager to forget everything else from the legion.

He slipped inside my thrust, parrying. "So, your boy wants you to go to Egypt."

"I'd ask how you know that, but you know everything."

He made a jab of his own, cat-quick. "If I know everything, then what do you think I pray for?"

My turn to parry. "You pray Jerusalem won't be rebuilt as Aelia Capitolina."

"What else?"

"That the Emperor will leave."

His next blow glanced off my shoulder. "I want more for Judaea than the Emperor's absence."

I knew what he wanted, but I wasn't going to say it. Saying it would have been treason for a Praetorian, or even just for a soldier of Rome. And habit died hard in me.

"'There shall step forth a star out of Jacob,'" Simon quoted, advancing on me, "'and a scepter shall rise out of Israel, and shall smite through the corners of Moab.'"

My relief in the simple pleasure of sparring drained away. This was no longer simple. "What's Moab?"

"You're a bad Jew, Vercingetorix." Simon's *gladius* flashed in a double strike. I parried the first, missed the second. "But the Lord our God can use bad Jews as well as good ones."

His sword tip rested at my throat. I felt suddenly very alert indeed.

"Mirah told me Antinous looked at you with tears in his eyes," Simon said as he lowered his blade and we raised our shields again. "As a straying son should look at a righteous father. I was a straying son. I strayed to the legions, but I found the path home."

Frustration was rising in me like a flooding sea. "What are you *saying*?"

"Follow your boy to Egypt." Simon's face was somber. "You might still bring him back."

A lump rose in my throat, and I stepped out of our hypnotic thrust-and-parry. "You're a busy man, Simon ben Cosiba. Traveling to Jerusalem, traveling to Lydda and Jericho and Jaffa. So why are you taking time from your afternoon to worry about a catamite?" I said the word harshly, because I knew he thought it. "Even if he is my son?"

"A catamite with the Emperor's ear." Simon blew sand off the edge of his blade. "Perhaps he might be persuaded to drop a word in that ear."

"What kind of word?"

"Leave Judaea for the Jews," Simon whispered. "Or we take it for ourselves."

I laughed. "Sounds to me like it would suit you better if I *didn't* retrieve my son from the Emperor's bed."

A shrug. "Such whispers likely won't work. According to my reports, Emperor Hadrian is a man of strong mind, unlikely to be swayed—"

"*Reports?*"

"—but everything should be tried, should it not? Everything peaceful." Simon looked contemplative. "Before the alternative."

"All right." I threw my *gladius* to the ground at his feet. "No more riddles. What are you planning? What are you *doing*?"

Simon held up his sword. "A good blade," he said. "There are smiths in Judaea who do nothing but forge weapons to supply Roman soldiers—and on the Emperor's orders, any blade that fails to meet standards is returned."

"I'm going to kill you," I warned, "if you don't talk plainly."

"What if I told you those inferior blades returned to all those smiths aren't scrapped?" Simon balanced his *gladius* against the sand, giving it a twirl so it spun on its point. "What if I told you they're reworked in secret, made into blades fit for any soldier? And then they aren't returned to the legions, but . . . hidden? Many, many thousands of them."

I stared at him. "Where would anyone hide so much weaponry?"

"Underground caches, perhaps." Simon smiled. "You'd be surprised how much of Judaea is hidden. Tunnels, passages, networks through the mountains. We have a history of being hunted. We know how to hide."

"You're mad," I whispered. "Rome's legions would crush you."

"Would they?"

I opened my mouth and closed it again. Because a fight through hidden city tunnels and mountain passes was not the kind of fight the legions trained for.

Simon spun his *gladius* about on its point again. "Of course, I'm not talking seriously," he said at last. "Just spinning clouds with an old friend."

"If I'm such an old friend, then why am I only hearing of this today?" My voice rose. "It takes years to build caches of discarded blades, and I'm only now—"

"Because I don't trust you," Simon said harshly. "You married my niece and you've lived here five years, and you've got more reason to hate Rome and its Emperor than most of the men I *do* trust. But you still shave your chin and speak Latin like a Roman, so why should I trust you?"

That hurt. I'd served Rome, yes—been loyal to her all my life, and I wouldn't deny that this flood of news raised the hackles on my neck. But I served my family too, and my family's people. Wasn't that worth just as much? "If you don't trust me, why tell me anything at all?"

Simon stepped close, and I saw the glitter in his eyes again. "Go with your son to Egypt. See if he knows what Caesar plans for Judaea. Then knock your boy on the head if he won't see the righteous path, drag him back to Bethar, and tell me what you've learned. Then maybe I'll trust you."

I stared at him. "And what happens then?"

"You get it *all* back. Have your son again. Be a soldier again. Fight a war again. But for God this time, not Rome." Simon bent and scooped up my *gladius*, offering it to me hilt-first. "And who knows? God is just. Serve Him, and He might even grant you the chance to kill Hadrian."

Fine words.

But it wasn't Simon who made up my mind for me, for all his hypnotic speeches.

It was Mirah.

ANTINOUS

It was a bad time to ask—Antinous could see that the moment he entered the room. Hadrian had one of his headaches; he was rubbing at his temple as he read his way through a scroll, and the groove between his brows was deep. Sabina sat at his side, sipping at her cup without speaking because she understood the pulse of the Emperor's moods as well as Antinous, and she knew when to be silent. But Antinous could not be silent tonight.

He came to Hadrian's couch, and he spoke simply. "My father wishes to join us when we leave for Egypt."

A peculiar silence fell. Antinous could feel the coil of sudden bright energy in Empress Sabina, though she didn't blink an eyelash; feel the hard watchfulness that spiked in Hadrian as his eyes traveled slowly—so slowly—from the scroll in his hand to meet Antinous's gaze.

Antinous cast his eyes to the floor. "With your permission, Caesar," he said, and knelt. "I ask this."

He had asked it before—when they had come to Jerusalem, when he had whispered to Hadrian across their shared cushions that he would be going to Bethar to see his father. "*What if he accepts my offer?*" he had whispered. Hadrian had only given a knife-edged laugh and said, "*He won't.*"

But the message had come today, just four words in that brusque scribble Antinous knew so well. Four words to send joy springing through his blood like divine nectar.

I will join you.

Hadrian looked at his wife. Sabina touched one finger to his hand as if to urge restraint, then rose to leave, her eyes flashing a warning as she passed Antinous. He heard the doors close behind her.

Hadrian erupted from his couch, scroll flying halfway across the room. He crossed the mosaics in three violent strides, jerking Antinous up from his knees. "Caesar," Antinous breathed, and Hadrian's mouth speared him. The Emperor's fists clenched in his hair, so hard Antinous gasped in pain, and Hadrian drank that pain down, his teeth scoring Antinous's lip brutally. Then his mouth and his hands both were gone, and he looked at Antinous with eyes remote and cold.

"Keep him from my sight," the Emperor said. "I do not wish to see him once, understand? *Keep him from my sight.*"

"Thank you," Antinous whispered. He tasted blood on his lip, and Hadrian raised a hand to touch it.

"My poor star," he said, and as fast as that, all anger was gone. "I am so sorry, I would not hurt you for the world"—and he said not one word more about Vix or any of the rest of it. It was only to Sabina that Antinous could talk of his father, and to her he babbled like a nervous bride.

"I've made arrangements for him to stay with the Praetorians. He can be inconspicuous there; they won't give him away to the rest of the court." When the Imperial cortege was on the move between provinces, the off-duty Praetorians traveled in their own phalanx of wagons and horses. Hadrian and Antinous traveled far away, at the heart of the whole procession, Antinous on his bay colt beside the Empress's palanquin, Hadrian either riding beside Antinous or lying with his head in Sabina's lap whenever they could bully him into resting. Around them the insulation of guards, secretaries, body slaves, dogs, and courtiers. No, Hadrian should not lay eyes on Vix at all. "As long as they don't *see* each other—"

"And as long as *I* don't," the Empress said, sounding wry. "Because the Emperor will be watching me, that I know."

Antinous winced. "I wish . . ."

"What?"

That you could be as happy as I am, he thought. *That the man I love would not be as unforgiving as a stone, when it comes to the thing that would make* you *happy.* Hadrian had softened toward his wife—they laughed together now, teased each other, argued books, shared a couch while working—but he had not softened *that* much.

"Wish for the moon," Sabina said lightly. "Hadrian will try to pull it down from the heavens to hang about your neck, I'm sure."

He'd find that easier than what I just asked of him, Antinous thought, rumpling a hand through his hair. "I'm nervous," he confessed. "We're to depart in two days. What if he doesn't come?"

But Vix came, his pack over his shoulder just like the old days when he'd swing through the door back home from the latest war. He looked as hard and awkward as he had that day in Bethar when all they'd been able to do was stare at each other and bleed inside . . . But he was here.

"Is he much changed?" Empress Sabina asked the next day. Looking very cool and remote about it all, holding her eyes closed so her little African maid could line her eyes with kohl against the sun's heat—but she still asked.

"He's leaner, maybe. A bit more gray." Antinous smiled. "No, not much changed."

Sabina kept her eyes closed. "And his wife?"

"She's in Bethar. I only saw her once. But she's—harder."

So am I, Antinous thought. You didn't spend five years gritting your teeth and keeping a smile nailed on while people called you a whore without getting a little harder around the edges. He had a little stony spot in his heart for Mirah, even after she'd given him her blessing. *You blessed me,* he thought, *but you turned my sisters against me.* Dinah and Chaya, who used to ride his shoulders, flinching away from him—sweet gods, but that had hurt! And it had been Mirah they looked at as they flinched, not Vix. *I want my father back.* Antinous sent the thought to his father's wife. *I will woo him back whether you like it or not, and then I will change Hadrian's mind about hating him. I will do it if it takes me the rest of my life.*

"You look rather grim." Empress Sabina looked up from her mirror, blinking kohl-rimmed eyes. "Does it worry you, having Vix here?"

"It's such a chance, that's all." Antinous smiled. "I don't want to ruin it."

"You won't. Egypt is a land of magic and healing—anything can happen there."

"Maybe Egypt will heal my father and me." Antinous felt his smile disappear. "Maybe it will heal fate."

Sabina cocked her head. "Whose fate?"

"Never mind." Antinous still thought of the swirling blackness he'd seen at Eleusis; the terrible conviction of death on the mountaintop with the smell of lightning in the air. *Hadrian's death.* "If Egypt is truly a place of healing, we must get the Emperor to see some of the native doctors in Alexandria. I don't like the way his headaches are coming back . . ."

Egypt. They approached it by the coastal road, from Gaza to Pelusium lying fortified and remote between the marshes of the Nile and the lapping blue waters of the sea. Shining Alexandria, the famous lighthouse piercing the blue dome of summer sky, the natives cheering their Emperor so wildly that Antinous was deafened for hours after. "Of course they cheer," Lucius Ceionius said. "The Emperor here is not only emperor but Pharaoh. Pharaoh and God!"

"What do they call the great-nephew of a pharaoh?" Pedanius Fuscus wanted to know. He'd joined the party at Alexandria in a toga so new and stiff it almost creaked, edging up to Hadrian whenever he saw a chance. "Does a pharaoh's great-nephew get to be a god as well?" the young man asked hopefully.

"He at least gets a statue," Hadrian said, looking tolerant. There *had* been a statue to Pedanius Fuscus erected in Greece, Antinous remembered, a handsome marble boy carved optimistically to look like a young emperor. In the flesh he was no boy but a young man, burly and charming with a self-deprecating smile. "I suppose I should not hold it against him that I dislike his grandfather," Hadrian had said, raising a brow over the latest nagging letter from Servianus. "The lad seems intelligent enough. Perhaps he will make a suitable heir, after all."

"I don't like Pedanius Fuscus," Antinous confessed, not to Hadrian but to Vix. Safe topics of conversation had to be saved up for those precious hours in the evening when he would leave Hadrian to his work or perhaps depart a banquet early, and go share a quiet cup of wine with his father in the Praetorian barracks. He'd have rather talked about Hadrian, about Empress Sabina, the people most important in his life, but his father could not hear either name without looking shuttered, and Antinous learned to speak of others. Pedanius Fuscus was a safe subject. "Mind you, he was only a boy when I saw him last. But he was trying to beat Titus Aurelius's daughter into a pulp."

"What?" Vix lowered his cup, scowling. "That little bastard!"

"I wouldn't say he succeeded. She was going at him like a clawing whirlwind." How old would little Annia be by now? Twelve, thirteen? "I suppose it prejudices me against him. Still, not all bullies grow up bad."

"I was a bully when I was young," Vix admitted. "My father had to beat me to a pulp a few times before that lesson sank in."

"You never beat me to a pulp."

"Never had to, never wanted to."

"Maybe once," Antinous said lightly, deliberately.

Vix looked away to stroke the black dog's ears. "Do you know if the Emperor plans to go back to Judaea?" The kind of abrupt change of conversation that happened if Antinous made even an oblique mention of Hadrian. *Gently does it,* Antinous thought, letting himself be steered to the rebuilding of Jerusalem as Aelia Capitolina and how the Jews were in uproar over the idea of having a temple of Jupiter built over their own altars. More safe subjects. He had learned not to nag Hadrian if he wanted to make his point—just talk mildly around the edge of the matter until things sank in. His father was just the same.

More time, Antinous prayed. *Give me more time.* Because his father wasn't happy in Judaea, no matter how much he talked of his wine shop and of Judaea's unrest. He looked uneasy and somehow shamed when he spoke of those things—Antinous saw it every time. *Don't be in a rush to go back. Just give me time.*

Canopus next. The long stretch of water that Hadrian at once swore to re-create at his villa, here illuminated at night till it sparkled. The waterway was crowded by little gliding pleasure crafts bright with gilding and curtained with silk. Hadrian's small barge lay moored beside the jetty, and the Emperor lounged on a pile of cushions, half-dozing against Antinous's shoulder. Sabina sat cross-legged on Hadrian's other side, perusing a scroll. "It promises to teach me to read hieroglyphs." She frowned. "I have my doubts . . ."

"Do you mean to go back to Judaea, Caesar?" Antinous was asking. Vix's questions recently had made him curious. "After Egypt?"

"Why should I?" Hadrian's eyes were still closed. "I have achieved everything there I meant to. And there is no reason to go for pleasure, considering the province has nothing to offer but hot wind and stubborn people."

"We might see the rebuilding of Aelia Capitolina, Caesar." Vix had mentioned how much opposition there was to the city's new name. "Maybe let it stay named Jerusalem?" Antinous suggested.

"A gesture of goodwill, eh?"

Sabina frowned at her hieroglyphic scroll, turning it upside-down. "This is utterly useless. I can't even tell which way the characters go . . ."

"I'd rather talk about Cyrenaica than Judaea." Hadrian waved a hand sleepily. "Did you hear there's a huge lion ravaging the country there? We could mount a hunt, my Osiris." He'd taken to calling Antinous his Osiris as well as his star, after the reborn god of the ancients.

"I would very much like to see you hunt a lion, Great-Uncle," Pedanius interjected. He'd been trying his best to cuddle up to one of the half-naked Egyptian courtesans, but Lucius Ceionius had floated past on his own pleasure craft and the girl took one look at his aquiline profile and hopped lithely from one boat to the other. "My grandfather says I throw a hunting spear almost as well as Caesar himself," the Emperor's great-nephew persisted, but Antinous put a finger to his lips, silencing him. The Emperor had dozed off.

"Let him sleep." Antinous stroked the Emperor's hair. "He stays up half the night working; he may as well doze when he can."

"Of course." Pedanius did his best to be polite to Antinous, but his gaze always slid away quickly. "Will you have me fetched when Caesar wakes, Aunt?" he asked Sabina. She was his great-aunt, at least by marriage, but he always called her aunt. Possibly to make the Imperial tie sound closer; possibly because he thought no woman wanted to be called Great-Anything. "I have so little chance to make an impression on him. Perhaps you might speak to him about letting me come on that lion hunt . . ."

"Perhaps." Sabina looked amused as Pedanius went clambering out of the little pleasure craft. "Probably looking for another courtesan," she said to Antinous. "Shall we wish him better luck? He seems a nice boy. He's polite to you, which makes me think better of him."

Polite to me when you or the Emperor watches, Antinous thought. But it was not his place to disparage the Imperial family, so he dropped a kiss on Hadrian's temple where the pulse beat fast even in sleep, and changed the subject. "Stay with him, Lady? I want to walk."

Hadrian stirred but continued to doze as Antinous slid free, and Sabina tugged the Emperor's slumbering head down on her own shoulder instead. Antinous meandered up the jetty, taking no particular course, just looking at the stars overhead and the warm glow of lamplight reflecting on the Canopus waterway. *Beautiful,* Antinous thought, and wondered why he felt melancholy. Egypt was everything he had been promised, a place of magic and healing. He had his father with him, and he had Hadrian; he was *happy.*

The gods are jealous of happiness, Antinous thought. *So they send melancholy thoughts and dark dreams.* It was something to be borne, that was all. Payment for bliss.

"Feeling wistful, boy?"

He thought for a moment it was Vix, because his father called him *boy* when he was teasing, but Vix never drawled like that. Antinous turned to see Lucius Ceionius lounging against a pillar, all in matching shades of green tonight with a synthesis of sage-dyed silk and jade bracelets with slave girls in matching jade beads. "I thought you had a courtesan to entertain, Lucius."

"A pretty girl, but dull. I prefer women of intelligence as well as loveliness, and such are few." Lucius joined him with a languid look out toward the Emperor's barge. "You seem on cozy terms with Empress Sabina, young Osiris. What can I say to get her into my arms? I swear, the woman is impervious."

"You live dangerously." Antinous laughed. "The Emperor's wife—"

"A collector of beauty must be willing to take risks." A sigh. "She is older than I, but she carries it with *such* elegance . . ."

"Give up," Antinous advised. "Because I'm afraid she won't have you."

"What a blow to one's confidence." Lucius shrugged, not looking too heartbroken. "Well, at least you're honest. I shall be honest in turn, Antinous."

His attention sharpened. "Do you want to tell me I am a disgrace, a he-whore, a blot upon the morals of the Empire? Believe me"—a smile of steel-edged pleasantness—"I have heard it all before."

"Not at all." The kohl-lined eyes crinkled. "I don't care if the Emperor is mounting you. You're lovely to look at, even to someone like me who doesn't care for male flesh, and you're more intelligent than people think. You're even rather good for that uncertain Imperial temper of his. But how old are you—twenty?"

Antinous spoke tightly. "Twenty-four. What of it?"

"Ah . . . That's worse than I thought, then. You look younger." Giving a nod to the mop of curls Antinous had let grow long. "You were still a boy when you left Rome with the Emperor. On the edges, perhaps, but close enough to count. Not by the time we return to the Eternal City. If you think the disapproval was bad before, it's nothing to what will be waiting when we return."

"I am used to scorn—"

"Gods know you should be by now, but the scorn won't be for you. It will be for the Emperor." Lucius twisted a ring off his finger, admired it, decided it looked better on the other hand. "No one blamed him for humping a pretty boy, and if you were a slave or a native auxiliary or even a freedman, no one would care that you are twenty-four and still being fucked like a girl. But you're a citizen, a free man of Rome. An emperor who debauches a grown freeborn citizen of Rome, no matter how far beneath him in birth . . ."

Antinous let his voice grow cold. "There have always been men who formed bonds like ours."

"But not emperors. Emperors must uphold the moral principles of Rome, or at least the important ones. We don't hold a great deal sacred in the Eternal City, but the dignity of every free Roman is something we *do* take seriously."

"No one will dare mock the Emperor—"

"Not to his face. But behind his back, he will be denounced as a despoiler of Rome's sacred morals. That's how rumors against Nero and Caligula and Domitian started, you know. No one cared if they killed slaves or passed laws that made no sense. The denunciations started when they began either killing fellow senators or openly debauching Rome's morals. Emperor Hadrian seems to have reconsidered the wisdom of executing men of the Senate House, considering he hasn't done it for years, but the second?"

Nero. Domitian. Caligula. Emperors who had ended their days dead on the tiles, blood splashed around them. *Sweet gods, no. Anything but that.* Antinous had always assumed that the burden of shame and humiliation lay on his shoulders alone—not on Hadrian's. Never that.

But now horror curled through his stomach with cold claws. Death: death in the dark at Eleusis, near-death on the mountaintop. Could death be waiting not in the dangers of the east, not in Hadrian's unpredictable health, but in *Rome?* In the Eternal City, at the end of a knife?

"Enjoy your travels," Lucius said, and seemed to mean it. "Things are different in the east, aren't they? I enjoy the freedom, and so should you. Because when we all return to Rome, the Emperor—for his own good, whether he knows it or not—will have to give you up."

ANNIA

Rome

Evil worked better in the dark of the moon, everybody knew that. Annia waited, watching the moon shrink, and at last the night came when the house was asleep and she could sneak from her bed into the moonless gardens.

The voice called softly from the atrium behind her. "Where are you going?"

Annia turned around. "Marcus, go *away.*"

He came out from behind a pillar, dressed in a night tunic as she was, his hair rumpled. He was staying with them for a time; his dreary mother fancied herself ill again. "What are you doing awake?"

"What are *you* doing awake?" she countered.

"I'm an owl."

"You're an owl?"

"I'm always awake in the night. It's a fault, really. People should be larks, rising and falling with the sun, but as soon as I go to bed I'm just lying there awake, thinking. So I come out and look at the stars, and imagine I'm running with them." He pointed at the bundle in her hands. "What's that?"

"Nothing. I'm just going out to the garden for a moment."

"Even on her own grounds, a woman should be properly attended so nothing can befall either her, or her reputation." He came to her side. "What are you doing?"

"Working a curse. Are you satisfied?" She flung it at him. "I've made a curse tablet, like Empress Sabina did once. And to seal a curse tablet, you have to drive a nail through the lead and either bury it or throw it in a spring. So if you'll excuse me, I'm going to work some dark magic and then go back to bed."

She stamped off toward the *nymphaeum* at the end of the garden where there was a spring, choking back the hot tears that came to her eyes. The tears kept coming lately, but she refused to let them fall. *I'm not wasting one drop of salt on Brine-Face*, she thought viciously, and kicked a stone out of her way.

She hadn't been able to stop *thinking* of him, though. She couldn't stop herself from brooding, going over it all in her mind, bitterly calculating what she should have done different. Maybe the curse tablet would settle that.

Marcus fell in beside her. "Go away," Annia said, and dashed at her eyes.

"No," he said, and stumbled in the dark. "Who did Empress Sabina work a curse tablet on?"

"The old Empress. It worked, too." Maybe Aunt Sabina had some barbarian in her too, just like Annia. *The part of you that wasn't content to let an enemy go, but instead had to make him pay.*

"Who are you working a curse tablet on?"

"None of your business!"

They walked along in silence a little while. "It's Pedanius, isn't it?" Marcus asked, and stumbled again.

"Oh, *Hades*, just take my hand so you don't trip and break your neck."

"It isn't proper for a man to take a woman's hand unless a betrothal has been agreed on." His warm fingers interlaced with hers. "But I think a breach in decorum is allowable in this case."

"You're not a man, anyway." Annia knew she was being rude, but she couldn't seem to stop snarling at everyone. "You're still a boy."

"But you're a woman," Marcus said. "Legally, you could be married."

"Not at twelve. Nobody marries at twelve, even if it's legal."

"You still have the advantage over me. You're already a woman, but I won't be a man for another two years at least. So you don't need to fear me."

"I'm not afraid of anything," Annia spat, and her eyes pricked again.

They walked along silently, the trees black and rustling overhead. "Here," Annia said as they entered the grotto of the *nymphaeum*, and went to her knees beside the small cold well of the spring. She unwrapped the lead sheet of the curse tablet, fumbling for the nail.

"May I read it?" Marcus asked.

Annia looked at him a moment. Just a shadowy shape, but she'd know him anywhere by the attentive angle of his head, his relaxed stillness as he sat on his heels. She felt a lump in her throat, and she pushed the tablet at him.

He angled it under the faint starlight and read aloud, running a finger over the letters she had scratched into the lead. Annia hadn't needed any help wording the curse—she remembered that quite well, from eavesdropping on Empress Sabina. "*To the goddesses Diana, Hecate, and Proserpina. I invoke you holy ones by your names to punish and destroy Gnaeus Pedanius Fuscus Salinator for trying to take my virtue.*" A pause there. "*May he never prosper,*" Marcus kept on reading, and his voice had a note in it she hadn't heard before. "*May he never advance, may he never become emperor, and may I be the instrument of his downfall. May it be so in your names.*"

Annia's voice was rough. "Now you know."

Marcus was looking at her, she could feel it. She looked down at the spring, splashing the cold water.

"Pedanius attacked you?" he said quietly.

"Yes."

"Was it at his manhood ceremony?"

"Yes."

Marcus's voice got even quieter. "Tried to take your virtue?" he asked. "Or did?"

"Tried," she said, still splashing her hand in the spring, and somehow it all came out—running from Pedanius, having to get on her knees for him and tell him he'd be Caesar. That was the part that made her cheeks flush. Kicking him in the balls hadn't made up for it, not at all.

Her voice trailed off once it was told. She didn't want to look at Marcus.

There was a long inhale beside her. "Why didn't you tell your father?" Marcus said at last. "He would have believed you."

"Yes," Annia acknowledged. "But he'd have to do something about it, wouldn't he? So he'd go to Servianus, and Servianus would trumpet his grandson's innocence all over Rome, and my father would be shamed. Maybe more than shamed—the Emperor might punish him, for daring to accuse his great-nephew. Emperor Hadrian already dislikes my father; I can't give him any more reasons." She'd thought about it for so many hours, from every angle. *I cannot tell anyone.*

Except Marcus, whose eyes rested on her so steadily it was like a touch through the dark. "Annia," he said, "why won't you look at me?"

Because I'm ashamed! She wanted to shout it at him, and she wanted to cry. She swallowed down the little catch in her throat and spoke with dull flatness. "Everybody from my mother to the housekeeper to *Brine-Face* said I shouldn't go running about showing my ankles anymore, now that I was twelve and getting old enough to tempt men. I didn't listen, and look what happened."

"A virtuous man cannot be tempted to an evil act." Marcus sounded thoughtful, but very certain. "Therefore, the sight of your ankles or your anything else makes no difference: in acting upon his lusts, Pedanius proved himself as a man of no virtue. Well, we already knew that, didn't we?"

Annia stayed silent, turning that over. It sounded very well, but if this whole business came out to the world, *she'd* still be the one shamed. Not Pedanius. Annia knew that the way she knew dawn comes at the end of night.

"Pedanius is wrong about something else," Marcus added.

"What's that?"

"He said no one would marry you if he ruined you." Marcus sounded matter-of-fact. "But even if you hadn't fought him off—if he'd had his way—I'd still marry you."

She gave a harsh little laugh. "You're just saying that to be kind."

"No." His hand found hers in the dark. "I'm not."

"Ruined girls don't get husbands. Not good husbands like you, anyway."

"You think I'd be a good husband?" he asked, diverted.

She shrugged. "You're good at everything else, aren't you? Greek verbs and *trigon*, rhetorics and declamation, even your sword drills. You'd be good at husbanding too."

"Husbanding means the care and cultivation of plants," he began.

"Don't make me hit you," she warned, and tried to yank her hand away. But he held on, his fingers knotted warmly through hers.

"Pedanius couldn't take your virtue," Marcus said, and his voice was serious again. "Your virtue is already in you—it's in what *you* do, not what he does to you. I'd still want to marry you, no matter how he wronged you."

Annia looked at him a moment, and then she leaned forward and kissed him. She couldn't see as well in the shadows as he could; their noses bumped and she got his more of his chin than his lips. But it was still a kiss and she heard him inhale sharply. He smelled like ink and mint.

"I suppose you think that was improper," she said, pulling back a little.

"Nothing about you is proper," he said, and she could *hear* him smiling. "Maybe I'm going to be a good husband, Annia Galeria Faustina, but you're going to make me a very bad wife."

"Probably," she agreed. She felt light inside for the first time since Brine-Face grabbed her by the hair and told her to get on her knees. Just telling Marcus things and seeing him listen in that quiet way—it seemed to let all the wrath and the shame out. Ever since Pedanius had left for Egypt, Annia had been weighed down by the ball of rage burning in her chest.

Not now.

"Let's finish cursing this bastard," Marcus went on, and she gave his hand a squeeze to hear him swear. It was the kind of habit Annia felt she should encourage. "Because he's not going to be Emperor, even if he is Caesar's great-nephew. I'll hold him down in this spring till he drowns, first. I might just do that anyway."

"No, I will," Annia said. "I put it in the curse. I'm going to be the instrument of his downfall, remember?"

"Let me drive the nail into the tablet," Marcus proposed. "That gives me a stake in it, too. If you don't bring down Pedanius, I get a chance at him."

"You said curses were wicked," Annia said, just to tease.

"Oh, they are," Marcus said. "And I'll pray for his downfall. But if prayer doesn't work, well, 'if I cannot soften those above, I will provoke those below.'"

"You're going to tell me who said that, aren't you?"

"Virgil." Taking the nail from her hand, Marcus stabbed it through the folded lead tablet. "There," he said, and as he handed her the tablet, Annia heard that intensity in his voice again. "Gnaeus Pedanius Fuscus Salinator will never be Emperor. And more than that, he'll pay for attacking you. I swear it."

"I swear it," Annia echoed, and flung the tablet into the spring.

CHAPTER 13

VIX

A.D. 130, Autumn
Cyrenaica

The Emperor was hunting lion, and all I could think of was my wife. The hunting chariots, the horses, the bustle of the vast Imperial hunting party—none of it seemed as real to me as Mirah's blue eyes smiling at me as I told her I would join the Imperial cortège. Not because of Simon's words to me, but because of hers.

"Hurry up, Vix!" Boil's broad face was flushed with sunburn in Cyrenaica's brutal heat. "Don't you want to see the beast go down? It's as big as the Nemean lion, so they say! Been ravaging the local villages—"

I didn't care if the Emperor bagged his lion. He rode at the front of the hunt on his big black horse, Antinous a spot of blue on the horse beside him, and I heard Simon's voice in a whisper on the desert wind. *See what our Caesar plans next for Judaea.*

I didn't know how well I'd done at that. I was no subtle-tongued spy; I stumbled through my inquiries about Judaea with a flaming face. But my son seized my labored hints just because they carried words between us, suspecting nothing. Maybe he spoke to the Emperor, but I knew already there would be no change in Hadrian's plans for Judaea. Why should there be? He was an efficient bastard: He'd come to a troublesome province with a list of plans, he'd checked off every item on it, and he'd moved on. As far as he was concerned, Aelia Capitolina would rise over the ruins of Jerusalem, Greek-columned temples would crowd out the synagogues, and that was that.

And Simon, along with God knew how many men like him, would go on quietly counting the swords in those underground caches and training men to wield them, until someday there were enough of both.

"Caesar!" One of the huntsmen squatted beside a rocky outcropping. "Lion tracks. The beast has a paw big as a platter—" The whole party spurred ahead.

"What do you know?" I'd asked Mirah quietly the night Simon tried to recruit me, in the darkness of our bed where man and wife can murmur secrets unheard. And even so I whispered, because Simon's plan for me still pulled a reflexive cry of *Treason!* from the deep lairs of my mind. "What do you know of your uncle's . . . activities?"

"Nothing much. Nothing disastrous," she whispered back. "If I were forced to tell."

I felt a pulse of anger that Simon had entangled his favorite niece in such dangerous business. "How much is *nothing much?*"

"Enough." She cupped my cheek in the dark. "Will you go to Egypt with Antinous, Vix? Do what Simon asks of you?"

"Why?" I wanted her answer for that question. Not Simon's answer; hers. "Why do *you* want it of me?"

"Because I have watched you here for five years, and I see my husband in pain." There had been tears in her eyes. "You are half-alive, struggling to balance between Rome and Judaea, and there can be no more balancing. Come to us. Come to us, and let it be *done.*"

My throat closed.

"Rome is a disease." Mirah moved forward in our bed so her lips touched the hollow of my collarbone. I could feel the dampness of her lashes against my skin. "Cut it away from you, and you will be victorious."

"Victorious over what?" I closed my eyes, inhaling the scent of her hair. We'd touched less and less, over the past years—the fragrant softness of her flesh against me was making my heart race like a boy's. "Why does going to Egypt with the Emperor even *matter?* You truly think I can turn him away from these plans of his for Judaea, through Antinous?"

She pulled away from me, just far enough so that our noses still brushed. "No."

"Then why—"

"You have to prove yourself," Mirah said. "Do this for my uncle Simon, and he'll trust you. That's where you'll come back victorious. A man of Judaea at last."

I gave a harsh laugh. "Prove myself trustworthy? He once trusted me enough to guard his shield arm!"

"Don't judge him for growing hard, Vix. Hardness is what wins rebellions." The word was out, hanging there in the dark. *Rebellion.* And in my thoughts, something like an eagle's cry still shrieked, *Treason!*

"Besides, Uncle Simon is kind, too." Mirah's arm slipped about my waist under the blankets. "He's giving you this chance to save Antinous, before you break with Rome. And you'll succeed, I know it! You'll bring Antinous home, and I *want* that, Vix. I want him to come to God, so he can come home to us. So he can grow a golden beard, fall in love with a beautiful girl, dance at our daughters' weddings—"

My long resentment eased painfully in my chest when she said that. *You want him back, Mirah? Truly?*

"—and you'll stand by Simon when he takes arms against Rome," Mirah went on. "Vercingetorix ben Masada, my warrior for God." Kissing the center of my chest, she whispered in Latin. "*Judaea Victor.*"

I cupped the back of her head, twining my hand through her hair. "You see all that?"

"I do."

"When did you turn prophet?" I asked. But when had any of this happened, really? When had my friend turned from legionary to rebel? When had I turned from Praetorian to spy?

You have no more oath to Rome, I reminded myself. If I had, it would have been different—Mirah would never have asked me to break a sworn oath. But I had no oath to betray. Hadrian had made sure of that.

She was right. I was half-alive and more than half-crushed in this eternal struggle between Rome and Judaea; between my past and my family.

Time to choose.

"I'll go," I said, and moved over Mirah in our marriage bed and kissed her. We'd spent too many nights lately lying back to back in the darkness, but that night I made love to my wife, and it was like the old days. It hadn't been good between us since I'd stopped soldiering; that was the blunt truth. But now I'd be a warrior again, and for something better than the empty glory of Rome, and it was good.

"More tracks!" The cry of another huntsman broke my thoughts, and Mirah's smooth phantom flesh shivered away until I felt only the rough mane of my borrowed gelding. The Emperor's dogs were milling up ahead, and I saw Hadrian swing off his horse in an arc of purple cloak to peer at the ground. "The lion ate here!"

Just hearing his deep, self-satisfied voice made my blood begin a slow burn inside my veins. I hoped he wept tears of humiliation when Judaea went up in flames, when he was forced to give it up, forced to fail as he so rarely failed at anything. Because I didn't intend to fail. If I was breaking with Rome, I'd take a whole province with me.

Golden wings flashed through my mind, and I blinked away the thought of the Tenth Fidelis's eagle, so proud and unyielding in my hands. "If Judaea rebels," I'd whispered to Mirah sometime during that last tender night, "the Tenth Fidelis will march to crush the unrest."

"Then they'll die," she said quietly.

I tried to persuade myself that the Tenth could withstand any rebellious rabble . . . But men like Simon were not rabble. Men like Simon were trained and disciplined, and they understood very well how to fight Roman legionaries. "If the Tenth falls, so does her eagle."

Mirah pressed herself against me. "They aren't your men anymore," she whispered. "Or your eagle. I know it will still hurt, Vix, but it's the price. No one ever said cutting a disease out would be painless."

No, indeed.

"May I have first hit on the lion, Great-Uncle?" a boy's voice was saying eagerly. "I'm of the Imperial blood, I *should* have first strike after you—"

I looked at the Emperor's great-nephew: sweating in the sun, full of his own importance. "He should have been a tribune in the Tenth," I mused, still thinking of the legion's eagle. "We'd have knocked the bumptiousness out of him."

"Gods, yes," Boil said with relish. "Then picked our teeth with his bones. Tribunes are bloody useless."

"Most," I admitted. "Not all. Titus Aurelius—"

"No, he wasn't too proud for a patrician sprig." Boil cocked a blond eyebrow at me. "Hard to remember what a grand man he is now, when he used to share our sour *posca*."

I wondered what Titus would do, if he knew the decision I'd made. I saw his look of cool disapproval, the one that could shrivel gods on their thrones, and I blinked it away. Why should he disapprove? He'd do anything for his family, and I'd do anything for mine. Dinah and Chaya had stood to embrace me when I left for Egypt, and all the irritation I'd ever felt toward them when they fell into moody humors had blown away like chaff on the wind. Dinah was so beautiful, a colt-ish girl with a soft mouth made for smiles. Chaya had shy doelike eyes that would soon have suitors stumbling over themselves. I'd embraced them both fiercely, and Dinah had whispered in my ear, "Bring Antinous back, Father. I miss him." And Chaya had whispered in my other ear, "I'm sorry I was too nervous to hug him."

Antinous. He cantered ahead alongside the Emperor as the hounds gave voice. This was the first time I'd *seen* him at Hadrian's side, except at a very great distance—he'd been so careful to keep us far apart. I could see his blue cloak flapping behind him, see how he rode loose and easy in the saddle with his horse on a long rein. *Could* I bring him back, as my family seemed to think? Conversations with my son had gotten easier, but only if I kept off the subject of Hadrian. Just let me call the Emperor a raping bastard or a silk-tunicked turd, and Antinous's face hardened all over and the rest of the conversation was doomed. Maybe I'd have to choke him and throw him over a saddle, because I didn't see any other way of prying him loose from this cushioned whore's nest the Emperor had built around him.

I had to find a way. Because if I didn't, if I went home alone and threw myself into Judaea's struggles against Rome—well, there wasn't any way back from that. The path behind me would be burned away, no track even for a loving son to follow.

Simon won't care, a little voice whispered. *Antinous is a lure, something* to get you here in the first place. *Doesn't matter to Simon if you come back with the Emperor's lover or not.*

And some part of me suspected it wouldn't really matter to Mirah, either.

I actually closed my eyes at that thought, trying to shut out the thing I didn't want to think about my own wife. "What are you doing?" Boil laughed from his horse.

"Nothing," I muttered, and scratched at my jaw. "This beard's driving me mad, that's all." I'd left off shaving recently, thinking that if I was going to be a man of Judaea it was time I had the beard to match, and it was currently in the itchy stage.

I heard Hadrian's deep laughter up ahead, saw him extend his ringed hand out to Antinous so my son had to lean half out of the saddle to link fingers. "First blow against the lion is mine," Hadrian was calling out, ignoring his great-nephew's frown, "but I leave the death blow to you, Osiris!" I saw Antinous lift the Emperor's knuckles to his lips in thanks, and Hadrian smiled. He leaned forward in his own saddle to ruffle Antinous's hair, just like he'd ruffle one of his dogs, and I felt a surge of black hatred rise like a spring in the middle of my belly. *Why couldn't you have died on that mountain in Antioch, you bastard? Struck by lightning and cast down by your gods.*

The dogs were giving voice more urgently, seething and whining. "Close," the huntsmen muttered. "The lion's close, they've got his scent—"

The beast came from nowhere, a great leap down from a craggy outcropping of rock to the dry ground beneath. It gathered itself proudly as the dogs yelped and circled, the huntsmen shouted, and some of the more timid courtiers shrieked. I nearly shrieked myself because the lion was enormous: longer from snarling fangs to the tip of its twitching tail than I was tall, with massive clawed paws and teeth that could have punched through iron. My old lion skin had been a tawny thing, but this beast was darker, its short mane near to black. It gave a great slash at the ground and roared, no fear in its glittering eyes, and I remembered that this dark creature was a man-killer.

The Emperor raised his spear and charged.

"That rash bastard," Boil groaned. "Will he just wait for *once*—" Boil was already wheeling his horse along with the other Praetorians, and some part of me felt a nearly unstoppable urge to fall in protective formation alongside them. I reined back instead, my horse jostling that pretty-boy Lucius Ceionius, and I watched the Emperor. The lion screamed, making a lunge for Hadrian's horse, and the stallion reared. Antinous let out a warning cry, circling with his own spear ready and his reins doubled about one taut fist, but Hadrian just spoke a quiet word to his panicked stallion, never taking his eyes off the lion. As the stallion's hooves came down and the lion crouched to spring, the Emperor let fly with his spear.

In the breath of time it took the spear to fly, glittering in the sunlight and aimed for the lion's massive side, I had time to remember another hunt. That one had been in Mysia, and the prey had been a bear, and the Emperor had speared the bear in the side too before he had become aware of a golden youth on the far side of the clearing . . . *Full circle*, I thought as Hadrian let out a shout of triumph, his spear spitting the lion in the ribs, and kicked his horse in a dash past the beast as it screamed in pain.

"For you!" he yelled at Antinous, and his teeth gleamed in the dark thicket of beard. "I've blooded him, my star, now he's yours!" Antinous was already spurring forward, his eyes all taut focus and his spear like a streak of lightning ready to fly, but the lion, which had whirled to follow Hadrian, now whirled back, blood spilling like rubies from its side, and it flew forward with a great rake of its claws and another maddened roar. The dust billowed up, and by the time I'd kicked past Lucius, the horse was on its side and shrieking, haunch opened to the bone, and Antinous had tumbled free.

No. Not free. The fallen stallion had trapped his leg against the ground, pinned my son helpless.

The horse. I shot the thought at the lion like a spear of my own. *Go for the horse, not my son*—but this monster was a killer of men, and it stalked toward Antinous with a snarl. Antinous, struggling to free his trapped leg, struggling to reach his spear, which had fallen a dozen feet away, and a wave of stark, blind terror swamped me.

I was off my horse and unsheathing my dagger, pushing through the pack of yelping dogs, but I'd never get there fast enough. Never in this

world. In one horrific flash I saw my son die under the lion's claws, die as
lion bait like a gladiator in the arena, like I should have died, oh God, *no*—

Antinous froze where he lay trapped, staring as his death came for
him, wide-eyed as the little boy who had ridden my lion-furred shoulders. Another lion was coming for him now, claws raking, and I would
never be there in time. But the scream that was just forming in my
throat came roaring out of Hadrian instead.

I never saw a man make a leap like that in my life, the leap that the
Emperor of Rome made as he vaulted off his horse very nearly over the
stallion's head, to land square on his feet between Antinous and the lion.
Hadrian never stumbled, just cocked his arm, and I saw the muscles
bunch clear across his back under his cloak as he hurled his second
spear. The lion screamed again as the blade pierced its broad chest, and
Hadrian was already flying forward, sword leaping from its scabbard.
"*Caesar*—" Antinous shouted, not frozen anymore, trying to pull his
leg free from the struggling horse, but Hadrian never looked back. He
just slashed, opening another red wound across the lion's huge shoulder, and another, and the lion batted him down with a rake of claws.
He rolled, all purple cloak and dark curls and more blood unrolling
across the packed earth like a royal carpet, and the Praetorians were
muscling in, but the Emperor never looked at them either. He came up
to one knee just as the lion flew at him, and somehow he was between
those massive paws, letting out a lion's roar of his own as he buried his
gladius hilt-deep in the beast's heart.

The lion collapsed atop the Emperor.

I was there a fraction of a heartbeat later, the guards a few steps
behind me, all our frantic hands rolling the beast away. It was dying,
the Emperor's spear in its side still pulsing blood and the Emperor's
sword in its heart pulsing very little. Its eyes were dimming, its claws
were still trying to find flesh to rend, but no one cared for the lion. The
Emperor's head lolled against my knee, loose, and my heart gave a great
thump. *He's dead*, I thought, *this time he's dead*. And the shriek went
up from one of the guards—"He's dead!"—and I leaned closer to put
my ear against his chest, feeling something wild and strange inside me
that could have been hope. I put my head to the Emperor's chest, and

before I could hear anything I felt the whisper of his breath past my ear and felt another violent squeeze of my heart.

He lived.

But he doesn't have to, I thought. My hand with the dagger still clenched in it was under his head—all I had to do was rake it across the back of his neck, out of sight of the frantic Praetorians. They were shouting for cloaks, for physicians, for bandages—one small motion of my hand would never be noticed. The wound would look like a slash from the lion's claws: Emperor Hadrian, struck down by a lion on a hunt. I could take my grieving son home with me, free from a madman's clutches forever.

I could kill him. I saw the slash in a heartbeat, felt exactly the degree of pressure the blade would need, how I could take off my cloak and slip it under the Emperor's head as a cushion, and do it right then with the cloth hiding my dagger. "*God is just,*" Simon had told me. "*Serve Him, and He might even grant you the chance to kill Hadrian.*"

Here it was. One stroke and I could save my son, kill a tyrant, and go home a hero to help liberate Judaea in the chaos of Rome's falling. My son had fallen prey to the Emperor's charm on one hunt—this hunt would see it done.

Full circle, indeed.

One stroke.

But—

But . . .

You saved my son, I thought. *You saved my son when I could not.*

"Hadrian," a voice was screaming, "*Hadrian!*" And Antinous clawed his way past the guards, pushed them bodily aside, and fell on Hadrian's broad chest. "No," he was shouting, "no, not like this—"

I still could have done it. Half the Praetorians were trying to pull Antinous back, the rest were running for a physician, and no one was paying attention to me. I could still have done it.

But Hadrian's eyes fluttered open, and they didn't even see me. They were all for my son, one desperate glance, and when he saw Antinous's face hovering over his own, I saw him squeeze his eyes shut, and I saw the tears that ran from the corners of his eyes into his hair. "Thank the gods," he whispered, and he pushed himself unsteadily up to a sitting position. His neck, that strip of unarmored and vulnerable neck, glided away ghostlike from my hand, and he sat up to grab my son in a great bear hug. "My star," he said unsteadily, "oh, my star—"

"I killed it!" a voice said triumphantly. "The lion, Great-Uncle, I finished it off!" Pedanius Fuscus, the Emperor's great-nephew, standing over the lion, one foot posed carefully on its massive shoulder, his spear stabbed down into the beast's throat. "It was still moving," he explained, but no one was paying any attention to him. Antinous was sitting in the dust, tears running down his face.

"Caesar," he said hoarsely. "You saved me—you shouldn't have saved me, you—"

Hadrian rose, just as unsteady on his feet, and pulled my son up into his arms. They clung together, gripping each other tight, and I saw uncomfortable glances between the Praetorians and courtiers. I saw disgust, too, on more than one face. Young Pedanius Fuscus looked peevish, standing so artfully posed over the lion.

"Sweet gods, Caesar," Antinous said, cradling the Emperor's face in his hands. "Why did you jump in its way? It could have killed you—"

Hadrian's voice was low, his mouth pressed against Antinous's curls as he crushed my son against him. "I'd die in a lion's mouth for you," he murmured. "I'd die in its teeth and let the Empire burn after me, if it meant you lived."

"No," Antinous cried, and his eyes were wild. "That's not how it works, I offered my life for *you*—"

"Shut up." Such an expression on the Emperor's face as he looked at my son: a relief so deep it bordered on agony. I knew that expression, because I'd worn it myself the day I'd thought Mirah lay crushed to death in the great earthquake of Antioch years ago. I'd thought her dead and then I'd heard her voice calling me, live and well. The relief had brought me to my knees with that same anguished look of joy Hadrian now wore.

Because I loved so deeply, and losing that love to death would have crushed me.

Hadrian and Antinous held each other for a long time after that, grappled chest against chest and still shaking, the lion dead beside them. And I watched them as my golden chance crumbled away, and with it all my hopes.

ANTINOUS

Egypt

"Now, this is absurd," Hadrian said irritably. "Acclaimed in Carthage as a god because of a perfectly coincidental rainstorm—and here I am a *cursed* god because I cannot make the Nile rise?"

A chill ran through Antinous despite the heat that had collected under the canopy of the Imperial barge. "Don't say that, Caesar—'cursed.'"

"I *am* cursed," Hadrian grumbled. "Cursed by Egyptian peasants who think I have merely to wave a hand, and then the river will rise and fertilize their wretched fields!"

"Give the Egyptians their superstitions, Caesar." Empress Sabina sounded lazy, reclining with eyes closed on the next couch. "We Romans are no better, always peering at cow entrails to try to see Fate."

"I gave the peasants here enough of a concession just delaying this trip up the Nile at all." Hadrian glared about the deck of his gilded barge as if not pleased with the cushioned couches, the autumn breezes that flapped the striped silk canopy overhead, the green waters of the Nile slapping against the hull below. A far bigger craft than the little curtained vessel where they had floated in Canopus; almost a floating palace—but to Antinous it felt like a prison. Perhaps because in Canopus you could step off that little pleasure craft at any time. Here, all was at the mercy of the surrounding Nile, even the Emperor of Rome.

It gave Antinous the shivers, but he tried not to show it. He twined his fingers with Hadrian's as the Emperor returned to his lapful of slates, stroking the swollen knuckles. *Ever since the lion hunt*, he thought—the swollen joints again, and those strange hardening pains returning to the flesh of his arms, and though Hadrian wouldn't say he had a headache, he was rubbing at his temple with a frown. Antinous touched the line between his eyes to smooth it away, calling for cold barley water.

"Perhaps you should rest," Empress Sabina said. Of course she had noticed the swollen fingers too, and the headache. But Hadrian only grunted, stylus tapping, and the Empress shrugged at Antinous as if to say, *We do what we can.*

I should do more, Antinous thought. But he gave her a smile, lowering his lashes so she couldn't see how the smile stopped short of his eyes.

The Empress stretched on her couch, propping her chin up for a look at the endless currents sliding past. In the barge's wake, a whole array of secondary boats drifted along in a flotilla. "I love this river," she observed. "Can we keep sailing forever?"

"It's beautiful," Antinous said honestly enough. The Nile seemed like a living thing, a green serpent sliding through the land, the ripples of the water almost lazy under the autumn sun, which still shimmered down with such fierce heat. It made for strange whimsical daydreams, but it made for black-fanged nightmares too, and Antinous hated this river no matter how beautiful it was. Because the dreamlike haze of heat and water, the blue lotuses and the liquid-eyed birds watching the barges slide past—they all hid danger. Look at a muddy log, and suddenly it blinked alien eyes and turned out to be a crocodile. Admire the innocent-looking hippopotamus fussing over her young in the shallows, and the guide from Alexandria laughed and said that the beast could sink their barge and everyone on it . . .

Danger here, Antinous thought, and he tried to mock himself but the foreboding would not leave him. It sat in his bones, watching like the crocodiles. And why not? Twice Hadrian had narrowly dodged death—from a storm's lightning, and from a lion's claws. *What if there is a third time?*

There would not be. Antinous told himself that fiercely. But he still wished they could leave this beautiful, treacherous river.

Lucius Ceionius was speaking, tickling the Empress's ankles with a feather fan and saying something flattering about how if the Emperor was Pharaoh in Egypt, then she was First Wife. "Better than being any kind of goddess," she said, nudging his hand away with her henna-patterned toes. "I wouldn't dare proclaim myself a goddess on this river—it would eat you for being presumptuous; you can just feel it. First Wife is good enough."

"And Antinous as First Concubine," someone snickered almost

inaudibly behind them. Hadrian was coughing in quick dry bursts—the cough was new, what did it mean?—and didn't hear the muttered insult. Antinous did. He'd heard far worse, but it wasn't the joke that hung and resonated in his mind. It was Lucius's warning voice from Canopus.

If you think the disapproval was bad before, it's nothing to what will be waiting when we return.

To Rome. Where there was also danger, just like this beautiful river—just danger of a different kind. *Because Hadrian will not give me up,* Antinous thought in stark honesty. He had seen that when his lover flung himself between Antinous and a lion. *And if he will not give me up, what will it cost him?*

Hadrian was still coughing, and Antinous pushed the thoughts aside to thump him on the back. "Breathe, Caesar—"

"Cease worrying," Hadrian said between coughs. "If I die on the Nile, at least I will be resurrected."

"So the story goes," Antinous temporized. "And then the river will rise—"

"The sacrifice works best if it's a beautiful boy!" Lazily, Lucius snapped his fingers for wine from his slave girls, twin Greek beauties identical to the last freckle. His latest craze: *"I shall be served henceforth by nothing but twins!"* Antinous would have found it funny if the girls didn't have such sad eyes over their permanently smiling mouths. "A boy's life given to the Nile; I hear it's an infallible spell for prosperity and health—"

"I am not throwing my beautiful boy into a river for *any* reward." Hadrian pulled Antinous's attention to the slate in his hand. "Tell me what you think of this, Osiris—an arch in Rome to commemorate our great lion hunt! The two of us, standing with our feet upon the lion's mane . . ."

More glances from the courtiers, and this time the Emperor saw them too. Hadrian stared around him with a gaze of long challenge until every eye dropped to the deck. *An emperor's bedmate carved upon an arch,* Antinous thought. *How that will shock Rome.* Only those of power and rectitude were relegated to triumphal marble.

"I'd rather not be put on an arch, Caesar; it wouldn't be well looked on." He saw the Imperial brows begin to draw together, and added, "And if you don't care for that, well, you know how I hate sitting for sculptors."

"Do it to please me, then?" Hadrian wheedled. "There, you have made your Pharaoh beg! Perhaps a statue of you as Osiris, too. I'll commission both, as soon as we return to Rome."

"Return?" Antinous looked up at him. ". . . When will that be, Caesar?"

Not yet, he thought in a pang of pure fear. *Sweet gods, not yet!*

But you were just praying to get off this river, another voice mocked in his mind. *The gods were listening after all!*

"We'll go to Thebes, first, and Philae." Hadrian was sketching again. More of his architectural jottings for the great villa outside Rome—at the rate he was designing additions and improvements, it would never be finished. "After that, it's time to return home."

Antinous looked from Hadrian to Empress Sabina. "Home," he echoed, turning the topaz ring around his finger where Hadrian had placed it. Home was here, in the world enclosed between their three points. But how much longer would that go on? Rome's scorn or the lash of the Fates who had already swiped twice at the Emperor—what would bring it to an end?

The Empress smiled. She slid off her couch and settled onto theirs, folding up her feet and leaning her head on Hadrian's shoulder, reaching across him to match her fingers against Antinous's. "Home is wherever the three of us sit, Antinous. So *home* will come back to Rome with us, won't it?"

His voice was almost mute as he squeezed her hand. "As you say, Lady."

VIX

When I found my son in the moonlight, he was trying not to weep.

The Nile at night is a sight that could bring anyone to tears. The danger that runs under the lazy surface during the day was sharper at night—the slap of the river's currents against the barge's hull came clearer in the dark, and the splash of the water warned of lurking crocodiles when you weren't being lulled by sunlit water lilies floating so serene on top. But despite all the dangers, it's the beauty of Egypt's great river at night that cuts like a knife and brings tears to the eyes: the thousands and thousands of stars overhead; the silver fullness of the moon; the warmth of the autumn night that still felt like summer.

But I didn't think it was beauty that brought my son to the brink of tears. Antinous sat at the stern of the barge, his feet dangling over the side like a child's, his shoulders slumped in utter misery. Beside him, his black dog whined and wagged its tail.

I padded across the deck and sat down beside him. He gave a start, turning his face away and trying to hide the anguish in his eyes. "I didn't see you there," he said, and began to pointlessly rewind the white bandage about his thumb. He had sprained it on the lion hunt—his only injury, thanks to Hadrian.

"What are you doing out here?" I asked, and tousled the dog's pointed ears.

"Thinking. Thinking of nothing very much." His face was still turned away from me. "The Nile has so many legends attached to it. Anyone who throws themselves into the Nile will save the life of a loved one, did you know that?"

"Morbid." Were we going to keep playing this game, the game we'd been playing all the way from Judaea? The game where we danced around each other's bruised feelings, never saying anything important? Hell with that; my son was in *pain*. "Why are you so nearly weeping?"

He gave up pretending and bowed his head into his own hands, shoulders heaving. I sat, waiting. Most of the Imperial barge slept. The Emperor had moored his barge on the riverbank tonight, the rest of his flotilla clustered around him, and there had been music and merrymaking on the cushioned decks: a whole golden entourage laughing and throwing carved dice, watching the Emperor's copper-skinned acrobats tumble to the beat of their drums.

But the Emperor had retired early, complaining of a headache, and the barge was quiet now except for the shuffle of the sailors as they moved about their duties. It was the hour my son and I usually met to talk if he wasn't still attending in the Emperor's bed . . . A good many nights I'd had to ponder that thought, waiting for him, but now he was here with me, not Hadrian.

"All right," I said at last. "Let's have it."

Antinous was silent, his head still hanging low. He wore one of those Egyptian kilts that didn't look nearly so well if you had a battle-scarred body, like I did, or if you ran to fat, like many of the courtiers. Antinous had covered the kilt with a pelt around his shoulders, the skin of the lion we had hunted in Cyrenaica. The Emperor had had the pelt tanned, and draped it around Antinous's shoulders with his own proud hands.

"So?" I persisted. "What troubles you?"

Antinous looked at me over a fur-draped shoulder, and his eyes were sunken and miserable. "We go back to Rome soon," he said starkly, "and I think it will be the end of me."

I blinked. "Has someone *threatened* you?"

"Sweet gods, no." He gave a hollow little laugh. "I wish they had."

"Then what?"

He stared at the black water with its reflected stars. "Here," he said, his voice halting, "it's different. In the east, an emperor is free to climb all over everything without risking his dignity, an empress can paint her eyes and show her shoulders without being a harlot . . . and a man like me finds less condemnation."

"Not everywhere in the east," I said, thinking of the epithets I'd seen scrawled on alley walls in Bethar about the Emperor. "Not in Judaea."

"Why do you think Hadrian hated Judaea?" An attempt at a smile. "He said later—'If they'd wanted me to look kindly on their demands, they'd have thought twice about the things they said of you. They sullied your name. So I took away the name of their holy city.'"

I didn't think that was advice that Simon and all the firebrands like him would find acceptable, once I went back to Bethar. "When *do* you go back to Rome?"

"A few months, and I'm already dreading it." He took a ragged breath.

"For every kind man like Titus Aurelius there's another like old Servianus who looks at me like I'm filth. And for every one like Servianus, there are two more like that young bully Pedanius to spit on me openly if the Emperor isn't watching. Hadrian shields me as much as he can—and Empress Sabina, what I'd do without her I don't know." A short laugh, and for a moment I saw real tenderness. "She's like my Praetorian, standing guard and skewering anyone who even gives me a look."

A queer feeling skewered *me* that moment. Sabina, looking out for my son. I'd resumed my old habit of avoiding her, which was a trick on an enclosed boat, even such a large one as this, but I'd done it. The closest I'd gotten was watching her enter the temple at Arsinoe from a distance, the only one in Hadrian's entourage brave enough to feed the sacred crocodiles, pulling her Egyptian dress around her bare brown legs as she tossed the great beasts their wine-soaked honey cakes.

The black dog whined, butting Antinous's shoulder and interrupting my bemused thoughts. Antinous scratched the dog behind one ear, struggling to keep his voice from breaking. "It's bad enough what they'll say of me in Rome. I could endure that. It's what they'll say of him, for debauching a man of my age and station. I'm twenty-four. There's no pretending I'm seventeen and a fit age to do what I do, even if I keep my hair long to look like a bed-slave—"

I swallowed rage. My son, tarting himself up to look pretty when he was so much more—

"I could endure what they'll say of me. I'm used to it. But what it means for him—Lucius Ceionius says—"

"Lucius is a prancing idiot," I growled. Him and his twin slave girls and his pretty tunics.

"He's a vain fool, but he's right when he says that Hadrian will have to give me up." Antinous stared at the water. "Once he returns to Rome, I'll have to go."

My heart thudded in my chest then. "What does the Emperor say?"

"I don't even have to ask him." My son was still as a statue. "He will die before he gives me up—I saw that at the lion hunt. So it will have to come from me. At some point when we go back to Rome, I'll have to leave him. And sweet gods, Father, it's going kill me."

Father. He'd finally called me that. My thudding heart nearly stopped altogether.

He wept silently, tears running down his carved cheeks like rain off a statue. The lion skin slid from his shoulders to the deck, and I put my arm around him, my throat thick.

"He can't afford the kind of trouble I'll bring him." Antinous's voice came stark through his tears. "He puts on a good show, but his health is getting nothing but worse. He'll have his hands full just settling the succession when he gets home; he doesn't need to face scheming from the Senate because I've blackened his name. I close my eyes and I see him *dying*—"

"Dying?" I said sharply. "How?" Under my knife on a lion hunt?

"I see the lightning striking him dead. The lion tearing his throat out . . ." Antinous raked a hand through all that curly hair. "He's dodged death twice. What if the third time is a knife on the Senate floor, because of me?"

I couldn't say my son was wrong to fear that. I couldn't even say I wouldn't rejoice if it happened. I paused, looking out over the river to the nearby bank and its pathetic settlement of mud huts.

"I have to give him up," my son said bleakly. "It will break his heart, and it will break mine because I would rather be dead than be without him. But he's my world. And I will not be the thing that brings him to ruin."

"Turn around," I said.

"What—"

"Turn around, boy." He just stared at me with tracks of silver marking his face, so I went to kneel behind him, drawing the knife at my waist. I gathered the mass of curly honey-colored hair in my hand, and I sawed through it at the nape of the neck. He sat unmoving, crying the last of his tears away as I tossed the silky handful into the Nile and then trimmed the rest ragged and close to his head, short as my own. I sheathed the knife and came back to sit beside him, taking a deep breath. *Hear me,* I begged my son silently. *If you have ever listened in your life, listen to me now.*

"Look at me, Antinous."

He raised his eyes, no longer crying. Without that tangle of curls, he looked older. No less handsome, but harder around the edges. "You look like a man," I said with all the vehemence I could summon. "Not a bed-slave. Not at all. God knows I wish you'd give the Emperor up and come home with me, but you're a man grown and you make a man's choices."

His voice was low. "Father—"

"If you come back to Judaea with me, Antinous, I'll sing the whole way. But if you go back to Rome with the Emperor, don't go to them a painted catamite with curls, trying to look younger. Throw it in their faces. Let them see you a man to equal any other."

"I can't." He began to shake his head.

"You can, if that's what you want. Because you *are* a man to equal any other. And the Emperor will take any chance of danger to keep you by his side." I seized my son's lean bare shoulders. And said it. "Because he loves you."

Antinous's head jerked up, and I made myself look at him with steady eyes. Love: the thing I'd finally seen, that day on the lion hunt. Maybe Hadrian *had* only been caught by my son's good looks, in the beginning. Maybe there *had* been a certain dark satisfaction in bedding the son of a bitter enemy. But when the Emperor of the known world flings himself under the claws of a man-killing lion, risks his own death so that a humble Bithynian boy escapes with nothing more than a sprained thumb . . . Hell's gates, what else can you call that but love?

How the gods must be laughing. My enemy and my son, united as true as any set of lovers who ever lived. The thought of it still brought a bitter taste to my mouth, but I'd been wrestling with what I'd seen ever since Hadrian's neck escaped my knife at the lion hunt. If I'd killed the bastard, I'd have lost my son forever.

What does it matter? I'd thought bitterly, all the way up the Nile past the wonders of Gizeh and its pyramids, Arsinoe and its temples. *You'll lose him anyway, the moment you go back to Bethar to fight.*

Maybe not. Maybe he'd weigh his choices—Hadrian's love, or Hadrian's duty—and come with me, after all.

But it was his decision.

He looked up at me and he had tears in his eyes again. "I don't know," he whispered, and I bled for him. That's what you do, when your children grow up and you can no longer slay their demons for them.

I seized his hand and pulled him to his feet. "Whatever you choose," I whispered, "you are my son, Antinous. *My son*. True as blood. And I love you more than anything on this earth." I pulled him into a hug. My son, who I hadn't held since Bethar when we'd embraced more in anger and in grief than in hope. It was hope I felt now as I cupped the back of his head with my hand, as though he were just a small boy again, and he hugged me back so hard my ribs creaked.

My son.

"I gave you a terrible haircut, Narcissus," I said as we broke apart, and the radiance of his smile almost made me break down in tears.

"Don't call me Narcissus," he said.

"Never again," I promised, and I never did.

He smiled at me. A sweeter smile, all wistfulness in the moonlight. "Thank you, Father."

I kissed him once on the brow and I left him, padding back across the deck toward the steps that would take me belowdecks.

I turned back just once before I went below, and I saw him gazing up at the stars: a lean silvered figure in his kilt and his cropped head, every long smooth line of him carved in the silver light.

My son.

ANTINOUS

Beside the moon-glossed Nile, Antinous drew a shaky breath. His heart hurt, torn open by too many tears and too much love. A good pain, clean as a knife slash that drained a festering wound. *I have my father back*, he thought, and the words brought such an agony of joy that he almost wept again. *I am my father's son.*

His head felt curiously light, and he ran a hand over the ragged chop his father had made of his hair. *Hadrian will like it.* He should go back to Hadrian's bed, take him in his arms and whisper to him of

Rome. Of serene days in the Emperor's ever-expanding villa, where Hadrian would do nothing more taxing than begin the memoirs he was always talking about writing, and Antinous would sit at his side.

For how long? he could not help thinking, and still felt a shiver of superstitious fear: Hadrian dead with a knife in his back.

But didn't that fate wait in the shadows for every emperor, not just Publius Aelius Hadrian? For one reason or another, and usually far more sinister ones than love?

The Emperor will take any chance of danger to keep you by his side. Antinous heard those words in his father's voice. *Because he loves you.*

Antinous took another long and shaky breath. *We will have years,* he thought. *I must believe that.* And even if it was not years, it was enough. Love that challenged lions and empires and death itself was enough, in whatever measure it graced a man's life.

He raised his eyes to the heavenly sky, drinking it in. Would he ever see Hadrian and his father smile at each other? Probably not.

But a man could dream.

Antinous made a wish on the moon, the same moon he'd seen tangled in the tree branches at Eleusis on the night he'd first held Hadrian in his arms. He heard footsteps behind him and began to turn, when a blow to his head shattered the world, sent it flying around him like pieces of black glass.

Dark, he thought, too confused to be frightened. Swirling dark like he'd seen in the *kykeon* the second time. A dizzy moment as he felt himself being tugged, hoisted under the arms, lifted up. Then the dark was gone and the stars were rushing at him, reflected in the Nile.

So beautiful, Antinous had time to think. And then he was falling among the stars.

CHAPTER 14

SABINA

"Is Antinous with you?"

Hadrian stood at the threshold of Sabina's chamber, barefoot and rumple-haired in his sleeping tunic as though he'd barely risen from his own bed. Sabina blinked, managed to unstick her eyes. "It is *dawn*," she yawned, sitting up from her rumpled cushions. "Why in the name of all the gods would your lover be in my bed?"

"I thought the two of you might have tiptoed out again to watch the sun come up on the river. Otherwise he always wakes *me* when he rises."

"We're trying to get you to sleep more. It's a dire plot we cooked up between us, I confess it." Sabina swung her bare legs out of her sleeping couch, reaching for a robe she'd been given in Alexandria, embroidered all over in lapis-beaded eyes of Horus. "If he left your bed this morning and left you behind to sleep late, well, he's just doing what the physician said was best for you, so don't scold."

Hadrian was already stamping off. Sabina smiled at her little African maid, who had come forward with a cold mint tisane, and the Empress was stirring it in its agate cup and wondering when they would reach the wonders of Thebes when a shout split the morning bustle.

Not a shout, Sabina realized. A scream.

She kept hold of her cup as she ran out on deck, her many-eyed robe rippling behind her, and she thought perhaps one of the sailors had fallen overboard and given a shout of alarm. Or someone had spotted a crocodile again—there was Julia Balbilla giving her fluttery shriek, standing at the gilded railing of the barge, pointing into the waters beside the bank.

"What?" Sabina laughed, coming up beside her. "Goodness, the crocodiles can't harm a barge this size, it's the hippopotami that go after boats—"

But it was no crocodile with its lidded reptilian eyes that Sabina saw in the Nile's idle green swirls when she followed Balbilla's gaze. It was a tangle of branches and dead leaves from a fallen tree on the bank just a few yards distant, a tangle of debris that the river hadn't yet swept away. And among that clot of branches, limp and shockingly white, was a man's hand.

"Oh, gods," Balbilla said shakily. "Forgive me—I know peasants drown in the Nile every day, the currents are so fierce—but it startled me, that *thing* poking up from the water like it was beckoning to me—"

Sabina's fingers suddenly opened and the agate cup tumbled from her hand to shatter on the deck at her bare feet. Ice crawled through her bones. "No," she whispered. "No."

That dead hand showed a flash of white against the dead leaves. A bandage wound neat around the thumb, the linen sodden from the water, but Sabina could remember Hadrian tying it off with his own hands. "We should be lucky you escaped the lion with nothing more than a sprained thumb, my star."

Sabina found herself bent double, her head shaking violently back and forth. "No—" she said, "no—no—" So much *no*, and all the *no* in the world would do not one bit of good. Not against that dreadful sight. "*No*," she wailed, and she went on screaming because she wanted to drown out the sounds of the boat around her, the cries of alarm and the cries of warning that were just beginning to burgeon. She wanted to drown out the world. But most of all she wanted to drown out the sound that Hadrian would make when he came up on deck in his tunic and his bare feet and his night-rumpled hair, when he heard her screaming, when he came half-alarmed and half-irked to her side at the barge's gilded rail—

When he looked down and saw Antinous lying dead in the arms of the Nile.

It was no sound at all at first. The world had faded to utter silence in Sabina's ears by the time Hadrian came beside her at the rail, half-running from belowdecks at the sound of the commotion. His hand rested beside hers on the railing, and she felt the heat of his swollen fingers. She looked up at her husband, his deep-set eyes that had already left her and were speeding swiftly across the water, and she had a mad urge to clap her hands over his eyes because as long as he didn't see, then his world wouldn't end.

But he saw, and she had time to feel the flex of those swollen fingers as they convulsed about the gilded rail. And there was still no sound, not a sound in the world except the Emperor vaulting over the side of the barge and landing with a great splash in the river. A moan went up from the watchers, seeing the currents seize their Emperor, and one of their Egyptian guides began to mutter prayers against the treacherous eddies of the Nile. *No*, Sabina could have told the guides, her wails trapped in her throat by now. *The Nile has already claimed its sacrifice today.* Hadrian was already swimming against the current, pulling himself through the water in strong scything strokes.

It seemed only a moment before Hadrian reached the tangle of dead branches and rotted leaves that leaned from the bank. He tore at the mess of it, and he was making a sound, his frozen silence gone. "Antinous—Antinous?" He sounded almost bemused. Rotted leaves and globs of mud spun through the green waters, splattered the Emperor's face like blood splashing up from a mortal wound. *Mortal wound*, Sabina thought, *mortal wound*, and felt such a stab of agony through her body that she nearly cried out again. All as Hadrian tore at the leaves and kept asking "Antinous?" as though it were a question that had any kind of answer.

And then the white face appeared. *When did he turn so white?* Sabina thought. Antinous had been made of gold, a creature of sunlight and swift motion, but as he emerged from the grip of the branches that had trapped him against the bank, he looked to be made of marble instead. White and cold and smooth and wet, one hand thrown loose across his broad unmarked chest, the other with its sodden bandage trailing loose, fingers mooring the water . . . His profile like a drowned god's, pale and peaceful, lashes gleaming like wet gold against his cheek, the strong column of his throat utterly unmoving.

"No," Hadrian said, just as Sabina had. "No—" The limp golden head lolled against his shoulder, in the same place where Sabina had so often seen Antinous curl close under his Imperial lover's arm, and Hadrian smoothed the cropped hair. Smoothed it over and over. When had Antinous cut his hair? "No," the Emperor said, voice rising. "You have to wake, my star. Osiris woke after he was sunk in the Nile. You have to wake, too. *Wake*—" and he shook the corpse, but Antinous's head flopped backward like a dead fish, and his eyelids slid back grotesquely to reveal blind staring eyes. Dead eyes, corpse eyes, and that was when Hadrian howled.

He howled like a beast, like a thing from behind the gates of Hades, and the howl would not end. It went on—and on—and on—as he rocked Antinous against him in the shallows of the Nile, rocked him and smoothed his hair and howled and howled and howled, and a recoil of horror went through the chorus of watchers around Sabina. *Chorus,* she thought. *That's what we are—the chorus to a Greek tragedy, and the last act is upon us and all we can do is react.* She staggered away from the crowd, pushing through them, and the first person she saw through her swimming eyes was Vix. Vix, puzzled and alert, his russet hair gleaming in the morning sun, one foot still balanced on the top step where he'd come from belowdecks. Drawn, no doubt, by the Emperor's animal howling, and his gray eyes were already going to the railing where the crowd milled and jabbered.

Vix had time to take two steps toward the commotion before Sabina slammed into him. She half-lunged and half-fell against his chest, her knees giving out, and Vix caught her just in time, his arm hard around her waist. "Hell's gates—" he began, but Sabina's hands were at his face, trying to cover his eyes.

"You can't look"—she was weeping—"you can't look, promise me you won't look!" She hadn't covered Hadrian's eyes in time; Hadrian had seen and now he was making that terrible bestial cry. If she let Vix see, he was going to go utterly mad. "You can't look," she cried, and tried to cover his eyes, but he had seized her wrists and moved her bodily aside, sprinting for the railing, and this time there was no shocked silence. There was just a bellow like a bear who had been gored—"*Antinous!*"—and then another splash as Vix too vaulted over the side of the barge, making a neater dive into the waters than Hadrian, and Sabina bent over retching, her stomach turning itself inside out even as she wept. She heard the energetic splashing of Vix's arms as he swam to join the Emperor in a few swift strokes. And then more shouting, "Let him breathe, Caesar, you bastard, he can't breathe with you clutching him like that! He can't breathe, Hell's gates, he can't *breathe*—" And then Vix just roared, a long wordless roar that went into a guttural sob, and Sabina staggered to her feet and fell against the railing in time to see Vix's head drop and his arms convulse around his son's still, white body, as Hadrian still made his animal howls into Antinous's wet hair. The three heads together just above the water: Hadrian's dark, Vix's russet, and Antinous's fair, a terrible tableau of agony against the lazy green ripples of the Nile.

Later she realized it couldn't have happened that way. There were others in the water by that time—sailors in the swift little reed boats that had been lowered from the deck to assist; slaves swimming out with lines; Praetorians splashing toward the Emperor. But somehow all she saw was Vix and Hadrian cradling Antinous between them, and she bowed her head then on the railing and felt the great crack of something breaking inside.

"Gods," someone said at Sabina's elbow, and through the fog that unsteadied her eyes she saw Lucius Ceionius, looking stiff and uncomfortable. "Caesar weeps like a woman!"

Sabina gave him a ringing backhanded slap before she even realized she was moving. Lucius stared at her, openmouthed, the print of her hand rising scarlet on his cheek. She wanted to hit him again but the guards were shouting, and she pushed her way farther down the railing as Boil and the other Praetorians hauled the weeping Emperor limp and unresisting back on deck. He collapsed boneless to hands and knees, his breath coming in shallow pants, and he looked up slowly around him, and his eyes were blind. "Antinous?" he said. "Where is Antinous?" And Sabina felt a sob in her own throat, because there was hope in his eyes. Hope that this was nothing but a dream, a *kykeon* dream where nightmares became flesh. A dream that could be dispelled if only Antinous would come bounding up from belowdecks, laughing and gleaming and shaking his head at all the fuss.

But Antinous was being winched up to the deck in a loop of rope behind the Emperor. Vix climbed that railing first, soaking wet and granite-faced and utterly mute after his one guttural roar, and he pushed the helping hands away. Vix alone lifted Antinous over the railing, arms straining, cradling that long body against his chest as though it were a child's.

"Antinous," Hadrian whispered.

Vix laid Antinous on the deck. The Nile's fierce currents had stripped that beautiful form naked, torn the kilt from his hips and the topaz ring from his left hand. Antinous was naked as an infant in his father's arms, and Sabina saw Vix's chest heave as he straightened those long limbs. But Vix's stone face never moved at all. He just bent forward and pressed his lips to that pale forehead. As a father would kiss a child after a nightmare, Sabina thought, and the stab of agony went through her again. *Not Antinous*, she howled inside. *Anyone but him!*

His little black dog came trotting up, whining somewhere in the back of its throat. He sniffed at his master hopefully, tail wagging, and that was when another howl came from Hadrian as he collapsed across Antinous's unmoving chest, weeping and weeping as if he would flood the Nile with grief alone. Sabina stumbled, going to her knees beside him, her hands slipping through his curly hair. "Hadrian—" Her eyes filled with tears as she remembered the bathhouse in Antioch where she and her husband's lover had lain in the curve of Hadrian's arms, all three of them so happy. "Hadrian—"

But the eyes that found hers were tear-drowned and savage. "*Get away from me*," he hissed, and her vision exploded into sparks as he slapped her away across the deck. Sabina heard a moan from the watching crowd, and through her unsteady eyes as she pushed herself up on one side, she saw the look in their eyes change. Not just shock or sadness as they watched their Emperor huddling over his lover's body. Not just unease as they heard his cries rise up to the wheeling birds overhead.

Fear, Sabina thought, the whole side of her head ringing savagely from Hadrian's hand. And she felt the same fear rise through her, clawing and choking, because the Emperor's cries no longer sounded human at all.

VIX

I howled like a wolf when I found my son. Just once, shouting his name—but within my skull, the cry went on and on.

Antinous. When I closed my eyes, I saw the silvered figure I'd left on the stern of the barge last night, the boy who stood living and beautiful beneath the moon. *Alive.* Not that empty naked shell I helped pull from the Nile.

I remember nothing after that. The world went away from me. When it came back I was on my sleeping pallet in the barge quarters where the Praetorians slept, and I was alone. Alone and huddled, gasping for breath. I closed my eyes and Antinous smiled at me on the back of my eyelids. I made a strangled sound between my teeth, and the world went away again. It kept doing that. I came to myself once to realize I held my naked sword across my knees, clinging to it as Boil tried to wrest it away. I resisted, but he shouted for the other Praetorians, and then things tilted again and when I woke it was night and my hands were empty. I could see moonlight coming from somewhere, and I nearly went blundering up on deck to see if I could find Antinous at the stern with his shorn hair and his tender smile. But he wasn't there; he was dead. He was dead, oh, my son was dead, and I could not weep.

"Vix."

A voice.

"Vix—" A woman's voice. "Look at me."

I didn't want to look at anyone. I wanted to die.

"Vix, please listen to me. Go to Hadrian." Her words came tear-clogged. "Vix, he won't let anyone touch Antinous's *body*. It has been four days, and he won't let any of us touch it."

Four days. Four days? How had it been four days?

"Four days in this heat. Please, Vix. Go to him. Make him see reason. Make him send Antinous to the gods. *Please*."

My eyes opened, but Sabina's bruised and pleading face was just a hovering blur.

Four days in this heat, I thought, and then somehow I was sitting up. Sabina looked at me through tear-swollen eyes. "Vix?" She reached out, but her fingers dropped before they touched my arm. I would not have touched me either. I was filthy, unshaven, and sticky, and in my head there was still a resounding howl of utter agony. My eyes burned tearless. My voice was a croak.

"Take me to him."

The Emperor of Rome just stared at me as I banged into his private quarters. It was night, the indeterminate blackness between the fall of the sun and the rise of dawn, but he didn't look surprised to see me appear unannounced. He stood barefoot and wild-haired in the same sleeping tunic he'd worn when they first hauled Antinous from the Nile, beard untrimmed and stubble growing down his neck, and his eyes were vacant pits. "Vercingetorix," he said vaguely. "I felt you coming."

I looked about the chamber for my son's body, but it was not there. I heard the doors close behind me—neither Sabina nor the other Praetorians dared follow me inside. "Where is my son?" I demanded.

The Emperor ignored that. "I always know when you're near me. Something about the mortal enemy side of things. You put the hairs up on my neck. Probably because you're looking for a chance to cut it."

"I almost did cut it," I said. "On the lion hunt. *Where is my son?*"

"In my chamber next door, laid out on my sleeping couch beneath a sheet of gold cloth." The Emperor flung himself down on the nearest couch, draping one leg over its arm and not seeming to notice that all the cushions had been torn off. Antinous's dog had made a nest of them, sleeping uneasily in the corner. "Sit."

There was no room anywhere to sit. His private chamber was a wreck. I looked around the morass of torn hangings, spilled wine, and toppled statues, and finally perched on a carved chair with a splintered leg. Hadrian pushed a silver cup at me. "Drink. I'm tired of drinking alone."

There were no slaves, so I mixed the wine myself. I filled Hadrian's cup as well, and we tossed it back in identical sharp swallows. My tongue burned, and my stomach growled. How long had it been since I'd eaten or drunk anything? My throat was scratchy and dry, demanding more, and suddenly the stench of the room rushed in on my numbed senses. I smelled the sharp sourness of the wine, the tang of sweat and tears, the reek of urine from Antinous's dog pissing in the corners—and something ranker, riper.

That smell. That *smell*. I kept my eyes stubbornly on the carpet, away from the door at the chamber's other end. His bedchamber, where my son lay under a sheet of gold.

Four days in this heat. I looked up at Hadrian's haggard face. "Let me have Antinous's body," I heard myself saying in my raven's croak. "Let me lay him to rest."

Hadrian poured more wine for us both. "What gives you the right to do it?"

"He was my son."

"Not by blood."

"No. My wife bore me girls—and do you want to know the truth, Caesar? She hated Antinous for it." *No*, I thought even as I said it. *Not hated. Resented. Envied.* But my world had become a black and absolute place and had no room for any feelings but absolutes. Hate. Love. Pain. Death. "I didn't sire him, but that makes no difference to me. I loved him more than my life."

Hadrian looked at me over the rim of his cup with those pitlike eyes. "So did I."

"So get another lover," I flared. "An emperor can always get another bedmate. A father can't get another son."

"You think love is something that can be *replaced*?" Hadrian bolted down his second cup of wine. "If you sired another hundred sons, they would never replace the one you lost. If I took another hundred lovers, not one of them would be my star. No one can *ever* replace Antinous."

"No," I said, and as fast as that my anger died.

"You're the only one on this boat to love him as much as I did," Hadrian said, and toasted me. "Maybe that's why I'm drinking with someone who nearly cut my throat."

We made a bitter toast to that. The wine roiled in my stomach like poison. "I cut his hair, the night he died. I've been cutting his hair all my life—it's something a father does. So won't you let me tend his body, Caesar? Because a father should do that, too."

Hadrian gave a sharp shake of his head. "You repudiated him, and so did the world. Everyone but me. In death he is mine."

"So for the love of God, put him on a pyre and burn him!" I could smell my son rotting in the Egyptian heat—rotting, all his golden beauty. It would drive me mad. "Send him to the gods, Caesar!"

"I will." Hadrian sounded fierce. "But not by fire. Not on a pile of wood like an ordinary mortal, to be reduced to common ash. He's to be mummified. His body preserved, wrapped in gold and resin. Then I'll build a great tomb, and erect a statue of him as tall as a god, and every day I live there will be offerings at that statue. At the tomb of Antinous."

"Mummified?" I said, stupidly.

A wave of the Emperor's hand. "I've sent for the priests from Hermopolis. The ones who know how to do it."

"Doesn't it take months?" I had no idea, really.

Hadrian was indifferent. "Then we stay here for months. Rome can burn for all I care; I will not put him on a pyre."

More silence. We drank, and through the shutters sealing in the room's stale stench, I saw a sliver of moon. Waning now, its fullness disappearing. My last glimpse of Antinous had been under that ripe moon, every line of him etched in its silver light. My last glimpse, before I'd seen him wax-pale and dead in the Nile's waters. How could that be? How could he be so vibrantly alive one moment, warm in my arms, his hug crushing me with its force, and then be . . . gone?

My eyes stung. If I could weep then perhaps I could rest, but I deserved neither.

"Lucius Ceionius tells me a new star has been spotted in the heavens," Hadrian said, his gaze drifting after mine to the shutters. "A star of Antinous, he says. A sure sign that he has risen into the heavens, to blaze with eternal light like all the other heroes of lore."

"Do you believe that?"

"I think Lucius is a flattering fool worth no more than his embroidered tunics," Hadrian said. "But I will name the star after Antinous, anyway. Why not? He deserves a star."

We clinked cups again, drank again.

"You know when he first made love to me?" the Emperor asked softly. "It was in a grove of lemon trees just outside Athens, after the Mysteries. Gods know what excuse I made, to get you away and him alone. He wore a blue tunic, and he looked at me with such clear eyes, and the sight of him made me tremble like a boy."

I curled my fingers tight around the wine cup, feeling its carved acanthus leaves bite into my flesh. "I don't want to hear how you and my son made love."

"I could hardly summon the courage to touch him," Hadrian said as though he had not heard me. His eyes stared blind into the past, a warm Greek day all fresh and fragrant with the scent of lemons. "I looked at him and I tried to tell myself he was just another plaything. Unworthy of me. Something pretty to be used and tossed aside."

I bolted to my feet. "I said, I don't want to hear—"

"But he looked at me and he smoothed my hair and he laid me down under the lemon trees," Hadrian said, "and I knew I was the one unworthy."

I flung the wine cup across the room with a clatter. "If you were unworthy, why didn't you leave him be?" I snarled. "A madman like you, drawing him into your nest—"

"He was my chance for light." Hadrian looked at me. "My one chance."

"And he *died* for it!" I roared. "God *damn* you, Caesar! God *damn* you! He died because of you—"

"Did he?" Hadrian came off his couch in a sudden leap, fingers digging into my shoulders. "Was it because of me, Vercingetorix? I know he had his dark moments; I *know* he dreaded going back to Rome. He thought death marked me, and he said after the lightning strike that he'd told the gods to take *his* life if they would spare mine—"

I hesitated.

"You hate me," Hadrian pleaded, husky-voiced. "Hatred doesn't lie. Hatred doesn't tell soothing stories. You'll tell me true. Did he fall into the Nile by accident? Or *did he jump?*"

I still hesitated.

"Tell me," Hadrian begged, hanging on my arms. "Tell me. And if he killed himself for me, to spare my life from the Fates or to spare my reputation from the gossip, then give me that sword of yours and I'll fall on it."

I had another chance, then. The Emperor's eyes were full of fire, his voice clotted with anguish; he gripped me as though he'd break me—but I could break him, and with just one word. *Yes,* I thought. *Yes, he threw himself into the river because of you. Say it, Vercingetorix.* The Emperor dead, my old enemy, the man who had debauched my son, whose death would probably even free a rejoicing province of Jews. *Say it.*

"No," I said. "No, Caesar. He didn't die because of you. He died because of me."

Hadrian didn't even hear the last words. His face crumpled in agony and in relief, the moment I said no, and his head came forward against my shoulder as he wept. I put my arms around his shoulders to keep him from falling, my eyes burning again like salt and fire as I remembered that last night with Antinous. His wistful voice echoed in my ears.

Anyone who throws themselves into the Nile will save the life of a loved one, did you know that?

Why hadn't I paid closer attention? He'd said himself how worried he was for the Emperor, for his health, his headaches and his fevers, for his reputation once he returned to Rome. But I'd been so cocksure, telling him to make his choice like the man he was. Thinking he chose between life at Hadrian's side and life at mine. Never thinking he might have chosen no life at all.

My son, fearing for Hadrian's good health, his good name, his *life*. My last glimpse of Antinous alive on this earth, and he had been gazing out at the Nile's seductive waters. Perhaps he stood there a long time after I was gone. Or maybe he dropped into the water and let the currents take him before I was even back in my pallet that night.

My fault. Mine alone. I wasn't going to hang that about Hadrian's neck, good as it would have felt. He'd loved Antinous. I'd been the one to fail him. I'd failed him again and again and again, until he died.

Hadrian pushed away from me with a sudden shove, digging at his weeping eyes as though he wished he could gouge them out. If he wanted to, I wouldn't stop him. "Not just a tomb," he said savagely. "Antinous will have more. Games in his honor, held on this site."

"Yes." Maybe I should give myself up to fight in those games. Die as a gladiator in my son's honor; die in blood on arena sand with my heart speared on a trident fighter's triple prongs. It had a certain fitting ring; my wasted manhood ending as it had begun. *Full circle.*

"And not just games." The Emperor was ranting, striding up and down the room on a weaving path. Antinous's dog whined from its pile of cushions. "I will make him a city here, opposite Hermopolis. He will have an entire *city* raised to his glory, a city to rival Rome. Antinoöpolis. I will see the foundations laid before I leave Egypt, laid in stone and marble for all time—"

No, I mused, *not a gladiator's death.* With my luck, I'd probably survive Antinous's games. I needed something more certain than a gladiator's end, some better way to make sure I died howling and bleeding and battling. Rebellion ought to do it. *Go home, join Simon and his friends, and let their firestorm of liberation kill you.* Mirah could at least live on with the dignity of being a martyr's widow.

"A temple," Hadrian was saying, his hands building pillars and columns and domes in the air. "A temple in his name, to grace the center of Antinoöpolis. And another temple in Rome to the glory of Antinous the God—"

"The god?" My wine-fuddled thoughts swam hazily back to the dark room, the fetid air, the Emperor looking at me with his wild beard and his glittering eyes. "My son is a god, now?"

"He was *my* god," Hadrian said, and all his manic grandiose energy seeped out of him. His legs gave out and he dropped to his couch again.

I moved more slowly, creaking back to my own chair like an old man. God knows I felt like one. "Antinous the god," I said, sounding it out. "He was just a boy, Caesar. A good boy who grew into a fine man—"

"And do you know how rare that is? Goodness. True goodness. He even made me good." The Emperor ran a hand through his hair. "You will never know how hard I worked to be worthy of him."

"You failed," I said.

"But he never knew I failed." I heard a fragile pride in Hadrian's voice. "The performance of a lifetime, and he never knew it. To be emperor I made myself look like a good man, on the outside. But for him, Vix, I wanted to *be* a good man."

Vix. Hadrian had never called me Vix. Just Vercingetorix, or before that, the ever-mocking "Tribune." I gave a bitter bark of a laugh, and we clinked cups again. We were drinking it straight by now, not bothering to mix water in, and it was fire on the tongue.

"And now," Hadrian went on, musing, "I've gotten used to it. Pretending to be a good man. First for my Empire, and then for him." Hadrian turned his cup upside down, watched a drop of wine collect on the silver rim and fall to the floor. "But why should I bother anymore?"

"Antinous would want you to carry on as you were—"

"*But I don't want to!*" Hadrian flung his wine cup across the room in a clatter of metal. The dog flattened his ears. "I don't care if Rome burns. I'd light it on fire myself and lay it on Antinous's tomb as a tribute. Burn it all with him."

I wasn't afraid. I should have been, but I wasn't. I looked at the Emperor and I just repeated, "But he wouldn't want that."

"I know. Oh, I know. So I'll build a city for him instead of burning an empire. But, gods—" Hadrian closed his eyes with a shudder. "I pray someone tries to kill me. I pray someone tries to plot against me. I pray someone makes *war* on me. Because it's not in my nature to build and preserve, and gods know you're aware of that even if Antinous never was. I have a black soul, and I feel like giving it free rein."

I stared at him, at his set face and his pit-dark eyes and the fist clenching and unclenching in slow rhythm at his side, and dread mounted in me like a wall, brick by remorseless brick.

I pray someone makes war on me.

Oh, no, I thought. *No—*

Hadrian moved unsteadily toward his chamber. His small *tablinum*, where I presume he curled up to sleep since my son occupied the bedchamber. "Need sleep," Hadrian said not too clearly, and struck open the door. I paid no attention. I was echoing all over with dread.

I pray someone makes war on me.

Well, Hadrian was about to get his wish. But I didn't think Simon would get *his* wish, for a free nation of the Jews.

Mirah had mocked Hadrian as a coward who didn't fight. Simon judged him better, as a practical man who would not fight without good reason. *We make Judaea too much trouble, and he will let us go,* Simon had said. But that was when my son had been on hand to temper Hadrian's darker urges.

I didn't see the stone-faced madman in this room weighing practicalities if he heard Judaea was in open rebellion. I saw him burning the whole province to the ground.

You're drunk, I told myself. *You're drunk, and your son is dead, and you're seeing doom in every corner. That's all.*

"Vercingetorix," Hadrian said, and my eyes jerked up to meet his. He hadn't closed the door of his chamber yet; he stood swaying on his feet, but his gaze on me was steady. "What was your old legion? The one Trajan gave you, as commander?"

The dead legion, I almost said. Because if rebels like Simon didn't level the men of the Tenth, Hadrian would when he threw them into the fight. "The Tenth Fidelis," I said instead, hoarsely. "Stationed in Judaea."

"I give it back to you," he said. "It's yours, Legate."

I was on my feet, and I didn't know how I got there. "*What?*"

"You aided me tonight." His eyes were unblinking. "For that I owe you. I don't like owing you. I'd rather hate you."

"You can't make me legate," I said, dry-mouthed. "You stripped me of rank for debauching your *Empress*; the Senate won't—"

"The Senate can piss down their own throats," Hadrian said clearly. "And I don't care if you bedded my Empress. I don't care about anything. The Tenth is yours, Legate. Good night."

He banged the door, going to his lonely couch and his oblivion, and I stood there in the stinking filth of the room and I began to laugh. Not because it was funny, although it was. Because would the bastard never stop screwing me over?

The Tenth is yours, Legate. The doomed Tenth, stationed square in the middle of the firestorm that was about to erupt in Judaea. Africanus and the men who had bought me drinks and looked at me with such admiration. The eagle I had carried so proudly. All of them doomed, and I had just about wrestled myself to the conclusion that Mirah was right; that it was the price that had to be paid. For a province to be freed, men had to die.

Not my men.

They aren't your men, I thought.

They are now.

Not yet! I screamed inside. *Turn the appointment down. Go home!*

Too late. I could feel the tattoo on my arm burning, the crude X I'd inked just below my shoulder the day Trajan had given me the Tenth for my own. I'd felt it prickling every time I thought about the men of the Tenth dying in the streets of Jerusalem as they tried to hunt down rebels, prickling me in reproach—but I'd always been able to stamp it down. For Mirah. For Simon. For the girls.

Now it burned me.

Two different men had asked me to fight for them. Two brilliant, bearded men with deep-set eyes and ruthless visions of the future. One I loved, and my family stood on his side. One I hated, and my legionaries stood on *his* side. I didn't know which man was right. I didn't know anything anymore.

Except that my son was dead, and the Fates were cruel.

Hadrian had smashed almost everything in the room that could be smashed, but there was a polished silver mirror canted sideways against a wall, still intact. I righted it as my son's dog watched me with anxious eyes, as I looked at my own reflection. My new beard had grown in since I left Judaea, and it was finally past the maddening itchy stage, thick and red-hued. Mirah would like it.

But I didn't look like a man of Judaea, even with the beard. I didn't look like a warrior for God. I looked like a soldier of Rome, and God help me, that was what I was.

"Legate Vercingetorix," a familiar voice said behind me.

I turned. Sabina came slipping into the wrecked chamber, her eyes shadowed, the great bruise still showing along the side of her face where Hadrian had struck her away. "You overheard?" I said stupidly.

"Yes. Your promotion, and his plans for Antinous's body." She went to listen at the door of Hadrian's bedchamber. There was an indistinct rumble of snores beginning, and her face softened. "He'll sleep for hours now," she said, and looked at me. "Thank you for helping him. I hope he helped you."

I couldn't answer that, so I gestured at the bruise on her face. "He hurt you," I said, and heard the growl in my own voice.

"He didn't mean to. He sobbed apologies into my lap afterward."

"But he hurt you, and you still tend him?"

"At least I know how to handle him. The slaves aren't really safe around him in these moods."

"Sabina—"

"You have the Tenth Fidelis," she said, calmly dismissing my pity. "I'm glad. The men will be safer when the fight comes, if you're leading them."

"There's a fight coming, is there?"

"Isn't there?"

Did she know about the unrest in Judaea? I thought she did. Sabina knew things like that. Hadrian and Antinous had been too dazed in their happiness to see much of anything going on around them, but Sabina had always been clear-eyed. She came toward me, running a fingertip over the Mars amulet at my neck. "That should keep you safe, if the Tenth comes to any trouble."

"I don't want to be safe." My throat was full of thorns, the amulet like a weight about my neck. "Why didn't I give it to Antinous? Then it would have kept *him* safe."

Her voice was gentle. "It's just a token."

"A token." All the tokens I'd gathered over my wandering life— from my father, from Trajan, from Mirah—even one from Sabina, long hidden away. "Why don't I have a token from Antinous? Why didn't I give one to him? *Why?*"

Sabina eyed me for a moment, and then she stood on tiptoe and untied the amulet's cord from around my neck. I didn't stop her. "Wait," she said, pressing her fingertips against my chest, and carried the amulet to the room's other door. She slipped inside, and I gagged at the smell. My golden son was in there, rotting. I wanted to scream. I wanted to die.

Sabina came back and she had something over her arm, I couldn't see what with my wine-blurred, grief-blurred eyes. I felt her light touch as she draped something about my shoulders, and I felt the familiar weight of fur. "I burned my old lion skin," I said. "I burned it in Judaea, when I vowed—" When I vowed I was turning my back on Rome for good.

"This is the pelt of the lion Hadrian slew in Cyrenaica." She pinned it about my shoulders. "The one he killed to save Antinous. It will keep you safe, in place of your Mars amulet. And I laid the amulet with Antinous's body. When he's mummified I'll see that it's woven into the wrappings over his heart." Her eyes were so clear. "Part of you, with him always."

My eyes burned. The embrace of the lion's fur felt like Antinous's arms. I hunched into it like I'd been stabbed, my whole body shaking, and Sabina opened her arms. I dropped into them, crashing to my knees.

"Ssshhh," Sabina said, fingers slipping through my hair, and her touch destroyed me. I gripped her, drowning, and I wept at last for my son.

Then I rose, and I wiped my eyes, and I went to war.

HADRIAN'S VILLA

Look back over the past, with its changing empires that rose and fell, and you can foresee the future, too.

—MARCUS AURELIUS

CHAPTER 15

VIX

A.D. 131, Spring
Bethar

All my life, I'd wanted to ask my wife one question: *What do you see?* That girl Mirah had been, the girl who danced among the vines at Tu B'Av with sloe blossom braided in her bright hair, merry and light-footed and laughing, her blue eyes somehow only for me—what had she seen when she looked at me? I had always wondered.

She only laughed whenever I asked her, shaking her head in puzzlement. "I saw you, of course!"

Did she?

Because I knew what she saw when she ran to greet me in the small courtyard of our house in Bethar. I knew very well.

Somewhere on the journey between Egypt and Judaea, I shaved off my beard. I took it off in short brutal strokes of the knife, standing naked before a bowl of tepid water in some decrepit roadside inn. Then I attacked my russet hair with its graying streaks, taking it down to the bare scalp, and left my head bleeding in half a dozen places. I put aside the nondescript tunic and cloak I'd been traveling in, and put on for the first time my full regalia as legate. The breastplate, the sword belt, the scarlet cloak. The mementos I'd accumulated over my life, the ones I'd laid aside when I came to Judaea, reasoning that they had no part in my new life—I drew them out, one by one. The string of campaign tokens I'd won in Dacia and Parthia, strung once more across my breastplate. The gold ring engraved with the letters PARTHICUS, given to me from Emperor Trajan's own hand, pushed once more into place on my first finger. Antinous's lion skin, pinned about my shoulders. The blue scarf Mirah had been wearing when she survived the great earthquake in Antioch, stuffed under my shoulder plate with a caress of the worn cloth.

I looked bare and brutal, blood still trickling down my neck from the nicks in my shaved scalp. I looked like the man who had killed a rebel king in Dacia, who had clawed his way red-handed from legionary to aquilifer to centurion to tribune to legate. I looked like a man to be feared.

That was the man Mirah saw striding across her courtyard, his boots slapping harshly at the stone. She was watering the small orange trees in their pots, and her head turned at the sound, and for a moment she didn't know her own husband. I hadn't been able to tell her of my promotion by letter—during those long winter months I'd spent in Egypt at Hadrian's side after my son's death, I must have written and torn up the words a hundred times. She'd sent me greetings of her own, warm sympathies written in a scribe's hand when she heard of Antinous's death, and I had not been able to reply, not when I couldn't tell her the whole truth. And now I wished I had found some way to do it, because she looked first alarmed and then puzzled as I took off my helmet and tucked it under one arm.

She took a step as though to embrace me, but my somber face stopped her in her tracks.

My voice was hoarse as I asked the question. "What do you see?"

"I see you," she said, just as she had long ago.

"And who am I?"

"Vercingetorix ben Masada," she said. "Warrior of God." She looked at my armor and perhaps she thought I had earned a post with Hadrian so I could report on him. After all, I had left her so I could spy on the Romans.

But I had returned as one of them.

"Vercingetorix the Red," I said, and took a deep breath. "Legate of the Tenth Fidelis."

Mirah looked at my armor again, and a leaf drifted down past her head, that bright hair hidden away behind another blue scarf. The girl who had twirled and spun through the vines at Tu B'Av still had freckles that danced across her nose like flakes of gold. *What do you see?*

My Roman son, my father had said.

You are of Rome and your wife is of God, my mother had said.

They knew me better than my wife did.

Mirah's eyes crawled across my breastplate, rose to my shaved jaw and shaved head, and she read my expression for what it was. Her whole face convulsed. She put a hand to her mouth, her head shaking from side to side.

I took a step forward. She backed away from me, her head still shaking back and forth. "Mirah," I said helplessly, but what could I say? *Mirah, I am lost here. Mirah, I am not born to run a wine shop or help free your province of the Jews. Mirah, I do not know what you see when you look at me, but see what is there: a man made to harvest the souls of Rome's enemies.*

And Mirah, I love you.

But I saw no love in her eyes that day, as I stood in my legate's armor, in my Roman boots made for stamping on Judaea's rebels. Her blue eyes filled as she stared at me, but not with tears. With revulsion.

She gave a swift lunging dart of her chin, and she spat at me. Her spittle landed on my polished breastplate. And though there were still so many bitter words to be said, so many things to be screamed and argued and wept, that was the moment when my heart broke.

SABINA

A.D. 131, Summer
Rome

The Empress of Rome went straight into her sister's arms. She felt like a child in need of rocking, and though Faustina was the younger, she must have known that. She held Sabina tight, murmuring soothing wordless nonsense as she'd have done to Annia. And Sabina felt a man's arms slide around them both, shielding them like a warm wall, and heard Titus's quiet voice. "How bad is it, Sabina?"

"Oh—" She lifted her head to him, wiping at her eyes. "It is so much worse than you could imagine."

He made no reply, only stepped closer. Sabina stood a moment, cocooned safely between her sister's soft breast and Titus's lean shoulder, their arms sheltering her from the world, from the curious eyes of the slaves. It felt like that moment in the bathhouse in Antioch with Hadrian and Antinous, the three of them standing wrapped together in such companionable affection. *Only Antinous and I were allied in fear for Hadrian,* she thought. *Hadrian and I never dreamed of ill fortune for Antinous.*

She stepped back from her sister and her brother-in-law, giving a watery smile. "So much for the Empress's grand return to the Eternal City," she said, looking down at her travel-stained *stola* and ruined cloak. The seas had been ferocious all the way from Egypt, even the usually placid waters of the Tiber. Not a soul on Sabina's ship had come off its decks less than hollow-faced and covered in grime. Summer was only beginning to turn to fall; the seas should still have been calm, but Sabina didn't question the ill winds or the ill luck. There had been no good fortune at all since Antinous had died, and that was all there was to it.

"You've gotten thin," Faustina scolded, pulling back to look her sister over. "Do you truly grieve so much for Antinous? He's been gone nearly a year."

"I will miss him always," Sabina said, and the pang of grief stabbed her just as sharply as it had when she saw him lying in the Nile. The shock had gone, but not the grief. "But it's not just Antinous. I miss my husband."

"You've only been parted from him since he left Egypt for Syria—"

"Oh, I was missing him long before that." Sabina felt her smile turn mirthless. "The moment they dragged Antinous out of the Nile, Hadrian was gone."

The Hadrian she had grown accustomed to, anyway. The man who could be teased and scolded, who would debate new laws and Greek philosophy and architectural principles until dawn, the man with a smile never far from his face. That man was lost into a grief fathoms deeper than her own. He worked the days and nights round without caring for sleep, did his Imperial duties with savage precision, lashed his grief-gaunt body into vicious morning hunts followed by immobile public appearances followed by nights of feverish writing, writing, writing. "What are you writing?" Sabina had asked.

"The legacy of Antinous," Hadrian responded. "A great city named Antinoöpolis erected on the bank where he fell—two colonnaded thoroughfares crossing at the center, with a shrine in his name. Yearly games to be held in his honor. Temples, epic verses, statues to be commissioned in every corner of the Empire—" The Emperor finally looked up, his gaze red-rimmed. "He will not be forgotten. His name and his face will live forever, I swear it. My legacy will be his."

"What of Rome's legacy?" Sabina had asked, stroking his hair.

Hadrian returned to his feverish writing, ignoring her touch. "Burn it all down, for all I care."

Now, Titus steered her from the brightly painted atrium into the sunlight of a little walled garden, ordered cups of barley water, and dismissed the slaves. "So, the real news about the Emperor. Let's hear it."

Sabina cradled her cup. "What have you heard already?"

Titus looked up at the cloudless sky as if searching for tactful words. It was Faustina who said bluntly, "That he thinks his lover is a god."

"True enough," Sabina said. "By the time I left Hadrian's entourage, Antinous's worship was already spreading in the east. Hermopolis, Alexandria, Lykopolis—they all have temples. More are planned."

Faustina sighed. "I'm not saying the boy wasn't a gift from the heavens—we all know what a balm he was for the Emperor's temper. But a Greek-blooded common-born boy worshipped like a Bacchus or a Mars?"

Sabina shrugged. "Perhaps he deserves to be deified. Certainly they believed so in Egypt—the river began to rise as soon as his body was taken from it, as if in homage." And then there was Hadrian's renewed and savage burst of good health. *Anyone who throws themselves into the Nile will save the life of a loved one . . .*

There were already rumors that Hadrian had had his beloved sacrificed, a dark bargain with the gods for renewed health and long life. *Fools.*

"Whether he deserved deification or no," Titus said in austere tones, "a catamite has never before been entered into the realms of the divine. I say it not out of insult," he added, noting Sabina's frown, "but so you may imagine the Senate's reaction."

Sabina drew herself up in a flash of cold anger. "If it will assuage Hadrian's grief to have his beloved remembered as Antinous the God rather than Antinous the Catamite, then the Senate may hiss like ganders."

"You've got a glare that could crack marble," Titus said, looking her over. "What an empress you've become, Vibia Sabina. I remember when you were a barefoot girl with your hair in your eyes, sprawled on the floor with a map."

"And I remember a gawky boy who came to propose marriage to me." Sabina looked at her brother-in-law: long, lean, quiet, commanding, with smile lines about his eyes and hands so still that their smallest gesture made illustrious men scurry. Titus Antoninus Pius, they were calling him now; one of Rome's most honored sons, cheered by all. "How old were you then? Sixteen?"

"And now I'm well past forty." Titus ran a hand through his hair, silvering about the ears. "And sometimes feel as old as Servianus."

"Some parts of you are still just as active as they were at sixteen," Faustina murmured. "What?" she said at her husband's glance. "I meant your stomach, of course! You should see him fall on Alpine cheese," she told Sabina. "It's like lions falling on gladiators. Or Annia falling on her water flask when she comes back from her run—"

This time, the pang in Sabina's chest was pleasure rather than pain. "Where is Annia, anyway? Running?"

"Of course." Titus gave a fond shake of his head. "Though I restrict her to no more than four miles a day."

"I long to see her." See if her hair had darkened from pure red to Vix's russet, see if she had grown out of her freckles . . . Sabina smiled involuntarily, and Titus and Faustina smiled back. *We three,* Sabina thought. All her life, it seemed, she had been one of three. As a girl it had been herself and Vix, forever tearing gaps in each other until Titus arrived to complete the triangle and cement the peace. Then there was herself and Hadrian, ever an ill-matched pair until Antinous came to make it three against the world. Now Antinous was gone, but there was still Titus and Faustina to complete a new trio.

One of three, Sabina thought, looking at the way her sister's hand twined with Titus's. *Never one of two.*

Their smiles all faded, as though her melancholy had crossed the table. Faustina sighed, and Titus's fingers started to drum against the carved arm of his chair.

"Will Hadrian be satisfied with making Antinous a god?" Titus asked at last. "With founding him a city, holding games in his honor, endowing him with priesthoods?"

"He will never be satisfied again," Sabina stated. "There will be more temples, more priesthoods, more cities renamed Antinoöpolis—"

"That will not please the Senate."

"Then Hadrian will have their heads."

"Can't you stop him?" Faustina jabbed a pearl pin more deeply into the blond coils of her hair. "You have some influence, surely."

"He pushes me away. He pushes us all away."

Sabina had stayed at Hadrian's side through it all—fits of weeping where he'd fling cups and furniture at the walls; feverish days of writing and planning. She'd stood at Hadrian's side this spring in the new-rising Antinoöpolis, dispensed prizes to the victorious gladiators celebrating the games of Antinous in blood. She'd veiled herself in black when Antinous's mummified body was released by the priests, and his soul sent into immortality. But Hadrian had turned to her afterward and said with blank exhaustion, "Go back to Rome, Vibia Sabina."

"Let me stay to help you—"

"I go to Syria next," Hadrian said, cutting her off with a sharp gesture. "To deal with Judaea. I mean to do bloody things there, things not fit for your eyes. Go home."

And that had been that.

"So, Antinous's influence is passed," Titus said. "And for the moment, so has Sabina's. Is there anyone else who can check the Emperor?"

Vix? Sabina thought. Vix, who had spent most of the winter drinking wine with Hadrian, pouring him into bed at the end of the night whenever he fell soddenly unconscious, getting more and more impatient about departing to his precious Tenth Fidelis. You couldn't say Vix had any influence over Hadrian, exactly, but Hadrian certainly let him get away with more than he allowed from anyone else.

But Vix was gone, dismissed like Sabina herself when the Imperial party left for Syria—he'd flown like an eagle for Judaea, his new commander's regalia slung across his saddle. "No," Sabina said. "No, there's no one. Lucius Ceionius hangs on Hadrian's arm day and night, flattering and joking, but it's nothing." Lucius was just a pretty face. He could not replace Antinous, or do what Antinous had done for Hadrian.

"The Emperor," Titus said, "is in danger of losing everything he has built. If he continues to anger the Senate, they will cross him in retaliation. And if he then begins to hand out executions—"

Faustina squeezed his hand fiercely. "Not you. I will *not* stand by again and watch you march into a cell!"

"I shan't give the Emperor any cause to send me to one." Titus smiled, giving her fingers a squeeze. "But someone must persuade Hadrian to leave off building temples to a lost lover, and come back to Rome. He should settle here, smooth some ruffled feathers, and for the love of all the gods, deal with the succession."

"He doesn't care who inherits the Empire," Sabina said. "As long as it still resounds with Antinous's name."

"I hope he's satisfied with Pedanius Fuscus, then, because the boy has been acclaimed all over the city since returning from Egypt, and the longer Hadrian goes without contradicting that—"

"Leave the matter of the succession for a moment," Sabina said. "There is one thing that might bring Hadrian out of this cloud he's in, and set him back to himself. And that's vengeance."

Rouse the worst side of his nature deliberately, she thought with a twist of her mouth for the irony of it. She'd spent so many years helping him suppress his temper, and now she wanted to inflame it. *If anger will bring him out of this mad spiral of grief, then I'll stoke him to a fury.*

"Vengeance against whom?" Titus was asking. "Whatever poor slave catches his eye at the wrong time? The Jews, for refusing to allow a temple of Antinous in Jerusalem?"

"No." Sabina finally released the suspicion that had been growing in her for months. "I cannot prove anything, but . . . what if Antinous did not drown by accident?"

Faustina and Titus exchanged glances. "You mean suicide?"

"No." Sabina spoke tersely. "What if he was murdered?"

She left her sister and her brother-in-law feeling rather foolish. Faustina's shudder had been instinctive—"I can't bear to think someone might have heaved that gentle boy into a river like so much trash!"— but Titus's arguments had been logical. "Before we cry murder, surely there must be a *reason* for it. Who would benefit from Antinous's murder?" The answer to that would appear to be no one. Antinous had not had a real enemy in the world; he was either loved or despised, but even those who despised him as a womanish whore would not likely have risked Hadrian's wrath to harm him. There was no value to killing him except perhaps to rid the Emperor's reputation of an embarrassing blot, and who would risk Hadrian's vengeance for something so insubstantial?

"It must have been suicide," Titus concluded after his calm appraisal of the facts. "He feared the return to Rome. You yourself said he was gloomy in his last days. A moment's despair may well have driven him to the irrevocable."

"He had a bump on his skull . . ."

"And you say the physicians dismissed that. He might have struck his head on the railing of the barge as he fell."

Sabina could not say that was wrong. Suicide was the logical answer—or at most, an accident.

But.

The following morning, an ancient freedman came tottering into her atrium: a Greek tightly wrapped in a long gown, head crowned with thinning white hair. He had a name, but nobody outside the Imperial family knew it.

He bowed very low before Sabina, who had donned Imperial purple and wig for once and sat on her couch with her spine straight as a spear. "You summoned me, Lady?"

Sabina lifted a hand to the roomful of slaves, attendants, hangers-on. "Leave us." She waited until the room emptied, then spoke crisply. "When I was first made Empress, you came to me and said you had spies in every important household in Rome. Is that still true?"

He did not look at all surprised by her question. "It is."

"Despite the fact that I have made little use of you, since I inherited you from my predecessor?"

"That makes no difference." His tone was placid. "I was trained by old Emperor Domitian's wife, and it was her belief that an empress must have her own sources of information. What she did with that information would be entirely her own affair, but Domitian's Empress contended it was best to *have* it." He gave a reminiscent sigh, as if remembering fondly the kind of use Domitian's Empress had made of his information. "I have always been prepared to inform you, Lady, should you wish to be informed."

Sabina rose. "I want every courtier, every freedman, every senator, and every slave who was present on the Imperial barge in Egypt a year ago investigated."

The old man's brows rose. "Investigated for . . . ?"

"Someone may have pushed the Emperor's favorite to his death. I want to know for certain."

"Few things in my arena of work are certain, Lady."

"Understood. But if there are answers to be had, I want them."

"Such searches prove expensive, Lady. The bribes alone for such a wide search—"

"My private purse as Empress is at your disposal. Let it be known there will be rewards for even the smallest piece of information." Sabina gave a nod of dismissal. "Report to me, and only to me."

The old freedman nodded, then doddered out looking frail and harmless. Sabina smoothed the folds of her *stola*, sitting again and calling for her steward. *One way or another*, thought the Empress of Rome, *I will know. And if you murdered Antinous, whoever you are, I will hunt you down.*

VIX

A.D. 132, Summer
Judaea

When the storm clouds of revolt finally loomed on the horizon, I took one last journey from the Tenth Fidelis to the house in Bethar. The courtyard was full of abandoned furniture and half-filled boxes. "Going somewhere?" I said, and Mirah didn't even look up.

"Get out." She went on stuffing clothes into a pack.

"It's my house."

"Not anymore." She had a point—I'd only spent a handful of nights here since returning from Egypt. It hadn't taken long for the shouting, the tears, and the stubborn brick-wall madness of our entrenched and opposite positions to drive me to the Tenth Fidelis. I'd moved my meager possessions into the legate's quarters.

I wanted to tell her how I'd missed her. The words were on my tongue, but Mirah glanced up, her hard gaze sliding past me to the four men at my back. Two were guards; the third was Africanus, dark-faced and lithe. The last was Boil, big and red-faced as ever, who I'd begged permission to yank from the Praetorian Guard and transfer to the Tenth as my second. Mirah showed no fear at the sight of them, just allowed her lip to curl and repeated, "Get out."

I took a deep breath. "Where are the girls?" Hell's gates, let me not be too late.

"They don't want to see you."

"I don't care what they want. Where are they?"

"Gone," Mirah flung at me, but she was lying. I caught sight of two pairs of liquid-dark eyes, watching fearfully from the shutters of the house.

My heart eased. "Where are you going?"

She said nothing, just jutted her jaw. She looked thinner.

"You go to Simon?" I persisted.

"Yes." She threw the word down like a challenge.

"Where is he?"

She smiled, and it was the kind of smile she used to give me across a pillow. "I wouldn't tell you that if your thugs there put a spear through me."

I made myself shrug. "Doesn't matter. He's with the rebels, wherever they are. Underground, I reckon." I ran a hand along the trunk of the little potted orange tree that stood beside the courtyard gate. It was high summer; the fruit was ripe and the smell came to my nose mellow and sweet. "We found the tunnel networks outside Jerusalem, Mirah."

A faint widening of her eyes.

"Quite impressive," I said. I'd set my engineers on the hunt the moment I took control of the Tenth, finding at least a few of the rebellion's old hiding places: an infrastructure of tunnel complexes, of wine cellars and oil presses, new storehouses linked to ancient burial caves. And the chilling part was that the structures we'd found were abandoned, swept out, not so much as a rusted sword to be found. Whoever had used them had long moved on.

I'd have kept on looking, but then the Roman engineers hard at work raising a city called Aelia Capitolina over the ruins of Jerusalem had clumsily managed to collapse the ancient tomb of King Solomon in their efforts to lay foundations for a temple, and that was the flame that lit the tinder. I started to get dispatches of towns being seized somewhere near the border by Egypt. I'd wasted no time warning that ass of a provincial governor to summon the Twelfth Deiotariana to back us up—and I'd taken my four men to Bethar for Mirah and the girls.

"So the rebels are moving." I took a step closer. "It doesn't matter. You know they won't catch my men unawares."

"You won't find anyone to fight, *Legate*."

"I can always find someone to fight," I said with complete truth. "If there's anything you can say about me, Mirah, admit that I can always find a fight."

"Not this time," she said. "Uncle Simon trained with your legions, spent his youth learning what Rome has to teach. He won't let it be wasted. He'll run rings around you—"

"So he's high in the rebellion's leadership." I felt a sinking feeling in my chest. Hell's gates, but I didn't want to face my friend across a field of blood.

Mirah laughed as though reading my mind, and it was a mirthless sound. "He's not Simon ben Cosiba anymore, Vix. He is Simon bar Kokhba."

"And what does that mean?"

"You'd know if you ever bothered to learn our language." A shake of her head. "That should have told me something."

I took a step closer. "How were you supposed to meet Simon?"

"You think I know? I join him in stages, and no man knows more than the next waypoint. We all made sure we knew nothing worth telling." My wife stood there with her head thrown back, small and unflinching in the middle of the ransacked courtyard, her blue eyes glittering and her freckles standing out like a sprinkle of ginger across her upturned nose. Her lovely hair was wrapped tightly away and her face was thin and stony, but she was still beautiful to me. Everything became my Mirah: sloe-blossom wreaths and happy smiles; matronly headscarves and fanaticism.

"Take her," I said quietly.

She didn't struggle when one of my legionaries came and took her arm in a firm grip. She didn't struggle until the other legionary went into the house and came back pushing my daughters in front of him, crying and clinging to each other. "Don't touch them," Mirah cried, but I paid no attention. I turned and strode out of the open gate, and my men dragged my family behind me.

There was one neglected shrine to Juno in Bethar. It had been defaced, scrawled with obscenities and stinking of piss. There was a turd sitting on the altar, but it didn't matter, it was still a Roman altar, and I marched my daughters up to it. "Boil," I barked. "Africanus."

They already knew what to do. Boil stepped forward to Dinah's side, and Africanus took his place beside Chaya.

"No," Mirah shrieked, and it took both of my ox-built legionaries to hold her back, writhing and cursing, but I ignored her. I stood with a hand wrapped around Dinah's arm on one side and Chaya's on the other, while they married my officers. *Ego tu Gaius, ego Gaia*, the Roman vow for brides went. *Where you are Gaius, I am Gaia.*

Mirah would never have said the words. She'd have glared murder and sealed her mouth like stone. Dinah gave one shake of her head, trembling all over, but I just gave her a fierce glare and she wilted, stammering through the vow. Boil slid an ill-fitting ring over her finger, murmuring his part—*Where you are Gaia, I am Gaius*—and then it was Chaya's turn. She didn't even need a glare from me; she hiccupped the words out between sobs, giving a whimper of terror as she dared look up at Africanus's night-dark face.

There was no sacrifice, no ritual cake, no feast, no procession to the bridal home. But by Roman law, it was a wedding. "There," I said over Mirah's cries, and sent my daughters stumbling into the arms of their new husbands. "You're Roman wives. The rebels won't touch you because you're daughters of a Jewish mother, and the Romans won't touch you because you're the wives of Roman officers."

They didn't seem to care for their newfound safety, weeping and clinging to each other, but it was the best I'd been able to devise. I'd seen Roman legionaries on the march through foreign lands, and there wasn't a pretty native girl anywhere who would go untouched. Even the daughters of a citizen like me, if they were found with the rebels—well, there wasn't any proof, was there, of who their father might be? But Roman wives with rings on their fingers and marriage contracts with their names—contracts I'd already had drawn up . . . It might be a paper shield, but even a paper shield was better than none. I'd arranged to have them taken clear out of Judaea into Syria, where there was a house waiting with a high wall and guards to man it, but I knew enough to make legal plans in case the rebellion spread as far as Syria.

I let the girls weep in each other's arms. "Thank you," I told my men, not that they had much choice in the matter, but being legate had its advantages. *You're getting married, and that's an order.* "I'm grateful," I said, "but remember that if either of you lays a finger on my girls, you're a dead man." We'd already discussed this part, but it had to be clear. "When this revolt is over we'll have a pair of divorces with no one the worse off. But if they tell me you deflowered them, I don't care if it's your husbandly right or not. I'll geld you."

They both gave me curt nods, Boil with a glare—he had been my friend since Dacia, after all. It had still needed to be said where the girls could hear it. I hoped it would give them some measure of comfort, but Chaya was sobbing hysterically, and Dinah held her in shaking arms. I could have wept for the distrust in my daughters' huge dark eyes, but I hardened my heart. They could feel whatever they liked about me—it didn't matter, as long as they were safe.

Mirah was still hurling curses at me like nails. I came toward her, gesturing at the legionaries to let her go, and she flew at me like a tigress. I let her get in one hard-fisted blow that snapped my head back, and then I seized her and held her at arm's length, letting her fists flail uselessly. "They're going away from here," I said over her screaming, "and not to Simon. They're sitting this war out in safety, and so are you."

"*I am not!*" Mirah screamed. "You can't stop me from going to my family, you can't—"

"I can. You and the girls are going out of danger if I have to have you dragged every step of the way." I had my doubts about leaving her with the girls—what if she tried to escape with them into the war-torn countryside?—but I was already tearing my daughters away from everything they knew. I couldn't take their mother away as well; I'd just have to see they were all under guard. "After this whole doomed revolt is done, you can do as you like," I told Mirah. "But until then, I'm locking you up and keeping you alive."

"You think I'll ever want to lay eyes on you again?" she cried, still struggling against my grip.

"Once the rebellion is over, Judaea will either be free or in ashes," I said. "Frankly, I think the ashes. And when that happens, I'll come back for you. I'll always come back for you."

"I am no longer your wife! I will not be the wife of a Roman tyrant—"

I gave her a little shake, cutting her off. "You will always be my wife." *Because I miss you*, I wanted to cry. *Even like this, with you shouting and cursing my name, I miss you.* "You hear me, Mirah? Until one or both of us is dead, you are my wife."

"Then I pray death comes to one of us." She stared at me with tearfilled eyes, but she wasn't crying from grief. My wife was crying because she hated me utterly. "Dear God, but I should have stabbed you while you slept long ago."

My broken heart spasmed in my chest. *Oh, Mirah*—I could see the girl in white, dancing at Tu B'Av. I could see her in every detail, right down to the smile in her blue eyes.

"Then hate me," I said. "As long as you survive."

I returned to the Tenth to find a heap of hysterical dispatches. Towns were being seized openly along all the borders, and I had incoherent lists of the dead and even more incoherent reports of the rebellion's leadership. "It's said they cut off the little finger of one hand as a sign of loyalty to their leader. He's not hiding anymore—sent signed dispatches all through the province, inciting rebellion. He goes by the name of Simon bar Kokhba."

My stomach sank as though it had been filled with lead, but was I surprised? Not really. "What does that mean?" I asked. "The name."

"Son of a star. He changed his name to match a prophecy. 'There shall come forth a star out of Israel—'"

Behind me, Boil sucked in a breath. He'd loved Simon too, in the old days in the ranks. Africanus gave a low whistle. "Sir, if this is your wife's uncle, we should question her. Gently," he added as my head whipped around.

He meant that it would look bad for me, my wife being so close with the rebels. But I knew where my loyalty lay, and I wasn't having Mirah questioned just to allay doubts. She had nothing to say to me, and I had nothing to prove.

Simon ben Cosiba, turned Simon bar Kokhba. His men were soon moving through the narrow mountain passes, moving to cut us off. "Let them come!" one of my tribunes trumpeted. "We'll show them what a Roman legion can do!"

"They know what a Roman legion can do." I looked at my officers. "We retreat. Now."

That was a march from the gates of Hell, looping north from Jerusalem with what felt like most of Judaea on our heels. I marched the men at double pace, marched them till they were tumbling down in the road, screamed at them to get up, ordered the centurions to lay on them with vine sticks until they got up and limped on bloody-soled.

I lost a whole cohort at the rear when screaming rebels came out of the dark in fast-moving formation, came from the midnight black and massacred them before they had a chance to form ranks, and I lost another cohort over the following two nights in a pair of vicious dawn attacks. Over a thousand men, gone.

Boil cursed and my tribunes pleaded with me to turn and stand ground, turn and fight, but if we did I'd have a whole legion of dead men. "Give the Twelfth time to get here," I said, staggering from lack of sleep. "That's when we fight."

But we ended up running clear to the border of Judaea, because the Twelfth didn't even get halfway to Jerusalem before Simon and his nine-fingered rebels fell on them. Fell on them and slaughtered them to the last fucking man.

Mirah's words whispered to me: *This time we've learned.*

We ended up wintering—where? I can't remember. I had a single half-shattered legion; I could do nothing but fortify our camp and wait for the Emperor, praying we'd still be alive by the time he arrived.

Black days.

Hadrian was preparing to return to Rome, but it didn't take him long to head for Antioch and summon me. "You look like every rebel in Judaea marched over your face on the way here," was his greeting.

I shrugged. I was winter-starved, ashen, taut, and feral; close to tears and just as close to fury. I walked straight across his chamber, helped myself to a cup of unwatered wine, tossed it down, and sat without permission. He had advisers there—commanders, Praetorians, the odd senator—and they looked at me as nervously as though a wolf had stalked into their warm enclave. "You don't look too pretty yourself, Caesar," I observed. He looked thin, and his eyes were red-rimmed. He sat still, none of his old restless gestures, and he had Antinous's black dog across his lap. The animal never left his side.

"Life feels like death," he said, stroking the dog's pointed ears, "without Antinous."

"That it does," I agreed, and I saw his advisers shifting uncomfortably. *Such grief is womanish,* they were likely to say when Hadrian could not hear. I'd heard plenty such whispers on the barge back in Egypt, with Hadrian howling and weeping his nights away.

I liked his grief. I still wept for my son, too, and I didn't care if it made me womanish.

"How bad is it?" Hadrian asked bluntly. "In Judaea."

"Bad," I said, just as blunt. "They control all the territory south of Jerusalem and running along the sea. They've established it all as a free state, under Simon bar Kokhba." I used the new name. Thought it might make him seem like a different man. So far it wasn't working. "The Twelfth Deiotariana is gone. I lost a quarter of my legionaries just getting to Caesarea—"

"Outrageous," one of the senators harrumphed.

I just gazed at him. "You try marching twenty hours straight with ten thousand well-armed nine-fingered lunatics on your heels every step of the way."

Hadrian lifted a hand before the senator could bristle. "What do you advise, Legate?"

"Let it all go?" I suggested. "Let them keep their damned free state?"

What Mirah prayed for, what Simon hoped for. Sometimes, even now, I dream about what would have happened if Hadrian had said yes. But—

"No," he said, and there was a glitter in those lifeless eyes. A fathomless black rage that would see the whole province burning like a pyre.

So be it. I shrugged. "Then we take it all back."

"You think that's so simple?" the new Praetorian Prefect drawled.

"Simple, yes," I said. "Easy, no. Move every man you can spare into the province and stamp until everything that hits back is gone. It's hard to *do,* not hard to understand, you shit-brained wine-sack prick."

"See here—" he bristled, but Hadrian interrupted, eyes never shifting from me.

"What will be required, to subdue Judaea?"

"I'll need new men in the Tenth. To replace my losses." God, so many losses!

"I'll have the ranks filled with sailors and marines from my fleet, to make up the ranks until new legionaries can be conscripted. What else?"

"At least eight more legions." I braced myself for refusal. I needed those eight badly, but it was so much to ask for—even at the height of Trajan's Parthian wars, had such a massive force ever been summoned for a single threat? Hadrian might very well laugh in my face.

"Make it twelve legions," he said. "What else?"

"More commanders," I rallied. "I can't do it all, not something this size. We'll need good competent men, not pride-stuffed peacocks thinking only of their own reputations."

"I'll summon Sextus Julius Severus from Britannia. He's my best. The governors of Syria and Arabia as well."

Someone else spoke up. "It'll take time, assembling them—"

"See it done," Hadrian said, and that was how a whole war was charted: a few terse lines between two old enemies. I looked at the Emperor, and he looked at me. I remembered the hatred I'd felt when I found him with Antinous, when I ripped across the room roaring for his blood. I remembered the rage I'd felt when he gave me the Tenth back in his drunken haze of grief, setting me on the course that ruined things for good with Mirah. I remembered the rage and the hate, but I couldn't feel either. God knows I didn't have any love for the bastard, and Hadrian had none for me either, but he trusted me utterly. All the facts and figures I'd gathered to beg my case today, and he hadn't asked for a one. My opinion was enough, and the war was mine, and all with hardly a word being said. And I felt one last spasm of grief for Simon, because I could so easily have been his general instead, sitting at the right hand of my friend who was another bearded, brilliant, enigmatic man like Hadrian.

But I was bound to the Emperor instead: two angry, aging men locked together in a shared grief.

He held a hand out and I grasped it, feeling the strength of his grip as he felt mine. We looked at each other, hands locked not in enmity but in accord, and he dismissed me with a thought rather than a command. *Bring me blood, Vercingetorix*, I imagined him thinking.

Gladly, Caesar.

All through the war it was like that, the complicit silences. I swear I heard his orders before he ever voiced them, and he knew my actions before they were ever taken. I was his dog of war, and he let me off the leash. Black days, yes. But days with a strange bitter exhilaration, doing the job I knew how to do, and doing it so well. Love it or hate it—and mostly I hated it—I was made for this.

Close to a year and a half it took to assemble the army we needed. Near to thirteen legions. Sextus Julius Severus arrived, and he grunted to meet me. "Heard of you," he said, looking me up and down. "Nothing good."

"It's all true," I said, and I liked the man. God knows he was a brute; he thought nothing of tacking a villager up on a cross as an object lesson to a whole town, and his men would rape anything that had a hole in it. But he told foul cheerful jokes, and he bullied me to eat when I forgot, and I'd long since abandoned the whole puzzling conundrum of how a savage brute could also be a man to be liked. I was a brute myself, those three years. I drove my men hard, I handed out punishment freely, I gave the courageous no more praise than a nod and shamed the cowards as viciously as I knew how. I was Vercingetorix the Red, Hadrian's dog, and I gave a dog's howl inside at the river of blood I unleashed.

"I have done what I can to see you all prepared." Hadrian summoned all four of his commanders, but he spoke mostly to me. "I return to Rome. Tell me when it is ended."

"It'll be over in a matter of months, Caesar," Severus predicted. "How long does it take to put a pack of cockless Jewish bastards down in the gutter?"

"A year," I guessed. "A year at least." Because I knew how Simon and his men would fight—and they did. They fought like gods, they fought like savages, they fought like fanatics. They fought like men I'd have been proud to call my own, like men with a cause worth dying for. Like men with a cause worth killing for, and my men died. So many!

But we took our own price in blood. More than half a million Jews dead.

I cannot believe that number. Surely there were never so many rebels in Judaea to begin with? And there were so many survivors, the ones who escaped the purges and the raids and the battles to fight us again. Surely five hundred eighty thousand dead cannot be right. On bad nights I sat up doing my figures, reviewing the lists of the dead over and over, trying to work out a better number. But there was no better number. Five hundred eighty thousand.

We had thirteen legions divided among the four of us; we had four hammers made of steel-clad men, and we hammered at anything that moved. We hammered that land until it was nothing but bloody scraps. My war was a straight brutal drive south toward Jerusalem. If I found a village, I razed it to the ground. If I found a fortified town, I surrounded it and starved it into submission, and then I razed it to the ground. If I found rebels, I fought them and then I executed them. It was, God help me, the only way of winning this war.

And I still didn't know if we *could* win, because Simon's rebels were the rock and sometimes my hammer broke against his rock. I lost a cohort and very nearly Boil along with them in a sudden attack just past Neapolis; he came staggering back on a half-dead horse, a bloody stump where his shield hand had been. Severus captured one of the rebellion's leaders—not Simon; a holy man—and had him flayed, and a few days after that my first century and two others were razed and the rebels flayed all the centurions. Flayed men look all the same; just bloodied dolls. Without his shining dark skin I wouldn't have recognized Africanus, but he lay atop the heap in his regalia. *Chaya is a widow,* I thought stupidly. But why would that matter to her?

So many dead, but soldiers still touched my lion pelt as I passed, because somehow they believed I was *lucky.* "Vercingetorix the Red doesn't lose," I heard one of my centurions boasting to a newcomer. "Bastard's got Fortuna herself at his back, cooing and spreading her legs for him whenever he wants." Maybe he was right, because I didn't take a scratch through that whole savage campaign, but what kind of luck was it that made sure I survived when so many of the men I loved died?

Three years. Three years, and we appeared to be winning, if you could call such bloodily bought victories *winning*. Simon's men were at last on the retreat, fighting like wolves. My legions were driving toward Jerusalem, my co-commanders veering to join me. One final convergence, driving the scattered remnants before us and leaving ash and blood in our wake, or at least that was how we planned it, though I was nowhere near so confident. Simon and his dream would not die easy. *He will take us all with him*, I thought. *Or at least me.*

I wasn't really surprised when I learned where Simon and the core of his fanatical nine-fingered heroes chose to make their stand.

Where it all began, of course.

Bethar.

Chapter 16

ANNIA

A.D. 135, Spring
Rome

"Gladiatorial games," Marcus declared, "are crass and vulgar and bring out the worst in man's nature."

"How do you know?" Annia looked up at the great round shadow of the Colosseum rearing up before them, roaring noise to the sky as more and more plebs flooded eagerly through the entrances. "You've never been, either!"

Marcus grabbed Annia by the elbow so the pair of slaves he'd insisted on bringing could clear a path. "Gladiatorial sport is doubly unsuitable for a woman's eyes—"

Annia let him lecture as they pressed inside behind the slaves. The day had dawned warm and heady: Veneralia, a spring day filled with rose garlands and sighing women. The day when the statue of Venus Verticordia would be taken from her temple, and a cluster of female attendants would bathe it and dress it in new finery. Those girls not at the temple were waving garlands and getting their stars read to see who they'd marry, and the boys got to ignore all the silliness and go enjoy themselves at the games. *I wish I were a boy*, Annia thought, and then hastily amended the wish for any gods who might be listening. *If I can't be a boy, can I at least be grown?* A grown woman could just announce she was attending the games instead of the temple rites—a girl of seventeen had to resort to an absurd amount of sneaking.

"Don't worry, we won't get caught," Annia told Marcus, who was still muttering objections. The vast buzzing of the Colosseum's throng rose around them as they climbed the marble tiers inside, as though they were rising through an immense beehive. "My parents are attending the rites—they think I have a headache, and my little sister is covering for me." Annia didn't like sneaking, but that didn't mean she wasn't good at it.

"We'll never get away with this," Marcus groaned, but Annia stopped listening because they emerged into the vast oval of the Colosseum. An expanse of raked sand stretched below, and tiers of seats rose clear up to the sky where brilliant awnings offered shade from the delicate spring sun. So much bigger than she had imagined! Annia laughed, scarcely hearing herself over the roar of bets being shouted and bouts being called, and slung a happy arm about Marcus's waist. "Let's find a seat!"

He shook off her arm as fast as possible, but took her formally by the elbow afterward as though they were about to enter a palace. He was always doing that lately: flinching if she gave him a casual hug or tickled his ribs, then offering his arm whenever she came to a step. Like she had the plague and shouldn't be touched, but was incapable of going up a flight of stairs. "Women shouldn't sit with men at the games," he was worrying now. "But that's more the rule for well-born women, and you look like such a pleb in that dusty tunic, I don't see anyone trying to separate us."

"Thank you," Annia said as they beat a path to the seats his two slaves had found. "Thank you very much."

He shook his head at her sarcasm. He looked especially handsome when he was annoyed, Annia always thought—something about the way he squared his shoulders like a statue, and his eyes sparkled outrage. "He's grown, hasn't he?" Ceionia Fabia had whispered not long ago. Under those demure downcast lashes, she never missed a thing, especially if it was male and eligible. "Rather handsome . . ."

He's more than handsome, Annia thought, not that she'd ever tell Ceionia that. Marcus had shot up in height, one of the rare boys just as tall as Annia, and his face was strong and sunburned under its faint new stubble. He still wore the tunic and the *bulla* amulet—his grandfathers had absolutely Republic-era ideas about boys being given a toga too young—but he looked a man, not the skinny boy Annia had known all her life.

A man who always seemed to be hectoring her lately, and that Annia didn't find quite so charming.

"I don't see why you felt the games were more important than the Verticordia rites," he was saying in that disapproving tone she now heard so often. People were surging to their feet, clapping and shouting for the opening speeches, but Marcus was oblivious. "You could have been chosen as one of the attendants to Venus today! Ceionia Fabia was chosen, and she felt deeply moved—"

"Did she cast her lashes down and say, 'I am not worthy of the great honor bestowed upon me'?" Annia fluttered her lids extravagantly.

"Ceionia Fabia is a girl of most appropriate behavior."

"What you mean is that she's pretty."

"She *is* pretty." Marcus gave an obedient clap as a team of rangy leopards came prowling onto the sand for the first of the wild-beast fights. "It's not an opinion; it's a verifiable fact."

"She's also hates me like a plague. Don't tell me that's not a verifiable fact."

"No," Marcus admitted. "She does dislike you. Because you have more suitors."

Annia felt a flush mount in her cheeks, and kept her eyes on the arena where a herd of fleet gazelles had just been released for the leopards. She *did* have more suitors than any girl she knew. As soon as she'd turned fourteen, the men started to pay court. "You're the Emperor's niece by marriage," Annia's father had said, "and his approval will be required for any match you make. But I see no reason you may not have your choice within those boundaries."

Annia shrugged. She was going to marry Marcus, of course. He'd proposed it long ago, and it had seemed silly at the time, but she'd had years to get used to the idea. He was clever and serious and good, even if he could be a prig, and she knew how to push him around a bit, which every woman agreed was essential in a husband. But Annia couldn't marry Marcus until he was at least a few years older, so until then she had to be an obedient girl and put up with ridiculous men who pretended it was Annia and her reddish hair and her long lanky body they wanted, and not her dowry and her Imperial connections. It could have been funny, but Annia found it all a little depressing. A part of growing older that she did *not* enjoy.

The leopards were making short work of the gazelles, all that lithe, long-legged grace shredded into bloody heaps on the sand. "I don't like this part," she said, averting her eyes. Those poor, fast, graceful things.

"I don't, either." A bull was herded into the arena next, a bull with horns that had been sharpened and tipped in steel for a duel against a bear. "Was it Aemilius Scaurus I saw calling on you yesterday? Girls think he's handsome."

The bull rushed the bear, and Annia surrendered to the temptation to tease just a little. Maybe she intended to marry Marcus, but he didn't need to know that yet. "Aemilius Scaurus *is* handsome," she said primly. "It's a verifiable fact."

Marcus scowled. "You're teasing again."

"Don't be so easy to tease," Annia retorted, and she might have kept on, but then the bear made a swipe of its massive claws and tore the bull's throat open. Much of the crowd seemed to find that hilarious. "Oh, *Hades*," Annia said, and tried to ignore the queasy roll in her stomach. "I don't like this part, either."

Parades followed, and then the *bestiarii*, teams of animal fighters pitted against snarling striped cats . . . Annia was squirming sickly in the middle of all the cheering, wondering if it would be a mark of squeamishness to leave early, when she was arrested by a mutter of gossip from the seats behind her.

"—the boy's late!" a man was saying drunkenly behind Annia. A deep voice, a rough Subura accent. "Can't abide an emperor who misses his own games!"

"Boy's not emperor yet."

"He will be . . ."

Annia looked up toward the Imperial box and felt a lurch in her stomach. Pedanius Fuscus had just entered, giving a hoot of appreciation for the tigers dying in the arena. Pedanius Fuscus, taking his place on a golden chair.

"Didn't you know?" Marcus asked. "He's sponsor of the games today. His grandfather paid for everything, but officially today's celebration is a gift to the city from Pedanius. With the Emperor in Judaea again, he's the natural choice to take Hadrian's place . . ."

Annia couldn't stop looking: Servianus beaming with pride beside his treasured grandson, who had grown into a burly young man in his twenties, carrying the crisp folds of his toga in flawless pleats, raising his hand to the crowd. A roar went up for the perfect young prince with his easy smile, and Annia felt a surge of such acrid nausea that she had to put her head between her knees.

"I didn't know it was still so bad for you." Marcus's voice was quiet, not reproving anymore. "Seeing him, I mean."

"I don't see him often." Annia sat upright, forced herself to shrug. "He's a man grown. Too busy for girls like me anymore, thank the gods."

The midday executions were beginning, lines of shackled prisoners shoved out onto the sand. Normally Marcus would have been considering their plight and saying something about the nature of justice, but he was looking at Pedanius instead. "He can't hurt you, you know—you shouldn't be afraid."

"I'm not afraid!" Annia's head whipped up. "I'm *angry*, Marcus. Everyone looks at him like he's the dawn, like he's the whole promise of tomorrow wrapped up in an Imperial purple ribbon. Why don't they see what he is?"

"Because most people only see what's on the surface?"

Annia had always known that—just as she'd always known that most people didn't want to know what you saw if you *did* look under the surface. But that didn't make it any less maddening. "People are sheep."

The first prisoner died swiftly, a bent-backed woman folding into the sand with a *gladius* through her throat. Pedanius was applauding up in his box, but desultorily. Slave executions were such dull entertainment, after all—half the crowd was chatting, and the other half getting up for a cup of wine. Annia ignored the laughter and the chatter, feeling her jaw set as she watched another prisoner fold up onto the sand. She didn't want to watch them die; the sight made her ill, but someone in this arena should watch their lives end as if it mattered. She and Marcus watched it all in stark, sick silence, until the last tottering figure had fallen.

Why did I come here? Annia thought. *Why?*

The wailing of reed pipes came then as the bodies were raked away. Pedanius came forward to announce the comic acts that would finish the midday interval—an elephant that danced to lyre music, a tame pair of tigers that could be ridden by acrobats. Annia did not think she would ever laugh again.

Marcus was looking up at the Imperial box, some of the color back in his face now that the killing was done. "The Emperor hasn't *officially* chosen Pedanius as heir yet," he said as though trying to distract himself.

"But the Emperor hasn't excluded him, either. And if he doesn't bother picking anyone else, it might very well *be* Pedanius. Because he's family." Annia gave a bitter laugh. "So maybe we should make another curse tablet."

"Maybe we should grow up."

"What's that supposed to mean?"

"Well—curse tablets? That's a game for helpless children and slaves."

"And women." Like the woman who died first in the line of executions. "Women are helpless, too." The Colosseum rocked with laughter for the capering elephant in the arena, but Annia's stomach roiled bitterly. *Pin all your impatience on growing up*, she thought, *and then you learn it gets no better when you're grown.*

Marcus was looking quizzical, and Annia fumbled for the right words. "Everybody's helpless when they're a child. But at least boys get to grow into men and become useful. Girls just grow into women, and they stay helpless forever." Looking up at Pedanius Fuscus where he sat tossing coins to the elephant's trainer. "He grows up and becomes powerful, and I just grow up and become—nothing. And all I can hope is that the bastard goes lion-hunting with the Emperor again, and the next lion eats him."

It was one of Brine-Face's favorite stories, now that he was back in Rome: telling, with becoming modesty, how his spear had finished the lion that had so nearly claimed the Emperor's life. "Pedanius Fuscus hasn't got the guts to kill a frog," Annia had snorted, but no one listened. She was just another useless girl growing up into a useless woman, and Brine-Face was the golden boy, the future Emperor.

The elephant lumbered out of the arena to a scatter of applause, and Marcus sent his slave boy off for barley water. "Do you want some food too?"

"I'm not hungry."

"If you don't want food, you shall at least have a wreath." Marcus gestured for his slave girl. "Two myrtle crowns for Veneralia!"

He was trying to cheer her, Annia knew that, but she felt more mulish than cheered as the slave girl swayed off with a smile back over her shoulder at Marcus. "She's flirting with you," Annia observed.

He looked embarrassed. "I know."

"Actually, I think your slave boy was too." A fair-haired Greek who gave Marcus an open-lipped smile before going off for barley water.

"I know," Marcus repeated.

"You're blushing." Annia surveyed him, forgetting for a moment about Pedanius up in his golden chair, laughing at the tame tigers in the arena. "Are you bedding one of your slaves? Which one?"

"Annia Galeria Faustina!" Marcus's voice had long broken to a smooth tenor, but his words scaled up in a squeak, and he flushed. "You cannot possibly ask such things!"

"Well, are you?" The thought gave her a prick of jealousy, but she didn't show it. Girls had to be pure as Vestals when they came to their wedding beds, but not boys. They could bed as many slaves as they wanted. "Tell me!"

Marcus ran a hand through his hair. "The boy is Theodotus and the girl is Benedicta, and they were given to me for my *toga virilis* ceremony next month. That is all."

"Gifts to make you a man," Annia said flatly. "Well. Brine-Face's manhood present to himself was me, so I suppose yours are an improvement."

Marcus stared stubbornly out at the arena, empty now that the tame tigers had been herded out. "I may not be a man yet, but I am old enough to know that it is unseemly to submit to some vulgar fit of passion."

"Why?" Annia couldn't help asking. He clearly wanted to, and that gave her a different kind of pang—because he'd never looked at Annia's hips like he had the slave girl's, with that flash of something hungry and hot. She gave her dusty dress a tug, feeling like a street urchin.

He sat for long moments with his lips clamped shut as the crowd roared for the upcoming gladiator bouts. Annia waited. Marcus could never resist the urge to pontificate, even if the topic was one to make his ears burn.

"Just because one has a passion doesn't mean one should give in to it," he burst out suddenly in that pedantic tone he still couldn't shake when he was nervous. "It is a principle at the very core of Stoicism: control of one's baser thoughts and emotions. Look at the way people still laugh about Antinous—because the Emperor didn't control his passions at all. His love *or* his grief."

"Anybody would grieve for Antinous." Annia could see his statues all through Rome, and every one made her furious, because even the finest marble didn't have life in it. Didn't have that vivid laughing expression she remembered from the very last time she had ever seen him—the night he'd hauled Brine-Face off her and Marcus, and then cuffed him for spitting insults about the Emperor . . .

"But one's passions should never gain control over one's life." The gladiators had begun their slow purple-cloaked parade around the arena, the crowd roaring and surging to their feet, but Marcus argued on, oblivious. "An emperor's bedmate deified? That's why people laugh when the Emperor isn't listening."

"They laugh because Antinous was a free man of Rome," Annia pointed out. "But bedding a slave isn't base. You could do it if you wanted to." The slave girl was wending her way back with two myrtle wreaths over her arm, hips moving as fluid as a snake. Annia gave her dress another tug.

"Putting a pretty slave in a boy's bed isn't what makes him a man." Marcus was the color of a pomegranate. "It takes more than a moment's friction and sweat to do that."

"What does make a man, then?" Annia crammed her myrtle wreath down over her unraveling braid.

"When I think of the man I want to be," Marcus said seriously, "I look to your father. He said he would sponsor me when I put on my toga next month—if I could be a man like him . . ."

"He is wonderful," Annia agreed. "Do you really put your toga on so soon?"

Trumpets blared as the gladiators disappeared below, and Marcus had to raise his voice to be heard. "My grandfather wanted to put off the ceremony until the Emperor returned, but he's still sieging Bethar. Thank the gods. Emperor Hadrian terrifies me."

"But all through his travels, he wanted those reports on your studies. He likes you."

"I wish I knew why." Marcus grimaced. "I know I'd never get through my first speech in a toga if I had him staring me down."

"Well, now you don't have to." Annia grabbed hold of his hand, impulsive. This was the Marcus she liked best, not the one who preached about proper behavior. "If you get lost in your speech, just look for me."

Marcus looked at her strangely. "Things will change, you know. When I've put my toga on, I can't be running about with you anymore."

Annia blinked. He'd dropped her hand like it was a dead frog. "Why?"

"After I'm a man, I won't have time for such things."

"You really can be insufferable, you know that?" Annia whipped her gaze back to the arena, clamping her teeth on more hot words. Two Thracians had been matched for the first bout, and everyone was shrieking for their favorite—she was damned well going to watch. Pedanius gave the signal to begin, looking lordly, and Annia wished she could see him on the arena sand. *I wouldn't be satisfied with first blood then*, she thought. *I'd put my thumb out for a death blow.*

Most bouts only went to first blood, but there was one death that afternoon. A *secutor* with a heavy shield raked his blade across a trident fighter's gut, and it should have been a shallow cut, but the man didn't retreat fast enough. He fell with a scream, blood spilling through his fingers, and the *secutor* didn't wait for the signal from the crowd. He made a fast thrust through the heart and then saluted his fallen opponent, full of somber pride, and the screaming crowd hushed a moment in reverence.

"I don't like this," Marcus said. "It's barbaric."

Annia watched the victor's proud strut through the Gate of Life. Before now she'd stayed seated as the rest of the Colosseum stamped and roared, but now she found herself on her feet with everyone else, banging her hands together. "It's terrible."

"Then why are you smiling?"

She hadn't realized she was. She looked down and realized her palms stung from clapping. "I don't know. I don't really like that I'm enjoying this part, but I am." She tried to make sense of it as she sat down, watching another pair begin to circle each other. "I didn't like the prisoner executions, or the animal bouts—it's not like the animals or the prisoners have any chance. But the gladiators . . ."

"You'll watch a gladiator die, but not a few gazelles? That makes no logical sense."

"Well, most of the gladiators don't die, do they?" The trident fighter below took the bout in a thrilling sweep of net, spilling his opponent to the ground and then raising a fist to the sky, giving his victory to the gods. "They're brave," Annia said, and felt a fierce thrill curl through her like a flame. "I like to see courage."

"Most of them are slaves. Just as helpless as those prisoners earlier."

Maybe, Annia thought. But at least the gladiators were dangerous. You couldn't be utterly helpless if you had a sword in hand and the skill to use it. *I wish I could use a sword*. She curled a fist and imagined it, a blade like a natural extension of her arm.

"You'd be down there if you could, wouldn't you?" Marcus looked disgusted. "A gladiatrix with an Amazon helmet!"

"I would." She leveled her imaginary *gladius* at Pedanius in the Imperial box, as though they faced each other across a stretch of bloody sand. "Annia the Amazon! Annia the Barbarian—"

Marcus snatched her arm down. "Must you make such a spectacle of yourself?"

She yanked away. "If I embarrass you so much, why are you here?"

"Duty," Marcus bit out, and that stabbed. Annia looked back at the arena, ostentatiously sliding away from even the brush of his sleeve, and Marcus stared too. Brine-Face was shouting up in the Imperial box, myrtle wreath cocked over his head at a rakish angle.

"Look," Marcus said at last. "I'm taking you home."

"No." She still didn't look at him. "There's another *secutor* fight. I think I like them best." Maybe she'd lay a bet, too. Everyone around them was busy arguing odds.

"This isn't proper for you to be seeing at all." He took her hand, tugging her up.

"You're not my father, Marcus Catilius Severus." She pulled away. "No matter how hard you try."

Marcus gave her a cold look. "I'll leave Theodotus to see you home safely. I have more pressing matters at hand than watching men bleed and trying to get you to behave."

"You're a pompous ass," Annia said.

"You're a silly child," he returned.

"And you're not a man yet!" she shouted after him as he went stamping off down the marble steps, slave girl swaying along behind. Her and her hips. He'd probably give in to all those passions he was so proud of controlling, and take her to his bed. "Go ahead," Annia muttered. "She'll tell you you're wonderful, and you'll get even more pompous than you already are."

Brine-Face was still whooping in his golden chair. *I kicked you in the groin,* Annia thought. *I put you on the ground screaming.* But what did that matter? She might have won the battle that day, but Brine-Face would still win their war. He would always win, because he was a man and because he was going to be Emperor.

Annia put her head down on her knees, ignoring the surge of shouts as the gladiators flew at each other. *Antinous*, she thought, somehow. *It all started with you.* Antinous died and Emperor Hadrian went mad, and ever since then it seemed to Annia like the whole world had gone mad with him. Marcus had grown into a stranger, Pedanius Fuscus would grow up to be Emperor . . .

And what will he do to me then?

SABINA

A scream brought the Empress of Rome bolt upright in her litter. She had been half dozing, on her way back from a late banquet after yet another temple dedication, sliding into a dream of Antinous's golden hair in the Egyptian sun—*how did you die, please tell me*—but she brushed the dream's threads away and drew back the litter's silk curtain. "What was that?" she called to her bearers.

"Just a brawl, Lady."

Another shout came, stifled this time in a groan of pain. Sabina heard gasping, the thud of what sounded like booted feet against flesh. She squinted into the darkness—a half moon lit the broad street, and she could just make out five or six hulking shadows buffeting and kicking at a limp shape. "Run them off, Centurion." Sabina's official uses might now be limited to dedicating temples and dispensing charity, but the Empress of Rome was not about to glide past in her litter as murder was done.

The thugs ran at the first sign of lowered Praetorian spears. Sabina slipped from her litter and crossed the stones to the young man huddled in a bundle of bloodied toga. "You poor boy, how badly are you hurt?" she began as her Praetorians rolled him over. Then she blinked recognition. "Pedanius?"

Her husband's great-nephew looked like a slab of meat on a butcher's table. Both eyes were purpled, his nose flattened and smashed, and his mouth—his mouth was a gory mess of broken teeth and torn lips. "Lady," he managed to splutter through a mess of bloody spittle and tooth splinters.

"Don't speak," Sabina ordered. "Don't move, either. Praetorians, be gentle." She had him lifted into the litter; they weren't far from his grandfather's villa. "Let me see . . ." She prodded carefully under the folds of his toga as the overburdened litter rose beneath them. She was no medicus, but no one could travel with so many of Hadrian's hunting parties and legion inspections without knowing something of cracked ribs and smashed noses. Poor Pedanius groaned in pain as she touched his ribs—something broken there, very likely—but he didn't seem to have been stabbed. The blood was all from his nose and his destroyed mouth. "You'll live, never fear!" She smiled reassurance at him. "I suppose they followed you home from a wine shop to rob you?" One didn't usually see gangs of street thugs in this refined quarter of the Palatine Hill.

"Set on me," he mumbled thickly, and she heard his outrage even through the slur of his blood-filled mouth. "Set on *me!*"

"I'm afraid Imperial blood is no protection against fists and boots." Sabina eased a cushion under his head. "Better to learn that, if you ever do become Emperor."

Her litter-bearers bore Pedanius into his grandfather's house. Servianus was busy thundering, "Sad times we live in, when an emperor's heir can be robbed and beaten in the streets!" so Sabina gave orders for the Imperial physicians to be called. "I will visit again tomorrow," she promised as the slaves dabbed at the boy's bloody face, and took herself off feeling rather invigorated. Gods knew she wished no harm on poor Pedanius, but it felt good to do something *useful* for a change. Lately her days had been nothing but waving to crowds or brooding alone. Even reports from her ancient freedman and his net of informers provided no distraction, because all those discreet inquiries about those who might have wished Antinous harm had led exactly nowhere over these many months.

It felt satisfying to deal with something as straightforward as a bloody nose and a boy's comfort.

Poor Pedanius still looked like a butcher's mess the next morning, but he rallied his gallantry as the sight of Sabina. "You are very kind, Aunt," he said, or at least Sabina thought that was what he said. He had been bandaged and splinted, but there was no splint for his mouth; his front teeth had been knocked cleanly out, and the remaining teeth splintered so badly they looked like broken road markers.

"*Four* broken ribs, three broken fingers, broken nose—" Servianus shook his head.

"But he'll be mended soon enough," Sabina pointed out. Antinous had been pulled from the Nile perfect and smooth-skinned as a statue, and yet his soul had flown. "I'll visit again soon, I promise."

"Perhaps you might bring your niece, Annia Galeria Faustina? The sight of her would cheer my grandson. I hope for a marriage there, of course—"

Astounding to think that her daughter was old enough for marriage. Annia had grown abruptly in the past few years, not so much lengthening in height but growing into the height she already had: skinny limbs turning sinuous and firm, bright hair darkening to a coppery russet. She moved with a light-footed swagger, shoulders swinging and hair flying, either scowling her black glare or shouting her raucous laugh, but never still. Not what girls of good birth were supposed to look like, smooth-haired creatures like Ceionia Fabia with their meek smiles and downcast eyes. Annia was something far better than that, something made of flame and wind. *My daughter.*

"—but it is not just an alliance I think of," Servianus was saying. "My grandson is *quite* infatuated with the girl."

Sabina raised skeptical eyebrows. "With Annia, or with her lineage?"

"Her lineage makes her my choice as a wife for him," Servianus said without embarrassment. They both knew how the game of alliances was played. "But Pedanius wants the girl for herself. I see the signs; his eyes follow her constantly. I tell you, he is in love. Perhaps you might speak to your brother-in-law . . ."

Pedanius Fuscus and Annia? Sabina mused on that as she went home. The boy had been all eagerness-to-please during those months he traveled in Egypt. Perhaps a bit puffed up, but he had cause to be: birth, charm, *and* good looks (at least before he lost those teeth). If Pedanius had the sense to admire Annia for her fire as well as her lineage, perhaps he warranted more consideration . . .

A drawl greeted Sabina as she entered her own atrium unwinding the veil from her hair. "How many *In my days* did Servianus sprinkle on your visit?"

Sabina smiled at Lucius Ceionius, lounging in wait with his dazzling smile and glossy hair and gleaming beard. "Only six."

"Six? How lucky you are. I called upon young Pedanius earlier this morning, and Servianus gave me a full fourteen." Lucius shuddered. He was all shades of gold today in a spring-yellow tunic embroidered with topaz beads, flanked by a pair of identical blond slave boys in yellow-dyed wings like sun sprites.

Sabina's African slave girl came to take her mistress's *palla*; she was no longer a child but a lissome young woman, and Lucius eyed her idly. "Are you willing to sell that one? I could pair her with a delicious little Nubian of mine, 'twin handmaidens of Pluto—'"

"She's to marry a scribe of mine who is working to buy his freedom," Sabina said. "When he does, I'll free her as a gift to them both. So, no, you may not have her. What brings you here, Lucius?"

"Is your company not reason enough?" Lucius's eyes swept approvingly over her *stola* of silver tissue, the silver loops about her wrists and toes, the fan of brilliant scarlet-dyed feathers, which she used to brush his hand away as he reached for hers.

"I think I am past the age for such flattery—especially for a man who has so many delicious little slave girls on hand."

"Slave girls are but a rinse of barley water to cleanse the palate, Lady. Not a mature and complex wine to be savored."

Sabina laughed outright, and he feigned hurt, hand on heart like a young swain. "Why do you mock? Have I not long been your admirer? You put the young wives of Rome to shame—I should know; I've had most of them. Subtlety is what I admire in a woman. Elegance. Intelligence—"

"Enough." Sabina waved a hand, amused. "I still think you have a reason to call besides paying me compliments. Though I'm sure I don't know what it could be—I'm Empress of nothing, living in an empty villa with a few polite slaves and aging cats while my husband slaughters Jews at the edge of the Empire." Sabina added a silent prayer to that, the one she said every day. *Keep him safe. Keep him safe.* Always twice, because one "him" was her poor maddened husband and the other was the name that came blood-tinged from the battles of Judaea: the Emperor's favorite commander, Vercingetorix the Red.

She banished both from her thoughts, waving Lucius to a seat beside the central pool as the African girl brought chilled mint infusions in silver cups. "What may I do for you?"

"Bluntly?" He gave a smile to make it charming instead of blunt. "Support me as Imperial heir."

Sabina burst out laughing again. "Is that all?"

"Why not?" He grinned, not remotely offended. "Someone has to be heir. Why not me?"

"You have shiny hair, and great knowledge of wine and women." Sabina tilted her head. "I think an emperor needs rather more."

His smile shone out unwinking as a lamp. "What does that matter if the Emperor finds my other qualities more important?"

Sabina considered, tapping her fingers along the cup. "Is that your way of hinting that you have become my husband's lover?" She knew he wasn't, but she wanted to see his reaction.

"Gods, no!" He looked startled. "I'd be yours any day you asked me, my dear lady, but not the Emperor's. I'm no Bithynian love slave!"

Her voice chilled. "I will not hear insults against Antinous."

"Nor would I dream of offering any." There was a bust of Antinous in rosy marble on the east side of Sabina's atrium, placed directly opposite Hadrian's where their stone eyes could easily find each other. Lucius wandered to the bust with its Greek fillet and curly hair and gave the aquiline stone nose a careless pat. "I liked Antinous. Most decorative, and rather more intelligent than one expected of a catamite—"

"This is not the way to seek my favor," Sabina said crisply.

"But the Emperor's favor is with me now." Lucius wandered back, sinking onto Sabina's couch this time. "Not as a bedmate, of course. No, no. I do but flirt, and make him laugh, and for a lonely aging man it is sufficient. Few people make him laugh these days. Am I wrong to hope his gratitude will stretch . . . far?"

Sabina regarded the glossy curls and shining eyes. True; during Hadrian's time in Rome between sojourns in Judaea, she had seen Lucius at the Emperor's side a great deal, forever laughing and making graceful witticisms. Maybe Hadrian *had* found a new favorite. "Then why are you not in Judaea?" she asked. "Making the Emperor laugh and incurring more gratitude?"

"It's all blood and mud in Judaea." A flick of the well-tended fingers. "No, I thought to stay here: the companion to welcome him back, a balm after all that bloodshed. And I use the time to obtain support from those who count."

Sabina spread her arms at her empty atrium. "Do I look like I count for very much these days?"

"You have always counted." Lucius captured her hand, his smile glittering and his eyes all cool speculation. "For all the Emperor's periodic rages at your . . . hmm, *indiscretions* . . . well, he's never divorced you, has he? And at times, you've stood in very high favor indeed. You could again, with me as your ally." His thumb brushed along her knuckles.

"Could I?" Sabina swirled the wine in her cup idly, alert to the last fingertip. "And how would you make an alliance with me? I have no daughter for you to take as your empress." Not that he knew, anyway. "And I hardly think you will offer to wed me, no matter how much you like to flirt."

"Oh, my wife will make an excellent empress, if a rather *duller* one than Rome is used to. And my children will find other advantageous marriages; I have one or two ideas there. For you?" Raising her hand to his lips. "I have in mind the role of adviser. You have advised two emperors already." He turned her hand over, lips brushing the inside of her wrist. "Why not three?"

"Adviser? That sounds like the kind of role my husband promised

Empress Plotina, Lucius. And he threw her away like a worn-out old slave."

"Plotina was utterly useless," Lucius dismissed. "A rigid old cow. You, my elegant lady, are somewhat more . . . supple."

He took the cup from her hand and set it aside, drawing her into the curve of his arm. Sabina allowed herself to be drawn. Her skin was prickling all over with sudden attention, and not from Lucius's smooth touch.

"Think on it, dear lady." His breath feathered across her bare arm. "Those Jews cannot last much longer, and when they are done, the Emperor will return home and give some thought to the succession." He bent his head, lips grazing the line of her shoulder. "Servianus is too old to serve as heir"—Lucius's mouth brushed higher—"and his grandson might have been a possibility, but with those teeth knocked out he sounds a lisping fool. In the Senate House, he would be a laughingstock." Nibbling along the line of her neck. "A laughingstock can never be Emperor."

Sabina allowed him to tilt her head back. "Is that why you called upon Pedanius first thing this morning? To assess your competition?"

"Naturally." Against Sabina's jaw, Lucius's mouth curved into a smile. "The boy is finished, whether he knows it or not."

And who finished him? Sabina thought as Lucius's lips traced up to her ear. A pack of determined thugs venturing all the way into the Palatine to deliver a beating: bent on robbery, or hired by the man sitting opposite?

"Think on it, Lady?" Lucius asked, and then he kissed her. Sabina let him, partly because a man like Lucius thought kissing a woman was the best way to persuade her to anything, and partly because he was good at it. *It has been a very long time since a handsome man kissed me.* No woman in Rome would want to be Empress if they knew what a cold bed generally came with it.

"So," Lucius murmured, withdrawing. "You will think on my offer?"

For a moment, Sabina toyed with the thought of allowing him to seduce her. Who knew what she might be able to get out of him over a pillow? And it would be pleasant work, judging from his kisses. But she felt no yearning at all as his smooth hand dropped away, and Sabina smiled faintly. *It seems time has made a loyal heart of me.* She knew the only man she wanted, and all she could do for him was offer a daily prayer of *Keep him safe.*

"I'll think on everything you've said, Lucius." She gave a little laugh as he brought her hand to his lips, to make him think a few caresses and some flattery had bought him everything he wanted. "I intend to think *very* hard indeed."

Her ancient freedman had arrived before her golden guest was gone an hour. "Lady, there has been no news—"

She cut him off, no longer smiling in the slightest. "Tell me again what you found of Lucius Ceionius's activities the night Antinous died."

"Lucius Ceionius?" Casting rheumy eyes up to the inlaid ceiling. "By all reports, he was bedding down with two slave girls. Twins, of course."

"Did you have the girls questioned?"

"I could not. He sold them immediately afterward."

Sabina sat back. "Does that strike you as strange?"

"No, Lady. My reports say that the man is easily bored. He changes slaves as frequently as his tunics. Or his bedmates."

"Find the girls," Sabina said. "Find any slave he had on that barge."

The freedman went so far as to blink. "That will be difficult, Lady. Even for me. To track a few slaves sold years ago, and far away in Egypt—it will take many months, if they can be tracked at all."

"I have nothing but time. Cease all other inquiries but this one."

"You believe Lucius Ceionius may be . . ." The freedman thought her a fool, she could tell. Sabina did not care. Her blood was sounding the alarm. Lucius: such a pretty, glossy fellow, hardly to be taken seriously . . . Except that he was just a step from the purple. All on the basis of a handsome profile, a few jests, an emperor's loneliness.

Did you create that loneliness? Sabina wondered. *Just so you could be the one to fill it?*

I liked Antinous, he had said. She did not think he was lying. But to have the purple within grasp, and all for a shove . . .

A shove. And perhaps a hired beating for yet another handsome boy barely into his twenties.

"Bring me news from Egypt," she told her freedman fiercely. "I don't care how long it takes. Just find it."

VIX

A.D. 135, Autumn
Bethar

"Mirah is gone."

I stared at Boil, just returned from Syria. He was gray, tired, thinner than the blocky, fair-haired Gaul I had known for so long, and he wore a leather cap over the healed stump of his shield arm. "What?"

"Gone. For three months."

"Three *months?*" I repeated, and found myself shouting. "Why in hell's gates am I only hearing about it now?"

"Your daughters said she'd sworn them to secrecy. And the guards didn't dare tell you until they could find news of her. They thought you'd kill them."

"I *will* kill them. One task, that's all they had! How did she get away from—" But did it matter how Mirah had slipped my guards? She was a resourceful woman; intelligent; driven. Walls wouldn't hold her, not if she was determined.

I didn't bother asking where she'd go. She'd gone to join her family. Left the girls in safety, and for that I was glad, but she didn't care anymore for her own safety. Not Mirah.

I squeezed my eyes shut. One more thing on top of this hellish siege, this desk of mine piled with reports and blades, with lists of wounded and lists of dead. "I'll put out people to look for her. In Jerusalem, or . . ." I trailed off, and didn't bother picking the thought back up. Boil just waited. A tribune with an armload of dispatches poked his head in, opening his mouth, then just backed out again.

"The siege," Boil said at last. "Any progress?"

"Not much."

Boil tried for a smile. "Not like Old Sarm, eh?" Sarmizegetusa; the fortress in Dacia where Trajan had laid siege many years ago. My first real campaign, and I'd made a name for myself in that siege, helping smash the city's pipes so thirst would drive them to open their gates. I didn't see the rebellion of Simon bar Kokhba and his men ending quite so easily.

"Been a long time since Dacia." Boil turned to go, then hesitated. "You, me, Simon—even Hadrian. Same players, really. Just a different stage."

He ducked out, shaking his head. I stared at the latest list of the dead, and then I shoved it aside and went to look out over my camp. The legions had dug in for the last fight: a small city of men clinging grimly to the dark earth of Judaea. Bethar loomed sullen and black over the ashy ground, just as Old Sarm had loomed over green hills.

Wars are colored things. That Dacian war was green and gold, all sunlight and forested slopes in my memory: an Emperor I revered at the head of a legion I loved; friends about me in the tent every night. Simon ribbing Boil mercilessly over that girl who had left him for a flute player; all of us laughing. Can a war be golden? I think it was, at least for me, though it probably wasn't so sunlit as I like to remember.

And the war in Judaea? Black and scarlet. Blood and ash, from border to border of the province, nothing but blood and ash and bitterness, and Bethar piercing its heart like a thorn.

All through that summer and fall, we sieged Bethar. Hadrian stalking back and forth along our siege wall in his breastplate and purple cloak, graying head glinting like steel under the whirling clouds. Me pacing at his heels, right alongside my son's dog. Outside the final stubborn problem of Bethar, the slaughter was mostly over—and all over Judaea, the survivors were being rounded up. Children and women for the most part, because the men of fighting age would have been killed and most of the elderly would have succumbed to famine and fever. So the rest came to me: children with the same huge terrified eyes Chaya had as a child when she screamed for fear of monsters in the dark; women with the kind of blank faces and limping steps that meant they'd been raped too many times to count. So many prisoners, the east would have drowned in them.

"Sell them," Hadrian said. "They cannot rise again if they are enslaved."

"No," I agreed bleakly, "they can't."

I looked at him and he looked at me.

"I forgot how much I dislike this place," he said at last. "It's ugly here."

"We made it ugly," I said, and he nodded. We sat drinking wine for a silent hour, and then I rose and dealt with the slaves. Throughout the whole war, that was the one time I disobeyed Hadrian's orders. I sent a good many Jewish prisoners to be sold at the great markets in Hebron and Gaza, enough to satisfy the records—but after so many years doing the Praetorian Guard's endless paperwork, I knew how to falsify reports. A good many of those captive Jews never made it to the auction blocks. I funneled them onto ships and into wagons, into any vehicle that would take them to Syria, to Arabia, to Africa and Numidia. To anywhere, as long as they were gone and free. I diverted supplies too, supplies to keep the prisoners fed and clothed until they could be delivered to their new lands. I suppose a great many died on those leaking boats and creaking wagons, and the ones that arrived would have arrived threadbare and homeless—but it was a chance. A better chance than a slave block, or so I told myself.

I did my best, I swear it. I wish I could say it was pure kindness on my part, or whatever was left of kindness in me. It wasn't. It was the guilt and shame that stabbed me when I thought of my mother, of the bitter sorrow I'd see in her eyes if she could see me selling the remnants of her people, and I made my amends in whatever small way I could. Although it wasn't all for my mother, or for my own shattered conscience.

I hoped I'd find Mirah among those broken survivors.

But I didn't find so much as the gleam of her hair or the whisper of her name, not in all the reports or in all the wagonloads of hunched figures—and while I spent that summer and autumn disposing of Judaea's survivors, Bethar fell.

Fell in a welter of betrayal and starvation, in blood and in desperate back-alley fights. Precious few left alive there for me to save with my paper tricks. I suppose you want battle heroics, something rousing and noble for the brave rebels who had played their desperate game to the end, but I didn't see much of that, and anyway, my final part in Judaea's rebellion didn't come until the end. Just like at the rebellion of Dacia.

Two rebellions: so different. But at the end of each was a siege, and a doomed warrior . . . and a fight to the death at my hands.

Hadrian had no interest in watching the captive rebel leaders die. Would I never understand the man? I didn't think he had interest in anything *but* death anymore. Maybe it was because he'd had another of his troubling nosebleeds that morning, and he could do little except sit leaning back in a chair with red rivulets running down his throat as his dog whined and his physicians fluttered. He summoned us four commanders for no more than the barest of instructions.

"Kill them quickly," he said, one fist curling and uncurling on the arm of his chair.

"You don't want to march them back to Rome in chains, Caesar?" Severus sounded disappointed. Captives in chains always looked well at a triumph, and all the commanders were hoping for a triumph.

"No." Hadrian sounded curt around his bloody nose. "Kill them here, and do it quickly. Just bring me the head of Simon bar Kokhba when it is done."

I felt a chill, because those had been Emperor Trajan's orders in Dacia for another rebel king—and those had been Hadrian's orders to me at the start of his reign, when I'd had to bring him four heads in a sack. Echoes and echoes. Is the past ever truly done with us?

"'Kill them quickly,'" Severus said with disgust as we retreated to the open square in Bethar where such executions were best conducted. "I was hoping for some crucifixions at the very least! Flaying bar Kokhba alive, would that count as quick? I could skin him fast . . ."

"If you want the Emperor to skin *you*."

It was a cold winter's noon when the rebellion's final act began to play, the sky blue and hard overhead, the square a blinding white in the grim sunshine, lined by my legionaries in their battered armor. Blood underfoot, dried between the stones from the city's fall, and curls of smoke still rising into the air from buildings that still smoldered. I wondered if one of them had been my wine shop.

Eight shackled prisoners marched into the square, shoved into a rough line. Such flinty pride in those straight shoulders and bloodied, bearded faces—though the only face I really saw clearly was Simon's. Severus read out the list of their crimes and the sentences to be passed, voice booming, and I didn't hear a word because I was looking at my old friend. Simon was gaunt from Bethar's months of starvation inside the siege wall, pared down to bone and sinew and whipcord muscle. His beard had gone wild, and his eyes still glittered with calm watchfulness. He turned his head, looking down the line of crested helmets and gleaming breastplates until he saw me, and then his eyes stopped. I swallowed, realizing I'd broken into a sweat under my breastplate.

Finish it, I prayed. *Just finish it.* But even if Hadrian had decreed speed and mercy in their executions, the executions must still happen, and seven others would precede Simon to their deaths. Die they did, as swiftly as a sword could strike their heads from their shoulders.

Then Simon's turn came.

He stepped forward among the heads of his comrades, shackled hands folded before him, and a stolid soldier stood by with a bloodied sword. The men shifted, eager to see the great "son of a star" whose prophecy had crashed to the earth instead of soaring to the heavens— and I hadn't planned to move, but somehow I was stepping forward.

"Mirah," I said low-voiced, and my mouth was dry. "Do you know what happened to your niece?"

Simon's eyes connected with mine slowly, as though he were dragging himself away from some inner citadel. "Mirah," he repeated, and his deep voice vibrated me like a lyre string.

"If she made her way to you from Syria," I said, "tell me."

"Yes," he said. "She made her way to me. A woman of God, worthy of all honor."

Severus was coming toward me with a puzzled frown, but I saw nothing but Simon. "Where is she?"

"Dead."

Some part of me must have known it. *Until one or both of us is dead,* I had told her when we last spoke, *you are my wife.*

Then I pray death comes to one of us, she had hissed at me.

Her prayer had been answered. Not mine.

Mirah. My Mirah, only she hadn't been *my* Mirah for a very long time. I bowed my head, my eyes dry and burning, and I wished I could tear the heart out of my frozen chest. "How did she die?"

For the first time, Simon smiled.

"How?"

"Aren't you going to kill me now?"

I drew my sword. "Tell me how she died."

He bared his throat for me.

"Vix?" Severus tramped up to my side, scowling like a jowly hound. "Why are you mucking about?"

I reached for the *gladius* at Severus's waist and unsheathed it in a quick yank. "He's going to fight me."

Severus's hand caught mine over his own hilt. "What?"

"Let him fight like a gladiator," I snarled. "They think we're barbarians for our gladiatorial games? Let him fight in one."

"Have one of your legionaries do it—"

"No," I said. "Simon bar Kokhba fights me."

Severus grinned. "Just don't let the bugger win, will you?"

He stamped back to the side, and I turned in one motion and tossed his sword to Simon. He caught it with a quick swipe, still fast despite the shackles, and I didn't give him a chance even for a practice heft. This bloody square had become arena sand, and there wasn't room here for pity. "How did Mirah die, Simon?" I snarled, and made a savage stab toward his belly.

"She was caught in our retreat past Jerusalem by a party of Roman sentries." He sidestepped my thrust, parried it, and began to advance on me. "Men from your precious Tenth. They raped her to death and left her to rot under a tree. Maybe that's how it happened, Vix. Or maybe not. Why should I tell you?"

I came for him again, short brutal jabs that could have disemboweled an ox. He had no shield to catch them, but a chunk of charred wood lay discarded in the bloodied square, remnant of some burned house—he snatched it up, and there was enough length in the chain between his wrists that he could hold it as a shield to parry me. "Tell me!" I snarled.

"Maybe she died of a fever in Bethar." Block again, and then he was the one attacking. Advance and thrust, crisp as the legionary he'd once been. "Maybe I buried her somewhere in these walls and said the mourning prayers for her." His sword rang against mine, and he was starved and beaten but he was ferally strong. I heard a growl from my legionaries as I retreated before those vicious stabs. "Or maybe she starved to death when your siege wall went up."

I stabbed at his makeshift shield, seeing charred splinters of wood sift down on the blood-flecked stones. "Or maybe she still lives."

"No." Simon's voice lost its mockery. He stepped back a moment, lowering his *gladius* just a touch, and I stepped back too. A moment of stillness, both of our chests heaving. We were neither of us young, like the men who had marched together in Dacia. "No. She's dead. That I do promise."

"And why should I—"

"I swear it in the name of the kingdom of Israel that was mine for two whole years before you came to tear it down." He said something else in Hebrew, and it had the sound of an oath. "My niece is dead, and I wept for her. But you'll never know how she died, Vix. Never know how she spent her last hours. Never know where her body lies. Not ever." He spat between my feet. "Consider that your punishment, you dog-whipped, Roman-veined *traitor*."

When I was young I would have roared. Young men always roar. Old men lack the breath, and I just flew at him in bitter silence. *Gladius* met *gladius* as we clashed and parried, and over the pounding of my own blood I could hear my men cheering me. Simon's lips skinned back from his teeth. Maybe it was rage powering him or maybe he really was the son of a star, because his sword was like a wall ever blocking mine. We had sparred together in Bethar for so long, and he must have thought he knew all my tricks.

"You know what your trouble is, Simon?" I panted. "You fight like a fucking Roman."

"I am not a Roman," he snarled.

"But you fight like one," I said, and with that I tossed my *gladius* from my right hand to my left.

Roman legionaries are all trained to fight the same way. Sword on the right, regardless of which hand they favor. Keep behind the shield; short jabbing strokes; the point beats the edge—everything that had been drilled into Simon and me during our legionary training, and that was how we'd always sparred together because it was all he knew. But legionary training hadn't been the beginning of my partnership with a sword, as it was his. I'd been trained first with the left hand, by Rome's greatest gladiator who also happened to be my father. The left hand recognized no rules, fought in no formations. *The point beats the edge*, the right hand said. *Hell with that*, the left hand thought.

It was how I'd destroyed a Dacian king's escape at the end of another siege. Echoes and echoes.

"You fight like a Roman," I taunted again. "That's one *Roman* part of you that never died. You've got Rome in your veins, same as me." He came after me like the legionary he once was, teeth bared. I abandoned all my careful footwork in an extravagant sideways leap, spreading my arms wide like a gladiator taunting his opponent in the arena. He made the stolid lunge that I wanted but I wasn't there, I was sliding away in a half turn, and my sword came around in one whistling-fast sweep, and it opened Simon's belly from side to side.

His sword dropped. His guts dropped. And he dropped, ashen-faced, blood pouring over the stones in a viscous flood, and I leveled my *gladius* at his eyes. "Tell me," I panted, and the roars of my legionaries were just a dull roar behind the hammering of my own heart. "Tell me how Mirah died."

He stared at me, holding his own guts. Just stared. "*Sh'ma Yisrael*," he managed to say. "*Adonai Eloheinu Adonai Eḥad.*" He drew out the last word in a hiss of agony, his eyes full of hatred for me and everything I was. "*Sh'ma Yisrael Adonai Eloheinu Adonai Eḥad,*" he repeated louder. The final prayer that is supposed to be the last words of any Jew. And I drew my sword back and I took his head in one sweep that dropped me to my knees. I stayed there, kneeling in Simon's blood, head bowed and eyes stinging, his head lying beside me and his eyes still open.

Echoes and echoes.

Full circle.

When I killed King Decebalus, I had let someone else take his head to the Emperor. But I took Simon's head to Hadrian myself.

He would not look at it. "I have lost my taste for taking heads," he said, staring at the smoking city.

"So you make me do it for you?" I flung the head at his feet. "May your gods rot your bones."

"They are." His eyes turned to me, tired. "I know what you did, Vercingetorix."

"What's that supposed to mean?" My men were celebrating and the other commanders getting drunk, but I paced back and forth in front of the Emperor, blood roaring in my ears and blood drying on my face. "What do you mean, you know what I did?"

"The Jews intended for the slave blocks. All the ones you spared."

I stopped pacing. I scrubbed my bloodied hand off on Antinous's lion skin. "Do you care?"

"At the beginning, I wanted every rebel in Judaea sent down to Hades. But now?" Hadrian's hand stroked the dog in his lap. "Let the survivors alone, so long as they make no trouble. I merely want to go home."

"Well, we can. Because it's finished, all of it. I finished it for you."

"I am thankful."

"Thankful for your victory?" The word was bitter in my mouth.

"Thankful there will be no more bloodshed."

"Didn't think you would ever have your fill of blood."

"I didn't think so, either." He picked up a letter he had apparently been writing. "To the Senate," he said, and read, "'If you and your children are in health, it is well . . .'"

I finished it, the traditional opening of any letter from an emperor at war to the Senate. "'—because I and the legions are well.'"

"That is how it should go." He laid the letter down. "I find I cannot write the second part. The legions are not well."

I couldn't argue with that.

"I have never seen such casualty lists..." He shook his head. "Enough bloodshed."

He sat in silence, stroking my son's dog, and I stood picking at the flakes of blood drying on my hand. I couldn't think of what else to do, so I stood there.

"You should eat," said Hadrian, surprising me.

"I'm not hungry, Caesar."

"You look thin and sharp as an overhoned blade, and about as likely to snap in half. Sit and eat with me."

I was too tired to object, so I sent for a plate of bread and cheese and dried meat, and divided it in two. He looked at his share with as little enthusiasm as I had for mine, but he picked up a lump of cheese. "Tell me of Antinous."

"Tell you what?"

"Something I don't know. Something from his boyhood. Something good." The Emperor stared at his plate. "I must hear something good today."

I looked at my own plate. Something good? Was there anything good left in this world?

"Antinous had two mothers," I said slowly. "The Bithynian girl who gave him both life and her beauty. And the woman who raised him, who bandaged his scraped knees and taught him to play gently with his sisters..."

The woman who resented him and loved him both.

Hadrian smiled. "That is a good memory."

I picked a chunk of bread off my plate, throat thick, and heard myself saying a few rusty words of Hebrew, words I remembered Mirah saying many times.

"What words are those?" Hadrian asked, the flare of his endless curiosity lighting his eyes just for a moment.

"The Hebrew prayer for bread," I said. "My wife taught it to Antinous."

And I ate my punishment.

CHAPTER 17

VIX

My daughters.

I cannot think of them without wanting to weep, without seeing them as they stood that last afternoon in the courtyard of the house in Syria. The walled and guarded house that had been their prison, from which Mirah had fled and never returned.

My girls stood like a matched pair, arms about each other's waists, not girls any longer but women grown. Dinah with her fall of shining hair, Chaya with her rosebud mouth, staring at me with identical dark eyes as I removed my helmet. They moved not one muscle to embrace me when I spread my arms. I ached as though my heart had been punched out of my chest, because all I wanted was to hold them. But they just stood, staring, as I lowered my burning eyes and stammered out the news that their mother was dead.

I'd vowed to tell Dinah and Chaya myself, to be there when they wept for their mother since I had been gone for so much of their young lives. But Dinah only fixed me with a stare like Mirah's, a stare full of soul-devouring hatred, and said, "We know."

She led her sister into the house, and they shut the door on me. If any tears came from those enormous eyes, I never saw them. I had always thought my girls petal-soft in their souls, but rebellion and loss had put steel in their spines. They knew that Roman law meant I could do as I wished with their futures: marry them off again to men of my choosing, haul them back to Rome to keep house for me, anything— but they turned their backs on me.

"I warned you," Boil said quietly at my side. "Not to expect too much."

"Would Dinah stay wed to you?" My one frail hope, grasping to take root in all this wreckage I'd made. Boil wasn't a Jew, and he was older than my elder girl by some years, but he was such a *good* man, solid and kind and dependable as a rock. I had a sudden, desperate little vision of him taking Dinah back to Rome. Settling with her, raising children with her, somewhere I could visit now and then and at least see my daughter was happy.

"She hates me," Boil said, and my hope died.

I found myself staring at my hands, roughened and raw, a soldier's hands like any other, and yet everything that came from these hands turned black. The price I'd paid, maybe, for my legendary career: the common legionary rising to become hero of Rome. Severus and the other legates were already talking of the rose petals and honors to be heaped on us all.

My stomach clenched at the thought. I'd risen through the ranks like a gleaming star, trod a golden path that my men in the Tenth spoke of in hushed envy . . . But every person to love me paid the price.

Mirah. Antinous. My daughters, made into bitter crones before their time.

I tracked down Mirah's mother—the sole survivor, from what I could find, of the warm and expansive family I'd married into. Once she'd been a rosy matriarch with laughing eyes who loved to scold me and stuff me with roast lamb. Now she was a bent-backed old woman, and the day Boil brought her to the house, she began to scream curses at me. I let her say it all, standing numb. But I had words of my own when she was done.

"Be a grandmother to my girls," I said. "See them married to good men of their own choosing." I couldn't stay in Judaea—and if I tried, Dinah and Chaya might be dragged down with me as the daughters of a hated man. I knew what to say; I just had to close my eyes a moment before I could get it out.

"I'm returning to Rome."

The arrangements were made in a matter of days. Money for the girls' dowries, the dissolution of Dinah's forced marriage. Mere days. I opened my arms to them both when I bid my last farewell, but they made no move toward me. I stepped forward and gathered them close anyway. Those slim bodies went rigid in my arms, and I wanted to howl because I remembered the rosy, radiant little girls who ran to the door for my kisses. Who clung to Mirah's skirts sucking their thumbs. Who rode Antinous's lean young shoulders.

"Live well," I whispered to the last of my family. "Live happy."

I prayed for that, as I turned from their unyielding faces and walked my Roman boots out of their young lives. My poor, blighted daughters.

I pray for them still.

SABINA

A.D. 136, Spring
Hadrian's Villa

Sabina's first glimpse of her husband after his final return from Judaea was of a bowed and solitary figure mirrored in a long pool. "Hadrian," she called softly, but he did not lift his head.

She waved her attendants away and walked toward him, bare feet noiseless in the grass. Hadrian had re-created Canopus here, the floating golden city in Egypt where they had all dallied just before that doomed journey on the Nile ... A long canal with a curved marble loggia at one end, at the other a temple with a great scalloped semi-dome. Everything a frame for the massive statue of Antinous, marble head bowed toward the bent figure of the Emperor hunched at his pedestal.

"Welcome home," Sabina said.

Hadrian raised his eyes. Dear gods, such changes—his gaze so sunken, his hair almost entirely gray, his skin ashen. *He is only sixty,* Sabina thought. *Just sixty, and he looks a hundred.*

"Vibia Sabina." His voice was deep as ever, but so listless. "I did not summon you."

"If my husband returns home, my place is at his side."

He did not reply, just reached up and stroked Antinous's stone foot on its tall pedestal. "The priests say you arranged for his rites to go on through my absence."

"I had offerings made every day."

"Sacrifices?"

"No. Antinous wouldn't have liked lambs slaughtered on his altar. I bring cups of that Nomentan wine that was his favorite, and I bring skinny old street dogs and promise him they'll be fed. And I bring flowers." She touched the bank of rosy blossoms massed at Antinous's stone feet. "Especially these lotuses you had dedicated to him."

"Thank you." Hadrian touched a lotus, his swollen fingers caressing the petals. "A poet brought me the first of these, did you know? Claimed he found it at the site where Antinous and I hunted the lion in Cyrenaica, where it sprang up out of Antinous's blood. Hence the rosy color."

"Do you believe that?"

"I think it's a second-rate piece of poetic drivel. But I still commissioned the poet to write a Homeric epic of the lion hunt. Most of the idiots I rule prefer second-rate drivel to genius any day, so a good second-rate Homeric epic should spread the name of my star far and wide." Hadrian stared up at the statue. "I've had him carved so many times. Antinous as Hermes in winged sandals—as Dionysus in a crown of grape leaves—"

"Osiris in headcloth and kilt," Sabina contributed. "I'm fond of that one."

"But they all look somber." Hadrian looked at her, eyes pleading. "Why can I not have him carved laughing?"

Sabina touched his hand where it still lay before the bank of lotuses. "Antinous's most beautiful smiles were always for you. Keep them for your memories, not for marble."

"Laughing or grieving, the world will know his face." Hadrian's fingers clenched through hers. "He will spring up behind me, everywhere I go. His temples. His shrines. His face. Across the spread of my empire, he will be remembered."

Sabina could feel a feverish heat radiating from Hadrian's hand. *His old rashes and fevers and aches, but far worse.*

"There are other things to talk of besides Antinous, now that you are back." She kept her tone gentle, returning the squeeze of his fingers. "You have conquered Judaea—"

"Syria Palestina." The passion went out of Hadrian's voice as soon as they left the subject of his dead lover. "There is no more land named Judaea. I have redrawn the borders and renamed the entire province." A shrug. "The Jews will give Rome no more trouble, that I swear."

"Future emperors will thank you." But it was a bleak kind of victory. Sabina shivered inside her ice-blue *palla*. "You're to celebrate a triumph, I hear?"

"My generals deserve it. They performed magnificently."

Triumphal honors for Vix. He had always dreamed of that, as long as she had known him. She wondered if it would please him at all. *Oh, Vix*—and a stab of pure longing went through her. Strange how it did not diminish through the years. She had not seen him in so long, and now he would be back in Rome. But Sabina pushed the thought aside, giving Hadrian's hand another gentle squeeze. "I look forward to presiding over the triumphs with you."

"Lucius Ceionius will preside with us as well."

Sabina glanced up sharply. Hadrian still sounded listless, and his eyes still rested on the lotuses. "Why?"

"He amuses me. Difficult to do, these days."

"He is ambitious." *You do not know how ambitious.*

"Does that matter? He tells me jokes and makes me smile. I need to laugh."

Sabina hesitated. The words hesitated on her tongue: *After Antinous died, Lucius sold every slave attending him on the barge in Egypt. Not just the girls who were his bedmates that night, but every single one. As though they might have something to tell about their master.* That much she had been able to glean from her old freedman over the past months. "Trace them and buy them," Sabina had ordered. "The twin girls especially. Send them to Rome."

"It will take a great deal more time," the freedman warned. But Sabina did not want to come to her husband with anything less than facts straight from the mouths of their source, and there were no facts yet. So she kept silent.

"Vibia Sabina," Hadrian said, his tone formal now. "Preside with me at the triumphs. I see it as one of the final great public appearances I shall make. Afterward, you are free to do as you please."

"What do you mean?"

"You have been my empress more than fifteen years." Hadrian broke a lotus off its stem. "But I no longer require an empress. I have ruled longer than any emperor since Tiberius, and I do not think there is much time left for me."

"May Caesar live forever," Sabina intoned like a flattering poet, but Hadrian did not smile.

"I don't want to live forever. Not without Him. I might wish to see Athens one more time, or my wall at the north of Britannia—it would have been pleasant to see how it looked when finished . . ." Hadrian looked briefly wistful, then shook his head. "But my traveling days are done. That bloodbath in Judaea was my final performance as the traveling emperor. So after the triumphs, I shall retire to my villa here among the statues of my beloved and write my memoirs. And you"—he tucked the lotus behind her ear—"may go free."

Sabina felt her lips part. "You mean you wish to divorce me?" she managed to say over her suddenly racing heart.

"I will set you aside if that is what you wish." His voice was still lifeless, but his hand lingered on her cheek. "Divorced or no, I mean you to take the rest of your life and do with it as *you* please. I am dying. You are not. I have used up your youth up in my service. Take the years you have left as your recompense. Travel, take lovers, remarry, do good works, bury yourself in seclusion in the provinces, run away with your barbarian ex-legionary if he still wants you . . . But please yourself."

Sabina felt a thrumming in her heart like a pair of wings. *Go free*, the words echoed. *Go free*. And she saw herself walking the great wall in Britannia again, running this time, glorious under the moon. Vix at her side, perhaps—she could feel the touch of his hands so strongly against her skin that she shivered in a flash of utter longing.

Go free. No more prying eyes; no more wearisome, endless duty.

She looked up at Hadrian, his eyes holding hers. She remembered how he had kissed her in the bathhouse in Antioch, looking at her fondly instead of coldly. That had been the kindling of affection between them, all because of Antinous. In Hadrian's savage moods after Antinous's death, she had feared that affection utterly dead.

But he stood here now with his hand cupping her cheek, telling her to go free.

"What if I wished to stay with you?" Because she could not stop thinking of the look Antinous's beautiful face would wear, if he knew she went dancing off to freedom and left Hadrian to the care of indifferent slaves, ambitious courtiers, and voracious Rome itself. "What if I wished to look after you?" she heard herself asking.

"Chain yourself to a useless invalid with a murderous temper?" Hadrian sat on the marble bench beneath Antinous's statue, moving stiffly in his purple-bordered toga. "I would think you mad."

Sabina sat beside him, claiming his hand between both of her own. Gently, because of his swollen knuckles. "We have sometimes been enemies, you and I, but we started out as friends. Remember? You wed me because I was Trajan's great-niece, and I wed you because I wanted to see the world, but it was more than that. We'd stay up late arguing whether Ennius was superior to Virgil, and you took me with you to Pannonia when all your officers said a woman shouldn't go . . ."

"And then I became Emperor." Hadrian looked at her. "And I was not kind to you."

"No," Sabina acknowledged. "And I hated you. But Antinous came, and I loved him, and he loved you. And we became friends again, didn't we?"

"What do we have now that Antinous is dead?" Hadrian sounded curious.

"Fate, perhaps." Sabina gave a half smile. "You never divorced me no matter how much I angered you, and I never left you no matter how much I loved another. What does that tell you?"

He sounded very dry. "That my wife has turned seeress?"

"It tells me that the Fates twined your thread with mine, and made a great many knots. I do not think they would be pleased if we tried to cut those knots. And neither would Antinous." She took a breath and reached up, stroking his worn, bearded cheek. "Thank you for my freedom, Hadrian. But I am going to stay. I am going to take care of you."

His brows creased over his nose. Fond or not, he did not like to be contradicted. "You are a stubborn woman!"

"Always. But I can help you." She smiled. "Because we are not done yet, you know. There is Rome's future to settle."

"I find it hard to care." His gaze drifted out over the still water of the canal. "What have I done for her so far, Vibia Sabina?"

"How can you ask that?"

"I think it. Every night I think it."

Sabina supposed every emperor must think such thoughts in dark hours of the soul. The ones humble enough to admit they could fail, anyway. *Publius Aelius Hadrian, showing a drop of humility.* She would never in all her life have imagined that.

He was still waiting for an answer.

"Remember the plans you laid out for me in Britannia? Your plan for Rome?" She listed them off on her fingers. "You wished to end the constant expansion of an Empire already quite unwieldy enough. You wished to ring that Empire in walls, so that all emperors of the future would know *This is Rome*, and go no farther. You wished to raise temples and columns through every province so the whole Empire would be left more beautiful than you found it. You wished to remake the legions and bring prosperity to your citizens, as a father does his children." She folded her hands, enclosing within them Hadrian's list of gifts to his people. "You have done all of that, husband. Hadrian Caesar, Father of Rome."

"I slaughtered half a million of my children in Judaea." His voice was harsh.

Sabina reached up to tug his head down, wondering if he would lash out at her as he had done when he grieved Antinous on the Nile.

But he did not. Perhaps those half-million deaths in Judaea had exhausted him, because her husband allowed his head to drop onto her shoulder, burying his face in the curve of her neck. His skin was hot against her throat, and his shoulders heaved under her circling arm.

"For better or worse, the business in Judaea is done." Sabina rubbed his shoulder, back and forth as she'd soothe a trembling dog. "You still have work to do. At the very least, you must name an heir and begin preparing him for his duties."

"I am tired," Hadrian whispered. "So tired."

"I will help you. As I've always done." She kissed his forehead. "Even when we were enemies."

They sat on the bench a long time. *Peaceful*, Sabina thought, and smiled. She never would have equated such a word with Hadrian.

He straightened at last, rising in a stiff movement. "Will you excuse me?" he said formally, his hand still resting in hers. "I have been a long time abroad . . . I will require a long stint in my Hades."

She returned his gaze, asking the question she had long wondered. "What is in your Hades, Hadrian?"

"I would rather not say." His gaze was straight for once, no ironic gleam or faint smile or any of his other masks. Just naked honesty. "You have retained a good opinion of me somehow, though I don't understand why—I would not want to lose that good opinion now."

"As you please." She inclined her head. Perhaps she was never going to know what was in his Hades. If it was the price for truth between them, she was more than willing to pay it. "I will see you this evening, then?"

"Yes." He snapped his swollen fingers for his dog to follow him. "Will you see that Lucius Ceionius joins us? After my Hades, I will need to laugh."

Sabina hesitated. *Lucius Ceionius*, she thought again, but Hadrian looked so terribly worn, visibly pulling his pride and his dignity around him. *When I have proof*, she thought, and rose. "I will summon Lucius."

"Thank you." A nod, deeper than usual, and then his fingers slid away and he went stalking off along the still canal, dog trotting in his wake. Head bent beneath the fading light, but not defeated. Not yet.

I will save you, Sabina thought. She plucked the lotus from behind her ear and twirled it between her fingers, feeling steady and serene and lighter than air. *I will save you whether you wish to be saved or not. Call it Fate, call it love, call it my final duty as empress—but I will find proof that Antinous was murdered, and I will bring you back to life.*

Go free, Hadrian said.

This felt like freedom to her.

VIX

Rome

Blood, I thought, inhaling deeply. *Sweat, dirt, marble . . . Stray dogs, frying meat, cheap perfume . . .* "You old bitch," I said aloud to the Eternal City. "I'd know you anywhere by your smell alone."

I was home, swaying and tired, heartsick and just a little water-sick too as I disembarked onto the docks. And smiled for the first time in what felt like months, because someone was waiting for me. A tall man in a spotless toga, graying elegantly about the temples but otherwise untouched by the passing years, giving me his quiet smile. "Hello, Slight," said Titus Aurelius.

"You bugger!" We clasped hands in a grip that left our fingers bruised, both of us pretending our eyes weren't full of tears. Titus seemed to know without a word being spoken that I was lost in Rome, that I might have a legion but I no longer had a home, that I was slinking back to the Eternal City unheralded because I couldn't bear the fuss people might have made over me. He led me back to his quiet villa on the edge of the city, where his wife eyed me as though I were a wild wolf but told me there were rooms readied where I could stay as long as I liked. I sank into that luxurious bed and prayed for numbness or death, whichever came first and ended my black dreams.

I'd been staying in that villa ten days before I laid eyes on her. A delicious hot afternoon, the sky blue and cloudless overhead. A fine day to celebrate, and Rome was celebrating. Titus and Faustina had gone to join the hubbub, begging me along, but I declined. I took a jug of wine down to the little vineyard at the edge of the villa, halfway to drunk and aiming to get the rest of the way there by sundown. Out here I had no company but the budding vines, the birds wheeling overhead, and a moss-grown statue of Priapus, who leered over the vineyard with his huge jutting phallus. Randy old bastard. "Send a woman my way," I said, toasting him. "Been a long time since I've had one." How long? Months before Bethar fell, surely. Executions, siege walls, and cartloads of wretched slaves hadn't really put me in the mood for bed-sport.

Priapus sent me a woman, all right, but that donkey-pricked god had a sense of humor because the one he sent was hardly out of girl-hood. She was just a spot of dark green speeding through the vines, and I squinted because I was halfway down the jug by that time and couldn't really focus until she came skidding to a halt in front of me. "You look familiar," she greeted me without preamble. "Who are you?"

"A conquering hero," I answered, "or so they tell me."

She evaluated me as she stretched the arch of first one bare foot and then the other. A tall girl, maybe seventeen or eighteen, with reddish hair stuck in sweat-damp tendrils to her neck. She wore a rough green tunic kilted up for running, showing a pair of hard and muddy feet. Not a pretty girl, but she looked like an Amazon: slim-hipped, broad-shouldered, long-legged, sweating, and fierce. "Are you Vercingetorix? The one staying with us?"

"Us?"

"I'm Annia Galeria Faustina the Younger." The memory surfaced even as I heard the name—the memory of a little girl with a *trigon* ball and a bloody nose.

"You've grown." I ducked my head in the best bow that I could manage while sitting down. "And yes, I am Vercingetorix."

A huge grin broke over her face. "I'd have recognized you sooner if not for the hair!"

"It's growing back." I had prickles of reddish stubble all over my head now that I'd stopped brutally razoring my scalp. "I'm surprised you remember meeting me. You were only seven or eight."

"You're the one who started me running!" She bounced a little on her toes, as though ready to sprint off through the vines again. "It does help me keep my temper, you were right about that." A lightning flash of a scowl. "Most of the time."

I tilted the jug, filling my cup. I was still stuck at the faint-blur stage of tipsy, and what I wanted was serious-blur. What I wanted was *numb*.

"You've been staying with us near ten days." Annia tilted her head. "Why haven't I seen you before now?"

"Because I'm avoiding people in general and your mother in particular."

"A conquering hero of Rome, terrified of my *mother*?" Annia bent down to touch her toes in a quick stretch. Always moving, this one. "You're the terrifying one. The slave girls say you ravaged every third virgin in Judaea, and killed every second man."

"Maybe I did."

"I doubt it." Annia flopped down cross-legged like a boy. "Why are you here?"

"In Rome? Because the Emperor ordered it." I took another long drink, holding the fiery wine in my mouth to feel the burn. I didn't even know if the Tenth Fidelis was still mine. My orders when I was done finishing my sad business in Syria hadn't been very extensive—return to Rome for the triumphs. Maybe afterward I'd be relieved of command. I didn't really care.

"No, I meant why are you *here*?" Annia twisted her sweat-damp hair into a rope, lifting it off her neck. "The triumph is going on right this moment. The chariots should be making their way to the Temple of Jupiter Capitolinus—the whole city's turned out to celebrate the victory over Judaea. They've turned out to celebrate *you*, you and the other commanders. So why are you getting drunk in a vineyard?"

She had big blue-gray eyes with red lashes, like a sword blade with a fan of blood on it and every bit as piercing. I rotated the cup in my hand. "I declined the triumph."

"Why?"

I gave a bark of a laugh. A triumph—the highest honor a soldier like me could ever dream of. I'd marched in a triumph behind Trajan, and I'd ached to stand where he stood: the victorious commander in his chariot laden with charms, his face daubed by red paint and his head crowned by a victory wreath; rose petals in his path and cheers deafening his ears.

Well, today it could have been me. But I'd told Hadrian I'd rather be buggered with a rake.

The Amazon was still waiting for her answer, and not too patiently either.

"I want nothing," I said at last around my blurring tongue, "except to forget every single thing I did in helping to crush that rebellion. Every death, every execution, every battle, every massacre. I won't ever forget, but I'll be damned if I celebrate it."

Annia pointed at my wine. "Can I have some? My mother won't let me try unwatered wine." She saw me hesitate. "If we're talking about massacres, I'd like a drink."

"Can't fault your logic." I poured a measure of wine into the spare cup. "Just a sip," I began, but she tossed it all down the way she'd seen me do it. A minimum of spluttering, too.

"Ugh." She passed the cup back. "Thank you. I can understand why you wouldn't want to march in the triumph, but doesn't that mean you'll never be honored for the *good* things you did? It can't all have been bad. My cousin Marcus says only those recorded are remembered—if you aren't recorded in the triumph, no one will remember you were a hero in Judaea."

"Suits me fine if history forgets I was ever there. God knows I never will." Another swig. I really had to be drunk by now, even if I didn't feel it. Because I hadn't talked this frankly even to Titus. "I lost everything I had in Judaea."

"What did you lose?" Annia flexed her muddy feet one at a time, the afternoon sun dappling her freckled skin.

"My friends died. My wife died. My girls . . . are gone." I drank again for Dinah and Chaya, another of my endless prayers for their happiness. "So you see"—I tried to muster some kind of smile for Annia that didn't make her recoil with its bitterness—"you see why I'm damned if I'll take a triumph celebrating everything I've lost, eh?"

Annia considered that, regarding me with her sword-colored eyes. "But Judaea had to be subdued. We heard terrible stories, the atrocities. Well, nobody told them to me, but the slave girls get positively ghoulish when they think no one's listening."

"There were bad things done," I acknowledged. "On both sides. Tell it truthfully, maybe we *didn't* have to put down Judaea. But they couldn't have timed their rebellion for a worse moment. Hadrian had no mercy in him right then, not at the beginning."

"Because of Antinous?"

"Did you know Antinous?"

"I loved him." She smiled, and both the smile and the words pierced me. But this was a sweet pain rather than a thorned one. "He always said I was the first friend he ever made in Rome. And he saved me and my cousin Marcus from getting beaten to a pulp by Brine-Face—"

"Brine-Face?"

"Gnaeus Pedanius Fuscus *Salinator*." She drew out the last name scornfully. "The golden boy."

"No, he's not." The very thought offended me. *Antinous* was the golden boy, not that arrogant little prick. "Pedanius Fuscus is a sack of shit in a silk tunic."

"Oh, I like you." Annia grinned and looked at the wine again. "Can I have some more of that?"

"You shouldn't."

"Why, because I'll get tipsy and then you'll try to ravish me?"

"No!" I said in horror.

"Well, good. You couldn't, anyway." She tossed down another swig, slanting a brow at me in warning. "I know exactly where to kick you if you try."

I felt a smile tug at my lips, the first one I'd felt in quite some time. "So why aren't *you* at the triumph?" Didn't girls her age like the chance to dress in their finest, go out into the city, get admired? With Titus's heaps of gold and her mother's bloodlines, surely every young buck in the city was groveling at her feet.

Annia grimaced, taking another sip of wine. "I'm avoiding my cousin Marcus. He's become an utter ass ever since he put his toga on. He'll spend the whole triumph dancing attendance on my father—hours and hours of seeing him nod like a donkey and pontificate like an old man. Ignoring me."

"Ignoring you, eh?" I tilted my wine cup at her, since she had the jug, and she filled me up. It soothed me somehow, talking of a girl's innocent problems. "Why does he ignore you?"

"Because he's an ass? We've been playing together since I was four years old—he'd come toss a *trigon* ball with me, and we'd do lessons together, and we made a curse tablet—and the moment he put on a toga he turned into a bundle of starched laundry. He just looks down his nose at me and avoids me." She grimaced, taking another swallow of wine. "This is disgusting."

"There's a reason civilized people water it." The sky was swimming over my head, and I was definitely at the blurred stage of drunk now— but curiously, I no longer felt quite so much like falling on my *gladius*. I rolled my head at Annia. "So, this boy just became a man—"

"He thinks so." Her gaze was looking just a bit glassy. A good girl like her wouldn't have my tolerance for strong wine. I made a note to haul her back inside before she fell unconscious or I did, because then Faustina really would think I'd gotten her daughter drunk and ravished her. God help me then.

"So your friend Marcius—"

She giggled. "Marcus."

"Right. Won't look at you anymore, won't visit."

"He's got more *important* things to do." Annia slid down on her side, propping chin on elbow, and I saw the flash of hurt on her face.

"Suitor?" I guessed. "Not just friend?"

Her head jerked up and she glared. I raised my eyebrows. Finally she shrugged, taking another gulp of wine. "He always said he'd marry me someday. But we were just babies. He doesn't want to anymore."

"Yes, he does."

"What?"

"You're a clever girl, but you don't have a man's perspective." It was the least I could offer after she'd succeeded in lifting my despair. "You want to know why your Marcus avoids you? Because he doesn't trust himself to keep his hands off you."

"Not Marcus. He's a Stoic." She had some trouble with the S. "He believes in controlling the passions of the body."

He sounded a proper little prig to me. I let out a snort. "If there's anything that's all but impossible for a boy of sixteen or seventeen, it's controlling *anything* when a girl like you is nearby."

She laughed, and then she hiccuped. "I don't think so. He models himself on my father!"

"You think your father didn't feel the same at that age? He kept a mistress—that skinny housekeeper of yours, in fact."

Annia dropped her cup. "*Galeria Lysistrata?*"

"She had a different name, then. She took your mother's appellation after they married, as a sign she wasn't cross the affair was over. They all stayed good friends."

Annia looked stunned.

"Young men take mistresses, or they visit whores, but good girls like you they can't touch. So your friend Marcus stays away." I looked at the jug and saw we'd killed most of it. "Just ask him. Watch his ears turn scarlet."

"They do turn scarlet when he's embarrassed." Annia giggled, and her chin slid out of her hand. She held out her wine cup. "This disgusting wine is growing on me . . ."

"That means it's time for you to go back to the house, Annia Galeria Faustina."

I stood up a trifle unsteadily and hauled her to her feet. She staggered, hiccupping again, and I had to sneak her into her chamber and pour her into her sleeping couch. She slid almost instantly into sleep, and I stood looking down at her. She slept on her back, her feet twitching even in slumber. If her Marcius or Marcus or whatever his name wasn't throwing himself at her feet, he was a fool.

I tucked a coverlet around her shoulders, a little awkwardly. I'd never tucked my own girls in, and I'd certainly never tucked my girls in when they were drunk. I wished I had.

Annia started to snore. I smiled a little, rustily, and then I padded out and headed for my own bed. I slept on my back too, and I could hear my own snores begin before I even dropped off—but curiously enough, I slept without dreaming. I didn't stir till Titus and Faustina returned that night.

For the first evening since I'd arrived I didn't stay in my chamber like a surly bear curled up for the winter, but tugged a fresh tunic over my head and went downstairs to join the bustle of welcome. Annia stood in the atrium, and Titus had paused unwinding his toga and cupped her cheek in his hand, turning her face toward the lamplight. "Annia," he was exclaiming, "your eyes are red as fire. Are you ill?"

"Can you dim that lamp?" Annia winced, and massaged her head through a tumble of sleep-tousled hair. "Ow . . ."

"How was my triumph?" I said hastily. "You two look very fine!"

Titus was still looking at Annia. He looked at me, and when he spoke his voice was ominous. "Vercingetorix," he said, "is my daughter *hungover?*"

I looked at Annia and she looked at me. A mistake, because she started to laugh. She had a raucous, rough-edged shout of a laugh, and the sound of it sent a grin spreading slowly over my face. She leaned against a pillar, shaking with laughter under her father's disapproving eye, and I . . .

I felt those barbs of agony and guilt and accusation recede, just a little. Just enough to let me smile at the red-haired girl whose company had made my sleep dreamless.

There was the faintest quiver of mirth around Titus's eyes, but his face remained stern. "Vix?"

Still smiling, I moved past him to where his wife stood tall and beautiful in midnight-colored silk and sapphires, her eyes as sparkling blue as the jewels. I seized her hands, and I bowed over them. "Faustina," I said, and I put the smile away to give her every drop of honesty I had. "Your daughter is indeed hungover. She came to no harm, but it was my fault entirely, and I ask you not to punish her. I offer sincere apology." A deep breath then. "I would apologize as well for hauling your husband away to a cell on your wedding night. I swear to you on the gates of Hell, I will die on a blade before I ever see harm come to your family—even if the Emperor himself stands in the way."

I lowered my head and I kissed her astonished hands, sealing the oath. Because it *was* an oath—I'd never let the black fate that took my wife and daughters touch my friend's. Never.

Then I moved past Annia, who was still laughing and wincing and rubbing her head all at once. I tousled her red hair in passing, and I headed for the bathhouse. I still felt sick and heartsore when I thought of Judaea and all that passed there . . . but I also felt like a bath and a shave.

ANNIA

A.D. 136, Autumn
Hadrian's Villa

"Dear gods, what are you wearing?" Those were the first words out of Aunt Sabina's mouth, when Annia alighted in the gardens of the Emperor's villa.

"A dress." Annia looked down at herself, feeling mulish and embarrassed all at once. "Mother said I was old enough to be choosing my own."

"And you chose *that?*"

"Ceionia Fabia helped . . ." Ceionia always looked perfect, after all: a luscious little thing with her smooth hair and dimples, and she had condescended to lend Annia her expertise. "A girl with red hair must wear *nothing* but green. This shade, something pale. Girls our age must wear pale colors, or we look vulgar. And you have such a long face, you must balance it with curls on either side." Ceionia patted her own hair, smoothed into a knot with just one curl dropping over her shoulder. "Goodness, our first party at the Emperor's villa! My father says my little brother and I must be the picture of poise; he says the Emperor has *quite* the surprise planned for our family . . ."

Annia didn't care what the Emperor planned. She only wanted to waylay Marcus and see if *any* of what Vercingetorix had said could possibly be true.

"I think Annia looks lovely," her mother said loyally. "She'd look beautiful in anything."

"Faustina, you're a wonderful mother but a terrible liar," the Empress of Rome retorted. "That sickly green makes Annia look like a month-old corpse, and if Ceionia sold her on it, then she's a clever little tart who was trying to eliminate the competition."

Should have known I'd get it wrong, Annia thought dismally. She'd always prided herself on being a Spartan sort of girl, all steel and gravitas—it was embarrassing how much she simply wanted to look *pretty,* but the thought was there anyway. *I want to be pretty for once. I want Marcus to look at me.*

Her Imperial aunt must have caught her expression, because she did a swift evaluation of the bustle behind her. The slaves were still dashing about with garlands of ivy and roses for the Emperor's vast outdoor banquet; the festivities wouldn't begin for the better part of an hour. "There's time," the Empress decided, and crooked a finger at her niece. "Come with me."

Annia found herself whisked into a sumptuous windowed series of chambers that could only be the Empress's private apartments. "My mother said that at my age, I really should know how to choose my own attire. But I don't know *how*."

"The trouble with your mother, may all the gods bless her, is that she looks marvelous in absolutely anything. So it never matters what she wears." Aunt Sabina surveyed Annia with a critical eye. "Those like you and me with less in the way of raw goddesslike beauty must work a little harder."

"But you're beautiful too." Her Imperial aunt had a midnight-blue gown embroidered with silver stars, and more stars strung about her neck and her hair and her ankles on loops of silver wire. She looked like a night sky and about as all-knowing.

"What a nice thing to hear, and at my age, too." Aunt Sabina smiled. "But I assure you, it's all illusion. You'll learn to cast one, too. Ceionia has good cause to be jealous of you, if you only use what you have."

"Definitely not green," a tall African slave girl said, wrinkling her dark nose.

"No. That flame-colored silk I had as a present from the merchants in Alexandria . . ."

Annia felt herself whirled and stripped, pinned and discussed. "The gold sandals lacing up the shins? And gold bracelets, delicate ones, and a belt of gold cord—"

"I feel like a slave getting oiled up for the auction block," she complained, and Aunt Sabina's painted eyes held hers.

"That is what an empress feels like at times, my dear."

"Really?" She cocked her head. Aunt Sabina with her oceans of poise and endless elegance?

"Oh, yes." Her aunt sat Annia down on a carved ivory stool and with her own hands started to comb out the horrible ringlets. "Because an empress really *is* like a slave at an auction block—she stands there as crowds of people ogle her, and she stares over their heads with a fixed expression. An empress's appearance is an Imperial duty. But you, on the other hand, wish to look beautiful tonight for a rather more personal reason, I think?"

Annia felt herself blushing, thinking of Vercingetorix the Red's blunt words about boys of Marcus's age. *"Good girls like you they can't touch. So your friend Marcus stays away."* Annia didn't quite share his certainty, and before she could really summon the courage to ask him again, he'd moved on from their villa. Besides, you couldn't really go up to a hero of Rome, to a *man*, and ask—

"What do you wear if you want to make someone seduce you?" Annia blurted out. And immediately wanted to die.

One of the slave girls lifted a hand to smother a giggle, but Aunt Sabina just looked thoughtful. "That depends," she said. "Do you actually want to *be* seduced, or are you just hoping to raise the notion in his mind? Actual seduction is going to be rather difficult to achieve at a banquet this crowded."

Annia felt herself going scarlet. "Just—raising the notion," she whispered. Dear gods, let Aunt Sabina not ask who.

And she didn't. Annia's mother would have at least smiled knowingly, and her sister Fadilla would have clapped her hands and started reeling off names, but Aunt Sabina just fetched a little pot from one of the slave girls and sprinkled a pinch of something over Annia's loosened hair, wavy from the ringlets but no longer bunched on either side of her face. "A combing of gold dust through your hair to make it gleam, I think," she murmured. "And a pinch massaged into the skin . . . You'll glimmer under the light, and no one will quite know why, but they'll be drawn to you." Pushing Annia straight when she strained for a glimpse in the glass. "Not yet, you aren't finished."

"Like a roast?" Annia muttered, still feeling her cheeks flame, but she was starting to get interested in the process despite herself. Finally Aunt Sabina tugged her to her feet, gesturing the maids to hold up a glass.

Annia stared at herself. "I don't look—proper."

"I thought you wanted to raise thoughts of seduction, not propriety,"

Aunt Sabina pointed out. "And really, you aren't showing any more flesh than prim little Ceionia."

"But . . ." Fiery orange-red silk sluicing down her body, a webwork of gold covering her ankles and her bare arms, gold dust making a faint gleam at her eyelids and the hollows of her collarbone. Maybe it was too much. "I look like an eastern—something-or-other," Annia fumbled. "Not like a Roman girl should. They'll call me a harlot."

"Let me tell you something, Annia Galeria Faustina." Aunt Sabina tugged a strand of gold-dusted hair over Annia's shoulder. "Don't waste yourself worrying what the proper Roman girls say, because you will never look like them. You look *better*—a fire nymph and an Amazon rolled into one, and they know it. Maybe it's all that running you've done, but you don't mince when you enter a room, you *swagger*. So put those splendid shoulders back and swagger into that atrium like the goddess you are, and if anyone flings the word *harlot* at you, crush it under your heel like the nonsense it is. Because there is no man in Rome who would not choose you over boring little Ceionia and her properly folded hands."

Aunt Sabina looked quite fierce suddenly, but did she have *tears* in her eyes? "Did they call you names when you were my age?" Annia found herself asking.

"My predecessor Empress Plotina loved to call me a whore," Aunt Sabina said, and the shine in her eyes must have been a trick of the lamplight because now she had her usual expression of faint amusement. "But I never paid such barbs any attention, nor should you. So why don't you be just a *little* scandalous and loop the end of your skirt up over one arm to show a flash of ankle? They're splendid ankles; you should show them off."

Annia was beginning to smile. "That will make Servianus hiss."

Aunt Sabina tugged the gold-embroidered hem a little higher. "Good."

The atrium with its rose-garlanded pillars was mostly filled with muttering senators clustered like hens, taking sidelong glances at the Emperor where he sat looking drawn and irritable in a gold chair, fingers drumming. "His heir," Servianus was saying, "he must announce an heir soon, his health . . ." And whenever anyone spoke of the Emperor's health the whispers faded off into even more inaudible mumbles. Servianus was too preoccupied to notice Annia or her ankles, but as Annia stood looking about for her parents—all right, looking for Marcus—her gaze swept right across Pedanius Fuscus, standing with a cup of wine in hand, and his gaze was going up and down her body and then back again. *He didn't look that hungry when he was trying to rape me*, Annia thought, and a spasm of disgust went through her, coiled around with fear. She stamped down both, putting up her chin. *I'll die screaming before I show you one drop of terror.*

He crossed the mosaics: a handsome young man in a fine synthesis, but somehow not quite the golden boy of Rome anymore. He'd changed since that beating he'd taken. He looked twitchy now instead of confident, eyes sliding off to the side instead of resting firm during a conversation, his smile nervous instead of charming . . . And of course, as soon as he opened his mouth to speak, his new lisping splutter sealed the whole dismal impression. Those *teeth*—Annia wanted to beam whenever she saw those gapped and broken-off teeth that turned every word he said into a hissing mess.

"Brine-Faith," she greeted him, mimicking his lisp with a lift of her eyebrows.

"You look like a whore." His eyes slid over her again.

Maybe it was just because Aunt Sabina had been called a whore in her day too, but Annia threw her head back and laughed. Real laughter—the spasm of fear in her stomach was utterly gone. "And you look like an idiot," she returned. "But you *are* an idiot, and we both know I'm not a whore."

She patted his cheek and moved off, partly to irritate him and partly because she'd just seen Marcus—lean and serious in his own perfectly pleated synthesis, standing at the Emperor's elbow. One of Hadrian's quizzing sessions, probably, where he fired question after question at Marcus as though looking for chinks in his defenses . . . Annia didn't know if it was the gold dust and flame silk that made her confident, but she slid through the crowd and came right up to Marcus's elbow. "—no power over what the Fates put in our path," he was saying in response to some question of the Emperor's. "But a man does have power over his own mind, and in the end—" He saw Annia and stopped a moment, and her heart fluttered in her chest, but his face never moved even as his eyes traveled her whole flame-wrapped length. "Control over the Fates is impossible," he said, turning back to the Emperor. "So control over the mind is the best man can hope for."

"Well put," Hadrian said, and turned a moment as a steward tugged at his sleeve with a murmur. Marcus gave a little bow, still ignoring Annia, and she narrowed her eyes. *I will get a reaction out of you if it kills me, Marcus Catilius Severus.*

She made her own curtsy to the distracted Emperor, looking for a way to slide out of the crowd with Marcus, but some senatorial colleague of her father's spoke up—"Titus Aurelius's daughter, isn't it? The one who runs like a little wood nymph"—and that provoked the kind of slightly derisive laughter that gritted Annia's teeth. Servianus shook his head nearby.

"A disgrace," he said, eyes fastened disapprovingly on Annia's ankles. "Your father is far too indulgent. Girls of good birth should spend their days learning to manage a household! If this is how the daughters of Rome fill their hours—"

"On the contrary," Emperor Hadrian said, and Annia's eyes flew to him in surprise. He was surveying her too, not with Marcus's expressionlessness or Pedanius's hunger, but with a sort of objective approval. "The women of Sparta ran races to prove their fitness as the bearers of strong sons. The fleetest were prized as wives and mothers alike. Was that such a disgrace?"

"Sparta is not Rome, Caesar."

"And Rome has always looked to the glories of Greece for improvement. Why not in the standards of our womanhood? I do not see disgrace here." Hadrian leveled a finger at Annia. "I see a future mother of warriors."

Annia bobbed another curtsy. "Caesar," she managed to say, but felt pride in her like a warm bubble as Servianus's chin jerked. *Take that, you old goat.*

"That reminds me," the Emperor murmured, his gaze sliding past Annia again. "I must speak with your father about you—if the steward will fetch him . . ."

Annia seized on his nod of dismissal, sliding her fingers through Marcus's elbow. "Come with me," she whispered, and stalked (swaggered, Aunt Sabina said she swaggered—did she?) out through the pillars of the atrium to the cool autumn night.

The air in the gardens was dark and lemon-scented from the numberless trees. Annia could see peacocks wandering, and more guests, but she didn't pay attention. She just led Marcus around a dark hedge until she couldn't see anyone, and then she turned and arched her back a little in that catlike way she'd seen the Empress do, feeling bold and reckless and altogether heady.

"So," she said without preamble. "You don't have to marry me."

He started. "What?"

"You've been saying you were going to marry me as long as I can remember, but you've evidently changed your mind in the past year. Since you're the honorable sort who wouldn't break your word"— Annia forced herself to shrug—"I release you."

Marcus's mouth opened and closed for a moment. "I can't talk about such a matter with you," he said finally. "One talks about marriage with a girl's father, not the girl herself."

"And now you don't have to talk with my father," Annia said. "Never will. Free at last."

"We shouldn't be alone like this together, either," he went on, eyeing her. "It's not suitable."

"What, the dress isn't suitable?"

"Well, you could drop the hem. I can see all the way up to your ankles."

"Empress Sabina says I have lovely ankles."

"You do," he bit off.

"Brine-Face said I looked like a whore." Annia took a step closer, her heart thrumming. "What do you think?"

His face changed. "Pedanius said what?"

A shrug.

"He needs another lesson." Marcus's voice was clipped.

"What do you mean, a *lesson?*"

"We should go back inside."

"So go," she challenged. "You don't owe me anything anymore, Marcus."

He didn't move. "You think I don't want to marry you?"

"You haven't spoken two words to me since you put on that toga! What was I supposed to think?"

He started to turn away. "I'm taking you back to your mother."

"No," said Annia, and she reached out and dragged his head down and kissed him. The first time she'd kissed him—at twelve, over a curse tablet—she'd mostly gotten his nose. This time her teeth scored his lip as their mouths clashed. She wouldn't have been surprised to see blood by the time they pulled apart. His hands had found her waist, heating her skin through the silk, they were both trembling like leaves, and Annia's blood roared so loud in her own ears she could hardly hear her own voice.

"I don't care what your precious Stoics say," she told him shakily. "Perfect control is boring."

"You think I have any control at all?" His hands made fists in the silk at her back, and he yanked her against him. Annia felt the prickles of the hedge on one side, the movement of the night breeze on the other, but Marcus was long and warm and hard against the whole length of her, and he was growling something into her hair.

"I'll tell you how much control I have, Annia Galeria Faustina. I got so angry that day we went to the games—"

"I know you did, I—"

"Shut up!" He gave her a little shake that somehow wrenched her onto her toes and closer up against him. "Not at you. At Pedanius Fuscus, because just the sight of him in the Colosseum made you so bitter and helpless. I went home early, and I counted all the money I had, and it wasn't enough. So I sold my two slaves—I never touched them, and I never will because I sold them away, and the day after my manhood ceremony I went out and I hired thugs. The expensive kind who won't get drunk and botch the job. And I hired them to beat Pedanius Fuscus to a pulp."

"Marcus—"

"I told them to spoil his looks." The words kept tumbling. "Because it's what he had, that golden confidence and the looks and the birth to go with it. That's what made people think he was a young emperor in the making. I told them to spoil his looks, take his confidence, because I thought maybe it would be enough to stop him from becoming Emperor. Hadrian's as vain as Venus, he'd never choose a successor who looks ridiculous. An heir who can't give a speech at the Rostra without lisping and spluttering? People would laugh. Hadrian's too full of pride to pick an heir people would laugh at. At least I hope he is, because I fear for you if Pedanius Fuscus ever becomes Caesar. He hurt you once, and if he's emperor no one will be able to stop him from doing it again. So I stopped *him* first."

Annia's throat was thick. She could hardly see Marcus's face through the melting shadows; she didn't know if he looked grim or exultant or despairing. *For me.* She reached up and touched his cheek, fresh-shaven and smelling of bath oil and the dye that edged his synthesis. *For me.*

"You probably despise me because I should have beaten him up myself," Marcus finished in a rush. "You would have done it yourself if you were a man. Well, I wanted to. I wasn't even afraid to try. But I didn't want to just *try.* I had to be sure—and I didn't know if I could do it, with him so much bigger and more vicious. In the end, it was more important that he be put down, no matter who did it.

"So, if you want to know how much Stoic control I have," he finished, "I'll say it. None. I couldn't stop thinking about Pedanius Fuscus till I'd put him in his bed with four broken ribs and a broken nose and all his teeth smashed in. And I can't stop thinking about you at all. I can't be *around* you at all. Just the smell of your hair, and I want to drag you off behind a hedge."

"We are behind a hedge," Annia whispered.

"That's why I should take you back inside."

But neither of them moved.

"I'm working," Marcus whispered into her hair. "I'm working so hard—trying to be worthy. The kind of suitor fathers don't laugh off, when you turn up and start talking betrothals when you're nowhere near twenty. Lucius Ceionius says he might be able to get me an appointment as Prefect of the City, and that would be prestigious—I'd be a man on his way, a man with a career. I thought I could ask for you then. But I never stopped *planning* to ask for you." His fists uncurled from her crumpled dress, one hand curving around her hip, the other sliding up her back. "I've been practicing the speech since I was twelve."

Annia's voice didn't work for a moment. Then all she could say was, "How's it coming along?"

"Fairly well." His hand was winding deeper into her hair. "Do you want to hear it?"

"I'm going to hear it tonight anyway," she whispered. "When you approach my father."

"I'm too young and unestablished for a wife, he'll never—"

"I'm an Amazon, Marcus. We do things differently. We don't wait for our men." Annia took his face between her hands again, yanking him down so close their lips brushed. "If you don't ask for my hand, I'll storm in there and ask for yours."

They were kissing again, kissing and kissing, Marcus's hands tangled deep through Annia's hair, her fingers laced at his neck. "We should go in," Marcus said, and began kissing his way across Annia's throat.

"Right away," she agreed, and discovered that she could stop his breath altogether just by nibbling along his ear.

"No, really." He sounded a trifle strangled as he dropped his lips into the hollow of her collarbone, right where Aunt Sabina had massaged gold dust. "I really can't take responsibility for what my hands are going to do if I ever get them untangled from your hair."

"Promise you'll ask my father tonight?" Annia pulled back just enough to catch Marcus's eyes. "He won't say no, he loves you like a son—" And now Marcus really *would* be a son, in a way. Gods, her parents were going to be so happy! *Not as happy as me*, Annia thought, and felt a bolt of pleasure clear down to her toes.

"Tonight." Marcus pulled back, bumping his nose against hers, giving that smile that lightened his serious face like a shaft of sunlight. "It really is a good speech I prepared."

They went on kissing for a while and then Marcus groaned. "We really *do* have to go!"

"One more kiss—"

"No, someone's calling my name from inside!"

They disentangled fast and bolted for the atrium, sliding up the rear entrance into an empty anteroom beside the triclinium. They caught a glimpse of each other and burst into horrified giggles at the same time. "You've got gold dust on your lips," Annia gasped. "Quick, use my hem to wipe—"

"Your hair has thorns in it—"

They pulled and tidied at each other in the deserted anteroom, kissed some more, yanked apart, and slid into the crowded atrium precisely ten heartbeats separate. Annia still thought anybody would be able to guess, looking at them, exactly what they had been doing. Marcus wore an enormous grin like a fool, and she guessed she did, too. *I am going to marry Marcus Catilius Severus. I am going to marry Marcus Catilius Severus . . .*

An irked-looking steward found Marcus. "You are late," he snapped. "The Emperor has summoned you. No time now to speak with him privately, he's already begun his address—"

Marcus made disjointed apologies, and Annia put a hand up to cover her mouth and went sliding the other direction, through the throng of curious senators as the Emperor began one of his formal, graceful speeches. "Where have you been?" her mother whispered as Annia slid up to her side. "Your father has been trying to find you—one of the Imperial stewards was speaking to him about you. I hope you weren't off sneaking unwatered wine again!" But her mother didn't look overly cross; in fact, she was looking over Annia's dress with approval. "Whatever did Sabina put you in? It's rather dashing. Though your hair is a *mess*—"

Annia let her mother pluck and smooth at her wild locks. Hadrian was droning something about the future of Rome, looking tall and gaunt beside handsome Lucius Ceionius, who he was praising for his *great and honorable service to the Empire*. That was a joke, but nobody was laughing. Lucius just looked triumphant, standing there with his head thrown back and his eyes gleaming. His dumpy little wife stood beside Empress

Sabina looking colorless and nervous next to all that sinuous starry flash, and his children too: Ceionia and her smooth hair, eyes demurely downcast, and her little brother Lucius, almost six years old and squirming at his sister's side. *I want to have a boy like that,* Annia thought. She had always liked Ceionia's little brother, a lively, wriggling sort of boy. He often asked Annia to help him hunt for bugs to put down his sister's neck, and she never said no. *Marcus and I will have a son like that. Though no son of Marcus's would ever pick his nose in public . . .*

A ripple went through the crowd, bringing Annia out of her happy musing. "I cannot believe it," she heard her father murmur, his lips not moving at all, but others didn't have the control he did. Servianus was white and openmouthed with shock—and Aunt Sabina looked frozen.

"Lucius Ceionius?" Annia's mother whispered. "As Imperial *heir?*"

"In replacement of the son the gods have not seen fit to give me," the Emperor was saying in his fine deep voice, "he shall be known henceforth under the name Lucius Aelius Verus Caesar . . ."

The new heir gave a small nod to the crowd. A scatter of uncertain applause rose, but there still seemed to be more shock than anything. Annia didn't think he looked much like an emperor, even if he had changed just for the announcement into an Imperial purple synthesis embroidered all over in little Roman eagles. A man who cared for nothing but fashionable clothes and other men's wives—what kind of emperor was someone like that supposed to make?

She saw Pedanius Fuscus standing absolutely rigid with shock, white-faced and astounded as his grandfather, and a bolt of superb, glorious satisfaction shot through her. *You had no idea you were being shut out,* she thought, nearly bouncing on her toes in glee. *Neither of you!* And Marcus was right: Hadrian had not chosen an heir who lisped and spluttered through broken teeth, an heir who could not even mingle at a party anymore and look confident doing it. Gnaeus Pedanius Fuscus Salinator was finished—and all because, in a way, he'd told a girl of twelve to get on her knees and call him Caesar.

Full circle.

"—and to bind his family all the more closely with my own," Hadrian was saying, his eye going over the crowd as if to mark who was not smiling, "a pair of marriages. For his son—" Little Lucius was picking at a scab on his elbow, and his mother had to swat him. Annia stifled a giggle.

"—a betrothal to be sealed at once with my own niece, Annia Galeria Faustina."

Annia's head jerked up as all eyes in the atrium went to her.

"And for my heir's daughter Ceionia Fabia—" Ceionia continued to stand with her eyes demurely fixed on the floor, but Annia could see her nostrils flare like a hunting dog that had just caught the scent. "—a betrothal to be sealed between herself and a young man most dear to my heart—"

No, Annia thought. *No.* Because it wasn't Pedanius—Pedanius had already been discarded.

"—and most vital to the future of my Empire—"

No!

The Emperor finished affably. "Marcus Catilius Severus."

CHAPTER 18

VIX

"Lucius Ceionius, eh?" I asked the Emperor when I next came to visit—something that had somehow (and I wasn't sure how) become habit.

"Yes. Lucius Ceionius." Hadrian slanted a warning brow, clearly not desiring my opinion on his recent choice of heir.

"Curious pick," I said. What was a man like that going to do as Emperor: theme the Empire into coordinating colors? Dress the legionaries in eagle wings? *Not my legionaries.*

"Lucius entertains me. For that alone, I'm inclined to reward him." Hadrian moved a game piece on the board between us. "Since it's so nakedly clear what he wants, he may as well have it. Your move."

I shrugged, not really inclined to give the new heir any more thought. It was not my business anymore. I lived in a strange kind of suspension, isolated from the restless pulse of Roman life. I was still commander of the Tenth, but the Tenth was quiescent, refilling their depleted ranks and training the new men back in the east. Nothing required my presence—God knows, after all my drilling, they knew how to train new men. So I left everything to my seconds and remained in Rome.

What a strange time that was.

The Emperor had smiled when he heard me say so, the very first time I came to see him at his villa. "Why?"

"For so long"—I'd been fumbling to find the right words—"my life was tied to yours, Caesar. Smoothing your travels, guarding your back, waging your damned wars." Hadrian's will was my life; the pulse of my veins beating to the same rhythm as his. "Now, my life is my own."

"So why did you answer my summons?" We'd been sitting in the tiny *tablinum* of his private moated villa inside the vast one, a space big enough for two men and a game of *latrunculi* if they didn't mind having the board jammed tight between their knees. The same chambers he'd shared in solitude with my son, and part of me thought that if I just listened hard enough, I'd hear Antinous's golden ripple of laughter. "Why did you agree to come see me if I no longer own you, Vercinge-torix?" the Emperor wanted to know, and he sounded genuinely curious.

I turned the board's one blue piece over in my hand. "Part of me thinks I'm cursed," I heard myself saying. Not in rage, just in calm bitterness. "I can't fail at war, but everything else I touch turns to shit. So if I'm going to spread my bad luck to anyone else—"

"It might as well be me?" Hadrian looked amused. "I assure you, I am quite as cursed as you are."

He didn't look well, that was certain. Thinner every time I visited him, frequently fever-flushed, sitting almost motionless because he hoarded his energy now for public appearances. "You look like Death," I told him, two days after he chose Lucius Ceionius as heir, and he laughed outright.

"Clearly my wits are going the way of my health, because I find myself enjoying your rudeness these days. I hardly ever feel like order-ing your tongue sliced out anymore."

"I may be insolent, but I'm not boring. You're bored these days, Caesar. That's why you keep sending for me."

"Are you bored too, in all this newfound peace?"

"I like boredom."

I had long moved myself out of Titus's sumptuous villa, taking rooms on the Esquiline. I didn't want the official quarters I could have leveraged as legate—bare rented rooms were good enough for a lonely man with nothing in the world but a few useless mementos. Spent my days rising early, partly from habit and partly because of the dreams of Judaea, of Mirah, of Antinous floating in the Nile. I sweated through those dreams, went to the bathhouse and washed away the nightmares, and then I might spend the afternoon at the races or at the wine shops reminiscing with other soldiers. I pushed the pain and the rage back with slow, calm, clean routine. Visited Titus often, but he was a busy man; a happy man with a very full life. I was the one adrift.

So, I suppose, was Hadrian. Because he continued to send for me. I complained about that—"You realize that what with constantly trotting eighteen miles to your villa, Caesar, I had to buy a bloody horse?" But I kept coming.

A few hours a month passing conversation with the Emperor of Rome, and yet it was in the streets of Rome that I had to hear any news about him. He'd nearly died from a hemorrhage of blood, so the news went from the wine shop—no doubt that news was greeted with joy in the Senate, but in the streets I heard nothing but prayers for the Emperor's health. The common Roman thought only of peace and prosperity, and Hadrian had given them nearly twenty years of both. He would be missed when he was gone, and that was an odd thing to admit about a man I had once hated so passionately. I could not really hate him any longer, perhaps because I was so numbed I could barely manage to feel anything.

Except a certain stubborn ball of resentment at my core whenever I looked over the *latrunculi* board at my dead son's marble face, and wondered if Antinous would still be alive if he had never shared the Emperor's bed. If he would have lived happier in obscurity, never driven to drop himself into the Nile and drown his grief.

"Tell me another story of Antinous," Hadrian commanded, and I had the absurd image of Antinous himself as a boy, begging me for stories of heroes and gods. Hadrian had the same eager expression, and my resentment faded a little.

"You've heard every memory I have." I moved one of my white pieces on the game board. Hadrian always played black, of course.

The Emperor moved my piece back. "Not that one! I'll win in four moves. Slide it here"—demonstrating—"then tell me about the day you gave Antinous his first sword."

I surrendered. "He was just a scrap of a thing, all curly hair and scraped elbows, and he'd been begging over a year for his own blade . . ."

That, of course, was the real reason the Emperor sought me, and why I went to him. To no one else could we speak so endlessly of Antinous.

Empress Sabina slipped in quietly at the end of my story, and I jerked a little in my recitation. The first time I'd seen her up close since Egypt, when I departed to Judaea and she to Rome. She was a jolt to my eyes, lithe as a spring flower in a pale yellow *stola*, her cropped head and narrow arms bare, and she carried a cup to Hadrian's hand. "Drink," she ordered the Emperor. "From your physicians."

"They are useless, and so are their potions. I want to try that wise-woman who came to the villa with a good health charm—"

"She was a fraud. Drink, please."

"Do not give me orders, Vibia Sabina," Hadrian grumbled, but he drank as I sat there feeling awkward. Sabina's eyes met mine, and I looked back at the *latrunculi* board. A moment later I heard her footsteps retreating.

"I really should have forced her to leave me," the Emperor mused, moving another game piece. "When it comes to my health, she is an even worse bully than Antinous."

I stared at the board, feeling an awkward flush heat my neck. It was inside this little moated villa that I'd dragged Sabina up against me in a vicious embrace and thrown our old intimacy in Hadrian's face, in front of my son. She could have been dead that day because of me, dead at *his* hand—I didn't want to sit here under a marble copy of my son's face, listening to Hadrian complain about her as any man would complain about a wife who scolded him.

I had no idea if he felt any of his old rage that I had bedded her. He didn't seem to—he seemed as numb to violent feelings as I—but who knew with a man like him? Who *ever* knew?

All I knew was that I did not think it wise to lay eyes on Vibia Sabina.

But I did, on and off as I continued to visit, because though gossip said she lived separate from the Emperor, she evidently visited often enough to tend him herself despite his army of physicians. She forced potions into his hands, she touched his forehead as though checking for fever—and Hadrian might give her fingers an absent squeeze when she excused herself. She never had a word for me. The last time we'd really spoken had been that day on the Nile a few years ago when I'd gotten the Tenth back and I'd wept in her arms. Now I saw her every month or so, and we didn't speak at all.

Not until the year turned, well after Lucius Ceionius had been chosen as heir.

"I saw Servianus turned away at the gate." Sabina spoke unexpectedly, interrupting our silent game as she came to mix Hadrian's wine. "I suppose he's come to harp again about the slight given to his overlooked grandson?"

Hadrian shrugged. "I have informed him my mind is made up. The boy is thoroughly unsuitable. He used to be quite charming, but after that beating he took, he is a figure of fun."

"So is Lucius Ceionius, in a different way." Sabina was turned away from us, stirring Hadrian's cup, and her voice had a note that made me glance up despite my resolution not to look at her. She was gazing at the Emperor, and her eyes were oblique. "The silly costumes on his slaves, his ridiculous dinner parties . . . You might have considered other names besides his."

"I would have chosen young Marcus Catilius Severus were he older," Hadrian mused. "A brilliant mind and a humble soul; it's a rare combination. But he's too young. Pity."

"So why not consider—"

"I do not wish to discuss it, Vibia Sabina. Lucius is my heir. I will be sending him to Pannonia soon, so that he may act as my deputy and receive the homage of the legions. That is an end to it." Hadrian did not quite snap the words, but there was an edge to his voice that told me they'd had this discussion before. "Your move, Vercingetorix."

Sabina retreated in silence. I moved my piece; Hadrian beat me in eight more exchanges, telling me how he had replaced the water in his moat around the villa with Nile water brought from the banks of Antinoöpolis—"It seemed appropriate to encircle myself in grief and love together." No more was said of Lucius the future Emperor, and soon enough Hadrian began to doze and I slipped away over the wooden footbridge.

"Vix."

I stopped, halfway through the peristyled tree-dotted courtyard that abutted the moated villa. Sabina drifted out from behind a massive statue of Neptune, wrapped against the last of winter's chill in an ice-blue *palla*. She'd waited outside to catch me alone, and waited quite some time too. "Lady," I said finally.

"I need your help. Walk with me."

"Is that wise?" I could not tell what she was thinking.

"Hadrian no longer questions the company I keep."

"Even me?"

"Even you."

I wasn't sure I believed her. I started to walk, winter-dry grass crunching underfoot, and she fell in beside me. *Go away, just go away.* I liked my life numb and uneventful. Nothing Sabina put her cool hands on stayed uneventful for long.

"What do you think of Lucius?" she asked.

Of all the things I thought she might have asked me, that would not have made my list. "I don't think anything about him," I said finally. "Don't have to."

We passed under another of the ever-present lemon trees, all but alone. "Most of Rome flocks around the rising sun rather than the setting," Sabina said, noting my glance around the largely empty sprawl of grass and statues. "Lucius's atrium is very full these days."

"Stop doing that."

"What?"

"Reading my mind."

"I wish I could read minds," she sighed. "If I could, I'd have the proof I need."

"Proof? Of what?"

"That Hadrian has made a grave mistake." She looked at me, breath rising in a white mist on the air. "And if his health continues to decline, he will die before he can correct it."

"How do I help with that? *You* persuade him he's made a mistake. You two look amicable enough these days." I saw it, those small touches of her hand to his forehead or his lips to her knuckles in absent greeting. There was something like affection there, and that dumbfounded me. Affection, after everything that had passed between them?

It was not jealousy. It was incomprehension. It was also no business of mine, so I told myself not to think about it.

"Hadrian will not listen to me on this," Sabina said. "He is tired and he only wants the matter settled. He chose an heir; now he'll put the problem aside as solved and spend his days remembering Antinous."

I heard the grief in her voice, lingering like perfume over that name. However I had wronged the Empress of Rome, she had loved my son.

But her voice when she spoke again was hard. "I want Lucius gone, and to be rid of him I need proof. That is why I need you. Help me question him."

"Why do you need me for that?"

"I need answers. I'll get them any way I can. If I don't have your help, I'll probably have to seduce him." She looked at me, her gaze straight as a sword. "I'd rather have you."

For what? I almost asked, but I wasn't getting sucked back into an empress's games. Not again.

I lengthened my stride, leaving her behind me. "Seduce that buffoon if you want," I threw over my shoulder. "I don't care. None of this is my business."

"It *is* your business." Her voice fell behind me as she halted. "He killed your son."

SABINA

"Lady—" Lucius's steward greeted Sabina, but she sidestepped him, stalking to the atrium of the vast overdecorated house where the Imperial heir held court in a crowd of petitioners. The walls were lined with page boys in eagle-feathered wings—evidently the tableau of the day was Jupiter holding court in the heavens, for in the middle, the man her husband had chosen as heir reclined in a gray tunic embroidered in lightning bolts. And his smug face grinned out under a fillet of Imperial purple.

"Empress Sabina!" He came to her with outstretched arms, kissing her hand with the easy intimacy of a friend. Of a *family* member. "Naturally I am delighted—is the Emperor's cough troubling him again? Do tell him I will call upon him, some business we must discuss before I depart for Pannonia—"

Sabina filled her lungs and said, "*Out.*" And glanced at the man hulking behind her in his most imposing armor. Vix had already seen Lucius's Praetorians and was glaring them out of the room with a scowl like death. They looked to their master for orders, but he gave a light laugh and nodded.

"Not contradicting your Empress," Sabina said as the atrium emptied. "Wise." And when they stood alone and Vix had barred the doors, she hit the new Imperial heir fast and savagely across the face. Not a woman's slap, but a tight-fisted hammer of a blow Vix had taught her years before, the kind of blow centurions dealt out to legionaries who had earned a flogging. From the corner of her eye, she saw the savage flare of approval in Vix's eyes.

Lucius's head snapped back. "Lady—" He paused as he fingered his jaw, caught somewhere between indignation and laughter, between brazening his new status or laughing it all off as some odd jest.

Sabina turned away. "Legate," she said crisply, "put him on the ground."

Vix came forward, stone-faced and blazing-eyed in his breastplate, every bit the ruthless killer who had flattened Judaea under his boots. Murder came off him in red waves, raising the hair on Sabina's neck as he brushed past, and Lucius froze like a mouse before a cat. Vix looked at him for a silent burning moment, and then he chopped Hadrian's heir in the throat with the side of his hand, folding Lucius over gasping. Vix flipped the other man down to the mosaics flat on his back and held him there—then looked up at Sabina.

"I'll beat the truth out of him," Vix had said in Hadrian's gardens the previous day. "I start smashing the joints in his arms one by one, and he'll tell everything we want to know."

"It may come to that," Sabina said. "But let me try first."

She knew what it cost him to stand back now and let her ask the questions. But he stepped away, clenching the hilt of his *gladius* and giving her a nod.

"Lady!" Lucius rasped.

Sabina ignored him, shrugging off her *palla*. She returned Vix's nod and stepped deliberately over Lucius. He tried to rise, and she put a foot on his chest and pushed him back down.

"You may be heir," she said, gazing down at him, "but I am still Empress of Rome. If I like, I can squash you like a spider."

"Lady—"

"Shut up. I would be careful, if I were you, what you said to me, Lucius Ceionius."

His bearded chin jerked up as he stared at her. "Lucius Aelius Verus Caesar," he said. "That is my name. By the Emperor's orders."

"You are still Lucius Ceionius to me." She pressed her foot harder. "We will leave aside for the moment your ridiculous appointment to the purple, and we will leave aside as well the matter of my favorite niece marrying your *six-year-old son*. Not," Sabina added, "that I will ever permit that." Her glorious Amazon of a daughter was going to marry whomever she damned well pleased, whatever lucky boy she'd tripped out to inflame in her gold finery. Not some sniveling child a third her age. But that was a matter for the future. "I am going to ask you a question, Lucius, and unless you want to see your own blood on the tiles, you will not lie."

Lucius's eyes flashed to Vix. "You would not dare harm the future Emperor!"

Vix just smiled.

Sabina slid her toe to Lucius's chin and nudged his gaze back toward her. "Concentrate on me, not him. I want to know how you murdered Antinous."

A silence filled the atrium. Sabina heard the splash of water dripping from the roof gutter down into the central pool. Lucius swallowed, his eyes suddenly cautious. "I did not murder him."

Sabina looked at Vix. He unsheathed his *gladius* with slow, ringing menace, and Lucius's eyes flew to it. "Do not lie to me," she whispered.

"I'm not, I—"

Sabina lifted a finger, and the *gladius* tip flashed up to Lucius's throat.

"You're mad," Lucius gasped. "When the Emperor hears—"

"I am his wife." Sabina stepped over Lucius, a foot to each side of his waist, and slid herself slowly down over his whip-tense body, eyes never leaving his. "And he lets me do whatever I like."

"He favors me—"

"I could have you cut to pieces on the mosaics right here." She pressed her fingertips into his chest right over the heart. Vix still held the sword at his throat, and she could feel the pulse of her old lover's rage like the beat of her own blood. "If I tell Hadrian it was revenge for Antinous, he would do nothing but thank me."

Lucius repeated, "You're mad!"

"No. I am *Empress*. I learned under Plotina. I learned under her predecessor Domitia. You know what empresses are, Lucius? We are plotters. We are schemers. We are survivors." She smiled. "And sometimes, we are killers."

Lucius tried to jerk his head away from the *gladius*, but he couldn't jerk his gaze from Sabina's. "I did not kill Antinous."

"You did." She slid her fingertips slowly up his chest, lowering herself closer. "I've had you investigated. You were with the Emperor on the barge that evening, being entertained by a troupe of dancers—and when the party was done, you took two slave girls to your bed with you. Twins, of course. Beauties, the pair of them, and very valuable. So it's curious you had them sold just two days after Antinous died—not just them, but every slave you had with you."

"Lady—"

"I had them tracked," Sabina whispered. "And that did take time. I couldn't find all your slaves, but I found one of those twin girls. She whored for a priest of Anubis for a while, but he freed her eventually, and I had her brought to Rome. What an interesting tale she had to tell."

He swallowed. "What could she possibly have to say?"

To Sabina, nothing at all. The girl had arrived a month ago, terrified, crashing to her knees at the Empress's feet. To all Sabina's questions, she would answer only a shake or a nod of the head, too petrified to speak a word. "You try," Sabina had told her African maid. "She won't dare speak against a former master, not to the Empress of Rome, but she might talk to a fellow slave. Wheedle it out of her, and I'll grant you your freedom on the spot."

It had taken most of the month.

"She told me you went back up on the deck of the barge," Sabina said. "You took her and her sister with you, one on each side. You saw the Emperor's favorite on the stern, speaking to a bearded soldier." From the corner of her eye, she saw Vix's jaw clench—that soldier had been Vix, of course. The last time he'd seen his son alive. "They embraced, and the soldier departed. Antinous was left behind, standing by the railing looking out at the water. And you dismissed both your slave girls—abruptly—and they went below. Leaving the Emperor's favorite alone at the rail, and you staring at him."

"Did the slut see me push him?" Lucius flung back. "No. Because I did not!"

"You made sure she did not. And you sold her away before anyone could question her." Sabina wished there were more—she'd consulted with her ancient freedman, seeing where inquiries might next be directed. But then Lucius Ceionius had been elevated as heir and Hadrian was making plans to send him to Pannonia, and there was no more time for lengthy inquiries.

Time was, in fact, running out. So she had decided to beard the beast in his den.

"No one benefited from Antinous's death but you." Sabina spoke softly, pressed up against Lucius's whole length. "There were those who despised him for being the Emperor's lover, yes, but they wouldn't have risked Hadrian's anger harming him—not for mere moral outrage. And everyone else loved him and would have moved the heavens to keep him at Hadrian's side." A memory flashed of Antinous's face, so young and golden and full of light when he smoothed the worry lines away from Hadrian's brow. "You dared risk it because you saw oppor-

tunity. You became the Emperor's new favorite and you parleyed that
into a new name and the Imperial purple."

Lucius tried for contempt. "This is all very thin, Lady. You think
you can hang an unseen murder about my neck on the word of a slave
bitch?"

"But you weren't *planning* to kill him, were you?" Sabina moved her
face closer, hovering just over his. They might have been fond lovers
pressed together in a bed. "You were hoping Hadrian would tire of him,
of course. But you would have been content to bide your time, if you hadn't
seen him unaccompanied that night. He was so seldom alone. What a
chance." Running a fingertip down Lucius's cheekbone and feeling the
film of sweat. The sweat of guilt, or just terror? "Admit it, Lucius. You
didn't plan it. You just stepped from the shadows and gave him a shove."

"I—"

She saw him swallow. "You've always admired me." Lowering her
face closer. "You even tried to seduce me. I almost let you."

A faint sound from Vix. She wondered what he thought of her for
such an admission.

"I have nothing but admiration for you, Lady!" Lucius had long
forgotten about Vix—his panicked stare was all for her. "A very lovely
woman—"

"I liked you, Lucius." She wrapped her hands about his throat, light
as feathers. "But I *loved* Antinous. You killed him, a boy I loved. And
you turned my husband into a walking dead man. But I will be merciful. If you confess that you shoved him into the Nile, I'll give you time
to run before I tell Hadrian. And you can spend the rest of your life
running, because he'll never give up trying to find you. Personally, I'd
head north of the wall in Britannia and keep going."

Vix spoke. "And I'll find you even if you run that far."

Lucius made a twisting lunge as though to get out from under her.
Sabina locked her hands and her thighs both, rolling him. Now she
was beneath him, but she reared up snake-fast so her eyes captured his,
and Lucius froze. As much from her gaze as from the tip of the *gladius*
Vix poised again at his throat.

"I'm not finished with you yet," she said, fingers locked hard about his throat. "Try to flee again, and I'll begin to scream. And every sycophant in your atrium will rush in and see you trying to rape the Empress. That I *can* get you arrested for."

"I'll bear witness," Vix agreed, *gladius* never moving.

Lucius stopped struggling. He looked as though he'd been mesmerized by a snake. "*I didn't push that boy into the Nile.*"

Sabina pulled him slowly down against her, fingertips digging deeper around his throat, grinding her hips under his. As terrified as he looked, she could feel his body responding against her, and she gave a benign little smile. She doubted this was how he'd ever envisioned himself entwined with the Empress of Rome. "Convince me," she whispered, and reached down to grab him where it would hurt the most if she squeezed hard.

"I admit I told him stories!" Lucius's voice scaled up in a yelp. "I'd hoped he'd leave the Emperor's side, maybe commit suicide—he was starry-eyed enough to believe that nonsense myth about sacrificing yourself in the Nile for a loved one, when I told it to him—"

Vix made a low sound like a growling cat. Sabina squeezed her fingers just enough to make Lucius gasp. "You'll regret that. But do continue."

"I did not push him." Tears were starting to spring up in Lucius's eyes. "I will swear any oath you please, Lady. I saw him on that night, and I even *thought* about pushing him. Which is why I let the slave girls go below. But I didn't lay a hand on him—didn't think I could get him over the railing unseen, truth be told. I saw an opportunity when he turned up dead, and gods know I used it, but that is all!"

Sabina looked at him a moment longer, evaluating. She looked up at Vix. Vix was staring at Lucius, eyes like slits, but he spoke to her. "I believe him, Lady. I tortured men in Judaea—I know what the truth looks like."

Sabina looked back at her husband's heir, trembling teary-eyed over her. She nodded, and Vix's *gladius* withdrew. "Get off me, Lucius."

He scrambled up. Sabina extended a hand. He helped her to her feet, bowing almost double. She took some time brushing off her *stola* before she gave him leave to rise from his bow. "Apologies," she said, no apology in her voice. "But I had to be certain, and there are times an empress must be ruthless. Emperors, too. Remember that, if you follow Hadrian."

She turned to go, tugging her *palla* over her hair, when she heard his quivering voice rise behind her. "Assault a man of Rome, the Imperial heir, for a *catamite?*"

Vix whirled, his sword coming a hand-span out of its scabbard before Sabina's fingers caught his wrist. He could have flung her off like a feather, but his knuckles just clenched until they went white. She waited until she was sure he wasn't going to spill Lucius's guts across the floor, and then she turned a smile on the Imperial heir that made him take a step backward.

"Something else you should know about empresses," she said. "We never forgive an insult. Call Antinous a catamite one more time, and I'll come back and finish the job I started."

She could hear his gulp behind her as she stalked from the atrium. The crowd of his well-wishers outside took one look at her face and fell into bows, heads dropping when she passed as though they had all been scythed.

"He was telling the truth." Vix sounded tired. "God damn him, he was telling the truth."

"I know."

Vix glanced at her. "You were terrifying."

"I know." But the grim amusement of Lucius's fear had faded away, leaving a taste in her mouth like ash. So much time, so many inquiries—she had been so certain, and it was all worth nothing? If not Lucius, who? No one else had profited by Antinous's death; no one. Sabina came to a halt on the steps before Lucius's vast house, and suddenly she wanted to lay her head against Vix's breastplate and weep. "How did I get it wrong?" she cried. "I was *certain!*"

"Your evidence looked likely." Vix's voice was flat and lifeless again, as it had been for months whenever she heard him talking with Hadrian. "But it didn't add up to piss. My boy drowned himself, and there's an end to it."

"I hoped—" She swallowed disappointment. "What a thing to hope for. *Hoping* he was murdered . . ."

"Blaming someone would help." Vix glanced back at the lush facade of the heir's house. "Killing someone would help."

"Yes."

"I still wanted to kill him," Vix said softly.

Sabina looked up at her old lover. A shell of a man again, an empty statue dressed in armor. An hour ago he had been blazing with rage and life, a sight to take the breath away. *That's what Hadrian will look like*, she had dared to hope. *When we bring him Lucius's confession, and he realizes it is not his fault Antinous died.*

But there was no confession, and Vix had become a walking corpse again, and Hadrian would stay one. Because she had been wrong.

ANNIA

A.D. 137, Spring

"I'd rather go to work in a salt mine than spend an afternoon with Ceionia," Annia said flatly.

"I know," her mother agreed. "Spiteful little cow."

Ceionia had come swishing into the atrium yesterday taking precedence over Annia and her mother both as though she were Empress of Rome already. "You must come weave with me in the afternoons, Annia. I'm going to weave my Marcus a wedding tunic. You could make a start on your bridal veil!"

"Just go string a loom with the girl," her mother advised. "It will be good practice keeping your temper."

"I'll have to keep my temper with her the rest of my life, if she's going to be my sister-in-law." Annia glowered. "Must I start now?"

"Don't write off the rest of your life just yet, my love. Little Lucius is only six. He won't be ready to marry you for at least another nine years, and that's a long time for things to change. So bite your tongue, and bide your time." Annia's mother gave her a shrewd look. "I thought you'd be pleased. You didn't seem chafing to marry anyone, and at your age most girls are already giving birth to their first child. At least this keeps you unattached a time longer." Another look. "If that's what you want?"

What I want is to tear the hair out of Ceionia's head every time I hear her coo, "My Marcus," Annia thought. *Because my wedding has to wait, but she could marry him tomorrow if the Emperor decides he wants it done.*

In the end, Annia was glad of the daily trips to weave with her future sister-in-law. Because she always walked; a point of pride after all Ceionia's little hints about how it was unwomanly—"Imperial women are always above the crush, Annia, you must take a litter!" So Annia started *running* the distance between, just to be as unwomanly as possible, and she was taking a fast jog away from the house of the new heir, wishing she had a fleeter set of slave girls for attendants, when someone fell in beside her.

"The Pantheon," Marcus breathed, pretending to bump her and veer away. "Tell them you want to pray!" And Annia made for the Pantheon, that cool pillared place where her father had taken her and Marcus when it was being built, her heart pounding in her chest like a beat of thunder. She left her maids at the steps outside with a few coins and ducked into the marble gloom, making for the watery splash of sunlight on the floor where light came in from the space in the coffered dome. She didn't have to wait long.

"You should see how you glow in here." The voice came low behind her. "Your hair drinks up all the sunlight from the oculus."

She turned and looked at Marcus, standing with a fold of his toga pulled over his head and his face somber. She wanted to see him smile, so she said, "What's an oculus?"

"The opening at the dome's apex. It allows a source of natural light and drainage for—" Marcus broke off, and that was when she got her smile. "You're teasing me."

"Always." She wished she could take his hand, but there were worshippers all around, hurrying to the statue of their favorite god or goddess. Annia and Marcus just stood, staring at each other. "You don't have to sneak to see me, you know. We're cousins—you could just *visit* me."

"But we're both betrothed, and not to each other." Bleakly. "People would be watching."

"People are already watching me," Annia said, attempting levity. "Lucius Ceionius, for one. Ever since he saw me in that orange dress, he's had a light in his eye. He's just the sort of father-in-law to have wandering hands."

"He hasn't—"

"I'm not afraid of Lucius Ceionius. I'll just smack him off, Emperor's heir or no." Ceionia's father was too insubstantial, too utterly frivolous to frighten Annia in the slightest. "He's off to Pannonia soon anyway. Imperial business. How are *you* faring, Marcus?"

"The Emperor keeps summoning me." Marcus nibbled a thumbnail. He had ink under his nails, Annia saw with a little pang of tenderness. "He keeps outlining courses of study with my grandfather. I'm to be made Prefect of the City; that much has been decided. And he's told me to increase my training with the sword, so he must have some military post in mind at some point. He watched me do my sword drills yesterday . . ." Marcus tore a hand through his curly hair. "I still don't know what he meant, that I was 'dear to his heart.' I'm not—the most complimentary thing he said about my *gladius* work is that I had very little enthusiasm, but a quick wrist! If all I have in my favor is a quick wrist, how can he call me 'vital to the future'—"

"He's grooming you," a harsh voice said, and Annia turned fast, ready to run or strike out or both as Pedanius Fuscus strode forward. Time seemed to tilt, and she remembered him as a sturdy nine-year-old trotting through this same temple at his grandfather's side, the three of them eyeing each other in the same hostile little triangle. Only now it was hatred, not just childhood wariness. This was hatred leaping thick and silent between the three of them.

"I was hoping you'd meet the whore somewhere more private," Pedanius told Marcus, jittering a little as he always did now. Tall and nervous in a bright blue tunic, sweaty as though he'd just come from the bathhouse. But it was the sweat of nervousness, not a steam room. "I've been following you on and off, you know. Hoping to catch you without all the Imperial slaves and tutors the Emperor has around you most of the time."

Marcus drew himself up. "And why would you follow me?"

"Because it was you." Pedanius stepped closer. "It was you who set those thugs on me, wasn't it?"

Annia drew swift breath to lie, but Marcus spoke without a qualm. "Finally figured that out, did you?" he said in his most overeducated drawl. "Really, you are slow."

"You made me look ridiculous," Pedanius hissed through his ruined teeth. "You stole the Emperor's favor. You're *always* stealing something from me, Marcus Catilius Severus. First you got to join the Salian priests; then you got the Emperor's favor; you'll get Prefect of the City—you've probably already gotten this whore's virginity, too—"

"Hold your filthy tongue," Marcus warned, dropping the drawl.

"—and you can have all that, but you're *not* going to be heir. No matter what your thugs tried to do to me. I will see you dead first."

Annia gave a contemptuous laugh. "He's not *heir*, you thickheaded lout! Lucius Ceionius is, or were you even listening?"

"Lucius? He won't last the year. Probably diseased already from all his whores, and even if he isn't, no one takes him seriously. It's just a sop for him because he tickles the Emperor's fancy and his balls. He's supposed to keep the chair warm for *you*." Pedanius jabbed a finger into Marcus's chest. "The Emperor said himself when you were just a whining little brat and he found us all outside his Hades—he said you reminded him of himself."

"Because I *bored* him," Marcus said flatly. "I have no Imperial blood, and at best I'll make provincial governor of somewhere backwater like Pannonia. To think I have any chance at the purple is absurd. And to base such a theory on a few childhood recollections is the act of a poor theoretician."

"I should have killed you when we *were* children," Pedanius whispered. "I wish I'd done it in this temple, the day we met."

"You're mad," Annia threw at him. "You really are mad, you know that? Following Marcus about like some crazed dog, following me about just to call me a whore—can't you find some new pastime, you ivory-skulled ass? Why do you keep tormenting us?"

"Because he stole from me." Pedanius's eyes shifted from Marcus to Annia. "But you unmanned me. You know what happened, the day of my manhood ceremony when you kicked me? You burst one of my *balls*."

Annia's breath froze in her throat.

"I had to say a horse stepped on me. The medicus had to take it off like I was a damned eunuch, and my grandfather had to bribe him to keep it quiet." There was a furious shame in Pedanius's gaze, as though he wished he could stop the words from spilling, but the old rage had burst like a torrent and taken his shameful secret out with it. "I'm half a man thanks to you, you vicious bitch. I lay there under the knife and I swore I'd pay you back—"

Annia wanted to step back from the hate coming off him like boiling black smoke, but she held her ground. *A reason*, she thought. Finally, a *reason* for his unrelenting hatred all these years. *I burst one of your balls*. With one ferocious stomp of a kick. She still wanted to step back, but a bolt of savage vindication shot through her, and she threw her head back and let him see it.

"Come near me again, and I'll stamp the other ball flat too," she snarled. "Leave Marcus and me alone. Go plot against Lucius instead, you gelded freak."

"Oh, I am." Pedanius smiled. "I'm still taking what's mine. And when I have it, I will come for you both."

"Oh, Hell's *gates!*" Annia cried, borrowing Vix's favorite curse. Children's rivalry, escalated to this horror of retribution—where in the name of all the gods was it going to *end*?

When one of us dies, the thought came whispering back.

"Know something else—when I come for you both, I'll do it myself." Pedanius fished in the pouch at his waist, taking out what looked like a ring. A flash of gold that he twisted slowly onto his middle finger. "Marcus here had to hire someone to beat me to a pulp. Me? I do my own bloody work."

"Then I won't be caught alone again," Marcus said, infuriatingly mild, and took Annia's hand. "Come along, Annia. We have no time to yammer about childhood slights."

Pedanius's fist shot out toward Marcus. But Marcus was already moving, and Annia was yanking him backward at the same time, and the ringed knuckles only grazed Marcus's nose. Annia tensed, ready to swing, but Pedanius only aimed the one blow.

"I killed a man with this fist," he whispered. "Killed him. Took his life and took this ring off his dead hand. And next I'll kill you, and I'll take something of yours." He pointed at Annia. "I'll take her. And she'll make me a man again."

"Try," Annia grated. Marcus squeezed her hand, so hard her knuckles ached, or she might have flown at Pedanius right there in the middle of the Pantheon among the crowd of oblivious worshippers.

Marcus touched his own face. The gold ring had drawn a single drop of blood. "The only blood of mine you'll ever get," he said calmly, flicking it to the floor between Pedanius's feet. "Good day."

"Well," Annia breathed as they retreated outside, trying to slow her thudding heart. "That was a surprise."

"That he means to see us dead? Not really."

"No, that I cost him one of his balls." Vicious satisfaction was still curling through her stomach at the thought.

Marcus frowned, too distracted to reproach her for foul language. "Do you think he meant it, that he's killed before?"

"I wouldn't put it past him." They'd stopped under the pillared portico leading to the outside, people pushing all around them.

"But why would he carry that ring about with him? Sheer idiocy—"

"It makes him feel like a man," Annia guessed. "Because killer or not, he's still a half-gelded coward."

"Don't underestimate him," Marcus warned.

"If you're so wary, why did you admit you were the one who had him attacked?" She could have groaned, hearing him say those words. "Why didn't you lie?"

"We're bound by Fortuna." Marcus shrugged. "All three of us. Somehow. We should accept the things that the Fates bind us to, even

Pedanius Fuscus. He might as well know as not—it doesn't make any difference to fate."

"You're an idiot."

Marcus smiled faintly and smoothed a lock of hair back behind her ear.

"He might be right, though," Annia said, trying not to curl her cheek into his hand. Her maids were standing at the other end of the portico, and they were definitely peeking. "Maybe Hadrian *is* grooming you. Maybe he does want you as heir—you to follow Lucius Ceionius."

Marcus shook his head. "Lucius will want his own son to be heir. You're more likely to be Empress than me to be Emperor."

"I might be Empress," she said flatly, "or you might be Emperor. But not each other's."

They looked at each other for a while. There were clouds gathering, shadowing the street. Another spring rainstorm on the horizon. "Have I mentioned how much I dislike Ceionia?" Marcus said eventually. "She tells me she's weaving me a tunic with her own hands, and she looks offended if I don't comment at once on her wifely diligence. And every time I express an opinion, she agrees with it. I have deliberately stated two contradictory opinions in a row, just to catch her out, and she agreed with both. Women should make themselves agreeable to their husbands, but not that agreeable. I cannot *stand* her."

"Good." Annia felt a little bloom of relief. Ceionia was very pretty, after all, and very suitable. "I hate her, too."

"Well, her father is in no rush to see us married." Marcus blew out a breath. "I think he believes she can do better, once he's emperor. Thank the gods, whatever his reason. We've got time . . ."

Annia leaned against him, not caring if the maids saw, and buried her nose in the hollow of his throat. Marcus's arms went around her, and they held each other desperately tight for a moment.

"I will never, ever weave you a tunic with my own hands," Annia whispered.

"Good."

VIX

"Odd to see you so idle," Titus observed as spring melted toward summer. "I could get a different post for you if you wanted it. Another legionary command somewhere, if you don't wish to return to Judaea?"

"No." This was all I had left in my life: quiet days while I waited to become an old man. I'd found brief, furious purpose in the thought of bringing my son's killer to justice, but there was no killer. That business was done, and so was I.

Lucius Ceionius had gone off to Pannonia. "He'll stay a few months longer than I planned," Hadrian said, frowning over our last game of *latrunculi*. "Officially, because the Pannonian legions need further inspection. Unofficially, because he fell ill just before he left Rome. Collapsed with his lungs wheezing and bleeding, and the physicians say the colder northern air will do him good."

I hoped he would die there. He might not have killed my boy, but he'd still *used* his death—tried to manipulate him into throwing himself from the barge. *May his lungs rot for that*, I thought, but it was dulled rage. I looked at Titus's daughter sometimes, young Annia with her firestorm of hair and limbs, and Hell's gates, but I couldn't imagine ever having that much life in my veins again!

She was wretchedly unhappy, I could see that clear enough—disappointed over her betrothal to Lucius Ceionius's snotty-nosed brat, or so Titus said. Annia didn't get mopey in her wretchedness. She got vicious, spending her energy in lung-breaking sprints, and on the days I came to visit her father and he wasn't there, I'd visit Annia instead, let her beg me for stories of the legion camps.

"I think I'd like traveling with the legions," she decided one dusty afternoon, snagging the *trigon* ball from my long toss into the air. Her golden-haired little sister, Fadilla, had joined us to make a third, bouncing up and down—*me, me!*—as Annia arced the ball gently for her sister. "You'd always be on the move with a legion, always seeing something new."

"Maybe you'll see a legion someday," I offered as Fadilla ran for the catch.

"Can you raise children in a legion camp? Because I like children and I intend to have a whole flock." Fadilla took a tumble over a stone, and Annia veered off to raise her up. "You're not going to cry, are you? That knee's barely even bumped! Let me see—"

I smiled, watching how deftly she inspected the scraped knee, blowing kisses over it until Fadilla was giggling. If Annia wanted a flock of children, she'd be a good mother to them, and I said so.

"Lucky for me," Annia snorted, "my future husband *is* a child."

"I could marry him for you," Fadilla volunteered, but even she looked dubious. "If he didn't pick his nose all the time . . ."

I laughed. "No need to sacrifice yourself. I have absolutely no doubt your big sister will be able to ditch that little bastard without any help from you."

Annia gave me her tilted grin, slinging the *trigon* ball aside. "Race you to the edge of the vineyard?"

"I'll win!" Fadilla shouted, and took off in a streak of blond hair. Annia ran behind in exaggeratedly slow strides, and I heaved my grizzled bones into a lope in pursuit.

"Faster, Legate!" Annia shouted over her shoulder, and I put my head down and pretended to run faster. Everything about this girl made me smile: her swagger, her fast feet, her shining devotion to her little sister . . . Titus was lucky in his daughters. Far luckier than I had been.

My daughters. No letters from them, but I hadn't expected any. I did get one stiff little note a few months ago from Mirah's mother, telling me the dowries I'd settled on the girls had gotten a wine merchant for Dinah and some kind of scholar for Chaya. Good matches both, and I was glad.

"Down to the edge of the vineyard!" Annia shouted. "Or it doesn't count!"

She was already twisting vine leaves into a wreath for Fadilla's hair—"A crown for our victor!"—by the time I pulled up at the stone wall at the hill's bottom. "Race back?" she suggested, bouncing on her toes, and Fadilla clamored agreement under her wreath.

"Allow me some time to die." It was a hot day for spring; I put my hands on my knees and bent over wheezing.

"You're old," Annia scoffed, stretching down to touch her toes.

"Not too old to lay you over my knee and beat you, girl."

"You'd never catch me!" Dancing out of reach. "At least take off that lion skin, I don't see how you can go slogging about in *fur*—"

I made a swipe for her flying red braid and missed. "I'm used to it." My one token of Antinous—I slept under it even in the growing heat, and sometimes it gave me dreams of his golden hair. *Don't call me Narcissus . . .*

I looked away from Titus's daughters, hiding the bitterness that creased my eyes, and that was when I glanced over the wall marking the border of the vineyard. I'd never run all the way to the bottom, not this far. "I didn't know there was another villa so close to yours." Small but rambling; terraced gardens dropping down to a vineyard of its own that ran right along this one.

"The Empress's villa," Annia said. "She watches me go by on my morning run, if she's there—I'll generally run across our vineyard *and* hers."

Fadilla bounced, waving a plump hand over her head. "There she is!"

I'd already spotted the distant figure in white, standing like a slim marble column on the terrace overlooking the gardens. It was too far away to see a face, to see anything distinguishing at all—but I still knew it was Sabina. I saw her arm rise, answering Fadilla's wave. "I thought she stayed at the Emperor's villa," I heard myself saying.

"She comes here a good deal. Whenever the Emperor gets in a temper and tells her to stop nagging." Annia snagged her little sister midbounce, replaiting Fadilla's fraying braid. "They're an odd pair. I used to think they hated each other, but sometimes I see them lock eyes and it's like they're reading each other's minds." Tying off the plait, she dropped a kiss on her sister's head. "Shall we race back?"

"You two go," I said, and swung over the wall and made my way toward the Empress of Rome.

She met me halfway, coming down through the terraced gardens.

As she drew closer, I saw she was wearing one of the Egyptian-style sheaths she'd adopted in Alexandria, white linen tied between her breasts in some complicated knot that left her shoulders naked. Barefoot, bareheaded, coming to a halt before the orderly rows of vines. I halted too, wondering what she saw as her eyes traveled over me. Vercingetorix the Red, the man who had butchered Judaea? The brash ass of a boy who had once fought a duel to win her garnet earring? Or a grizzled legionary with gray-shot hair and a shoulder-load of bad dreams?

She smiled, crinkling the corners of her eyes, and I saw the girl I'd found in her father's atrium, blinking up at me with those same blue eyes as her finger held her place in a scroll. "Hello," she said.

I said just as simply, "Hello to you, my lady."

We walked beside the rows of vines, and our words came slow and cautious. Bit like our aging selves, really. I had not seen her since our failed interrogation—what did we speak of, after a disappointment like that?

"I come here when I'm not required for Imperial functions," she said, nodding out over her villa. "Or if Hadrian wants to be alone. More and more frequently, these days—he's becoming a recluse."

"So are you, by the looks of it." Not so much as a page had approached the Empress out here with a dispatch or a visitor. Whenever I'd seen Sabina before, these months past, we had been insulated by marble and formality: her rank, Hadrian's presence, slaves and hangers-on. This solitary silence wrapping the two of us away from the rest of the world was unsettling.

"I do live very quietly here," Sabina said. "Just a few slaves and guards, and they know to keep their distance. I like it. I used to have an atrium crowded with petitioners, but the wives of dying emperors don't have so many of those."

I could not help asking. "You've not heard anything else, have you? From these informers of yours—if Lucius didn't push Antinous, perhaps it could have been someone else?"

A mute shake of her head.

Of course not, I thought, and wondered what I was doing here, walking beside her.

She made a tilting motion of her shoulders as though sliding the matter of Lucius and our failed accusations away. "Titus tells me you live in the Esquiline." Speaking lightly. "I thought you must be returning to your family in Judaea."

I could say it now without feeling the prick in my eyes. "I have no family anymore."

A breath came beside me, but she didn't ask. I knew she wouldn't. Vibia Sabina, soul of tact. I told her anyway.

"My girls, married and gone. My wife, dead."

"I am sorry," she said quietly.

Another silence. She turned away into the vineyard, trailing between the vines to give me time to swallow my sadness, and I was grateful. A hawk winged overhead through the sunshine, and Sabina arched her neck to follow its flight.

"This is where Annia runs when she comes cutting through." Sabina looked at me over her shoulder, a white shape moving down the orderly rows, bare toes curling into the earth. I followed the Empress into the vines, running my hand over the first tight buds of the unripe grapes to stop myself from tracking the sway of Sabina's hips through sunlit linen. Those Egyptian shifts didn't really hide anything. I remembered how she had slithered catlike under Lucius Ceionius, purring in his ear as she threatened his life and his balls.

I cleared my throat. "Yes, Annia's a fast one. And fierce."

"Very." Sabina glanced over her shoulder at me, her gaze guarded. She'd lined her eyes in crushed lapis, and they looked enormous. "My sister tells me you've grown fond of her."

"Of her and her sister both." Though it was no real secret Annia was my favorite. "Maybe it's because of my own daughters. I miss them, but at the same time . . ."

Sabina turned to face me. "What?"

I halted in the middle of the vineyard, staring down the row. "They're *better* without me. I was a piss-poor father, and I ruined them, and Antinous too. Everything that comes from me—anything that isn't blood and death, because those are the only things I'm good at—everything that comes from me gets ruined. Including all my children."

A slow, silent breath from Sabina. "That's—not—true," she said slowly.

I gave a bitter little laugh. "Yes, it is."

Her eyes lowered, then lifted back up. She took a breath. "It's time I told you something."

"What?"

She didn't answer at once. The sun beat down, and I could feel a trickle of sweat making its way down my back under the heat of Antinous's lion skin. She looked at me with her lapis-blue, lapis-lined eyes. "I don't know how to begin, exactly."

I raised my eyebrows.

She drew a gulp of a breath. "It's Annia. She's not Titus and Faustina's daughter."

I stared.

"She's ours."

Somewhere behind me, a bird exploded into the sky with a buffet of wings. "Ours?" I repeated dumbly, and my voice came out in a whisper.

"Yours." Sabina rested her fingertips against my chest in supplication. "And mine."

I could hear her voice explaining, the words spilling like they'd been upended from a jug corked for nearly twenty years. Explaining a deception wrought, a secret kept from the Emperor and the whole world—but it was all happening somewhere distant, the words coming fogged and half-heard to my ears.

I had another daughter.

Annia of the red braid and the ferocious scowl and the long, long limbs. Annia Galeria Faustina . . .

"Mine," I whispered, "*Mine*—" There was no disbelief. The truth of it called to me in Annia herself, her freckles and her temper and her restless energy just like mine. The truth had called me from the day I met her, a savage little girl of seven cuffing blood off her lip and telling me she never cried. I'd loved what she was right then and there, and I loved the fleet young huntress she'd become who had been able to make a heartsick old soldier laugh.

My daughter, I thought again, utterly stuck on that one precious, incredible thing. Somehow I was on my knees between the vines, gasping like I'd run a mile. The world swirled around me; sights, sounds, scents, so bright and beautiful when everything had been so gray and meaningless—

"Vix—" Sabina went to her knees too, seizing my hands, and her eyes were full of tears. "I'm sorry."

"Sorry?" My heart and mind all whirling. "Sorry—*why?*"

She bowed her shorn head, narrow fingers wrapping mine tight. "Sorry I never told you."

Time was I'd have flung that apology right back in her face. Hated her for keeping yet more secrets, just as she'd kept Antinous's love for Hadrian a secret. But what kind of secret-keeper had I ever been? The day I found Antinous with Hadrian, I flung the secret of Sabina's long love for me in the Emperor's face. What if I'd done even worse? What if I'd thrown Annia at Hadrian too? Would I have burned my youngest daughter's life up in an emperor's rage, just to hurt her mother, if I had known the truth?

I don't know.

I don't know, and I'm glad I never will know. Because there would be no way in this world or the next to make that right.

My hands tightened on Sabina's until I could feel her rings pressing my skin. "You were right not to tell me."

She laughed a little through the tears in her blue eyes. Blue to my gray—that was where Annia got the sword-steel flash in her gaze; in the combination of our eyes. The thought gave me exquisite pleasure. "It feels *good* to tell you."

I'd have been half an empire away once Sabina realized I'd left a child in her belly. I was off rounding up Hadrian's enemies for him as she shouldered everything alone. "Why didn't you wash her out of you with some potion?" My voice was hoarse. "Hadrian's temper back then, he would have killed you if he found out. It would have been safer."

"Even when she was just a flutter inside me, I loved her," Sabina said. "Because she is *ours*."

My carefully hoarded numbness shattered all around me. My forehead dropped against Sabina's shoulder, and I trembled all over as the world rushed at me, full of light and sound and color again. Different from the brief surge of life I'd felt when hunting for my son's killer, because that surge of life had come on a red tide of rage. This—this was rebirth. I smelled rich earth and budding grapes, leaves and sunlight and the must of wine still contained on the stem. The tears that sprang to my eyes were a balm, sweet joy and sweet relief. That black certainty that everyone I touched was doomed—

Everything that comes from me gets ruined, I'd told Sabina bleakly. *Including all my children.*

Not quite, I thought now, and my shoulders heaved in a sob of relief. *Not quite.*

Maybe only because I hadn't raised Annia. Maybe only because she'd been reared far away from me and my turmoil, raised by my best friend, who was a far better father than I ever was.

But that didn't matter. What mattered was that at least one of my mistakes had turned golden instead of black. I'd taken the Empress of Rome in my arms on a dry island, and that colossal recklessness had not for once brought death and misfortune in its wake. It brought one joyful, gleaming miracle of a girl.

My daughter. She didn't make up for the children I had lost.

But she was still a miracle.

"You know—" Sabina lifted my face from her shoulder, cupping my cheek in her hand. "Annia looks so much like you. Every day I've seen it, watching her grow. Your hair—" Fingers sliding back into my hair, over the spot where one obstinate lock kicked up. "Not just the color. That one wild bit in the back; Annia has it, too."

"She has your eyes." I traced my thumb over Sabina's lashes. My senses were drinking the world in; drinking her in—the softness of her skin, the smell of her perfume, the pool of her eyes. "Bluer than mine."

"Your height." Sabina stretched toward me like a willow. "Your temper—"

"Your—" I couldn't think. I couldn't think, but it didn't matter because Sabina kissed me.

It was all storm when we came together and made Annia. Here under the blue sky and blazing sun, it was tentative, my lips brushing hers as though they'd forgotten how to kiss. Her cool hands linked behind my neck, pulling me closer, and that was when I felt fire licking through my veins. My unfeeling body roaring to life, and all because Sabina's mouth was opening under mine like a lotus. The cool sweet taste of her, the feel of her hands pulling me closer, the smoothness of her skin against my rough jaw—she lit a firestorm in my veins with one kiss.

Mirah, I couldn't help thinking, because she was the last woman I'd kissed in passion—but Mirah's bitter shade was gone. Even her living presence hadn't banished Sabina from my bones. Mirah had belonged to her God, but I belonged to Rome, and Sabina *was* Rome, the Empress of Rome and the mother of my only remaining child, back in my arms where she belonged.

I was crushing her against me and ravaging her mouth for more, her bare shoulders like flame under my hands as I pulled her down to the rich earth between the green vines. She was stripping the lion skin from my shoulders and I was tearing at the knot of fabric that held her dress together. Her small breast was honey and silk in my rough hand, and it was a good thing we were off in the vines, off in the middle of nowhere where no prying eyes could find us, because I couldn't have stopped if one of her Praetorians had leveled a spear at my throat. I spread the lion skin down over the earth and spread her on top of it, and then it was nothing but her limbs coiling about mine, entrapping me length against naked, sun-warmed length.

She slid her hand along my shoulder, caressing an old scar she knew was there and chuckling low in her throat in the way that had always seized me. I never knew another woman who laughed so much in bed. "Passion"—she murmured into my mouth between kisses—"is for the young."

"Bugger that." Ever since Judaea I had felt old, an aging man with nothing before me but regrets. But now I had fire in my veins instead of blood, and I could have conquered Parthia with nothing but a single sword. I could have raced my youngest daughter across the length of the Empire and won at a sprint. I could have strode out onto the sands of the Colosseum and taken on every champion my father had ever bested. I was Vercingetorix the Red, and I was no longer a dead man.

I buried my lips at the base of Sabina's throat in the spot that had always made her gasp, and she gasped now, her whole supple body arching around me as I slid home into sweet, familiar flesh. I knew her so well; I knew every inch of her skin as though it were my own. I'd had her more times than I could count; I'd loved her and hated her, wept with her and fought with her, but I had never stopped *wanting* her. I'd wanted her when I watched her writhe over Lucius as she threatened him; I'd wanted her in the perfumed and magical dark of Eleusis; I'd wanted her when she was a long-haired girl in her father's house. I'd wanted her when I was just a grubby slave brat first laying eyes on a pearled doll, wanted her without being old enough yet to know what I wanted her for. She was poison in my blood, poison so fire-sweet a man would be happy to die in it, right here in this green haze of vines under a blazing sun. My Empress.

She never stopped kissing me even as I moved in her, that sweet mouth drinking me savagely as though she could draw the soul out of me and into her own, and maybe she had. I made a noise against her mouth, half curse and half groan as I pulled her long thigh around me. "Hell's gates," I breathed, moving deep, moving slow. "What do you do to me?"

Her eyes in their lapis lines were an endless drowning blue. "I love you," she said against my lips. "I love you"—as the edge of pleasure rushed at us—"and you love me."

She said it again late that night in her chamber, the moon high in the sky and throwing silver shapes through the window across our tangled limbs and tangled fingers. She said it matter-of-factly, her sleek head tucked against my chest, and I laughed.

"Love never worked very well with us, did it?" I pointed out. "Always leaving each other for one reason or another—"

"Adventure." Kissing my chest. "Or ambition." Kissing my throat. "Or power, or war, or marriage." Kissing her way up toward my mouth. "Do you see any of those reasons here now, Vercingetorix?"

I pulled her over me, moonlit and beautiful. She wore nothing but the single garnet-and-silver earring I'd taken from my pouch and hung back beside her throat where it belonged. "I see you," I told her. "Empress of Rome and Annia's mother—and I'm not sure which is more impressive."

"And I see us two," Sabina said, giving an odd little inward smile. "At last I am just two, not three."

I cocked my head. "What does that mean?"

"It means I will not leave you again," Sabina said quietly. "Not for any reason, Vercingetorix. Hadrian gave me my life back, what there is left of it, and I swear by all the gods that I will share it with you."

CHAPTER 19

SABINA

A.D. 137, Six Months Later

"Can't you be the one to tell her?" Sabina begged. "I'm a coward."

"You're the Empress of Rome," Faustina said. "Act like it!"

"You're the one who should be Empress," Sabina muttered, and it took a whole half year's worth of bullying before Faustina wore her down. A half year of tending Hadrian's fevers and nosebleeds and going home to Vix's arms in private—watching Lucius Ceionius return from Pannonia, oddly thin and still coughing; hearing Hadrian complain about him—"He spends most of his time in the bathhouse trying to sweat out that cough! Does he think he can rule an empire from a sweating room?" Half a year, and Faustina had worked on her every day, never pestering, just tilting her head to one side in that charming way of hers and *insisting*. And somehow the Empress of Rome found herself standing in her emptied villa in a state of pure panic, waiting for her illicit daughter.

"I have stood before crowds of thousands," Sabina said aloud, pacing the length of the atrium. "I have traveled the wildest wastes of the Empire, I have marched in the blood of a conquering army, I have survived decades as Empress of Rome." Turning on her heel, pacing the other direction. "How is it possible that I am terrified by a mere *conversation*?"

"Who are you talking to, Lady?" Boil's voice came from behind. It had been Vix's idea for her to hire his old friend into her guard. "He's been struggling lately," Vix had said. "Says he'd rather eat his own spine than go back to Judaea. He'd guard you well, and keep our secrets, too." It had been a request she was happy to grant.

Sabina turned. "Has my niece arrived?"

"Saw her coming up through the vineyard at a good clip, Lady." Boil smiled. "And the villa's been emptied. The slaves were happy to get a day to themselves."

"Thank you." Sabina did not intend to have eavesdroppers. She'd have given Boil the afternoon away from the villa as well, but he refused. "I'm not leaving the Empress of Rome without a single guard," he said flatly. "Vix'd flay me alive."

A smile. Vix was here more days than not, and of course Boil knew why. They were discreet—even if Hadrian no longer paid any heed to his wife's bed or who slept there, Sabina saw no reason to cause gossip—but guards knew everything. Boil kept watch on the nights Vix stayed, to keep the other guards and slaves from knowing.

Annia came up the terrace, taking the steps two at a time. She wore a blue tunic tucked at the hips, and her breath puffed in the cold air. She snapped off a legionary's salute to Boil, the one Vix had taught her, and sailed into the atrium with a grin and a curtsy for Sabina. "You're alive!"

Sabina blinked, knocked off guard. "Was I supposed to be dead?"

"You haven't come to a single dinner party or public festival all summer *and* autumn," Annia said. "There's a rumor going about Rome that the Emperor had you chained up and is starving you to death. I'm glad he's not." Another curtsy.

Sabina nodded dismissal to Boil, repressing the urge to fidget. Vix hadn't been keen on Faustina's notion to bring their daughter into the secret. "The fewer who know the better! It's for her own safety."

"At the beginning," Sabina pointed out. "Hadrian was different then. Now I think if I told *him* he'd just blink and say, 'How careless of you.'"

"And you'd risk that?"

"No. But to tell Annia seems a risk worth taking. She's old enough to hold a secret, and she should know her own blood."

Vix had looked absolutely petrified. "I'll be there if you wish it," he gulped, "but Hell's gates, I'd rather charge a field of Parthian savages."

"I'll get her used to the idea," Sabina said with a kiss to the side of his neck. "And send her to talk to you afterward."

Now, looking at Annia's candid blue-gray eyes, Sabina wished she'd made Vix stay by her side.

"You've gotten me out of an afternoon at the theatre," Annia was saying, oblivious. "For which I thank you."

"You don't like the theatre?"

"I'd have to sit with my betrothed." Annia made a face. "And people stare at little Lucius and me, and they laugh. We look ridiculous."

"I doubt you'll ever have to marry him." Knowing she was stalling, Sabina sank down on a couch and indicated the other end for Annia. "Was there someone else you were thinking of? Hoping for?"

"Maybe." Annia flopped down, curling her long legs to one side. She avoided Sabina's gaze, her voice bleak. "But I can't have him, not if the Emperor wants otherwise. Girls don't usually get what they want, not when powerful men have other ideas."

"Oh, I don't know." Sabina found herself smiling. "I've usually found a way to get what I want, in one way or another."

"What did you want when you were my age?"

"Adventure. Travel. The world." And she'd gotten those things, if not quite in the way she'd imagined.

"And now?"

Vix. Vix giving her his tilted grin over a pillow, Vix's hard chest at her back through the night, vibrating heat as though his blood burned hotter than an ordinary man's . . . Just Vix.

Annia was still looking at her, quizzical. "What I want now," Sabina said, "is to tell you something—"

"Lady?" Boil's voice interrupted, apologetic. "A visitor to see you."

"I am not receiving visitors today."

"I told him, Lady, but he insisted upon waiting. Gnaeus Pedanius Fuscus Salinator."

"Tell him to return tomorrow." Sabina looked back to Annia, and saw an odd expression flit across that freckled face. "What?"

"What does Pedanius want with you?"

"He still wants to be Imperial heir instead of Lucius, of course. His grandfather has been on a rampage about it, with Lucius returning from Pannonia so ill. Pedanius probably hopes I will speak with the Emperor on his behalf."

Annia looked strangely stiff. "Will the Emperor—"

"No, he won't change the succession. At least not yet." Hadrian in his fading health was stubborn as an ox—"*I can hardly put Lucius aside because he coughs too much!*"

Something occurred to Sabina, and she looked at her daughter. "Pedanius isn't the one you have a liking for, is he? From what his grandfather once told me, he's quite infatuated with you." Pedanius wouldn't have been Sabina's first choice for her daughter—he was so twitchy and nervous now, and then there were his ruined looks. But Annia was hardly the kind of girl to reject a man just because his smile had been spoiled. "If you welcomed his suit, I might be able to suggest a betrothal—"

Annia erupted from the couch so violently she nearly fell over backward. "I'd rather eat a snake!"

Sabina rose. "I didn't mean to—"

"The Emperor isn't going to give me to *Pedanius*, is he?"

There was such blind panic on the girl's face, Sabina laid a hand on her shoulder. "No."

"Good." Annia's mouth pressed into a hard line, just like Vix when he was chewing on hatred. "I'd marry a little boy over that foul coward any day."

"What happened?" Sabina's prepared speech had fallen aside. "What's so terrible about Pedanius?"

"Never mind." Annia's shoulders rose and fell in a remarkably cynical shrug. "No one ever believes me."

"I will always believe you," Sabina said quietly. "Tell me."

Annia hesitated.

Sabina cupped her daughter's face in her hands. "Tell me," she repeated, and felt her heart thudding.

Another shrug. The casual shrug this time: Vix when he was about to underplay something. "Pedanius tried to rape me when I was twelve." So flat, so matter-of-fact. "I kicked him in the groin, so hard he—well, let's say he's half a eunuch, I kicked him so hard. And it got me out of trouble that day, but ever since, he's been swearing up and down that someday he'll be emperor and then he really *will* get to rape me. As many times as he wants."

A long pause.

"I see." Sabina fought to keep her voice even. "And you thought no one would believe you? That your *father* wouldn't believe you?"

"Oh, he'd have believed me," Annia acknowledged. "But he'd have tried to *do* something about it. Go to Servianus, and you know that old bastard—" She broke off, biting her lip. "I'm sorry, I shouldn't—"

"He is an old bastard. Go on."

"Well, *he'd* have just said I was a lying little harlot. And he'd go trumpeting his grandson's innocence to everyone, and they'd believe his version because he's a man. I'd be disgraced and so would my father, so . . ." Annia trailed off.

"I see." Sabina exhaled a sigh so slow and rage-filled that it was nearly motionless. "You could have come to me, however. Not only would I have believed you, I could have done something about it. It's one of the nice things about being Empress, Annia. You have guards who, if ordered, will haul someone out into a gutter and eviscerate him. No matter whose great-nephew he is."

Annia gave a crooked smile. "I was a little nervous of you back then."

"Not anymore, I hope."

"No, I think you're rather splendid."

Sabina wanted to pull her daughter into her arms, but Annia would just get irked and pull away scowling. Vix-like. She settled for dropping one fierce kiss on Annia's forehead and released her. "Well," she said, and struggled to keep her voice even. "You have no more need to fear that vicious gap-toothed bastard, I promise you that. Even if the Emperor *does* seek an heir to replace Lucius, I swear it will not be Pedanius."

"Good." Annia hesitated. "It's not just what happened to me, you know. People don't see what he is, because he's handsome and charming. Well, he used to be, anyway. But he can drop that charm like a mask and that's when he's bragging about the men he's killed—"

"Killed?"

"He was boasting." Annia wrinkled her nose. "He bragged he'd killed before, and he showed me a ring he took off a man's body as a prize, and said he'd get his hands bloody again if it would make him emperor."

Sabina felt her heart begin to pound, and for an entirely different reason. "Annia," she said, "did Pedanius say *who* he killed?"

"No." Annia looked scornful. "He's stupid, but he's not *that* stupid. He's careful never to say anything he can't deny. He's very good at not getting caught."

Dear gods—oh, dear gods . . . "This ring he showed you. What did it look like?"

"Just a ring. He hit Marcus with it—"

"Think, Annia. Any detail. Anything you remember."

Annia chewed her lip. "Gold," she said. "With a yellow stone? Not very large."

"It wouldn't be," Sabina said faintly. Because he didn't like gaudy baubles, so Hadrian had said, *"A topaz, then. The color of your eyes."*

Oh, dear gods.

"Aunt Sabina?"

The Empress found herself sitting on the end of the couch, her breath coming in short silent gasps, Annia's anxious hand on her shoulder.

Pedanius Fuscus.

"Aunt Sabina?"

Pedanius Fuscus.

Currently outside her atrium, waiting to speak with her.

Sabina looked up into Annia's worried young face. "My dear girl," she said, and managed a smile. "I had something to tell you today, but you ended up having something to tell me instead. Something far more important, so the chat I planned is going to have to wait. I want you to—"

"Aunt!" The impatient voice came at the end of the atrium, and Sabina saw the hatred prickle through Annia's whole body before she even saw the boy in his purple-bordered toga. "You'd keep your favorite great-nephew waiting?" Pedanius said, trying an ingratiating smile. His broken teeth looked like fangs.

Sabina rose, smoothing the folds of her *stola*. She turned her head to Annia, speaking very, very low. "Run home. Don't walk, run. Tell your father there is a ring that should have stayed on the hand of Antinous, and now I know where it is."

"But—" A glance at Pedanius, and a blanch of horror that Sabina hated to see on such a young face. "You mean—"

"By the time you come back," Sabina said even more softly, "he will be in shackles. Go, my love."

Another narrow look at Pedanius, and Annia was gone through the other end of the atrium. A flash of blue linen and russet hair—and Sabina turned back to her guest. To her husband's great-nephew, whom she had always rather liked. Whom she had saved from his beating, and carried home with a pillow beneath his head.

"Aunt," he said again, spreading his arms as though for an embrace as he came closer. "Why send Annia away? I have a few words for her—"

But Sabina stopped him in his tracks with an upraised palm. "Gnaeus Pedanius Fuscus Salinator," she said like a judge. "Did you push Antinous into the Nile?"

His arms dropped.

"Did you?" Sabina repeated.

He ran a tongue over his lips, and one foot tapped against the mosaics.

"Answer me," Sabina said coldly. "Did you kill Antinous?"

He shrugged, looking petulant. "Yes."

Sabina exhaled. Felt the prick of tears in her eyes—tears of relief? Of rage? She had no idea. "Why?"

Pedanius was pacing back and forth a little, eyeing her. "Not good," he muttered. "Not good . . ."

"You could say that." Sabina raised her voice. "Boil!"

"I didn't plan this," Pedanius said rapidly. "I was supposed to be here with you when the news came—innocent, you know. The dutiful heir with the Empress of Rome, it looks right, us together when the messenger arrives—you could be first to acclaim me—"

"News of *what?*" Sabina felt as though her skull were going to explode. "Acclaim you as *what?*"

"Emperor," Pedanius said, as though that were obvious. "It all happens today."

He was still pacing, little useless steps. Edging closer. Sabina stilled herself, nailing him with her eyes. "What. Happens. Today?"

"Everything." A vague wave of the hand. "I didn't count on this. On Annia . . ." Gnawing his lip, he looked like a little boy suddenly. "Whore," he muttered. "Doesn't matter, no one will believe her."

"I do. You knocked Antinous over the head, you took the ring from his hand, and you pushed him into the river. You showed Annia the ring. It was a ring I knew well. And if you think Hadrian will not have you killed, you are a fool as well as a murderer." Sabina raised her voice again. "*Boil!*"

"If you're calling for your guard," said Pedanius, "he's dead."

"I do not believe that for a moment." Vix's enormous, rock-hard right-hand man could never be taken down by a boy like this. "*Boil!*"

"He caught me eavesdropping." Pedanius hedged closer. "I was just hearing bits, but Annia was telling you about—well. I wish you hadn't sent her out, but I can find her later. She's not as important as she thinks she is." Another step. No one appeared in the doorway behind him. "I'm sorry, Aunt. I was just supposed to be sitting with you this afternoon, when the news arrived. I really was. You were supposed to be my witness."

"What did you do to my guard?" *My* only *guard.* The thought went through Sabina like a spike of ice. She had wanted an empty house to speak to Annia of her true parentage, a house where there would be no listening ears . . . And now there were no listening ears when she needed them so badly. "*Boil!*" she shouted again, but no huge comforting shape in Praetorian armor loomed between the columns.

"He said he'd lead me to the other atrium to wait. I got him in the neck, from behind." That was when Pedanius drew a dagger from the folds of his toga—a blade with a fancy gold-tooled hilt. Such a silly weapon, Sabina thought, to kill a man like Boil. A man who had survived three separate wars in three separate corners of the Empire, only to be killed by a boy with sweat on his upper lip and an overdecorated dagger.

A boy advancing on her, blade in hand. "I'm sorry," he said again, and sounded nervous. "You were supposed to live through it all. Blame that bitch Annia—"

Run. Sabina sent the thought after her daughter like an arrow. *Run like the wind, Annia. Because I can't.* She was no fleet young Amazon, and Pedanius would be on her like a cowardly dog the moment she showed him her back. Just as he'd done with Boil.

She put her chin up instead, stared him down. "So your plan has changed." Coldly. "You'll murder the Empress of Rome rather than escape what's coming to you?"

"Nothing's coming to me but the purple. As long as Hadrian doesn't find out. And he won't. He'll be dead first."

"You stupid child." Sabina loaded every word with scorn. "You might be able to kill a lone woman in an empty villa, but the Emperor will not be such an easy target. You think your little plot can get through all the layers that surround him?"

"I've got someone with him already." Pedanius threw it at her. "Someone he'll never suspect. He'll be dead before he hears a word about you."

"Who is with them?"

Pedanius smiled, but sweat ran down his face despite the cold. "I'm not telling you."

"*Who?*" A Praetorian who had been bribed? A slave with a smuggled sword? Emperor Domitian had been stabbed by a freedman with a dagger hidden in a false sling; Emperor Caligula by his own Praetorians. If some bribed killer got close enough, what would they find? Hadrian, sick at heart and sick of body, retreated into the inner sanctum of his villa like an old tortoise pulled into its shell. A bitter, aging man wrapped in furs: an easy target.

Pedanius came a step closer. Sabina gazed at him unblinking.

"Who have you bribed to kill the Emperor?"

Pedanius swallowed, raising the dagger and leveling it at her. "Don't look at me."

"Will it be poison for him? Or the sword?"

"Shut your eyes."

"If you want to kill me, child, you'll have to do it as I watch."

"I said, stop looking at me—"

"*No.*" Sabina snapped her voice like a whip as she advanced, stalking him until she could feel the dagger's tip prick through the silk of her *stola*, right over the heart. She grabbed the blade roughly, redirected the point higher to the bare flesh above her breast and below the shoulder. Squeezed the blade's edge until it bit into her flesh, and did not let go. "You fell on Antinous from behind, and Boil too, but I refuse to make it easy for you. You look me in the eye while you kill me, you murdering little *coward.*"

She stared at him with eyes of ice. Pedanius's gaze wavered. She could feel the blade quiver, feel blood begin to seep through her fingers from the edge. For a moment she thought she had won, that he would fall to his knees at her feet. That she could take the dagger from him, bind him, run to warn Hadrian of the danger that stalked within his own villa—

Then Pedanius Fuscus gave a watery little sigh, and he pushed the blade through her fingers. Pushed it home.

VIX

"Father!"

I heard the pounding of footsteps coming up through the gardens, and Annia's voice calling. "*Father!*"

I'm here, I thought, and swallowed hard. She'd come back from Sabina's villa sooner than I thought.

Annia came flying into the atrium and skidded to a halt, hair flying all about her. Just the sight of her made my heart squeeze. My daughter filled me with the sort of foolish urges that usually assail fathers with their first children, not their last. I'd missed so much of her life, and now I wanted to buy her jewelry, teach her how to form a proper fist, tell her to drop her hems lower because she kilted them far too short for my liking when she went running. Mostly I restrained myself, because in the eyes of the world Titus was her father, and he'd stay that way even if Annia knew I had sired her. Sabina and I made her, but we hadn't raised her—and I wouldn't encroach on that.

I rose, marshaling soothing words if she was angry, comforting words if she cried—but her eyes passed across me. "Where's my father?"

Whatever Sabina had planned to say, she hadn't said it. Part of me felt relieved at my reprieve.

Annia groaned. "They're all at the theatre, why did I forget!" She dropped a string of curses that would have done any legionary proud. "We need to send a message to my father, he has to come *back*—or I need Marcus, oh, gods be damned, Marcus is with the Emperor at the villa—"

"What's happened?" My daughter's face was bone-white and deadly serious.

"Pedanius Fuscus," she said, gripping my arm, and there was a spill of words. Pedanius and Sabina and Antinous, and something incoherent about a ring. "I didn't want to leave Aunt Sabina, not alone with Pedanius—"

I didn't understand her panic. "Sabina could flay that little pustule with a glance."

"But she asked me about the ring from the man he said he killed, she said—"

"Besides," I added. "She has guards. One guard, anyway."

"Yes, and he'll seize Pedanius, but the *ring*, she said to tell my father—"

Annia's worry was starting to infect me. "Did you see Boil? A big Gaul—"

That was when Annia flung her head back and let out an earsplitting shriek. "*Would you shut up!*" she roared. "*Pedanius Fuscus murdered Antinous, and the Empress knows it!*"

The silence after that was deafening.

"Antinous?" I whispered, my heart suddenly a crushed and frozen thing still trying to beat in my chest.

"Antinous," Annia said. "I don't know *why*, I don't know anything, but Aunt Sabina does. She knows it all somehow. Because of the ring

Marcus and I saw, the one Pedanius showed us when he boasted that he'd killed before." Her hand tightened around my arm, only to jerk away a moment later. Because I was running, yelling for Titus's grooms. "My horse!" I shouted, because it would get us there faster than a run on foot across the vineyards. I was in the saddle in an ungainly scramble, Annia flying up behind me, and I kicked the mare into a gallop before I felt her arms lock about my waist. We were flying along the road toward Sabina's front gates, breath puffing cold on the winter air, and it still wasn't fast enough for me.

"He'll be in shackles by the time we get there," Annia panted behind me, "you'll see—" but I wasted no breath on words. Sabina's front gates loomed, the rise of marble steps behind, and I came off the horse in a leap. I took the steps up into the villa four at a time, and the mangled place in my chest was trying to expand. *Antinous. Antinous.* My son, not dead of his own hand after all. Sabina had been right—he had been murdered. Just not by the hand we supposed.

My son's name beat in me like a drum, until I came to the wide atrium where I'd spent so many quiet evenings with Sabina this past summer. We'd sat laughing in each other's arms night after night, but I wasn't laughing now. Because Boil lay on the step just outside, facedown in his Praetorian armor, one massive arm with its leather-capped stump outflung. His other fist was curled about the hilt of his *gladius*. He'd managed to do that much, before succumbing to the neat little stab wound down into the back of his neck.

"Dear gods," Annia whispered.

Boil. Boil my second, Boil the last of my *contubernium*, dead on the mosaics with his eyes glazed over, but I was already springing across his still body. Up through the pillars of the atrium, seeing the pool, seeing the gray winter light through the open roof, and I saw her. My Sabina.

She was on her knees, slumped against the couch. Her sleek head was bowed and her hands pressed against her own breast. She wore the single garnet-and-silver earring that had been her gift to me and then mine back to her when I reclaimed her, and it trembled against her throat. Her blue silks gleamed sapphire in the light from the roof, except where they were stained by blood. Because she knelt in blood, a lake of blood, a sea of blood spreading on the mosaics around her. So much blood, a pulsing ribbon of it coursing dark and fast from under her hands, from her breast down the length of her slim trembling body to the floor.

She looked up, and I saw the stark whiteness of her face, her blue eyes gone blank and dizzy with pain. "Oh," she breathed, and her hands fell away from the wound and reached for me, narrow hands painted scarlet, and I caught her before she fell into the lake of her own blood. I caught her and turned her against me, moving somehow even when my mind was one long howl.

It was Annia who howled, who flung herself forward reaching for her mother and shrieking like a fury. She looked like a fury, hair flying out around her like snakes, hands curled like claws, face stretched with a rage too great for curses, a rage I understood because I felt it too. But I'd ridden the crest of so much rage in my life, I knew how to shove it back to a place where it wouldn't harm anyone until it was needed. I reached out and slapped Annia across the side of the head even as I was lowering Sabina to the floor.

Her roar cut off. She sat back on her heels in the blood, staring at me, tears springing to her eyes, and I was already snapping orders. "Get me cloth, curtains, anything, and then see if there's a slave *anywhere*, a groom, a page—" Annia sprinted into the next room, leaving bloody footprints behind her, and I tore Sabina's gown open to see the wound and she was trying to grip my hands in her blood-slippery ones.

"Pedanius—" she said, or I thought she was saying. Her voice was a thready blur. "Fuscus—"

"Breathe, don't speak, just breathe—" Hell's gates, so much blood! Her gown ran dark with it. *Not Sabina*, something in my head was screaming, *not my Empress*, but I had no time for screaming. She was clawing at my hands trying to get me to listen.

"Pedanius—"

"Pedanius Fuscus killed Antinous." Annia's voice, tear-clogged but swift as she crashed to her knees beside me with an armload of cloth, a huge heavy drape she'd ripped off a couch or a doorway. "We know he killed Antinous. We will tell the Emperor—"

"Hadrian—" Sabina was trying to swallow. Why couldn't she swallow? The pulse in her throat was fast and light under my bloody hands, like a panicked bird's. "*Hadrian—*"

"We'll tell him," Annia said desperately. "Pedanius will never get away with it—"

"*Hadrian,*" Sabina was insisting. I could see her eyes wandering, fighting for focus. She was trying so hard, and I was swabbing at her breast with a fistful of clean cloth, trying to see the wound. "Not the lung," I told her, "not the heart, either. Far too high—he missed—"

"Panicked," Sabina said, the word coming so clear I could see it all. She lifted her hands and I saw slashes across her fingers—she'd fought him, maybe seized the blade, and she must have deflected the *gladius* over her breast rather than through it. The blade had gone through high, punching all the way through her back, and then he'd tried a second time and got her in the shoulder. Two wounds straight through, four places for blood to leave her body—

"Pedanius might have panicked and run, but he still thinks he killed her." Annia's voice tumbled. "How can he think he'll get away with it, when he knows I saw him here? When the Emperor finds out—"

"*Hadrian,*" Sabina said again, and her whole body arched up against my arm in urgency. "*Villa.*" I looked into her pleading eyes, those blue eyes I knew so well. "*Another.*"

"Someone's already at the villa," I guessed frantically, "trying for Hadrian? Another plotter?"

Sabina's bloody fingertips fluttered against my chest with even more urgency.

"Today? Someone is there *now?*"

Her head drooped in a nod, and kept right on drooping.

"Who? Sabina, *who?*"

But Sabina couldn't tell me that. Maybe she didn't know or maybe she just couldn't say it, because she was going from me, falling down the dark well, slipping away. "No," I snarled, and I was wrapping her in cloth by the arm's-length, strapping her wounds in layers, anything to close those four gaping holes in her body. She went limp against me, the bloodied silver of her earring swaying against my fingers. "No," I breathed, "no, not you, *not you*—" Her eyes had fallen closed, but my wet scarlet fingers still found a rise and fall in her ravaged breast.

The villa could have fallen down around me and I wouldn't have heard. I ripped at the pile of cloth for more bandages, striking Annia away as she reached to help me. "Warn Hadrian," I rapped out. "He has to be warned, he could be killed at any moment—"

"But Pedanius is *finished*. Even if he has a guard or slave bribed to kill the Emperor, we'll know he was the one who—"

"He doesn't know that!" I lifted Sabina's limp form. The floor looked like a butcher's yard. "You're the only one who knows, and he thinks you're a stupid girl who can be dealt with later. He didn't know you'd come find me. If his man at the villa isn't stopped, the Emperor dies."

Hadrian, Sabina had whispered. *Hadrian*. Maybe the last word I'd ever hear on her lips, and I had a spasm of hatred for the Emperor. He got everything, maybe even the last moment of Sabina's life.

But if Hadrian died, God only knew what would happen. That bitter old bastard was all we had, the wall holding out the bloodshed like those white walls he built in Britannia to keep out the chaos.

"He'll never believe me," Annia was arguing, her voice rising in blind panic. "I'm just a child to him, you should be the one to warn him—"

"*Do you know how to bind a sword wound?*" I shouted. "*I stay with your mother!*"

Annia didn't even hear my slip of the tongue. She was shouting over me, "But the Emperor won't listen to a word out of my mouth! If I had my father, if I had Marcus—" That was when my daughter stopped, blood draining from her face. "Oh gods, Marcus is *with* him. He went to give the Emperor his report as Prefect of the City—"

"Then he might die too." I had Sabina in one arm, but I managed to unbuckle my sheathed *gladius* and slap it hilt-first into Annia's hand. "Take this, get on my horse, and carry warning to the Emperor. *Make* him hear you."

"Vix—" Annia took a step toward me, clutching my sword. A girl, just a girl in a blue dress, wide-eyed and bloody-kneed and so young. My daughter.

I rose fast and hard, so fast she recoiled from me. "*Annia*," I roared, and her eyes flickered over the blood on my hands, the body lying limp at my feet. "*Annia, run!*"

And Annia runs. So fast, just a streak of blue fading away from me, and I wonder, *Can she outrun death?* Because if she can't, if she fails to carry the warning in time, an empire falls. You'd think the fate of the Eternal City would depend on someone like me, a warrior with bloody hands and a bloody sword. But it will rise or fall on a woman—and maybe it always does.

There are hoofbeats outside, and then I am alone. Alone with the woman I have loved all my life, more than my life. More than Rome, and she is white and waxen and slipping away from me. "Sabina," I whisper, going to my knees in her blood and tearing at her bandages again. "Hell's gates, do not leave me now."

ANNIA

Eighteen miles, Annia thought as she flew down the steps in her bare, bloodstained feet. *Eighteen miles to the Emperor's villa.* An hour's ride at a gallop—surely no more— She hauled herself into the saddle, slung Vix's *gladius* across her back, and banged her heels into the mare.

She nearly fell off on the first lunging stride, clinging to handfuls of mane as the horse bolted down the road. Dear gods, why had she never learned to ride a horse? Because girls of good birth didn't *ride* horses, they rode in litters or in covered palanquins with cushions, but why hadn't she learned anyway? She'd never before been stopped from doing things just because they weren't *done*. But she'd always preferred her own two feet to take her anywhere she wanted to go, not four hooves that bounced and jolted and sent her teeth crashing together with every rattling stride—

She reached the road, hooves ringing on stone rather than dirt.

Eighteen miles down the road to the Emperor's villa outside Tibur. Just eighteen miles.

Marcus, she thought. Marcus who smelled of linen and ink, of wax for writing tablets and the mint he liked to chew. He'd have begun this morning with a mint infusion, worrying over his diction and his declamation as he went to make his report to the Emperor, never dreaming that the afternoon would bring horror and conspiracy and a lake of blood. Just as Annia had begun the morning with a lighthearted dash across the vineyard because her Imperial aunt wished to speak with her.

Whoever Pedanius had poised to strike at the Emperor—would they kill Marcus, too? She could see him lying limp like Empress Sabina, face gray-white as this winter sky, eyes glazed and dead—

No. Annia flung the word at the Fates like a spear. No one would die today. Not Marcus, not the Emperor, not even Aunt Sabina lying so pale and blood-spent on the floor. Vix would fight off Charon the Ferryman himself if he came in his long black barge for the Empress, and Annia would save Marcus and Emperor Hadrian both.

Marcus.

No. Don't think of him. Just the road ahead.

Marcus—

No. Road.

It was the road that brought her down. A rut between the stones that caught the mare's hoof and sent her stumbling to her knees. Annia went flying as though she'd been fired from a bow. She was rolling as soon as she hit the ground, gasping with pain and gasping for breath. *Please*, she prayed, staggering to her feet and clutching for the *gladius* before it could slide from its scabbard, *please let the mare not be lamed!* And that was the prayer the gods decided to answer, because the mare most definitely wasn't lamed; the mare had recovered her balance, veered off the road, and was now galloping across a field of weeds. Annia shouted, but the mare was headed for her stables or for Rome or for damned *Carthage* for all Annia knew, and she was going there far faster than even Annia could run. One flip of the tail and the mare disappeared into a line of scraggly trees.

And Annia looked all around her.

The winter road was utterly empty. Not a way station in sight—and there wouldn't be one for twenty miles at least, because she remembered Marcus droning on about road systems and how each traveling station was spaced precisely a day's journey apart. Not a farmhouse or a shack to be seen. Nothing at all, perhaps, between her and the Emperor's villa but twelve miles of road. According to the mile markers, she had come only a third of the way.

She looked down at her bare feet. Long, strong, capable feet. Muddy, still splashed with the Empress's dried blood. She stretched them, going up to her toes slowly and back down. "Twelve miles," she said aloud. "Just my daily run."

Three times over.

She shook her hair out of her eyes and began to run.

SABINA

Save me.

When Sabina was a child, she'd suffered from fits of epilepsia. "Like Julius Caesar," her father had said, trying to cheer her, "so you see you're in good company." But the fits had not felt like a blessing. Her head would clamp, and her vision would shatter into a thousand pieces, and before the fog descended and her father tried to cushion her fall, she would have time for a silent cry of *Save me!*

She had been stabbed through the breast. She remembered the blade going through her, very clearly—but this still felt more like a fit of epilepsia than a wound. The shattering of consciousness, the fog claiming her mind and her vision, the dimly felt panic as loving hands cushioned her.

Save me.

Someone *had* saved her—Sabina remembered that. She had not had a fit of epilepsia since she was twelve; she'd been cured by that oldest of remedies, a gladiator's blood painted on her lips and on her temples. Vix's blood, a boy gladiator freshly wounded from his first bout. Even when they were children, the Fates had tied their lives together. Vix had saved her.

Save me now, my love.

Her head hurt. How did her head hurt more than her torn and bleeding body? Hurt like the old fits, reality flying away in shards. Shards that would cut you if you tried to gather them; Sabina remembered that. Never stopped her from trying. You could see things in those shards, disjointed things, things that made sense if you could only remember them afterward. She never remembered.

Save me.

Disjointed images, and she didn't know if they were dreams she saw or just flitting shards of glass. A riderless mare cantering over a field. Hadrian laughing—"Well put, young Verissimus! Tell me more"— while a bent figure in a toga looked disapproving; she knew that stoop-shouldered figure, who was it? But the image was gone. Emperor Domitian was dying in a room full of blood and moonstone, then it was Trajan gasping his last on a rocky island, and now it was Hadrian's turn. But he couldn't die yet; they had to warn him, and Sabina wanted to scream as she saw Hadrian's fingers drumming against his chair and a man's voice saying, "Some wine to take into your bathhouse, Caesar?"

"I will finish telling Marcus about my Parthian days, first—" came the absent response. And a gnarled hand cradled a vial under a fold of toga, but now that image was gone, too. A girl came next, a girl running like the wind, and she turned into Vix at thirteen, circling on arena sand. The boy Vix became the man, cradling her in his bloodied arms. "Sabina, Hell's gates, don't leave me now—"

Then save me, she thought, but the world was going away.

ANNIA

Twelve miles. Twelve miles of hell.

Annia ran through the afternoon, legs flashing, hair flying. Ran too fast at first, her heart pumping panic and Marcus's name pulsing through her with every step. She tried to pace herself, but her steps kept speeding until she was flying, sprinting down a line of winter-bare poplars. She might have sprinted herself blind and crippled but she tripped in a rut just like the mare, went down on her knees and scraped them both so badly the blood ran down her shins. She screamed, more from fury than from pain, and her galloping heart caught up with her and she vomited into the bone-white dust. Her stomach jerked until there was nothing left in it, and she screamed again, a challenge of pure rage to the Fates. "*Why?*" she shrieked, and the ravens went flying up from the leafless poplars, and there was no other answer. She swiped an arm across her soured mouth and started running again, and this time she paced the miles off one by one, baring her gritted teeth at every new marker.

A cart will come, she thought at first. *A messenger.* She could see the messenger so clearly, an Imperial courier on a fleet horse, carrying a bag of those endless dispatches constantly being sent from Rome to the secluded Emperor. The messenger would halt at her hail, and the rest of the journey would disappear in a flash. But no courier stopped. She saw three that afternoon, galloping past on their fast horses, and she screamed at them but they didn't stop. *Bastards*, she thought, *you oblivious bastards*, and kept running alone, Vix's sheathed blade bouncing against her back. So few people traveled in this time of flat, short-lived days before Saturnalia. There was a wagon with a pair of drovers who whooped at the sight of her, but she flashed past before they could scramble down. After a while she stopped craning her eyes to see if there was anyone else on the road, because they were shades slipping into the past, choking on the dust from her flying feet.

Fourth mile marker. Mouth burning, but there was no water, not until Annia caught a glimpse of brackish puddles gleaming in a plowed field. She flung herself on them, drinking what little there was straight from the earth. Annia Galeria Faustina the Younger, daughter of one of the richest men in Rome, niece to the Emperor, drinking from a puddle. She looked down at herself, covered in mud as well as blood and dust, and kept running.

Six miles. Her feet were bleeding. Marcus's name kept going through her like a sword, making a cadence she tried to pace her feet to. The pain had shifted from her feet to her knees, throbbing with every step.

Eight miles. Twice her usual run; another still to go. *I will never make it.* She knew that in her bones; she was weaving all over the road. *Don't fall, you weak girl.* Her stomach roared, and she let herself hobble a few paces. Throat burned. *I will never make it.* She kept running.

Tenth mile marker. Something Vix had said over the Empress's limp body. *I stay with your—* But Annia hurt too much to pull the rest of his words into her mind, and they went slipping away.

Eleventh mile.

The first buildings appearing—the turnoff toward the vast complex that was the Emperor's villa. The outlying buildings; the Praetorian barracks, the slave quarters. Annia stopped, gasping, pain knifing down each thigh, hair lying in sodden strands across her sweat-soaked back. She'd long since stopped feeling the cold. How long had she been running?

Forever. Forever and a day, and she still wasn't there yet.

She lurched into motion again. The last mile, up the long terraced rise toward the crown of marble that was Hadrian's massive domicile. The earth pulling on her feet with every step; a boulder sitting on each shoulder—oh gods, her *knees*—but the green of the gardens stretched ahead . . .

"You, girl!" An imperious freedman put out a hand, but Annia shoved past. She had run twelve miles in well under two hours, judging from the sun's slant; she was not stopping now. The grounds ahead stretched flat, the killing incline finally leveling out, and she was suddenly flying. She aimed for the Emperor's private quarters, that tiny islanded villa at the center of the whole nest of temples and gardens and audience chambers. That was where Marcus had said he was summoned to make his report. Her legs flashed beneath her, her feet screaming relief to be running on grass rather than stone, and she flung it all into this last sprint. Praetorians stood like pillars around the tiny moated villa, spear-heavy, frowning. "The Emperor," Annia shouted with the last breath she had, "the *Emperor*—" She gathered herself for the wooden bridge spanning the moat, but a heavy hand seized her arm and brought her up in a violent yank. Sparkles of pain shot down her scalp as the guard seized her sweat-soaked hair and snapped her head back. "Where do you think you're going, girl?"

"The Emperor," she gasped, "there is a plot against the Emperor—I am his *niece*—"

But she didn't look like an emperor's niece, she looked like a beggar woman, and the Praetorian just chuckled. "And I'm Queen Cleopatra."

Annia pivoted around the grip turning her elbow numb, bringing her free fist up in a clip that glanced off the guard's forehead. "Let me *go*—"

The chuckles stopped, and her knees hit the marble with a slam that brought a howl of agony surging up her throat into the gate of her clenched teeth. A guard wrenched Vix's *gladius* off her back. "Come for the Emperor armed, and you think we'll let you through?"

The *gladius* was gone, and she had a hand at each elbow wrenching her arms out of her sockets and dragging her away, but Annia filled her lungs and screamed, "Marcus!"

Dear gods, please let him be alive.

Silence from the tiny moated villa, and for one horrific moment Annia envisioned him dead already, slumped beside Emperor Hadrian with a knife in his heart or poison curdling his veins. Dead, dead, and all her speed wasted.

"MARCUS!"

And he was there, coming quick and alarmed out of the tiny *tablinum*, tall and straight in his immaculate toga, which did not have one drop of blood on it. Not one, and Annia released a sob of relief. And then, joy. Because the Emperor was coming out behind him, Emperor Hadrian who had obviously been preparing for his bath because he was barefoot and stripped to a tunic. The Emperor, very irritated and very, very alive. "What is the meaning of this?" he demanded, and Annia saw herself as he must see her: a tall girl slumped between two Praetorians, made unrecognizable by mud and blood, lower than the lowest dirty slave in this entire gracious villa.

"Just a half-mad slave girl, Caesar," one of the guards began, but Annia straightened as much as she could while hanging between them, and summoned Sabina's Empress voice. That imperious ring of steel that could drop grown men to their knees. "I am your niece, Caesar, and I have come to bear witness to a plot against your life. Enacted by Gnaeus Pedanius Fuscus Salinator."

"Absurd!" another voice harrumphed before the Emperor could do more than look puzzled, and Annia's breath froze in her exhaustion-withered throat. Ancient Servianus, wizened as a turtle in his toga and waving an agate wine cup, came stumping out of the *tablinum* behind the Emperor—and he was leaning on the arm of his grandson. Pedanius's eyes met Annia's across the narrow moat that the Emperor had filled with Nile water in memory of his beloved. And Antinous's killer blanched white.

"The girl slanders my grandson," Servianus was trumpeting, and somehow Annia was being marched across the wooden footbridge by one of the Praetorians who still held her by the elbows. "She may come from a noble family but she is a known whore and liar—"

"It's true," Pedanius said quickly, eyes still darting over Annia in disbelief. Marcus was staring at her too, but she couldn't rip her eyes from Pedanius, his hair glinting in the sunlight, his immaculate toga with its touches of Imperial purple. The same one he'd worn when Annia saw him enter her aunt's atrium—dear gods, could it only be a few short hours ago? Not a drop of blood on him. Annia saw a sick flash of Empress Sabina clutching at her ravaged breast, and felt a wave of hatred so strong she nearly vomited. *I will rip you apart with my bare hands*, she had time to howl inside the furious confines of her own skull, even as another panicked part of her was shrieking, *Why, why is he here?* His plan had been to wait a safe distance away as the Emperor was killed, wait in conspicuous innocence for the news to arrive.

But the plan had gone wrong, and of course Pedanius wouldn't have a plan in reserve. He'd just go running to the villa in a panic to see if Hadrian was dead yet. See if his grandfather had killed the Emperor. Because of course it was Servianus. Just because a man was ancient and withered didn't mean he couldn't kill.

But Hadrian wasn't dead. Somehow he was still alive—and he was listening, however impatiently, as Annia was dragged to stand before him. "Caesar," she said, and she swayed in her exhaustion like a spear-shot gazelle, but she had to make him believe her. "Caesar, I come from the Empress. Pedanius Fuscus has already made an attempt on her life, and now he has come to—"

"I have been here with you, Caesar," Pedanius interrupted quickly. "I joined you and my grandfather while cousin Marcus here was making his report!" He clapped Marcus on the shoulder as though they were the best of friends. "Forgive me, but your niece lies. She has hated me ever since I refused to consider marrying such a dishonest slut, and she seeks to slander me—"

"I am not lying!" Annia shouted, even as Marcus said quietly, "She doesn't lie." But Servianus was thundering again, and the other Praetorian was presenting the Emperor with Vix's *gladius*—"She came armed, Caesar"—and Pedanius was protesting his innocence at the top of his voice. "The ring," Annia tried to shout, "he has Antinous's *ring*, he killed Antinous—" but they drowned her out with their noisy outrage. Marcus was trying to defend her, and the Emperor was tapping his foot and clearly ready to have them all tossed out of his presence. Annia could have sobbed with fury. It was all for nothing: Pedanius Fuscus and his hateful grandfather stood there impeccable and virtuous in their pristine togas, and she was a filthy, lying barbarian of a girl. She might have unmanned Pedanius Fuscus, but she would never beat him—because the Emperor would never believe her.

Make him listen, Vix had said.

The Praetorian's grip on her arm had loosened. She was the Emperor's niece, even if she was a lying slut, and he didn't want to hold her too roughly. Besides, she was just a girl, and girls were no threat to anyone. She tore her elbow out of his hands and made a desperate lunge, barreling past Servianus. He reached for her and she batted him aside, knocking the agate wine cup from his hand and hearing it shatter on the marble. Twelve miles she had run, and yet it was the final twelve feet that mattered. Annia summoned the last breath in her chest, the last burst of strength in her body, the last drop of speed in her blood, and flung herself at Pedanius Fuscus. The Praetorians snatched at her, Servianus stretched out his arm, Pedanius twisted to get away, but they were all too slow. She came at him like a burst of desert wind and rammed the heel of her hand toward his broken mouth. Even as he dodged, her other hand darted snake-quick for the pouch at his waist. She tore it loose and hurled it toward the Emperor in one fluid motion. And prayed.

Please let him still have the ring.

The pouch seemed to fall slowly, bouncing at the Emperor's feet. It fell, disgorging a rattle of small things: a few sesterces, a token for the bathhouse, a whetstone . . .

And a gold ring with a gleaming topaz.

Everything seemed to stop at the sight of that ring. Pedanius Fuscus opened his mouth, but his voice choked in his throat. Servianus's ancient wattles quivered. Annia flung her head back and stared at the Emperor, her chest heaving like a bellows . . . And Hadrian stared, slowly turning wax-pale. He was still holding Vix's *gladius*, which the Praetorians had stripped from Annia, but now he passed it to Marcus standing beside him and bent to gather the ring into his cupped hands. Annia had never heard such a silence.

Marcus broke it. "Caesar," he said, and his voice was cool and quiet. "By the name Verissimus, the nickname of Truthful One which you yourself gave me, I bear witness that Pedanius Fuscus showed me that ring and swore he killed the man who wore it."

"And I bear witness as well," Annia rasped before Pedanius could ever, *ever* drown her out again. She strode forward over the lake of spilled wine from Servianus's shattered cup, feeling the broken shards cut into her lacerated feet, but the pain was nothing. She crushed the broken pieces underfoot, striding blood-shod toward the Emperor, where she went to her knees before him. And somehow—around the roar of agony through her lungs and her feet and her whole pain-racked body—she found the right words. The words to make an emperor listen. "I bear witness for Empress Sabina, who this moment lies bleeding at the hand of Pedanius Fuscus, that this ring belonged to Antinous."

Hadrian's eyes dragged slowly from the ring. Annia could see the burning weight of his gaze like a heap of red-hot stones, as his head turned slowly toward his great-nephew.

Pedanius let out a snarl and made a panicked lunge. *To flee,* Annia thought from her knees, but he lunged toward Hadrian, not away. His hand flashed beneath his toga's folds, and she saw the dagger appear in his fist. A dagger with a blood-dark blade, Empress Sabina's blood dried to crusted streaks, and it scythed toward Hadrian. One lunge—perhaps Pedanius still thought he could win it all if he just swung fast enough. Perhaps he thought it was still possible: Emperor Gnaeus Pedanius Fuscus Salinator.

But the Praetorians shouted, yanking the Emperor back out of reach, thrusting their armored bodies in front of him, and Marcus darted forward to intercept the blood-dried *gladius*. "*Marcus*," Annia screamed, trying to scramble to her feet, but her legs finally failed her, gave out useless and spent. She would never reach him, and the blade was coming down, and Pedanius's face was a rictus scream of hatred. For the Emperor, or maybe just for the rival who had taken so much from him: the Salian priesthood, Hadrian's favor, Annia herself.

Marcus unsheathed Vix's *gladius* in one motion and brought it up in a swift ring of steel on steel. Annia had time to think how slight he looked against Pedanius's overbearing bulk, and the bright blade slid away, disengaging from the blood-dark one and coming back in a short thrust. The Emperor himself had noted that Marcus had a quick wrist.

He spitted the would-be Emperor high between chest and shoulder. The same place Pedanius had stabbed Sabina.

Pedanius looked down at the blade, and the expression on his face matched his grandfather's: utter disbelief. Surely the gods would never allow any harm to come to the golden boy, the prince of Rome, the future Emperor. Neither of them believed it, even when Pedanius stumbled two steps backward and lost his balance on the marble lip, falling with a splash into the Nile-green waters of the moat.

Only then did he scream.

Praetorians were jumping down into the water, Servianus was screeching something, and Hadrian limped forward, but Annia had eyes only for Marcus. He was standing like a granite statue, bloodied sword in hand, staring at the blood spreading in the roiling water. He looked numb, horrified, dumbfounded, and all at once he flowed to his knees. Annia crawled to him, putting her arms around his neck. He clung to her, his breath warm against her cheek, but his hands ice-cold. And he never let go of the *gladius*.

"I love you," she whispered as they rocked back and forth on the lip of the moat, the world exploding around them in bloody confusion. Annia shut her eyes. Her body was empty of everything but pain and racked by violent shivers; she was suddenly freezing cold and felt every muscle stab like an individual blade—but Marcus was alive inside her arms. He was gripping her so hard she hurt even more, but that didn't matter. She could have died right there, closed her eyes and happily just died.

"Caesar!" The harsh shout of a Praetorian, grating against Annia's ears. "Caesar, what do you want to do with this one?"

Annia felt Marcus shudder in her arms. They both looked up to see Pedanius Fuscus sagging in the water between two Praetorians, blood coursing down his chest. He suddenly looked like a child to Annia's eyes—bewildered, wet, no more dangerous than a half-drowned rat. Yet he had almost killed the Emperor. Might have killed Empress Sabina. *And we know he killed—*

"Antinous." The Emperor's voice was husky. He was still gazing at the topaz ring in his hand.

The Praetorian waist-deep in the water shook Pedanius back and forth like a bundle of bloody rags. "He'll live if we bandage him, Caesar. Long enough for a cell and a sword."

Servianus moaned, crashing to his knees. Pedanius stared up at the Emperor, chin quivering. He let out a choked sob, but Annia could not summon one drop of pity. *You killed Antinous*, she wanted to scream, still shuddering with that paralyzing cold, and now that Marcus and Hadrian were safe, her mind was full of the golden boy she had loved since she was a child. *You killed Antinous.*

"Why?" said the Emperor, and Annia thought it too. *Why?*

Pedanius opened his mouth, but the only thing to come out from between his broken teeth was a line of spittle as he hunted for words. "Grandfather wanted it," he finally said, and Servianus let out another moan. "And I—I didn't like that Bithynian he-bitch. He was just a whore, and he swatted me on the ear like a slave. I was supposed to be *Emperor*, and he—" It occurred to Pedanius all over again that he was never going to be Emperor now, and the tears started running down his cheeks.

Now he believes it, Annia thought, and still she felt no pity. Even as she watched him weep.

"Shall I haul him out, Caesar?" the Praetorian asked. Pedanius sobbed, and his grandfather clasped his gnarled hands and began begging for mercy. Annia looked up at the Emperor, at those deep-set eyes glittering with tears. Looked at the extraordinary mix of hatred and grief, vindication and vengeance that rippled over that immobile face.

"Drown him," said Hadrian.

A fierce shudder went through Annia as the guards thrust Pedanius screaming and struggling down into the water of the Nile. He managed a final scream, and then his madly jerking head was thrust under the surface. Servianus was tearing at his own hair, mouth working in soundless agony. Annia felt her muscles spasm in a violent jerk as she watched, not knowing if it was relief or disgust, joy or plain exhaustion. All she knew was that she could not look away. *I owe him that,* she thought, though she couldn't say which *he* she meant. The dead and beautiful Antinous? The enemy who had told her to get on her knees and call him Caesar? Caesar himself, or Marcus, who held her so desperately tight?

All of them, Annia thought.

Pedanius thrashed a long time. Annia felt nausea rise like poison in her throat, but she never looked away, nor did anyone else. They all watched, until Pedanius stilled in the water. Until the guards turned him over, showing his vacant, water-bloated face, and the Emperor gave a great sob. "My star," he whispered, "oh, my star!"

And Annia saw twilight's first star reflected in the dead eyes of Antinous's killer.

CHAPTER 20

VIX

Rome was awash with rumor and revelation. The Emperor's great-nephew had been executed. The Emperor's brother-in-law had been arrested. The Empress of Rome was dead.

How I had wept, these past four days.

Four days—that was all it took for the word to spread through the Eternal City. And the reckoning was not nearly done yet. The city trembled, waiting for Hadrian's vengeance, every goose-necked, pale-livered senator going to ground and waiting for the bodies to mount.

My eyes burned, and so did my heart.

It was a strange tribunal that gathered under the half-domed vault of the Canopus. In the center, the massive statue of Antinous, his curly head bowed, his marble lips curved in a smile, painted with such wondrous lifelike delicacy that he seemed ready to step off his flower-massed plinth. To one side of him stood five of us arrayed like judges. Titus, stern-faced in a purple-bordered toga; Faustina at his side, jeweled and silent. Another pair beside them, not so perfect yet in their control: my Annia and her Marcus, welded together at the hand. Marcus was hollow-eyed the way boys are when they first swing their swords to draw blood, and Annia was still too exhausted to jitter in place as was her wont.

And completing the tribunal, me. I'd been summoned by Imperial courier just the previous night, and here I stood, sword back at my waist and eyes sunken from grief.

Opposite us, on the other side of Antinous's statue, stood one solitary figure between spear-braced Praetorians. The accused.

A beautiful morning. Mist hovered over the long stretch of the Canopus's waterway, wreathing the marble nymphs who stretched away in two serene lines, their images doubled in the pool below. A pale winter sun already risen, promising a blue day—a cold day. The smell of Antinous's lotuses rose rich and heady from their mass at his marble feet.

We waited.

The Emperor came slowly, and he came alone: a tall man, iron-haired, bearded, bent-shouldered, his toga tightly wrapped against the cold. My son's black dog ghosted along at his heels. His once-strong arms were gaunt, his immobile face had sharp hollows, and even from a distance I could see the swollen joints of his hands. But as he halted and fixed us in his bottomless gaze, he had only to raise one finger and we all went to our knees before him.

All but Servianus, who stood as proud as though he had the whole Senate at his back and not a set of leveled spears. "Caesar—"

"Silence," Hadrian said. No more than that, but the old man's jaw snapped shut. Servianus, the most moral man in the Empire, who had incited his grandson to murder *my* son. I stared at his wizened face, and my hand clenched on the hilt of my sword.

We all rose, and Hadrian's gaze traveled over his old rival. "You will follow your grandson to Hades within the day."

Servianus bowed his head, tears springing to his eyes for the boy who had been drowned. I had no tears. I had already wept myself dry these nights past for those Pedanius Fuscus had harmed. Antinous. Sabina.

"But before you die, I will hear you speak." Hadrian opened his hand in invitation.

The rheumy old lids opened again, slitted as an ancient tortoise, and I wondered if I would be called upon to force the confession from him. But his grandson was dead and his own life forfeit—he had nothing left but words, and he gave a faint shrug of acquiescence.

The Emperor saw it. "So. You meant to kill me?"

"Not you, Caesar. Lucius Ceionius. Your head was turned by a pretty profile, and you appointed a fool to the purple. I could not have that."

"Lucius's illness at the year's beginning—poison?"

"Applied in the steam of his bathhouse. A poison that could be breathed—it destroys the flesh within the chest, over time. The effects mimic half a dozen chest ailments."

"Not very effective, considering Lucius isn't dead."

Another shrug. "He went off to Pannonia before a second dose could be administered. Most of a year lost."

"I assume you saw he got that second dose once he returned?"

"Yes. He will still die, Caesar—his physicians informed me not a month ago that he was coughing blood and would soon be confined to his bed. That vain, useless layabout will never wear the purple."

"I regret his illness, but I am not altogether sorry he will not be Emperor. He was," Hadrian acknowledged, "an overhasty choice on my part."

"Yes, Caesar." Servianus gave a little bow. They might have been two old men discussing the weather.

"Not that your grandson was much of a choice, either." Now the Emperor's voice had the whip-crack I knew so well. "And at some point, you finally got it through your ivory skull that I would never appoint him."

"For a few missing teeth you would cast aside your own blood—"

"A few missing wits as well. Your grandson was bested four days ago by a boy half his size and a girl with fleet feet." A nod to Marcus and Annia. Marcus looked somber. My daughter jutted her chin. The rumor was already spreading through Rome that Hadrian's life had only been saved because the goddess Diana herself had run wild-haired from the heavens, blowing into his villa in a cloud of flame to bring him warning. I looked at Annia, and I could believe it.

"The girl is nothing but a whore," Servianus snapped, his calm fraying. "And the boy attacked him most dishonorably!"

Marcus started to speak, but Hadrian gave another of those tiny gestures that silenced everyone. "Still," he said, "the young whore and the dishonorable boy were not part of your plans, Servianus. You sought merely to dispose of me. More poison?"

"In the steam of your bath, as with Lucius. A much larger dose, to ensure faster results." A disapproving glance at Marcus. "If you had not insisted on arguing Stoic philosophy with that boy all afternoon, you would have been in your bath and dead long before the whore arrived!"

"See, Verissimus?" Hadrian looked at the tall boy at Annia's side. "Philosophy does have its uses."

Marcus gazed stony-faced at Servianus. "Call her a whore again, and I will run you through as I did your grandson."

"He can call me what he likes," Annia said before either Servianus or the Emperor could answer. "We defeated him *and* his grandson."

She had a glitter of pure contempt in her eye as she looked at the old man. Looked down at him, because my girl was tall as a goddess and now she held herself like one, exhausted as she was. I was used to seeing her swing between unconscious swagger and self-conscious awkwardness, confidence melting to uncertainty, exuberant motion to nervous stiffness. Not anymore. She stood tall and proud and still, and she had the assurance of an empress. My daughter, standing below the marble statue of my son. Strange that of all my children, the two who held my heart the tightest were the son I raised but didn't sire, and the daughter I sired but didn't raise.

Antinous was dead, but at least Annia was alive. Vibrantly alive, the girl whose bloodied feet had saved an emperor's life.

"I had just entered my bathhouse and its poisoned fumes when the commotion outside began," Hadrian said. "Had Annia Galeria Faustina been slower, I might be dead." He accorded my daughter a nod, and my battered heart was glad. She nodded back.

The Emperor resumed his tribunal. "You were to kill me," he said to Servianus. "Perhaps hoping to pass it off as a mere illness? That's how I would do it. A frail old man succumbing to a winter cough is innocuous enough. And when the news spread to my shocked and grieving great-nephew, who received the message with my shocked and grieving widow—why, you would hoist your frail bones to the floor of the Senate to put forward that Lucius was far too ill from his life of depravities to don the purple. You would urge your fellow senators to appoint the Emperor's closest living relation. Emperor Gnaeus Pedanius Fuscus Salinator."

A calm nod from Servianus. "I serve the Empire." His voice had the round tones of a formal oration. How often had the old bastard practiced this speech? He meant to give it, whether to a victorious Senate or to our tiny tribunal. "I serve the Eternal City. I only sought to remove a tyrant, a debauched madman who had dragged the morals of our illustrious past through the mud. I serve the Empire, as true heroes of Rome have done before, in my day."

Hadrian shrugged. "I am certainly a tyrant, and I will not quibble at charges of debauchery or madness, either. I don't take it amiss when an idealist tries to kill me." A shake of his head. "But I'm old and ill, Servianus. I have only a year or two left, perhaps less. Why take the risk of murdering a man already dying?"

"Dying?" Servianus's calm mask cracked for a moment to show true rage. "Do not talk to me of *dying*, Caesar. I have more than ninety years to my name! You would cling to life out of spite, just to see me in my grave first. I wanted to *see* my grandson take the purple, see it while I was still on this earth!"

A little silence fell. Titus broke it, speaking for the first time. Quiet words, because he did not need to orate to make you know their power. "You are a disgrace to Rome, Lucius Julius Ursus Servianus—in your day, or any other."

Servianus bristled, absurdly offended, but Hadrian held up a hand. "We have one more point to discuss," the Emperor said in a knife-edged whisper, and his whole body went rigid. "Antinous. Why did *you* want him dead? Your grandson had some petty grievance to nurse, but why were *you* so eager for the death of a good-hearted man? He was no threat to the Empire; he was not even a concubine who might have borne me a son to cut Pedanius out of the succession, so *why?*"

More silence. I heard the lonely trickle of water in the Canopus's waterway, the caw of a raven. Antinous's dog whined, looking up at the Emperor.

"Antinous was a blight," Servianus said as though it were obvious. "I told my grandson that an honorable man would naturally seek to remove a blight from the honor of Rome."

Hadrian's eyes never shifted. "Is. That. *All?*"

The ancient face was seamed in malice. "He struck Pedanius. My grandson told me. That he-bitch struck the future Emperor of Rome like he was a dog, called him bully and child—"

"We *were* children." Young Marcus spoke up, hard-faced. "Dear gods, that was *years* ago! The night after the Salian rituals when Antinous caught us fighting—"

"He did not have the right! He was nothing, and he dared strike my grandson!"

"You old snake." I spoke without intending it, and Servianus's eyes jerked toward me. "You had my son killed for *spite*?"

"Pedanius saw a chance in Egypt to avenge his honor." Servianus drew himself up. "To strike the catamite over the head as he himself was once struck, and toss him into the Nile. And I thank the gods for it."

There was another silence, this one broken by the Emperor. "Vercingetorix." Looking at me. "Is there anything else you wish to ask? As Antinous's father, it is your right."

I unsheathed my *gladius* in one slow movement and came forward, my footsteps silent on the grass. "Tell me one thing," I said harshly, and my blade was still edged with his grandson's blood after young Marcus had returned it to me. "Did Pedanius tell you what my son was doing before he was knocked unconscious? What he looked like, standing at the railing of the barge?"

I had just left Antinous behind, that night. Had he been praying in the moment before his death? Weeping? Gazing into the water, measuring a jump? Because the guilt still scourged me: that my grief-haunted son had sought his own death.

Servianus shrugged. "Smiling," he said indifferently. "Pedanius said he was gazing at the moon and smiling."

Smiling.

I bowed my head, feeling tears in my eyes. Surely my son would not have been smiling at the moon if he was contemplating suicide. Surely.

He chose to fight grief. Not succumb to it. That was something.

It was enough.

Servianus spoke past me to Hadrian. "You'll have your barbarian here take my head off, will you? What will the Senate have to say about that?"

"I do not care what they have to say," Hadrian replied, and turned to me. "You are no longer my dog of war, Vercingetorix. I will spare you this duty, if you do not want it. But it is your right to carry out the sentence, should the prisoner fail."

I let the word out like a scrape of metal on bone. "Yes."

"So be it." Hadrian stared ahead as blind as Justice with her shrouded eyes and her scales. I saw Titus looking on with a face like winter, saw Faustina swallow hard but stare without wincing, saw Marcus and Annia stretch their heads higher in the same unflinching gesture. Antinous gazed over all our heads, faintly smiling. *Oh, Antinous!*

"Lucius Julius Ursus Servianus," Hadrian said. "You are a killer and a traitor, but I will permit you to die as a Roman. Return to your cell, and you will be allowed to take your own life." Servianus's chin jerked. Hadrian looked at him directly. "But if you are not dead by sunset, I send Vercingetorix the Red to your cell. And his will be the last face you see on this earth before the ferryman carries your worthless soul to join your foul little grandson."

Servianus looked at his Emperor. I'd wager anything I had that he would muster the nerve to open his own wrists, ninety or no. All I'd have to do at day's end was collect his head, as I'd taken Simon's head in Bethar. And as in Bethar, I'd bring the traitor's head to my Emperor.

Echoes and echoes. The past is never truly done with us.

The senator known as the most moral man in Rome stared at Hadrian as the Praetorians took rough hold of his ancient elbows. "May you linger a long time, praying for death," Servianus said, "but be unable to die."

Hadrian inclined his head. "I am sure I shall."

Then they were gone, a hunched shadow stumping away between his guards. He departed like a wisp of poisonous smoke, and in this pale pure dawn, I was relieved to sheathe my sword.

Titus had pulled a fold of his toga to cover his head, a sign of formal mourning. Faustina murmured a prayer. Young Marcus was white-faced but composed, his hand never releasing my daughter's. *Marry Annia*, I thought. *Please marry her.*

Hadrian stood looking down at Antinous's ring. It sat tightly under his swollen knuckle. Hadrian kissed the gold stone, murmuring something, and when he finally looked up at me I saw tears in his eyes.

It is done.

But he was Emperor, and Emperors are never done. There is always more work to do, and with my son avenged, Hadrian steeled his spine to do it.

"I need a young arm to lean on," he said, and looked at Marcus. "Walk with me, Verissimus. And you, Titus Aurelius—I summoned you this morning for a reason."

My friend nodded. "To stand as witness."

"To stand as heir. I once asked why you were still alive. Now I know. You are destined to succeed me as Emperor."

SABINA

"Am I still dead?" Sabina wanted to know.

"It's the prevalent rumor." Faustina slid an arm around Sabina's torn and bandaged shoulder with exquisite care, helping her sit up. "Though nobody seems to know what killed you. Everyone knows Servianus and Pedanius were executed, but nobody's quite so certain how *you* died. My maids heard rumors about poison, hired killers—and coming first, of course, that Hadrian had you executed too, for having some part in Pedanius's plot."

"Gods save me," Sabina sighed. "I really should make some sort of public appearance. Or nobody will believe it's me once I actually turn up alive."

"It's only been five days since you were stabbed," Vix growled, entering her chamber with a brimming cup. "Plenty of time to correct misapprehensions later. For now, lie still and take your draught."

"It makes me drowsy," Sabina complained. She didn't want to sleep; she'd been lost to black and uneasy dreams for five days and nights after she'd slid into oblivion in a pool of her own blood. By the time she'd wakened, Pedanius was drowned and Servianus dead by his own hand, and the world was a different place.

A world where apparently, Rome believed her dead too. *That* was entertaining.

"I don't care if the draught makes you sleepy. It also kills the pain, so drink it." Vix pushed the cup into her hand. Sabina made a face at him, but drank. As a nurse he was a horrid bully and a terrible fusser. But he clutched her hand as though fearing she'd still slide off to death if he wasn't watching every moment, and he looked at her as though she were beautiful—although one glance in a glass was enough to tell Sabina she was pale as unpainted marble. *I'll die if I lose you,* Vix had whispered in her ear while she was barely conscious, and she had followed the sound of that whisper out of her black dreams like a thread winding through a labyrinth. *Do not die, Sabina. Not now.*

Sabina had no intention of dying, no matter what Rome thought.

"Satisfied?" she asked, finishing her foul-smelling draught. And Vix finally consented to carry her out of her chamber to the atrium, where Titus and the children waited, and where Faustina had already plumped a couch high with cushions and furs. Vix fussed some more, piling pillows behind her head and settling her feet across his lap, and Sabina looked up at this room filled with so many of her loved ones. Alive and safe, all of them—except Antinous.

And at least he is avenged.

"I hate this room." Annia limped like a lamed colt around the central pool, her feet still bandaged from her sprint to Hadrian's villa. Afterward, according to Faustina, she'd slept the day and night round, only rising to eat everything in the house and discover that her run down the hard stone of the road to Hadrian's villa had broken two of her toes. But her restless energy was clearly springing back. "I can't look at this floor without seeing a lake of blood in the middle," Annia continued, scowling at the mosaics.

"I like it," Sabina decided. "The scene of our victory. And the blood's all cleaned away—"

"How is the pain?" Titus asked in his quiet voice. "And don't be stoic, please; I know you far too well for polite lies."

"It's bad," Sabina said, matter-of-fact. Her whole right side from shoulder to breast was a mass of flames. "The physician is still looking worried. He mutters about the dangers of infection—"

"Damned know-nothing," Vix growled. "I'm getting you a legion medicus. What do those court potion-makers know about wounds?"

He captured her hand possessively, and Marcus raised a hand to shield his eyes. "*Must* you?" he pleaded. "It is highly improper for a guard to be so familiar with the Empress of Rome!"

"But Empresses of Rome may do whatever they please," Sabina said. "You have many years ahead of you to learn that, Marcus."

Annia grinned, flopping down beside him on the third couch. "He learns fast."

They all laughed but Titus. He had lapsed back into silence beside Faustina, head bowed. Sabina risked the stab of pain through her shoulder to reach out and touch his knee. "When does the Emperor want your decision?" she asked.

"As soon as possible." Titus looked up. "*Me*, as Emperor of Rome? I have nothing to recommend me. The most anyone can say is that I'm unobjectionable—never made any enemies, never landed myself in any scandals, never made any spectacular mistakes. And that is enough to qualify me for the purple?"

Marcus spoke with quiet sincerity. "I can think of no one more suitable, sir."

Titus ran a hand over his hair, and with a wash of love Sabina saw the lanky boy he'd once been. How that boy would stare, looking at the man he became!

And the man he could become: Emperor of Rome. *Oh, Hadrian, this time you chose well!*

"It would mean a great change for our family." Titus looked at Faustina and Annia. "I turn it down, and the life we have goes on unaltered."

"Can you be sure of that?" Faustina countered. "If you turn it down, whoever Hadrian chooses instead will always be nervous of you—"

"And you *should* have been Emperor all along," Vix said from Sabina's feet. "Trajan wanted you for his successor—Hadrian and his scheming did you out of twenty years on the throne. This is his way of apologizing, and Hell's gates, he never apologizes for anything. You really want to throw it back in his face?"

Titus sighed.

"My darling." Faustina laid her arms about his neck, her golden hair glinting and her eyes amused. "There is no man in Rome who would make a finer emperor. So for the sake of all the gods, just breathe deeply and say yes. As for what it means for us, well, we shall manage. Annia may have to do her running with a Praetorian in tow, but frankly I think I shall make a *splendid* empress."

"Far better than me," Sabina agreed.

Titus took a deep breath. They all waited.

"No announcement unless poor Lucius either succumbs to his ill health or is formally set aside." Titus looked up. "I will not have him humiliated on his sickbed. Surely Hadrian will agree to that."

"Until then—" Vix swung Sabina's feet out of his lap and rose, giving a slow, perfect salute. "Hail, Caesar."

The solemnity held for a moment. Titus's face was somber, Imperial. Vix was proud and fierce-eyed, and Sabina felt a thrum of sweet pain that wasn't her wounds. How proud Antinous would be—he had always revered Titus. *Did your death bring this about?* Sabina could not help wondering. She would not have traded that golden life for anything in the world . . . But it was something, to know that at least one consequence from that terrible day on the Nile was one Antinous himself would have cheered.

She could see him now, springing up with his enchanting grin to wring Titus's hand in congratulations. Maybe Vix saw it too, because his solemnity cracked and he yanked Titus into a bear hug. "You long-winded prig," Vix said as Annia cheered and Faustina beamed. "Now you get an entire empire to bore!"

"You could lead my Praetorians," Titus offered. "Prefect Slight, this time around."

Vix shook his head. "There won't be a duller job in all the Empire. You'll be so damned popular, no one will ever try to kill you."

"Let me give you one order, at least. Come with me to the Emperor this afternoon, when I give him my answer?" Titus made a wry face. "I may need you to drag me the last few steps, when my courage fails."

Vix glanced at Sabina. She smiled. "I shan't stir off this couch until you get back, I promise."

"Go on!" Faustina shooed. "Marcus, go with them."

"Me?" Marcus rose. "Why?"

"Because the Emperor said something to me when he made his offer," Titus said. "When he sent you off to fetch wine for us. He told me that I was destined to succeed him, and that *you* were destined to succeed me."

Marcus looked like he'd been turned to stone. So did Annia, frozen halfway through replaiting her untidy hair, and Sabina laughed silently.

"Me?" Marcus said at last, stunned.

"Hand him an empire and he looks like you handed him a bag of spiders!" Vix hooted, but Titus's face showed that he understood everything.

"I am to adopt you as my son and heir," he said gently, coming to lay a hand on Marcus's shoulder. "It was a condition of my acceptance, and it's one I wouldn't dream of arguing."

"You will want your own heir—" A panicky look at Faustina, looking on serenely. "A son of your own, surely the gods will bless you both—"

"I am not to have sons of my own blood," Titus said even more gently. "The gods decreed that, and I will mourn my two boys always. But the place of son and heir, it seems, was always intended for you. And I am honored to act as your father."

Marcus looked away then, hiding his face. Titus put an arm about his shoulders: two men, tall and lean and scholarly-looking, who might have *been* father and son.

"Come see Hadrian." Vix smiled. "He'll talk the ears off you both, finalizing all the details." Titus and Marcus turned to follow, both looking grave at the future that faced them rather than elated. *A man who does not really want the Empire is the best man to rule it,* Sabina thought. *And somehow my husband found two of them.*

There was a clatter of boots as the men swung out, Vix banging into something because Vix couldn't go anywhere without banging. Titus's voice floated out, musing: "I shall grow a beard. A sign of filial admiration for Hadrian . . ."

As their footsteps faded, Sabina called for wine. Her villa was still empty, guards and slaves still dismissed, which probably contributed to the rumors that she was dead, but she had her African girl—freedwoman, now. "Three cups of the good Nomentan, and don't bother watering it. While Hadrian and Titus are busy laying all their important plans for the future," Sabina said to her sister and daughter as the African girl whisked out, "we may as well lay some of our own."

Annia was still looking stunned. "My father, Imperial heir," she said slowly. "And *Marcus?*"

"Titus will have to take over Imperial duties soon," Sabina warned Faustina. "Hadrian really is quite ill."

"Titus can shoulder a great deal of the burden. And I can take over duties for you."

"Good." The cups arrived; Sabina passed one to her sister and her daughter. "You already know my routine, but Annia should learn it too."

"Me?" Annia's red-lashed eyes blinked.

"If all goes according to plan, you will be Empress someday, too." Sabina smiled. "Marcus's."

Annia looked stunned all over again, and Faustina laughed. Sabina wondered if she hadn't seen some flying, splintered image of the three of them while she was lost in her feverish wound dreams that had felt so like an epilepsia fit. Wondered if she had not seen the three of them, sitting here like a trinity about this same couch. The Empresses of Rome—past, present, and future.

"Just think," Sabina mused. "It would be the first time in Rome's history that a daughter followed her mother as Empress . . ."

Annia's eyes flared. "You know," she said slowly. "Vix said something to me, the day . . ." She didn't have to specify which day. "I didn't notice it at the time, but I woke up last night remembering it."

She looked at her unwatered wine and tossed it down in a single gulp. She looked from Sabina to Faustina, and Sabina felt her heart begin to pound under that straight, questioning gaze.

"So," said Annia. "Which of you is my mother?"

ANNIA

Annia's mind was reeling by the time she escaped her mother and her—other mother. She wandered out into the garden, shaking her head a little, and found Marcus by the fountain, shoulders outlined dark and bowed against a blue afternoon sky. Was he returned from the Emperor's villa so quickly?

He looked up at the sound of her footfall. "What is it?" he asked, seeing her bemused expression.

It hovered on the tip of Annia's tongue. *I have two mothers, Marcus. And two fathers.*

And though the thought was astonishing, she was somehow not shocked—not deep at the core of her. Aunt Sabina's watchful eyes all through her childhood, the thrum of instant liking she had felt the day Vix appeared in his lion-skin cloak . . . No, Annia was not really surprised. Nor distressed.

More than anything, the thought made her smile.

I have two mothers, one the kindest woman in Rome and one the cleverest. And two fathers: one the wisest man in Rome and one the bravest. What other girl in the Empire was so fortunate?

But Annia rather thought Marcus *would* be shocked, and he'd had enough surprises for one day, so she tucked her astounding new secret away to tell him later.

"I think we should run away," she said instead—though the thought of *running* anywhere at a pace greater than a gentle amble was horrifying. She was still so muscle-sore and foot-weary that she hobbled like an old woman. "Go to Britannia or Hispania or somewhere, before we get just as crazy as our elders. I left my mother cackling away with Aunt Sabina, getting tipsy and telling horror stories about empresses of the past. You would not *believe* the things they were saying. All I can conclude is that ruling an empire turns you utterly mad, so let's run away before it happens to us."

"Don't tempt me." Marcus scuffed the path with one foot, head still hanging.

Annia came closer, setting her own revelations aside for his. ". . . So it's settled?"

"Nothing's settled. How can it be?" Marcus started to pace, restless. "The Emperor said he always wanted me for his heir. I was too young, so he was planning to have Lucius Ceionius adopt me, only now it's to be your father instead." Marcus looked up at Annia, and she saw his eyes were wild. "I don't understand. Why did he choose me?"

"Who knows why Emperor Hadrian does anything?" Annia shrugged. "He's got a mind like a maze. But he's decided you're the one, and he's right." If she knew nothing else—and her world had tilted so many times today, her mind was spinning—she still knew that.

"He made your father swear a solemn oath on every god in the heavens that he would name me his successor as soon as he took the purple." A gulp. "All I wanted was to serve the Empire, maybe write a philosophical treatise or two in my spare time. And now I'm to be Marcus Aelius Aurelius Verus Caesar: heir to the throne."

"That doesn't please you?" Surely Marcus had to know he was *born* for this.

"How many promising boys in the past have been groomed for the purple by hopeful emperors?" Marcus cried out. "They just get killed! Whenever an emperor dies, the gods toss a coin, and we all hold our breaths. Peace or chaos, no one knows what will come. Not even Hadrian or your father can guarantee I'll ever be Emperor. I might as well have a target painted on my heart—"

"Stop right there. All those promising young heirs who died young? They mostly got killed off by the same Imperial family who elevated them. But this is my *father* we're talking of, not some ambitious upstart being asked to keep a throne warm for a rival. My father keeps his oaths. And he loves you." Coming closer. "Emperor Hadrian did his best to safeguard you—he eliminated every rival in Rome who could oppose you, and he set my father to guard your future. That's about as certain as any mortal man could make it, Marcus." Annia paused a beat, feeling a great swell of tenderness. "Emperor Marcus Aelius Aurelius Verus Caesar."

His chin jerked.

"I've never liked *Aelius*," Annia decided. "Perhaps I can just call you Emperor Marcus Aurelius?"

"Aurelius like your father." Marcus's eyes met Annia's, and they were full of tears. "I admire him more than any man I have ever known, and now he'll be my father in truth." A breath. "Father and father-in-law."

"I know. My mother told me." Annia couldn't resist a laugh. "Ceionia will be furious. I think I'll break the news to her myself."

She did, too—and she enjoyed every moment, two days later, when she watched Ceionia lose her fabled decorum entirely and rip that half-finished wedding tunic off the loom, shrieking.

Marcus leaned his forehead against Annia's, his hands warming her waist, and they stood quietly in the waning afternoon. It was fiercely cold, and Annia's body still ached so badly from her twelve hellish miles, but in Marcus's arms, she felt neither pain nor cold. She felt warm as a fire, and full of hope.

"Vercingetorix wants to speak with you," Marcus said. "He said he and the Empress have something to tell you."

"The Empress already did," Annia said. "So let them wait. I want to be here with you."

"He's her lover, isn't he?" Marcus's brows puckered. "You're not going to be taking up with guardsmen when you're Empress of Rome, are you?"

"Why would I bother? I'll have Emperor Marcus Aurelius, and he's enough for me."

"I had a dream last night." Rocking his forehead gently against hers, smoothing his hands up and down her back. "I dreamed I had shoulders made of ivory, and I heard Hadrian's voice telling me I would need those shoulders, because they would carry a heavy burden. This morning, I didn't know what that dream meant . . ."

"And now you do," Annia whispered.

"Even with shoulders of ivory, I don't think I can carry an empire," Marcus whispered back.

"I'll help you, I swear it." Annia cradled his face in her hands. "And this is all a long way off, you know. It's my father's turn, first—we have so much time to learn."

Their lips touched. Annia felt Marcus's taut body against her relax, just a little. What a worrier he was! "And since we have so much time ahead of us," Annia added, suddenly playful, "I don't think we should marry right away."

He frowned. "What?"

"I know you, Marcus. The moment we marry you'll start ordering me about." Annia felt warmth running through her like a ribbon of flame, right where his hands were still stroking her back. "I'll only marry you once you've finally figured out you will *never* be able to get me to behave."

"I already know that." He frowned, distracted just as she hoped. "We'll marry at Lupercalia."

"See? You're already giving me commands." Annia slipped out of his hands, backing away with a grin. "Maybe you're going to be Emperor, Marcus, but I'm going to be Empress. And an empress of Rome *always* gets her way."

He smiled. "Annia, *must* you?"

He seized her around the waist again, but she slid free before he could kiss her. "Catch me," she breathed, and those twelve miles and two fractured toes hadn't stolen her speed after all. She ran like the wind, relishing the pain in her bandaged feet. It was a pain that meant *victory*, and for the rest of her life, Annia Galeria Faustina would feel that victorious ache come back at odd moments. When the twins were teething and she was walking up and down with a baby on each hip long after the nursemaids gave up—when she dozed by light of a lamp, waiting to see if the legions would come back victorious—when she finally persuaded her husband to give up his writing for the night and come to bed . . .

Shining moments—hopeful moments—that was when she'd wince and feel the ghostlike pain of her feet the day she ran them into blood, gritted her teeth, conquered the agony, and sprinted on. The day she saved an emperor, brought down an enemy, avenged a friend—and won Marcus for her own.

She laughed whenever she felt that reminder of pain. Laughed in triumph and in happiness, just the way she was laughing now as she sprinted off into the twilight with legs flashing and hair flying, future Emperor Marcus Aurelius chasing behind.

VIX

A day later, I stood under the massive statue of Antinous and watched the Emperor burn all records of Servianus and Pedanius's plotting. The smoke rose, wreathing my son's marble face, and I hoped those two were writhing under the whips of the Furies. *Die*, I told their shades. *Fade into history—my son will live on.*

"There." The Emperor heaped the last scroll on the brazier. He looked thinner than ever outside the layers of his toga; just a collection of bones in a tunic of undyed wool. His only ornament was Antinous's ring on one swollen finger.

"What will you do now?" I asked.

"Write my memoirs. And poetry, of course. I scribbled a verse at dawn this morning that I think Antinous would have liked."

"Let's hear it," I said, because he'd recite it whether I asked or not. Some things never changed, and Hadrian's vanity was one of them.

"*Little soul,*" he quoted slowly, "*you charming little wanderer,*
My body's guest and partner,
Where are you off to now?
Somewhere without color, savage and bare;
You'll make no more of your jokes once you're there."

"I like it," I said, and I did.

"It came from a dream of my star." Stirring the crisping parchment in the brazier. "I saw his soul fluttering, the color of gold. Waiting for mine."

I didn't say it out loud because I knew he'd mock me—but I was thinking of writing my memoirs, too. The life of Vercingetorix the Red: soldier, and gladiator, and general who had traveled the length and breadth of the Empire, served three emperors, loved one empress and fathered another. Hadrian would preserve my son in his memoirs, god and beloved—but what of the others who had crossed Hadrian's path and mine over the course of our long and complicated lives? What about Titus, friend and future Caesar? Young Marcus, Imperial heir and future son-in-law? And all those women, the women in blue: sinuous lapis-eyed Sabina, bitter-edged Mirah in her blue scarf, merry sapphire-decked Faustina, and fleet-footed Annia running in a blood-stained blue tunic to save the Empire?

If Hadrian will not tell their story, I suppose it will be up to me.

"You look tired, Caesar." Sabina tilted her head at Hadrian as we rejoined her. She had insisted on coming back to the villa; I had insisted she was still too weak to be moved, and we both know who won that argument. She looked so white and drawn on her couch that my heart clenched. I thought I saw glints of silver in that silky cap of light brown hair where there hadn't been any gray even days ago. But her blue eyes gleamed, and bundled in her silver wolf skins with my garnet earring swaying beside her throat, she still had the mischievous look of a child bundled for a snowstorm.

I settled beside her, putting my arms around her since Hadrian did not seem to take offense anymore. Even if he had, I could not have stopped holding her. I did not think I would ever be able to stop holding her. Sabina had become a part of me, flesh of my flesh during those long hours I spent cradling her in a drying pool of her own blood. A part of me I could not lose, and I had so nearly lost her! Those hours were the stuff of nightmare: rocking her limp form, talking to her, sobbing for her, praying over her. Knowing in that bleak hard core of me that if I lost Sabina I would have fallen on my own sword.

I had lost Antinous. Mirah. My girls. Simon, Boil, so many friends. But not Sabina. She nestled a little into my arms even as she was asking her husband, "Are you in pain?"

"Agony," Hadrian said shortly. "My limbs swell, my heart throbs, and I wake at night gasping for breath."

"You should rest."

"I will rest when I am dead, and I am certain that will be soon."

We might as well have been the only people left in this huge marbled place. The Imperial court had been banished the day of Servianus's arrest and not yet called back; they clustered in Rome trading wild rumors. I supposed it would soon enough sort itself out. Hadrian seemed in no hurry, nor was I.

Hadrian was gazing around him at the massive grounds he had built, the smoke from his burning scrolls still curling up into the sky. "You know"—surveying the vast gardens, the huge colonnaded stretches of marble—"I think I shall leave this place. I meant it for my crowning achievement, but now it has the feel of a tomb."

"Where will you go?" Sabina asked.

"Baiae, perhaps. The small villa by the sea—I can write poetry there, washed by the waves." He smiled a little, and I imagined he was remembering the sea at Eleusis. Me on one side and Sabina on the other as we plunged into the cleansing ocean . . . And Antinous, tossing his salt-drenched hair out of his eyes and laughing.

"We will accompany you," Sabina said, but the Emperor shook his head.

"I go alone."

"Why?" she demanded, but Hadrian looked at me.

"Where would you go," he asked, "if you could go anywhere?"

Britannia, I thought at once. I'd been thinking of Britannia a great deal lately. My parents had found peace there, and peace had bored me when I was young, but now I thought of the mists and the rains, the black silk sky pricked out with thousands of stars, the white ribbon of Hadrian's great wall . . . And Titus had dangled a tempting proposition before me just yesterday. "You could take charge of the legion there, Slight. Keep the men fit; make repairs on the wall when needed; keep peace in the region. Think on it."

I'd thought I was done with the legions, but maybe not. When my daughter was Empress, she'd need someone in that troublesome corner of the Empire to keep the peace. Since I'd already pacified the east, I might as well make sure of the west. Annia already had a far better and more civilized father to train her for the work that lay ahead here in Rome—but Rome could always be threatened by danger rising in the provinces. Who better to stop it than her barbarian of a second father, ready to march with his legion wherever she needed me?

I had been Hadrian's watchdog for so many years. Now, perhaps, I could be my daughter's.

I didn't voice my thoughts, but Hadrian saw that I'd thought of something. "Go there," he said, "wherever it is, and take my Sabina with you."

The word broke from us both. "What?"

He looked mildly irked. "Must I make it an Imperial order? You, Vibia Sabina, will do as I ask for once and leave me. You, Vercingetorix, are to spend the rest of your days as Imperial guard keeping her safe."

"I will not leave you to die alone," Sabina stated, but Hadrian's eyes just met mine over her head.

Persuade her.

God, but I wanted to! If I had my way, I'd take the woman I loved from this cesspit of a city to some distant, beautiful place where no one on earth would recognize or search for the Empress of Rome, and keep her safe till the end of her days. The whole city still buzzed with the rumor that she'd been killed—I had half a notion to let them go right on thinking it, and take her for my own. Because what held us here in Rome? Our daughter was grown, soon to marry and launch into her future under the care of Titus and Faustina—and they in turn had an empire to lead until it was Annia and Marcus's turn. That was their path. Perhaps the path for Sabina and me led to Hadrian's wall, both of us hand in hand under the moon, gazing at those stars that had so long led us in opposite directions.

A trickle of smoke from the burning brazier had been threading its way up toward the sky, but now it was gone. Hadrian looked at the empty sky for a while, and then he turned back to Sabina and me. He said simply, "Have I ever shown you my Hades?"

We glanced at each other. "You have never shown anyone your Hades, Caesar." Which had not stopped the Empire from gossiping about what happened there.

"Come." He led the way, stiffly. I followed, carrying Sabina because she still had no strength to walk any distance, and Antinous's ancient gray-muzzled dog creaked along behind his master. We descended stone steps to the black iron doors set below the ground. Hadrian unlocked them with a small iron key, flung them wide, and went in without turning to beckon us.

"I think I should be on my feet for this," Sabina said, and I set her down. Her hand slipped instantly into mine, and I admit I swallowed hard as we followed Hadrian into the dark corridor.

Light flared, orange and hungry. The rough stone walls were spaced with brackets, each holding a lamp in the shape of a screech owl, and Hadrian went down the row lighting each one. "I require light," he said without turning. "I keep the horror of all horrors in this private hell of mine, and such things must be seen clearly."

Sabina's fingers tightened through mine, and I swallowed again. A stone chamber at the end of the passage, and two more lamps. Hadrian lit them, and there was a flare of reflected light that dazzled me for an instant. When my eyes cleared, I saw the Emperor's Hades.

A stone chamber, empty but for a great chair of wrought ebony, its arms worked all over in tiny howling faces like damned souls writhing in Tartarus. The arms of that chair had been scratched and worn smooth and scratched again, as though Hadrian had clawed at them over the years and years he had sat in it. He sat in it now, his fingers too weak to claw anything, and he stared at his horror of horrors on the wall, clearly illuminated by the lamps.

A mirror.

A great mirror of polished silver, giving back to him his own face.

Sabina gasped.

"I sit here," Hadrian said, "and I look on what I am. There is blackness in me, and I stare at it until I have beaten it back. Because you were right, Vibia Sabina. An emperor must be a good man if he is to stay upon his throne. I am not a good man, but I have worn the mask well enough. It would never stay on if I did not have a place to take it off in safety."

I remembered the tales of screams issuing from behind these doors, screams and curses and sobs. I saw the Emperor, clawing at his hellish chair, sobbing hoarsely before a mirror.

"I came here twice as often when I had Antinous." Hadrian's voice was a monotone. "How hard I worked, burying the darkness for him. He was the light, and I'd come sit here in the dark."

I didn't want to touch that writing chair, but my fingers found the high carved back and gripped hard. It was that or feel my knees buckle. I glanced at Sabina in the flickering light of the screech-owl lamps, and I saw tears running silently down her face.

"The gods are cruel," Hadrian said, staring at his own ravaged face. "Antinous is gone, and I am still here. The monster in the dark."

"You are not a monster," Sabina said, and she slipped to her knees beside his chair, resting her tear-wet cheek against his gaunt hand. "And you are not alone."

"I have always been alone," Hadrian said. "An empty shell in a good man's mask. You know why I truly chose young Marcus to succeed me? Because he does what I do. He agonizes to make himself a better man, and that is a good habit in an emperor. But he will not need a Hades to do it, because he already *is* a good man. I have never been anything but a monster."

"Monsters cannot love." My voice was hoarse. "And I know you loved my boy."

"I destroyed your life." The Emperor looked at me. "And yours"—looking down at Sabina. "And yet you are both still here."

"We stay because you are a great man." Sabina cupped his bearded cheek in her hand. "We stay because you are our Emperor. We stay because of love."

"I am not worth love."

"But I love you," Sabina said quietly, and I saw she meant it. She loved me but she loved him too, and there was a tiny stubborn part of me that resented sharing her. Just as I had so long resented sharing my son's love with this man, even if that was a far different kind of love.

"Antinous loved me," Hadrian said as though he had heard the name in my thoughts. "Servianus and Pedanius took him from me, and for that I should have wanted blood. I should have staked them out in their dying agony for all Rome to shudder at. But I did not. I let Servianus take his own life, and I drowned Pedanius in the Nile's waters as he drowned Antinous. They killed my star, and even that did not resurrect my appetite for blood." He looked up at me, and there was a child's bewilderment in his eyes. "Why?"

The words came from me slowly as I pieced them together. "Because . . . even if you were once a monster, you are no longer." I thought of the man who had tired of bloodshed in Judaea; who had released me from the task of killing his enemies and turned himself instead to befriending me over a game board. "You have spent so many years pretending to be a good man, Caesar, that I think you have become one."

His head fell, and his shoulders heaved. "I have tried," he whispered. "Gods know I have tried!"

He was weeping, and Sabina was weeping too, her face buried in his arm. And I took a shaky breath and realized that the defiant knot of resentment in me was gone. So many years I had hated this man, hated him and then resented him even as I admired his achievements and acknowledged his love for my son. I had held on to that last stubborn core of ill will.

But he wept before me now in a dark cell, and I felt no more hatred. Sabina had spoken true. He was a great man. He was my Emperor. And in my way, I loved him too.

I went to my knees at his side. I took his thin, shaking hand between my own, and I gripped it fiercely. "I am glad that my son gave you joy," I said. "I am proud to be your man. And until the ferryman comes for your soul, I swear I shall remain at your side."

And he whispered, "No."

"I swear it, I—"

"Take me from this place, Vercingetorix." His hand curved around Sabina's face. "Take us both from this place."

I raised Hadrian from his chair, and then I raised Sabina. I supported them, one arm about Hadrian's shoulders and the other about Sabina's waist, and they leaned against me as I led the way out of this foul place. I led us back into the light, where Antinous's dog looked up and wagged his tail. Hadrian straightened to lock his Hades behind him, as I supported Sabina against me before she could fall. She looked at Hadrian from the circle of my arms, and the silvery tear tracks still marked her face. "Wall up this place," she said. "You have no more need of it."

"I think you are right," the Emperor said, and tossed the key into the winter-dry bushes. "My villa in Baiae has no Hades."

"Let me come with you," Sabina began, but Hadrian cut her off with another of those perfect gestures.

"No."

"*Why?*" Sabina demanded fiercely. "Why?"

Hadrian looked at me, and somehow his words were in my mouth. "Because he no longer needs us."

"You have spent your life safeguarding my body—" Hadrian spoke to me. "And *you* have spent your life safeguarding my soul." To Sabina. "But death is the thing every man faces alone, even an emperor. I welcome it."

I looked at him. In his Hades I had seen uncertainty on his face, and the ravages of grief, and a terrible doubt. Now I saw weariness, and God knows he looked as ill as a man could look. But his gaze was sure and steady.

Sabina was still arguing. "I cannot leave you to die alone!"

"Something tells me I will not," he said, and he didn't. I did go to Britannia, and I did take the legion by the wall—but before Titus took the purple as Emperor, there was the inevitable day when I was called back to a seaside villa in Baiae, and I stood my last watch as the man in the bed drew his final tortured breath.

Sabina's head drooped, and Hadrian took a step toward her. I loosened my grip, and she went from my arms to his, resting her cheek against his broad chest. She stood between us, and I met his eyes over her head.

Persuade her, he told me again. *Let the Empress die to the world, and be reborn nameless with you.*

"I'll think about it," I answered aloud, with the edge of deliberate insolence that I knew had always made his teeth hurt. Just because I could—because soon I wouldn't have him to torment on a daily basis, and that saddened me. "No promises."

Sabina laughed a little, a watery sound as she lifted her head, and Hadrian sighed. "You will be the death of me," he said, and it warmed me through to hear the faint irritation returning to his voice. Some things never changed. Until that deathbed day arrived—and it was coming, not eight months in the future—Hadrian would always find me irritating.

But that day was not yet. And we walked away into the twilight, Sabina and I on either side of the Emperor we served, her narrow head resting on his shoulder and my hand steadying his arm.

Publius Aelius Hadrian is counted today among the Five Good Emperors, his twenty-one-year reign the centerpiece of Rome's golden age. His skills as an autocrat are undeniable: He was a visionary builder, a workaholic who made time to listen to even the lowest of his subjects, and a gifted soldier who understood the value of peace. He left Rome the legacy of a unified army, clearly defined borders, and codified laws. So why, during his lifetime, was he one of the most hated Emperors ever to wear the purple?

He had a dark side. The *Historia Augusta* records that he was "austere and genial, dignified and playful, dilatory and quick to act, niggardly and generous, deceitful and straightforward, cruel and merciful, and always in all things changeable." Even disregarding the more unreliable sources, Hadrian comes through history as a man who dropped his closest friends when they were no longer useful; a know-it-all who had to be the best at everything; a paranoid who hid his murderously short fuse under surface mildness; a vindictive brooder who could nurse a grudge forever; and a lover of display who faked modesty because it looked better for the masses.

He seems to have understood his own faults, because he exercised great control through most of his reign, sating his energy and his temper in non-stop work and travel. He indulged in one bloodbath at the beginning of his rule, condemning four political rivals and then blaming his Praetorian Prefect for carrying out the executions against his wishes. The Senate refused to believe the orders weren't his and never forgave their Emperor for forcing them to ratify the arrests.

Hadrian in his personal life is no less puzzling, his marriage to

Vibia Sabina full of contradictions. Their alliance was contracted for purely political reasons: Hadrian preferred male lovers, and married Sabina for her Imperial connections. There is clear evidence of acrimony between husband and wife; Hadrian reportedly found Sabina "moody and difficult," and she retorted that she would never bear him children because "they would harm the human race." There was also the scandal in which Hadrian dismissed his Praetorian Prefect and Imperial Secretary Suetonius because they were "too informal" with the Empress. Did she break her marriage vows, or did she just lack respect for her Imperial dignity as Empress? No one knows. But if Hadrian found his wife difficult, maddeningly casual, and possibly unfaithful, why did he never divorce her? He had no real need for an empress, having no desire for children, and yet he never raised the possibility of setting Sabina aside even when she disgraced him. Their marriage clearly had tense periods, but it also had times of accord: Some of Hadrian's writings refer to her as "my Sabina" with something like affection, and he frequently took her with him on his travels, as described by Greek heiress and amateur poet Julia Balbilla, whose atrociously bad verses written in Egypt still survive. Sabina and Hadrian's best years ended on that trip down the Nile, with the death of a certain Bithynian boy.

Antinous was undoubtedly the love of Hadrian's life. Had he been a woman, the romantic appeal of the lowborn beauty capturing the heart of an emperor would be a ballad for the ages, a real-life Cinderella story with a tragic ending to beat Romeo and Juliet. Besides Antinous's Greek blood, nothing is recorded of his family or background. He was likely educated at the *paedogogium* to become a court attendant, but we don't know exactly when he caught the Emperor's eye. At some point, Hadrian's lust for his beautiful bedmate flowered into genuine love, giving the Empire considerable embarrassment. Homosexual passion in Emperors was common, but open shows of adoration were considered distasteful, certainly for lowborn concubines who should be confined to the shadows and not flaunted as partners. There is also the possibility that Antinous's age caused condemnation: We have no recorded birth date for him, but however much he was called a boy, his statues show a young man in his prime rather than a lanky teenager, and Hadrian had been condemned before (ironically!) for preferring mature men as lovers rather than adolescent boys. If Antinous was older than the accepted age bracket for homosexual liaisons, as I decided to show him, then it was a serious violation of the code of Roman manhood—but not everyone was horrified by the affair. Empress Sabina evidently approved of Antinous rather than being jealous of him, and the trio traveled together in complete accord. Antinous's drowning on the Nile remains a mystery: accident, murder, or suicide? Who knows? Dark rumors swirled that Hadrian had his beloved sacrificed as an offering for renewed health, but the Emperor's grief was all-consuming. In Antinous's name he dedicated countless statues, multiple cities, and a religion that briefly rivaled Christianity. Hadrian also spiraled close to madness and stumbled into the worst disaster of his reign.

The Bar Kokhba revolt in Judaea was a genocide, a tragedy, and a catastrophic example of bad timing. Hadrian's peace policy was famous: He disapproved of expansion for expansion's sake and preferred to keep the peace within the Empire's existing borders. Normally he was an expert at keeping his provinces contented, but Judaea had been simmering since Trajan's reign, and finally boiled over into open rebellion shortly after Antinous's death. The grief-maddened emperor was in no mood for compromise: He decided to simply stamp Judaea flat, and imported three of his best generals to do it (I slid Vix among them as commander of the fictional Tenth Fidelis). The fact that none of the generals was placed in overall control indicates that Hadrian was present in Judaea at least part of the time to supervise the war personally. The brilliant rebel leader Simon Bar Kokhba fought Rome for a bitter three years but finally met his end in Bethar. Little is known of his background; my conjecture that he spent years in the Roman legions is pure invention, but he certainly had an intimate knowledge of Roman fighting tactics and how to counter them. Even Hadrian was appalled at the cost of victory, finding himself unable to give the Senate the traditional greeting of "I and the legions are well" once he had seen the lists of the dead.

Hadrian's assorted heirs make another batch of unlikely characters, but all are real historical figures. The Emperor had long been fighting ill health; he had recurring lapses of what was possibly erysipelas (an infection causing fevers, headaches, vomiting, and painful skin rashes), and when he began to suffer hemorrhages after the Bar Kokhba rebellion, Hadrian began looking for an heir. His great-nephew Gnaeus Pedanius Fuscus Salinator was the obvious choice, but Hadrian evidently did not think highly of him (one source records he was "erotic and fond of gladiators"). Hadrian preferred the future Marcus Aurelius, the young Verissimus whose scholarly development the Emperor had been following since childhood, but the boy was too young. Hadrian settled on an interim Emperor in the form of Lucius Ceionius, a man whose influence wouldn't challenge Marcus as he grew, since Lucius had little to recommend him except good looks, a love of other men's wives, and a habit of dressing his pages as wind sprites. Ceionius was duly adopted by the emperor, his children tied to the Imperial family with the pair of betrothals described here, but the new heir soon succumbed to illness—probably tuberculosis, though of course there were rumors of poison. (Mercury inhalation, which I have implied, mimics the symptoms of tuberculosis.)

Realizing his heir's ill health, Hadrian privately settled on a replacement: Titus, as I have called him in this story, though he would go down in history as Emperor Antoninus Pius. He was the perfect choice in Hadrian's eyes: modest, wealthy, popular, unambitious; a peaceful politician who wouldn't undo Hadrian's anti-expansion policy, a rock of morality who could be counted on to guard the throne for the young Marcus Aurelius rather than murder him—and Antoninus Pius accepted with some reluctance after Lucius Ceionius's lingering death. Hadrian had already, some months earlier, cleared the way for his intended successors with one more bloodbath, when the slighted Pedanius Fuscus launched a coup for the throne under the guidance of his grandfather Servianus. The plot's details did not survive, nor did the plotters—Hadrian had both men executed, sealing his dire reputation with the Senate, who were profoundly shocked to see a man in his nineties forced to the sword. Servianus cursed Hadrian at the last, praying the Emperor would beg for death and be unable to die—and his prophecy came true. Hadrian died the following year after a long battle with what was probably heart disease.

I for one hope that this troubled but ultimately brilliant Emperor did not die alone, and thus placed Vix at his deathbed. Vix is a fictional character based on several very real men: Praetorian Prefect Marcius Turbo, whose incredible military career launched him from common legionary to Emperor's bodyguard and right-hand man; Praetorian Prefect Septicius Clarus, who was dismissed for "intimacy" with Empress Sabina; Septimus Julius Severus, who spearheaded Hadrian's war against Simon Bar Kokhba. Empress Vibia Sabina was not present at her husband's deathbed; she reportedly predeceased Hadrian, but it's unclear where, how, or even what year she died. (And how odd that is, considering she was first woman in Rome!) Rumor whispered that she was somehow killed in the same conspiracy that claimed the lives of Pedanius Fuscus and his grandfather, but we don't know: Hadrian's enigmatic Empress remains elusive to the end. In my mind, she slips off to another twenty years with Vix at the north of Britannia, walking the famous wall built by her husband.

Rome enjoyed twenty-three more years of peace under Antoninus Pius, who was beloved by the Senate and the people of Rome. He may have been intended as an interim emperor, but his rule was unexpectedly long and very prosperous. He lost his wife, Empress Faustina the Elder, several years after his accession to the purple, and mourned her deeply, refusing to remarry. He took one of his freedwomen, Galeria Lysistrata, as a mistress and devoted himself to his Empire, his family, and the training of his adopted heir.

Marcus Aurelius succeeded his adopted father and became famous as the last and greatest emperor of Rome's golden age, combining the best qualities of the three men who preceded him: Antoninus Pius's kind nature, Hadrian's brilliant mind, Trajan's military prowess. He had to wait a long time in the wings for his turn on the throne, but there is no evidence of jealousy between him and his predecessor. They had a warm working relationship, and Marcus wrote a loving paean of praise to the man he revered as father and father-in-law in his most famous philosophical work: his *Meditations*. To this day, Marcus's collection of thoughts on Stoic philosophy, self-reflection, and man's capacity for improvement are revered as some of the most important philosophical writings to come from the ancient world. Marcus himself emerges clearly as a philosopher striving to perfect his thoughts; a scholar who could be repeatedly, endearingly pedantic; a man of the mind not too proud to admit struggling with the sins of the flesh (he gives a great "whew" of relief that as a young man, he was able to resist the temptations of a pair of slaves called Benedictus and Theodota!) Marcus writes little, however, about his wife, Annia Galeria Faustina the Younger. Advanced as he was in his philosophical views, Marcus had conventional ideas about how women should behave, and given that his much-loved Empress flouted most of them, it's possible that the great Stoic philosopher didn't feel up to the challenge of explaining that conundrum to posterity.

Annia was evidently an assertive woman and a controversial empress. Her marriage to Marcus Aurelius was long and happy, producing five living children, but the Senate was forever accusing her of political intrigue and affairs with gladiators—standard Roman insults for any female who dared to be unconventional! By contrast, the Roman legions adored her: She took on the role of Imperial Army Wife, toting her children along on Marcus's military campaigns and readily auctioning off her jewels when the troops needed payment. Annia's popularity with the common soldiers earned her the unprecedented title of "Mother of the Camp," and she was honored on more coins than any previous Empress in Rome's history. Marcus Aurelius always staunchly defended his free-wheeling wife, refusing to divorce her and refusing to remarry after she died (the long-jilted Ceionia Fabia offered her hand and was met with a resounding *No*). Marcus Aurelius himself died five years later, and the Empire (in the words of Dio Cassius) "descends from a kingdom of gold to one of iron and rust."

As always, I have taken some liberties with historical record to serve the story. The Imperial family tree has been simplified: Hadrian's sister and Sabina's extended family are not mentioned, and Faustina became Sabina's half-sister instead of her half-niece. We have no recorded birth date for Annia Galeria Faustina the Younger, but she was likely born some years later than the birth date given here (and of course, there is no mention that her parentage is anything illicit!). I have avoided any direct mention of Marcus's age, but he was about three years younger than I have implied for the purpose of this novel. The line of prayer from the Salian ritual that he translates as "A kiss to grief" was not translated until the Renaissance, but I allowed Marcus to be a bit ahead of his time.

Hadrian's execution of four political rivals at the beginning of his reign happened out of his sight, some weeks prior to his grand entrance into Rome—I moved the executions after his arrival to condense the timeline. Antoninus Pius was not under threat of execution with the other men; his inclusion as Hadrian's rival and Trajan's potential heir is my invention. A few details of Antoninus Pius's career have been changed to suit the story: His service as a tribune (it isn't known if he ever served in a Roman legion, though the office was a traditional rung on the ladder of the *cursus honorum*); the date of his consulship, which was moved a few years; his work on the rebuilt Pantheon; and his acquisition of the nickname *Pius*—historically he earned that appellation after Hadrian's death, when he deified his predecessor over the Senate's objections, and impressed them with his filial piety.

The order of events for Empress Plotina's death, the secrecy-shrouded Eleusinian Mysteries, the Bar Kokhba rebellion, and the Pedanius-Servianus executions is extremely hazy; I've done my best to tease out a narrative in each case, but dates and details are conflicting. Minor changes have been made to Hadrian's busy travel schedule: His bear hunt, his first round of journeying in Spain and Greece, and the incident in which he blinded a slave boy were moved by a year or two, as was the dismissal of Prefect Clarus and archivist Suetonius (author of the notorious *Twelve Caesars*, a work for which historical novelists from Robert Graves on down are fervently grateful!) Hadrian's lightning-struck visit to the shrine on Mount Casius really happened, but sources conflict about when he made that climb; I chose the date that better suited the story.

Finally, a note about the Emperor's Hades—Hadrian's enormous villa with its spread of gardens and temples, its statues of Antinous, and its moated private sanctum still stands today, a crumbling ruin outside Rome, and a mysterious snippet comes down through time about its construction: Hadrian reportedly built a Hades on the grounds, a subterranean entrance to the Underworld. What was this Hades, where was it, and why did Hadrian build it? We will probably never know.

Emperor Hadrian is the most complicated and fascinating of any emperor I have ever studied. He is probably best known to a modern audience through Marguerite Yourcenar's revered *Memoirs of Hadrian*, which puts a positive spin on most of his actions and portrays him as a saintly philosopher-king. Our perceptions now are more flawed and confusing, and yet it was a line of Yourcenar's that inspired my whole vision of Hadrian as he appears here: *The mask, given time, comes to be the face itself.* Hadrian wasn't a good man, but I think he tried to be one for the sake of his Empire, his Bithynian boy, and whatever stubborn friends like Vix who managed to remain at his side throughout his extraordinary life.

CHARACTERS

IMPERIAL FAMILY

*Publius Aelius HADRIAN, Emperor of Rome

*Empress Vibia SABINA, his wife

*Pompeia PLOTINA, his adoptive mother, widow of former Emperor Trajan

*Lucius Julius Ursus SERVIANUS, his brother-in-law

*Gnaeus PEDANIUS Fuscus Salinator, Servianus's grandson

ROMAN SENATORS AND THEIR FAMILIES

*TITUS Aurelius Fulvus Boionius Arrius Antoninus, nicknamed Pius

*Annia Galeria FAUSTINA, his wife

*ANNIA Galeria Faustina the Younger, their daughter

*Aurelia Fadilla, their daughter

*MARCUS Catilius Severus, a young cousin

*LUCIUS Ceionius, Roman aristocrat and dilettante

*Ceionia Fabia, daughter of Lucius Ceionius

*Lucius, son of Lucius Ceionius

ROMAN SOLDIERS AND THEIR FAMILIES

Vercingetorix (VIX), tribune in the Praetorian Guard, former officer of
the Tenth Fidelis

MIRAH, his wife

Dinah and Chaya, their daughters

*ANTINOUS, their adopted son

*Simon ben Cosiba, Mirah's uncle

Arius the Barbarian, Vix's father, former gladiator

Thea, Vix's mother, former Imperial mistress

Boil, a Praetorian guard

Africanus, an officer of the Tenth Fidelis

*Septicius Clarus, Praetorian Prefect

*Marcius Turbo, Praetorian Prefect

*Julius Ursus Severus, legionary commander

ROMAN CITIZENS AND SUBJECTS

*Julia Balbilla, Greek heiress and attendant to Empress Sabina

*Galeria Lysistrata (formerly Ennia), housekeeper to Titus and Faustina

*Suetonius, Hadrian's secretary and former archivist

*denotes historical figure

ACKNOWLEDGMENTS

Acknowledgments to my wonderful team of beta readers: my mother, Kelly Quinn, for her incisive editing; fellow historical novelist and marathoner Stephanie Thornton for her insights on the agonies Annia would have suffered during her half-marathon sprint; and most of all to brilliant duo Stephanie Dray and Sophie Perinot, who told me the book needed the viewpoint of the beautiful and doomed Antinous—how right you were.

Further acknowledgments to Anthony Everitt's brilliant *Hadrian and the Triumph of Rome* (my bible and security blanket); to my team at Berkley, including wonderful editor Jackie Cantor; my agent, Kevan Lyon; and the memory of my former agent, Pam Strickler, to whom this book is dedicated.